The Druids believed when we die
our souls return again in another form

Also By W. Ruth Kozak

Shadow of the Lion: Blood on the Moon
Athens & Beyond
Shadow of the Lion: The Fields of Hades
Songs for Erato

Dragons
in
the Sky

by
W. Ruth Kozak

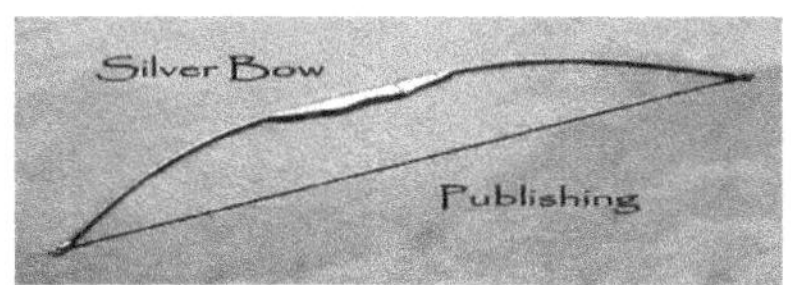

720 –Sixth Street, Box # 5
New Westminster, BC V3C 3C5
CANADA

Title: Dragons In The Sky
Author: W. Ruth Kozak
Cover Art: "Dragons In The Sky" image by Joseph P. McFarlane
Cover Layout Design: Candice James

© Silver Bow Publishing
9781774033296 print
9781774033302 ebook

Library and Archives Canada Cataloguing in Publication

Title: Dragons in the sky / by W. Ruth Kozak.
Names: Kozak, W. Ruth, author.
Description: Includes bibliographical references.
Identifiers: Canadiana (print) 20240498135 | Canadiana (ebook) 20240500962 | ISBN 9781774033296
   (softcover) | ISBN 9781774033302 (Kindle)
Subjects: LCGFT: Novels.
Classification: LCC PS8621.O97837 D73 2024 | DDC C813/.6—dc23

Dedicated to my parents and all my Welsh relatives

Author's Notes:

My father, Rev. Capt. R.F. Filer M.B.E., was born in Caerphilly so I have always had a connection to the Welsh. I have also lived in Greece and visited there many times. So, in many ways, this story is like a past life regression. It is true, that on my visit to Old Sarum, I heard the voice of Olwen telling me her story!

In researching for this novel I learned so many things about the Welsh (Cymry) people. The people of Cymru did not call themselves "Kelts," a name given to the northern tribes by the Greeks, but I have used that term in the novel for clarity. The name of the fierce tribe of the Essyltyr was later changed to the "Silures" by the Romans. The first recorded use of the name of Kelts (Keltoi in Greek) refers to an ethnic group by a Greek geographer in 517 BC, referring to people living north of Massalia, around the Danube and in the far west of Europe. The Kelts extended beyond the British Isles, from Spain to the Black Sea.

The ancient hill fort site of Old Sarum on the Salisbury Plain is the model for the tuath of Caer Gwyn as it had been occupied for thousands of years.

I have used the Greek spelling of the names such as "Filippos" and "Aristoteles"

I would like to thank U.S. writer, Scott Oden for his support, my beta readers Renate Ford and Mairona Liston, my Welsh connection, and Bruce Byfield for his tech assistance.

8

PART I

PART II

Was it the sound of the wind or the bird song from the meadow that brought Olwen's voice to me that day, as I sat on the edge of the earth mound at Old Sarum, on the Salisbury Plain, in England?

I looked through her eyes and saw life as it was then.

She spoke to me, telling me her story.

12

PART I

14

CHILD OF THE RAVEN

PROLOGUE

How do I tell my story? I am Olwen, daughter of the Raven clan, child of the Druid. I am a remembrancer, a seeress and a healer. I know how to read the runes and the secret language of the heavens. At night I study the patterns of the stars. My grandfather was a Druid and elder priest of our tribe. He knew the Mysteries of the heavens and the secrets of the forest and he taught me these things.

We are the Cymry. We lived on the southern plain of Albion, where the borders of our tribe enclose the Great Stone Circle and the hill fort of Caer Gwyn guarded the passages of the Chalk Trail. Now only a mound of earth rises out of the grassy fields like an inverted bowl, but when I was a child there was a greenwood and beech groves where I collected roots and herbs, and an oak grove where the Druids worshipped at a secret shrine. The Druids are the Oak Seers and they know all the Mysteries.

My people, the Essyltyr, left the green hills of our homeland, Cymru, to settle here on the plain. Our village, Caer Gwyn, was enclosed within a circular palisade of staves. It was a small village with wattled huts, like rounded straw stacks with low roof thatches. Inside the stockade, an outer circle of stables and cattle sheds ringed the craftsmen's huts; then the houses of the freemen. In the centre of the whorl, like the hub of a wheel, stood the timbered lodge of my grandfather, the elder priest.

Outside the palisade, the fields were bright with wild flowers. Our yeomen herded cattle that grazed in the lush green pastures along the muddy river bank, and raised small crops of barley and wheat. These were protected by the warriors of the ricon's Royal War Band who keep our borders safe from the raiders of rival tribes. The ricon, Madoc, ruled our tuath the same as a king.

In those days, Caer Gwyn's timbered hall rang with the bard's songs and, in the hidden grove, the Oak Seers prophesied fortune, war and death. Now the Council Hall and the ricon's lodges have decayed into earth. The mound is bare except for small shrubs and wild grasses. The oak grove that once held the mysteries of the gods has been burned and ploughed into the soil.

Here, in the summer afternoon, with the green-gold countryside whose air has the scent of fallow earth and meadow grass, one can still hear the gods speak.

Who knows the secrets of the Oak grove? The spirits of priests and kings are here. Listen to my story. I will tell it as the bards tell theirs. Listen to me. I am Olwen, daughter of the Raven clan, child of the Druid. I am an honoured child.

BALLAD ONE Olwen's Song

They say I am the fairest among flowers:
Daughter of the hawthorn.
Child of the Raven.
The Druid's child.

Listen to my song: I am an honoured child.

I am Olwen.

My voice is the bird's song: my music is the wind's harp.
I will be the pine cone clinging to the branch.
The wind will not dislodge me.
I will be the coral on the sea reef.
The waves will not displace me.
I will be the stone dolmen of the Sacred Henge.
Neither time nor elements will disturb me.
I will be the willow bending in the wind.
I will be the wave uncurling on the sea.
I will be the mountain, my pinnacle crowned with sun.
Steadfast I will stand.

A WINTER'S SONG

Stanza One:

In Ruis, the Elder month, it was our custom to make sacrifices to the Sun God at the winter solstice. The Druid slaughtered a white roebuck and divined the omens in the blood splattered snow. But that year, the gods were not pleased, and Boreas, the North Wind, blew down freezing blizzards across the Plain, burying our village in drifts that reached higher than the edges of the roof thatch.

We huddled in our huts around peat fires, wrapped in furs like hibernating animals, until finally some of us tunnelled out through the drifts to snare winter hares and to track white stag in the forest. Supplies of smoked meat and fish dwindled with each passing storm, and rafters that had been heavy with drying fruit and roots were bare. While we counted out the last of the bundles of food and herbs, we muttered oaths to the gods. It seemed we were not in their favour that year.

My guardian, Essylt, was a medicine woman and a high priestess of our clan. She was small and bright-eyed, ordinarily as lively as a sparrow, but that winter seemed to tire her. She began to look grey and care-worn. As the wind howled outside our hut I watched as she stared broodingly into the flames of the hearth fire, as though her thoughts had drifted off to other worlds. When the snow became too deep on the trail for her to struggle through, I made a child's game of it, keeping the pathway trampled clear. She kept me busy carrying votive offerings of dried berries, cups of grain, and sometimes a sprig of mistletoe to the woodland shrine.

Many of our people suffered from the winter's brutal cold. Almost every day, Essylt administered medicines, or said words of enchantment against the Raven of Death. We could not wait until the spring thaw to lay our dead in their barrows, so the bodies were burned on pyres outside the palisade. Most of the victims of the raw weather were the elderly, but once a little child wandered out into a storm and became buried in a snow bank. I saw them carrying him home, wrapped in a wolf skin. It grieved me for days. In spite of the wind and the drifts that reached above my knees, I struggled to the woodland shrine, bringing the last sprigs of vervain for a supplication to Arianrhod, our goddess protector.

I was turning fifteen. I had learned all the magic incantations before I was ten years old. Essylt, being a medicine woman who was also diviner of the auguries, was my teacher. I called her *modryb,* aunt, because she had nursed me from infancy. The Druid said that my real mother must have died in childbirth and someone had left me on the altar at the Great Stone Circle on the plain. If I had not been brought there, I would have been left exposed to the wolves.

The Druid, Maelgwyn, was an old sage, an elder priest of our tribe and one of the Sacred Brotherhood of Derwydds. To me he was Grandfather, my *tadcu.* During that winter, Grandfather's health started to fail. His bones became stiff and ached from the cold. He took to his bed, propped up on his sleeping pallet with heaps of woolly blankets. Essylt rubbed him down with camphor and fed him hot barley soup. I brought him cups of chamomile tea with honey. Scarcely able to walk, he stayed inside the Druid's lodge, surrounded by pots of burning myrtle oil, studying his star charts by the dim light of the cressets until he was too bleary-eyed to read the inscriptions. Then he would call for me.

I learned more about the stars that winter than I ever had known before. Grandfather showed me how to chart the constellations and to interpret the star signs, so I could watch the skies for him and divine their eternal secrets. He told me how he had found me at the stone altar one Midsummer eve. I was wrapped in a rough woven cloak, clasped with a brooch of a winged griffon, so he knew I must have been brought there by someone from the holy hills of Senghnydd.

"Our people are descendants of the ancient kings of Troy," Grandfather said. "The wisdom of our old priests comes from far beyond the place where the sun rises. We are as ancient and as noble as the spirits who dwell in the Sun God's temple on the Plain."

That year, for the first time, Grandfather missed the winter solstice rites. The snow was so deep on the avenue to the Great Stone Circle he could not venture there. Even though Lleu, his bard, offered to pull him by sledge, Essylt advised him against the perilous trek.

"Too many elders are already dead of the lung sickness. You mustn't go out into the bitter weather. You are too frail to risk it!"

So Grandfather Maelgwyn, who was as old as time itself, reluctantly sent the ricon's seer, a Druid known as Bedwyr, in his place.

Bedwyr was a man of shadowy reputation who had come to Caer Gwyn recently beguiling the ricon and the Royal War Band with his wizardry and glib tongue. It is true some seers are murderous and evil. There's good and evil in every one of us, and the Druids are not above reproach. Most of us trusted the priests who taught goodness. Until then, our ricon had always consulted Grandfather. Now the ricon's visits were rare, but Grandfather insisted once he was up and about again, things would change. Yet, somehow, Essylt and I sensed they would not.

Stanza Two:

The white bull with the gilded horns will herald the new year. Mithras, the Sun-god, is worshipped as a bull. The white bull must lead the herds through the fire ring into the summer pastures and must be offered to the gods.

I was a slight-built girl who looked younger than my years and would always be quite delicate. I was fair of complexion, with reddish hair, unlike the dark, swarthy people of my Essyltyr clan. That winter I reached the time when the moon-sickness told me I was a woman. Our bard, Lleu, teased me with a merry song about a little bud that blossomed into a brier rose. I blushed, because I was still shy and innocent as a child. While other girls of my age tended hearth fires and suckled infants, or learned the art of swordswomen, I spent my time on forest trails and communicating with the spirits in the oak grove. My only playmates were the wild creatures: the animals and birds that came to me, unafraid. Yet I knew, at Midsummer, I would take my final vows as priestess of the Raven clan and would leave Caer Gwyn to serve the goddess on the Holy Isle.

Essylt brushed my hair until it shone like burnished copper, and plaited it with bits of amber beads and rings of brass.

"There now, you're fitting for a god's child," she said, holding up her polished mirror. I gazed into it and saw a solemn face – a child's face, still, with serious grey eyes and the summer's freckles fading from across my tilted nose.

My cheeks were rosy in the firelight. It was a pretty face, although I had not paid too much heed before.

Lleu tweaked my pigtails and teased me. His eyes twinkled impishly whenever he smiled, and his face shone with laughter. He had been my grandfather's bard for as long as I could recall. He played the harp and sang for us. Often, I would follow after him like a small pup following its master. Sometimes I'd tug his tawny beard and rumple his hair, and then we'd wrestle like a pair of cubs. But now he drew back and I noticed Essylt watching me with a disapproving frown. Later, she took me aside and told me I must take care to be more graceful, for I was the goddess's acolyte. I must offer myself to the goddess unblemished. After that, I blushed when Lleu teased me and tried to act more seemly.

Essylt had spent the winter spinning flax and weaving at her loom. The threads were dyed a pretty blue to make a tunic for me. I had outgrown all my others and needed breeches too. She scolded me for putting out the knees of my old ones when I assisted Tog, the cattle steward, with the stable chores.

"It is time you gave up your boyish ways," Essylt scolded. "You are destined to become a priestess, after all!"

I pleaded that I only meant to help him with the Holy Herd. I didn't tell her Tog had given me the sacred white bull to tend.

Our herds had barely endured the long winter. They huddled under the shelters Tog had made for them, but even their shaggy, thickly matted coats hadn't kept them warm. Some perished from the cold; others fell prey to predators.

I spent some time with Tog, nursing sick animals and helping where I could. The Holy Herd was kept apart from the other cattle. Tog was the steward, appointed by the ricon, who tended and groomed them. He was a gentle man, though rough spoken, burly and russet-haired as the bulls. He had lived most of his life with animals and was somewhat coarse of manners. But he had a gentle hand when it came to calming nervous beasts and delivering new-born calves.

We kept votive lamps burning on the sacred altar, and left bowls of grain for the field spirits, so in the springtime we might see our herd replenished. But when the calves were born, one died – a breech – killing its mother; and all the surviving bull calves had shiny black or russet coats. `The only white calf in the herd that year was a yearling Tog entrusted me to tend.

He was white as hawthorn blossoms; his coat creamy and silken. From the first moment after his birthing, when he struggled to his wobbly legs and nuzzled to suckle, I loved him. I named him Mithras, though to speak aloud the sacred name of the God of Morning would be irreverent and profane. I meant no harm.

Being singled out and kept only for the service of the goddess and the holy shrines made me lonely. The calf was my friend, the playmate I had always longed for. I spent time with him every day braiding charms into his curly forelock, weaving garlands of flowers to place round his neck. I brought him barley treats, and even slept with him in the cattle shed some nights, though Essylt disapproved.

"You treat that bull as if it's your brother!" Lleu teased.

Grandfather reminded me, "Remember, my child, when it's a yearling it will be sacrificed."

I thought no more about this until Spring came.

Stanza Three:

Finally, Spring arrived. The snow melted and the first crocuses thrust their purple heads out of the thawing ground. Essylt and I were searching for roots along the forest trail when she stopped to rest. "Now that it's the Willow month, we will celebrate *Ysprdnos,* the Beltane Fires, and your white bull will be sacrificed," she said. "Are you prepared?"

I felt a little stab inside of me, and stopped beside the foxglove sprouts that had begun to peep out of the earth.

"A bull is always sacrificed at Beltane," Essylt continued. Her face crumbled with a frown as I continued counting the foxglove sprouts.

"Look, *modryb*! There'll be a fine crop of these this summer. A hedge of them along the trail." This meant more medicines for her basket to replace those we had used that winter.

She didn't seem to hear me. "The omens are adverse. We must sacrifice the white bull to assure good crops and productive herds."

I kept poking at the roots along the pathway with my digging stick, ignoring what she said about the bull and the omens.

"You mustn't spend any more time with Tog in the cattle sheds," Essylt went on. "He has stable boys to do that work."

"It's *my* bull!" I stabbed at a clump of last year's burdock. The prickly brown burrs caught on my tunic sleeve.

"The white bull belongs to the god. It will be slaughtered at Beltane," Essylt insisted.

I turned my back on her, so she would not see my tears. I felt a tug inside of me. A feeling of defiance knotted my innards. I jabbed so hard at the foxglove roots my digging stick snapped in two.

Essylt stopped me with a gentle smile. "Look now, child. You'll smash the new shoots." She showed me how to work the roots loose from the damp soil, and how to dig around them so as not to bruise the flesh. She put them into her basket, and we walked down the trail. For a while she was silent. Then she turned and faced me solemnly. "You're not a child now, Olwen. You are an acolyte of the Great Goddess, and you must remember that."

"But *modryb*, Tog gave the bull to *me*!"

Essylt's dark eyes sparked. She wagged her finger at me. "Remember who you are before you speak such nonsense," she scolded. "The white bull is sacred and belongs to the gods. Do not speak of it to me again!"

I trailed along behind her meek as a pup who'd been kicked by its master. I knew she was right. The white bull, *my* bull, would be sacrificed at Beltane. I vowed to offer the gods whatever I could if they would save Mithras.

Stanza Four:

The Willow month is the day of the Fires, *Ysprdnos,* the night of the spirits. It is the day we honour the Sun God Belyn. This is the first moon of Saile, and the herds must be led to their summer pastures. On every hilltop fires blaze. The sacred white bull with the gilded horns will lead them through fires of purification. Then, in honour of our bull-god Taranis, the white bull will be slaughtered. It is a ritual as ancient as the winter solstice rites. From time out of mind the fires have burned on the hills in the month when Guenhwyvar, the hawk, nests.

The first day of spring brought a deluge of rain which blew in from the sea and flooded the farmsteads. The newly seeded fields were drowned and it appeared there would be a scanty harvest that year. Grandfather said the rain was the tears of the Sun, and perhaps the gods were displeased with us, so we must honour them with sacrifices.

Grandfather was still ailing. The dampness made his joints so painful even the poppy tea we brewed for him did not bring him any ease. Essylt was kept busy tending him with medicines and magic charms.

The part of me that was still a child deliberately ignored what Essylt had said to me that day on the forest trail. I continued to visit the cattle sheds and sometimes Tog let me sleep there in the sweet straw, nestled close to my bull.

The cattle sheds were on the periphery of our village, close to the grazing lands. There were stables for the sacred beasts: bulls and lambs and goats all as unblemished and white as new snow. There were also cages of ring doves and brightly plumed cockerels. One year we had a great caged eagle with amber eyes and feathers the colour of honey. Someone had brought it down from the White Mountain where the storm gods dwell.

We kept the cows of the Holy Herd in separate sheds. These were tended by boys who served the king. Tog wouldn't let them near the sacred bull, and the boys watched me enviously as I followed him on his rounds, filling the grain baskets and bringing in armloads of fresh straw.

One night, Tog let me care for an ailing lamb, so I slept in the manger. I was wakened by the sound of men's voices. The stable was full of torchlight and three men stood by my bull's pen looking down at me.

"Who is this?" one man said.

"'Tis the Druid's child. She tends the bull." I recognized Tog's voice.

The man reached down and pulled me roughly to my feet. In the light of the torches I recognized him: the ricon's seer, Bedwyr. He was a thin, gaunt-faced man. His sharp, beaked features reminded me of a raven. He frightened me and I shrank away from him.

"Who tends the Goddess's altars while you waste your time in the stables?"

"May it please you, Druid," stammered Tog. "No harm is done here. The child cares for the sacred bull."

The Druid glared down at me with his cold eyes. "Let the stable slaves see to the animals and the priestess tend her shrines."

I cowered in the shadows, feeling comfort in the warm protective body of my bull.

Mithras balked as Bedwyr grasped his curved horns. "Perfection! The sacred beast is truly perfect for the sacrifice."

I threw my arms around Mithras's neck, but Bedwyr pushed me away. The other man came forward, dabbing at his eyes with the frayed corner of his cloak as he peered at the bull. He was Old Caradoc, the smith, a master craftsman and elder of our tribe.

"We will gild the horns, sire. I promise you it will be my finest work. You know my eyesight is failing, but my boy is well trained."

"You are the master, Caradoc," the Druid said.

Old Caradoc trembled. Even Tog seemed intimidated by the Druid's presence. The calves began to low. Mithras got to his feet snorting and pawing with his hooves.

I tried to plead for my bull. But even though I vowed to make special offerings, my appeals to save Mithras could not change the course of his destiny any more than I could change my own.

"See the animal is gilded and prepared!" Bedwyr said. He pushed aside the door skins and went out, leaving behind him a faint odour of musk. Tog and Caradoc followed and I was alone in the stable. I huddled close to my bull, feeling his warmth and comfort and I wept.

In the pale, grey light before dawn, I left the cattle shed. Two shadowy figures approached through the mist. I recognized Tog and Galen, the smith's apprentice. I knew why they had come. Tog was bound by duty to deliver the sacred bull for the rites. Galen would take my bull to the smithy where his horns would be gilded to make him beautiful for the sacrifice.

Galen was a slow-witted boy with the look of a scrawny rooster. His rusty, ragged hair stood up like a cockerel plume and he strutted arrogantly.

The hounds yapped round his feet and Tog lashed out at them until they skulked away whimpering.

Tog spoke to himself as he led my bull out of the cattle shed, "This bull is tame as a lamb."

Galen probed the bull with a stick. Mithras snorted and his hoofs pawed the ground. Anger surged in me as I stood protectively beside him.

"The masters promised a double ration of mead and venison if we please the Druids," Galen bragged.

Mithras tossed his great head and the magic charms I had tied on his forelock jangled softly.

"Here! What's this?" The smith's boy caught the charms in his hand and tugged at them, tossing them at my feet. "What talismans are these? A child's decoration for a holy bull? He shall have gold, and ribbons, not these tarnished bits of brass!"

The way he threw aside the little charms made me seethe inside. I felt as though an icy hand had gripped me, and I faced him defiantly, my fists clenched. His face reddened. He shifted his pale eyes as though he was afraid to look directly at me.

I spoke to him boldly: "I speak for Taranis, the Bull god, and I swear by the Earth Mother and all of the gods, if any harm comes to my bull you will burn in Taranis's fire."

It was the first time I had called a curse on anyone. It was a dreadful curse, one that demanded human sacrifice, a death by burning. I pushed by Galen and began to gather up the talismans.

Galen stood aside, hands trembling, he made a sign to ward off evil.

"She has called on the dark powers!" he stammered. His face had gone white as chalk.

Tog put his arm around me, but I pushed him away and ran until I was swallowed by the mist. Even when Tog shouted after me I did not look back. I had one single purpose in mind.

Stanza Five:

I ran from the stables to the Goddess's shrine, hidden among the bracken and sweet-brier, in the grove where the Druids performed their secret rites. The idol of the Earth Mother was carved of oak in the image of a raven woman, with feathery tendrils of hair flowing into the folds of her garment. Instead of arms, she had wings, and her feet were talons so she appeared to perch on the edge of the pedestal: a bird poised for flight.

Someone had placed a garland of spring flowers on her head, and at her feet were the offerings left by those who knew the shrine. My fingers trembled as I removed the amber beads and brass rings from my plaited hair. I placed them on the shrine, and spilled out the contents of my amulet bag: a sprig of vervain, a shiny stone, a pale blue starling egg and the brass charms from my bull. They looked tarnished among the bright beads and other treasures. I closed my eyes and recited the incantations, pleading with the Goddess to speak. But when I looked up at her, the unseeing enamel eyes stared blankly from the wooden face.

Until then, I thought her to be beautiful. I had not seen her before as a frightening bird-woman. She had always been a lovely goddess, blue-eyed and fair of face, with lips as red as rowan-berries. But as I looked at her now, the features changed. The eyes were as startling as a wraith's, and her red-tinted lips seemed like a beak dripping with blood.

I backed away from the altar, my skin crawling with horror. There was a frantic twittering in the brush beside me. A red-backed shrike had impaled a baby finch on the thorns and the nestling struggled to free itself from the shrike's strong, curved beak. I made the sign against the dark powers and tried to run, but the thorn bush entangled my tunic and held me, as though the Raven Goddess had caught me in her talons. The shrike scolded. The tiny finch was dead, its feathers oozing blood.

I felt the Raven of Death pursue me as I ran from the oak grove and fled to the sanctuary of my grandfather's lodge. Smoke curled from the chimney in the roof. I knew Lleu would be there, tending the morning fires.

"You must not trouble Grandfather," Lleu said as I entered the lodge.

I made the sign of the five-pointed star across my heart as I stepped into the round room. The oil of myrtle, burning in the incense pots, sputtered as the door skins fell back. Spirals of piney vapour curled up to the wooden rafters. The chamber was dark except for the feeble light from the small votive lamps on the shrine.

Grandfather was asleep on his pallet of white bull's hides. His shallow breaths sounded like the sleep of death. In the lamp-light, his face was pale, his white hair flowing around it like tallow.

Lleu was generally lighthearted and playful, but he looked grave. "Your grandfather has read an adverse omen in the stars," he said.

The menacing presence of the dark powers was like a mist clinging around me. I could not speak. Fear had silenced me.

As I left my grandfather's lodge, the wind gusted and tugged at the straw roof thatches of the round village huts. The sky was black with angry clouds. Freemen scurried for shelter and birds flocked into the greenwood.

A flash of lightning lit the sky, bright as fire and a great roll of thunder boomed. I reached Essylt's hut just as the sky poured down a drenching torrent. I ducked under the door skins into the warmth. The faggots on the cooking fire were smouldering and the iron cauldron steamed with the nutty fragrance of porridge.

Essylt was asleep close to the hearth. I knew she had waited all night for me. When I think of it now, I feel ashamed of how many times I had set her worrying. She was a kindly woman, and the only mother I ever knew.

She woke and scolded me as I stripped off my rain-soaked clothes. I dared not tell her I had spent the night in the cattle sheds. Instead, I said I had been tending the shrines. I hardly looked at her lest she catch my lie. She peered at me anxiously, then scooped some porridge into a bowl. I pushed it away. I had no appetite.

"I have been to see Grandfather," I said. "I'm afraid he is going to die." I could not tell her the Raven of Death had chased me from the oak grove.

Essylt drew me close to her beside the fire. "We will make votive offerings. The winter's chill and spring rains have weakened him, but he will recover." She shook her head. "He's a strong old man. He's favoured by the gods."

"Will he tend the Beltane's Fires?" I asked.

"No, but he will try to insist on it." She tugged at my hair with a bone comb, working at the tangles as she would the threads on her loom.

"I'm frightened, Auntie." I took her hand and held it to my cheek.

In the soft glow of the firelight, Essylt's face did not show a wrinkle, but she seemed sad and her radiance was dulled, as though an invisible veil had been drawn across her face. There was a distant, mysterious look in her eyes.

She said: "I am the sorceress, the High Priestess of the Earth Mother. You are her acolyte. Together, we will honour Her."

I remembered the first time she took me to the Great Stone Circle. I was only three years old, and to me the lamb's bleating had seemed like a human baby's cry as they sacrificed it on the stone altar. Essylt had comforted me. "You must not be afraid," she had said. 'Do not be afraid when they sacrifice the bull," she said now. She gazed straight into my eyes. "The omens will be adverse, just as they were before. The gods have brought you good fortune all these years, and they will in times to come." She tucked the wolf skin robe around me and crooned a little song as I closed my eyes.

Essylt's Song

My dreamy-eyed, enchanted child
What charms cast ye
That keep me bewitched?
What dreams spin ye,
my darling one?
Your laughter
is the sound of field spirits
piping melodic tunes,
making me dance.
You weave spells,
like gossamer threads
binding me.
Fair as sunshine
you are the daughter of the Hawthorn:
A fey spirit,
A wood nymph, a sprite.
You are Olwen, the Goddess's Child.

Listen to the wind sighing like a harp in the beech grove, and you will hear Essylt's voice. Listen to the trilling of the skylark. It is her. Her voice is the piping of field spirits and the tinkling of bells from the hillside. Olwen's song is a song of enchantment.

Stanza Six:

I dreamed I was dancing in the Circle of Great Dolmens on the Plain. I swirled and soared, buoyant as a seedling caught in the wind. In my dream-flight I began to ascend skyward, spiralling, circling the Great Stone Circle; soaring aloft, and plunging; sailing on the wind streams; flying into the sun.

A voice said: "I have come in peace, my child."

When I opened my eyes, I saw Bedwyr standing over me, making the sign of the pentacle. His eyes looked like those of the raven in the oak glade as he sneered down at me.

I buried myself under the warmth of the wolf skins to hide myself from his devouring stare.

"Why have you come here?" Essylt asked.

"I have come for the child," replied the Druid.

"Look here, she's just a child! She makes her final vows at midsummer. Until then you'll make no demands of her. She stands with no Druid except the Elder Priest, Maelgwyn, her kin."

Bedwyr was an eloquent man, but his cunning flattery masked more perverse intents. His charm was a guise he used with those he knew possessed the knowledge of the Mysteries. He may have feared Essylt, and dared not flaunt his wizardry with her. He spoke softly, with a sly smile, and made another sign of the five-pointed star out of respect for our house.

"To be sure. But is not the white bull her gift to the god? Then it is in her favour to make the offering in the field. On the eve of Beltane, she will stand beside me, in Maelgwyn's place."

I wished I could shrink from his sight, but his eyes caught me in their evil holding spell. "You are a beautiful child. When will you go to serve the Master on the Holy Isle?" he asked

"At midsummer, sire." I blushed at the way he was leering at me. His eyes flickered over me as though he could see into my soul. I dared to curse him in my mind, but outwardly I smiled sweetly to show him I was unafraid.

"You will serve the Master well." His tone suggested evil-mindedness.

I did not answer him but stared back at him defiantly until he turned away, sweeping out under the low lintel, his black cape swirling out behind him like the ruffled feathers of a bird.

The Druid can change his shape. The Druid is the Raven.

My hand trembled as I made the sign to ward off evil. Essylt touched the ash bows over the door and muttered an oath. "Protect us from dark powers!"

BALLAD TWO A Song For The White Bull

Listen to the chiming of the cowbells in the pasture.
Listen to the piping of the flutes
and the rhythm of the timbrels.
Listen to the lamenting of the harps.
It is a song for Taranis, the bull.
Listen to the bards sing praises
as he goes to his slaughter.
His horns are gilded with gold-leaf
as delicate as flower petals,
inscribed with crescents and vine leaves.
He has a hawthorn wreath around his great neck
and red ribbons braided in his forelock.
He is a creature of beauty and perfection.
He is Taranis, the Sacred White Bull.

YSPRDNOS: THE BELTANE FIRES

Stanza One:

At Beltane, the fires blaze on every summit and earth mound around the Plain. In my village of Caer Gwyn, the Druids prepared a pyre of oak logs in the centre of the hill fort. The postern gates were open to everyone. It was to be a night of feasting and gay celebrations but I felt only sadness because I knew soon they would sacrifice my bull.

Essylt laid out my robe of forest-green wool, the colour worn by ovates, the acolytes of the Druids. The edges were embroidered with gold vine leaves and the clasp was a crescent of gold, with a carnelian star. She fussed over me with the care a servant gives to a guest. My plaited hair hung heavily with the trinkets and ribbons she wove into it. I took the flat bronze hand mirror and patted my braids carelessly. It was a joyless occasion, my face looked pale and haunted, a tragic mask hiding my innocence.

"You must not be frightened. You will stand with honour beside the Elder priest," Essylt said.

Grandfather insisted he would attend the lighting of the Fires although he was so weak he had to be carried on a litter.

"You will stand beside him, not Bedwyr," Essylt said.

I promised I would act with a dignity, befitting an acolyte of the Goddess.

Essylt kissed me. "You are an honoured child."

I heard the Goddess speak: *You are Olwen, daughter of the Earth Mother. You must honour me.*

I responded: *I am Olwen, Child of the Raven. I wear the sacred gold torc of the Druid's Raven clan. I will honour the Goddess.*

The moon was full and lit the forest trail enough so that we did not need a torch to find the way. Essylt and I walked together up the rocky pathway to the hill fort. I tried to lag behind, plucking brambles from my cloak, and stopped to gaze at the stars. I had no heart for the festivities.

I am the Druid's child. Can I change my shape? Could I will myself to change into a bird and fly away into the night?

We crossed the drawbridge and entered the postern gate. The gates had been opened since dawn and, inside the timber stockade, coloured canopies were strung along the ramparts making shelters for wayfarers who journeyed for days to reach the fort. There were beds of straw in the compound for the animals, while the freemen unrolled pallets and blankets to set up small camps around the perimeter of the stockade walls.

A ragged gang of village boys gathered around the fire pits smacking their lips at the smell of roasting boar meat and cauldrons steaming with stews of venison and wild greens. The kitchen slaves bustled about tending the brazier and pouring mead into wooden flagons. It was a feast such as I had never seen before.

The chiefs of the Royal War Band strode among the crowd in their bright, yellow-checked capes. They were the sons of the ricon, and kin of the royal household. Their hands were on their sword hilts and their winged bronze helms glinted in the torchlight as they cast suspicious eyes among the jostling merry-makers, watching for vagabonds and thieves.

The freemen stood aside for us respectfully, making the good-luck signs. Some raised their flagons and implored Essylt for oaths to ensure them of charmed lives. They touched the hem of her cloak as she passed by and made signs to plead for healing or good magic. The children and young maidens stood back in awe and whispered blessings as we passed. A few women raised their swords and I made the sign of good fortune to them, and tried to smile. The swordswomen are the bravest of all. They are not afraid to follow their men into battle and many of them have scars to show for it. They are warriors; but they are wives and mothers too. I marvelled at their courage and thought,

I am the Child of the Raven, but I am a priestess, not a warrior.

The rumble of voices in the compound grew silent as Essylt and I crossed the circle toward the heap of oak logs where the Druids waited.

Grandfather was too frail to stand, so they propped him on his litter, draped in his crimson cloak, with the golden crescent of the lunula glittering at his throat. His white hair was crowned with oak leaves and his sceptre was a branch of mountain ash. I took my place beside him and waited for the rites to begin.

The oak pyre was circled by the members of the Sacred Brotherhood of Druthin. These were the white-robed Druids and the ovates and bards dressed in their sagums of green and blue, and the priestesses of our tribal cult. Essylt, the High Priestess, stood proudly in front of them crowned with her Raven's helm. Her indigo cloak sparkled brightly with its design of stars and spirals.

Bedwyr seemed dwarfed standing beside the massive hulk of the king. Madoc, our tribe's ricon, was taller than anyone in the circle. He was a formidable giant, a warrior who was honoured and respected throughout the land. He wore a diadem of bronze leaves on his head and a torc made of electrum which represented the Royal House of Caerh Gwyn. He and the War Band had left off their breast-plates and greaves but they carried the shields with the Raven crest; symbolic of the tribe. Their swords were stacked before the king, because, as in the law of all Councils, they bore no arms.

I saw Bedwyr watching me and held his gaze defiantly while Lleu helped Grandfather struggle to stand and make the sign of the pentacle.

"This is the feast of the Great God Bel. Light the fires to honour Him," he shouted in a wavering voice.

A young acolyte, an attendant of the Elder Priest, handed grandfather a lighted torch. Bedwyr turned and whispered to the ricon. Madoc nodded a consent and the Druid strode around the circle to face Grandfather who held the torch, ready to receive the Ricon's signal to ignite the fire.

In all the years I could recall, Grandfather had thrown the first torch into the beacon fire. This time, Bedwyr snatched it from his hand and tossed it upon the oak logs. The dried bracken, placed there for tinder, crackled in a blaze of flame. There was a moment of confusion and muttered curses because Bedwyr had deliberately slighted the Elder Priest. I saw the look of dismay on my grandfather's face, and noticed he was trembling. But he contained his anger and in his dignified way, said nothing.

Madoc's voice bellowed a joyous paean and his cry was echoed by the members of the Royal War Band and the crowd of onlookers who cheered: "Blessed be the Raven Clan!" He waited a moment, then continued, "We the Raven clan, the Royal House of Madoc of Caer Gwyn, honour thee Bel, Father of Gods. Bel, God of the Sun and all living things, bring us good fortune, peace and rich rewards!"

I cannot explain what forces propelled me to my actions in the moment that followed. Perhaps it was the hand of the god, or was it the Earth Mother who held me there as she had that day in the oak grove?

The image of my bull rose in my mind, and what would come tomorrow. I was mesmerized by the fire. The bracken sent a shower of sparks skyward like bright stars in the night. Ribbons of orange and blue flames twined and coiled like the spirals on Essylt's cloak. I reached out to touch them, feeling the searing heat as it burned my flesh. The smoke of the Beltane pyre swirled into misty visions, shifting and changing like ghostly spectres. I was so close that the flames scorched me, but I could not bring myself to move away. It was as if I was caught in some strange holding spell, waiting to hear the God's voice

I am the Oak God. I am He who sets the head afire with smoke.
I am the Eternal Flame.

I did not realize the cries and moans I heard were coming from my own throat. I felt drowsy and had the sensation of falling.

Someone lifted me up and held a vial of some bitter concoction to my lips. I tried to struggle, but gentle hands held me down.

"You have touched the fire. Your hands are burned."

It was Lleu, the bard, who bent over me, his face shrouded by gusts of swirling smoke. He appeared as though he were one of the spectres of my visions. I began to cry as he wrapped his cloak around me. I felt detached from everything; as though part of me was the smoke vapour rising above the flames on the oak pyre.

"Has she seen a vision in the fire?" questioned Essylt. "What have you seen, Olwen?"

I could not speak. Vaguely, in the distance, I heard the singing of a bard praising the goddess. Or was it just the wind's song in the oak grove? Out of the swirling blue smoke I saw the dark form of Bedwyr, the Druid, the sharp-featured face with the beak-like nose and cruel mouth and the eyes as red as fire coals.

I could not speak to tell them. *I saw the Raven of Nightmares, the Raven of War and the Raven of Death.*

Vaguely, I heard Grandfather say: "She has seen nothing. The fire frightened her, that is all."

The Beltane Fires began the loss of my innocence. The Goddess, who I always thought to be just and merciful, wise and benevolent, had shown herself as a sinister creature of the dark powers. I began to see *Her* as a terrible demon; half woman, half bird: the frightening spectre of nightmares, the Raven of pestilence and doom. And, as the little field daisy holds its golden heart up to the sun, then closes its petals as the darkness comes, so I began from that night on, to close my heart to all I had been taught.

Stanza Two:

The next morning, the Beltane processional left the hill fort. I walked beside my bull, trailing his tether in my scalded hand. In my mind I was leading him across the meadow as I did each day and had done since he was a newborn calf. I felt him close behind me, nudging me when my pace faltered. He followed me as trustingly as a dog follows its master. It was a game we always played together, but this time there would be no rewards of barley treats or clover.

We crossed through the compound between the circles of freemen's huts and the workshops, into the open market-place where traders had set up their stalls under bright awnings. They were selling shiny trinkets and clay votives representing the bull. There was a brisk trade at the bakery stall for wheat and honey cakes to offer at the shrines. A troupe of acrobats turned cartwheels, juggling coloured balls, while children squealed with delight. The amusement stopped as we passed by. Everyone watched solemnly, making the sign of the pentacle out of respect for us, and veneration to the gods. A little boy ran up with a handful of sweet grass to feed my bull. It was the last time Mithras would savour such a treat.

I kept my eyes on the footpath and followed the wheel ruts of the wagon track leading to the stockade gate. Beyond the gate, across a narrow wooden footbridge, the yeomen were waiting with their herds. They had forded the river farther downstream where it was shallow. The cows were left to graze along the riverbank where reeds were thick and new grass tender and green. A small crowd of yeomen and their families gathered to watch the processional.

As I led my bull across the footbridge, Mithras began to bawl anxiously. There were a hundred head of cattle, perhaps more, waiting to be led by the white bull through the fires of purification. They were stocky, shaggy-coated russet and black bulls, shy and nervous and easily frightened into stampeding.

There was an eerie stillness; I could not even hear the trilling of the white-throat and thrush that usually frolicked in the hedges. West of the muddy river, the downs unfolded into grassy slopes. The meadows were thick with golden-rod and clover. There were farmsteads scattered all along the boundaries of our *tuath*, fields tilled by the yeomen and seeded with barley and wheat and grazing lands for our herds. The pastures were fed by little springs and the streams flowed into a muddy brown river that separated the pastures from the enclosure of our village. At the edge of the downs were beech wood groves where men hunted deer and wild boars. Beyond this, the Plain stretched out on the horizon. These were our tribal lands, the lands of the Essyltyr. No raiders could steal our stock nor cross our borders, without being sighted from the ramparts of Caer Gwyn's hill fort.

This morning, even though the meadows were thick with thistles and clover, the droning of bees was silenced. The pastures had been enclosed with heaps of bracken; faggots of dry wood were banked in a circle around the perimeter. The Druids and their ovates waited in the centre of the field.

A high-pitched note sounded from a Druid's slender bronze carnyx. It was the signal for the fires to be set ablaze. A torch, thrown by an ovate, set the bracken smouldering; a sudden gust of wind fanned the heaps of brush and faggots into a blaze of crackling flames. Smoke thickened above the fields, drifting over the grazing cattle. The herd of bulls crowded uneasily. Mithras began to balk, shying away from the fire ring that blazed in front of him.

I clung tightly to his tether, but he lurched forward, knocking me aside. For an instant, it seemed as if he would run free across the pasture, away from the fire circle. He trotted a short way, stopped, then turned back as though he was waiting for me to lead him on.

As if an invisible force pushed me, I entered through the fire ring and Mithras followed me. I heard the bellowing of cattle behind me, and the soft jangling of their bells. I walked across the grassy circle toward the Druids, with Mithras trailing obediently behind me. Each moment seemed as though it were endless; each breath I took was suspended like a soughing wind. There were only the sounds of the crackling flames and the nervous lowing of the cattle.

Grandfather Maelgwyn stood beside the stone altar, leaning heavily on his oak staff. The king's seer, Bedwyr, stood beside him holding the golden scythe used for ritual sacrifices. As I approached the altar, the incantations began; the appeals to the gods to protect our herds and bring us bountiful harvests.

Grandfather's gentle voice quavered as he spoke: "You are an honoured child. Make your offering to the Gods, dear Olwen."

> *I heard the god's voice in the crackling flames, like the roaring wheels of war chariots and the snapping of his whips.*
> *The white bull is the God's tribute. I am Mithras, the white bull.*
> *I am Mithras, God of Morning.*

Mithras sensed the impending danger. He began to bellow, and struggled to break free of the tether.

Bedwyr scowled and handed me the scythe to make the ovation. It was a large scythe, the curving blade plated with gold and inscribed with magic symbols. It was heavier than I had expected, the handle moulded for a man's grip, so my scorched, blistered hands could scarcely hold it. I trembled and tried to keep my vision focused on the tufts of grey smoke billowing above the firering. Distanced from me, outside the circle, the throng began to scream an ovation to the gods. I raised the scythe in a salute, holding it up to the four corners of the grazing lands. Mithras stood quietly beside me.

Bedwyr's voice came to me, a hollow roar of the inferno as the wind gusted, fanning the blaze. *The white bull must be sacrificed.*

As I reached out to catch Mithras by his brass nose-ring, he moved toward me, nuzzling me just as he had always done when he wanted a reward of barley cakes. I hesitated, dropping the scythe from my hand. The smoke stung my eyes, choking me. I threw my arms around the bull's massive neck and cried aloud:

"If you sacrifice him, you can kill me too!"

Bedwyr snatched up the scythe and pushed me aside. The scythe flashed in one quick movement as Bedwyr wrenched the bull's head back. Blood spurted from my bull's throat, a crimson fountain saturating the Druid's white robe and splashed over me. Mithras struggled, then staggered and went down with a great bellowing cry. Bedwyr filled a chalice with the bull's blood, then holding it aloft, he chanted incantations to the gods and field spirits. Then he drank from it and spilled the dregs to the four corners of the field. Blood dripped from his lips like the gory beak of the Raven Goddess in the oak grove sanctuary. I screamed.

The cattle caught the scent of death and began to stampede through the embers of the fire ring. The throng of yeomen scattered in disarray, tumbling over one another as some of them were trampled beneath the hooves of the frightened herd. I ran until the voices of the Druids and the freemen were distanced from me and I could no longer hear the bleating of my dying bull.

In the dapple-green coverts of Caer Gwyn's greenwood where the shy deer hide, as a hind runs from the hounds so I ran, scudding through the bracken and the tangles of blackthorn as though I was being pursued by some wraith of the Otherworld. I lost all sense of direction until I found myself on the trail where a row of alders line the footpath to the Druid's sacred grove. I was near fainting; my mind and body seemed to have parted company and I would have rushed headlong into the three oncoming ponies had the riders not seen me first. I gaped at them, mute with shock, trembling with fright and stumbled into the thicket to let them pass.

The warrior reined his cob and dismounted while his companion waited on the trail.

"I smell the Beltane Fires and see the blood on you. The Raven of Death, is it?" He pointed at my torn and bloody tunic. "Beltane? The slaughter?"

I nodded mutely. My mouth was as parched as if I had swallowed gall. I waited timidly, afraid to step up to the path, afraid to look at him.

He was taller than anyone I had ever seen before, and I knew by his raven-black hair and swarthy skin he was an Essyltyr. By the dust and grime on him, he had been travelling for some days. I made a sign behind my back as he inspected me scornfully as if I was an errant slave or beggar girl. He had a cruel, thin mouth. A ragged scar ran across his cheek from nose to ear. Beneath his helm, his hair hung in thick plaits like twisted ropes. The helm he wore was bronze with a beaked Raven's head and outspread wings. It was the helmet of the royal War Band;. Around his neck he wore the electrum torc, twisted like a rope with the ends knotted at his throat. Only the sons of the ricon wore such torcs.

"I seek Madoc, the ricon," he said.

I motioned toward the village, gaping at him as though he were an apparition.

"Is she mute, poor thing?" asked one of the riders.

"Some scullery slave, like as not." The warrior reached out and pulled me by the arm, dragging me up to the path beside him. "Come here, then. Are ye taking advantage of the Beltane's feasting to make your escape?"

His companions peered at me curiously. I noticed one of them was a woman. I knew by her dagger and sword she was a swords woman, but from what tribe I did not know. She may have been one of the wild folk from the northern mountains. She was lean and brown as a man, dressed in hunter's leathers. She carried a bird that clung tenaciously to her gauntlet with wicked hooked talons, a falcon, with slate blue feathers and fierce dark eyes. It hissed and squawked. I was afraid it might fly at me until I saw it was tethered to her wrist.

I was frightened, but did not have the strength to run away, so I held my head as proudly as I could, not taking my eyes off the woman, although I was ashamed to be caught fleeing like a frightened doe, my tunic all splattered with blood and my face smudged with tears.

She began to laugh. "Look here, the child is wearing a Druid's torc. Are you a priestess then? Or are you one of Annwn's wraiths?"

The warrior chief lunged. He was a lewd, reckless rogue. Sensing his evil intent, I attacked him as a cornered vixen would, hurling an oath at him so he backed away and made a sign against enchantment.

"By the gods!" he muttered as he mounted his shaggy cob. "She's a fey young thing. A banshee, not a wood-nymph." He gave a lusty laugh as he rode off, signalling his companions to follow.

The swords woman tugged at the lead of the third pony. The rider stared straight ahead defiantly, not glancing my way. He was a thin youth with a sallow face and haunted deep-set eyes. Something foreboding made me whisper an incantation. There was wild look about him. He had swirls of woad tattooed on his arms and his wrists were bound with leather thongs. Was he some ragged thief the chieftain had captured on the Chalk Trail?

"Go in peace," I whispered as he rode past me. "The gods will go with you if you put yourself in their path." Then I turned and ran to the shelter of the woodland grove.

BALLAD THREE The Dragon's Fire

Who is the Star-son who twines himself around the universe like a golden serpent? Who is the Dragon who breathes fire across the sky?
   The God speaks and says: *I am the Star-son, the golden Dragon, the Fire-drake, the Sky Serpent. I foretell the births and deaths of Great Kings. Seek your destiny in the heavens*
   The Druid says: *Follow the Dragon's fire and it will lead you to your destiny.*

A MIDSUMMER SONG

Stanza One:

I always felt safe there in the bosom of the forest where only the wild creatures know the way through the honeycomb of trails. The trees are hung with shadows, and the dappled harts graze among the ferns; there are secret coverts where the wood nymphs dwell. Rabbits frolic in the sweet brier, and the red squirrels chatter from the pine branches. If you are very still, you will hear the evening song of the thrush and the sweet, sad treble of the wood sprite.

I followed the deer-trod path until it came to the rocky spur of the ridge below the hill fort. The bracken was as tall as my shoulders and a tangle of blackberry bushes scratched my arms and legs as I pushed through. I knew my way as easily as if I were a pied deer.

Up on the ridge, where the hill fort is hidden by a stand of junipers, there was a little cave, snug as a rabbit's warren, cozy and sheltered and known only to me. I often hid there, safe as a vixen in her lair. It was below the ramparts of the fort, and I could hear the muffled voices of the guards, and far away the village sounds; shouts of freemen and barking dogs. I hid there all day, while the Beltane's Fires smouldered in the pasture and the last dregs of mead were poured to the field spirits.

The sky had faded to grey, then darkened as the moon came up. It was a golden moon with a serene face, like a reflection in a bronze mirror. I watched as the sky filled with stars, I knew them by name: there was Arianrhod, spinning at her silver wheel; Alpheta, the hub star, bright as a beacon in the jet dark sky. And the others: the Hunter, the Twins, and the Great Bear. They were old friends who comforted me. As I gazed into the dark sky I noticed the constellation Taurus, the bull near Orion the Hunter.

I made a supplication to Latona, the Moon. Is she not the Sun God's mother? She who rules the Night? What are the stars? Are they the myriads of souls who dwell at the back of the North Wind? Is the bright star Alpheta their guardian? **The Druid's say the stars are the messengers of the gods.**

It was then that I saw what at first seemed to be a firebrand, a fiery arrow shooting from a bow. It arched across the eastern horizon, a pulsating. glowing ball with a tail that sparked and undulated, twining like a golden serpent across the heavens. For a moment, it hung as though it were suspended, then suddenly it was swallowed in the black abyss.

I clambered out of my hiding place, my heart pounding with excitement. What I had seen was the Dragon's Fire, a portent of rare beauty. The sight of it so awed me I forgot the chaos of the Beltane rites and the terror of the bull slaughter. A calm serenity enveloped me as though the Goddess herself had wrapped her arms around me; and I fell into a peaceful sleep on my bed of moss and boughs.

Early in the morning, when the sky was rosy with the dawn's light, I came out of my hiding place and climbed down the embankment into the glade. There was a small ring of stones set in the clearing, twelve granite uprights and an altar stone honouring Latona the Moon. It was the sanctuary where the Moon Maidens held their Spring solstice rites.

I picked some sprigs of vervain, and laid them on the altar. The glade was quiet except for the trilling of the birds. The bluish stones of the Circle winked as the shafts of sunlight glanced off their dew-wet surface. A starling flapped by me from the alders, so close I could feel it stir the air by my head, and I saw the glint of iridescent green in its dark feathers. It perched, scolding, on the Head Stone, then flew away into the trees.

It was quiet in the glade. The wind strummed through the alder boughs and I thought I could hear a harp's sweet melody and the wood-note treble of pipes. I listened to hear the bard's voice, but I heard only the wind and the birds and my heart beating like a small timbrel.

I moved around the perimeter of the stones. As I crossed the shadow of the uprights, the sunlight caught my movements, weaving a web of shadow and light. I began to whirl dizzily, as though in a dream-trance, my body empty as a shell, my spirit drawn out of me. It seemed I'd become a vapour. Everything that happened in the past was as distant as a dream. Then, as suddenly as I heard it, the music vanished, as though it had come and gone on the wind. Except for the gossiping of the starlings, the grove was silent.

I stood before the altar stone and repeated the incantations to Latona. The young spring leaves in the greenwood shuddered in a gust of wind. A raven's sharp cry startled the flock of starlings, scattering them. The raven made a swoop above the Stone Circle, then flapped away.

When I looked to see where it had flown, I saw the man. He was at the edge of the clearing with the slanting sunbeams shining on him. As he began to walk toward me, something shot through me, like a firebrand.

Who is he who stands, bathed in the sun's gold?

He came closer to the Circle, and then stopped as though he was afraid to enter the sacred precinct. I watched him timidly from the shadow of the altar stone. He smiled at me. He had a tanned, bonny face, but he looked way-worn and dust-stained from travel. His tawny hair was cut short, unlike the long tangled black manes or braids of our men from Caer Gwyn. I caught a glimpse of the green-gilt of his eyes; the way the sunbeams caught in his hair with a sheen the colour of honey. I was too shy to speak. We exchanged words with our eyes. Then he loosened the leather pouch from his girdle, and one by one drew out five pieces of gold. He held them out to me. I made no move to take them, so he tossed them at my feet. They scattered around me in the grass, glinting like the petals of buttercups.

"May the Goddess walk with you," I said politely. "I am not a Moon Maiden, but I will make the offering for you, as it is forbidden for men to enter Her sanctuary."

I picked up the gold pieces carefully as though they were talismans. I had never seen anything like them before. They were a thick, yellow gold, inscribed on both sides: one side was the profile of a man, though whether god or king I could not tell. The reverse was a chariot bearing a god-like creature surrounded by strange inscriptions, perhaps magic symbols such as those I had seen on Grandfather's star charts. They felt warm in the palm of my hand, as though they might melt.

"I will put them on the altar," I said.

"But they are for you," he said. "Take them." He had a shining smile. He shifted the bundle he was carrying from one shoulder to the other. "You dance as well as any wood nymph. Are you the spirit of the Fields or the Forest?"

I blushed to think he had been watching me dance. No man before had ever looked at me, nor smiled at me, in such a way.

"Who are you?" he asked, but I did not answer. I turned away and walked toward the altar stone. When I looked back, he was striding away. As he reached the edge of the clearing, where the trail leads up to the hill fort, he turned and looked back. The sun was on his hair, a halo of light like a diadem. I thought of the image on the golden talismans and wanted to call out to him, but he had stepped into the shadows of the woods and was hidden from my view. I put the talismans into my amulet bag, not knowing then, that their secret held my destiny.

I hurried to my Grandfather's lodge, dismissing the stranger from my mind. Grandfather was, as usual, at the table studying his star charts. He made the sign of the pentacle over me when I told him how I had seen the Dragon's Fire.

"It could be an adverse omen," he said solemnly. He bade me bring him the parchment rolls of star-charts from the big oaken chest.

"I saw a fire-drake too, some days ago," he said. He unwrapped the charts and laid them on the table under the light of the roof vent. I traced the path across the marks and symbols to show him in which direction the Dragon's Fire had fallen. He shook his head sadly.

"What does it mean, Grandfather?"

"The Sky Serpent foretells life or death. It may be auspicious or it may be ill-omened." He frowned and stroked his beard, deep in thought. Finally he spoke again. "There are two portents here. The Dragon's Fire I saw fell to the west, right over Caer Gwyn. That could mean a calamity for our tuath. The one you saw fell to the east, beyond the Narrow Sea means somewhere a king in the east will die and a new king will be crowned. Just as it is willed by the Gods: *As there is life so there is death.*"

Lleu, who was never far from Grandfather's side, brought a flask of cordial. Grandfather took it from him and held it shakily to his lips. He was so pale his skin seemed transparent. I had never seen him look so defeated and frail. It frightened me.

Lleu drew me aside. "He told me he has seen death in the stars," he whispered. "He has seen death for himself and for someone from a royal house."

He escorted the old man back to his sleeping pallet and covered him with the white bull-hide rug. Grandfather's breathing was raspy and shallow, his face ashen, faint traces of the bluish veins on his forehead showing through the delicate skin. He looked like a man who was weary after a long journey. It frightened me to think we might lose him. He was the Elder Priest, and our tuath depended on him. I knelt beside him, and took his limp, fragile hand in mine. I wanted to ask him more, but he had slipped into sleep.

Lleu spoke quietly so as not to waken him. "If the Dragon's Fire foretells of a new king, the Royal War Band will be displeased. They will take up arms, brother against brother. Old jealousies, suspicions, rivalries will tear our tuath apart. If Madoc thinks there is any threat to our clan, he will make war against the neighbouring tribes. Speak nothing of what you have seen. If by chance Madoc's seers have seen the Dragon's Fire too, then let them make the auguries. Look at your Grandfather. See how frail he is? If Madoc calls him into Council it will be the end of him!"

I sipped thoughtfully on the cup of honey mead Lleu had poured for me. My hands were trembling.

"There is talk that you called upon the dark powers and cursed the tribe," Lleu said sternly.

Until then, I had almost forgotten the past day's events. Lleu tipped his cup and smiled sympathetically.

"You are not a changeling, Olwen, nor a sorceress. I know you did not mean to curse the smith's boy. But he has made a thick broth of it and served it to all who will taste it. You had best not tamper with bewitchment. You are child, after all, not a fey spirit. I know you are innocent. But the Druid, Bedwyr, is like an adder hiding in a basket of fruit and his venom is as poisonous. He has made threats against you. You had best mind as you go. And remember, speak not a word about what you have seen."

"Perhaps the Dragon's Fire was a sign sent from the Moon Lady," I said. I told him about the stranger at the Moon sanctuary. Then, remembering the gold pieces in my amulet bag, I showed them to him. He handled each one with an in depth curiosity, but he laughed when I suggested they might be magic.

41

"Like as not the man was just a traveller passing through. These are not charms. They are things the traders use in exchange for goods. I have seen the ship men at the Narrow Sea. They say these are pieces used for barter in the lands across the water. They are of no use here. They are simply pretty trinkets."

"Is this not the image of a god?" I asked, showing him the engraved head. I remembered the man in the glade, how the sun shone on him so he seemed to be the likeness of the god. "Could it be he was sent to me by the Lady Moon?"

Lleu laughed as he tweaked my braids. "Man or God? Are they not often alike?" He poured more mead in my cup and we drank together, smiling. With Lleu, I could feel no sorrow. He was the dearest friend I had.

"Walk in safety, dear Lleu," I said.

"May you walk with the gods, little Olwen," he replied.

We tipped the dregs, then he picked up his harp and began to strum a tune for me.

Midsummer Song

In Duir, the Oak month,
I will wear a scarlet gown
and drink oak resin wine
that my voice will be sweet as the lark's;
that my lips will taste like honey;
that my heart will beat like a joyful timbrel.
May I be a wild rose blooming in the thicket.
May I be a lark singing in the meadow.
May I be a star when the moon wains.
May I be an island in the sea.
May I be a lamb safe in a fold.
May I be the shepherd who tends the flock.
I shall wound every man; no man shall wound me.

Stanza Two:

The Druid proclaims: *I am the Oak seer, the spokesman of the gods. The Sun God Bel does not find favour with the tuath of Madoc. The Child of the Raven has cursed us!*

The next morning a herald came, calling the people of Caer Gwyn to the Ricon's hall.

"Listen, O People of Caer Gwyn! *The Gods do not find favour with the tuath of the Raven.* The Ricon has called a Council. If you be son or kin or Chieftain of the Royal War Band. If you are Druid, bard or ovate, you are bid to come.

Listen, People of the Raven tribe: We will council with the Druid in the Great Hall."

Grandfather gave me his blessing as I set off for the hill fort with Lleu and Essylt. Grandfather was too ill to climb the steep path to the fort, so they would stand by me as I faced the Druid Bedwyr, and Madoc, the ricon.

We were met at the drawbridge by one of the ricon's sons, Ned, a wild young blackguard. He greeted us respectfully and made the sign of good magic. We followed him across the wide inner court where only days before the freemen of our tribe had gathered to celebrate the Beltane's fire.

I kept close to Lleu. He carried his clarsach under his arm and the strings of the harp trembled and sighed with each step he took. Ned looked back at us as if expecting we would vanish. He was a rough, tall youth with an unruly thatch of russet hair that looked like a tangled nest for vermin. Though he was just my age, it was well known he had already killed his first man.

He stopped us as we approached the door of the Council Hall. "We meet with you in friendship," he said. He unbuckled his scabbard and laid it down beside the door. No man could enter the Hall bearing arms.

"We have come in peace," Lleu replied, and we followed Ned inside.

The Council Hall was a formidable place. A feeble stream of sunlight filtered through the roof vent over the centre hearth and a few dim cressets lighted the timbered walls, casting long shadows off the weapons that hung along the beams. In the flickering light, the palmettes and foliated designs on the wall tapestries appeared to swirl and pulsate, coiling like live snakes and crawling creatures. A ring of spiked poles circumscribed the interior. From the tops of them, the skulls of dead warriors grinned and gaped in hollow-eyed silence.

Entering the Council Hall always made my heart quake. I had been there first when I was a little child and in my dreams I was often haunted by the memory of those spectral skulls. It seemed as though the spirits of the old ones were still there. Grandfather once told me he knew them.

"They were famous rival chieftains and renegades," he said. "It is our custom for warriors to sever the heads of their victims in battle."

The Hall was large enough to hold a hundred men or more, but that day there was only the Royal War Band and their escorts, some of the lesser chieftains who were guest friends of the ricon and the squires of the knights. I looked around the circle. The chieftains sat by the hearth-fire, the blazing flames colouring their dark, bearded faces and glinting from their polished torcs. The Druid, Bedwyr, was noticeably absent.

Madoc, rose from his wolf skins to greet us. Ned stood by him watching us furtively. The power of the Druids and the sorceresses was respected, and I knew he was in awe of us so I tried not to show I was afraid. Madoc towered beside him. He wore a fur tunic. His thick arms and bare chest were covered by a dense mass of black hair giving him the appearance of a great bear.

Lleu bowed graciously. "We serve the gods and thee, sire."

I could not take my eyes from Madoc's broad florid face. My gaze caught his fierce eyes and held there. He was the ricon, king of all the Raven clans, one of the bravest Essyltyr warriors my people had ever known. I gaped at him and Ned began to laugh, seeing my awe-struck look.

"Don't be fooled by that one, father," young Ned said. "She may look as delicate as a wood sprite, but she's bewitched. She's the one who cursed us, so Galen says. And by what we've seen at Beltane, there's no question about it." Ned was aggressive and taciturn, and known to emulate his father. He was never far from Madoc's side and there was talk that one day he would rule the tuath.

Madoc began to laugh too and took a step toward me putting his hairy hand on my head. I stood as proudly as I could without flinching. "Ye're a spirited lass!" he guffawed. "The Druid Maelgwyn's child, is it?" He beckoned to Lleu. "Here! Bring your harp, bard. We'll have a song or two before we feast. Then we'll council when our bellies are full!" He motioned for us to sit beside him on the wolf skins. Lleu began to strum the harp and sang a ballad about ancient warriors. His voice wavered and I knew his heart was not in it. He set the clarsach down after he was finished and begged the ricon's pardon.

"My Master, the Elder Priest is ill, sire. He cannot leave his bed. The medicine woman, Essylt, is there with remedies and potions, but all the charms she knows have failed to move the gods to heal him."

Madoc put down his wooden flagon and leaned closer to Lleu. He whispered so the others nearby could not hear. "'Tis said he's read a death sign in the stars. Could it be his own death he has foretold?"

Lleu did not try to hide the tears that brimmed in his eyes. "'Tis in the god's hands," he said.

I began to feel uneasy. If they knew about the curse, then perhaps they would learn that I had seen the Dragon's Fire too. I watched Lleu's face but it masked whatever fears he had.

Madoc called for more mead and food. His shouts sent the pantry slaves scurrying to bring trays of pork hocks and barley cakes. The Chieftains muttered exclamations of approval while their tankards were filled. Someone called for another song and the pipers droned some plaintive notes to stir the warrior's spirits.

I looked around the circle at the coarse, rugged faces of the men. Most of them were hidden behind dishevelled beards, and a few showed battle scars; a missing eye or a broken nose. They were the faces of men who knew death. I felt a chill run through me, as though a dead warrior's spirit had passed by. Behind the chieftains, like a renegade wolf skulking outside its pack, the tall, raven-haired warrior who I had met on the forest trail leaned against one of the skull-decked pillars. He was watching me.

"Who is that rogue?" I whispered to Lleu.

"That is Sholto the Tall, the ricon's eldest son," Lleu whispered back. "Seems he's again in Madoc's good graces. He left Caer Gwyn some time ago and became a hostage-guest of some northern tribe. It's an evil star that brings that scoundrel back here. Heed my words, trouble is never far off when that blackguard is around."

Just then the kitchen slaves came in with platters heaped with venison. The hungry chieftains clambered for the feast like a pack of hounds who have just brought down a hind. Madoc ripped at a steaming joint, tearing the meat with his teeth, and growled in satisfaction like a starving beast growls over carrion flesh.

"Do you believe my seers would make a false prophecy?" Madoc asked. He kept chewing at the meat, not taking his eyes from Lleu's face.

"I cannot say that sire," Lleu replied.

Madoc smacked his lips and wiped the grease from his mouth with the back of his hand. "Do you think Bedwyr is a charlatan?"

Lleu drew in his breath slowly, measuring his words as carefully as he would pluck the harp strings.

"If you doubt his prophecies, sire," Lleu answered," then you might council with the Elder Priest. We do not doubt Maelgwyn, sire. The gods have given him the Sight."

Those closest to the ricon listened to our talk. One warrior pointed an accusing finger at me and said: "What about this girl then? It is said she has called the dark powers on our tuath."

"This lass?" scoffed Sholto. "She's the one I saw running like a frightened hare on the trail. Don't fear her sorcery!"

I drew close to Lleu. I could hardly keep from trembling. How could I deny what I had done? I had made the curse impulsively and in anger, but the ricon's steward, Tog, had heard me too, and though he was my friend, he could bear witness against me.

"Have you cursed us?" Madoc questioned.

"Aye. She's cursed us, and desecrated the Goddess's shrine," a shrill voice replied.

Just then, as if he was an apparition, Bedwyr appeared from the shadows and strode into the midst of the circle, like a dark bird swooping on its prey. He carried a large bundle wrapped in skins which he set down at the ricon's feet. The chieftains began to mutter but were silenced as Bedwyr pulled away the covering of the bundle. He shook his bony finger at me. "See this, young witch! Your bewitchment has evoked a curse on the Raven Goddess!"

I stared, numb with shock, as Bedwyr exposed the contents of the bundle, the smashed remains of the Goddess's idol, charred and split as though they had been rent apart by a giant's mallet. Among the bits of splintered wood and broken clay were the beads and charms, the trashed remains of offerings and votive lamps, all smashed and desecrated.

A gasp of horror rumbled throughout the Hall. The eyes of everyone watched me, burnt into me like searing fire coals. I felt like a snared doe.

Bedwyr pointed accusingly. "You are the child who tends the shrine. Only the Druids know the sacred grove." He turned to the chieftains who were on their feet crowding around, clambering with excitement. "These are *her* offerings." He picked up a fistful of amber beads and brass charms and shook them in my face. "These are *her* trinkets!"

I caught in my breath. My heart was pounding. How could I answer his accusations? Perhaps that day in the grove, when I lost my senses, I had turned my anger on the goddess. Perhaps I had called down an oath so powerful the gods struck the shrine.

Hywel, who was one of the ricon's sons, came forward and poked through the remains of the broken idol. He picked up a piece of splintered oak. One of the Goddess's enamelled eyes peered up from his cupped hands. He shook his head in disbelief.

"Look here, Men of Caer Gwyn. This child could not have done this damage. See how it is charred and burned? No child's hand could do this. It was a god's hand did it. I swear by the god by whom my people swear: the God of Light has hurled his fiery spear and rent the shrine with his fire. It must have happened in the storm the morning, before the Beltane Fires."

The chieftains grumbled skeptically but Madoc silenced them. "Listen to him. This is my son, Hywel, your spokesman. He is favoured by the gods and his wisdom comes from them. Listen to him. He speaks the truth. Look here: no earthling could destroy this idol. See Druid? It's been cleft by lightning!"

Hywel held out his hand to me. "This is Olwen, the acolyte of the Earth Mother. We should not wrongly accuse her."

I reached out and took his hand for comfort. He was a gentle youth, soft-spoken and kind. There was an aura around him like the sunlight; a composure in his beautiful face that was serene and pure. I had heard he was an initiate of the ancient cult who worshipped the God of Morning and his mother knew the mysteries of the Moon Maidens. I knew him to be wise and just. He was the ricon's most favoured son, the pride of Caer Gwyn.

There was a white line etched around the Druid's mouth. Bedwyr's eyes blazed and he paced the Hall restlessly, his black cape swirling, fanning out like ruffled feathers. ***The Druid can change his shape. The Druid is the Raven.***

I wondered if anyone else saw him thus. I looked to Lleu for counsel, but he was stoic and composed. I forced myself to look back at the Druid, remembering the image I had seen in the fire. ***He is the shrike. I am the fledgling. He is the Raven. I am the Child of the Raven.***

Finally Bedwyr conceded. "It may be so, but until the Oak month, when the sun dawns on Bel's great temple on the Plain, this child will be in my charge. There'll be no more mischief, no time spent in the cattle sheds, no child's play with the sacred beasts."

I cringed under his baleful stare and Lleu put his arm around me.

"There's no need of that, Druid," he said. "She is kin of Maelgwyn, the Elder Priest and in his charge. She serves only him and the priestess Essylt. The child will take her vows at Midsummer. If she has spoken disparagingly, or acted impiously, it is the impetuousness of youth; a child, innocent and chaste. She is not bewitched by malevolent spirits, and she serves the Goddess well."

Madoc drew Bedwyr aside. They spoke secretively, glancing at me now and then. It seemed the time was endless until finally the ricon summoned me. I stood before him filled with apprehension. He loomed over me, a hairy giant as thick as a bear. He could crush me if he chose to. I was a small, timid nonentity beside him. I stood so close I could smell the rancid grease and peat smoke on him. Who was I beside this mighty warrior?

I am Olwen of the Hawthorn. I am the Druid's child.

The person of the Druid is sacred. No man must dare to harm him.

Madoc walked with us to the door and made the sign against enchantment under the lintel.

"Go in peace," he said in a gruff but kindly manner. He smiled at me in the way a sympathetic father might. "Look, lass, ye've put a fright in us with all this talk of oaths and bewitchment. Ye'd best leave the auguries to the Elder Priest. He's a wise seer; perhaps the wisest our tuath has known. I have always respected his word and I honour him. Walk in safety now. Go in peace."

We went out into the bright afternoon sunshine. Lleu took me by the arm. "Hold your head up and walk like a goddess's child, for that befits you,"

We stopped by the well and he scooped up some cool water in a wooden dipper and made me drink it. "You look pale as death," he said.

I leaned on him as we started across to the postern gate, but he made me walk ahead of him so I composed myself.

"It takes courage to put yourself in the gods' path, but they will walk with you if you do," Lleu said.

Each step Lleu took, I could hear his harp strings moan as though it sang a dirge. I felt cold at the sound of it. We crossed the drawbridge, past the scurrilous stares of the guards who made signs against enchantment behind their backs. Lleu walked silently beside me. It seemed both of us could sense something was amiss.

I kicked at the stones on the path and loitered, not wanting to leave the cool green shade of the woods. The glade was fragrant with the perfume of the first brier roses and finches trilled from the thickets. We dared not speak lest we disturb the peacefulness. A little boy came running up the trail to meet us. He was Grandfather's squire who Lleu had left to assist in administering grandfather's medicines. He stumbled and fell before us, his face streaked with tears, each breath a sob as he tried to speak. It was the news we had feared. Grandfather was dying.

BALLAD FOUR A Lament For Maelgwyn

I am Gwyn ap Nudd, ruler of Annwn,
the land of the departed souls.
I am the Raven of Death.
Listen, O People of Caer Gwyn:
Come and mourn your Elder Priest.
Come and pay homage to Maelgwyn,
For he has gone to dwell beyond the North Wind.

THE RAVEN OF DEATH Stanza One:

We drew the wicker shutters over the windows of the Druid's lodge and held the door skins closed with wooden pegs. Essylt placed a fresh sprig of rowan over the lintel and heaps of vervain on the threshold before the door. A gathering of freemen waited anxiously outside; some of the old crones had already streaked their faces with dirt and beat their breasts, moaning the dirge. A woman caught my arm and pleaded tearfully for me to make a charm. I made the sign of the five-sided pentacle over her. It was all I knew how to do for such a solemn occasion.

I followed Lleu faint-heartedly into the darkened chamber. The smell of lavender and rosemary permeated the room. Essylt had drawn a circle of chalk dust around Grandfather's pallet to keep away evil spirits. Inside the circle she placed votive candles and burned incense in a pot. She stood by the bedside and chanted incantations. She was wearing her ceremonial robes. The carnelian eyes of the raven on her small, winged helm glimmered in the lamplight.

Grandfather's body was covered with a stag's hide to secure his soul from demons. His face was sunken and grey like a death mask with a pentacle smeared in blood on his pale forehead. His breath was laboured, his eyes half open.

I stepped inside the chalk circle and knelt beside him. He lay still, his eyes intent on something distant. I touched the stag hide to my lips and cried to the life-giving gods, Peredur, god of healing, and Mithras, god of the immortal soul.

The old man stirred. His breath rattled in his chest. "Can you hear them?" he asked in a thin, trembling voice.

"I hear nothing but the wind through the roof thatch, Grandfather."

"No. Not that...the others...I hear them crying like lambs..." He lay still, his eyes intent on something distant. "Open the doors and carry me out where I can see the stars." His frail body shook. He turned his head feebly. "I must see it..." he gasped. "The Dragon's fire."

I took Grandfather's hand and pressed it against my tear-wet cheek. He sighed, then his eyes fluttered open. I leaned my ear close to his lips as he tried to speak again.

"Dearest Olwen," he whispered, "Go in safety, walk in peace."

Then he was dead, gone lightly as a shadow. As the chill of his dead soul passed by, I heard the fluttering of bird wings. The lamp flames sputtered as the grey smoke of the incense pots coiled along the surface of the reed-strewn floor and rose up like a grey dove to the roof vent clouding the stars.

One never knows when the gods will call or come for you but there are times when their presence is felt, and this was just such a time.

The God speaks and says: *Where else shall ye walk in peace?*
In what nobler land than Annwn, the Otherworld?

Essylt and I stripped Grandfather's lodge of all its tapestries and furnishings. These went to the Otherworld with him; with vials of myrtle oil, amphorae of sweet cordial and baskets of food. Even the ring doves from the roof thatch were offered as a sacrifice. I spilled their blood myself to speed his soul in safety to the Otherworld. Perhaps Grandfather's spirit would return to us in those same doves.

The funeral pyre was built in the town square where the ricon and all the townsfolk gathered to pay homage to their Chief Druid. It burned brighter than Beltane's Fire and Grandfather's soul became a spark which drifted heavenward to become a star to burn brilliantly in the night sky.

There would be rejoicing in the Otherworld when Grandfather's spirit joined his ancestors. We knew his soul would enter another's form, so we could not grieve too long for him.

Where else shall you walk in peace?
What other land than Annwn?
The Otherworld?

Stanza Two:

The God speaks and says: *Who but I know where the sun sets? Who but I know who dwells in the Halls of Annwn? As the storm clouds obscure the sun's bright face, So do the powers of darkness overshadow the radiance of virtue.*

In the days that passed, Essylt and I made sacrifices to the gods and kept the votive lamps lit on the shrines. We kept in mind the auguries, but soon it became clear there were other ill-starred omens about to be revealed.

One grey, cloudy morning, a stable boy was summoned to the smith's sheds. He said Old Caradoc, the blacksmith, was ailing. I prepared a basket of simple herbs and concoctions and went along to help Essylt. But it was too late for our medicines or magic. Before we reached the sheds, Old Caradoc

49

was dead. We could only sprinkle the hyssop around and make the sign of the pentacle in lamb's blood, as we had done for Grandfather.

The apprentice, Galen, knelt beside his master's body weeping as he clung to the smith's blackened apron. Caradoc had died right at the forge, the mallet still gripped in his hand.

The bellows boy, a small lad, with great sad eyes and matted flaxen hair, stood behind the forge weeping. He had been a foundling, or some captive from another clan. He wasn't more than eight winters old and had no master other than Caradoc.

Old Caradoc had made our tuath famous with his craftsman's skills. He was a noble man of high esteem and his death would be a loss to everyone. Every wall of the blacksmith's shed was hung with hammers, tongs and files; leather harnesses that shone with bright new trappings; swords of polished iron. Every corner of the workshop was stacked with iron bars ready for the forge. Galen had been with Caradoc nearly all his life, but he would never match his master's skill as a smith.

"It was your curse!" Galen sobbed. He cast an accusing look on me that made my flesh grow cold. I turned away as he spat on me.

Essylt tried to comfort him but he did not want to be consoled and pushed her away. He pointed to me and cried: "His death is on your hands, sorceress!"

I had forgotten the angry curse I had made when my bull, Mithras, was sacrificed, a curse on those who had let him be led to be slaughtered. Was it my curse that had caused old Cardoc's death?

Essylt put her arms protectively around me. "Sometimes things are said in anger that must not be held accountable. Death comes to us all when the gods see fit. Caradoc was at the end of his time, an old man in ill health. He was almost blind and crippled from so many years of bending at the forge. Even an oxen's heart is not so strong that it won't break. Let Caradoc's soul rest in peace until the gods free him from the Otherworld."

I wept to think the oath I had spoken in anger could have cause the death of our tuath's beloved blacksmith and keeper of the cattle sheds. Somehow I knew I must atone for the curse I made.

After I left Caradoc's smithy, I went to the woods where there was a rabbit's warren under the blackthorn thickets. I knew the times the colony fed.

I made a snare, weaving the thongs and willow staves the way Lleu had shown me. I remembered how he had teased me when I said I'd rather watch the rabbits play.

"Ye're too soft-hearted, Olwen," he had said. "I think ye'd try to tame a wild boar rather than to kill it."

I set the snare and waited for the doe and her young. The first rabbit came swishing through the meadow grass stopping to graze on the tender young shoots. It made a straight line toward my snare as it stopped now and then to feed. It was small and tawny-coloured, hardly more than a nursling. I held my breath as it came nearer and was almost tempted to frighten it away. But just then, as if some instinct told her to warn her young, the doe plunged out of the bracken and leapt straight into the trap. She gave a little cry, struggled, then lay quite still. I grasped her by the ears and tethered her with my sash the way Lleu had shown me. She was a plump doe, sleek and heavy as a sack of stones, and put up a valiant struggle.

I carried her into the sacred grove and placed her on the wet moss before the ruined shrine. I had no sacrificial knife. My digging stick would have to do; it had a point as sharp as a spear. I felt the fluttering of the doe's heart as I plunged it into her. I closed my ears to the sound of her frightened shrieks and stabbed until I felt the stick break. Her blood was on my hands. It seemed such an easy thing to kill her, even though weeks before I had watched her suckling her young. I placed the warm blood-soaked body on the altar stones.

"I beg you, O Mother of all Gods" I prayed, "If you must take another life, take mine."

Because of my curse, I blamed myself for Old Caradoc's death. His blood was on my hands, just as surely as now they were drenched with the doe's.

BALLAD FIVE A Ballad For Lovers

Fairest Lady,
fawn-eyed, gentle lass,
you came to me in summer,
smiling, with the sunlight
in your hair.
You lay with me,
beneath the hawthorn bowers,
sweet Lady of the Misty Lakes.
Your laughter echoed
in Caer Gwyn's valleys green,
a sound gay as the lark's song.
In Spring, our laughter
filled the valley, sweet as wine.
The hawthorn's fragrant flowers
made a cradle's bower.
But as the summer wind plucks
petals from the trembling boughs,
so you were plucked
from my embrace.

THE TRYST

Stanza One:

Where the river flowed brown and silent, Essylt and I collected sweet cress and hunted for the eggs of waterfowl. The meadows hummed with insects in fields that were bright with colour, a tapestry of green and gold.

We found a few eggs, those from late nestlings, and placed them in our baskets with the heaps of greens and reeds for weaving. I lingered near the water's edge and watched fish jump, leaving spirals on the still, rusty pools. In a little more than a fortnight, it would be summer.

Essylt laughed as she set her bundles down and watched me venture out into the stream. Near the narrows where there were trout and eels the village men would be setting their nets down. I had thought to ask Lleu to take me there. A day by the stream would please him. Essylt sat on a heap of last year's rushes like a moorhen on a nest. I caught her smiling at me as I waded through the reeds.

"You're a bonny lamb, child," she said. Her manner was so gentle and loving it brought a touch of melancholy to me.

Essylt had been preparing me for my journey to the Druid's Isle. On the new moon of the Oak month I would leave Caer Gwyn and begin life as an acolyte of the goddess. I couldn't bear the thought of leaving her when Midsummer came.

I flung myself down beside her, my tunic and breeches soaked, the water making puddles at my feet. Her dark eyes were serious; her smile faded like a shadow crossing light. I nestled close to her, smelling the fragrance of lavender and herbs.

"I'll miss you when I leave Caer Gwyn, dear Aunt!" I buried my face against the softness of her linen cloak.

"You'll serve the Goddess well on the Druid's Isle," she whispered. She stroked my hair as she held me close to her bosom. There was a sad look on her face as though she had seen some vision that made her turn within herself. Her eyes, grey as smoke, veiled her inner thoughts. She sighed as she picked up her baskets.

"Walk in safety, child, and keep yourself pure," she said. Then she walked away, down the towpath.

As I watched her go, I felt a wave of trepidation wash over me. The Druid's Isle was so far away. If I went there, how would I ever find my way back to Caer Gwyn?

I busied myself gathering flowers; their sweet fragrance made me forget my worries. There were harebells growing along the towpath where I picked a few pale lavender blooms. There were not many, but plenty of buds showed promise for the midsummer. The river widened as it curved beside the earth mound of the hill fort. I heard hounds baying across the plain on the other shore. The hunters had gone out that morning with their packs of deer hounds. There were pied deer out in the copses and the dogs always howled, catching wind of them. If it was a good hunt, there would be plenty of fresh venison to share among the village freemen.

A partridge startled me, flying into my path from the hedgerow. I saw the streak of grey-brown feathers flutter into the tall meadow grass. There would be a nest somewhere in the furze hedge and eggs were scarce. I set my basket down, parting the boughs in hopes of finding it. There was a nest with four eggs, but someone had already found them.

"They're the last you'll find this season," I said to the man who was stooping over to pick them up.

He looked up from his find; his eyes, green as spring moss, met mine. It was the stranger from the stone circle in the glen. I blushed and stammered, too shy to speak.

"I ought to let them set," he smiled. "The pair of them was guarding the nest. It might have been their last brood."

"You've disturbed them now," I said. "They won't set again."

"You take them then." He put the eggs carefully into my basket. "You are the little nymph who dances for the Moon Goddess. My name is Teag," he said. "I am a guest-friend of the ricon." He peered at me curiously and reached out to touch the brass rings in my plaited hair. I felt a tingling as his fingers traced along the designs of my neck torc.

"A priestess's torc." he said, with a look of surprise.

"I serve the Goddess. Olwen is my name," I said.

His eyes twinkled. I sensed he was a mischievous rogue, but something more than that as well. "Ah, sweet Olwen of the Hawthorns." There was a melodic lilt to his voice, an inflection of speech that differed from my own. I knew he was not of our tuath, but I knew the Northern tribes and he was neither Ordovice nor Dobunni either. "Where are you from?"

He made a sweep with his hands and laughed. "I'm from the north, the south, the east and west. A traveller. A craftsman."

I thought of the gold coin talismans he had given me with the mysterious inscriptions and the image of the man-god.

"Are you a goldsmith?"

He tugged at his beard. "Yes...that I am." Then he grinned. "Ah, yes. The gold *staters*. They are of no use to me here so I gave them to you. I got them in Massalia, in exchange for some work I did."

"Massalia?" The name had a ring of magic to it. "Isn't that far away? As far as Carnac's holy groves?"

"Yes, it's across the Narrow Sea. But it is in the south, farther away than Carnac. Ships come there from across the sea. It's a trading port." He began to speak in words I had heard my Grandfather use: names of mysterious countries that belonged to the dark-skinned traders who sometimes came to our sea coast; names as mysterious as those on the star charts. "Ships from Syracuse and Athens and Tyre." When he spoke to them, I felt my heart race with excitement, as though by naming them he invoked a magic spell, and I recalled Grandfather telling me how our people, the Cymry, had come from far away in the east beyond where the sun rose.

Curious, I asked: "Why have you come here to Caer Gwyn?"

"Fate led me here, I suppose," he teased. Then he sighed and smiled almost sadly. "I came back to Cymru, because I suppose it is a man's need to return home."

I asked him no more questions. I sensed he was like the wildfowl who would stay for a season then fly on. As if he guessed my thoughts he said: "I'll only stay as long as my heart wills it."

Our glances met, caught, held for a long time as though without speaking we knew each other's thoughts. The sunshine was so warm and bright I closed my eyes and heard the bees humming in the clover. His hand touched my cheek. I opened my eyes and looked into his, feeling something I could not understand.

"Will you walk with me?" he asked.

"I've shrines to tend," I stammered.

"Ah yes, you are the little goddess!" He was a bold rascal to tease me so.

I began to walk away. "Little goddess," he called, "You're more nymph than mortal. I believed that when I first saw you dancing in the stone circle. You are too beautiful, too enchanting, to be an earthling."

I smiled, remembering the day when I first saw him standing in the glen and had thought him to be a vision of the God of Morning. I turned to face him, my laughter turning to a sigh. He was like a god to me too, with the golden sunlight caught in his tawny hair, his eyes jewel-bright and clear as a crystal in which I might foretell my future. He took my hand to lead me across the footbridge. I could not walk away from him that day. I knew I never could again

Stanza Two:

The God speaks and says: *I am the Eagle who shakes the snow from the Holy White Mountain. I am the Hawk who hunts on the hill. I am the Falcon who circles the dolmens. I am the Raven who seeks and knows all.*

The melancholy that had beset me in the Willow month vanished as Midsummer drew near. The Oak month, I was sure, would recompense the adverse times that had befallen our tribe in the past.

Each morning Essylt sent me into the glade to replenish her medicines. Near the footpaths in the forest I knew the places where the mandrake grows. Often in the mystic rites the sorcerers concoct drinks of it that can induce visions and magic powers. I loosened the roots with my digging stick and filled my basket with them to use as potions, medicines, pain killers and drafts of sleeping potions. I collected yarrow, chamomile and comfrey, replacing the herbs and simples Essylt needed.

There was so much for me to learn before I left Essylt for the Druid's Isle. I had to learn how to mix concoctions and blend oils for salves, but sometimes I daydreamed over the jars and pots of mixtures and Essylt scolded me. I couldn't tell her I was absorbed in reveries about Teag. I dared not speak of him; it would be improper. As I meandered in the quiet groves picking herbs, I indulged in my youthful fantasies. I imagined Teag as godlike and charming; a champion, a warrior, a benevolent friend. It did not enter my thoughts that my life was predestined. I was blithe and frolicsome as a wood sprite humming tunes as I went about my duties, skipping happily on the forest paths.

I sang a merry tune as I picked the lilac flowers of the vervain. There is magic in the vervain, to ward off evil spirits. We hung it over the lintels of our huts and put some on the shrines to honour the souls of the dead.

In the grove the poplars were whitened by a gust of breeze and a bird's shrill cry disturbed the serenity. A falcon soared across the treetops, circling over the dell below the hillfort. A pair of rock-doves flew up from the copse as the falcon plunged, its wailing *kek-kek-ke-keeya* shrilling like a banshee's scream. It hit the grey dove like an arrow; pale blue feathers drifted like petals over the thicket. The dove's mate cried in alarm and flew into the trees. From somewhere in the shadows I heard a whistle, almost as shrill as the falcon's cry. The bird circled the dell once, then soared down, drifting as easily as a leaf to settle onto the outstretched gauntlet of a man who stood at the edge of the woods.

At first I had not seen him as his moss green tunic and russet breeches concealed him against the trees. The falcon ruffled its feathers and squawked as he stroked it.

"Well done, Corwalch!" the man exclaimed. He strode across the clearing to pick up the fallen dove. The tangle of his raven hair hid his face, but I knew him.

Sholto ap Madoc looked up and saw me. His eyes were as icy blue as a winter's sky. "Here, you! Priestess! Tie these for me." He had a clutch of birds slung from a braid of leather. He tossed them down at my feet and handed me the dove. Its little body was still warm. I set my basket down and tied it with the others.

He watched me with an amused smile. "Are you afraid of blood?"

I looked at my hands. They were sticky with the dove's blood. I remembered the day in the glade when I had killed the rabbit, but I pushed the thought quickly from my mind. Sholto sneered at me. The jagged scar across his cheek made him a fearsome sight. As he stroked the falcon's speckled breast the bird hissed a throaty sound, then stretched its wings and preened.

"You are no swords woman!" Sholto said.

I stood up to him with a proud toss of my head. I didn't like him or his hissing bird but I would not let him see I was afraid. I recalled what Lleu had said to me that day in the Council Hall: *Remember who you are!*

"I serve the Goddess," I replied. "I am Olwen, a Druid's child. Child of the Raven."

"Then you must learn to kill. The Raven is a War Goddess."

He must have seen the look of fright on my face and he began to laugh. I knew if I tried to run from him he would catch me and snap me like a twig. His bird had a beak as sharp as a scythe and talons that could gouge an eye out. I was afraid he would send it flying at me. I began to back away from him, wishing the bowers of the greenwood would swallow me so I could hide from him. I made the sign against the dark powers and began to run. Behind me, I heard him whistle and heard the gusting sound of a bird's wings as the falcon took flight.

That night, as I lay in my bed. I listened to Lleu and Essylt gossip, whispering by the hearth fire.

"Sholto ap Madoc has brought dishonour on the Royal House. He has coveted another man's wife and abused his privilege as a guest-friend betraying his Ordovice host."

They thought I was asleep, but I devoured every word they said with as much relish as I would listen to Lleu's tales of the ancient heroes. They said Sholto ap Madoc had stolen a chieftain's son away from a northern tribe, the Ordovices, where he had been welcomed as a guest-friend and had taken the boy as a hostage. It was a common thing among our tribes to keep another chieftain's child to ensure peace among the clans, but this was the Wolf Clan's favoured heir. The Wolf Clan was a savage tribe who practised the Ancient Mysteries and drank wolves' blood; a fierce clan who hid in the dense northern timberland where they guarded the passes to the sacred White Mountain.

Essylt's voice rang out with indignation. "Sholto also brought with him the wife of a Dobunni chieftain of the Horse Clan. He stole her too, though she seems a willing captor and mark my words, she's a right vixen to be sure!"

I uncovered my head from the sheep skins, the better to hear. It was a tale worthy of a minstrel's ballad.

"Now the hounds are barking at the door," Lleu mused. "The Wolf Clan and the Horse Clan vow to take revenge."

There was a damp chill to the air at night even though summer was near so Lleu threw more peat coals on the fire. He and Essylt clucked like hens around the fire. I wanted to join in but all the talk made me drowsy. So while the peat coals warmed the little hut with nuggets of light, I drifted off to sleep

It was a day when a damp south wind drifted the clouds like thistle-down when I met Teag again near the forest shrine. As we walked into the beech grove among the tumbled leaves and new blue sedge, a pair of jays squabbled over a nut and flew into the trees to scold.

We laughed and talked about our lives. Teag told me tales of travel to distant ports and tribes I never knew existed. He said he had travelled for years to learn the goldsmith's trade, apprenticing with the Masters of Keltic tribes. In Massalia he studied with goldsmiths from across the Blue Sea. He said there was more gold there than anyone had ever seen in Albion. When I asked him where his home was – the tribe he called his people – he told me he was born in the northern lake country, but he had been lured away when he was young by traders who took him across the Narrow Sea.

The beech wood was silent; the wind soughed through the treetops. We walked through the grove to the riverbank, by the edge of the grazing lands, where the willows dipped their boughs into the water and the pools sang with trout.

We stood together at the edge and saw our images reflect and tremble, one image melting into the other, the colours of our forms dappling the surface of the pool. It was cool under the shade of the lacy willow boughs. Teag stood so close to me our bodies touched and I blushed and drew away shyly. There was an awkward silence between us. For a moment I felt a surge of guilt. I was the Druid's child and I was chaste.

I studied the outline of his comely face, his dark straight brows and tawny beard, his eyes, green as moss. When I was with him, I forgot who I was. I was a woman now, not a child; a mortal woman, not the god's child.

"What made you come here to Caer Gwyn?" I asked.

"I can't explain it. Perhaps I'll know in time." He smiled and took my hand.

"Do you believe we can choose our destinies? Or have the gods predestined our lives for us?" I whispered.

"What do you believe?" He looked intently into my eyes.

"I was given to the goddess when I was a babe. My life is a gift from Her. I must serve Her until I die."

"Then, that is your destiny," Teag said.

I felt tears brim in my eyes. I could not tell him after the Midsummer rites I must leave Caer Gwyn. As if to read my thoughts, he said: "Your life is in the Goddess's hands. You cannot choose another destiny. You must be pure and chaste, a sacred vessel for the Earth Mother. You know you can never denounce Her."

Teag took my hands in his. His mouth tasted sweet as berries when he kissed me. We stood in silence, still holding hands, speaking only with our eyes. I looked into his face, his eyes, clear green, shone like jewels. I felt as warmed by him as if he were the sun. I had no desire to waken from that dream. I could not say "This is not right for me".

We were disturbed by the baying of hounds. They came tumbling from the copse, running wildly before the hunter. Even at a distance you could not mistake the mane of tangled black hair as Sholto the Tall whipped his pony to gallop abreast of the dogs.

The hounds scented us and came snarling up with the shaggy cob clamouring behind, and Sholto, red-faced from the chase. He cursed and snapped his whip at them.

"Down Gander, Lud, Samhain! Hush now ye black demon!"

The two pied dogs cowered at his command, but the black cur snarled viciously and bared its yellow teeth. Sholto leapt from his pony and in one quick movement had the hound down by the scruff of its neck. The beast yelped, then lay still. I was sure he had killed it, but in time it limped away and cowered by its mates.

"He's had the smell of blood and needs a whipping to keep him down," Sholto growled.

"Aye, but he's a good dog: a keen hunter, and spirited, to be sure," Teag observed.

"I've trained him from a pup," Sholto said. "Samhain will run a stag until it drops. His scars show how many wild boars he's cornered."

"Was it a good hunt then?" Teag asked.

"Aya!" Sholto shouted to his companions who had come into view. One was a young woman who led a chestnut mare with a deer's carcass slung over its back. I recognized her as the swords woman I had seen with Sholto on the trail.

The younger girl led her horse to the riverbank to drink and stooped to splash water on her face. I knew her to be the Ricon's daughter, Aeron, a graceful maid who often rode beside her brothers in the Royal War Band. She wore a man's short leather tunic and her bare arms and legs were scratched from the thicket branches. The strands of her white-gold hair clung damply on her brow.

"Ah, my lord Teag," she smiled. "Tomorrow, you must join us for the boar hunt." She called over to her companion who had dismounted and was letting her pony graze. "Tallia, this is my lord Teag. He is a guest-friend of my father."

I felt a little stab at the way she smiled at him, her violet eyes shining and her cheeks dimpled. She was a bold girl. She caught Teag by the arm, her eyes devouring him as though he were a battle prize.

"Father says Teag will be the new smith for Caer Gwyn. Is that not so, Teag? What this tuath needs is someone who can craft jewellery as well as weapons."

Teag seemed uneasy. "Your father has been generous to share his bread and board with me but I cannot stay."

"Nonsense! Don't think it, my lord. We'll talk some more in Hall. You'll join us for the feast tonight?"

"'Twill be my pleasure, Lady Aeron," Teag answered graciously.

"You are in the Royal War Band's favour," Sholto winked and smiled at Teag. "But mind that one. She'll trap you as sure as she can snare a fox!" Then he looked at me, curiously as if he hadn't noticed me there before. "The Druid's child, eh? Hadn't ye best be off to tend the shrines?"

"Mind she doesn't cast a spell on you!" laughed the swords woman.

I did not mean to fix a holding spell on her, but I couldn't take my eyes away. She was a huntress queen; a bronze goddess with taut oiled skin and small breasts curved like little cups. She was tall and lithe as a sapling, naked except for the ermine skins draped around her narrow hips.

She saw my dumbstruck stare and her dark eyes narrowed. I saw her make a magic sign, then she turned to Sholto and Teag. "My lord, I am a guest-friend of the ricon too, but I have not til now had the privilege of meeting you. You'll sit beside us at the feast tonight? Perhaps, if you are a master goldsmith, you'll have some wares to show us? Lord Sholto's sister tells me you are from Massalia? My husband, Lord Gwion of the Horse Clan, has bartered with traders from Massalia. I should like to know more of your travels. My lord, Sholto, can we make a place for Teag by our fire tonight?" The smouldering look she gave Sholto was dazzling and persuasive.

Sholto grasped Teag's hand. "We'll dine in brotherhood and peace."

"My pleasure, lord Sholto. Til then, walk in safety."

As we watched them ride away toward the stockade gates, I felt a little tug inside me and did not speak. Teag seemed subdued and thoughtful.

"I don't know what to make of it," he said. "I am just passing through."

There was no use asking if he would stay. He would. I knew in my heart it was his destiny.

The next morning, Madoc sent a herald around the tuath to proclaim Teag was named Master Blacksmith of Caer Gwyn. I drank each word of news about him like sweet cordial. Essylt scolded me for tangling the threads on the loom and rapped my knuckles with the distaff. We were weaving new cloth to make my garments for the journey to the Holy Isle.

"We've only weeks before the midsummer, so there is no time for idleness!" She felt my brow for a fever, thinking it was the ague that made me so dreamy. I insisted it was nothing but tangled the wool on the spindle again. I tried to make excuses for my clumsiness, but it would do no good to lie to her. I could not tell her about my trysts with Teag, although I felt some shame to know I was deceiving her. It did not seem wrong for me to love him. Just as the sweet briers burst into summer blooms, I had grown from child to woman.

I told her I could not concentrate for thinking of the Midsummer rites, but as soon as she was busy with her stew pots, I left the hut and ran straight to my shrine in the greenwood.

Stanza Five:

Lleu sat by the hearthstones, softly strumming his clarsach. His tawny hair was all askew and his grey eye reflected the fire's glow. His voice spiralled and soared like the wood-lark's blending like honey with the harp's song. It brought tears to my eyes to hear him sing.

You are a pure ray of the sun.
You are a white blossom.
You lie in glittering tears among the loveliest flowers.
Your spirit dances in the green fields of Senghenydd.
Where did you come from, little goddess?
Who left you alone on the altar?

The song made me think about my birth mother, and I wept to know her embrace. Sometimes in the quiet greenwood, or in the darkness near the hearth fire of our hut, I imagined I could feel my mother's spirit near, as though she watched me from the Otherworld. I knew nothing of my parents. If I questioned Essylt she would only tell me that my mother had died, and someone, perhaps my father, had left me on the altar at the Standing Stones.

Listening to Lleu sing, I wondered as a child will wonder, and dreamed of Senghenydd's emerald valleys, envisioning a life I had never known with my earthly parents. I wondered who my real parents were. Why had I been left at the Stone Circle? Had I been left there to give me a better life?

In the lamplight the bunches of dried herbs hanging from the roof beams, made intricate shadow patterns on the thatch. The hut smelled of wood smoke and lavender and the mutton stew that boiled in the pot.

Essylt piled more faggots on the fire and stirred the stew with her wooden ladle. Her grey hair was braided in a single plait and she wore a rag tied round her waist like a yeoman's wife. One would wonder at her being a High Priestess, yet there was always an aura around her, as though the Goddess was near.

Our days of sitting together around the fire were nearly over. I could not bear the thought of leaving as I began imagining all the years that would pass before I would tend the shrines at Caer Gwyn again. It seemed as though, in leaving Caer Gwyn, I was giving up my life.

I watched the fire, half hoping for a vision. a young girl's wishful thoughts, hoping my destiny could change. I sipped the tea of rose hips that Essylt brewed for me, and listened to the bard's song, dreaming I was just a village maiden sharing the cup of marriage with my lord Teag.

My dreams were scattered by the sound of hounds baying in the hazel grove outside our hut. Lleu set his harp aside and pulled back the door skins cautiously. It was a late hour for a caller. Essylt made a charmed sign as if sensing something was amiss.

"Who goes?" called Lleu.

"I walk with the gods," replied the intruder. I recognized the harsh tone of the voice, and made a pentacle sign across my heart.

Lleu stepped aside as Bedwyr's dark shadow filled the doorway. The Druid pushed aside the door skins and stepped across the sill, dragging a boy in after him.

"Look, Priestess!" the Druid said to Essylt. "Here's a mystery to untangle. Ye know the dialects of all the clans. See if you can solve this riddle."

He pushed the boy into the firelight. It was the youth I had seen with Sholto the day of Beltane's Fire. He stood speechless and dumbfounded, blinking against the light of our hearth fire. The Druid tore away his ragged jerkin, exposing the youth's pale skin which was patterned with designs of woad. He traced the mysterious patterns with his fingers. "What are these symbols?"

The lad stood silently, his face as blank as if he were both deaf and mute. Essylt took his arm and spoke in a gentle voice. "Who are you? What is your name?"

He stared at her dumbly. Then she repeated her questions using words I recognized as the dialect of the Ordovices, the mountain folk. I knew those guttural sounds. Grandfather had taught me a few words and Lleu had told me stories about their fierce clan. how many of them lived in caves like animals and worshipped gods of the old cults: the gods of thunder and wind.

"What is your name?" Essylt asked again.

The boy's composure changed when he heard the sound of his own dialect. He made a gruff sound. "I am Dafydd, Son of the Wolf"

Essylt repeated the question, slowly and softly. "Who are you?"

He looked back and forth at us like a trapped animal." I am Dafydd, son of Cymbeline. I am Dafydd, Prince of the Wolf Clan."

Essylt held the oil lamp closer and traced her fingers over the boy's tattoos.

"Here is the dragon's sign, the mark of royalty. And here is the mark of the Wolf clan."

The boy pulled away from her and made an angry growl. We had seen enough to know these strange marks were magic charms and tribal totems.

"I know of this Cymbeline," Lleu said. "He's a savage warlord. They sing his tales in Hall up in the north. If this boy is his son, there will be wolf packs howling at our doors as sure as I can swear on the gods of war."

"You must let him go," Essylt said to Bedwyr. "He bears the marks of strong magic. It is foolhardy to hold him. The portents are not good."

"He's Sholto ap Madoc's hostage," Bedwyr said. "He'll not be set free without a price." He slipped a leather noose around the boy's neck so when he tried to struggle it tightened until he nearly choked.

"Let him be!" I cried. Such cruelty seemed unwarranted to me.

The Druid turned a malevolent look on me as he pushed the boy toward the door. "You child, had best prepare yourself for Midsummer instead of mooning by the blacksmith's forge."

I blushed. *Did he know of my secret trysts with Teag?*

Lleu heaved a great sigh as Bedwyr left our hut with the boy. "That charlatan will bring the god's wrath on us with his evil ways," he said. "He conjures the dark powers and it chills my blood to think of what will befall Caer Gwyn."

"Aye," Essylt agreed. "He is a demon. But he is the ricon's seer." She poured some mead in Lleu's cup and some in mine. "Here lass, drink this. You've gone as white as chalk."

"What ails you lass?" Lleu said. He stooped to put his arm around me. I huddled near the peat coals, shivering and near tears.

"She's fretting about Midsummer," Essylt said kindly. But the long, perceptive look she gave me told me she knew more than she would reveal.

BALLAD SIX A Warrior's Song

Listen, O Chieftains of Caer Gwyn,
the wolves of Cymbeline are howling on the Plain.
Take up your bows and cudgels
we will hunt them down.
Call on Morrigan, the Raven Goddess of War.
She will ride with us into battle.

A CRY TO THE GOD OF WAR

Stanza One:

One morning, several days later, a rider brought word that a war party of brigands had been sighted just a few days ride from the borders of our tribal lands. The scout said they carried the banners of the Ordovices' Wolf Clan. There was no doubt they were Cymbeline's men. There were even rumors some of the Dobunni's Horse Clan's chieftains were with them. There was only one reason why Cymbeline's warriors had ventured this far south. They had come to ransom Dafydd, the hostage.

Our ricon, Madoc and his chieftains slaughtered a horse. After the Druid had consumed some of its flesh, they burned it on a pyre of ash bows to honour Morrigan, the Raven Goddess of War. It seemed a simple thing to settle. Madoc would council with the rival chieftains, the hostage would be released, and Tallia, the guest-friend of Sholto would be returned to her husband's tuath.

The Royal War Band was armed and ready, raving for a battle at any cost. There was a cry for blood from young blackguards who wanted to take more heads. The warriors of Caer Gwyn, who for so long had been content with border skirmishes and cattle raids, were thrilled at the opportunity to show their might as a fighting horde.

The War Band cried through the village for men to join them. Freemen, young and old, were willing to take up bows or cudgels for their ricon. Swords, rusting from lack of use, were polished and honed sharp; bows restrung, and weapons fashioned out of anything that could be used. Even the women armed themselves and young girls parried with swords in the marketplace. The scent of blood had set all the tuath howling like a pack of boar hounds on a chase.

It frightened me to hear them. I thought of the portents Grandfather had divined in the stars, and the Dragon's Fire I had seen falling from the sky the day he lay dying.

That night the moon was as red as a carnelian, an adverse omen. Daily, the tales about Sholto the Tall flowered like a bed of nettles. The gossips said he had left a maiden in the north who was with child by him. The boy, Dafydd, who Sholto had taken as hostage when he had left the Wolf Clan's camp, was said to be her brother. Now the Wolf Clan wanted revenge.

While passing through the Horse Clan's lands Sholto had consorted with the chieftain's wife, Tallia, who had followed him willingly. Our Chieftains could take as many wives as was the custom, but to covet a woman already bound by the cup of marriage was to dishonour her husband. Gwion, the ricon of the Horse Clan, meant to avenge it.

Despite the unsettling talk, I saw Tallia ride out with Sholto, proud as a queen on her dappled pony, her black hair crowned with hawk feathers, her body oiled and bronze. Everywhere they went, Sholto's sister, Aeron, was close behind.

In the past most of the War Band hated Sholto. He was an ambitious, insolent ruffian who would kill his own kin without any conscience and could not be trusted. Now it seemed some of them listened to his crowing when he bragged he would win them favour if they fought the rival tribes. The War Band was divided. Young Ned shadowed his father. Whatever Madoc ordered he would do. Madoc's other son, Hywel, kept silent. He was the Clan's favourite, their champion, and if he voted against warring, they would support him.

Essylt was worried by the talk. "Our people will pay the price if the hostage boy is harmed. He has the death sign on him."

Lleu shook his head gravely in reply. "Madoc is asking for a ransom. Bedwyr advised him thus. Mark my words, he's plotting with the ricon. There's surely treachery afoot."

It worried me what might become of our tuath if the other clans invaded us. I could only hope a peaceful solution would be found.

Stanza Two:

Each night we were kept awake by the din of mallets clanging on the blacksmith's forge. Madoc had ordered new weapons for his warriors. Teag was burdened with so much work I scarcely saw him during those days. But in spite of the Druid's cryptic warning, I could no longer keep away.

One morning as I passed by the smithy on my way to the grove to gather herbs, I saw the smith's boy, Galen, sitting on a stool beside the door. He was polishing newly forged sword blades. He looked at me with reddened eyes and a smug grin. "Master has no time for you. He's worked all night, see? Come back another time."

Galen rankled me. He was a lad with little manners and I found him brash and uncouth. It was difficult to keep a civil tongue with Galen. He always had a surly way with me. Perhaps he was afraid, because I had cursed him.

"I'm bringing potions and salves for Teag," I lied.

Galen glared at me suspiciously, then shrugged and moved aside to let me pass. As I went inside the darkened shed, he muttered an oath behind my back.

The fire was dying in the forge. Bran, the little bellows boy was asleep beside it, the bellows still in his hands. Poor lad, it was a miserable life for him. He was a child, but had no time for play. I counted my own self fortunate.

Teag was asleep in the back of the shed on a bed of furs. He hadn't even taken time to remove his leather apron or wash the soot from his face and hands. I felt a tug of remorse as I looked at him and meant to leave without wakening him. But just then there was a clatter of wagons outside the shed.

I shrank back into the shadows and willed myself to vanish, but it was too late. Sholto ap Madoc's gruff voice called out, asking for Teag. He swaggered into the doorway, his rough greeting waking the bellows boy who cowered with fright. I was certain he had seen me too, but he glanced past me quickly as though I were invisible.

Teag sat up rubbing the sleep from his eyes.

"We've come on the ricon's business," Sholto said. "See to it, will you smith? There's little time to waste."

His brother, the young prince, Hywel, and Galen struggled into the smithy, their arms heaped with old weapons and broken harnesses. Galen was red-faced and blustered, "This is more work than we can do!"

Teag ignored his protests and inspected everything as they set down their loads. "We'll do our best, that's all. You'll be a rich man in a fortnight, lad, and soon you'll be a master smith yourself when all is done." He set young Bran to work pouring the moulds and mending old trappings. "You and I can do the rest. You'll have an extra ration of ale when it's done."

Teag had not noticed me until then, but Hywel saw me hiding in the shadows. "Here now, what's this? You have a lass tending the forge?" There was mischief in his words. I wished I could sprout wings and fly away.

"She's the medicine woman, here with her salves and potions," smirked Galen. "Or are ye here on Druid's business, young witch?"

"Druid's business? Have you brought news from Hall then?" asked Hywel.

I stammered something to them about the omens – the blood on the face of the moon – and spoke of sacrifices to Morrigan. It was the kind of talk that stirred their hearts. All warriors like to honour our goddess of war, and they made the mystic signs as I spoke. Then, sweetly as I could, I offered Teag the potions and salves I had in my basket: concoctions of yarrow for healing wounds, bittersweet for compresses and salve of nard to sooth burned skin. Then I passed a little flask of juniper wine around. Teag drank it with a knowing wink at me, but Galen refused, as though he was suspicious I might have poisoned it with hemlock.

"Aye, death to the brigands!" shouted Sholto and raised his fist crying a war paean.

"Spill the dregs for Morrigan, little priestess," laughed Hywel.

The two brothers stood side by side: tall, arrogant Sholto, as wild and rough as a stallion and slender, graceful Hywel, a merry, gentle lad too beautiful to be a warrior.

As I poured the dregs in an offering to the gods, I felt a sudden chill creep up my spine. I remembered the Dragon's Fire, how Grandfather had said it could bode ill will.

Hywel's solemn grey eyes met my gaze steadily as I tipped the dregs in the god's honour. I wondered if he had felt the passing spirit as I had. I had sensed Death's presence there, just as I had the day Grandfather died.

BALLAD SEVEN A Paean For The War Band

> *Hear, O men of Caer Gwyn!*
> *The sons of Madoc will ride forth:*
> *Hywel, the favoured one, and Ned*
> *the Son of the Fox.*
> *They bear the ash bows as homage to Odin.*
> *They will counsel in peace*
> *with the wolves of Cymbeline.*
> *Hear, O bards of Caer Gwyn!*
> *Sing praises to our Princes.*
> *Honour the sons of the Raven Clan.*

A SONG OF WAR

Stanza One:

The freemen gathered on the trails to cheer and praise their hero warriors. Bards sang ballads telling the tales of their bravery. Essylt and I gave them talismans to bless their journey, and the Druid cut the ash boughs in honour of the God.

Their wicker chariots were decked with garlands magical rowan berries, and skulls, the shaggy ponies handsome with new polished trappings. The ricon's sons wore capes of red, their bronze helms gleaming in the sun. Hywel, flushed and beautiful astride his chariot, held up his sword to salute the crowd. Women wept as he passed by and threw flowers in his path. I watched him go, and made the signs for peace. Tears filled my eyes too.

Young Ned, insolent and cocksure, raised his sword and cried the war paean. The village youths envied him and wagered on how many heads he would take.

Sholto the Tall and his swords woman were absent from the ranks that day, but Aeron, dressed in bright blue with the raven crest on her shield, rode her dappled cob beside her brothers' chariots. She wore no helm; her white-gold hair was coiled and plaited. She made a pretty show, with a charming smile for all the village folk. She led the war chant as they reached the gates, then spurred her pony to ride ahead, leading them out across the Plain.

Stanza Two

I had not been to the cattle sheds since the day of Beltane, until one morning Essylt sent me with a basket of honey cakes for Tog, who tended the sacred cattle used for sacrifices.

Tog was squatting by the fire outside of the cattle shed stirring porridge in an iron pot. "What brings you out before the larks have sung?"

"I've come to see the new calves," I said.

He offered me a place to sit beside the fire. "Barley porridge," he said. "Share some with me, lass!" He scooped some of the steaming porridge into a wooden bowl and handed it to me. "Ye're thin as a rail and need to eat!"

We shared some together and then he offered me a honey cake.

"I have two new calves to tend," he said. "I wish ye could help tend them, but the Druid has sent a new lad to work in the stables with the Holy herd. A wild young colt he is, but I'll have him tamed in no time." He licked the honey from his fingers and patted his stout belly with a satisfied grin. "Come along! I'll show ye!"

I followed him into the stable. The shed was shadowy and damp. The empty stall where once my bull had been kept seemed so forlorn. Withered garlands still hung along the rafters where I had strung them. Where Mithras had fed on heaps of hay, there was a straw bed with a coverlet of wool.

'Ye've a good hand with animals," Tog said. "The new lad's not the help you were."

He lifted the bales and sacks of feed as easily as if they were feathers. There was no better steward than Tog, no man in the tuath whose heart was full of such goodwill. I watched him go about his chores and felt an ache as I remembered the times I had spent with him tending my bull.

"The new lad is hardy, mind, and shows some knack with animals. But he's vicious as a badger, a right young cur he is and fearless as a wild creature. The deer hounds eat from his hand. Even Samhain, that mean cur of Sholto's."

"Who is he then?" I asked. "Is he some kennel slave of Madoc's?"

Tog spat and scratched his tangled russet hair. "He's off with young Ned to trim the pony's hooves and harness them. Since the Royal War Band is riding to council with the Wolf Clan there's plenty of work for him in the stables. He's a bother to me, see? He must be tethered every night or come the morning he'd be gone. Then I'd have to answer to Sholto as well as the Druid." Tog leaned close to my ear, his gruff voice hardly more than a whisper. "'Tis the hostage lad. They've ordered he be kept here with the sacred beasts. So please the gods, I know not why, except he's like a demon and Madoc feared he'd put a curse on them. Truthfully, I fear the Druid is in this for his own evil intents."

"The boy is marked with the dragon's sign and other magic symbols to protect him," I said. "'Twould be best if they set him free." I told him how the Druid had brought the youth to Essylt. "He's Cymbeline's son. The son of the Wolf."

"I can't make out his gibberish," Tog shrugged. "He babbles in that northern tongue. The mountain men are savages and their habits are like beasts. I feed him the same as I would feed the deer hounds. He eats raw meat like a wolf. I keep him busy with work and see he's safe here in the night. If he breaks loose and runs away, I'll lose my hide, or worse!"

"Let me talk to him, Tog," I begged. "I know some of the northern dialect. I can understand enough to see if there is something he can tell us, some message he might send Cymbeline to stop the clans from fighting."

Tog looked aghast at me and shook his head. "Ye'd best not meddle in this, lass."

I coaxed him. He was always soft hearted with me, and finally he agreed

"Can ye tame the wild beast then?" he teased.

"He'll be gentle as a lamb with me. I give you my word."

"Will ye swear to keep your visits secret?"

I made a sign across my heart and swore an oath.

Tog led me to the back of the stable. The boy, Dafydd, was crouched in the corner of a cattle stall, blinking wide-eyed like a cornered animal. As I approached him, I took a sprig of vervain from my amulet bag, drew a sign with it, then tossed it at his feet. It was good magic. He snatched it up, his eyes cold as granite and expressionless. I felt my heartbeats quicken as my eyes caught his. The spell held so long it seemed as though even our breaths ceased.

There was a chalk-dust circle drawn around the perimeter of the stall where the boy slept, meant to keep out evil spirits. The Raven of Death could not enter it, neither could any mortal who dared to come to mock and abuse him. To the people of our tuath, the boy was merely a savage beast. In truth, it was because his ways were different from ours. They feared what they did not understand.

I stepped inside the circle unafraid. I did not take my eyes away from the boy's remembering all I knew of wild creatures. Even when he grasped my wrist so viciously it almost made me cry with pain, I did not flinch.

"I will try to help you," I said.

His vice-like grip began to slacken. "I am a son of the Wolf," he said.

"I am a daughter of the Raven, a Druid's child," I replied.

The fierce scowl on his face softened and his eyes lightened hopefully.

"You speak to me?"

"My grandfather's tribe was from Senghenydd," I said. "I learned your tongue from him. Tell me about the Holy Mountain and your tuath. Tell me about your father, Cymbeline the Wolf."

He leaned close and haltingly related the tale of how he had become Sholto ap Madoc's prisoner.

"Sholto was taken in a raid of brigands by the Wolf clan, but my father, Cymbeline treated him as a guest-friend." There was a bitter tone to his voice: "The cur defiled my sister. Then, knowing my father would kill him for it, he took me along as his hostage and fled. We are the Wolf clan, the hunters. My father will track this wild dog and kill him. My clan will make a sacrifice to Cerridwen, the Wolf-goddess. She will free me!" He spoke of Sholto with such anger it sent a prickling up my spine.

I told him how his clan was gathering on the plain near our tribe's borders. He began to smile and the hopelessness lifted from him; his eyes burned feverishly in his wan face. He showed me the blue woad tattoos that were his tribal marks; the wolf sign and the hunter's marks: the boar, the ram and eagle and the dragon, a mark of a king's son.

"Anyone who harms me will be cursed," he said. He told me tales of Cerridwen, the Wolf-goddess, an ancient cult, and how they drank wolf's blood and sacrificed at the full moon. "Our kings are chosen for their wiliness and bravery." he said.

We talked until the wicks sputtered in the oil lamps. Finally, Tog came, grumbling that I should be on my way.

"Ye'll be the death of me if Bedwyr finds you here," he said nervously. "Keep silent, lass, and mind as you go. Walk with the gods, go in safety."

I bade them the Earth Mother's blessings and set out on my way. Dafydd had enchanted me with his strange tales. Somehow, I felt kin to him.

Stanza Three:

The next morning, with dawn bright in the sky, I ventured past the smithy. When I saw the Royal War Band's ponies tethered there a feeling of foreboding came over me. I wished I had not come that way, yet still I was drawn to go inside.

Teag greeted me when I entered the smithy. I hesitated, seeing Aeron and the Dobunni swords woman, Tallia. She had a weapon in her hand, a long sword with a golden hilt fashioned of two stags' heads; the slender iron blade was patterned with foliated vines that coiled down the shaft. She thrust and parried as skilfully as a warrior, using the sword as though it were a willow bough, moving around the smith's shed gracefully, her long legs lithe and nimble as a dancer's.

Aeron laughed. "You're the queen of swords women, Tallia!"

Sholto the Tall stood by observing them, his arms folded across his chest. He bragged, "She'll meet any challenger! She's a brave lass, braver than most men. "'Tis a fine weapon, smith. I've never seen another better. It suits my lady."

"The sword will be a betrothal gift for Tallia," Aeron said. "We'll barter for some jewellery too, Teag," The way she spoke to Teag, and looked at him with limpid eyes, made me feel a surge of something I had never felt before.

"Those gold bracelets and rings with jet stone. My brother, Sholto, will pay a good price for those treasures. Anything you ask for shall be yours." She tossed back her checkered cape and stood with feet astride, hands on her hips. Her white tunic seemed as sheer as gossamer, showing the nakedness of ivory skin beneath it. Even her legs were bare, with sandal straps of leather laced up to her knees. I blushed to see such a bold display.

Aeron laughed, and watched Teag as a cat might watch a mouse. Then she moved closer, touched his arm, and smiled. "You're in my father's favour, Teag. There's profit in this for you."

Teag did not seem to notice when I turned away and left the smithy.

Galen snickered as I passed him on the pathway. "My master is the War Band's favourite now," he grinned mockingly. "You'd best not trouble him. Tend to the Druid's business."

That night I waited in my covert beneath the junipers on the ridge, but Teag did not come to join me. As I started down the trail, I heard laughter and saw two people walking arm in arm through the moonlit glade. The girl's pale hair shone like white gold in the moonlight. I knew at once it was Aeron walking with Teag. I watched them go up toward the hill fort trail. Willing myself to be invisible, I trailed them like a shadow through the trees. Then, cursing myself for my mortal foolishness, I raced away to hide inside the sanctuary of the stone circle, and wept as I watched Latona the moon.

That night I listened solemnly while Essylt and Lleu chatted near the hearth fire. I drank in the tales they told like potions, to soothe the ache I felt inside. I could not tell them what was troubling me, that a pain stabbed my heart each time I thought of Teag and the ricon's daughter. They thought it was the talk of war that had worried me. When Essylt saw I was crying, she fussed over me and wiped my tears away.

Lleu pulled his stool up beside me and put his harp across his knees.

"We'll sing some songs, lass," he said. Then he sang some cheerful ballads while Essylt poured bowls of steaming stew made fresh that day from wild hare and succulent meadow greens. I tasted it, but could not eat. Even Lleu's ballads could not comfort me. That night I cried myself to sleep.

The next morning dawned bright with promise. The air was fresh with the sweet fragrances of meadow grass and fallow earth and a gentle breeze ruffled the roof thatches. I lingered awhile outside the smith's shed, rehearsing what I might say to Teag. When I looked inside, the smithy seemed empty, so I crept inside silently lest Teag was asleep and I waken him.

To my surprise, he was sitting at his workbench in the corner, tooling a piece of copper. When my shadow crossed the patch of sunlight streaming in the doorway, he looked up with a startled expression. I spoke to him in jest, some girlish insolence, the way friends talk in private. He seemed displeased at my intrusion and frowned, then went back to his work.

From the shadows where the rafters hung with skins and harnesses, I heard another voice, one I knew. Aeron stepped out from behind the tapestry of Teag's sleeping alcove. She seemed as surprised to see me as Teag had been, and her manner was discourteous. She was dressed only in a doeskin loincloth with a tasselled fringe of beads. Her naked body was like an ivory statue, smooth and contoured to perfection. Her long fine hair hung loose and spilled in a shining wave over her bare shoulders.

Teag hardly glanced at either of us. She came to stand by him and pressed close against him shamelessly.

I felt a knot in my innards, like someone's fist had struck me. Without a word, lest tears should choke my voice, I ran out of the smithy.

Teag called after me, but I did not stop. He came after me and stopped me on the trail. I could not look at him. He cupped my chin and lifted my face up to his. There was an anguished look in his eyes.

"I've wronged you, little spirit. I do adore you. But it's Aeron I love."

I began to cry, angry I had allowed myself to be bewitched by him as if he was godlike. Now, in the brightness of the sunshine I saw him for what he was – a mortal man: an earthling as rough-hewn as the rest of the men in our tuath. I could not bear him to be so mortal.

"What will you do now?" he asked. "What have I done to hurt you, dear Olwen?" He looked pale and afraid, as though he knew my thoughts and was afraid I might cast a spell on him. I walked away from him proudly, but I felt cold and lifeless, like a leaf torn from a bough by a winter storm. I kept repeating to myself: *I am Olwen, Child of the hawthorn. I am the fairest flower. I am the Goddess's chosen one.*

I did not look back but ran straight to our hut.

"What is it, child? What ails you?" Essylt asked when she saw me. "You're pale as though you've seen the ghosts of the old ones."

I stared at her blankly, as dumbstruck as if I'd lost all sense. My mind was on the one thing that I could not divulge to her. To tell her the truth, to admit my indiscretions, would be a disgrace.

"Olwen you're trembling. What's wrong, dear child?" she urged.

I retched and heaved as though it were an ague. She brought cold cloths for my forehead and mixed a cordial of herbs. Then she wrapped me in her cloak and held me like a babe. I began to sob, and could not be consoled. Nor could I explain to her what had put me into such despair. The nightmare I had dreamed, the vision in the Beltane's Fire: the girl caught, pursued and dead. It now seemed true. There was no choice for me. If I did not die by my own hand, then the gods would see to my punishment. I could not hide from them.

I wept 'til I fell asleep, wakening when Lleu came into the hut to fetch Essylt.

"What ails Olwen"" he asked when he saw me.

Essylt shook her head. "It puzzles me," Essylt replied quietly. "She has no fever, yet she's beset by some strange ague. Poor child can barely speak and cried herself to sleep. What could have frightened her?"

"Could be an ill-starred omen," Lleu said soberly. "There's a dark cloud on the house of Madoc. Some poor wretch rode into Hall this morning. There's been a border skirmish. He escaped, but bore the bloody remnants of the Royal War Band's pennant. The Wolves of Cymbeline ambushed our men. There is death in the stars just as Maelgwyn predicted."

BALLAD EIGHT The Ballad Of Cymbeline

The Raven of Caer Gwyn is bloodstained.
Listen to her cry.
The Raven of Caer Gwyn is stained crimson
with the blood of her warriors.
Listen to her shrieks.
The Wolves of Cymbeline have swallowed
their gory drink.
The blood of Caer Gwyn's fairest warrior
is on their hands.

A CRY FOR REVENGE

Stanza One

The God speaks and says: *I am the Wolf who lives in a cave. I am the she-wolf who howls at the moon. I am Cerridwen, the Wolf-goddess; totem of my clan. The clan of the Wolf and the clan of the Raven will not council in friendship.*

Cymbeline speaks and says:_*We have eaten the flesh of the Raven. We have sacrificed to Cerridwen, the She-Wolf.*

The news swept through our tuath like the moaning of a death knell. Madoc's Royal War Band, riding in good faith to council with the rival chiefs, had been ambushed. As the cry went out, the clan began to gather at the hill-fort to hear the ominous tidings.

Lleu took his harp to sing laments in the Hall. Essylt hurried to the Druid's lodge to read the auguries. I huddled in my wolf skins near the smouldering fire pit in our hut, feeling numb, as though the life had drained from me.

By evening the wails and cries from the hill fort of Caer Gwyn echoed throughout the tuath. I roused myself, took the emerald cloak from the oak chest, and dressed in my ceremonial tunic of white linen. My fingers trembled as I fastened the clasp of the cloak – a sickle moon and golden star, the Druid's symbol. I knew I must join Essylt and assist her with the auguries.

I stumbled along the path following the laments of the mourners. The dirge grew louder as I neared the Druid's lodge. The freemen of Caer Gwyn were pressed around the entrance, some of them brandishing swords and crying the war paean. Others had torn their clothing and streaked their faces with ashes. They keened and wailed, calling on all the gods.

A cry came from the gates of the stockade. "The War Band has returned!" The freemen trampled each other in their haste. I followed them to the postern gate.

When the Royal War Band came straggling through the gates, the hysterical crowd grew silent. Young Ned was the first to enter. His face was bloodied, his tunic torn and soiled with grime. He stood astride his wicker war chariot and waved a clenched fist at the throng as he screamed the war cry. This put the freemen into a frenzy again. All of the chariots of Agrona, Goddess of War and Slaughter thundering across the sky could not drown out their cries.

The warrior chiefs and young men of the Royal War Band rode their ponies close behind Ned's chariot. Some were wounded, others pale-faced and mute. All bore testimony to that tragic day. Two score of Caer Gwyn's finest knights had ridden out to council with Cymbeline's Wolf Pack. Not more than half of them returned.

I heard a wail like a banshee's shriek, a terrible scream. A raven's cry!

I hear the Raven of War tonight: loud is her scream.
I hear the Raven of Death tonight: a heavy grief is on me.

Behind the warriors two stocky oxen pulled a groaning wain. It carried a bier bearing a shrouded body. The sobbing subsided into shocked silence as Ned dismounted from his chariot and strode along the ranks of men and stopped at the cart. He bowed his head for a moment in homage, then raised his sword and cried: "Death to the Wolf Clan! Death to the Wolves of Cymbeline! The Raven Clan will avenge this day!"

He pulled away the shroud to bare the corpse. It was his brother, Hywel.

I gasped and ran ahead to stand by Essylt. A woman screamed and fainted. Even the men began to weep. The Hope of Caer Gwyn lay dead on the bier. Dear Hywel, the bright Morning Star, the gentle youth who had made a pledge for peace and met with death instead. His beautiful face was pallid as tallow, his corn-gold hair matted with blood. They had wrapped him in his crimson cape and folded his hands across his chest with the bronze winged helm tucked under his arm. His sword and shield were at his feet.

I made myself stand straight, my chin held high. As I stood in shocked silence, I murmured a prayer and bit my lips to keep from weeping. I watched, feeling deep sorrow as men grasped the hem of Hywel's tunic and kissed it reverently, their faces wet with tears. Some impulse prompted me to take two of the gold coins from my amulet bag – those talismans Teag had given me which were engraved with a god-like man. It seemed Hywel was meant to have them for his journey to the Otherworld, a tribute to ensure his safe passage to Annwyn. I placed one over each of his closed eyes, then made the five-cornered star on his pale forehead with some of his own blood. I wept for him, for his noble purpose, and for the fate of us all.

Essylt raised her arms and cried out to the crowd. When she spoke, everyone fell silent.

"Listen to me! Peace must come to our land so we can dwell together side by side. I pray to the gods for such peace otherwise our world will fade into the mists of time and the gods and the Holy Mysteries will be forgotten!"

A silence followed. Then the men raised their fists and bellowed a war cry. "Death to the Dobunni! Death to the Ordovices!"

My heart leapt in my throat as I looked up to see the dark, ominous figure of Bedwyr standing by the bier. In one hand he held a white dove, in the other a ceremonial dagger. "Essyltyr, we must avenge our prince's death!" he cried. "We will spill this dove's blood and let it mingle with Hywel's so his soul may fly quickly to the Otherworld".

I saw the flash of the knife blade and the flattering of the bird's wings, then it lay still and Bedwyr placed in on Hywel's breast.

His shrill voice pierced the silence: "Death to the Dobunnis and the Ordovices! We will avenge Hywel ap Madoc's killing"

A silence followed, then the men raised their fists and bellowed a war cry.

As I listened, a cold chill came over me. What would happen to my people, our tuath, if these rabid warriors carried out their revenge?

Then Lleu plucked a string of his clarsach. The note reverberated sweetly calming the crowd's angry voices.

"Let me sing a lament for our ricon's favorite son, brave Hywel ap Madoc and how he won his honour-prize."

The angry voices stilled as the bard's words recalled their hero.

The men of Caer Gwyn rode out with the dawn;
swift were their ponies and glad was their war-cry.
The men of Caer Gwyn drank sweet yellow mead
and raised their swords to honour our war god.
As they spilled the dregs for the gods,
so they would spill their blood.
The men of Caer Gwyn will be honoured
as long as there is a minstrel to sing their song.
The War Band of Caer Gwyn rode out together;
they were the ricon's sons and fearless knights
of Madoc's Council Hall.
The War Band of Caer Gwyn raised their war cry;
short were their lives.
They would sooner the wolves had their flesh
than return to Hall without honour.
The War Band of Caer Gwyn will be honoured
as long as there is a bard to tell their story.
The warriors of Caer Gwyn feasted together;
they drank honey mead and supped together.

Two score of them raised their swords
in homage to Morrigan, the Raven Goddess of War.
The warriors of Caer Gwyn fought their foes.
Bright were their helms; keen were their lances.
Their swords were red with blood.
The warriors of Caer Gwyn
charged forward among broken shields;
they attacked together.
Although they were slain, they slew;
short were their lives.
Brave were their feats.
The Warriors of Caer Gwyn will be mourned
as long as there is a chieftain to chant the paean.
Weep, ye people of Caer Gwyn.
Weep ye maidens and widows and freemen.
Weep for your sons, your brothers and husbands.
For the brave warriors of Caer Gwyn will not
return to their Council Hall.
Mourn, ye people of Caer Gwyn
for your Hope is slain at the altar of the She-Wolf.
Weep for Hywel, your bright Morning Star,
for he has fallen by the sword-blade.
Weep for Hywel of the pure heart,
noble Hywel, who lies in his resting place
while Caer Gwyn mourns.
Weep ye people of Caer Gwyn.
Hywel the Morning Star will be mourned
as long as there is a bard to sing his lament.

Stanza Two

Listen to the gods speak: *Hywel, your fairest son, has been cut down and slain. Woe to those who have pierced him!*

Seven days of mourning were declared for Hywel. Those days are vague to me now, as though I had sipped the poppy tea and was in a dream-trance. In telling it, I am confused with details, though the words of Lleu's funeral lament have never left me.

He sang the song in Hall on the first day of mourning when the Druids had called a Council to determine the fate of our tuath.

It was a time of solemn decisions and sorcery. All the seers: ovates, priest-esses and acolytes, even the elder priests from the Great Sun Temple, would meet to invoke the gods and hear the prophecies. The fate of Caer Gwyn was in the hands of the Druids. If the auguries foretold we should make war, then we must follow the gods' will. If the divinations were for peace, we would obey in spite of the Royal War Band's cries for vengeance.

I tarried as long as I dared as I prepared for the Council. Essylt was impatient and scolded me as she laid out my ceremonial clothes. The turmoil that I felt provoked a stubborn streak in me and I refused to dress, rejecting the garment she lay out for me. I chose instead to dress in simple homespun and leather breeches rather than the white sagum and emerald cape of an acolyte.

Essylt reminded me: "You are the Goddess's child, not a herd-girl."

When I saw how regal she looked in her polished bronze helm and the garments she wore only for the Mysteries, I felt in awe of her. Essylt had served the gods for forty years and I wondered what it would be like for myself – to know no other life than to be the servant of the gods.

I did not need to look into her bronze mirror to know how dreadful I must appear. My pale face was smudged with mourner's ashes; my eyes swollen from weeping. Essylt's scolding prompted me to tears again and she drew me to her bosom, and crooned to me.

Stanza Three:

It seemed almost like a festive day with the freemen jostling for a better look at us as we walked through the village on our way to the Council Hall.

I caught a glimpse of Galen, the smith's boy, as he pressed forward and stood near the path. He glared at me with his all-knowing sneer. His sallow face smudged with soot, he had a defiant look in his narrowed eyes.

My heart quickened at the sight of him. I looked around, hoping for a glimpse of Teag, but the throng surged around us and I could only feel Galen's evil stare burning into my back, as though he meant to cast a spell on me. I kept close to Essylt, holding on to the edge of her cloak, protected from the presence of the dark powers that pervaded our tuath.

The day was bright with sunshine and the Council Hall did not seem so gloomy. Sunbeams streamed through the roof vents making crisscross patterns of light on the reed-strewn floor. The ring of posts with the skeleton heads, was hidden in the shadows. Although it was near the time of midsummer, a fire burned in the central hearth. The elder priests were placed in seats of honour around it, squatting on their heels or lounging on heaps of animal skins. All of them were dressed in white robes with collars of hammered gold. The bards sat among them with their clarsachs ready to sing the laments and record the day's stories in verse. Lleu wore his finest blue sagum, and sat in an honoured place next to the ricon's men. The young ovates from the Sun Temple carried branches of vervain and wore myrtle in their hair. They formed a circle around the Druids while the priestesses hovered in the background.

A priestess of the cult of Diva, Spirit of Rivers, had come out of the forest with her novices – little girls, some hardly past five summers old. The acolytes from the Sun Temple and the Moon Maidens were girls my own age. We would bed together at the midsummer rites, so we studied each other solemnly and curiously as we sat together on the white bull hides. Another time I would have talked to them, but this was such a joyless occasion we didn't even exchange smiles.

The priestesses took their places around the altar in the centre of the Circle. Essylt was resplendent in her rich robes, the crescents sparkling in an aura of purple and silver as the sunlight caught them.

The Hall was stifling from the fire. The scent of myrtle oil and musk gave the air a headiness. The children of Diva's cult began to fidget and complain. They wore rabbit skins and the flowers in their hair had wilted in the heat. Their priestess scolded them and one small girl began to cry. It brought to mind the times I had sat in Hall with Essylt when I was not much more than this child's age. Those happy days of innocence, even the times of small discomforts, had passed me by, and now I longed for them again. I held out my hand to the child, drawing her close so she could sit by me. She peered up at me blinking round blue eyes, her freckled cheeks wet with tears. She was a little tow-headed girl hardly more than a babe. I wanted to ask her name, but just then the bard announced the entrance of the Druid and the ricon.

Madoc stumbled as he walked into the circle. One might have thought he had partaken of too much mead, but I knew he was grieving. His hand trembled when he made the sign of peace. No matter how heroic and rough this man was, he was not afraid to show his sorrow. It made me feel sad again, to think of young Hywel, dead upon his bier.

Bedwyr, the Druid, swept arrogantly by the other priests and took his place beside the ricon. He made a show as if he were the Arch Druid not just the king's seer. He postured like an exalted noble, and primped like some court dandy. He had even worn a crown of oak leaves and a garment of fine linen worked with gilt edgings. It seemed an unfit costume for a burial rite. He was dressed more for a king's banquet.

There was furtive whispering when he took his place beside the altar. Many of the Druids watched with silent reproach, without giving him their greeting. Bedwyr drew a short sword from his belt, pointed it toward the four corners of the Hall, and proclaimed: "We meet in peace"

The other Druids repeated his words. "We meet in peace! Let the Council begin."

Bedwyr said: "The voice of our warriors is the cry of the Raven. And who but the Raven of War and the Raven of Death can free our sons from the tomb! Let us sacrifice a white dove for peace."

An acolyte brought the bronze libation dish and placed it on the altar stone to catch the blood of the offering. The Druids began to whisper solemnly among themselves.

Bedwyr's words silenced them. "Hywel, your fairest son, has been cut down and slain. Woe to those who have slain him! The voice of our warriors is the cry of the Raven. And only the Raven of War and the Raven of Death can free our sons from the tomb. Let us sacrifice to Morrigan, our Raven goddess of war!" He beckoned to one of his acolytes who came forward carrying a small black dog in his arms.

The clansmen raised their fists and bellowed a war cry as Bedwyr laid the animal on the alter stone. The chanting of the invocations began, the silver dagger flashed in Bedwyr's hand.

I watched dispassionately as the offering was made. I saw Bedwyr raise his sacrificial knife and heard the pup whimper and saw it tremble as Bedwyr slit its throat. Diva's child began to tremble and hid her face in my lap, sobbing just as I had the first time I saw blood spilled for a sacrifice.

Madoc's resonant voice broke the stillness. "Cold is my heart with pain and sorrow for the death of my son! Woe to us, for we have been besieged by the Wolves of Cymbeline. Woe to me, oh men of Caer Gwyn, for disaster has fallen on my House. Hywel pledged to council in peace but the Wolves of Cymbeline drank his blood." Madoc wiped the tears from his eyes. His hand was on his sword hilt as he tore at his leather jerkin and bared his chest so all of us could see where he had gashed himself in his grief. The children gasped in horror to see Madoc's hairy chest caked with the blood of his wounds. Some of the priests began to mutter.

"I have anger in my heart for this foul deed." Madoc cried. "I curse the Wolves of Cymbeline, and I have asked the gods for a sign. Grieve with me, Oh men of Caer Gwyn, for our Hywel who was slain by these wild mountain beasts. We have lost our Hope, our bright Morning Star, our prince. Lament with me, O Druids and men of Caer Gwyn. Invoke the gods and help me avenge my son's death." He pointed to the Druids. "See here, ye spokesmen of the gods," he pleaded. "Do not forget this day of mourning. Hwyel's life must be avenged. He was our pride. Yet those cunning wolves lay in wait for him and killed him ere he'd drawn his sword or announced his purpose – to council with them in peace. In the prime of his youth he was slain by his enemies." His deep voice broke with emotion and he staggered as though a dizzy spell had overcome him. "Now my tears flow, and I have gashed myself so that my blood flows for him. Honour him, O men of Caer Gwyn! Our beloved prince is dead. We must take the head of a Wolf for revenge!" His squire helped him to his seat on the stag hides beside the elder priests and handed him a goblet containing a potion. Madoc drank it quickly. Clearly, he was a broken man.

Bedwyr stood near the altar, eyes closed, his hands raised above his head. When the Hall quietened, he raised his shrill voice invoking the gods and the spirits of the dead. The Hall was still; the shadows lengthened, and a chill draft caught the embers of the hearth fire sending a veil of pale grey smoke swirling up to the roof vents. The hollow eyes of the warrior's skulls peered down. My spine prickled. The ghosts of the Old Ones were there. Perhaps it was their breath that had stirred the fire embers.

An old Druid from the Sun Temple stood to make his petition. He was frail and grey, as wizened as dried fruit. "I say we must council in peace," he said. "Vengeance will only reap more vengeance."

"I say we sacrifice for the Oak God!" called out one of the younger seers. "As they have slain our brave prince, so shall we slay theirs!"

The old Druid stood firm, shaking his bony finger at the Ricon. "Madoc ap Gwilym, your elder son has wronged this tuath. It is he who has brought down this pestilence upon Caer Gwyn. Sholto has dishonoured the House of Madoc and lost his honour. Because of him our tuath has been invaded. Look to your own house, Madoc, if you want revenge. One rat in the granary can spoil all the store." He was a man almost as old as time, thin as a stick with a face as gaunt as a skull, but power seemed to burn from him, crackling in his voice.

Madoc shifted uneasily and mopped his damp brow. He scanned the faces of the Druids as though he was waiting for their vote of confidence. The old priest squatted in his place again. Those around him raised their voices in agreement.

"Sholto the Tall has caused this blood-bath!" they shouted. "He has stolen the prince of the Wolf clan. He has cohabited with the woman of the Horse clan's ricon. Now these tribes have come to claim their own!"

The discussion grew so heated the small girls of Diva's cult stopped fussing and listened, wide-eyed, to the angry discourse. Throughout the argument, Madoc remained defensive, maintaining the woman, Tallia, was his son's affair and had come to Caer Gwyn of her own accord. As for the hostage, he assured them Dafydd was in safe hands and would not be harmed. Some of the priests agreed to this, arguing the boy was worth a ransom. "'Tis a small price to ask for those who died."

Bedwyr attempted to silence the clamour, turning his most malevolent stare on those who dared dispute. There were a few, old priests who knew the futility of wars and strove for peace. It was the younger Druids, those of the dark powers and the seers of Madoc's court who were eager for revenge.

"Sacrifice to the Oak God!" they cried.

I watched Essylt and waited for her to speak but she said nothing, though I saw her make the sign against evil. The cult of the River Goddess were peace lovers who did not even eat the meat of living things, but those of the Raven cult cried for blood to Morrigan, the raven goddess of war. I knew in my heart she would win. She was the Raven of War and Death and she would fly with our warriors into battle.

Then Bedwyr stepped forward, a dark, ominous figure. He stood by the bier, his dark shadow falling over Hywel's body. In one hand he held a white dove, in the other a ceremonial dagger.

He said: "We will spill this dove's blood and let it mingle with Hywel's so his soul may fly quickly to the Otherworld."

I saw the flash of the knife blade, and the fluttering of the bird's wings, then it lay still as Bedwyr placed it on Hywel's breast.

The Council ended on a quarrelsome note with men divided in opinions and the fate of our tuath left undecided. Bedwyr spoke convincingly of the fortunes in the coffers of the Wolf Clan: crystals and jet stones from the northern mountains, perhaps treasure of gold, too. I remember how Dafydd had told me Sholto had rejected that ransom once. Now men were clamouring for it like beggars after scraps. I knew the future of our clan depended on an omen from the gods.

Stanza Four

I went with Essylt to pay homage and view the body of our tuath's fair prince. Everyone from the humblest peasant to the richest chieftain had assembled at Caer Gwyn for the burial rites. Even the slaves were allowed to wander free that day. The entire clan was in mourning.

Hywel's body lay in state in the Great Hall, wrapped in fine linen and draped with the yellow and black checked cape of the Royal War Band. In the tradition of our ancestors we believed the souls of the dead travel to the Otherworld where their spirits rest. Offerings of apples, the fruit of immortality, rowan berries, oak and laurel boughs would be made to the gods, especially to Gwyn ap Nudd, the ruler of the Otherworld.

It was our custom to bury the dead in barrows. The barrows of the Royal House were in the fields below the hill fort, long, oval-shaped mounds heaped with shale, and earth that covered tombs beamed with oak and lined with field stones. The Royal War Band and the nobles of the ricon's house were buried there. In battles, the common foot soldiers were heaped in communal graves on the battlefields where they fell. Only the chieftains and royalty were buried with rich ceremony.

The funeral procession began from the postern gates with Madoc leading the way in his ornate wicker chariot, his black ponies decked in fine new trappings. He was dressed in mourning clothes of black leather and wore a winged helm trimmed with coils of brass. Ned rode beside him on a chestnut cob, flanked by his swordsmen. He bore the standard of the royal house: the Raven on a yellow field. Ned saluted the freemen as he rode by, showing on his face the festering wound he had received in the skirmish. Like his father, his bared chest was slashed and bloody to display his grief.

I watched from a place behind the royal escort as Sholto and Aeron took their places beside their father's chariot. Sholto the Tall was grim faced, his hair plastered with a thick wash of lime and spiked out like the mane of a ferocious beast. He wore leather armour and carried an oval war-shield, polished bronze with a design of vine leaves. Sholto seemed taut as a bowstring. There was a marked air of defiance and arrogance about him. Even his pony was nervous and wild. It pranced impatiently and showed the whites of its eyes until Sholto whipped it into submission.

His sister Aeron sat beside him on her shaggy dappled cob, erect and proud in the costume of the Royal War Band. She was not wearing mourning colours, but had chosen the bright scarlet tunic and checkered cape that distinguished her as a princess of the Royal House.

She spurred her pony suddenly, and darted ahead of Ned and Sholto, crying a shrill war paean. The sun caught the silver of her helmet, sparking off the tip of her sword blade as she raised it triumphantly over her head. I thought of that day in Teag's workshop and wondered what she thought now that Hywel was dead. She had lain with Teag the night her brother was slain. Did it weigh heavily on her mind that if she had stayed at Hywel's side that day, she might have died too?

The sight of her evoked unpleasant memories and I felt anger roil inside of me. Did I want vengeance? Or was it just the same quick passion that had aroused me to curse the smith's boy the day they had killed my bull Mithras? I turned my thoughts away from Aeron and grieved in silence for the golden youth who had died.

The wains carrying the biers of the dead rumbled behind the ricon and his Royal War Band. Hywel's bier was polished bronze and studded with jet-stone and amber. Madoc sent coffers of gold and all his best weaponry to be placed in the barrow with his son. Hywel was dressed in his armour and wore a helmet, shield and armour befitting his royal lineage. His body was accompanied by one of his young squires who was a willing sacrifice to serve his master on the journey to the land of Annwn in the Otherworld.

The aging Queen Gwyndolyn, Hywel's mother, walked by her son's bier escorted by her servants. She was regal even in her torn garments. Under the streak of ashes, her face still showed the beauty Hywel and Aeron had inherited from her. She had borne Madoc three children, but now she was old and not in his favour, though she still held a place of honour in Caer Gwyn's court. It was said she was blessed with the Sight and knew the Mysteries. She had been a priestess of the Moon Maid's cult before Madoc had taken her. As she cried out expressing her grief, her wails were so plaintive they cut through me. I had not seen such grief before. Hywel was her only hope to keep in Madoc's favour. Now he was gone, and Ned would take his place. Now Ned's mother was the ricon's favourite wife and gossips said she vied to place her own son on the ricon's throne one day.

The five warriors who had been killed with Hywel would be buried in places of honour beside him. All were laid out in ceremonial fashion, their bodies dressed with oils and perfumes, clothed in the costumes of the Royal War Band – bright linen tunics, leather breeches, checkered red capes and polished helms. Each warrior took with him his weapons and armour. These were stacked on the wood carts with the bodies. The ponies of the royal stables pulled the carts. They would be sacrificed in the barrow too, so they could pull their masters safely to the Otherworld. Every man went to the barrow with all his earthly treasures, not only weaponry but clothing and jewellery.

Madoc had declared the barrows should be stocked with amphorae of grain and joints of meat for the great feasting when their Shades should reach the Otherworld. Tankards of beer and honey mead and flagons of juniper wine were also provided for the revelry. All these libations were carried on carts behind the biers of the dead warriors.

The wooden wains creaked down the dusty track while the women of the Royal House straggled alongside keening and weeping for their dead. A procession of Druids followed Bedwyr and the seers of the Royal House. We walked in the order of our rank: first the Elders, the bards and ovates, then the priestesses and acolytes.

As the column of mourners filed down the trail we chanted and danced to the rhythm of timbrels and the mournful dirge of the pipes. The freemen of our tuath, the peasants, slaves and visitors from other tribes, watched silently with bowed heads as the funeral processional passed by.

When we reached the entrance to the barrow, the auguries were made and as Bedwyr placed oak wreaths on the altar to honour the dead, the bard sang:

> *We will light the candles on the shrines.*
> *We will spill the wine dregs to the gods.*
> *And after the wine-feast, we will weep for*
> *our brothers, and bury the dead.*

Annwn is not a place of gloom. We believe the souls of the dead will return to us when the gods see that the time is right. So, once the dead are safe inside the barrows, there is always rejoicing with songs and feasting. Yet I felt sick with gloom as I watched the carts being driven into the tombs.

The keening grew louder, the shrills of the weeping like a cacophony of ghostly sounds. I watched in horror as the wife of one of the dead chieftains fell on her own sword by the side of her husband's bier. The blood gushed from her, staining the grass as she fell, and she died before the wains were driven into the barrow and they put her body on the bier beside her husband so she could journey with him to the Otherworld.

Once the carts were driven in and all the treasures secured, the thick wooden doors of the barrow were closed and sealed with stones. It all seemed like an otherworldly scene to me. I stood mute, and spiritless, detached and drained of emotion. Essylt's voice brought me back to earth, reminding me the festivities were about to begin.

As the bards sang their songs to honour the dead, the sound of the laments caught me in their surge and carried me, trance like. I was in a mesmeric state, one I experienced when I danced in the stone circle, transported to another place, a dimension beyond my world, a dream-like, mystical place beyond the realm of reality.

Stanza Five

Madoc opened the gates of the hill fort for a grand feast to honour the slain warriors. The freemen gathered outside the Hall for their share of the spoils while the Druids dined inside with the Royal War Band and nobles of the king's house.

In spite of the grief shown earlier over Hywel's death, it was a merry event. The feast was dictated by the tastes of the dead: freshly killed buck and roasted pheasant, sweet cheese from the farmsteads and fruits imported from across the Narrow Sea. The wooden platters were heaped with steaming food. Even the pied dogs got scraps to grizzle over. Tankards were filled to the brim with beer and mead as the kitchen slave poured mugs for everyone.

As we feasted, Lleu sang a new ballad he had composed about the deeds of the brave warriors who had died.

> *Stand out, O maidens of Caer Gwyn:*
> *Dance to the funeral dirge: weep for your brothers.*
> *Weep for your prince, O Maidens of Caer Gwyn.*
> *The Hall of Caer Gwyn is dark tonight, without fire.*
> *There is only the sound of the maidens*
> *weeping for their fallen warriors.*
> *Listen, O men of Caer Gwyn:*
> *The heroes of our Royal War Band are dead.*
> *How bitterly we weep for them*
> *now they are dead, hidden under the earth.*
> *Our Hall is empty without them.*
> *Listen, O warriors of Caer Gwyn:*
> *Their death is our loss.*
> *Our ranks are barren without them.*
> *The wind laments their passing:*
> *The birds cry: Our grief is theirs.*
> *Listen, O poets of Caer Gwyn:*
> *The song of the birds is not heard.*
> *It is time for us to make music:*
> *Our harps will echo the voices of the dead.*

His song put me in the same mesmeric state I had experienced when I had danced in the stone circle – transported to another place- a dimension beyond my world, a dream-like, mystical place beyond the realm of reality.

I sat beside Essylt and other acolytes of the Raven cult. The older girls played games to amuse themselves, but the children of Diva's cult yawned restlessly. The little girl with the freckled face stayed close to me too shy to speak. She had brought a doll carved from wood which she wrapped in her cloak and cuddled it until she fell asleep.

I left my plate of venison untouched and sipped mead until I began to feel dizzy. Finally, I begged Essylt to let me leave. She wanted to send Lleu with me, but I preferred to go alone, to watch the moon and walk in the silence of the glade.

The night was sweet with berry smells and wild roses. Summer was in the air with crickets shrilling along the path. I felt strangely at peace as I made my way along the shadowy trail. The sounds of revelling voices from the hill fort were muted and indistinct as though coming from another world.

I dodged the tangled thicket and bracken like a doe hare returning to its warren. Once I reached my secret covert, I felt secure and safe. My nest of moss felt soft and dry, snug as a babe's cradle. The overhanging branches of the juniper hid me. I sat there, chin on knees in reverie. A thought came to me that if the goddess willed I should die, what better place could there be than in the shelter of my little cave. I thought of the woman who died on her sword and the sacrifices at the tomb. The thought of death frightened me, but if this should be my Fate then I would face it calmly, knowing the gods had willed it so.

It seemed I had dozed when someone called my name. I looked out, thinking Lleu had come to search for me, but it was Teag. In the pale moonlight he seemed like an apparition and I wondered if I was dreaming.

"I watched you go out from Hall and I followed you," he said.

He was wearing plain homespun mourning clothes. I had neither seen him at the burial rites nor noticed him among the guests in Hall. He knelt down and took my hand. My heartbeats quickened at the warmth of his touch and I trembled.

"Let me tell you this," he whispered, "You are the brightest star, the most fragrant of flowers and this is why the gods have chosen you. Can I hope you will forgive me? You knew it was impossible for us to be together. It was not meant to be. Olwen, sweet little spirit, I did not will it, but I have wronged you. I wish you will forgive me."

I turned away from him so he would not see my tears. He spoke the truth. There was no other way for us. Our destinies had been chosen long before the day we met at the stone circle. He took me in his arms and I began to weep uncontrollably, as if a storm had burst inside of me. I pressed my wet face against the soft wool of his tunic. He smelled of evergreen and peat smoke; I clung to him until a cracking in the brush and night sounds made him pull away from me. Still weeping, I covered my face with my hands. When I looked up again, he was walking away, his figure blending darkly with the shadows on the trail.

BALLAD NINE Song For A Swords Woman

Who is she who comes riding,
wearing ermine skins and hawk feathers
in her thick tresses?
Who is she who rides through the sedge,
a graceful huntress queen?
Sure-footed is her pony.
Sharp-pointed is her spear.
Leaf-shaped are her arrowheads.
Her bow is supple, made from a yew bough.
She rides, stately and proud,
a wild-eyed warrior queen.
Who is she who comes riding
on the spirited chestnut mare?
Who is this bronze-cheeked swordswoman
with hawk feathers in her hair?

A Homage to Lleu, the Bard.

Stanza One:

As I counted the days to the Midsummer rites, I stayed close by Lleu's side. There was comfort in his presence. His gentleness made me feel secure. He talked to me reassuringly about our journey to the Druid's Holy Isle. He said we would sing our way there 'til we reached the isle. I did not doubt him. His fame was known as far north as the White Mountain.

He told many tales from the Hall those days. He was more than just a bard. Because the ricon favoured him, he was invited to every feast and Council and after Hywel's burial Madoc had presented him with a fine gold torc.

Lleu was a gentle man with a serene face and genial smile. He had a gracious manner and each word he spoke was poetry. During the year he had been with Grandfather he became a *Gogynfeirdd* which was a high honour for a bard. It meant he received favours from the king and his knights, so though Lleu was not a wealthy man, he wanted for nothing. His ballads were known throughout the land. He played the harp with the skill of a master, plucking the strings delicately so each note was clear and pure. He sang the laments and recited the tales in a voice that trilled and soared as melodic as a lark's song. Often I sang with him and sometimes he allowed me to play his clarsach. I could sing the tunes harmoniously and learned every song Lleu composed. That is why I can sing them now and remember the tales of those days.

While Lleu made ready for the long journey to the Holy Isle, Essylt kept me busy collecting herbs and tending the oak-grove shrine. Each day I took fresh offerings: a wreath of oak leaves or a handful of grain. One day I caught a ring dove with down as white and soft as the first winter's snow. It was a fledgling and I couldn't bear to kill it, so I placed it on the altar with the grain and a few wild berries from the ripening vines. I prayed the Mother Goddess would take my soul and give it to that ring dove so if I should die my spirit would come back as pure and beautiful.

When it flew away it left some downy feathers on the altar among the chaffs of wheat. The down was stained red with the berry juice like blood spilled from a sacrifice. I kept the feathers in my amulet bag. And have them even now to remind me of those days.

Our tuath was still in mourning for the slain warriors. Every day new war parties rode out to scout the borders. Madoc announced he would council with the rival chieftains again. This time he would go himself, not risking his sons' lives. He rode off with an escort, a score of men with their banners unfurled and their armour polished and bright.

Rumours spread like fire in dry brush in the marketplace as gossips wagered whether Sholto would send his woman back to her people. Owion, the Hawk, chief of the Horse Clan had sent an envoy to meet with the ricon. Old women clucked behind their hands revelling in the scandal, not because it was unheard of for a swords woman to be as bold and indiscreet as Tallia, but she was the wife of a rival chieftain and even in our own clan, taking another man's woman boded dire consequences. Some freemen argued Cymbeline's revenge was cause for war because Sholto had dishonoured the Wolf Clan when he took Dafydd, Cymbeline's son, as a hostage and had refused to pay a ransom to secure the boy's freedom. But Madoc and the Royal War Band held firm. They would not deliver Cymbeline's son unless a ransom was paid.

I listened to the talk and waited for more news about Dafydd. The next day, when I took him honey cakes and berry cordial he seemed subdued, as if he had grown accustomed to his fate. I wondered if he knew Madoc had demanded a ransom for his return to the Ordovices, and I did not speak of it to him.

I went about my last days in Caer Gwyn tending to my chores. I tried to be cheerful, not protesting or complaining, resigned to my future as a servant of the Goddess. My life, like Essylt's was destined to be a life dedicated to the goddess.

I spent my days in reflection, retracing the paths I had walked with Teag, brooding over everything that happened between us. I tried to commit to memory every detail of him so I would always remember him: the texture of his tanned skin, the fragrance of him, his dazzling smile, his eyes as green as forest pools. He was the fair God of the Morning to me, and there could be no other who would take his place.

Stanza Two:

The gossiping of the village crones and the debates of the freemen did not seem to trouble Sholto and Tallia. I saw them every morning riding their ponies across the downs, sometimes armed for a hunt, other times riding out with Aeron and Ned or an escort of lesser chieftains.

I came across them once hunting in the beech grove. I hid in the bracken and watched how they challenged each other as if it was a child's game. Tallia was brave and fearless, Sholto watched her admiringly as she played with his falcon. She seemed unafraid of its sharp beak and vicious talons. She was as wild as the falcon herself and handled it as though it were as tame as a caged finch. While the hooded bird perched on a branch, Tallia and Sholto parried with their swords, then fell into the grass laughing. In my innocent eyes, it seemed certain to me they loved each other, and I wondered if Tallia would ever leave Caer Gwyn.

One morning as I walked along the towpath gathering flowers, I saw Tallia riding out alone. She was dressed in a hunting jerkin and leather breeches. She had a quiver full of arrows slung over her back and a bow in her hand. As she galloped her pony toward the stand of trees beyond the meadow, her thick black tresses streamed like the pony's shaggy mane. She whipped him on, then disappeared into the woods.

As I reached the footbridge, I spied another rider approaching from beyond the hill fort, leaning low over his horse's neck. He carried a bow, but there were no hounds running with him. It was too late an hour for tracking deer. The morning sun was bright, bees droned in the clover. A flock of starlings scolded in shrill voices then flew in disarray among the hedgerows as the rider and his pony neared the edge of the grove.

I watched the rider curiously. It was not Sholto. The bright sunshine gleamed like fire on the burnished colour of his hair. He rode along the edge of the forest, then gave a war whoop and disappeared into the grove in the direction Tallia had gone.

As I started down the riverbank, I saw the smith's boy, Galen. He had a net out and was trapping trout. When he saw me he scowled. I put my head down. He always made my emotions brindle up and I had to swallow what I felt like saying to him. As I passed by him, he said, in a mocking tone: "My Master will drink the cup of marriage with Lady Aeron after the Midsummer." His words unnerved me and I hurried past him.

Farther along the riverbank, the hurdle-maker and his boys were collecting reeds and willows. I greeted them, then stopped to chat awhile. They had heaps of withes and osiers, willow branches and reeds, enough to make a hundred baskets: perhaps withes for a hut or new wicker chariots for the chieftains. As they went about their tasks chatting with each other, a chance referral to the Midsummer rites set me wondering. The hurdle-maker laughed as he measured his tallest boy with the longest withe. The boy was a stout lad, almost as tall as a man.

"We need longer staves, my lads," the hurdle-maker said. "About a score will do. The cage must be big enough to hold a man."

My skin turned to goose flesh. "Why a cage for the Midsummer Rites?"

"For the sacrifice." The hurdle-maker hoisted the stack of withes across his shoulders, bent almost double with the weight of them. "The Druid ordered me to make it. I do not question why. He pays me well. I have two mouths to feed." He gestured toward the two boys. "They're good lads, mind, but have the appetites of boar-hounds." He gave me a toothless grin. He was not an old man; he was strong and muscular, but looked careworn from years of toil.

I watched him and his boys as they struggled down the path bristling like hedgehogs, laden down under their burdens of twigs and slender staves.

As I sat on the riverbank and watched the damson flies dance over the smooth brown surface of the water, a thought kept prickling me, like a bramble caught in my skin. No matter how I tried to dismiss it, somehow it loomed in my mind.

"For the sacrifice" the hurdle maker had said.

In all my life I had never witnessed a human sacrifice, though I knew of them. Grandfather talked about the Mysteries of the Oak King and the rites of Cyhyraeth, the death Goddess who demanded her victims be burned in a wicker cage. The rites of the Oak King were part of the ancient Mysteries, held at the Midsummer in honour of Belyn, the Sun God.

I knew of the rituals and the thought of them horrified me. A young man is chosen to represent the Oak King. He is plied with mead and oak-resin wine and paraded into the stone circle. There he is flayed and tortured, impaled with a mistletoe stick and hacked to death on the altar stone. After his blood is caught in a libation basin and the priests have tasted his flesh, his body is burned on a pyre of oak logs.

Grandfather had abhorred these sacrifices and while he lived, he would not tolerate such brutal acts. He taught that the taking of a human's life was not necessary to appease angry gods.

As I walked back along the towpath, the words of the hurdle-maker nagged me. A dull stillness pervaded the air, a bristling edge of expectancy, as though at any moment there might be a burst of thunder, yet the sky was clear blue and cloudless. Across the meadow from the beech grove, a raven cried in a shrill voice, its chilling sound haunting the stillness. I whispered a prayer and made the sign against enchantment.

Stanza Three:

The Druid speaks and says: *Kindle the fires of Midsummer with oak-logs. We will sacrifice to the Great God Belyn.*

That night as I sat near the hearth fire, I soon forgot the hurdle-maker and what he had said. Essylt stirred stew in the iron pot and Lleu put new strings on his harp while we talked about our coming journey to the Druid's Holy Isle.

Lleu was full of mischief and hummed tunes as he worked. He tilted his head to look at me with a sparkle in his grey eyes, and an impish grin.

"We'll make a joyful time of it, Olwen, and see the sights along the way! We'll walk Senghenydd's grassy hills. Perhaps we'll climb the Holy White Mountain too."

The Holy Mountain was the dwelling place of the gods where the great eagles shook the snow down in winter. It would be a grand adventure, one that few others ever experienced.

We laughed together while Essylt ladled the stew into our wooden bowls. It was sweet, steaming mutton in greens. We ate heartily. I felt content and happy in the warm glow of our little hut.

It was just before dusk when I heard the pack of hounds run howling past baying as though they had caught the scent of game.

Lleu set down his bowl and peered out through the door skins. "It's Sholto with his men!" He frowned and looked displeased.

"'Tis late for a hunt," mused Essylt. "Do you think there's word from the ricon?"

"Aye" Lleu pondered. "The men were armed with bows and cudgels. But why take the hounds to join the Council party? They must be tracking someone."

"Perhaps the hostage has escaped!" I had not seen Dafydd for several days and wondered if somehow he had managed to run away.

"Pity him if he has," said Lleu. "He'll not get far before those hounds will corner him. They're trained to kill and will rip a man's flesh to shreds in no time. Runaway slaves can never get far with Sholto's deer hounds on their trail."

"That boy is marked with death signs," Essylt added. She made a quick gesture of the five-pointed star against evil as she spoke. "Pray he walks the god's path."

I remembered what the hurdle-maker had said about the Midsummer sacrifice and repeated what I knew to Essylt. "Are they going to choose Dafydd for the Oak King's sacrifice? Will they avenge the death of Hywel by offering the son of the Wolf as the Midsummer sacrifice?"

Essylt looked downcast. "It seems our tuath is ruled by madmen and fools. They do not heed the oracles. They ridiculed Maelgwyn, their Elder Priest. They have set their sights on ill-starred fortune. In time we will see them turn brother against brother. The auguries have forewarned it. The seed of evil has been sown. A bloody harvest will be reaped." There was more truth in what Essylt predicted than we could realize then.

Several nights later, I was wakened from my sleep by a tumult at the stockade gate. The shouts were loud and clear as the village freemen tumbled from their huts still half asleep, wielding swords and halberds, crying for Sholto and the Royal War Band. The baying of dogs and clattering of weapons had alerted everyone.

Essylt and Lleu had wakened too, and we went outside to see what the commotion was. Half the village had begun to run toward the postern gates, believing we had been attacked. Hounds yapped, wild with excitement and snapped at the heels of the ponies. Amidst the shouts, the howls of the dogs and the nickering of frightened horses ran rampant.

Someone shouted, "'Tis not the Wolves of Cymbeline we need to fear now!"

Another man exclaimed, "There'll be more bloodshed now. Sholto ap Madoc will swear an oath to Odin for revenge."

A tall, chestnut-haired man stepped forward to speak. I knew him from the Royal War band. It was Ifor the Red, a kinsman of Madoc's house.

"They have found Sholto's woman, Tallia. The wolves had fed on her before we found her, but it was an arrow killed her, not the beasts. Someone dumped her body out on the downs, near the Dobunni's camp."

"Was it done by her husband, Gwion the Hawk?" shrilled an old woman.

"No," Ifor said, "'Twas another's arrow found its mark. One from our tuath."

The crowd gasped and fell silent with shock.

"Sholto ap Madoc has sworn to find his woman's murderer." In the torchlight, Ifor's hair blazed like a flame. He was a thin-faced man with a russet beard and bore a marked resemblance to the ricon's son, young Ned. He paced like a restless wild cat, his amber eyes shifting from face to face. It crossed my mind then, how that morning I had seen a bright-haired rider follow Tallia into the woods.

This man is cunning as a fox, I thought.

"This was clearly treachery!" shouted Ivor.

Horror-stricken and repelled, I watched as a stable slave passed through the crowd leading a sturdy pony that bore the body of the swordswoman. Tallia's corpse was wrapped in a bloodied blanket. Her long ebony hair hung tangled and matted, the graceful bronze limbs twisted and broken, her flesh torn by the wild beasts. One bare foot with a bronze anklet dangled limply from under the wrap.

"Who did this?" someone cried.

"One of us!" Ivor raised his halberd and shouted an oath. "There's death to the murderer and a reward to those who find him."

I wanted to blurt out how I had seen Tallia as she rode toward the beech grove, but something made me hold my tongue. I recalled the lone rider who had tracked her to the edge of the woods, remembered the burnish of sunlight in his flaming hair and the cry of the war paean as he raced his pony into the trees.

As I followed Lleu and Essylt back to our hut, I still did not speak of what I had seen that day. Perhaps I should have spoken out, but I did not want to wrongly accuse Ifor.

When I recall those perilous days, it makes my heart sad. It seemed our lives were like the Dragon's Fire, burning brightly for some time, then quenched as we plunged into the abyss fate had willed for us.

Stanza Four

A song for Gwion, the Hawk of the Dobunni Clan

Gwion, the Hawk of Dobunni is weeping tonight.
The heart's blood of Gwion has been spilled.
A heavy grief is on him.
The hands of Gwion, the Hawk are bloodstained.
The heart of Gwion is pierced with sorrow.
Alas, for he mourns his lost love.
Alas, how he weeps!
Gwion, the Hawk will break his war spear.
He will avenge his lady fair.

BALLAD TEN Son Of The Wolf

Cymbeline, the Wolf of the Ordovices is weeping tonight.
The heart's blood of Gwion has been spilled.
A heavy grief is on him.
The hands of Cymbeline are bloodstained.
His heart is pierced with sorrow.
Alas, for he mourns his lost son.
Alas, how he weeps!
Cymbeline the Wolf will break the war spear.
He will take revenge against his son's captors.

THE RAVEN OF NIGHTMARES

Stanza One:

The Druid speaks and says: *Who but the Raven of Death can free our sons from the tomb? The Oak King shall be sacrificed to atone for the deaths of our warriors.*

In spite of the draft of poppy tea that Essylt gave me, I could not sleep. I lay awake afraid to open my eyes, lest the Raven of Nightmares should be hovering over me. I was tormented by the phantoms of those who had died; memories plagued me of the vision I had seen in the Beltane's Fire: the girl caught in the thorn bush; the shrike and the fledgling.

As I finally drifted off to a restless sleep, I visualized the Oak King being sacrificed at the Midsummer's rites and could almost hear his screams as he was tortured and burned at the Sun God's altar. I recalled what Essylt had said: *Dafydd bears the sign of a prince, and a death sign. The omens are not favourable for those who harm him.*

I thought I heard a human cry. Imagining it to be Dafydd's voice calling for help, I sat bolt upright, my flesh icy as though a cold hand had touched me. I knew this was not an ordinary dream: it was the Sight, just as the vision in the Fires had been.

I rose from my bed and dressed quietly so as not to wake the others. I knew I must talk to Tog, the cattle master, and tell him about my vision. Tog was a simple man but he had the Sight. The Sight is a gift given to just a few. He would know the answer.

Lleu always slept across the door sill with his harp beside him. He said the clarsach could talk to him and helped to keep bad spirits out. I prayed the harp would keep silent, but every step I took toward the door it seemed to sigh. Lleu muttered something dreamily and the harp-strings trembled as I stepped across him. I lifted back the door skins carefully so the cool night air would not fan up embers in the hearth, but the sparks crackled in the charred faggots and I was sure Lleu would waken.

I crept out into the damp night, crouching under the edge of the roof thatch as furtive as a prowling thief. I waited, thinking I heard Essylt's voice, but neither she nor Lleu roused.

The moon was invisible behind a shroud of swirling clouds, the blackness edged with a ghostly silver light. From far across the downs the eerie sound of howling wolves turned my skin to goose flesh. I ran quickly, my heartbeats thundering in my ears, my bare feet not feeling the sharpness of the pebbles on the path.

Across the field, Tog's campfire was a winking light in the misty darkness. Tog always slept near his fire outside the cattle shed. He startled grumpily when I wakened him. He had his hand on his cudgel, ready at all costs to protect himself.

"What brings you out, prowling with the foxes among the herds?"

"I dreamed of the hostage, Dafydd. I thought, as you have the Sight, you might interpret it for me, and I must talk to him," I stammered. "I had a dream about Dafydd...that he was calling out to me!"

Tog grumbled because I had disturbed his sleep with what he thought was girlish nonsense,

I sat on a bale of hay and related my disturbing dream to him. Tog scratched his head and frowned. "I know not what to do, lass. He is in my safe-keeping for now. Do not worry, lass. Whatever is to be, it will be. He is the hostage son of a ricon. Surely Madoc will not allow harm to come to him! 'Tis best ye talk go talk to the lad. See if he really called out to you. 'Twas likely just a girlish fantasy."

The manger was shadowy and silent except for the low breathing of the cattle. There was one lamp burning but I could see nothing but the dark hulks of sleeping animals.

I did not have faith in what Tog said. "I must speak to him!" I said, and called out Dafydd's name. I heard his voice reply, soft and full of surprise as he sat up from his straw bed. He blinked sleepily as I knelt beside him and told him about my dream. He peered at me, his dark eyes burning in the lamp-light.

"I dreamed you were calling out to me, that you wanted me to help you," I said.

"I did call you!" His voice was as melancholy as a harp's lament. "'Twas in a dream. The men were chasing me. I called out your name because I knew you would help me." He spoke slowly, choosing words that were a mixture of his own dialect and ours, the way he had learned to talk to Tog and me. "I dreamed I was running along a riverbank. I could see the sunshine on the hills and heard the cry of wolves in the forest."

As he spoke, I felt like weeping, for the vision became clearer to me. I remembered seeing the hurdle-maker gathering withes to weave a cage for the Midsummer sacrifice. The Druid, Bedwyr, had said he planned to make a sacrifice to the Oak King and had proclaimed in Hall that the Son of the Wolf should die to atone for Hywel's murder.

In shock, I blurted out: "Bedwyr plans to offer Dafydd as the Oak King's sacrifice!"

"Then 't'would be best if you run, lad!" Startled, I turned to see Tog had been listening from the stable door.

"Look boy," he said. "I've grown to love ye like a colt. I bear no ill against ye." His voice was gruff with emotion. "Better the hounds or hunter's arrows than the fate the Druid has pledged for ye. I wish I could help ye, but the borders are guarded and anyone caught prowling at night risks death."

Dafydd had grown pale, but he spoke bravely. "They'll never lead me like some shackled beast to die on Bel's altar. My father will curse them. Cerridwen, the She-wolf is my clan's totem. She will protect me. Your warriors will cower like curs when Cymbeline's wolf pack invades." His eyes blazed with anger. He paced nervously, as though at any moment he might bolt and run.

Tog stood in front of him, blocking the doorway. Tog could wrestle wild dogs and snap their necks like twig. He had tamed Dafydd with the same ease that he gentled the mountain cobs or calmed rutting bulls. "We'll find a way," he said, "But not this night!"

I recalled the first day I had seen Dafydd riding with Sholto and Tallia. His face had been a mask of despair then. Now he bore himself courageously, stubborn, defiant and proud. He stood in the lamplight, and showed us the tattooed dragon sign, his mark of royalty, and all the symbols of magic, lines of blues and purples etched on his pallid skin like patterns on a silken tapestry: the symbols that would keep him safe from evil and enchantment. There was no mistaking that Dafydd was a king's son. No matter how our tribesmen thought him to be an ill-bred beast, he was a youth of noble bearing, his heart and spirit purer than those who sought to do him harm. He bore himself courageously, stubborn, defiant and proud. He was the Son of the Wolf, and he was too proud to run. He would face his fate bravely.

Stanza Two:

It was two days before the Midsummer and there had been no word from Madoc's council party. A herald of the Royal War Band announced that the pennants of the Raven of War were to be hoisted over the ramparts of the hill fort. A broken spear was displayed across the lintel of the Great Hall calling the chieftains to prepare for battle. An aura of doom hung over the tuath. While the Druids prepared for the solstice rites, the men of the Raven clan made ready for war.

I went about my tasks dispassionately. I felt numb, detached, as though life was unreal. I wished that I might waken to find it had all been part of my dream and clung to the hope that somehow Tog would find a way to help Dafydd to escape. Yet I knew it was as futile as the hope that I'd had when I had tried to save Mithras, my bull. I knew there was no way Dafydd could safely escape. All the borders of our tuath were guarded by the War Band. Since Tallia's murder, Sholto had employed men to patrol in the night with the order that anyone caught roaming after sundown risked death.

The day before the Midsummer Rites, I visited Dafydd for the last time. We met in gloomy silence. Dafydd listened impassively as I talked, trying to reassure him. We were both in the bloom of our youth, ripe for life and eager to live. He did not deserve to die.

"The gods will hear your plea," I said. "I will make a sacrifice on the altar for you."

Dafydd reached out and touched my sacred torc, tracing his fingertips over the raven's head and along the gold coil of the neck piece.

"I'd give my life for the god's service too, if you could make a supplication for me," he said. He took the sheep-shears from a hook, clipped a lock from his hair, and handed it to me solemnly. There was a peacefulness on his countenance as though he had resigned himself to his fate. His face glowed with an inner light. His eyes shone, bright and clear.

"Go to your shrine, little priestess. Place this on the altar Tell your Goddess my life is for her."

I took the shears and cut a lock of my hair too. The dark of his ebony curl entwined with the coppery gold of mine. "I will place mine on the altar too," I said. "It is the most we can offer together, a symbol of our friendship and trust." I took his hands and kissed him.

Before I put the locks of our hair into my amulet bag, we knelt together and said a prayer, pleading that Dafydd's life be saved.

He put his arm around me. "I am the Son of the Wolf," he said.

"I am the Child of the Raven," I replied.

I no longer felt afraid. I was certain the gods would hear my plea and save him.

BALLAD ELEVEN A Carol For Midsummer

She comes wearing a garment of crimson,
a golden torc round her neck.
Her hair is burnished as a crown.
Her lips red as rowan berries.
She is fairer than the Hawthorn.
Rosier than apples are her cheeks.
Her eyes blue as the primrose and
clear as Guenwyvar, the hawk.
There is no other child so lovely.
All who see her marvel at her beauty.
They shower her with flowers!
They crown her with hawthorn blossoms.
Wild roses are strewn at her feet.
They praise her with songs!
She is the Child of the Raven.
See the bright blush of the sun on her face?
She is the Goddess's child.
She is Olwen the Fair;
Olwen, Lady of the Hawthorn.

THE MIDSUMMER RITES

Stanza One:

On the day of the Midsummer rites, I would turn fifteen, the last year of my childhood. After the rites I would be sent with the other maidens to Mona, our holy island in the western clan lands of my people. It was on this island that Druids and priestesses dedicated themselves to serve the gods.

Several days before, I had wakened to the rhythm of Essylt's spinning wheel. The whirring of the wheel as she spun the yarn was like a song, one I shall never forget. The shifting of the warp sheds as she wove the threads of weft through on her loom; the tapping of the distaff melded with the lilting tune she hummed as she finished weaving the cloth for the tunic I would wear to the Midsummer Rites.

I had chosen to wear a garment of red for my initiation.

"Red is the sacred colour worn by the ancient kings of Senghenydd and reserved for the most splendid occasions," Essylt said.

Essylt and I had collected blood root from a grove. The blood root yields a fine crimson dye. I helped Essylt mix the dye and stirred the woven cloth in the bubbling cauldron until it was as rose-red as a bullfinch's breast and ready to dry in the sun.

She made my breeches of soft buckskin dyed bright purple, a rare dye Essylt had purchased from a trader from the east who came up the Chalk Trail with a load of exotic wares. She also bought some fine gold thread and paid him for a handful of polished jet stones for it.

We worked together at kneading and twisting the buckskin until it was pliable and soft as cloth. She embroidered spiral patterns on the hem of the tunic and braided cord ties with silken tassels for the knees of the breeches.

The morning of the Midsummer, Essylt fussed over me as I dressed in my rich garments. I stood before her feeling somewhat shy, imagining what it would be like to be one of the goddess's chosen ones. To be chosen to serve the goddess meant I must be chaste. I was afraid, knowing I was no longer the virtuous child she supposed me to be. From the moment I had seen Teag at the woodland shrine, I had lost my innocence. I remembered his words: *"You are the sweetest flower."* I rubbed my hand across my mouth, recalling the sweetness of his kisses, and wiped away the memory of my indiscretions. I thought about what life would be like on the Druid's Isle. Did I really want to give up my freedom?

A coldness brushed over me; a fluttering draft like the beating of a bird's wings. I thought: *From this day on there will be no turning back.*

Essylt helped me dress in my newly woven garments. As I stood before the mirror I glanced at the tear-shaped blue mark on my shoulder. "Bear this mark proudly," Essylt had told me, "For it is surely the mark of a tear shed by the one who left you on the holy altar!"

She was watching me solemnly. All the gaiety seemed to have gone out of her, like a cloud drawn over the sun; that dark, imponderable look I had seen before whenever she heard the gods speak.

"This day is the end of your childhood," she said. "As you were brought to the Sun Temple when you were a babe, now you shall return as a woman."

She straightened my golden raven's head torc. "There is no child as lovely as you, Olwen," she said. "I remember the babe, rosy and fair, that we found on the Earth Mother's shrine. Almost fifteen years have gone by as swiftly as the seasons change." She smiled at the memory.

From the time I was a toddler I had followed her into the sacred grove. She had taught me the rituals and chants and held me up to the idol in the oak grove so I could place votive offerings on the Goddess's shrine.

"You were never like other children," Essylt said. "Perhaps I should not have kept you away from the others." She held out an amulet of amber engraved with the symbol representing the Druid's wheel of life: Abred, the beginning of the soul's pilgrimage. Gwynfydd, the fulfillment of the pilgrimage and Cuegant, the Protector of Souls. "This will keep you safe," she said. As she put it in my hand I felt a sudden chill, a breathlessness that made my head spin. Why had she given me this talisman as a protector? Had she seen something in my future that foretold of some peril?

I will always remember how she had smiled as she placed amulet in my hand; the pensive look she had as she straightened my torc. I recall every gesture; the secretive knowing way she watched me. I could not hide anything from Essylt. She was more than the High Priestess. She was a mother to me. I did not doubt she loved me as if I were her own child. Yet I was an acolyte of the goddess and she would never allow me to forget that.

I turned to her with tears brimming in my eyes. I wanted to confess to her about Teag and how I loved him. She stopped me before I could speak.

"Dear child," she said gently, putting her finger against my lips. "In spite of everything, you have not loved the Goddess less. You are an earthling, after all. Perhaps the fault is mine for having raised you as my own. From the moment I found you on the Goddess's altar I wanted you to be my child. Was it my improprieties that made you so vulnerable? I know you belong to the Goddess, for it was to Her you owe your life. Now the time has come for Her to claim you, although it grieves me to see you go." Her eyes welled with tears and she began to weep. It was the first time I had ever seen Essylt cry. We fell into each other's arms. I clung to her, smelling the fragrance of hyssop on her garments, hearing the beating of her heart. I buried my face in her soft bosom as her trembling hands stroked my hair. I would never forget that moment and would conjure it in my mind whenever I needed comfort.

It was the custom, that on the morning of the Midsummer rites, the Druids made their offerings at the barrows of the dead. The Royal War Band had dispatched new scouts to search for the ricon, Madoc, and his escort who had crossed the border into Dobunni lands to bargain with the other warrior clans.

Lleu came to our hut and told Essylt that during the night a Dobunni herdsman had strayed across the border with his cows and was captured by the scouts who brought him back to Caer Gwyn.

"When the War Band examined him, they saw he had the mark of the gods on him — not only a cast to his eyes, but when they questioned him, his stammering speech betrayed him. The gods mark men in such a way," Lleu said. "The soldiers dared not harm him so they plied him with mead and promises that would suit a simple oaf. He told them all he knew, in his hesitating stammer. He said Cymbeline the Wolf was in counsel with Gwion of the Dobunnis. Their council fires had burned for many nights. They were camped on the other side of the forest waiting for a sign to attack."

Essylt frowned. "How do you know this?" she asked.

Lleu said that the man had rolled his strange eye round at them, staring with his mouth agape. "He said 'I have the Sight,' and peered at them until they shrank from his gaze," Lleu explained.

He went on to tell more of the tale, how their superstitions made the warriors believe the stranger could put an evil spell on them.

"The War Band dared not dispute his words, no matter how gawky and stupid he might have seemed," Lleu said.

"Aye. When the gods have marked a man it is best to be respectful," Essylt agreed.

Lleu accepted a cup of honey mead that Essylt handed him, took a long draught of it and went on with his tale.

"They questioned the man as they refilled his cup. The fool smacked his lips, wiped the spittle from his mouth and said, 'Eh? Your king?' Then Sholto cursed him. 'You fool! Yes. Madoc! Madoc, Ricon of Caer Gwyn!'"

He described how the man had grinned stupidly and accepted the steaming mutton bone they offered him. "He said: 'Ah, the Bear of the Atrebates? Madoc, you say. Now there's a man, I say. We raided herds together when I was young. Yes, Madoc. He's kin to me, you see." They filled his cup again and let him be," Lleu continued. "Later they sent him back with his herd, keeping only one of his cows for a tribute. But young Ned begged them to let him take a party of men and go after him, because he might lead them to the enemy camp. Sholto denied his request, said the fool was moonstruck."

He went on to relate how Ned had challenged his brother, but Sholto stood firm. "Without his father to bolster him, young Ned holds little ground against wily Sholto," Lleu said. "He pleaded with Sholto that maybe the man would lead them to their father, but Sholto laughed at him. "Kin, he says? Touched by the gods or not, he's a daft oaf. Take what he says as nothing more than the jabbering of a madman. We'll wait another day, then I'll go after him. No need for you to risk your neck, young Ned. You are father's pet, after all. He'll not have you harmed." So Ned stalked away mocked by Sholto's laughter.

Essylt frowned, and muttered a curse. "This does not bode well. Is it not enough that our clan is quarrelling with two others? And now there is obvious strife in our ricon's own family!"

A feeling of foreboding came over me. "What will happen *modryb*?" I asked.

"Nothing that is good!" Essylt said. "All we can do is pray somehow the gods will intervene and turn our Midsummer into the blessed celebration it is meant to be!"

Stanza Two

Midsummer is always a joyful time with dancing to the tune of pipes and clarsach and everyone merry. That year, in spite of the Midsummer rites, it was a time of war and the presence of the Dead was felt. Their spirits were restless. It was not a good omen.

Our solemn processional walked the Chalk Trail from Caer Gwyn, along the Sacred Way to the Temple of the Sun on the Plain. The Sacred Avenue led out across the downs, skirting the sloping hillocks and grasslands. The Ways from all the temples wind like serpent tracks across the Plain, joining at the Sun God's hallowed place.

The Order of Bards led the processional, followed by the Druids and priest-esses including Essylt. I walked with the young acolytes of the Raven cult from the High Place of Abiri, but I was the only honoured one from Caer Gwyn.

The trail was lined with the young and the freemen, some who were too aged or infirm to join the ranks. They cheered and cried out blessings as we passed by. Others joined us along the way, whenever we passed a meadow shrine or forest sanctuary. Druids and bards came from the citadels of Caer Badden and Caer Caint: from the places where the Arch Druids reside at Caer Evroc and Caer Llion. There were hundreds of ovates from the great citadel of Caer Troia where sons of Albion's noblest families live as guest-friends study-ing the ways of the ancient Mysteries.

The children of Diva's cult skipped out of the woods singing merrily, waving rowan boughs. To them it was a festive time. I caught a glimpse of the little one I had seen at the ricon's Assembly. Her freckled cheeks were as rosy as apples. She wore a new tunic of mossy green, and an amulet of a rabbit's foot on a leather thong around her neck. She caught me watching her and came up to me shyly. I took her hand. I longed to be her age again, to romp and play in the meadow grass, free as a young doe.

"What is your name?" I asked

She peered at me timidly, her eyes round blue as cornflowers. "Moina."

"Moina, sweet little lamb." I whispered.

Her chaplet of yellow field daisies was a bright contrast to her russet hair. I remembered when I was as small as she, crowned with daisies, eagerly following the crowds in the Midsummer processional.

I bent down and kissed her forehead. She blushed, then pressed her lips to my hand and skipped away to join her friends.

I watched her pensively, remembering when I was five years old, when Essylt first took me to the Midsummer rites. How I had cried when they said I couldn't ride with my grandfather! He had a special wicker cart, decked with floral wreaths and rowan boughs. He had looked so grand in his red cape, the golden crescent of his collar glinting like the sun's rays. He scolded me sternly, but I saw his eyes twinkle just the same. Then Lleu had come, hoisting me up on his shoulders, saying he would carry me all the way. He sang songs to please me. I wished I could remember them now. They recalled such happy times.

The trilling of pipes and hum of voices drifted lightly on the morning breeze. Ahead of us, I caught sight of Lleu; his bright blue cape fanned out as the wind caught its hem. His harp's song drifted back to me accompanied by the music of pipes and timbrels. As we came out to the open grassland, the distant glint of gold from the priest's luluna collars and the patches of bright crimson, green and blue of the Druid's sagums, coloured the Plain as gaily as meadow flowers.

Far across the downs, the stones of the Great Henge loomed, like a rank of old grey warriors, waiting in ominous silence as we approached.

The circle of bluish grey, rough-hewn dolmens is an awesome sight. The Stones have stood on the plain from time out of mind. Our remembrancers tell how giants placed them there in Bel, the Sun God's time. The old tales say Bel's mother, Latona of the Moon, was born there so every summer at the solstice Bel comes to visit her. There is no more magnificent a temple. It is the holiest of places. Priests and kings are buried there, their heads facing the rising sun. Those ancient shades haunt the place, especially at solstice. That is why we call this temple Cor Gawr, the place of the Holy, Anointed Ones. We have worshipped the Great God of Light and his mother, the Moon Goddess, since time began. He is the all-powerful, the Creator, the Savior and the Destroyer.

The long avenues from the High Seat of Abiri, straight across the Plain, were dotted brightly with the torches of the celebrants as they followed their High Priests toward the sanctuary, like shepherds leading their flocks to the shelter of the fold. Some of them had journeyed for days to reach the Great Henge. There were young ovates, boys in the prime of their youth who had devoted their lives to the service of the gods; bards and scholars of every age, who came from the high seats of learning; ageing white-haired priests, sages like my Grandfather, who had served the gods for all their lives. Priestesses came with their initiates to serve the shrines and share the wisdom the Earth Mother had given them.

There were even a few ancient seers from the god's Holy Mountain in Senghenydd, the venerable wizards who live their solitary lives high in mountain caves, worshipping the spirits of the timberland, and the gods of thunder and lightning who dwell on the summit of the White Mountain. Essylt told me they knew powerful magic, all the Mysteries since time began.

I gaped at them in awe. They were wizened, bent old men, clothed in ragged homespun robes, their bare feet gnarled as tree roots. Above their matted beards, dark eyes burned bright as fire coals. They possessed untold wisdom and magical powers beyond my comprehension

That night, we camped around the circumference of the trench in the shadow of the great blue stones. The gathering of Druids is a magic circle, keeping out the powers of evil. Only the most venerated ones: those of the royal house, the priests and ovates and initiates such as me, are allowed to join this camp.

I crept close to the campfire of the old mountain seers, listening as their bards sang mysterious songs in the peculiar earthy language they speak, which is as old as time itself. They possessed untold wisdom and magical powers beyond my comprehension. Essylt, who knew their strange tongue, translated some of the bard's verses, tales of mountain lore, werewolves and wood nymphs who cast bewitching spells on mortals. I longed to ask him to sing us the tales about the Wolf Clan, but Lleu had taught me it was impolite to interrupt a bard while he performed, so I held back, listening as dumb-struck as though he was a god speaking.

I lay on the rough white cowhides smelling the sweetness of the grass as I gazed up into the darkening sky. The happy voices of the bards singing to their harp's melodies washed over me as refreshing as a cool mountain stream. Although it was some time until sunset, Latona the Moon showed her mysterious pale face as though to smile at me.

The God speaks and says: *My Stones were hewn by ancient giants. Who but I knows the secret of the Place of the Holy Anointed Ones? This is the Place of the Moon and the Sun. This is the burial place of great chieftains and seers. Who but I knows the secrets of the dolmens on the Plain?*

All through the night our ranks were joined by the Druids and bards of Albion. They came from mountain citadels and the oak forests. The long avenue was dotted with torch-light as the celebrants followed their High Priests to the sanctuary. Some of them had journeyed for days to reach the Great Henge.

It was still dark when I was wakened by the sound of trumpets. The morning star was hovering high over the horizon, but the moon had waned slipping into the bosom of Earth. In the east, a faint tinge of pearly light heralded the dawn.

The holy seers and bards had gathered along the Sacred Avenue waiting for the processional into the Sacred Precinct. As the fanfare sounded from the curved trumpets, they began to file silently into the inner precinct of the great stone circle.

We didn't enter the precinct until the dawning of the midsummer sun rose over the bulk of the immense Sighting Stone. From this point, we would mark the beginning of the new season. Our processional entered from the northern arch of the Henge.

A light, cool breeze chilled the morning air. The massive dolmens loomed black against the lightening sky. We followed the priests and bards under the immense lintel of the entrance arch, dwarfed beside those colossal stones. As I walked round to take my place the great circle seemed to turn like a giant's wheel, and the illusion of it turning made me dizzy.

Within the centre of the uprights is the altar stone where the libations are made. I took my place beside Essylt. My hands trembled as I held the bronze, libation cup she had filled to the brim with resin wine to be offered at the Goddess's altar. I paced myself slowly, following behind her, careful not to spill the precious drops before the offerings were made. I tried to put my mind on other things, pretending this was just like any other day, when I made the offerings in the oak grove.

The sacred chants began: the liturgies to honour the Gods and the Earth Mother. I took my place with Essylt before the altar of the Mother Goddess. There were carvings on the stone that had been made in some bygone time. This was the shrine where I had been found as a babe. I gazed up at the great rock pillar and traced over the symbols with my fingertips. The goddess's voice came to me in the singing of the wind as it passed across the towering lintels.

The Goddess speaks and says:
> *I am a child in swaddling clothes.*
> *I am a sword in a warrior's hand.*
> *I am the cry of the raven in the field of battle.*
> *I am a maiden sweet and shy.*
> *Who is she with the crimson gown?*
> *Who is the fair-cheeked one who comes to honour me?*

I bowed my head and answered her:
> *I am Olwen, Child of the Raven.*
> *It is I who was the child in swaddling clothes.*
> *It is I who is the maiden with the crimson gown.*
> *I wear your golden raven's torc.*
> *I have come to honour You.*

As we gathered in the Inner Circle, the sun burst over the horizon like a beacon fire. I knelt at the foot of the giant heel stone and heard the cry of a raven as it swooped low over the pinnacle of stone. I put out my hand to touch the stone pillar; The stone was hot, and I felt a quick sensation, like the crackling of lightening.

As Essylt chanted the invocations, I stood, tall as I could, beside her. This was the moment of my initiation, the surrendering of my childhood for the service of the Goddess. I fixed my eyes on the strange inscriptions carved on the stone. I tried not to think of Caer Gwyn, of the greenwood, the willows dipping their leaf-tips into the brown pools, the place where I had sat with Teag. I dared not linger on those fleeting thoughts, for those were mortal pleasures and not befitting for this solemn occasion.

The Druids anointed me with water brought from the sacred spring of the White Mountain, and placed a wreath of ivy on my head. The cool water trickled over my face, mingling with my tears.

The sound of the carnyx heralded the rising sun of Midsummer. I raised my voice in a song of praise to the Earth Mother, giver of Life. The brilliance of the rising sun glittered from the rim of the tall blue Sighting Stone; it winked and radiated like a splendid jewel.

To the rhythm of timbrels and drums and the joyful singing of the celebrants, we danced around the inner circle of the sanctuary, first bowing at the shrine of the triple-headed god, the Trinity, our Great God, the essence of Light, circling the sanctuary as we sang praises of adulation.

**"Praise Him, for He is the Creator, the Conserver, the Destroyer.
Let God be praised in the beginning and the end."**

There was a large, flat altar stone just at the edge of the embankment ditch where we had entered the Sacred precinct. Near it, they had heaped oak logs, ready for the offering. The songs of joy died on our lips as a din of trumpets rent the air and a troop of seers led by the Druid Bedwyr entered the sacred precinct escorted by the warriors of Caer Gwyn's War Band.

I felt a chill when I saw his dark, foreboding figure. His voice was harsh, and shrill as a raven's cry

"People of Caer Gwyn, invoke the poet, that he may compose a song for you. Invoke the seer, so he may cast a spell. For I, the Druid, I am the Raven who flies with you into battle. I am he who foretells the secrets of the gods. For them I make these incantations. The god has spoken and His voice is the rumbling thunder!" He held up his arms, the black cloth of his robe fanning out like a predator bird's wings. **"Who is the god who sets the timber ablaze? Who is the fierce heat-giver? Duir, the all powerful; Duir, the Oak god. From Him none may escape. He is the god of the Sacred Fire. To Him, Duir, the Oak god, we will make our sacrifice."**

A loud wailing sounded when Bedwyr made his proclamation. I heard the din of a battle call and the frantic squeals of horses. A cry went out: "We must release the Son of the Wolf or our ricon will die!"

The night before our processional left Caer Gwyn, the sacred grove had rung with the cries of the Royal War Band who had gathered there to hear the Druid's divination. Oak resin wine had been spilled on the altar. Libations were burned, and the god had spoken. Now the War Band had come to the Midsummer Rites, their bright banners unfurled, the shrill sound of the Druid's carnyx mingling with their paeans as they pledged their allegiance to the God.

The warriors rallied, armed with swords and war axes and pleaded with Bedwyr to save Dafyyd and ask for Madoc's ransom. But Bedwyr had proclaimed: *"The gods have willed it. Their voice is heard in the crackling flames: hear ye, people of Caer Gwyn: I am the blaze that lights the heavens; I am the god who sets the head afire with smoke; I am Duir the Oak God. These are your portents. The Oak king must die!"*

Just at the entrance to the Stone Circle, I saw a wooden cart bedecked with flowers and wreaths. It bore a wicker cage hung with oak wreaths and glittering votive charms. A pair of great white oxen garlanded as beasts of sacrifice pulled the cart. The wheels groaned as the oxen lumbered slowly into the holy precinct. Behind it rode the Oak king on a war chariot.

The crowd began to close around, pressing closer to view the youth who stood astride the Oak King's chariot. It was Dafydd, dressed in a scarlet sagum, like those worn by the Princes of Caer Gwyn when they go into battle. A golden diadem of oak leaves crowned his head.

The Druid's voice was shrill, hysterical, above the shouts. "Kindle the fire. We will sacrifice to Duir, God of the sacred Oak tree."

A torch was thrown. A curl of flames began to rise from the heap of logs. I looked up at the youth on the Oak King's chariot. Dafydd looked down at me. Our eyes held in a moment of terrifying truth. My hands shook as I lifted the libation dish to honour him.

"The Child of the Raven honours you!" I cried.

He called back: "And I, Dafydd, Son of the Wolf, honour you, Priestess." He made a sign against enchantment as he passed by me.

"Who will be the Oak King's bride?" someone shouted.

The joyfulness of the day quickly changed and became a spectacle of riotous orgies. The celebrants had grown wild and shrieked as though intoxicated by the smoke from the sacrificial pyre. Guards from the Royal War Band pushed through and pressed the crowd back with their long oval shields.

"Make way! Make way for the Oak King's bride!"

A girl was led forward on a shaggy white pony. She was dressed in a sagum, pure as a field lily; her pale gold hair streamed over her shoulders.

I felt a stab, cold as a knife-blade going into my innards. It was Aeron, poised smiling, a cool expression on her face. I remembered that same look when she had stepped out from behind the tapestry in Teag's workshop. Where was Teag now while she paraded here, triumphant and sedate as a queen, playing the role of the Oak King's regent while they sacrificed Dafydd as atonement for her brother's death?

I made the sign of the pentacle as she passed by me. I felt numb with shock. Essylt found me huddled by the Sighting Stone. She took my hand and led me away from the sight of the oak pyre with its blazing heap of logs.

"They are going to kill him," I wept.

She drew her cloak around me, for though it was a bright warm morning, I was shivering with cold.

"Duir is the God of the consuming fire," Essylt said. "But He can create life too. Dafydd will die only if the gods will it."

I caught only a glimpse of Dafydd as he was borne away to the sound of cheering, trapped inside the ornamental wicker cage, carried on a cart pulled by two spirited horses. I do not think he saw me. If he did, he didn't appear to know me. He was intoxicated by the mead they had forced him to drink and exhausted by the endless hours of ritual and debauchery. He seemed spiritless as though his soul had already left his damaged body.

I made the god's signs silently as the cart rolled by. I recalled that night when he had said *"They'll never lead me like some shackled beast to die on Bel's altar. My father's gods will curse them."* My heart was wrenched by grief. If they killed him, would his clan retaliate? I felt so faint at the sight of him and sat by the roadside. Essylt stayed with me, not speaking, for there were no words left to express what either of us felt. She comforted me silently, as though I was still the small child she had nurtured at her bosom.

The war chariot bearing the lady Aeron and the king's seer, Bedwyr, followed behind the Oak King's cart. Aeron, the symbolic bride of the Oak King wore a crown of gilded oak leaves. She appeared as gay and charming as if she were on her way to a wedding feast, while the dark-faced Bedwyr grinned smugly and held aloft his serpentine wand, making the signs of blessing over our heads.

Essylt and I waited by the roadside until almost everyone had passed, then we made our way slowly along the Avenue, returning to Caer Gwyn with heavy hearts.

A Song for the Oak King

> *The seers rise early to perform*
> *the rites of the Oak King.*
> *There is dew on the Plain;*
> *the blackbirds are warbling.*
> *Every tree bows its head.*
> *The arms of the oak trees*
> *bend to the winds.*
> *In the sacred grove, the Raven cries*
> *a death knell to the Oak King.*

The curly-haired prince is a wild bird
trapped in a woven cage.
Swift horses carry him across the meadow
to the silent grove where the god's altar blazes.
The pyre of oak boughs,
cut from the bending tree
consumes him in its sacred flames."

Stanza Four

Three days after the summer solstice, our dismal processional left the Place of the Holy Anointed Ones. We made our way slowly along the Avenue, returning to Caer Gwyn with heavy hearts, walking to the pace of a drum's dirge and a pipe's mournful trilling, like a funeral cortege such as the one we had followed on the day of Hywel's burial.

Lleu was waiting for us at the outskirts of the village. By the sombre look on his face I knew something foreboding had occurred.

"You and Olwen must go straight to the cottage," Lleu told her. "On no account must you leave there. I am going to the Council Hall. Ivor the Red has returned to Caer Gwyn. He says the Ordovices are holding Madoc as ransom until Cymbeline's son is released."

My heart leapt with joy at the news. "Then Dafydd will be saved?"

Lleu shook his head. "No, Olwen. It is too late for that. They took him to the grove. The rites have begun. He has gone to his Fate."

My heart felt broken and I drew in a long breath. I remembered how Dafydd had borne himself so bravely. Why had the gods not saved him? He did not deserve to die. He was a noble boy, son of the Wolf Clan's ricon. They should have returned him to his people. Surely now the Wolf Clan would retaliate and what would happen to Caer Gwyn?

Essylt and I followed Lleu's orders and waited inside the hut. Outside I could hear women's screams and men crying out in alarm. There was a bellowing of horns and the clash of sword blades. The smell of smoke drifted in past the door skins. I peered outside and saw flames and smoke billowing from the hill fort.

Lleu burst in, his face pale and streaked with soot. "We must run for our lives!" he cried, waving his hand in the direction of the fort. "The Dobunnis and the Wolves of Cymbeline are at the gates!"

Essylt gasped with shock but stood her ground calmly. "The prophecies have been fulfilled. I will go to the Earth Mother's shrine and make a supplication to Her." She turned to me. Her voice was stern. "Olwen, you must hide. It is not safe for you here. I am an old woman; they would not dare harm a High Priestess. You, my child, will fall like ripe fruit into the hands of these howling curs. Hide away in your secret place. When the strife is over, Lleu will come for you."

"I can't leave you, *modryb*!" I cried. "Let me go to the grove with you."

Essylt was firm. "You *must* go, Olwen. Acolyte or not, you are a young, pretty prize that these savages will take. Hide yourself. Pray to the Earth Mother and I will offer her a caged dove for your safety."

She hurried back into the hut and put together a napkin of cheese and dark bread, and a little flask of goat's milk, enough to see me through a day or two. "Go quickly now. Let us hope that this pestilence will run its course as swiftly as brush fire." She hugged me quickly and kissed me. Her eyes were wet, but she blinked away the tears.

Lleu looked pale under the black soot smudges on his face. His hand shook as he made a sign against dark enchantment. It was the first time I had ever seen him without his clarsach slung over his shoulder, but there was no time to question him. When he hugged me, I could smell the burned timber on his clothing.

I wrapped the bundle of food in my cloak and ran as fast as I could toward the palisade gate. Before I reached the last ring of huts, a fire arrow hurtled over the wall, striking the thatch on a rooftop. It blazed instantly and the licking flames began to jump and dance from straw roof-cone to roof-cone until the entire circle of huts was ablaze. People were screaming with fright. Women with suckling babes fell on their knees appealing to the Earth Mother, their pitiful wail mingling with the sound of clashing swords and the roar of the flames.

The smoke stung my eyes and burned my throat. I darted past the crowds of freemen and ran out through the gates toward the lane of alders that led to the Moon Goddess's shrine. The tall, graceful trees bent down their heads to shelter me and muted the dreadful sounds of the war paeans that shrilled from the battlements of the fortress.

Just as I neared the glade, I saw two ponies tethered under an alder tree and heard the sound of angry voices. My heartbeats pounded like a timbrel beating to the frantic rhythm of a ritual dance. Not being able to distinguish the voices as friend or foe, I hid in the bracken and made myself as small and still as a doe hiding from hunters.

Through the leafy branches of the ferns, at the edge of the clearing, I saw two men wearing the checkered capes of Madoc's Royal War Band. The one who had his back to me had the same tousled russet hair and lanky build as young Ned. The other taller man was half naked and wore a thick leather vest girdled with a studded belt. He carried a long oval shield bearing the Raven's crest and his sword was drawn. Even at a distance I recognized the long-bladed sword with the stag's head hilt that Teag had fashioned for the swords woman, Tallia's, betrothal gift. Sholto's braided hair hung below his horned helm. His face was painted with swirls of blue woad; the scar across his cheek showed as a jagged line of purple. Brother to brother, they faced each other.

"I did not kill Tallia, Sholto. I swear by all the gods. It was not me!" Ned stepped away from him. His voice was shrill and quaked with fear.

"Ye're lying you cunning rogue! It was you who murdered Tallia as surely as it was your treachery that has brought this pestilence on the house of Caer Gwyn. Ye'll die for this ye loathsome bastard. Ye'll squirm on my sword blade like pig on a spit."

Ned put out his hands and pleaded, "No! I did not kill her. I swear on the name of our father, our clan."

Sholto held his sword pointed toward Ned's face. They were so close I could see Sholto's bright eyes, red-rimmed, blazing like a cornered boar.

"You killed my woman!" he shouted. "For what price? Did the Hawk Clan offer you a reward? What was it then? Half our tribal lands for the crown?"

Ned backed away, stumbling into the bracken where I was hiding. "I swear I did not kill her, Sholto!" he cried.

Sholto swung his sword back menacingly and advanced on his brother, his breath coming in loud gasps. "You lying blackguard! The smith's boy saw you riding into the woods that day. He watched you from the riverbank, you scurrilous cur. He saw you as you tracked my woman down. It was you who killed Tallia. I've proof of it."

"How much did you pay that swine to bear false witness against me, brother?" Ned cried. "Now our Hywel's dead and father is in the enemy's hands," he said. "I suppose you think the tribal lands will be yours. How much did you pay to buy off that wretched scum? Would you consort with jackals such as he, just to be ricon of Caer Gwyn? Ye'll never be a match for father, Sholto. Ye're not half the man he is." He stood boldly in front of his brother, his hand on his dagger.

Sholto gave a shrill war-cry; the glint of the sunlight blazed off the tip of his uplifted sword.

I remembered the burnish of the man's plaited hair as the sun had shone on it and how he had shouted a war-cry before he went into the forest after Tallia.

But the rider who had trailed Tallia was not Ned. The man I had seen trailing her was the same man who had brought her battered corpse back from the Plain: Ifor the Red, the king's most trusted knight. It was Ifor the Red who had murdered Tallia. It was he who had betrayed Madoc by escorting him into the enemy's hands. I wanted to cry out, but I was too afraid to speak and reveal my hiding place.

Ned fell to his knees in front of his brother, grovelling. "It was not me, Sholto!"

Gathering my courage, I leapt out from behind the bushes and screamed, "No! It was not him! It was not Ned!"

My warning was too late. Ned gave one last pitiful cry as Sholto's sword blade was brought down on him. With a sickening thud Ned's severed head fell from his shoulders and tumbled at my feet.

I recoiled in horror. "It was Ifor," I screamed. "Ifor the Red, your father's kin. *He* killed your woman."

Sholto stepped calmly over his brother's corpse, his dripping sword raised toward me. He towered over me as thought he was the transfiguration of the great war god. "So, I have been betrayed, by one of our own, Ifor the Red, Prince of Caer Gwyn? Who would have suspected it? Betrayed by my uncle!"

The sound of his crazed laugh chilled my blood. "Now the Dobunnis have come for their vengeance." He looked up toward the citadel that was still ablaze. On the ramparts near the postern gate, the raven pennants of Caer Gwyn had been torn down. One bearing a hawk and another a wolf fluttered in its place.

"Gwion the Hawk has had his revenge!" Sholto muttered. "He would never have been able to take the citadel without help from those Ordovice mountain curs." He slid his sword back into the sheath and stood gazing up at the billowing standards of the Hawk clan as they unfurled beside those bearing the Wolf's totem.

I chose at that moment to bolt and run away. Sholto gave a shrill whistle. I felt the fluttering of a bird's wings over my head and heard the shrill *'keeya'* of a falcon's cry as it plunged down on me. I fell and covered my head with arms as the bird attacked, its sharp talons grazing my flesh. Then the wicked bird with its yellow eyes and dreadful talons flew back to its perch in the alder tree.

Sholto stood over me, his sword blade pressed against my throat. I could not move, and as the blade grazed my flesh I felt myself lose consciousness; a spinning, giddy feeling, as though, like the hawk, I was taking flight.

When I woke, the words of a charm rang in my head like a knell, in rhythm with the jolting of cart wheels over an uneven track. *No man shall wound me.* It is a charm as ancient as the old tales; every child knows it. It was the last thing I thought of before I fell unconscious. The words clanged in my head, a sharp, jabbing pain. *I am not dead,* I thought. But when I tried to move I could not. My body felt numb and I was bound hand and foot.

I could not determine where I was, except to know that I was being carried on a wagon. There was a strong odour of hay and manure. Looking up, I could see the dark sky filled with stars, but I could not see the moon. By tilting my head; I could see the back of the lone driver, though it was impossible to make out who he was. Pain wrenched through my body, I lay still and squeezed my eyelids tightly closed, then blinked them open again, hoping I might be dreaming. The pain in my head was so fierce I wanted to scream; I tasted blood on my lips.

Thoughts prickled me, sharp as brambles. Slowly I began to remember. Was it the vision I had seen – the girl caught in the thorn bush? *Let it just be the vision. Let me be dreaming.* I tried to cry out. My throat ached. I could not utter a sound. I remembered a headless corpse, blood splattering the meadow grass, the flapping of a bird's wings. Could it have been the Raven of Death? *Am I dead!*

I listened for a sound that might draw me back into reality. There was only the dull rumbling of the cart-wheels. The night air smelled of damp, newly ploughed earth and the light scent of meadow grass. The driver began to whistle, a tuneless melancholy sound. I wondered if I might have been taken prisoner by the Wolf Clan and began to rehearse a bargaining plea.

I am a friend of Dafydd, Son of the Wolf...

Then why did you not save him? A voice in my head said. I didn't want to remember.

.   *Please*, I prayed, *let me waken in the Otherworld.*

Stanza Five

So it was that I drifted, protected by a mantle of unconsciousness. When I first opened my eyes and heard the sound of birds, I truly believed that I had become one of them. The rattle of the wagon wheels had stopped. Bright sunlight pierced my eyes with a sharp jabbing pain. I tried to move but could not. My body felt numb, as though I had no limbs. So I lay still, squeezing my eyelids tightly closed. The pain in my head was so fierce I wanted to scream. As the birds shrilled, I had a recollection of a falcon attacking me with talons as sharp and deadly as scythes. I struggled, tried to cover my face, but my hands were held fast. The more I struggled the more the pain enveloped me.

I listened for a sound, something familiar that might draw me back into reality. For a moment, the crying of the birds sounded like a woman's voice. I thought it was Essylt's voice calling me. I tried to answer, but I could not utter a sound.

Then I heard a distant soughing, a soft undulating roar not unlike the wind rustling through the oak grove. But it was not the wind. The air smelled damp, sharp with pungent odours unfamiliar to me. I gasped, drinking it I as though it were a reviving draft of water. My throat ached and my chest felt as if a weight were crushing it. I felt rough, dry earth and stones beneath me and realized I was lying on hard ground.

I thought I heard footsteps and when I opened my eyes again, someone was standing over me. First I saw his feet, then the soft leather boots laced to the knees of his breeches, above that the hem of a red tunic.

Sholto ap Madoc! I closed my eyes again, not wanting to remember. He kicked at me. I kept my eyes shut tight, dared not to breathe.

If I pretend I am dead, will he leave me?

I heard him laugh. He knew I was alive. When I finally dared to open my eyes again he was bending over me, his face still painted with the blue stains of woad, the livid scar across his cheek giving him a dreadful appearance. I turned my head away. A jumble of recollections began to explode in my head and I whispered an ancient charm:

> *May I be an island on the sea.*
> *May I be a hill on the land.*
> *May I be a star when the moon wains.*
> *May I be a lamb safe in a fold.*

I felt cold water splash on my face. Sholto knelt beside me and pressed a flask to my lips, forcing me to drink. The stale, bitter liquid could not have tasted better had it been sweet cordial. I began to revive and looked around.

We were in an open space, sand and rocks and tall reeds with a grassy heath sweeping beyond. I heard waves breaking over the stones of a long curve of beach. Sea birds, white as foam, glided and dipped over the surface of the glistening water. A damp mist swirled out across the undulating sea. I could only suppose we were by the Narrow Sea. But how did I get there? Beyond what had happened to me in the glade everything was as hazy as an old dream.

Sholto did not speak. He cut my bonds with his dagger and motioned for me to get out of the cart. I was too weak to stand alone and staggered against him. He pushed me away and prodded me toward a pony that was tethered nearby. My legs would scarcely hold me and my feet would not move. My hands were numb and there were deep welts where the thongs had cut into my flesh. I didn't struggle as he hoisted me up to straddle the pony's back. I was too weak to think about escaping, still unable to utter a sound. I was barely able to keep my hold on the pony's mane. My thoughts were muddled; what had happened to bring me there and how could I escape?

Sholto untethered the pony from the cart, and led the way on foot, leading his pony, while I rode on mine. We followed the rocky shoreline with the sea-birds crying in our wake, until we saw the thatched roofs and stilted houses of a settlement, a village of Shore People.

At the outskirts of the village we met a young lad with a bundle in his hand and a wicker basket full of fish slung over his shoulder. He greeted us. "From whence do ye come? Is it displeasing for me to ask who you are, sir? And who is your companion?" He peered at me with narrowed eyes seeing the bloody hawk's claw marks on my face. "Should she be in need of medicines, sir?"

"We are from Caer Gwyn," Sholto said. "The warlords of the Wolf clan have plundered our citadel and killed my brothers. The girl was wounded when we were attacked. I am Sholto ap Madoc, lord of Caer Gwyn. She is a priestess of our cult. I am escorting her to safety to the holy sanctuary of Carnac, across the Narrow Sea. We will make a pilgrimage on behalf of our tribe. I seek a vessel to make our way to safety across the sea."

All this I heard clearly but could not reply. Sholto lied glibly and I could utter no protest. It seemed as though I was still in the twilight of unconsciousness.

The Shore People are simple folk and the youth was somewhat in awe of us. "You must have spent the night in the woods and have no food or drink," he said. He offered Sholto his bundle. "Here are some barley loaves and cheese." Then in his courteous manner he offered to show us the way to the harbour where we might find a vessel to take us on our way across the Narrow Sea.

He led us through the village where the tall, stilted huts of the Shore People teetered like lanky birds on stilts by the water's edge. As we approached, the villagers came out and peered curiously at us. Some of them thrust out their hands and made signs against enchantment. They were gentle, simple folk and I wanted to cry out to them to ask for their help but my voice caught in my aching throat and it seemed my courage had ebbed out of me. The gods had spared my life, for that I was grateful, and I still had enough faith left in me to believe there would be some way I could escape from that bold, deceitful renegade Sholto without his murderous sword cutting me down. But the vision of Ned's headless corpse was enough to keep me silent. I would have to bide my time, then when the gods saw fit, I'd make my appeal to one of the friendly sea folk.

The shore was lined with dugout canoes and rafts and little skin coracles they used for fishing craft. Along a stone quay there were larger vessels; long, wooden-hulled boats with carved prows and leather sails, worthy ships used for making the long sea voyages across the Narrow Sea.

The boy pointed out the largest of the ships: a sleek black craft with a griffon carved on the bowsprit and yellow standards fluttering from its mast heads bearing the crest of a two-headed crimson bird.

"This is a sturdy ship, sir," the boy said. "I know the captain. For a small price he'll transport ye to your destination. The ship carries a cargo of iron bars to the trading ports on the other side. It's only a short journey if the tide's with you, longer if the sea is running high. But it looks like a fair wind, and she'll sail by noon if the cargo is on."

Sholto took off one of his brass armlets and handed it to the boy. "May you walk with the gods for your favour, lad," he said in his cunning, most charming way.

As we came toward the ship, I saw bare-chested sailors hauling the heavy cargo up from wooden carts. I had often seen those carts of ingots rumbling down the chalk trail from the northern smelters, as they passed by Caer Gwyn on their way to the sea port.

The boy called out a greeting to the men, and asked for their captain. While we waited I planned a way to call him aside and explain my plight. It was my only chance to escape.

The captain came up from the ships hold. He was a burly rascal with matted black hair that fell in locks of tangled curls to his shoulders. He looked ill-kempt and his doublet was stained with grease, but he had a ready smile and his booming voice was friendly. Sholto spoke to him in such a convincing way there was no doubt he would give us passage.

I hung back, waiting for my chance to speak. When Sholto's back was turned and he was laughing with the Captain over some joke they had shared, I signalled to the boy. He approached me shyly.

"You must go to Caer Gwyn," I whispered. "Tell them you have seen Sholto ap Madoc and the Druid's child. Tell them the Child of the Raven is alive!" Then I mouthed the words: "*I am his captive!*"

He hung back, a startled look on his face. I remembered the amber talisman Essylt had given me. and took it out of my amulet pouch. I pressed it into his hand. "Take this, I beg you. Make haste to Caer Gwyn. Ask for the bard by the name of Lleu or the medicine woman, Essylt. She is a High Priestess there. Show them this. Tell them what you have seen."

He hesitated before accepting the amulet. Perhaps he was afraid some evil curse might be on it.

"The talisman is yours, boy, if you do this for me. The gods will walk with you."

This pleased him, and he put the amber piece in his pouch and smiled at me.

Just then Sholto looked around seeming to sense something was amiss. The boy backed away and Sholto glared at me, then turned his malevolent stare on the lad.

He pushed me aside and said briskly "This maiden is in the god's service. It is best you do not converse with her; it goes against her cult. The master of this ship says he will take us across. We are pilgrims going to the holy sanctuary to appeal to the gods for our tuath. The port is near the oak groves of Carnac. With a fair wind we will reach there by tomorrow's sunrise."

I knew he was lying. What reason did a rogue like him have to visit the Druid's holy place? By now all the warriors and hunters with their hounds would be scouring our land for him because of the carnage he had brought upon our tuath. And if someone had taken word to Caer Gwyn that he'd been seen at the sea boarding a ship, perhaps they'd follow him.

He lowered his voice. "Go on board now."

I flinched as his hand gripped my arm like a vice.

"And mind your tongue, girl, or ye'll feel my steel again, only the next time I'll slit your throat." He pushed me roughly toward the gangway, then turned to the captain to negotiate the price of our passage.

A swarthy crewman helped me up the narrow plank and showed me a place to sit among the bales of cargo on the deck. From the dockside, the Shore boy watched me with wary eyes. He was a hardy lad, open-faced and straight of character. I trusted him to deliver my message to Caer Gwyn. Mostly, I trusted the gods would walk with me and save me from Sholto's treachery.

PART ONE EPILOGUE

A LAMENT FOR CAER GWYN

The fierce wild men of the mountains
rode their chariots into the charred ruins
of Caer Gwyn's noble citadel.
Their naked limbs were tattooed with patterns of woad,
their faces smeared with blood.
They wore wolf skins and carried halberds and swords.
Warriors and priests fell in their path.
Freemen cringed before them and begged for mercy.
They were cut down as swiftly as a reaper scythes his crop.
The ground was soaked with their blood-bath.
The air rent by their piteous cries.
But the gods did not hear them.
The great warlord, Cymbeline, rode into Caer Gwyn
Dressed in a leather doublet, wearing a wolf's head for a helm.
On the end of his long spear was a bloodied head.
"Here is your ricon, Madoc!" he cried.
'Impale his head on the stakes in your Hall.
Remember him well.
Here is Madoc, ricon of the Essyltyr,
the great chieftain of Caer Gwyn.
I swear by the gods no man of Caer Gwyn
will remain alive until you deliver my son to me!

PART TWO

THE VOYAGE

The Keltic Lands of Northern Europe
And
Greek Makedonia

122

BALLAD TWELVE The Ballad Of A Stolen Maiden

*On the day of Midsummer
where the totems of the Raven clan
guard the shaded paths of the woodland grove,
Sholto ap Madoc, son of the brave Ricon of Caer Gwyn,
stole a pretty maiden and carried her off across the Narrow Sea.
She was a gay, young girl of golden locks,
skin whiter than the foam of a wave,
red as foxgloves were her cheeks.
All who knew her were filled with love for her.
She was the fairest and the loveliest, a most perfect child.
Olwen was her name, blessed child, a child of the Druids.
As the renegade warrior snatched her away, she cried:
"Farewell my beloved modryb Essylt,
My eyes will never see you again.
Farewell Lleu, no longer will I hear your bard's song.
Farewell Caer Gwyn,
I will never walk your forest paths or verdant fields
or dance again in your sacred circles of stone."
The maiden despaired, wished she had drowned in the sea,
better than being killed or ravished by her murderous captor.
Sholto ap Madoc fled with her far from the woods of Carnac,
across the lands of the Belgae.
The maiden cried: "Woe is me, gods, that I am still alive!"
Dismal was her life, a hostage,
running like a frightened hare over the land,
traversing green-swards, roaming through the gorse,
sleeping at night in the dark wood without a soft bed.
It was a great grief! A wicked fate was hers,
without relief from fear and weariness.*

*Weak and trembling, gloomy and sad, she rises early,
hears the melodious piping of a thrush in the tree-tops.
Beyond the trees is a lake where slender fish leap in shoals.
Yellow primroses grow on the banks, delicate and bright.
Fragrant is the air with herbs and meadow-sweet grass.
Weeping and treachery are unknown in this pleasant land.
There is no harsh sound, only the sweet music of the birds.
The loveliness of this wondrous land quiets the maiden.
She listens to the sweet bird-song and hears the voice of the god.*

OLWEN'S LAMENT

Stanza One

The ship with the double-headed griffon set sail from Albion in the oak-god's month, five days after the Midsummer rites. As the long craft slid out of the little harbour, and the rowers began pulling at their oars, a fair wind came up. The sailors scrambled to raise the sail, and the oarsmen fell back to rest. The breeze caught the great sail so it billowed out with the crimson standards flapping from the masthead.

A flock of seabirds cried in the ship's wake as the shoreline began to recede. I watched that beautiful green land with the shell-strewn beaches and lush forests fade from my sight. The sea rolled, grey and empty, in every direction until Cymru's lovely shores were just a misty outline. Salt spray mingled with my tears, and I thought of the bright groves and grassy meadows where I had spent my childhood. As my homeland vanished from sight, I felt as though my life, all fifteen years of it, was over. I remembered leaving my cloak in the glade where Sholto had struck me down. Surely by now, someone would have discovered it there beside the body of young Ned. Would they believe I was dead too? I wept bitter tears as I wondered what had become of Essylt and Lleu; if the Wolf Clan had ravaged our village. I despaired, believing I would never see my home and loved ones again.

The wind picked up and the sea became choppy. The ship plunged into the waves, rolling and heaving so the motion of it churned my innards until I could not move from my place without feeling as though I would be torn apart. I lay on the deck between bales of cargo, so dizzy and ill I began to wish myself dead. One of the sailors brought me a bowl of gruel but I sickened at the sight of it, heaving until I thought I would turn inside-out. All the while, Sholto sat beside me, his sword across his knees, laughing to see me in such a wretched state.

The ship rode low with its heavy cargo of ingots. The crests of the waves dashed over the stern spewing foam across the deck soaking me to the skin. I could taste the salty water that stung my eyes and chilled me to the bone. I lay there shivering, not even able to lift my head.

It seemed most of a day passed before the gentle touch of a hand on my shoulder roused me. A young lad who I had seen attending the captain had brought me a cup of steaming broth. He propped my head with his hand and lifted the cup to my parched lips. I swallowed it down gratefully, then lay back as limp and lifeless as a drowned creature. He brought a blanket and put it over me and wiped my face with the sleeve of his tunic.

"The sea can be unkind when ye're not used to her," he said. He had the same gentle lilt to his speech the Shore boy had. "Ye've only a short journey though, if ye're heading for Carnac. In this wind it will be a day, no more. See over there? By morning ye'll see the shoreline. 'Tis a lovely land: oak groves and pleasant streams jumping with fish. There's a good track that leads to the Holy Place. Ye'll have no trouble finding the way." He smiled wistfully. "'Tis not for me, that Holy Place. I'm born to the sea, and I'll not leave her. But I know about Carnac because we often take pilgrims across: Druids, and those like yourself, and some plain folk who go to see the oracles. What favour will you ask?"

He motioned to Sholto with his thumb. "I see your warrior is still wearing his cuirass and his face is all painted for battle. He says your hill fort was attacked. How does it come that ye're the only two to reach the sea?" He peered at me suspiciously and pointed to the wound on my throat. "Who did this? Ye're wearing a priestess's torc and someone dared harm ye?"

"It was..." I propped myself up on my elbow and struggled to sit up but a wave of nausea overcame me. I wanted to tell him all, but Sholto was watching me, his hand on his sword hilt.

"I'll bring ye medicines for that. It's beginning to fester. Ye'll have a nasty scar otherwise," the youth said.

Sholto stood and stepped between the boy and me. He glared at the boy with a menacing look. "Keep your distance from this girl," he warned. "No filthy sea-swine will handle her, ye hear? She's a priestess of the Sun God's Sanctuary, under my protection, to be taken to Carnac. So stand your distance boy and tell your mates Sholto ap Madoc has warned ye."

The boy scrambled away without a backward glance. Sholto stood over me, the sword blade pointed in my face. I recalled the bloody scene in the glade and fell back, shutting my eyes from the sight of his cruel face.

Stanza Two

When I opened my eyes, the last of the stars had faded from the heavens and the sky was tinged with the rosy grey of dawn. During the night, the wind had ebbed. The oarsmen pulled at their oarlocks, bending to the rhythm of the oar master's chant and the cracking of his whip. In the hissing of the waves I heard the strong, calm voice of the god calling to me from the sea depths.

I am the strong wind on deep waters. It is my voice you hear in the breaking of the waves...

Sholto was snoring in a deep sleep so I crept carefully over to the deck rail. In the distance, the dark bluish outline of a shore was visible through the morning mist, and the raucous cry of seabirds heralded our approach to land. The damp, salty-sweet spray of the sea foam was enough to revive me.

The captain's boy came out of the galley cabin and approached me cautiously. When he saw that Sholto was asleep, he beckoned to me and set down a bowl of porridge. Before I had a chance to speak, he disappeared back into the cabin but returned a moment later with a water flask and a small basket containing jars of salve and clean cloths.

With a tender touch, he cleaned the wound that Sholto's sword blade had left on my neck. We dared only to whisper lest Sholto waken.

"Where did you learn your skills?" I asked.

He smiled and said, "My grandmother was a medicine woman. I would have followed in her profession, but the sea called me. Now I look after the men, binding up blistered hands, cleaning the wounds made from the oar-master's lash. It is a useful skill. See here now, ye'll be right in no time and with luck there will be no scar. It would be a shame to mar such a pretty maiden as you!" He drew his hand away with a shy smile. His eyes grew dark and serious. "May the gods walk with ye, lass," he said. "Ye've had a terrible fright, to be sure. I wish ye the god's speed on your way to the holy Place."

I wanted to blurt out the story of how I came to be with Sholto, but before I had mustered the courage to say a word, he dashed away in answer to his Master's call.

I watched the distant shoreline draw nearer. The swirls of mist cleared, and the first pale rays of the dawning sun shone on white banks and tumbled rocks that rose from a long, sandy beach. Grey waves hissed over the pebbles, un-curling in a rim of foam. Above the cliffs, a dense grove of trees hid the slope of the land beyond. It was not so unlike Cymru. I felt some comfort in knowing somewhere beyond the forest, there was a sanctuary in the Holy Place called Carnac. Did Sholto really intend to take me there, and why? Sholto was a man with no mercy. I had seen that in the woods when he murdered his own brother. Would I be offered as a sacrifice like they had offered Dafydd?

Stanza Three

The long ship skimmed along the shoreline until it came to a small bay. A settlement of mud huts and little stone-built houses with low roof thatches and market tents were scattered along the beach. The oarsmen heaved up the oars; there was a scramble as the sailors dragged the ropes and pulled the ship alongside the quay. When the anchor was down, the captain barked orders. I heard the crack of his whip and the cursing of men as they hurried about their tasks unloading the cargo.

Curious people clustered along the quay getting under foot and calling to the sailors. There was a din of noise; fishmongers hawked their morning's catch and peddlers sold their wares. The smell of fresh barley bread from a nearby baker's oven mingled with the pungent, salty odour of the fish and with it the fragrance of pinewood. Pied dogs barked and snapped at the heels of the strangers who had set foot on their land.

I waited nervously while Sholto led the ponies safely ashore. The little cobs had fared well on the sea voyage, but the noisy crowds made them skittish. Sholto had a struggle to hold them while the captain's boy escorted me down the plank and onto the quay. I could still feel the roll of the sea when I stepped onto the land, a peculiar sensation, unfamiliar to me. I looked back at the ship, wishing I could have stayed aboard her.

The villagers pressed us from every side. Sholto put on a good show and told them he was a visiting knight who was escorting me, a Druid priestess, to Carnac's holy sanctuary to plead for the safety of our tuath that had been attacked by northern warriors.

Would they guess the truth? They treated me with reverence and more than once someone called a request for a charm. I made the signs of good fortune politely and kept a clear mind for a chance to explain my plight. How could they guess I had been stolen and was in jeopardy? Druids are in the god's hands and exempt from harm; we can travel into any land without fear. So, I smiled bravely and held up my head, remembering who I was.

The captain had been watching us. He signalled the boy and gave him an order.

"My captain says I should lead ye to the Carnac trail," the boy said.

I expected Sholto to protest but he seemed to think better of it and motioned for the boy to take the pony's reins while I mounted. I looked anxiously around me, hoping I might see some way to escape now we were safely on the land. I couldn't risk calling out, because Sholto was always watching me, his hand on his sword hilt, glowering a warning as though he knew what was on my mind.

He took the reins from the boy and told him to walk in front of us. The ship's boy led us along a maze of cobbled alleys, through a village unlike any I had seen in Albion. The stone and wattled houses were crowded closely together with the doorways opening onto lanes where the gutters ran with filthy waste filling the air with a dank, acrid odour. There were crowds of freemen everywhere; the alleys jammed with ox-carts and people jostling by, with baskets and bundles, hurrying on their way to the market. Grimy children squatted under the roof thatches playing at their games. They shouted greetings as we passed and the small boys ran alongside Sholto, gaping at him curiously while their rowdy dogs snapped at the horses' hooves.

The village was protected by a stone wall that extended from one edge of the port to the other, with a tall gate and a watchtower. At the village gate a toothless old watchman surveyed us suspiciously and put out his gnarled hand for alms. We had nothing to give him, so I made a sign of the pentacle and gave him a blessing. He grinned, muttered his gratitude, and let us pass.

Outside the walls, the land stretched out in a low plain. There were well-tilled fields of tasselled corn and grassy pastures where shaggy cattle grazed. Across the fields, the scattered groves of birch and ash trees became denser, forming a forest of dark pines and evergreens. The road forked there; one track, well travelled and rutted by cartwheels, turned eastward. The other was little more than a footpath that led into the forest. A heap of stones marked the entrance to the trail; a rough- built shrine of a traveller's god.

The boy stopped there. "Here is the way," he said. He pointed toward the distant trees. "The track is marked clearly. There are many shrines like this one. It is a full day's journey to the Holy Grove. Ye'll find a hermit's cave just off the pathway before you reach the Sacred Way. The old man will give you food and drink, and bed you down for the night."

I knew this was my last opportunity to appeal for help and had enough courage to speak up.

"We must make a libation here at the god's shrine," I said.

Sholto did not protest, even as I dismounted and went to the heap of stones. I had nothing to offer, not even a crust of bread, but this was my only hope. So I bowed my head and repeated every charm that came to mind, pledging my service to the gods if they would help me.

As I stood there, I wondered desperately what I should do. The ship's boy pressed something into my hand. "Take this!" He glanced over at Sholto who was still astride his horse. "It is a sailor's talisman to ward off evil. If you pass safely to Carnac, give this to the old man at the cave so he will know the gods are with you. My ship will anchor in the port for four days. I believe this man, Sholto, has evil intent. If you are in danger, do not be afraid because I will follow you."

He was a brave boy to make such a gesture. I felt a great sense of relief, as though the gods had already answered my pleas.

I looked over at Sholto who was standing by the shrine, head bowed, as if he was making a supplication to the god. I dared to reply to the boy and whispered, "If you can, send a message across the sea to the hill fort of Caer Gwyn. Tell them you have seen the Druid's girl, Olwen."

The boy made the sign of the pentacle. "Go in safety, walk in peace,' he said. He whispered, "I will follow you some of the way." Then he hailed Sholto and went on his way back toward the village.

We turned down the narrow track toward the forest trail. I mounted my pony, ready for the unknown journey ahead. Had Sholto heard my conversation with the boy? I dared not to look back lest he suspect something. The boy had said he would follow us; I could only hope he would stay well hidden.

Stanza Four

The forest was filled with black shadows, the trees so tangled and dense the sunlight was blocked out. We had gone a short way, when suddenly Sholto wheeled his pony round and shouted for me to follow him. He drew his sword from its sheath and peered around as though he was listening for something. Silence engulfed us eerily; even the birds seemed to have stopped twittering. He ordered me to dismount and prodded me ahead of him at sword point. I was filled with terror, believing he intended to kill me in that desolate place where he might hide my body in the underbrush.

I stumbled ahead of him, trying not to cry out. Suddenly Sholto stopped. I heard the crackling of twigs in the underbrush, then the startled cry of a partridge alerting its mate as it flapped up out of the thicket. Sholto pushed me aside and darted off the path into the brush. Someone scrambled out of the bracken, leaping over the windfalls into the dense underbrush. I caught a glimpse of a boy's tawny hair and the bright blue of his tunic. It was the ship's boy!

Sholto shouted as he charged into the thicket after him. I heard the slashing of the sword, then a small, thin treble cry and the thrashing sounds of branches breaking as the two of them struggled. I held my breath and stifled a scream. I wanted to run into the brush after him and help the boy. I stood frozen in fear. I held the talisman the boy had given me tight in my hand and said a prayer that he would escape and his life would be saved.

Then Sholto came out of the brush and I saw the blood on his sword as he slammed it back into the sheath. There was blood on his hands and splattered on the front of his breeches.

"Now then," he growled, "Ye'll have no other warnings."

He grabbed me, grappling with me roughly. "Give it to me now, or I will cut ye're hand off so ye'll remember this lesson." He snatched the talisman the boy had given me out of my clenched fist and threw it into the bracken. "They will never find the lad," he snarled," and they will never find us. So, mind — Druid priestess or ye'll die here with him if ye try any more tricks."

His hand was on my throat, squeezing the breath out of me. I felt myself grow faint. The blood pounded at my temples and everything became dark as I fell to the path at his feet.

When I opened my eyes again, Sholto was bending over me, his face still flushed with anger, the red scar livid across his cheek, his eyes fiery with rage. I thought he would kill me then, but he pulled me up and hoisted me onto the pony, tethering it to his horse. I was mute with fear as he led me out of the forest, back toward the cornfields.

BALLAD THIRTEEN A Captive's Lament

How sad is my heart;
I weep for the dark halls of Caer Gwyn.
I weep for the sunny woodlands of my home.
A longing comes over me.
How sad is my heart;
I long for my loved ones.
No more shall I hear the sweet songs of Lleu's harp.
No more shall I walk the herb-strewn paths with Essylt.
Caer Gwyn, my village on the green plain, I shall see no more.
What ill-luck caused the gods to take me away?
Woe is me, gods, that I am still alive.
Woe is me that I will nevermore see my lovely land.

THE JOURNEY

Stanza One

The way led to the east, through villages and past sedgy flatland, isolated farmsteads and wild, dense forests inhabited by foxes, bears and stags. Sholto had acquired a bow and arrows, so he shot game, small deer or rabbits, which he butchered and roasted over a campfire. After the ship boy's murder I could neither eat nor sleep; in truth I willed myself to die. He pushed me on relentlessly, leading me on horseback by day and tied to his side at night, treating me in the same rough manner he would handle his hunting dogs.

Since the ship boy's killing, I dared not defy him and became as passive as a slave, obeying him dutifully and mutely. At night I lay awake bundled in a sheepskin, conscious he was watching me, too terrified to move, gripped by the fear he might molest me. It seemed as though my wits had become dulled by the shock of all that had happened. I knew when Madoc learned Sholto had slain his brother he would send men to scour to the ends of the earth for him. But would they search for me? Did they know Sholto had stolen me?

A few days later, on the trail to Carnac, we encountered a ragged band of men on the road. I thought they might be brigands but none of them appeared to be armed other than the daggers at their belts. They greeted us and eyed Sholto warily. A chill crept over my flesh and I made the sign against evil. *'Please Gods, avert the bad spirits.'*

"Who are ye? From where?" one of the men asked. His tongue had some of the same sounds as our language, but the accent was slurred and strange.

"We're going to Carnac. We're travellers in search of good fortune," Sholto replied.

The man eyed him suspiciously. One of the other men said, "Ye're going to Carnac? You'd best be gone from here if you want to save your skin. There are ship's crew about searching for a man who killed their captain's boy."

A man with a jagged scar across his cheek leered at me. "The girl? How much for her?"

I felt a surge of terror but stifled it.

I saw Sholto stiffen. "The girl's not a chattel. She's a Druid priestess. We are travelling together to Carnac."

The men talked freely among themselves. I kept my eyes lowered and listened.

One of them approached close to Sholto, eyeing him suspiciously. "We are Belgae. What tribe are ye from?"

"We come from Cymru, across the Narrow Sea," Sholto said. I saw his hand on the hilt of his sword. "The girl's a Druid's child. I'm taking her to Carnac. Now, stand aside and let us pass."

The man peered closely at Sholto and stepped closer. "The rogue they are looking for is Cymry."

"Stand aside!" growled Sholto. He leaped off his pony and unsheathed his sword, brandishing it at the man. "I'll have yer head if you make a move closer." He stepped forward menacingly and the other men backed away, scurrying into the bushes.

The man stood his ground, boldly facing Sholto. "Ye're the filthy rogue, aren't you? The one who killed..."

The words were barely out of his mouth before Sholto swung his sword. I watched in horror as the man's headless body crumbled and fell to the ground.

"Now!" Sholto said, as he mounted his horse. "We'll take another road. Not to Carnac. Not if the ship's crew are looking for us!"

I wondered where he was taking me, but I dared not ask. He pushed on relentlessly, leading me on the pony by day, tied by his side at night. He treated me in a rough manner, snarling and threatening to whip me if I dared disobey him. I could not imagine what he might do to me, and I knew somehow, I must try to escape. I could barely utter a sound, existing in a dream-like trance. One day passed into another, until I lost all sense of time and direction.

At night I watched the stars and looked for a portent. Only the phases of the moon indicated that a full thirty days had gone by from the time the griffon ship had deposited us on this alien shore.

We travelled for days, usually avoiding the settlements along the way unless Sholto needed food or drink. One day we came to a pond and Sholto stopped to water the ponies and bathe himself. I was too afraid to strip out of my bedraggled clothes to wash off the grime. When I caught a reflection of myself on the surface of the pool, I saw how thin I had grown, my long hair matted and unkempt. I looked more like a beggar or a slave than a Druid's child. I wondered, if once we were far enough away, Sholto would decide he had no more need of me. What would happen then? Would he let me go? How

131

would I find my way back home? In despair I waited for that day to come, all the while wondering if he would just kill me and leave my body for the vultures.

Seizing my chance, while Sholto bathed, I broke away and dashed into the thicket. Sholto yelled and I heard the splash of water and the sound of his footsteps crashing through the brush. He caught me from behind and threw me to the ground, his foot on my chest.

"If you ever try to run again, I will kill you!"

With each word he pressed his foot down harder on my chest until I could scarcely breathe. I saw the madness in his eyes, and cringed under his malevolent glare. "W-where are you taking me?" I gasped.

"I'm going to the ends of the earth, to seek my fortune. And you, little priestess, are my luck charm." He reached down and pulled me to my feet. His hand gripped my arm like a talon as he pulled me close to his naked body. "I will not do you harm if you obey me. But if you try to run, or seek help, you will die – and anyone who tries to help you - like the foolish ship's boy! You can live or you can die," Sholto warned. "I can keep you as my luck-charm or sell you. A pretty girl like you, a Druid's child, will bring a good price. Decide your fate, girl. And don't work your magic spells on me or you'll feel my sword on your neck. If you try to run again I will kill you!"

After that, Sholto kept me close beside him, tethering my pony to his, watching every move I made. He had a savage, cruel nature and I dared not defy him, so I followed him dutifully like an obedient slave. He rarely spoke to me.

At night, bundled in a sheepskin, I lay awake, conscious he was watching me, too terrified to move, always gripped by the fear he might attack me, ravish me and then kill me. It seemed as though my wits had become dulled by the shock of all that had happened.

Stanza Two

The God speaks and says:_*Who made the ruggedness of the mountains? Who but the gods know where the sun shall set? I am the wind soughing through the pines. I am an eagle on a cliff. Who but I know the secrets of the uncharted paths?*

The summer sun was hot as we travelled across the hills and plains. Two moons had waxed and waned since I had been taken. Soon our way was blocked by the towering heights of a mountain range whose massive granite walls rose into the sky with snow-crested summits shrouded with clouds. Were these the formidable heights where strange gods dwelt?

We began our journey through the Alpine mountains early in the morning, cloaked in a swirling mist. The way was marked with boulders up a rocky spur.

Our sturdy sure-footed ponies picked their way carefully around them and down through the thick pine forest.

Sometime during the day the mist turned to rain, and by nightfall we were soaked to our skins, so Sholto said we would make camp for the night. He snared a rabbit and roasted it over the fire. Filling the empty gnawing of my stomach seemed less important than being warm and dry.

While he built a lean-to shelter to protect us from the rain, I collected dry faggots for a campfire. I was numb with cold and could hardly bear the pain in my bones. I dreamt of bathing in a cauldron of steaming hot water and bargained with the gods to allow me such a luxury.

We set off early the next morning. The rain had stopped, and the fog lifted. Sholto was wary of dangers as we headed through the dense woods. There were wild animals prowling, so we kept to a track where the sun shone through the green leaves and the wind whispered in the branches. Sholto always kept one hand on his sword hilt, as if at any moment he expected we might be ambushed and attacked. The thought caused my skin to prickle with fright, yet what was worse: death by Sholto's hands or a stranger's? In truth, I had come to accept this would be my fate.

We travelled for days, not meeting a soul, hidden in the dense brush by day, hovering near the campfire at night while I prayed the flames would scare off beasts and spirits. At last we came to a valley where sheep grazed in verdant meadows. It seemed a peaceful place and the fears I had felt during the mountain trek were eased by the tranquil scene that lay ahead.

We rode on across the patchwork of fields where occasionally there were villages with clusters of stone huts. Long-horned sturdy cattle grazed in the grass and lowly folk gleaned late summer harvests.

As we went across the fields, Sholto waved and call out a greeting to some men who were working in the field. "Who are you?" he asked.

"We are Ligurians," they replied. "And who are you?"

"We have come from the east," Sholto said. "Carnac. He turned to me and said, "These people are peasants, so they will be friendly folk, but you must not speak. Understand?" He drew his hand across his throat.

"Where go ye?" the men asked.

"To seek our fortune in the south where I am told there is much wealth."

"Ah, ye're heading south?" one man said. "They say there's a king in the south who is recruiting men for his army."

"Yes! We are going there!" Sholto said and spurred our ponies forward.

The sun was high in the sky above us. We came to a stream that burbled between a stand of willows and we stopped in the shade for a meal of stale bread and mouldy cheese, all that was left in Sholto's kit.

I lay on the riverbank to rest, and closed my eyes. A clatter of waterfowl took off downstream and an arrow whizzed into the startled flock. I heard Sholto shout and when I looked, I saw he had shot one of the birds.

"Duck for our supper!" he said, as if it mattered to me whether I filled my empty stomach when it meant only another day as the hostage of this despicable man.

I walked to the water's edge. The river ran swift and when I stepped into its cold stream it made rivulets around my ankles. Small fish crowded around my feet, nibbling at my toes. The coldness of the water made me gasp as I plunged under, my feet on the pebbly bottom, my arms spread wide letting the current tug at my clothes, cleansing me of the filth of travel, of Sholto and his sneering evil. I said a prayer to Diva, goddess of rivers, and let my breath out in a stream of bubbles as I submerged my head. Perhaps I would let myself be carried away by the current. Perhaps I will drown here, I thought as I let myself sink. A euphoric feeling came over me, a feeling of peace, but something made me push to the surface again gasping for breath. Circling around me was a cob of swans. Had our swan goddess, Alarch, sent them here to protect me? When I emerged from the water, it startled them, and they paddled away downstream.

I pulled myself onto the warm shore to dry my sodden clothing in the sun. Exhausted, I lay listening to the gurgling of the stream and the sound of trilling birds in the willows. I let myself drift into a quiet reverie until I heard Sholto's voice. When I opened my eyes he was standing there looking down at me.

"You do not wish to eat?"

I turned my head away. "No."

"I have roasted the duck."

The thought of it made my stomach clench. "No. I do not want to eat."

"As you wish," Sholto said, "but food is scarce on the journey."

I would rather starve than live another day as your captive, I thought. Instead, I tried to sound brave and wise. "We Druids travel under the protection of the grey mantle of Mona and the gods of the Holy Isle. We will be fed as if we come from the gods."

He reached down and grasped me by my hair. pulling me to my feet. I tried to wrench myself free but he pressed against me, his mouth crushing on mine. I smelled the rankness of his breath, the stench of his unwashed flesh.

"Yes, little priestess," he said with a crooked smile. "With you by my side, I am protected. We will not be harmed by warriors of any Keltic tribes. They will see you wear a Druid's torc. You are my luck charm." He pulled me close and I wrenched away bracing myself for what would come next. If he wanted to, he could snap my neck like a rabbit's. Instead, he released me and stepped back, laughing. "Not just yet, little one. I must not harm the Druid's child so long as I need the god's protection."

Stanza Three

We made our way through mountains that towered as high as the clouds, following a deer-trodden rocky spur into a perilous forest, hinds scudding through the pines at the sound of the horses' hoofs. I had been taught to have no fear of wooded places and followed Sholto in silence along the tracks through the woods and across fields with the stubble of newly harvested wheat. There were shepherds on the hillsides tending their flocks and they waved as we passed by.

At night, to pass the time, Sholto liked to tell tales. At first, they were warrior tales and I listened with my mouth clamped shut, his voice pounding my ears like drum beats. Then, as the days passed, I softened and even shared a few of my own, though Sholto jeered and said they were maiden's tales. Still, he listened, sometimes even smiled, and I felt his demeanour soften.

He began to be less watchful, perhaps knowing I'd never dare run away. For where could I go without him to protect me? We were far from the Narrow Sea, traversing wild lands where savage beasts roamed. Sometimes we met suspicious, threatening strangers and I feared they might seize me and sell me into slavery. Sholto, my captor, had become my protector. I dared not leave his side.

As much as I despaired, I lived day by day, grasping what courage I could in spite of the many times I was certain that soon my life would end and I would find myself in the cold embrace of Llud-Nuatha, lord of the Otherworld. At night, the harvest moon hung full and orange in the dusky sky. I turned to the moon for solace and lay staring up at the black night. The moon had not risen, and the stars shone so clear and bright I lifted my hand as if to reach out and touch them. I remember the god's words: ***The gods only go with you if you put yourself in their path and that takes courage. You are on a dangerous journey, and you must chart the way yourself, remember every mountain track and farmstead, each barrow and hill fort. The path will lead you to your destiny.***

Then, one night, I saw it-- the dragon's fire, falling toward the south. An omen. What did it mean? I recalled Grandfather's predictions that night in Caer Gwyn when we had seen the dragon's fire in the sky.

It often portends the death or a victory of a great man or king, he had said. *It can bring good luck or bad.*

Sholto was sitting at the far side of the fire. The dim light cast a dark shadow over him except for the flickering of the flames washing over his face. Behind the shadow-play of light I saw his grim smile. I knew he was watching me. My stomach knotted. I could only guess what his plans were for me, and the thought of it kept me lying awake far into the night. I wished *he* would die! I knew only one thing: I must learn to live with my fate or I was the one who would not survive.

As the days passed, we travelled farther and farther, traversing more high mountain passes, fording rivers, crossing valleys where there were settlements of people who called themselves the Salt People. They were rough, burly men, their pale hair swept back, hanging loose to their shoulders. They spoke a dialect of our Keltic. Sholto said there were salt mines in those mountains, and they traded it to other tribes who needed it to preserve meats. To Cymry people, salt and oil were more precious than gold.

One day as we crossed a valley, we came upon a humble shack built of mud and stone where goats and a few ragged sheep grazed in the field.

"We'll stop here awhile," Sholto said. He dismounted and went toward the shack calling a greeting.

A wrinkled old woman came out to greet us. "Where have you come from?" she asked.

"We came through the woods yonder," Sholto replied in his gruff way. "We are from the tribes of the north beyond the Narrow Sea, in the green lands of Cymru."

"And where are you bound for?"

"We are going south," he said.

She peered at him suspiciously with rheumy eyes. "To seek your fortune?"

"Aye."

"And what is this fortune you seek?"

"I am Sholto ap Madoc, the son of the ricon of Caer Gwyn. Our tuath was burned by our enemies and a great calamity befell our people. There is wealth in these southern tribes. We are going to the land beyond the mountains where I am told there are tribal lords who will pay me well to fight for them."

The woman came close and poked at me with a bony finger. "Who are you child? You are as frail as a bird."

I grasped the first thing I could think of to say. "I...I am Olwen, child of the Raven." I pointed to my Raven torc of twisted gold braid. Before I could explain, Sholto shot me a warning glance and said, "She is a child of the Druids." He put his arm around me as if to feign affection. "She is my protector on this journey."

The old woman sighed and looked at me with reverence "Ah, a Druid's child, eh? A young priestess then! Surely you must walk with the gods, for these are wild, dangerous lands."

I wanted to blurt out: *I am the hostage of this wicked man who has stolen me from my home!* but when I saw Sholto glowering at me, my courage failed, and fear froze the words on my lips. As if he knew my thoughts, Sholto stayed close, and watched me, his face engraved with a hard expression. What would he do should I tell the kindly woman the truth? I swallowed hard and stared at the ground so she would not see my fear or detect Sholto's falsehoods.

The crone clicked her tongue and scowled at him with a gaze so fierce Sholto seemed cowed, as if she had cast an evil eye on him. "You must come in by the fireside. Come, and share a meal with me. Let me at least feed the child. She looks half starved!"

Sholto agreed and we followed her inside. As we entered, I detected the sweet odour of incense. and noticed bundles of herbs hanging from the mantle where dozens of small ceramic jars were arranged along the shelf. Could this old crone be a sorceress or healer like my *modryb*, Essylt?

She motioned for us to sit on hides by the hearth. The aroma of stewing meat and the fragrant scent of herbs from a pot simmering over a small fire was like a life-giving ambrosia to me.

The crone ladled some into a wooden bowl and offered it to me. "Eat! Eat!" she commanded.

The stew was made with chunks of meat and vegetables, food such as I had not tasted for months. Still I was only able to eat sparingly while Sholto consumed everything with the voraciousness of a hungry wolf. He scooped the meat into his hands and licked his fingers. When he was finished, he smacked his lips and expelled a great growling belch.

The crone offered him more. He had become almost docile and I wondered if she had cast a spell on him.

As I savoured the hearty meal, I grew more curious and bold enough to speak. I pointed to the collection of clay jars.

"What are those?"

"Herbs. Medicines," she told me.

I felt my heart quicken. I had sensed from the moment we entered her hut the woman was a healer. There was something eerily familiar about her and now I had no doubt.

As we readied to depart, while Sholto went to fetch the ponies, the crone brought me a warm cloak. As she wrapped it round my shoulders, she whispered close to my ear, "You have been sent here so I may help you." She grasped my hand with her bony fingers.

I knew she understood what I was afraid tell her. She hobbled to a wicker chest in the corner and opened it, sifted through its contents, and picked out a small vial that she put in a black silk bundle and slipped it into my amulet bag. "You will find the right time to use it." She peered deeply into my eyes. "It contains a powerful potion. It will numb a man's wits, or it will kill him. Use it wisely." She glanced outside where Sholto was waiting and cast a gaze toward him so fierce I knew she meant it as a curse.

"I was taught by a sorcerer, a man of great wisdom," she said. "Say the charms and make your supplications. Watch for the signs. You must listen and, look for the signs!" She stood still, her eyes closed, as if she was drifting into a trance. "I see a place...a clearing in the forest where wolves prowl in the shadows like great brindled dogs. Water gushes from the rocks into a pool. This is the place...the enchanted place where you will make your offerings. May the goddess protect you and return you safely to your people." She leaned toward me and kissed me. "You will know what to do. Mark your way. When the time is right, make your escape." She put her hands on either side of my face and kissed me on the forehead. "May the sun and moon be on your path."

She reached in the amulet bag that hung round her waist and took out a delicately carved piece of bone shaped like a horse strung on a silken cord which she slipped over my head. I stumbled for words to thank her.

"It is Rhiannon, the horse goddess, a luck-charm," she said. "Keep it with you. She will bring you luck. Say the charms and make your supplications. Rhiannon will help you find your way back."

I clasped her hand, to let her know I understood, then I made the sign of goodwill and peace, and went outside where Sholto waited with the ponies.

As I mounted my pony and rode away, following Sholto toward the vast unknown wilderness of the mountains, the crone's words stayed with me: *Read the signs. They will help you find your way back.*

I felt suddenly stronger, more assured all would be well, knowing the goddess was with me on this journey, and she would keep me safe.

Stanza Four

The weather had turned fine and the snow we had encountered in the heights was melting. The trails ran with mud and fog lay softly over the slopes. We rode our horses, following a mule track through a gorge when we heard the barking of dogs and hoof-beats cantering on the trail behind us. Alarmed, Sholto's hand clasped his sword hilt.

A black-haired youth mounted on a solid bay gelding accosted us. He carried a bow and quiver of arrows; his javelins were tied across the saddle-cloth. He sat quietly on his mount and looked steadily at Sholto. I took careful note of him— his bright checkered cloak, the style of the brass torc and patterns of woad etched on his bare arms. My hands tensed on my pony's reins, and I scanned the track way behind him to see if there were others, but he seemed to be alone.

The hounds ran up as soon as Sholto dismounted from his pony. They crowded around him snuffling and gnarling. Sholto pushed his way through them muttering gruff threats. The dogs backed away showing their sharp teeth.

The young hunter swung his fist up, giving the salute of a warrior. "Where are you bound?" he asked. He spoke a Keltic tongue, one different from ours yet easy enough to understand.

"South," Sholto said. "And who are you?"

"My name is Ban," the youth replied. "I am from a tuath of Dardanians. These are Illyrian lands. And you? From which tuath?

"I am Sholto ap Madoc. We are Cymry, from the northern lands. We have travelled far."

The hunter glanced over at me. "And the maiden?"

"She is my sister," Sholto lied. "She's a priestess of our clan, a medicine woman."

"Why have you have come so far to our land?" He inspected Sholto and pointed at his sword. "Are you a warrior?"

"I have heard there are tribal lords here who will trade with us and hire strong men to fight for them," Sholto said.

"Then you must go south to Makedon," the hunter said. "There is a mighty king in the south who has conquered all these lands. The Makedoni, they make trade with us. You can make good trade with this king. Keltic arms – swords, daggers."

"Who is this king you speak of?"

"He is named Filippos. His army numbers tens of thousands. He is a fearsome warrior and has conquered all the lands from one sea to the other." He swept out both arms. "Illyria, Epirus, Thrace. All are his." He waved his hand eastward. "Now he will go far away to the east to fight the mighty armies of the Persians. You should go there, to Makedon."

Sholto weighed the hunter's words. "Is he generous, this king? Does he pay his warriors well?"

"Yes. This king is very rich," the youth continued. "There is much gold and silver in Makedon. They say he is recruiting men to go on a conquest east."

"Is that where you are bound, to join this king's army?"

"No, but if you need food, fresh weapons, I can take you to my tuath," the hunter offered. "My father is a tribal chief. My people will welcome you."

"How many days before I reach the lands of the warrior king?" Sholto asked.

The youth squinted up into the sun and calculated on his fingers. "If you keep to the valley, perhaps ten more days. There are tribes along the way, friendly people who will take you in. If you meet anyone, show them this," He took off one of his arm bracelets and handed it to Sholto. "Tell them you are a friend of Ban, son of Tagos. "He smiled and nodded toward me. "What will become of your sister if you join the king's army?"

Sholto shrugged. "She'll bring a good bride price."

Horror swept over me when I heard Sholto say those words: *A good bride price.* I would rather die than be sold as some man's chattel. Until then I had been useful to him, protected by my birthright as a Druid's child. No one had dared harm us as we had passed through the Keltic lands. But now we were in the land of strange, fierce tribes who did not honour our gods. Sholto was a warrior, and here he could find his fortune with this foreign king who traded with the Kelts and needed men such as Sholto ap Madoc for his army. What was to become of me then? Was I to be given as a dowry price to some alien chieftain, sold as a hearth slave? Or would he abandon me here now he had no more need of me?

Goddess, mother goddess, I thought, *please protect me from such a fate.*

No matter what, I knew I must heed the old crone's warning and try to get away. Once we reached the country where that fabled king was recruiting his army, Sholto would have no more need of me except as his bed partner or slave.

BALLAD FOURTEEN The Samhain Moon

The God speaks and says:
There will come at sunrise a fair man.
Sure-footed is his steed.
He lights up the lands as he rides.
Thousands of brightly clad warriors are waiting.
On the day of battle he rides his steed into the sea
and it becomes blood.

THE FATE OF THE GODS, CALAN GAIA: SAMHAIN

Stanza One:

We travelled south to what Sholto said were Illyrian lands. Whenever we met the Illyrian clansmen, Sholto questioned them and always the reply was the same: "Mind as you go. Filippos the Makedonian has conquered our lands. He is a fearsome warrior. He has married our women and taken our young men as hostages. He thinks ill of Kelts, so unless you have something to barter or trade it's best you do not venture too far south."

Their warnings did not deter Sholto, so we kept going. All along the way, whenever we stopped, I made offerings of whatever I could find: smooth white stones on which I scratched the symbol of the pentacle for good fortune, rowan berries mixed with a pinch of salt for luck.

We followed a well-trodden trail used by the people who lived in those mountains. I had memorized the crone's words and paid heed to the terrain, the lay of the land and shape of the hills, the height of the mountains, every turn in the path, each place we made a camp for the night.

Mist wreathed over the low pastures. The moon shone pale through the branches of the trees. At night I watched the stars, noted their position in the sky and the waxing of the moon. The Goddess of the Moon is gifted with magic and has power over the dead. Soon she would shine her brightest for our festival of Calan Gaeaf, Samhain, the night when the sun descends into darkness and the Earth, our Mother, dons her garments of mourning. and our ancestor's voices whisper in the wind. Our goddess Cerridwen, Keeper of the Sacred Cauldron, comes close to us on that night. I would invoke her and ask her to protect and guide me. Perhaps the spirit of Grandfather Maelgwyn would also come to comfort and guide me with his wisdom. I had watched for the signs as the old woman had told me, waiting for the time to be right when I could flee from my captor.

I rode in silence following Sholto in the falling dusk. Fog began to blow in wisps across our path as we made our way through the dense forest. The eerie howling of wolves sent a cold shiver through me that prickled my skin. At last we came out of the dense thicket and found ourselves in a clearing free of the forest's sombre shadows. We were in a small break in the woods, a grove half encircled by a rock outcrop. At one end was a small spring that gushed from inside the rock.

We are here! I thought, and a chill ran down my spine. I felt my heart-beats quicken as I remembered the words of the seeress: *"I see a place...a clearing in the forest where wolves prowl in the shadows like great brindled dogs. Water gushes from the rocks into a pool."*

On one side of the clearing, a cascade of water splashed from a cleft in the rocks into a pool. It was just as she had described. I knew this must be the place— the place where I would make my escape, where I must make the offerings, and put the potion in a drink for Sholto.

The crone had told me: *It can make a man sleep. Or it can kill him!*

I felt a chill at the thought. Did I have the courage to poison Sholto? Or should I just give him enough of the potion to put him into a deep sleep?

"We will stop here for the night," Sholto said.

We dismounted in the glade. Sholto tethered the horses and set about to build a fire in the clearing, kindling it with pieces of dry bark until the fire blazed.

"This will be our Samhain fire," he said with a wry smile. "Do you think it will keep the spirits of the prowling dead away?" He began to gather dry bracken and threw the sheepskins over it. "We'll sleep together close to the fire. It will keep the wolves away."

I shivered, not just from the chill of the late afternoon, and drew my cloak tighter around me. The light was fading rapidly, and dusk filled the grove with shadows. I looked up at the sky through the trees and saw the pale blinking of the first stars and the moon, shining like a bronze shield above us. The gods have the power to delay the moon's course, to spin a single night into the length of many. I prayed it would be such this night.

Sholto sat on the sheepskins near the fire, his sword beside him.

At home they will be slaughtering the cattle, I thought. Calan Gaeaf was always a day of blood and frightening spirits as the dead return to haunt us. What good was Sholto's sword against the demons of Samhain? Flames flickered across his face, and he looked as fierce and frightening as Llud Nuatha, lord of the Otherworld.

I knew what I was planning was the right thing, but still — to kill a man with poison? Could I do that? Would I be haunted forever by his evil spirit?

I went to the spring and filled a pot with water from the cascade's pool which I brought to heat on the stones by the fire. I tossed some rose-hips and crushed herbs from my amulet bag into the pot and while the water began to steam and bubble, I gathered sprigs of rowan berries and boughs of fern and juniper to toss into the flames. As the fragrant smoke rose, I laid the sprigs of rowan berries beside the fire with some wild garlic from my amulet bag and I whispered a prayer to wise Cerridwen, one Essylt had taught me.

"In the presence of the Goddess I bear offerings. From the Earth, her never failing presence; from the Holy Kindred these gifts I offer. From all that is given, I give in return. By fire, the fruits of the rowan tree and boughs of the evergreen, I beg you Goddess, give me knowledge and strength to do what I must. Show me the omens. Help me find my way home again!"

After the infusion of herbs had steeped awhile, I tipped some into two cups. In the one for Sholto, I poured in a handful of potion the crone had given me. *How much should I pour? How much will stir his ardour? How much to make him sleep? How much to kill him?*

The crone had said; "You will know". But I did not.

I managed a courteous smile as I handed the cup to him. "Here is some herb tea to warm you. Have some to brave the night. It's our night of Calan Gaeaf and though we are far from home, we can at least honour the spirits and celebrate together with tea instead of mead."

It had been too cold to take off our furs, but now the fire blazed bright so I shrugged off my cloak and sat beside him, humming a quiet tune to ease the tension I felt.

Sholto warmed his hands around his cup and slurped a mouthful of the tea. He peered at me, brows furrowed, then winked at me and said, "It tastes almost as good as mead."

Was he suspicious? Did he know I had poured what might be a lethal concoction into his drink?

I drew in a long breath, then calmly took a sip from my own cup. "Do you fear this night?" I asked. On Calan Gaeaf night even dauntless warriors like Sholto, who fear nothing, are afraid of the dead souls who come prowling.

A black scowl crossed his face and his eyes glistened. He glanced at me swiftly and swallowed another great gulp of the tea. "I am a chieftain. The demons delight in attacking royalty on this night."

I took two smooth white stones from my amulet bag. "Here, then. We'll make an offering. Then we'll see if the souls of the departed ones come to warm themselves by our fire."

I gave him one of the stones and we each tossed them into the flames. I said a prayer to the spirits of the dead ones, to Grandfather and brave Hywel and even to Ned whom Sholto had so brutally killed.

I wondered: *Was it true if one of the stones was missing in the morning the person who threw it would die?*

For a while Sholto and I sat silently watching the flames and the blue smoke drifting into the darkening sky. As the fire dwindled, my eyes closed in half-dreaming. The ground beneath me was soft with moss and fallen leaves. I might have drifted off to sleep, but just then Sholto reached out and lifted a lock of my hair, running his fingers through it. His touch woke me from my reverie.

"Have you cast a spell on me, little one?" He looked at me with glinting eyes and a careless smile, then tipped the cup and drank the rest of the potion.

I heard the slur in his voice and knew the potion had swollen his tongue. His hand touched my thigh and he looked at me the way I had seen men in Hall leer at the serving girls. I scrambled to me feet. "I... I'll put more wood on the fire."

Sholto groped toward me, then gave a sigh and fell back with his arm thrown behind his head like a pillow. His eyes were half closed. He mumbled something, then lay still.

The fire had died and the wind soughed through the trees in a low moan. Past the tops of the trees I could see the face of the moon shining in a big silver globe. Sholto didn't move and it wasn't long before he began to snore. I knew the potion was taking affect. How long would it be before the poison would seep through his veins and stop his heart?

I must leave now! The thought made my chest rise and fall rapidly as if trying to keep pace with my thoughts. *It must be now!*

I gathered up my cloak and moved into the shadows away from the campfire.

'*Raven of Panic, do not let me fail!*' I whispered.

I crept toward the edge of the clearing. My movement made the ponies restless so they snorted and tugged at their tethers.

I must escape! I knew that it would cost me my life if I didn't.

Just as I reached the trail I heard the scuffing of footsteps behind me and Sholto's angry snarl. "You put an enchantment on me, didn't you? You damnable witch!" His voice was measured and deliberate. "I will punish you for this!"

Why had the potion not worked? Had I not put enough in his mead to paralyze a steed?

He came stumbling toward me like a rutting boar. His hands tore at me, ripped at my clothing. I struck back at him with my fists, but his attack had been so sudden I felt helpless as a trapped doe. One of his hands was on my throat squeezing the breath out of me, while the other clawed at my breasts. "No more of your witch's games, little one. You served me well as my talisman. Now you will serve my lust!"

I shrieked at him. "If you dishonour me you will be punished! You are cursed, Sholto!" I tried to push him away, but he held me fast. I beat him with my fists and clawed at his face as he pressed his body against mine.

He seized my wrist in his hands. I yanked away against his grip. He was built like a bull. I was no match against his hulking frame. I writhed and struggled, but he was too strong. Gathering what strength I had to fight him I prayed any charms I said would protect me, but I wondered if the gods wished to punish me. Was this my destiny, that he would rape and kill me and leave my body here for the wild animals to plunder?

143

I spat in his face. "May the hounds of Calan Gaeaf devour you!" It was the worst curse I could utter. My screams startled the ravens who flapped out of the trees squawking in alarm as they circled above me. Was it an omen sent from the goddess?

With a furious oath Sholto threw me to the ground. I landed heavily with him on top of me. In a swift motion he pinned me down, his knees straddling my body. He was a man whose girth I could not encompass with my arms, a man strong as a bull. I will never erase the memory of his scarred, wicked face; the thick hot saliva as he covered my screams with his mouth and shoved his tongue into my throat until I gagged. I felt the cold blade of his dagger against my neck. I truly believed my life was over then, that he would violate me, then kill me.

Stanza Two

Vaguely I became aware of the baying of hounds, and a whooshing sound. Sholto gave a great gasp and I heard the quick huff of his breath as it was driven from him. He shuddered, then went limp. There was a voice somewhere above me. Everything seemed to swirl and dazzle. Pain seeped over me as the weight of Sholto's body was lifted off of me.

Beside me knelt a youth. I pushed myself up until I was able to sit. My head was aching; fresh blood soaked my tunic. I recoiled, thinking the youth meant to harm me, but instead he spoke quietly, as if to soothe me. My ribs stabbed and burned, sweat beaded my forehead. I struggled to get to my feet but my knees crumbled. The youth caught me, holding me against him until the dizziness passed.

I stared down dumbly at Sholto who lay face down, the long slender shaft of a spear firmly embedded between his shoulders. A great brindled dog, its hackles bristling, snuffed around his body, lapping at the blood that seeped from his wound. *Was this one of the hounds of Samhain?*

The boy was looking at me with such burning eyes. He appeared to be about my own age, dressed in a loincloth with a spotted animal skin for a cloak. A tangled mane of coppery hair fell over his face. *Could he be one of Samhain's wraiths?*

I was mute with shock and trembling so much I could hardly stand. A stiff-coldness seeped over me and a great heave of nausea. I swallowed to keep from vomiting. I would have screamed if my throat had not closed over with fear. Instead, I made a half-strangled yelp, like a kicked pup, and scrambled backwards.

The youth spoke softly, as if he was calming a frightened beast. He must have seen the fear in my eyes, and he put his hand on my arm as if to reassure me. Then he took off his cloak and placed it around my shoulders in a gesture of such tenderness that suddenly tears gushed from my eyes and I began to weep. He put his arm around me and spoke in a language I had never heard before. He pointed to the blood on my clothing and muttered something I could not understand. His hand brushed over my bruised cheek. I flinched, expecting a blow, but when he had noticed my raven torc, he examined it with a show of great curiosity.

"*Magi?*" he asked.

Did he recognize from my torc that I was a Druid's child?

He looked inside my amulet bag, sniffed some of the dried herbs and roots I kept there, and weighed the bag in the palm of his hand.

"*Pharmako?*"

I was so frightened I could not answer him. He pointed to himself and spoke slowly. "*Alexandros. Ego Alexandros.*" He repeated the words until I realized he meant his name. He spoke to me softly, like you would talk to a frightened child. I did not answer, did not move, still terrified. Then I pointed to myself.

"Olwen."

"Ol-wen?" he repeated.

I nodded and said slowly, "My name...Olwen."

He drew a rough diagram in the dirt with a branch, indicating a large, circled area.

"*Makedon,*" he said, and pointed again at himself. "*Alexandros. Makedoni.*" Then he drew another circle just above the other. "Illyria?" He pointed at me. "Illyrian?"

I shook my head. "Cymry."

"Ah! Cymry. *Keltoi!*" He peered quizzically at me. "*Keltoi pharmakes!*"

He took my arm and led me to sit on the sheepskins beside the dying embers of the fire. I watched, numb with shock, as he yanked the spear from Sholto's back and struggled to remove the electrum torc from Sholto's neck. When he found it impossible to remove, he picked up Sholto's sword. I hid my eyes, thinking he meant to use it to cut off Sholto's head. Instead, he held the sword aloft to admire it and traced his fingers over the intricate designs, exclaiming over it in his strange language. He parried with it, tested its balance and flexibility, and grinned with pleasure. He said something, perhaps asked a question, but I was so frightened I could not answer. The dogs began to bay and run about. From the forest, I heard men's voices calling his name. I closed my eyes, felt the earth spin, and the sounds faded away.

Stanza Three

The heat of flames roused me. The crackling of burning wood and smoke tingled my nostrils. I was lying on the ground covered by an animal hide near a bonfire. I heard the sound of laughter and through the haze of the smoke, saw a group of youths gathered under the trees. The forest was dark, but the light of the flames illuminated them so that I recognized the fair youth who had rescued me from Sholto.

My head was spinning dizzily but I propped myself up so I could see. They were a band of young huntsmen, to be sure. They spoke a rough tongue I had never heard before, talking freely as they passed around a leather satchel and examined its contents. In the centre of the group my saviour, Alexandros, was brandishing a sword, laughing as he parried and lunged. The firelight glinted from the blade. *It was Sholto's sword.* Vague memories came back to me of the scene in the grove – Sholto lying dead, the youth seizing his sword, admiring it, snatches of conversation, my fear, the youth's comforting reassurance.

He mocked a lunge at a tall youth, then laughed and handed him the sword, saying something in that strange language he spoke. *"Yeia sena, Hephaestion!"* Then he reached into a satchel and from it took a dagger. I recognized it was Sholto's satchel!

The youths gathered closer, admiring the dagger, exclaiming over the jewelled hilt and engraved blade.

I heard Alexandros say. *"Keltoi"* Then he handed the dagger to a brawny, dark-haired youth then he yelled, *"Pausanias, yeia sena!"*

The young hunter admired his gift, parried with the dagger, and playfully lunged toward Alexandros. Then laughing, he sheathed it in his belt.

I watched as Alexandros distributed the contents of the satchel – Sholto's dagger, a pewter drinking mug, a belt studded with amber. Each of the hunters was given a treasure. Would he keep nothing for himself?

The hunter named Pausanias pointed my way, saying something that made the others laugh raucously. I huddled under the hide coverlet trembling. Was I to be Alexandros's prize? Had he saved me from Sholto just to take me as his own – to enslave me, perhaps, or to use me for his wanton desires then cast me out.

I shut my eyes tight, pretended to still be unconscious. I heard footsteps come close, then Alexandros's voice – soft, not menacing as I had expected. He spoke a few words, leaned down to draw back the covers from my face then spoke to the tall youth behind him who handed him a wine flask.

Surprisingly, Alexandros said a few words in my own language – halting but discernible. "Drink. Wine. No fear. You safe here."

I took the wine skin from him and drank, the tart wine quenching my thirst. He reached out his hand to help me up. My head spun, I felt bile rise in my throat. I could not stand and collapsed back on the ground feeling myself drift once again into the black depths of unconsciousness.

Out of the darkness came a grey fog. I floated up through the fog, and the farther up I floated the worse the pain in my head. I struggled to get back but my struggle seemed only to drive me further into the abyss. The memory of the last night broke over me in a wave. I let out a weak cry and surrendered to the darkness.

BALLAD FIFTEEN Apollo's Child

Ode to Apollo

Beautiful Apollo, god of the sun, music and poetry.
Was it you who rescued me
that night in the forest?
Apollo, redeemer and pacifier,
you were my protector, my saviour.
Beautiful god, crowned with laurel,
you rescued me from the Darkness
and brought me into the Light.

THE PHYSICIAN

Stanza One.

I woke in a strange bed, in a dark room lit only by the faint guttering light of a small oil lamp that was held by a man who was leaning over me. When I saw the kindly face framed by greying hair and a flowing beard, I first thought that my Shadow had passed over to the Otherworld and I had found my Grandfather. I tried to speak but was too weak to utter a sound. Great shudders wracked my body. I felt cold, so cold. The man peered at me anxiously. I felt his hand against my brow and sensed it was the touch of a healer. Warmth enveloped me in drowsy waves and I let myself drift back into the dark abyss.

When I woke again, the room was brighter. Pale sunlight streamed through the latticework of the window dappling the room with patches of sunlight and shadow. The man still sat beside me and smiled when he saw I was looking at him. I tried my voice again. This time I managed to whisper: "Grandfather?"

He took my limp, cold hand in his. The warmth of his touch surged through me. "You may call me grandfather," he said.

It startled me to hear him speak my own language. In my euphoric state I believed I was indeed home in Cymru. Yet, when I opened my eyes again, this time focusing more clearly on the man and my surroundings, I realized everything was quite unlike anything I had seen before, and the man was not a Cymry or a Kelt, but a stranger.

He was a small man, with strong aquiline features and thick brows that arched over deep-set blue eyes. He was dressed in a simple homespun tunic girdled at the waist with a leather cord.

I glanced around me. The room, and all its furnishings were as simply clad as he; a small, rectangular room with mud-brick walls and a ceiling of cedar beams thatched with strips of bark. A strong fragrance of the bundles of herbs that hung from the rafters permeated the room. Nearby, a rough-hewn table was cluttered with jars, cruets, baskets of herbs and a small heap of parchment scrolls. The only other furniture was the low bed I was lying on, and the stool on which the man, beside me, sat.

The door was ajar, and from outside I heard the sounds of clucking and bleating; the breeze brought in the pungent odours of a farmstead. The dirt floor was strewn with sweet-smelling reeds; several goatskins were placed around a small stone hearth in the corner.

I wanted to ask him where I was, but he silenced me gently, motioning I must not speak.

"Lie still, little one. You have been very ill — more dead than alive — but now you are safe." His gentle hands lifted my head on the pillow.

"Drink this," he said, and held a cup to my lips. "The fever has lifted, and soon you'll be strong enough to leave the bed. Rest now, for you have been through a terrible ordeal — beaten and half-starved. Lucky the hunters heard your cries and you were rescued in time."

He rubbed salve on my forehead. *Valerian, balm oil of spikenard.* The scent of it brought back a dream-like memory of the mosses at the river's edge where Essylt and I gathered cool cress and herbs. My body was stiff and sore, but the pain had calmed to a dull ache. My mouth was swollen and tasted of the sweet remnants of the potion. I realized I had been there a long time, and vaguely recalled drinks poured down my throat, strong drinks of bitter herbal remedies.

I had no recall of what had happened, or how I had got there. Sometimes a lack of memory can be merciful. I believed for a while I was on the edge of the Otherworld, but the aching of my bruised muscles and the fierce pain in my head told me the living world still held me and the voice I had heard murmuring to me was human. Had I cried out the name of Sholto? I wanted no more to think of him, in life or in death. I tried to open my eyes but drowsiness weighed me down, so I let myself drift.

The gentle touch on my head was the touch of a healer. His voice was calm and gentle. As if he knew my questions, the man said, "Your captor did not violate you. As for what happened, we will speak of it another time when you are stronger. My name is Theon. I am a physician. The hunters brought you to me. Young Alexandros has looked in on you almost every day. We were afraid you might not live. You have suffered through a long ordeal, but you have a strong will. In spite of everything, you will survive."

I opened my eyes and he smiled reassuringly and tucked the blankets around me with caring hands.

I smelled steaming broth and pork fat boiling in a cauldron over the fire. He ladled some into a bowl and brought it to me. "Eat this," he said. "It will give you strength." Like a nurse feeding a child, he scooped spoonfuls into my mouth until I felt my strength returning.

"Are you a Kelt?" I murmured. My throat was dry, my voice hardly more than a whisper.

"No. I am a Greek, a Makedoni. But when I was as young as you, I travelled and spent many months in your lands. I know your people. I lived in the mountain caves with your wise men and priests." He pointed to my raven torc. "That is a Druid's torc. Your totem is the raven," he said knowingly. "You are a daughter of the Raven clan? And what is your name?"

"My name is Olwen. I am from Cymru. I am a Druid's child."

I told him the story then, exactly as it had happened. As I recounted it my memory began to clear. I told him about the Midsummer rites and the murder I had witnessed, and how Sholto had taken me captive. I shivered recounting the long journey across the Keltic lands, tales of terror and magic, how the crone had given me the potion so I could escape from my captor.

"I wanted to kill him but I wasn't certain of how much it would take. He went to sleep — or so I thought. But, as I was gathering my things to run away, he woke up, and that is when he attacked me."

"He was a wicked man and deserved his fate," Theon said.

"He took me away from Caer Gwyn because I saw him slay his brother. He had done great harm to our tuath. That is why he was running away."

"He would have slain you too, if Alexandros hadn't heard your cries " Theon said.

"Alexandros?" I had a vague memory of a young hunter who had burst into our encampment just as Sholto was about to violate me.

"Yes, Alexandros. He and his friends were hunting in the woods and he heard your cries. He is the one who brought you to me."

"Does he live here with you?"

"No. He lives in Pella, the royal city."

"Royal city? Where?"

"You are in Makedon now," he said.

Makedon? It was all too much for me to comprehend and I drifted off to sleep again.

Theon would not let me leave my bed, but continued to tend my needs as he had done all the days I had lain helpless, delirious with fever. He had taken all my clothing and wrapped me in clean linens that smelled of herbs and fragrant musk. Sometimes he bathed me with cool water, anointing my skin with oils and soothing liniments. He brewed succulent broth in an iron cauldron over the hearth fire and brought me steaming herbal teas in little clay cups. Some of the teas he said he had picked from the mountains.

In the daytime, I watched him at his work, grinding roots with a stone mortar and pestle; sorting herbs into bundles, and mixing some of them in pottery vials. He was surprised when I named them: hyssop, chamomile, mandrake. There were a few I did not know. He told me their names and said when I was better he would show me where they grew in the forest near the farmstead. He was surprised I knew so many things about the medicines. I told him these were mysteries Essylt had taught me when I was still a small child.

"Medicine is a noble art," Theon said.

He asked me to tell him about Essylt, but I could not speak of her without feeling tearful. After a while he did not question me more, but I saw him watching me many times when he thought I was asleep. I knew that, like my beloved *modryb* and my *tadcu,* Grandfather Maelgwyn, he was a man of great compassion.

At night, when the fire burned low in the stone hearth, we sat together on the goatskin rugs and Theon told me about his youth.

"I went to sea on a merchant ship, paid my way by tending sick crewmen. We sailed all the way across the sea, through the Stone Pillars, until we came to Ocean. It was a hardy trader ship with a crew of Phoenicians. They carried a cargo of faience and gold ingots and amphorae of sweet wine. It was summer, and the sea was running high with a good strong wind. We made the south coast of Britain in three months' time. I put off there and followed the Chalk Trail north."

I wondered if he had gone past Caer Gwyn.

"I went all the way north to Caer Troia, in Llandin where the Arch Druid sits in his Holy Place," Theon said. "There I followed the great river, by coracle, and walked across the Plain. I spoke to the seers of the Sacred Circles in Abiri and Cor Gawr, then I went back to the Narrow Sea and found another trader sailing across to the Belgae lands."

I told him about the ship with the double-headed griffon. He listened intently, his eyes seeming to drink every word I said. I spoke haltingly. It was like remembering a frightening dream. Everything seemed so long ago, vague in my memory, as if I was trying to see through a thick mist.

"Sholto told the ship's captain we were going to Carnac," I told him.

"And did you go there?" he asked.

I stopped speaking then. Something caught the words before I could form them. I sat silently awhile staring at the licking flames. "I knew he was lying," I said finally.

Then Theon told me he had visited Carnac; the oak groves, the sacred circle of dolmens. He spoke about it as though he had been there yesterday.

"It was a happy, mystical time for me. I was only a youth then, but the memory of it is still vivid."

I told him about the Midsummer day when I had turned fifteen years old.

"What do you remember about that day?" Theon asked.

The orange flames curled around the pine logs. Little sparks cracked in the greyish smoke.

"We went to the Stone Circle. There was a great oak pyre. They were going to sacrifice to the Oak God, Duir. The white oxen were flayed and the Druids burned them. And there was a wicker cart, all garlanded. The Oak King's chariot."

The resin on the logs hissed and sizzled. Somewhere in my mind I recalled the smell of burning flesh.

"Who was the Oak King?" Theon asked.

The words caught in my throat and I slipped back into silence, unable to speak Dafydd's name. It was a dark refuge where I might hide from the visions that the curling, bright flames brought to my mind. Theon did not press his questioning but helped me back to the bed and tucked the sheep's wool blanket around me.

Once the fire died, it was cooler in the hut; there was a crispness to the night air. Theon pulled the shutters tight to keep out the draft.

That night, images came, beginning like dreams. I recalled Dafydd and our final parting. I remembered seeing him in the wicker chariot. I lay awake, the flicker of firelight dancing off the walls around me in ghostly shapes. It is one thing to have the gift of seeing the spirits and hearing them move about, but it is a gift of darkness as well as light. I was haunted by the past. The shapes of death came to me as clear as those of life and I dared not think of my future.

Stanza Two

Early one morning, Theon brought me my clothes. They had been washed and mended and had the sweet fragrance of cedar on them. He had mended all the little tears, and repaired the snags in the embroidered threads. The colours had faded, but they were still the beautiful garments Essylt had made me for the Midsummer rites.

Theon said: "Fresh air and sunshine will heal you quicker than my medicines."

He turned away while I dressed. I had grown thinner; the crimson tunic and the purple breeches hung off my frame as though I had shrunk down to the bones. I tied the sash as tightly as I could. Even my amulet bag weighed heavier than before. I felt awkward and gangly, like a small child dressed in a woman's garb.

"There!" exclaimed Theon when I was ready. "You are beautiful! You look fine!"

I brushed down the folds of the tunic. The cloth was still the bright crimson dye but there were darker patches near the hem. My hand brushed across them. I remembered. something that made my heart-beats quicken. For a moment a giddy feeling washed over me.

Theon caught me as I swayed. "Perhaps it is too soon," he said.

I could not take my hand away from the dark stains. Theon watched me, his brow furrowed.

"It did not wash out!" My voice trembled and the words caught in my throat. "The blood did not wash out!"

"Never mind," Theon said lightly, steering me toward the open door. "We will get you some new clothes."

"*His blood!*" I repeated dumbly. I had a vague recollection of Sholto's tumbling body; his blood spurting like a fountain splashing over me. My heart beat so furiously I felt as though I might choke and I struggled to regain my composure.

"The sun is bright," Theon said. "We will go as far as the plane tree. Tomorrow you might feel strong enough to walk to the waterfall. Come along, Olwen. I have fixed a place for you to rest in the sunshine."

The door of the house opened onto a clearing where the parched grass had been trampled in a wide ochre space of farmland. Beyond this, the fields rolled out over a plain, bordered by a curling lip of barren hills. In patches across the plain, there were silvery groves and occasionally the landscape was broken by towering spires of cypresses that jutted into the cloudless sky. The sunlight streamed down in a white brilliant light drenching the fields and hillside, but there was a touch of brisk coolness in the air.

I took Theon's arm and leaned against him weakly as we stepped outside into the hard, bright sunlight. My eyes ached in the glare of it and I put my arm across to shade them. Theon waited, holding me until I was able to adjust to the clear, open light of the outdoors.

It was near winter judging from the leaves that had fallen from the trees and the dusting of snow on the mountains. I had lost all track of time. The branches of the oak and maple trees scattered among the juniper and black pine were almost bare. Farther up, where the ridges of granite rock rose up in rugged steppes to the mountain tops, rowan trees blazed with brilliant golden foliage among the terebinth and firs.

Theon led me across the yard toward a gnarled old tree. The branches spread wide from the thick, knotted trunk. The dry leaves, touched with the yellowing of the season, rustled in the breeze. He had placed the sheepskin rug under the tree, and a low table was set with a small jug of wine, a loaf of sesame bread and a chunk of white cheese.

While I sat under the tree, Theon went about his chores. Chickens clucked around his ankles and the goats nuzzled to be petted. I watched him fill a clay amphora from the stream and throw grain from the baskets which the scolding hens fought over. Out beyond the farmstead past a stone sheepfold, the sheep grazed, turning away from the sun. A little brown donkey stood patiently by in the field waiting, watching, nodding its head now and then to shake off a swarm of flies.

I counted the moons. It was well past Samhain, but still the month when the wind whistles through the dried reeds on the river bank and the screech owls, their eyes shining in the night, call out their messages from the death goddess.

So much time had passed, yet I could remember little of it. I had no idea where I was, or the location of this farmstead. I recall the young hunter who had rescued me had said *"Makedon!"* as mysterious a place to me as the names I had read on grandfather's star charts. I only remembered the long, relentless trek across the towering mountains where even in the valleys there were traces of snow and the nights were bitterly cold, and Sholto watching over me, his eyes burning like the fire-coals.

"You have not even taken a bite of your food!" scolded Theon, startling me out of my reverie. He watched me, his arms folded, peering at me like a stern father. He handed the plate of cheese to me. I broke off a piece and tasted it. It was tangy with salt, goat's milk cheese that he said he had churned himself. The wine tasted strong and fresh. I felt the colour return to my cheeks.

"See here!" exclaimed Theon, "I've forgotten the olives. You must have them with the cheese."

He bustled off toward the cottage and returned with a pottery dish heaped with small, oily black fruit. I had never before tasted such a delicacy. The flavour clung, tingling to my palate. I ate several of them and more of the cheese and fresh bread he had baked that morning in his stone oven and washed it down with the tart red wine.

Theon turned away and stared out over the open grassland toward the distant hills. "He will come today," he said, shading his eyes against the glare of the sun. "Alexandros. He has not passed this way for a fortnight. But I expect he will come today."

"Alexandros?" I asked. We had not spoken for some time about the young man who had brought me to him, who was part of the blurry past.

"Yes," Theon said. "He and his friends hunt boars, and he will come a day ahead. Alexandros likes to spend time alone in the forest. It settles him. He has much on his mind these days."

I was about to ask Theon to tell me more about Alexandros, but just then he waved in the direction of the field and exclaimed, "There! You see? I knew he would come today!"

I could barely make out the distant speck of a lone rider. As he got closer, I could see the tousled burnish of his hair. He was bent low over the neck of a sleek black horse, riding at a fast gallop. When they reached the pasture, the sheep fled with frightened bleats, and when he galloped into the farmyard, the chickens flew up squawking in a cloud of drifting feathers.

The horse had a white blaze on its forelock and a mane as shiny as polished ebony. There was foam on its bit. It snorted and reared as the young man drew in the reins and took some time to calm it. He was flushed, breathing heavily as he dismounted.

He spoke softly to the horse. "*Ela, ela* Bucephalus!" He held tight to the rein and pulled the horse's great head down so he was nuzzling against its broad cheek. The horse's wide eyes rolled back showing the whites. Soon it stood quietly, head down. When Alexandros dropped the reins, the horse trotted off toward the edge of the clearing where the golden hay was ripe for grazing.

He greeted Theon and the two spoke together quietly, then Alexandros looked over at me with a smile, his grey eyes shining. "*Chairetai!*"

I smiled back at him, shy and afraid to speak.

He came close and looked me over as if appraising me, then spoke again to Theon in their own language.

Theon said, "Alexandros says my medicines have performed another miracle. I told him that the autumn sun, good food, clear mountain air and the company of friends are the healers. I am only the gods' servant." He motioned for us to sit. "I will bring fresh wine and cheese," he said, and he walked away toward the cottage.

Alexandros had a quiver of arrows over his shoulder, and a small bow. Several brown speckled birds were tied to a thong hanging from his waist. He laid the birds beside me on the grass.

I remembered a day in the greenwood at Caer Gwyn. Sholto. A brace of rock doves; a fierce, golden-eyed hunting falcon. "You must learn to kill if you are the Raven's child," Sholto had said.

I studied this young man, Alexandros. He was smaller than what I remembered from that night in the grove, not much taller than myself, and of a light, wiry build. His face had the open serenity of a child's yet there was something strained in it; a bruised look around his eyes; a furrow to his brow. His eyes were dark, slate grey, but when he smiled a light went into them.

He sat down beside me and took some of the bread and cheese, handing some to me. His skin was tanned the colour of polished bronze. He had beautiful hands, long fingers; he was wearing a ring on the little finger of his left hand — a rich blue sapphire set in gold, his only adornment. He wore a short tunic of soft, ivory kid-skin with a plain corded belt. His sandals were laced to the knees. His legs were very strong, the muscular calves had a light growth of fine golden hairs. He seemed a very simple youth; his style was ordinary. I took him to be a country lord's son.

I did not know his language and felt shy, not knowing what to say to him.

He pointed at himself. "Alexandros."

I nodded and said, "Olwen."

"*Ah-wen. Keltoi?*"

"I am Cymry," I repeated. "My people are the clan of the Essyltyrs. My name is Olwen. You are Alexandros?"

"Alexandros, *Makedoni*. Olwen, *Keltoi*." He gave me a quick, bright smile that made me feel at ease.

Theon came back with a tray of fresh food and another jug of wine. They spoke quietly while Theon poured the wine into our cups. Alexandros had a light, soft voice. I noticed when he listened to Theon he would incline his head to one side. He never interrupted but would wait until the older man had finished speaking then reply in a clear, true-ringing voice. Once in a while he glanced over at me and smiled.

"Tell him I am grateful he rescued me. I owe my life to him," I said.

"Alexandros would like to learn your language," Theon said. "He is eager to know about your people. You must learn to speak with him. He is Makedoni and he speaks Greek. He is a bright young man. Would you like to be his teacher?"

I blushed. It was an unusual request, and one I had not expected to be made of me. I was, after all, an alien in a land I knew nothing about.

"He says you will be his guest-friend," Theon said. "Of course, you do not have to leave here until you feel well enough. And he says you may choose where you will stay. Here? Or do you want to go to Pella?"

"Pella?" He might as well have asked if I would like to go to the place where the white mists drift out to Ocean.

Theon noticed my confusion and laughed. "He lives in a city to the south."

"Is he a tribal lord's son?"

Theon chuckled. "Well, yes...that he is. He's the son of a noble family." He patted my arm, "Never mind, Olwen. You will stay here until you are stronger. Then we will decide. Alexandros, drink the wine! Enjoy the food!" He lifted up his cup and touched it to the rim of Alexandros's cup. Alexandros lifted his and took a long drink of it then tipped the dregs.

"We Cymry spill wine for the gods too," I said. "In this way, our languages are the same!"

Stanza Three

My convalescence was a time of rebirth for me. Theon was not only my physician, administering potions to heal my ills, he was my protector, guiding me through the dark moments when I would lapse into melancholy. He was skilled in the practice of medicine. He told me that after his youthful adventure to Britain, he had studied the healing arts at a sanctuary dedicated to the Greek's healer god, Asklepios.

"My teacher was the eminent physician, Hippocrates," he said. "From him I learned all about the art of healing."

Theon became both a friend and counsellor; he soothed me when I awoke, frightened by the presence of the Raven of Nightmares; reassured me and comforted me. His little house became my sanctuary, and as the days passed, I began to be myself once again.

Every day I helped with chores, churning the thick goats' milk for cheese and creamy curds, grinding wheat to make the flat bread we dipped it in. I followed Theon along the forest trails where we gathered firewood and collected sweet chestnuts to roast over the fire at night.

The trees were vivid with the russet and yellows of autumn and the woods smelled pungent with damp earth and decaying leaves. I thought of the beech groves of Caer Gwyn. They would be a blaze of golden colours now and Essylt would be collecting hazelnuts. The fields would be ripe with grain; and the harvesters mowing and reaping. The men would have driven the cattle herd to their winter grazing within the stockade enclosures before the first snowfall. I felt sad when I thought of home. And yet, it was still like a murky dream — as if I had truly died and left that life for this new one, though Theon said in time I would remember everything.

Alexandros came by more frequently those days. It was boar hunting season and he usually came a day before, shared a meal and sat with us by the fire. With Theon's patient tutoring I began to learn their language, though I would never master it. Alexandros was much quicker to learn mine. He already knew some words, picked up from captive warriors and slaves. When he came to visit we would sit out under the plane tree and communicate in halting sentences in the simple country jargon of the Makedonians that Theon had taught me, but when he talked to Theon he used the pure, soft-sounding Greek which lacked the throaty earthiness of my own speech. We devised a way of communicating with bits of this and that described in pantomime. Soon we were able to understand one another quite well.

Our conversations were simple. We talked mostly of things that were at hand. Sometimes when he visited, Alexandros and I walked around the farmstead and traded words for objects, pointing to things and exchanging pantomimes to explain others. In no time the words came easier to me.

Any discussion about our lives was vague, although Theon translated when we could not make ourselves understood. I felt it was important to ask Alexandros questions about his family. When I finally did, he said he had a mother and a sister. When I asked about his father, he replied bluntly, in his own tongue, so I did not understand. His eyes slid away from mine. He seemed startled and uneasy and stared, chin on fist, into the fire.

After few moments he replied, "My father has much land!" He turned his head and winked at Theon. I supposed they had a secret between them and felt too shy to question further. Later Theon told me, "Alexandros's father is not in his favour." I did not ask why.

Theon explained to Alexandros that I had come from a place called Cymru, neighbours of the Britons. "Long ago, the Cymry came from a country in the East and settled there. They are different from the other Kelts of Britain. Olwen was raised by a Druid star-seer, in the care of the medicine woman and High Priestess. She is an acolyte of the Raven's clan."

Alexandros was fascinated with this and questioned me about it. I explained my duties as an acolyte to him. He wanted to know every detail and would not let go until I described them.

I told him everything I knew, beginning from the time I was a little girl. He asked me about our gods. We compared each one with the gods he worshipped. Many of them were the same except for their names. With Theon's help interpreting, he told me curious tales of mortals who mingled with the gods. He said he was a descendant of the god-hero Achilles who was the hero of the Troy Wars.

"My mother worships the cult of Dionysos, the wine god. She is a priestess of that cult and has been since she was a young girl. My father found her at one of the rites," he said. "She was just fourteen then; a princess of Epirus."

A dark shadow crossed his face when he spoke of his mother. He looked into the fire and there was a long silence before he spoke again. "The rites of the Dionysos cult are secret," he said. "I have only seen them once."

"I should like to see them some day," I replied.

He shook his head. His eyes, in the shadows, seemed to have sunk deeper; his face looked drawn. "No, you shouldn't!"

I could see my suggestion had disturbed him and wondered what dark mysteries this cult had.

Theon poured more wine, then Alexandros brightened and took a long drink, and settled back. He asked me about the Midsummer rites. With Theon's help, I explained them to him, recalling how I had been destined to make a holy pilgrimage to the Sacred Isle, but how fate had placed me here instead. I felt bewildered and detached as I talked about it. I could not remember much beyond the sacrifices as though a shroud was pulled across my memory.

"Do you know why the Fates have sent you here?" Alexandros asked.

"No," I replied, and slipped back into the security of silence.

"There is a purpose for everything," Alexandros said. Then, seeing I had withdrawn, he smiled and put his arm around me as a brother would to comfort his sister.

"Your *moira* is this," he said. "You have been sent here to teach me! It is your fate!" We both laughed, and I began to feel better.

I looked forward to those visits and watched eagerly for Alexandros to come riding across the fields. Usually he arrived by mid-morning just as Theon and I were finishing the farm chores. We would see him galloping wildly past the distant olive groves. Bucephalus always put out a great burst of speed when they reached the edge of the fields and came clattering like a whirlwind into the farmyard scattering all the animals and chickens in fright. He was a fine horse, the most beautiful horse I had ever seen, tall, fine boned and long-legged. His coat was shiny black, pure ebony except for the white blaze on his forelock that gave him his name.

"Bucephalus means Oxhead," Alexandros explained. "I won him in a wager with my father. The horse was uncontrollable and none of the men could break him," he said. "I was only twelve years old then, but I was determined to have him. The horse had cost a fortune in gold. My father said it was too wild to be broken, but if I could tame him, I could have him."

He told me how he had watched the horse for days and discovered that Bucephalus was frightened by shadows.

"You must always keep to the side of him," he said "If you cross him, he will rear. He is a strong horse. He almost killed a man who tried to break him. Look here, I will show you."

He demonstrated how when he stepped in front and his shadow fell across the horse's path, Bucephalus would roll his eyes and rear, thrashing the air with his hooves. When he approached from the side and gentled the horse with a quiet voice and soft touch, Bucephalus stood by calmly.

"He is a good horse, a brave horse," Alexandros said. "And one day I will ride him into battle!"

He said it with an air of arrogance. I saw the fierceness in him, yet it was hard for me to imagine a gentle youth like him would one day become a warrior.

Stanza Four

One morning Alexandros arrived later than usual. He had been hunting by the lake and had brought along his hunting dog, a tawny-coloured hound, that raced beside Bucephalus yapping with excitement.

He dismounted and handed Theon a brace of waterfowl. "We shall have a fine feast tonight!" he exclaimed. He was flushed, and his eyes shone. The dog leapt up eagerly as if trying to snatch the prize.

"Down, Peritos!" Alexandros scolded. The hound quietened and lay obediently at his feet. "Peritos is a good dog, a faithful companion," Alexandros said. "He knows how to obey!"

He explained that Theon had given him the dog when he was just a little boy. "My mother would not allow Peritos to be kept in my room, so I had to sneak him up the back stairs from the kitchen. When my mother found out, she punished me and made Peritos stay outside in the stables. One night I crept out and slept with him. My nurse was beaten for it, but after that mother gave in, and Peritos has shared my quarters with me ever since."

Alexandros let his horse out to pasture, and I showed him the little table we had set under the plane tree. I had helped Theon bake flat bread. It was still steaming, right from the oven. I told Alexandros how we had gone to harvest the olives from the groves.

"Theon showed me how to knock them down from the trees with the long stakes," I said. "Then we carried them back to the cottage. While I pounded each one with a stone, he made the brine in tall pottery crocks. Theon says we must crack the olives open to the pits in order to take out the bitterness. Afterwards, we put them in the brine where they will soak for a few weeks. Then we'll put them in oil mixed with herbs and garlic."

Alexandros listened, his head tilted, and watched me with a curious smile. "You see, little farm girl, your *moira* is not to be a priestess. You will make someone a good wife one day."

When he said that, I had a fleeting vision of Teag and remembered how I had once dreamed of exchanging the sacred marriage vows with him. The thought brought a lump to my throat, so I quickly pushed the memory aside.

We were sitting under the plane tree. The hound was teasing the chickens and Theon came out of the cottage to scold it. He waved at us, then went back into the cottage to stoke the fire so we could roast the birds. A thin stream of smoke curled from the chimney.

"I have brought you something," Alexandros said. "It is a talisman." He handed me a raven's feather, black as jet, from his kit bag. Its iridescence caught the sunlight. "When I was hunting by the lake, your Raven goddess sent me an omen."

He told how he had sighted a flock of waterfowl and was preparing his bow, when a great raven had appeared and scattered the flock. I had told him about the goddess who often took the raven's form and flew into battle as the Raven of War, scattering the enemy hosts and causing frenzy and confusion. He wanted me to have the feather that had dropped from the raven's wing.

"Surely it is an auspicious omen, foretelling good fortune for all of us," I said.

"It means the Makedonians will be victorious in battle," he replied.

The sunlight slanted through the leaves of the tree. Alexandros had a braided ribbon with gold threads tying back his hair and in profile with the sunlight catching his auburn curls, he looked like someone I had seen before. I remembered the gold image of a god on the coins Teag had given me. I took one of the coins out of the bag, placed it on the palm of my hand to show him.

"You are like this god!"

Alexandros took the gold piece and held it up to the sun. "That is Apollo, the sun god!" he said. Then he flipped the coin over and traced out the name that was inscribed under the charioteer "*Filippos*. Yes. I know him. Where did you get this?"

"From a gold-smith I knew. It came from Massalia," I said. I could not take my eyes from Alexandros's face. "Who are you?" I asked again. "If you are not Apollo, then who are you?"

He winked and gave me a secretive smile. "I am Apollo's child," he replied.

Stanza Five

The reed moon waned to its last thin sickle. Now it was Ruis, the Elder month when the chestnuts fall and shed their yellow leaves. There was a fresh dusting of crisp snow on the crests of the mountain. We kept the fire going most of the day. Theon gave me one of his own cloaks to wear over my woollen tunic. The air was so frosty in the early morning my breath came in misty puffs.

"We will have an early winter, I think" Theon said. He pointed up to the ridge where the snow line had reached the timber. "One good storm and we will be snowed in."

We gathered firewood along the edge of the forest. Theon said we must bring as much as we could carry every day because the winter might be long, and would certainly be cold. I told him about the winter in Caer Gwyn, when the little child had frozen in a snowdrift and we had to tunnel our way out of the huts through the drifts. Theon said he had once lost an entire flock of sheep in a winter storm. He wondered if this year might be the same.

It was past midday; the sun well beyond its zenith. Alexandros had not come that day. I watched the horizon across the fields anxiously. A light wind was beginning to stir. Theon said he would go back to the hut and stoke the fire. I was preoccupied with thoughts of Alexandros as I followed him. I placed my armload of faggots on the pile beside the hut then walked out to the edge of the field. Beyond the pale golden stubble of the fields a lip of foothills unfolded, a dark rim against the clear sky. I had grown accustomed to Alexandros's visits and anticipated each day with pleasure because of them.

I waited the whole morning before I finally saw him riding across the field. The wind whipped back his cloak as he rode, so he appeared to be astride a great black winged creature —similar to the winged horse, Pegasus, in the tales Theon had told me.

He rode up, the picture of a young nobleman dressed in a short tunic, dyed a deep blue, girdled with a gold-tussled belt. He looked down at me and though he smiled, his eyes were dark and his face seemed pale. As he dismounted, I saw a polished dagger strapped to the knee of his high kidskin riding boots. The haft was carved with a swirling Keltic pattern. A sudden memory made my innards twinge. I thought of Sholto—his dagger—and remembered that night when Alexandros had held it in his hand admiring it.

He swung his cape aside and greeted me as usual, in my language. "Well, sweet Olwen, how are you this bright day?"

"Fare well," I replied. We had taken to greeting each other like Cymry and I made the sign for peace and friendship.

He tethered Bucephalus under the tree. "I cannot stay long," he said. "My companions are probably looking for me. I stole away from them, so I must ride back before nightfall".

Theon came out with a tray of dried figs, sweet honey cakes and cups of berry cordial.

"*Chairetai*, Theon!" Alexandros took a cup of cordial but graciously declined the sweets. As he sipped the drink, he seemed distant, preoccupied. He spoke to Theon in the quick, soft Greek they used for private discussions. I understood the words 'Chieftains' and 'soldier' and something about 'a matter of great importance to the Makedonian people'. It sounded like Council talk, and from the stern look on his face, I supposed there was some trouble within his tribe.

Alexandros set the cup back on the tray and turned back toward his horse. Theon seemed as disappointed as I was that he could not stay.

"Will you return soon?" I asked.

"No. I have important matters to attend in Pella." He looked up toward the granite pinnacles beyond the forest. "There will be much snow," he said. A frown creased his forehead. "Theon, you must think about what I said. Your old bones will not withstand another harsh winter."

"Alexandros wants us to come to Pella," explained Theon.

"I will send a boy — the best steward I have," Alexandros said. "You need not worry about your flocks nor the farmstead. Will you come?"

Theon would not answer forthright. I hoped he would agree. I would miss those fireside chats with the young lord's son.

The stern look on Alexandros's face softened and he smiled at me as he mounted his horse.

"Go in safety, Alexandros," I said.

"Walk in peace, little Kelt," Alexandros replied. Then he and his fine winged steed rode away.

Stanza Six

True to his word, the next day Alexandros sent a boy with a wagon and supplies. The boy was a simple fellow with a gap-toothed smile and easy manner. Theon took to him, in spite of his earlier reluctance, and later told me he never doubted Alexandros's choices. Because of this he was willing to leave his flock and farm.

We left the farmstead while it was still dark, making our way across the fields on a track well-used by travellers and farmers, marked by many shrines for the wayfarer's gods. We offered at the first one. I placed some sheaves of wheat on the altar and said some words to see us safely on our way.

Both Theon and I fell silent as we trudged along the trail, the little donkey bearing all our possessions trotting dutifully behind us. I knew Theon felt the same reluctance as I had at leaving his cozy farmstead.

"Never mind, we will go back in springtime," I said, trying to sound cheerful.

There was no sound as we crossed the open fields except the swishing of our footsteps through the tall, unmown grass. It was still too dark to see the olive groves. Later we heard sheep bleating and as we neared the foothills, the distant tinkling of goat bells came in waves like the siren voices of field nymphs. I made the luck signs and whispered charms to the field gods so we would not be enchanted by them.

The sky lightened, and as we came up on the crest of a low hillock, the sun burst over the tops of the mountains in the east, the bright beams sweeping down across the sleeping land, glancing across the surface of a distant sea. It was a dazzling sight. Along the curve of shoreline was the outline of a city's walls and just above the walls the glint of gold refracting off something that looked like a gleaming sunburst.

"There is Pella!" Theon exclaimed.

I was speechless with wonder at the beautiful sight. I had never seen a city such as this and did not know what to expect of Pella. Until then I knew only hill forts like Caer Gwyn – timbered fortresses high atop earth mounds, or stone citadels perched on mountain crags. Most of them were inhabited by tribal chieftains, some who called themselves ricons. Others were estates owned by rich land barons who ruled their serfs and freemen just as though they were monarchs.

Pella was larger than any settlement I imagined existed, though Theon said it was not quite as grand as the Hellenic city of Athens.

"Most of the freemen lived outside Pella's walls on farmsteads, or along the shore in fishing villages," Theon explained. "Only merchants and wealthy noblemen can afford houses within the city walls. To be sure there are some plain folk, artisans and craftsmen. I dare say we might even see a beggar or two. Cities are made up of all sorts."

I stammered in surprise, confessing to him that I thought Pella would be a simple, rustic fortress such as the others I had seen in the northern lands.

Theon smiled, "Yes, Alexandros would prefer that. He likes the homeyness of timbered halls, and if he had his way, would rather live at Aigae. The palace there is very old, built long ago by the ancient kings of Makedon. It has strong thick walls of stone, and timbered halls, much more to Alexandros's liking. His taste is quite spartan, actually, and he is not given to the airs of his family's nobility."

I had not realized until then that Alexandros was not just a country baron's son. Now I saw with my own eyes he was much more than that.

"Who is his father?" I asked. "How rich a tribal chieftain he must be to own all these lands!"

Theon, sensing my bewilderment, said gently. "Did you not know? Alexandros is a prince. His father is Filippos, king of Makedon. All the lands across the northern borders are his."

Seeing the look of astonishment on my face, Theon laughed. "Alexandros is a good prince and one day when he is king, he will govern well."

It came clearly to me then. "*I am Apollo's child. This is my father.*" Alexandros had said when he had shown me the name inscribed on the gold coin. I had thought it was a jest.

The rising sun flooded the city lighting the buildings with the pastel colours. As we drew nearer, Theon pointed out the palace that towered above the low flat rooftops of the houses.

"It is not as opulent as other palaces, "Theon explained, "The old king, Archaelaos, who built the palace was mad for gold and wanted to impress the Athenians by somewhat overdoing things." Theon explained. "Filippos owns all the eastern gold mines and wanted to show the Greeks he is not the rustic mountain barbarian they claimed him to be. The palace was built some few hundred years ago, but Fillipos had it rebuilt to suit his purposes. It does have some delightful features; there are beautiful gardens within the inner court, and some of the wall frescoes are splendid!"

I felt overwhelmed, thinking of how many people lived within the humble walls of Caer Gwyn's hill fort. This city and its palace were vast.

We stopped to rest on the hillside while the donkey grazed in the grass. It had been a long journey across the valley and Theon leaned heavily on his staff as I followed him down the path toward the city gates.

The city walls were made of field stone, and wide enough for men to walk along the tops. There were watchtowers on each side of the portals. The gates were made up of thick beams on iron hinges; there was no trench or moat to cross, the road led straight in.

The gates were open letting in the trickle of peasants who entered with their ox-carts and donkeys laden with bundles and produce from their farmsteads. Theon greeted the watchman at the gate and waved to the soldiers on the watchtower. One called him by name and came down to greet him, kissing Theon on both cheeks.

He was a tall youth, simply clad in a brown tunic, but his crested helmet was as beautiful as a brightly plumed bird. I stared at him with such round eyes that Theon began to laugh. The boy stood a good head taller than Theon. He could not have been much more than my own age. He was clean-shaven, or perhaps his beard had not yet grown;

"I delivered this young man when he was born. His mother is of hardy peasant stock; his father was a hoplite in Filippos's army but was killed in battle. Now young Cleomenes has filled his father's boots, and very well I would say!' He smiled at the young man."We are bound for the palace," he explained. "Send word to your good mother that once I am settled here, I will come out to your farmstead for some of her fine cooking!"

"To be sure, Theon, sir," the youth replied. He may have been a country boy but he did not lack manners. I thought of the uncouth ruffians that made up Madoc's band; the thought brought a quick glimpse to mind of young Ned which I pushed away quickly. This was not a time to think of adverse things.

The road into the city was paved with wide blocks of stones that sloped toward the centre where a trough of running water carried refuse. At each corner, the drains poured into deep terra-cotta cisterns where the refuse was washed away. The buildings seemed to press upon each other; houses built of mud bricks and stone, public houses and shops, all crowded close together. Here and there was a touch of colour from late-blooming flowers that clung to walls and balcony railing in bright hues of crimson and magenta. Some of the buildings had colonnades and terraces hung with vines. Most of the streets seemed so narrow only a donkey could pass, but the road we entered on was wide and the pavement worn with ruts of carts and chariot wheels. It opened onto a central market square where hundreds of people jostled in a colourful throng plying their baskets of wares. I could not believe my eyes. There were rows of gay striped awnings as though all the freemen of the city were congregating in that one spot. I thought perhaps it was a festival.

"This is the *agora*— a meeting place for merchants and tradesmen. Those buildings on the other side are for the city magistrates where all the business of the city is transacted. There, at the law courts and money exchange."

The market was a myriad of wonders. Theon pulled at my arm as I stood there gawking. He waved across the road at a young man who was standing half-hidden in the shadows of an overhanging balcony. A dog, a lanky brute, larger than any of the village pied dogs I had ever seen, ran up to Theon snuffling. It stood almost as tall as my chest and pushed its wet nose up under my chin.

"Peritus!" Theon laughed. The dog quaked with excitement to hear its name called.

I thought the dog looked familiar, but I did not realize at first that the young man was Alexandros. He was dressed in a simple brown tunic, like a country boy. It was only when I saw the tangled mane of chestnut hair, and then the cape – the same one he had worn that day at the farmstead when he had come riding up with Bucephalus, looking like a god on a winged steed, that I realized it was him.

The dog wagged its long tail and had its paws on Theon's chest. It frightened the donkey which began to bray.

"Peritos! Come!" Alexandros called, and the dog went obediently to stand by him.

"Welcome to Pella!" Alexandros greeted Theon with a kiss on both cheeks and put out his hand to shake mine. "Your old quarters in the palace are ready for your arrival." He smiled at me. "Have ever seen such a city, little Kelt? It's bigger than the Greek's Athens. My great-grandfather made it the biggest and best city in the world!"

We followed him with the dog trailing along obediently at his side. The rising sun flooded the city lighting the buildings with pastel colours of the sunrise.

Theon pointed out the palace, set on a knoll in the centre of the city.

"See the corner terrace, facing north toward the sea? Those are Alexandros's quarters. The women's are on the other side. The lower floor has the Great Hall and lodgings for the Royal Guard, nobility – anyone of consequence. There are kitchens too, and a bathing room." He pointed out the top-most tier. "The king's rooms and library are there. It's full of books and scrolls from all over Hellas and the eastern lands."

Library? I did not know about such things as books. My people's language was not written but told by remembrancers and sung by bards. We had no scribes to set things down for us.

"And there's a room for observing the heavens," Alexandros said. "*Astronomia* is the word we call it. Our seers are called Astronomers."

"We call ours *seronydd,*" I said. "My grandfather was a star seer. He taught me some of the heaven's mysteries."

"Alexandros has a keen interest in such observations," Theon said. "Perhaps you might share what you know with him."

Ahead of us there was an open square in front of the polished stone steps that led up to the palace gate. Enclosing both sides of the palace were walls of thick stone. Flowers, bright yellow as the sun, clung to the buff- coloured walls. Just inside, where the great oaken doors stood open, I glimpsed a courtyard where a sparkling fountain glistened among the rich foliage of a garden. At the entrance was a shrine with a statue freshly garlanded; it seemed to be the likeness of Alexandros. Vines spilled down from the high terraces in scarlet and russet hues bright as flames against the marble facade. Above the red-tiled pediments at the peak of the roof, a starburst of hammered gold blazed, reflecting the sun.

We followed Alexandros into the wide courtyard. Several richly-dressed men were gathered under the trees in the courtyard. They looked up from their discourse when they saw us and studied us with curiosity. Some of them called out greetings to Alexandros.

I felt uneasy and realized how out of place I was there. The tunic I wore was coarse grey wool, and much too large for me. I must have looked a sorry sight – like an unkempt, ragged waif. My hair was still in plaits, the Keltic style, but I had lost most of the amber beads and brass rings that were usually braided into it. I still wore the raven torc though, so I lifted my chin proudly in spite of my embarrassment. Theon was acceptable in his simple garb. People would recognize his serpent pendant and know him to be a servant of Asklepios. Some of the men in the courtyard acknowledged him with friendly gestures. One or two winked knowingly at Theon when they saw me. I supposed they thought I was his servant.

On the upper terrace, a woman leaned over the balustrade. She shaded her eyes with her hand and waved. Alexandros waved back to her. As we came closer I saw she appeared to be quite young. She was tall and slender, her auburn hair tumbling loosely over her bare shoulders. The sun shining on her made her seem as though she was dipped in gold.

She peered down at us, measuring us haughtily with her head tossed back. As the light caught in her glossy hair, bright-coloured as the golden tassels of ripe harvest corn, I could see a resemblance to Alexandros. She called out something, but Alexandros had turned away and did not return her greeting.

"Is that your mother?" I asked. He did not reply.

"I will fetch a boy to stable your donkey," Alexandros said to Theon. Then he went off, leaving us standing there while the woman on the balcony continued to watch us, still as a statue.

"Who is that woman?" I asked Theon.

"That is Alexandros's mother, Olympias!" Theon said.

"She looks very young!"

"Yes, she has kept her age, to her advantage," Theon's voice was unusually terse and sharp. "She bore him when she was as young as you."

Alexandros returned soon with a little, brown-skinned boy. "Here is Ahmed. He'll take your donkey to the stables."

The boy had a sad, pinched face, old for its age, and he did not smile. Without speaking he took the donkey's reins and went off with a curious backward glance.

The woman from the balcony had come down to the portico and stood beside the rose-tinted columns. She had a disdainful air about her and hardly took her eyes off of us. Alexandros saw her there, excused himself, and went to join her.

"Come along, Olwen," Theon said. "I know the way to the royal guest house. We need not wait for Alexandros."

"Should we not wait for him to show us in?" I asked.

Theon chuckled, "I have known this palace since his grandfather's time."

As we walked through the palace grounds, Theon explained. "I was born near Pella in a village called Stagira. You may have heard Alexandros speak of his tutor, Aristoteles? Aristoteles was a boyhood friend of mine. His father, Nichomachos, became the court physician here. I chose to serve Asklepion too and took the vows of chastity and served at the sanctuary of Epidauros. Aristoteles chose to follow a different path, the school of philosophers. He has made a name for himself as Alexandros's teacher."

"Then why does Alexandros come to you for counselling?" I asked.

Theon said, "Alexandros knows he can trust me to give him wise advice."

"Does he heed you?"

Theon chuckled. "He's a headstrong boy. He'll do what he wants. But if I can steer him on the right path, then he'll at least make a wise decision. To be sure, Aristoteles has left his mark on Alexandros. When it comes to the healing arts though, Alexandros always comes to me. That is why I am often invited to stay in Pella as a guest-friend, and sometimes aid the palace physician." He smiled, "The first time I came to stay at the palace, his father, Filippos, was still a young man. He never lost his country soul, even when he came to power. He might be a crude sort — some think he is a drunken bully — but he is a crafty statesman and a brilliant commander who never puts himself above his men. I should hope that Alexandros will learn the art of war from his father. He is a good boy with a pure heart. It is the mother one must be wary of." He stopped and looked down at me with the sternest look I had ever seen on his face.

"Whatever happens, Olwen," he said. "Remember you must never be at cross purposes with Olympias!"

Stanza Eight

Theon led me along a path that skirted the wall on the east side of the palace, through a small portal. An old gate keeper greeted him. The man ran a curious rheumy eye over me and lifted a bushy eyebrow. Theon spoke to him quickly. The porter gave a wide knowing smile and let us through. We entered through the portal and stepped into the lush gardens that were enclosed behind the palace. Everything seemed to sparkle. With the sun full on the palace it gleamed like molten gold. The garden was a paradise of trees and plants such as I had never seen before. I truly could not believe my eyes! Surely this must be like the Otherworld where the gods dwell.

The flowerbeds were still brilliant with colour. Among the shrubs were statues; and fountains spurted water from the mouths of lions or strange mystical beasts. Others sprayed silvery jets that caught the sun and reflected with rainbow colours.

There were shrines everywhere. I could not believe so many gods existed! Some were simple altars with offerings still smouldering in marble libation bowls; others were images of beautiful creatures both male and female; some of them garlanded, all of them gilded and painted with life-like glass eyes set in their comely faces. One would think they were actually alive!

Theon pointed them out to me by name: "Mighty Zeus; Apollo; Athena, holding her little owl; Poseidon, the sea god with his three-pronged trident; lovely Artemis carrying her bow and arrows; Dionysos whose altar was heaped with fresh fruits. Our gods were not like these noble, beautiful man-like beings. I could not help but think of our humble shrines in the oak groves of Caer Gwyn.

We passed the garden of shrines and entered a paved avenue lined with statues of the god-heroes. Theon told me their names: Herakles, Perseus and the brave Achilles. This avenue led to a wide court where shade-trees lined the paths paved with smooth river stones, placed in designs of black and white. Across the court, under the shade of a wide-spreading tree a man stood holding a conference with a group of young boys who crowded around him.

The man's head was bent in thought while he listened to the words of a youth who was speaking to him. They were too far away for me to hear, but the hum of their discussion reached me when the speaker had finished his say: they all began to talk at once, until the man held up his hand to silence them.

"That is Alexandros's tutor, Aristoteles," Theon explained. "Those boys are his students, the *ephebes.*"

"Are they princes too, like Alexandros?" I asked.

"Most of them are sons of noble families and there may be one or two who are hostage-princes, the sons of kings from lands that Filippos has conquered," Theon explained. "These young boys will one day serve in the Royal Guard.

They are hand-picked, and if they are lucky they may be chosen as the Companions of Alexandros.

"Like our Royal War Band," I mused

"Just so," Theon agreed.

"We have nothing such as this in Caer Gwyn," I exclaimed. "The king's sons, if they are favoured, and the sons of tribal chieftains and knights, are sometimes sent to the *cyfaiths* — those cities where the Druids have their studies."

I was curious about these boys and their teacher.

"They will study with Aristoteles until they are old enough to become officers in the king's guard," Theon explained. "Aristoteles is a philosopher. The boys' lessons include sciences, mathematics and rhetoric. They attend the gymnasium too. There is also a theatre, where great dramas and comedies are performed. Alexandros is a lover of the arts, you see. Some of his closest friends are actors and poets. The darling of the court these days is an actor named Thetallos. He's in great demand and performs in all the famous theatres throughout the country."

I listened, fascinated by Theon's stories. The only theatres I knew of where the travelling troupes of mimes who sometimes came through the villages at festive times, though I had heard sometimes jugglers and acrobats performed for the ricon at his feasts. Of bards I knew many things from Lleu who had taught me how to strum his harp and sing the songs.

"I come from a family of remembrances," I said.

Theon smiled. "Then perhaps you can learn to sing the songs about our people too," he said.

When we came out of the gardens, my head was throbbing as though it might burst. How could I fathom such a way of life as this? It was beyond anything I had imagined. Life in Caer Gwyn had been so simple; this was a world of kings and noblemen with riches beyond belief. I fairly trembled at the thought of it. What would become of me I could not know. I felt as insignificant as a speck in the vast heavens' grain. I fell silent, speechless with wonder and contemplation. Even so, I did not feel a sense of adversity. If this was to be my fate, or *moira,* as Alexandros had said, I would accept it gratefully.

We had come to another portal, this one leading into the palace buildings. A tall guard wearing full armour stood, still as one of the garden statues, with his shield on his arm and a long spear held erect. He held his pose though I saw his eyes follow us as we passed.

A tall, stately man approached us as we entered through the gate.

"Is he the king?" I asked.

"He is the regent, Antipatros," Theon said. "While the king is away on campaign, Antipatros rules in his stead."

As he drew near, the man opened his arms in a gesture of welcome to Theon. The two men greeted each other with a hearty hand-shake and kissed each other on both cheeks.

"My good friend, Theon! How long it has been since you have visited us. Are you well? Have you come to stay a while?" The regent was most regal, a well-seasoned man with a neatly trimmed beard and silver-grey hair. He had a handsome face, stern yet smile-lined.

"So, Theon, is this is your new servant? Alexandros told me you were coming and bringing a maiden with you." He appraised me with keen eyes.

"Olwen is not my servant, sir," Theon said. "She's a healer like me."

Antipator's eyebrows raised in surprise. 'Well then, young maiden, welcome to Pella!" Then he turned back to Theon and they continued their discussion.

As the two men spoke, a scrawny, pale-faced youth came running through the gate and up to the regent. "Father, Aristoteles says I must..."

Although I could not hear their words. It was clear the boy was agitated and I saw the regent's face flush.

"I ordered you to do it and you will obey me!" the regent snapped.

"But father..."

"If Aristoteles says you must pay heed to your studies, then you will do it." The boy walked away, casting a sullen glance back over his shoulder.

Antipatros shook his head and shrugged. "That boy!" he said. "He always tries to avoid his training. Of all my sons, Kassandros is forever a thorn in my side." He slapped Theon's shoulder. "Now then, I have had the servants prepare your rooms. It's been so long since you occupied them, but they are still much the same as before. The girl will stay with you?" He peered down at me with the hint of a sly smile. "Or will she reside in the women's quarters?"

"For now, Olwen will stay with me," Theon said. He put his arm around me and drew me close. "Olwen tends to me like a daughter would for a father. Until she learns the palace ways, she will stay in my care."

"Well then," Antipatros said. "I will let you find your way. Until we meet again, the god's blessings on you both."

Theon led me down the long, dim corridor, then past a cavernous room from which drifted the aroma of roasting meat. I glimpsed inside and saw an immense fire-pit with steaming cauldrons big enough to hold a man. A flock of bustling servants ran to and fro with platters heaped with food and clay jugs of wine. There were pantries and kitchens in Caer Gwyn's hill fort but this one was large enough to prepare a meal for an entire army!

The corridor opened onto a pillared court plainly landscaped with wide, flat paving stones around a central well framed by terra-cotta pots with flowers in bright autumn hues; climbing vines wound around the squared pillars and clung to the stone walls. A number of small rooms opened onto this courtyard. Theon explained these were the quarters of the palace stewards, those in charge of the kitchens and administrators of the small army of slaves who were at the service of the royalty.

"It is the oldest quarter in the palace, and one that the king did not renovate," said Theon. "I have always preferred it. I suppose it reminds me of when

I was first a guest-friend at the Makedonian court. They have always kept my room here for me."

He led me into a small cottage off the courtyard, simply furnished with a thick oaken table and several stools. The mud-brick walls were plain and un-adorned by tapestries or frescoes; but there was a small niche by the hearth – a shrine to the house gods- with a little painted votive lamp. I cupped the lamp in my hand, quite taken with its intricate design of florets and wheat sheaves.

There were four rooms in the house, one where Theon could treat his pa-tients, the main room where we would prepare our food and two others for private sleeping quarters.

In the centre room, two low couches covered with white sheep's skins were strewn with brightly woven pillows. In the corner was a carved wooden chest on which the boy had left our bundles. Over the table hung a bronze candela-bra; there were clay oil lamps on the sideboard too, and a jug of wine chilled in a bucket of fresh snow that Theon explained had been brought down from the mountain. A plate of fruit had been set on the table beside a rich yellow round of cheese and bread, still steaming, from the oven. The stone hearth had been swept clean and a basket of firewood placed nearby.

There was a shuffling at the door, and someone tapped to get our attention. A girl with arms laden with bundles waited to be admitted. She hesitated at the door sill.

"Please sir, I have brought you gifts from my lady the queen."

"From Olympias?" Theon said. He took the bundles from her, frowned, and held them out carefully as though he was suspicious of their contents.

"They're for you and the young maiden, sir; my lady Olympias sent them as a welcome gift for her son's guest." She looked at me shyly and said, in a soft voice "I am Arsinoe. My lady has put me at your service, for your bath."

She was a young girl, dark-skinned with luminous brown calf-eyes and shiny hair that hung in springy black tendrils. Theon whispered to me in my own language, so the girl would not understand. "Olympias has probably sent her to spy on us. Olympias does nothing unless it suits her purpose."

"I will pour your bath now," the girl said. "You will follow me."

"First, let us have a look at these!" Theon said. He handed me one of the bundles tied with a silver cord. I gasped with surprise when I opened it, and saw Theon give a knowing smile.

Inside was a gown of saffron made of a silky material as fine as gossamer; sandals of soft leather with golden buckles, and a little box of inlaid wood containing earrings shaped like delicate gilded birds. I stammered my thanks. The girl smiled, showing a dimple in her cheek.

Theon unwrapped his bundle which contained a tunic of fine white linen. "Well now," he said. He cleared his voice and looked down his nose in an im-perious expression. "I think we shall look quite presentable for the royal court with these splendid garments." A smile tugged the corners of his mouth even though he tried to appear stern. "Tell the queen that we gratefully accept her gifts." He nodded his approval for me to follow Arsinoe to the bathing room. There was an amused twinkle in his eyes as if it gave him pleasure to see me so indulged.

Stanza Nine

The bathing room was part of the women's quarters and was for the use of the courtiers or courtesans.

"The queen has her own private baths in the royal pavilion," Arsinoe said. "This bathing room is for guests."

We conversed in a hesitant mixture of gestures and Makedonian. She said she was from a far southern island called Krete and served Olympias.

"Of course," she admitted smugly," I have served other noble masters before that. In fact," she said, tossing her head so the ringlets danced around her small brown face, "I was a gift to Filippos from a Kretan nobleman." She spoke the name *Filippos* with a hiss of disdain. "When he grew tired of me, he gave me to Olympias."

I remembered what Theon had said about Olympias having 'spies'. I also remembered he said no one must ever be at cross purposes with the queen. It curbed my curiosity and I did not question Arsinoe. I knew of the intrigues within the timbered halls of Caer Gwyn's hillfort, so there was no telling what went on here in Pella. It was beyond my imagining.

We passed through a maze of corridors and entered a courtyard which was enclosed by flowering hedges. In the centre was a fountain with a plump little winged boy carved in pink marble holding a bow and arrow. Just off the courtyard, behind a colonnade of rounded arches and potted plants, was the bathing room.

As soon as I entered the room I felt as though I was being plunged under water; everything shimmered in the tones of aqua and pink such as are found inside a seashell. The floor was pearly with crushed shells and the walls painted with murals of lovely sea-nymphs riding on the crest of waves, and leaping fish — little blue creatures with smiling faces. Arsinoe said they were called 'dolphins'. The room was small with only one bath made of faience tiles that reflected a bright bluish-green like the sea. Arsinoe said it was a Kretan bath. "The Kretans have many bathing rooms such as this in their old palaces," she said.

While I disrobed, she called the other attendants, girls of various ages, some of them dusky-skinned like herself, others fair like me, but all of them spoke Makedonian, mixed with some of their own strange languages. They stared at me, tittering behind their hands and rolling their eyes as though I were a peculiar thing, like some mongrel pup cast out of its litter. They took my clothing gingerly, holding their noses in disgust. I realized in that damp room filled with the fragrance of rose-scented oils, that my garments reeked of the animals and wood-smoke smells of the farm. I covered myself shamefully, conscious their eyes were inspecting me. My skin, where it had been exposed to wind and weather, was tanned and freckled while all the rest of me was white as milk and all of my bones stuck out through the flesh.

Arsinoe hid an amused smile and pointed to my raven torc. I removed it reluctantly and handed it to her. She turned it over curiously in her hands then said something to one of the attendants who was holding my soiled garments. I realized they meant to discard my belongings. Before she could give the torc to the slave, I snatched it back with an oath that made her withdraw her hand as though my words had bitten her. She widened her eyes and stepped away from me. It must have been the look I gave her. She spoke sharply to the slave and they put my garments and the torc outside on one of the benches. None of them dared touch them after that.

I stepped into the bath and sank into the steaming water. I closed my eyes and let the fragrance of roses and the soothing warmth of the water envelope me. Arsinoe poured in a vial of fragrant oil and began to scrub me with a large rough object riddled with holes that she called a 'sponge'; she said it came from the sea. I thought she would rub my skin away.

When I finally stepped out of the bath I was scrubbed red as a new-born and my blood prickled at my skin. The attendants wrapped me in a soft cotton sheet and I was told to sit on the low marble bench while they untangled my hair, searching through it as though they expected to find vermin, then brushing it until I thought they would pull it from its roots. They oiled it and wrapped it in a steaming cloth. I rested there dozing, revelling in the luxury of this new experience. The slaves chattered among themselves. Sometimes I caught a snatch of words I could understand – a phrase or two in the slow, simple Makedonian dialect Theon and Alexandros had taught me. It was mostly tidbits of palace gossip and I suppose they did not know I could understand some of what they said. Once one gave me an artful look and whispered something about *'to Filippos's liking'* and *'like the father, so is the son'*, but Arsinoe hushed them.

When I said demurely "I am the guest-friend of the king's son," in the most perfect Makedonian I could manage, the girls blushed red as crimson.

Arsinoe brought me the new garments and dressed me with careful attendance. The gown felt soft, cool against my flesh; Arsinoe explained the colour, a rich blue, had been chosen especially to compliment my fair hair.

She clasped the jewelled pin at the shoulder of the gown and tied the braided girdle so it would show the contours of my slender body. Then she stood back to inspect me and shook her head. "You do not have the fullness of breast, nor the contour of hips to give credit to the style," she said. When I blushed, she said, "Never mind, we will fatten you up."

I heard one of the girls snicker. "She doesn't have much more shape than a boy." The others laughed and Arsinoe scolded them.

172

After my hair was dried and curled with heated iron tongs, Arsinoe twisted and pinned it up with combs. When she handed me the gilded mirror, I hardly recognized the face I saw. The loose tendrils of my hair shone and the pretty golden birds glinted from my ears. My skin was powdered and my cheeks tinted to give them more colour; my eyes were painted too, like the eyes of the sea-nymphs on the wall fresco, luminous and soft, the eyes of a stranger.

Arsinoe handed me my torc and I saw how tarnished it was beside the bright yellow-gold jewellery Olympias had sent for me. So I agreed, with a reluctant sigh, that I would wear the plain twist of gold chain instead. It was the first time I had never worn my Raven torc.

"Now you look like a princess!" Arsinoe exclaimed.

She escorted me back through the labyrinth of halls to where Theon waited. He was wearing the new white tunic and the barbers had trimmed his hair and beard. When he saw me, his eyes went round as an owl's. At first he was speechless but before long composed himself and I felt uncomfortable and blushed. Then he said, in his droll way, "Well now, a vision of Aphrodite you are! You look respectable enough to grace the royal chambers!"

He poured me a cup of wine. "We shall drink to good fortune," he said.

"And to Alexandros," I said." I lifted the goblet to my lips, then remembered to spill a little to the gods. Whatever gods they were, I thanked them.

Arsinoe stood in the doorway waiting to be dismissed. Theon waved her away with a reminder to take her lady our regards and gratitude.

"We shall have our evening repast sent into the palace gardens — a fitting way for you to spend your first night as a royal guest," he said. "Alexandros has not summoned us, so I expect he is detained. You do look like a vision of Aphrodite!" He looked at me with a quizzical expression. I felt my cheeks grow hot. Perhaps it was the wine.

Stanza Ten

The late afternoon sun slanted between the pillars as we walked down the long portico. Theon showed me the beautiful wall frescoes with scenes of the heroes and gods and paintings of battles and hunts. The Great Hall was barred by a polished door bolted into place with a bar of hammered brass. The guards stood stiff as statues and wore their full armour.

Theon said we could not go into the Hall unless we were summoned. There were always guards posted by it to keep out those who did not have an audience with the king.

I asked him if Alexandros would join us.

"Alexandros is busy with palace affairs and I do not know how long it will be before we will see him again," Theon said.

I felt a tug of disappointment but dismissed it.

173

We stepped out into the lush greenery of the garden. Inside the inner court; the garden was surrounded by open porticoes on each side. Three tiers of terraces looked down on it. The air was fragrant with plants and the sweetness of flowers. Carved benches were set around an oval fish-pool, heaped with soft cushions where we could recline. A table was set with cups of cordial and a tray of honey cakes.

I had never tasted such sweet morsels. I licked the honey from my fingers and took the cup Theon offered me. The cordial was sweet with the delicacy of fruit.

"Ambrosia for the goddess," he said.

The meal was simple served on silver platters. There was roast kid; wild thistles steeped in oil with herbs; and various other appetizers none I had ever tasted before, all of which were delicious. We ate with our fingers; I should not have known what to do and would have wiped them on my lovely gown but Theon called the serving boy who brought water in a basin with rose-petals floating on top.

I was enjoying myself so much I did not notice the sky had grown dark; the stars twinkled in the vast dome of the heavens. The slaves lit the cressets along the portico. Everything glowed with a soft light. Somewhere I could hear the strumming of music; I thought it was a harp but Theon said it was called a *lyra*. I longed to hear Lleu's voice and the ballads I knew. I drifted into these thoughts when I heard Theon exclaim and saw Alexandros peering down at us from the terrace above.

He ran down to join us, greeting us courteously. I thought he seemed tense and had a strained expression on his face; his voice did not ring with its usual cheerful tone.

I suppose he did not recognize me as I reclined on the bench. He looked past Theon, frowned and then the smile faded from his face. I heard him mutter a word, *"Hetaera!"*

I stood up and greeted him. "A god's blessing on you, Alexandros," I said. The disapproving look left his face and he gave me a fleeting smile. "I did not know you. Your face was in the shadows, and..."

"Arsinoe's work!" Theon said. "But doesn't she look like beautiful Aphrodite?"

"You are as lovely as the goddess," Alexandros said, but I detected a tone of disapproval in his voice. He excused himself and said he had an audience in the Great Hall — something about his father, and some ambassadors from the north. "I will send for you just as soon as I am able," he said. "These affairs of state must be dealt with quickly before the winter comes making it difficult for ambassadors and delegations to travel to and fro." He appeared edgy and there were shadows under his eyes.

Later Theon remarked how Alexandros was 'strung tight as a bow string' "It is to be expected. He has much to think about. His father is away putting down a rebellion in Thessaly and word has come from the east that there is more trouble brewing with some of the Thracian tribes."

As we walked back to our chambers I asked him, "What is a *hetaera*?"

Theon's brows lifted. "*Hetaera*? Why that is a woman, usually very beautiful and independently wealthy, educated, talented — often dedicated to the service of Aphrodite, the love goddess and paid for her services. There are several here in the palace. They are the only women who are invited to share the men's couches at the feasts. Why do you ask?"

"I heard Alexandros say the word." I felt a twinge somewhere inside of me and my cheeks burned.

Theon must have heard the tremor of my voice. He patted my arm. 'Never mind," he said, "I am certain he did not mean that *you* looked like a hetaera!" Then, under his breath I heard him mutter, "I'm quite sure that is just what Olympias had hoped for!"

The next morning as Theon and I shared a meal of flat bread and cheese, we were disturbed by someone rapping loudly on the door. When Theon opened it, I gasped, thinking it must be an apparition. The man at the door was a giant with skin as black as ebony; only the whites of his eyes and his gleaming ivory teeth showed in his face. I almost screamed with fright, but Theon invited him in.

"Gods, Xenon!" Theon exclaimed. "You have grown as large as a bear since last I saw you!"

The giant laughed, a low grumbling sound like a wild beast's roar. He wore brass rings in his ears the size of bracelets and was naked except for a white loincloth. His skin glistened as though it were oiled.

"Xenon is a Nubian," explained Theon. "He comes from a far country where everyone is as black as he is."

Truly, the world is such a strange place. In just one day I had seen people coloured every hue, like the flowers in the garden.

"Xenon has been a slave in the palace for as long as I can remember," Theon said. "They are cheerful, trustworthy people, the Nubians, and gentle as foals in spite of their size!"

I stared with round eyes at Xenon. He wore jewelled bands on his wrists and ankles; his arms were thick as tree trunks. I was certain he could lift an ox! He carried a chest polished and rosy with carvings of flowers on the lid which he put down in front of me.

"My lord Alexandros sent this for you," he said in his rumbling voice. He bowed his head to me. His hair was tightly curled, clinging to his massive skull like sheep's fleece.

"Go on!" Theon said, "Let us see what treasure the young prince has sent to you."

I opened the lid of the box slowly. Theon and Xenon watched, Xenon's wide mouth curved upwards like a crescent moon, Theon's face wrinkled with a grin.

I gasped with surprise at what I found inside the chest; garments like those I had worn for the Midsummer rites: a crimson tunic of finer cloth than Essylt's homespun but embroidered with gold threads in a pattern much the same; breeches of soft kid dyed rich purple with tassels at the knees; high laced riding boots of soft leather. These were wrapped inside a cape of red fox pelts that had a gold neck clamp shaped like the Makedonian starburst. Theon said I would need them for winter. In another little painted box I found amber and faience beads and brass rings like those I used to plait into my hair. These were far grander gifts than the silken gown and trinkets Olympias had sent me. I was overcome with delight.

"Alexandros wanted to surprise you, "Theon said.

I thought again about the look on Alexandros's face when he had seen me in the garden. Did he know his mother had sent me the other garments?

"Alexandros wishes you to have your own attendant," the Nubian, Xenon said. He went to the door and called to a young girl who had been waiting outside. "This is Aricia. She will look after your needs," Xenon said.

"Aricia is a tribal hostage – one of the king's war-prizes," explained Theon. "Alexandros has placed her at your service. She will tend to your baths, wait on you, run errands, escort you wherever you go. She is yours while you are guest-friend here."

She was a plain girl with straw-coloured hair braided in a simple style. She had a solemn face and looked frightened. "Aricia, miss." she said. "I am your servant." She spoke in a dialect of a northern Keltic tongue I recognized.

I put out my hand to greet her. "My name is Olwen" I said.

"I am at the king's bidding," she said. "He has been kind to me but he has no need of me now." She looked at me with sad brown eyes. "I come from a noble house, even though it is a Triballi one," she said. She lifted up her chin and I saw she was near tears. "My father was a king in our land." She told me she was the daughter of a chieftain who had been killed when the Makedonians invaded her tribal lands. She had been taken as a battle-prize although she was considered hostage rather than slave.

I thought of the green lake in the Triballi lands where Sholto and I had camped and how the chieftains had brought us into their village and shared their meal with us. I told her about Sholto even though I found it difficult to speak his name. Having been taken herself as hostage, she knew, I suppose, that it was a dark corner I had chosen to forget. She did not ask me more.I told her I was grateful to Alexandros for his kindness.

Aricia said, "He treats me kindly too." She helped me bathe and dressed me in my new garments, then she combed out my braided hair, carefully curling it so it fell in soft tendrils. She held up a copper mirror.

"See? Now you are like a Child of Aphrodite!" she said.

I glanced in the mirror, but the face looking back at me was not my own. It was a beautiful face, rosy-cheeked, framed with copper-coloured curls.

"I am the Child of the Raven," I said. "I can never belong to Aphrodite!"

BALLAD SIXTEEN A Song For Filippos, King Of Makedon

This is a song for Filippos, son of Amyntas
that noble warrior of Makedon
whose bloodline comes from Herakles.
Warriors, shout a paean for him:
Raise your swords to honour him.
Musicians, play for him
on your sistrum, cymbals and drums.
Maidens, dance for him.
Singers, laud him,
for he is Makedon's invincible hero.
He is fearless and energetic.
He is cunning and wise.
Poets, tell his tale.
Strike up your harps in praise of him.
There is no other man who can compare
with Filippos, the Lion of Makedon.

ODE TO THE KING

Stanza One

Before the first winter snow, the king returned to Pella. Aricia was showing me how to tie threads on a loom when Theon came with the news.

"Filippos has arrived back from Thessaly. There will be a grand celebration to welcome him."

I had heard the king was a boisterous fellow with a penchant for raucous carousing and an appetite for maidens and fresh young cadets. Theon said there would be sacrifices and feasting but only women, such as those Alexandros had called *hetaeras*, attended events held in Pella's royal hall.

It was a sharp, wintry day with a north wind blowing. Storm clouds loomed over the distant hills. We waited in the palace forecourt near the entrance gate where a troop of armour-clad soldiers stood guard. I looked for Alexandros and saw him standing on the upper portico beside his mother. His bright hair was crowned with a diadem of gold, and he wore a purple tunic. Beside him stood Olympias, splendid in a gown of saffron wool with a fox cape around her shoulders. She stared down into the crowd below, a fierce scowl on her face.

On one side of them a white-haired man stood beside a stocky youth. The elder man bent to speak to the youth who nodded and stared down into the crowd, his mouth agape.

"That is Alexandros's half-brother, Arridaios." Theon explained. "Poor boy was poisoned as an infant – so it is believed. He hasn't any more wits than a three-year-old. Alexandros protects him, takes him riding sometimes. But mostly he's kept out of sight in the care of his keeper. He's an embarrassment to the king. And as for the Queen..." Theon's brows lifted and he shrugged, clicking his tongue. "There is reason to suspect. You see, Olympias won't tolerate any rivals to the throne."

I felt a shiver at his words, but before I could question him I heard the roars outside the palace walls as the Makedonoi welcomed their king home. Outside the palace walls, the streets of Pella were jammed with people. As I listened to their cheers and the stomp of marching boots. I thought back to the day when the Royal War Band of Caer Gwyn had brought the body of Hywel the Fair home from battle. What a solemn occasion that had been! Not a joyous homecoming such as this.

Soldiers and palace people milled about the forecourt, hailing each other. I kept a pleasant face, though I felt fearful and nervous as we waited to greet the king.

"You are anxious," Theon said. He laid his hand on my shoulder. "I understand. This is all strange to you. But do not worry, Olwen. I have known the king since he was your age. He's a man of great renown now, but he is still Filippos, a shrewd but fair man, one who loves to sing a skolion and drink a hearty draft of wine with his friends. Hear how the people love him! He is their champion."

The king arrived, riding up the steep path to the palace gates. A roar went up from the soldiers who guarded the gates and the people in the courtyard began to cheer. Filippos sat on his steed in a commanding posture, waving to the eager crowds. He was a stocky-built bearded man, war-scarred, with sun-browned weathered skin. He was surrounded by a retinue of burly soldiers carrying gold standards, dressed in leather jerkins and burnished helmets crested with red plumes

"Those are his generals," Theon said. He pointed them out by name. "There's Amyntas and Attalos and Parmenion all of them are formidable warriors, and the young, fair-haired man is Eumenes, the king's royal secretary. He's a Greek."

When they entered the gate into the courtyard, a great cheer went up. A tall youth, darkly handsome with a neatly trimmed beard and hair cut to the nape, broke from the line of guards and ran up to take the bridle of the king's horse. The king dismounted and greeted him, kissing him full on the mouth.

"That is Pausanias, the king's bodyguard." Theon's voice had a tone of disapproval.

The name, *Pausanias,* stirred a memory in me of that dark night in the forest glade and the hunters gathered around the blazing fire. I remember Alexandros handing around Sholto's weaponry. Pausanias was the one to whom he had given Sholto's dagger!

I thought it strange to see the king make such an intimate gesture toward a youth who was under his command. Our warriors never greeted each other with such intimacy, the way a man would greet his woman.

I watched the two as they stood together. The youth was taller than the King, indeed a handsome young man, who carried himself as regally as a prince. *Pausanius, the king's attendant.* Where was Alexandros? Why had he not come to greet his father?

I stared at the youth, his haughty manner, his fine-woven clothes. And yes! There was the dagger tucked in his belt. Even at a distance I recognized the amber stones inset in the hilt. Something came to me, bristling the hairs on my nape, but I said nothing and threw off the feeling.

Pausanias led the king's horse away, and Filippos strode with a demeanour of authority into the forecourt. The palace people swarmed to look, calling greetings to their king and his attendants. Among the men were women in twittering clusters, well-dressed hetaeras, those expensive girls who Theon said came from Corinth and Ephesus to serve the officers. Some of them threw garlands of flowers and waved branches of myrtle.

The king was surrounded by his welcoming admirers, generals and guards. Beside them he appeared small, yet he exuded power. He was short and broad-chested, gnarled and scarred as an old oak that's been hacked by woodsmen. He must have been handsome once, but an ugly scar ran across his right eye from brow to cheekbone giving him a fearsome look.

"How did the king lose his eye?" I asked.

"It was in a battle," Theon said. "They say it was portended by the oracle at Delphi that he would lose an eye. You see, he had spied on his wife, Olympias, saw her caressing her serpent in her bed. The oracle warned him that he would be punished for spying on the mystical rites that only those initiated into the cult must have knowledge of." He paused and mused a moment before continuing. "She's a strange woman, Olympias, possessed by the dark arts. And she has tried to impart that strangeness to Alexandros by convincing him he was conceived by a snake – the golden snake of Ammon. From his infancy, she has filled Alexandros's head full of these mystical stories."

"And he believes her," I said. "He told me he was the son of Ammon."

"It's all nonsense!" Theon exclaimed impatiently. "Ammon is an Egyptian god. Alexandros is Filippos's son, in spite of palace gossip. Olympias is a dangerous woman. She uses snakes in her cult worship. Filippos has grown to detest her because of it." Then he stopped speaking. His face was flushed as though he was embarrassed by what he had said. He ruffled my hair and managed to smile. "You're just a child still, dear Olwen. These tales of palace intrigues must not be believed or they will corrupt your innocence."

A loud cheer from the crowd interrupted our conversation. Alexandros had come down from the portico and strutted up to greet his father. Everyone's eyes turned toward him. He stood out like a bright flame amid the crowd of leather-clad soldiers. He and Filippos shook hands and Filippos stood a moment, his good eye scrutinizing his son. Then he clasped Alexandros into an embrace. Another cheer went up from the soldiers.

"Filippos! Alexandros!"

Then another cheer, louder than the first, from a group of youths who had pushed forward and cried eagerly: "*Alexandros! Alexandros!*"

Of all the boys, Kassandros, the thin, freckled youth who was the regent Antipatros's son, was the only one who held back, scuffing the dirt with his toe. He had that same sullen look on his face I had seen him give his father.

The other boys crowded around Alexandros eagerly, cheering louder than they had for his father. They greeted him with the same reverence as if they were in the company of a god-hero. One, a tall, tawny-haired youth, had brought a wreath of laurel to place on Alexandros's head. I supposed he must have been a favourite because Alexandros stopped and embraced him.

"Those boys are Alexandros's Companions," Theon explained. "When he becomes king, they'll be his generals."

I remember how Alexandros had said to me once, "I will be greater than my father. The gods have ordained it." I had thought this a boastful statement, but recalled his tale of Achilles, how the gods had told Thetis, his sea nymph mother, he would outshine his father. I wondered if Alexandros's mother, Olympias, was more than mortal? Could it be true, her story that Alexandros was conceived of a god? I had listened to Alexandros's tale as though it was a fable, how his mother claimed the golden snake of Ammon had visited her the night she had conceived him. It did seem certain that Alexandros possessed something more than most of the mortal boys who surrounded him, but was he truly the son of a god?

Everyone swarmed forward, closing around Alexandros and the king. Soon I lost sight of them as they were surrounded by the soldiers, and the crowd pressed into the Hall.

Stanza Two

What Theon had said was true. The king liked to celebrate. The revelling went on for several days. Even from our house in the back of the palace the sound of rowdy singing and howls of laughter carried and continued through the night.

A few days later when all was quiet again, Filippos sent a message for Theon.

"The king wants to see me," Theon said. "Alexandros told him I was here. You will accompany me."

I felt reluctant, but Theon insisted I must go with him. I felt shy, and honestly afraid of facing a man such as King Filippos. Alexandros had rarely spoken of his father, and when he did I sensed an edge of resentment in his tone. The serving girls gossiped of family feuds and heated quarrels between the king and queen. I had learned to stay out of Olympias's sight since that first encounter. The girls spoke of the queen's fearsome temper and jealous rages. Anyone who stood in the way of her son suffered for it. And Filippos was a man of heated passion, taking wives for every conquest and lovers at any whim — both boys and girls, they said.

Theon sensed my trepidation. "Filippos is interested in the Kelts and no doubt will want to question you," he said. "He speaks a little of your language and what you don't understand I will interpret."

I had often been in our ricon's presence in Caer Gwyn, but I had never been in the presence of a fabled warrior king such as Filippos of Makedon.

"Remember, you are my assistant, and a respected acolyte, so no harm will come to you," Theon said. "In fact, I'm quite sure the king will be pleased to have you in his court."

We were led through the palace by a servant, down halls with painted walls and floors paved with river stones in intricate designs. Theon explained the library was a place where poets and philosophers gathered. I had expected a quiet sanctuary, but as we approached the thick oaken doors, I heard the sound of angry voices, two men shouting. Theon seemed alarmed too and stopped outside the door. I could not understand everything I heard but I knew the words *betrayal, promises, jealousy, forsaken* and I clearly interpreted what they meant.

I heard a man growl. "Leave me!"

The doors burst open and the same youth I had seen in the courtyard the day the king returned from his campaign, rushed out. It was Pausanias, the bodyguard Filippos had so boldly kissed. His face was set in an angry scowl, his dark hair dishevelled. He was clearly agitated and trembling, his face flushed red. He pushed past us rough and rude, without a word, and ran down the corridor.

Theon looked down at me, his brows furrowed. He glanced at the servant who had led us to the library, and shrugged, but said nothing. The servant stepped cautiously into the room and announced, "The physician, Theon, is here, sir, as you have bidden."

I followed Theon into a massive room painted with a mural dedicated to the Muses. Shelves of scrolls with tooled bindings and gilded cases lined the walls. A dazzle of sunlight splintered through the half-open shutters. Filippos sat on a chair with carved lion's heads on the arm rests. He got up from his writing table and put out his hand to greet Theon.

"How long has it been, old friend, since last we met?" There was no hint of the anger in his voice I had heard coming from the room earlier. The king seemed calm and relaxed, undisturbed by whatever had passed between him and the bodyguard. He gave me a brief glance, then motioned for Theon to sit on a stool next to the table. "Alexandros says he invited you to spend the winter here."

"That is so, sir," Theon said. "He thinks I'm too old to withstand the winter at my homestead. We are grateful for your hospitality." He nudged me forward. "This is Olwen, sir. She is a Kelt from the northern lands. She is an acolyte priestess and healer."

Filippos's good eye slid over me. "A little Kelt, eh? One who has the powers of medicine and magic?"

"Yes. I...I was sworn to be an acolyte of the goddess, sir," I stammered, and put out my hand to greet him. My palms felt sticky with sweat. His strong, calloused fingers squeezed mine tight.

"Welcome, little Kelt," Filippos said, flashing a charming smile. He scanned me from head to toe with his baleful eye. "You must tell me about your people. I know there are strong tribes in the north, fierce warriors." He waved his hand toward the divan. "Sit. Tell me where you are from. What is your tribe?'

Theon sat on the stool beside the king while I took a seat on the divan as he had commanded. Filippos sat back on his high-backed carved chair and folded his arms across his chest waiting for me to speak.

"I am from the north, sir, from Cymru. I am an Essyltyr, from the clan of the Raven. On my fifteenth birthday, at the Midsummer, I was to begin my service to the goddess at our holy isle..."

As I related my tale to him I felt overwhelmed with sadness, remembering the thatched domes of our village houses nestled below the hill where Caer Gwyn's stone fortress stood guard over the Plain. I told him of our sacred groves, the woodland shrines where the Druids worshipped the mighty oaks, the great stone circle where omens were foretold at the summer solstice.

 The king settled back in his chair and cast a long glance at me. "You have the poise of a priestess, yet you are still a child. How old are you, girl? And what do you know of the gods and magic?"

I stammered my reply," I grew up in the house of a Druid, sir. My grandfather was a star seer. My *modryb*, Essylt, is a priestess and healer. I learned everything from them."

Filippos beckoned me closer. "Tell me about your king. What kind of fortress does he have? How many men does he have in his army? I want to learn more about the Kelts. We call them Hyperboreans – people of the north wind. I have heard how they are fearsome warriors who paint themselves and fight naked, fierce as wild beasts. I know there are tribes to the north who have threatened to invade our borders. What can you tell me about your people? It is true your warriors take the heads of their enemies?"

I described the hill fort of Caer Gwyn to him; how rough and simple it was compared to the royal palace of Pella. I told him about the council hall and the tall posts decorated with the skulls of vanquished enemies.

Filippos listened, his hand stroking his beard, his good eye peering at me intently. When I finished my tale he asked: "What is the name of your king?"

"We do not have a king, sir, though our ricon is the same. Madoc is his name. It was his son, Sholto ap Madoc, who took me from my home." My voice sounded thin and tiny in the high-ceilinged room.

Filippos leaned forward, peering at me with furrowed brows. "Speak up, girl! So you were taken as a hostage? Why? What were this man's intentions? To collect a ransom? To sell you? Or..."

"He was a renegade, sir, an evil man who had caused great harm to our tuath. I saw him kill his own brother..."

"Aha! So he took you as a ransom because you were a witness to this killing, and because you are a pretty girl, one favoured by the gods."

"A traveller needs only to be in the company of a Druid to be safe, sir," I said. "The person of a Druid is sacred. And I am a Druid's child."

"I was told Alexandros found you in the forest. Well then, child. Now you are here in Makedon. What will become of you?"

"I am fortunate, sir, that Theon has taken care of me. For this I thank the gods – mine and yours."

Filippos looked up at Theon. "What do you intend to do with her?"

"She will live with me, Filippos," Theon looked over at me and smiled reassuringly. "She knows the healing arts and what she doesn't know I will teach her. Olwen is safe with me, safe as any daughter, or grand-daughter would be. I have lived a lonely life all these years and her company has truly brought me comfort."

Filippos chuckled. "Ah yes, Theon, every man should have a fresh young maiden to sweeten his elder years." He reached out to touch me and I pulled back.

Theon's face reddened. "I needed a help-mate and Olwen has been that to me. She is a bright child and has been well-taught by her aunt who is a medicine woman, and her grandfather who was an elder priest of the Druids. She is a blessed child, sir, and will serve us as she would serve her own people."

"It seems the Keltic kings are beset by the same problems we have. I no sooner finish with one pesky rebellion, before there's another." Filippos said. He gave a deep sigh. "The Greeks are stirring up unrest in Thessaly. I fear it will one day come to an all-out war to put them in their place. And now that I've returned home I have word from the east there are revolts in Byzantium."

"When will you go to Byzantium?" Theon asked.

"I can't wait until Spring to put things right. I must go east before the winter snows close the passes, I've already sent for my ships. I'll leave the boy in charge. With Antipatros's guidance, he'll learn how to keep order here." He brought his fist down on the table with a thud. "It is time Alexandros assumed some responsibility. Life is not all hunts and games. There's been a lack of discipline and he's too much under the influence of his mother. She has him decked out like a fancy boy. I hear he's spending too much time in the theatre with his actor friends and not enough time on the drill field." He stood and began to pace. "The witch has him playing the lyre and singing sweet as a girl!

I had hoped the years he spent with Aristoteles would have done more than enrich his mind. Olympias has made a delicate boy out of him, not a warrior as he should be!"

"Alexandros is only a youth, still an *ephebe* like the rest of them." Theon said. "He's a good hunter, I know that. He has visited me many times on my farm, brought me fresh venison and boar meat. Alexandros rescued this girl, you know. Her captor would have violated and slain her had Alexandros not heard her cries. He killed the man and brought her to me."

I dared to speak up again, "Yes, sir. I owe my life to Alexandros."

"Well then," Filippos said. "My son is more of a man than I thought he was."

"He is," Theon said. "And you should be proud of him." He got up from his stool and put out his hand to shake Filippos's. "We'll take our leave now, sir, and let you tend your business." He motioned for me to come by his side. When I did, the king held out his hand and took mine, drawing me closer to him, so close I could smell the acrid tinge of wine on his breath. He reached up and stroked my hair. "Fine as silk," he said. He scanned my face with his one eye, "You are a pretty girl, little Kelt, but you are too shy!"

I shrank back at his touch. There was something in his manner that repulsed me.

Filippos looked up at Theon and smiled. "She will make a pleasing companion for you, my friend."

Stanza Three:

The next morning I woke to the soft sounds of Theon preparing our breakfast. He preferred to make our meals as he was accustomed to, rather than be waited on by the palace kitchen slaves. Even when I offered to help, he shooed me away.

"I've lived on my own for long enough I don't need an extra pair of hands meddling in my kitchen," he scolded. Then he smiled at me. "You can fetch the honey pot and put the kettle on the hearth for our tea."

I brewed some tea from the camomile we had gathered on the mountain while Theon stirred the pot of barley porridge. A fire blazed on the hearth; and we sat beside it with our bowls of hot porridge and sipped the fragrant tea from small clay cups.

We spoke little while we ate. Theon seemed intent on some inner thoughts, and I went back in my mind over the meeting with the king the day before. What had the king meant when he said Alexandros was more of a man than he thought he was? A strange thing for a father to say, I thought. From what Filippos had said to Theon about Alexandros spending too much time with his actor friends and being under the influence of his mother, I assumed the relationship between father and son was strained. A pity, I thought. To me, Alexandros was a fine young man, one a parent should be most proud of.

After we ate, we worked together sorting out vials of infusions and bundles of herbs we had collected on our morning walks. I felt safe when I was with Theon. It was good to have a friend like him and except for the fact I still longed for my old home, life was pleasant in the palace. The corridors and great Hall were populated with charming people. The ladies of the court were magnificent in their jewels and finely spun gowns, and the men handsome, with trimmed beards and colourful tunics, their arms shining with gold bracelets.

There had been none of this extravagance in Caer Gwyn. I recalled the ricon's great hall with its massive pillars capped with the skulls of dead enemies, the rough-hewn furnishings and animal-skin rugs, the half-naked warriors with their tattooed bodies and long manes of hair. Still, I longed for home and the old ways I had learned from my childhood with the Druids. But I was safe here, so I tried to content myself.

Theon was explaining to me the uses of the various medicines he had stored in cruets and vials on the shelf, when there was knock on the door. He looked up from his task and called, "Come in!"

Alexandros paused at the door, outlined in the stone frame. He was not alone. With him was the tall, handsome youth with the tawny hair and a kindly face. I recognized him as the Companion who had crowned Alexandros with the laurel wreath the day the king had returned to Pella.

Theon stood to greet them. "Alexandros, Hephaestion, *Xairete!* Greetings to you, young sirs."

"The royal ships are in port," Alexandros said. "Father wants you to go to the harbour. One of the mariners on the royal trireme has fallen ill."

Theon's brow creased with a worried frown. "How ill is he? Is it a fever?"

Alexandros shrugged. "A winter's chill, most likely." He turned to his friend and I saw how he stepped closer and slipped his arm around Hephaestion's waist. "We'll go ahead. Shall I tell them you are coming?" He glanced over at me and smiled. "You will come too, little Kelt? You've not seen anything so grand as the royal fleet."

Theon nodded his approval. "Olwen, fill your basket with infusions and what other medicines we might need."

"Shall I send a carriage for you?" Alexandros asked.

"No need, Alexandros," Theon said. "Olwen has not been to the harbour or explored the city. The walk will do us both some good."

After Alexandros and Hephaestion had left, I said to Theon, "Is that youth Alexandros's favourite?"

Theon looked at me in thoughtful silence, then said: "Yes. Some say Hephaestion is Alexandros's shadow. He's a young lord's son and the two have been inseparable friends since they first met at Aristotele's school in Mieza."

The morning was grey and chill with a hint of snow. I pulled my woollen cloak closer around me and followed Theon out of the gates and down the palace steps.

It was a long walk from the palace to the vast market area that lay at the foot of the hill. We shouldered our way through the throngs crowding the market place Theon called an *agora*, continuing past workshops and imposing buildings where Theon said the business of the city was transacted. The narrow-cobbled streets beyond the agora were lined with brightly painted two-storey houses with shuttered windows and terra-cotta roofs.

As we neared the harbour, the chill in the sea air was invigorating and I could smell the rich tang of freshly caught fish coming from the small craft tied by the quay. The royal fleet was beached along the banks of Pella's wide lagoon — long war galleys, some with twenty or thirty oars sticking up like the quills of porcupines. I had never seen ships like that before. The boats we Kelts used to cross the Narrow Sea were smaller craft, called *caracols*. These mighty ships had prows carved into the shapes of gods and formidable battering rams jutting out to stave and sink a ship easily in a sea battle.

"Those are triremes," Theon explained. "They've come from Byzantium to replenish stores and take on new crew. They are the king's warships."

The lagoon was dark green, ruffled with frothy waves. Overhead, the sky filtered sunlight casting a silvery glow across the surface of the water. On an islet in the middle was a stone tower. Theon said it was a treasury but it looked more like a prison.

One ship was tied up to a small stone jetty at the shore. A seaman stood on the deck and hailed us as we approached. "Are you the physician?"

"Yes, I am he. The king asked me to come," Theon said. "Where is the mariner I am here to tend?"

"Come aboard," the seaman said. He was a young man of middle height, slender and graceful, with olive-coloured skin and black curls that fell to his shoulders. He was dressed for the cold in a woollen cloak. He held out his hand to help Theon up the plank. "My mate is there." He pointed to a small shelter at the rear deck where a man lay under a heap of sheepskins.

I stepped onto the plank to follow Theon, and felt it shift as the ship rolled with a wave. When he saw me teeter, the seaman reached out and grabbed my arm, holding me until I regained my balance. "Let me help you, pretty maiden. Are you the physician's daughter?"

"I assist him," I stammered, feeling shy and out-of-place. "I have the medicines here in my basket."

"Ah...so you know the healing arts?" He gave me a smile and the day seemed suddenly brighter. His hand was still on my arm and I felt the warmth of his touch seep into my chilled body. My heart almost ceased to beat. I studied his face, saw the weathered lines made by a sailor's life. I met his eyes, dark as a stormy sky, creased at the corners from long gazing at the sea.

"My name is Olwen," I said shyly. "I am Cymry, from the land of the north wind. Theon, the physician, is my guardian."

His dark brows drew together. He muttered something in a language I did not know, and when he spoke again I sensed an inflection in his voice revealing he was not a Makedonian or a Greek.

"My family comes from the east, from a place called Phrygia."

I recalled Grandfather Maelgwyn telling me stories of the ancient star seers that had come to our land from a far-away place in the east bringing with them the knowledge of the heavens. My people were descended from them.

"My name is Elidi." the seaman said.

Then something happened that was strange indeed. When he said his name, *Elidi,* it was almost as if I knew it before it was spoken. There was a familiarity about him that made me feel comfortable, as though he was an old friend. When I repeated his name, "Elidi" it was as though, in some hidden corner of my mind, I already knew him.

He took my arm and guided me onto the deck. "I'm the helmsman of this ship," he said. "My trierarch has gone to meet with Prince Alexandros." He led me to where Theon was kneeling beside the ailing sailor.

He was an old man with weathered skin and matted grey hair. His beard was speckled with vomit. From the rank stench, I knew he had dirtied himself.

"How long has he been like this?" Theon asked. He looked worried.

"He fell ill on the voyage," Elidi said.

"Have others fallen ill?" Theon asked.

"None yet..." I saw the dark look of concern on Elidi's face. "Could it be the *plaga*?"

"We must hope it is not, or it will be a disaster — for you and your shipmates." I had never seen Theon look so grave. I knew he was worried and the very words "*the plaga*?" sent chills through my body.

I took a step backwards. *The plague!* I had heard of this pestilence, Essylt had been fearful of it when so many people from our village had fallen ill. She told me it had ravaged Caer Gwyn when she was a child and all the elders and many of the young people had died from it.

"What if it is?" I stammered. "Can you cure it?"

Theon frowned. "There is no cure. It is a serious illness, borne by rats and the bites of fleas or other infected animals. It spreads quickly and it's deadly." He turned to Elidi. "Bring me hot water and a basin. The fellow has a fever, but it may be nothing more serious than an ague from the winter's cold."

I had never seen Theon so concerned before. He stood with bowed head, taking deep breaths as he tried to calm himself. I heard him murmur a prayer to Asklepion, the healing god, under his breath.

When finally he spoke, he said: "Once the plague devastated the whole city of Athens and much of the countryside. That was after the Peloponnese Wars and they think it came into the city from Pireaus, the seaport. It spreads quickly and there is no medication or balm that will ease those who fall ill." He bent over the man and examined him closely. "The plague symptoms are fever so intense that people will go naked and bathe in icy water. The eyes and throat are infected and there is vomiting. The body often breaks out in pustules and ulcers." He knelt beside the ailing seaman and touched the man's forehead. "This man has a fever for certain, but perhaps..." He stopped speaking and shook his head. "We must trust the gods and pray it isn't the *plaga* or we could all be doomed!"

I shuddered at his words and backed away, afraid to come too close to the infected man. Under my breath I said a prayer to Airmed, my own healing god, and tried to gather myself as bravely as I could to face whatever might be the consequences of this terrible disease.

Elidi returned with an ewer of steaming water and basin which Theon set down beside the ailing man. He poured the water and pulled back the blankets. The stench overpowered me as he removed the man's soiled garments, and I gagged and turned away.

"If you wish to be my assistant, Olwen, you must learn to abide far more dire things than the stink of a man's excrement," Theon scolded. He instructed me to choose certain herbs and potions from my basket: a jar of *propolis*, a sticky bee's nectar; sea-buck thorns; bilberry to treat the man's diarrhea, powdered *species* of eucalyptus and grape leaves; dried chamomile and thistle to make into infusions of tea.

I caught Elidi watching me and my cheeks reddened, so I focused my attention on the sick man as Theon examined him. "His humour is somewhat choleric," he said. "Olwen, see the slight bluish cast to his skin? It may be *cyanosis* — a lung disease." He held his ear close to the man's chest, noting the rasp of his laboured breathing. "Has he vomited blood?" he asked Elidi.

"No sir," Elidi said. "No blood in his phlegm, or vomit."

"That is good then." Theon pulled the sheepskins up under the patient's chin. The man uttered a weak thanks. "Move him to a warmer place and keep him on a diet of liquids for a few days," Theon said. "I'll leave you these powdered herbal *species*. Make him hot infusions of chamomile to drink with them. Then after a day or two, feed him some *ptisan*. The barley gruel will help him regain his strength."

"Thank you, sir," Elidi said. He glanced at me and smiled. I was certain he was as relieved as I was at Theon's diagnosis.

"Let me know in a day or two how he is," Theon said. "And do not worry. I don't think it is the *plaga*." He turned to me and smiled. "You have proven to be an able assistant, Olwen. Your Aunt taught you well. I see you understand many things about the healing arts, and I will teach you even more. I have need of an assistant and it was good providence you were sent you to me!"

This pleased me, as I knew Theon saw how frightened I had been. I murmured a prayer of thanks and smiled at him with relief. He put out his hand and patted me on the shoulder. "You are a brave girl, Olwen. You have indeed been given the gift of a healer."

I followed Theon back down the plank to the shore. When I looked back, Elidi waved at me. I wondered if I would see him again.

BALLAD SEVENTEEN A Hymn To Poseidon

I sing of Poseidon, ruler of the Sea.
You help us, great Poseidon, Protector of all waters.
In storms you save us, give us safe passage.
Highest of gods, Earth Shaker, Lord of the Sea.
Be kind, noble Poseidon.
Save our ships from the jagged reefs.
Steer us safely to shore.
Guide us with your brazen trident, O Sea god!
Great Poseidon, Horse Tamer,
whose white steeds save us from the depths.
On this day, Thee we invoke.
Grant us a successful voyage
in Praise of the Sea God.

Stanza One

One morning when I woke there was snow on the ground, soft and white as lamb's fleece. During the night the hag, Cailleach had arrived, that blue-faced goddess with silver hair, who brings the long, freezing nights of winter. Until then, the days had been crisp and clear but today there were icicles on the eaves and the bushes in the courtyard sparkled with frost.

I thought, *It is the time when the sun stands still bringing darkness, a time to cut the mistletoe that grows on the oak trees and give it blessings. It's the time we Kelts light fires to banish the darkness and bring us luck for the coming year.*

As I recalled my last winter at Caer Gwyn, a wave of melancholy engulfed me. I remembered how Boreas, the North Wind, had blown drifts of snow as high as the roof thatches and a child had frozen to death in the drifts. Essylt had gone out to administer to the sick. Many of the old ones had died that winter. The crone, Cailleach, the fierce goddess of winter, bringer of death and endless freezing days, had been cruel that year.

How long had it been since I was taken from my home? I counted the passage of time on my fingers, from Midsummer until now. Eight full moons had passed, though it seemed a lifetime. Today Essylt would be in the forest collecting laurel and evergreen boughs. Her basket would be full of bayberry and the blessed thistle. Druids would be gathering in the sacred oak groves to cut the mistletoe and haul in a yew log for the solstice fire.

As I stood at the window watching the soft flakes drift down, Theon came to stand by me. I didn't refuse the fur cape he offered me. He must have sensed my sadness, because he tweaked my braid and put his arm around me.

"Tomorrow is a big festival," he said. "You must not despair. It is great celebration of Poseidon our Sea God, a joyful time to celebrate the winter!"

The following day, at mid-day when the winter sun was still high above, Theon and I joined the royal processional that began at the palace gates and wound its way down the acropolis slope, past two-story private houses and an elegant estate he said was the Regent's.

The streets were jammed with people garlanded and dressed in their best clothes. I wore the fine-woven Keltic clothes that Alexandros had gifted to me, and my raven torc. Theon, dressed in white chiton, wore a crown of ivy. He looked as regal as Asklepios himself.

We walked ahead of the royal entourage. Behind us, I could hear the loud shouts of praise when the king and his escort approached. The processional made its way through the agora with its columned stoas, past the long colonnaded gymnasium and theatre. Some of the people had climbed onto rooftops, the better to see. Everyone cheered as we passed. The soldiers' armour shone, the plumes of their helmets bright against the winter grey of the sky. They sang a hymn to Poseidon Hippos, the Horse Father as they marched, stamping the beat with their feet and banging their shields.

Crowds of people lined both sides of the wide paved avenue that led toward Pella's harbour. Since this celebration followed the rites of Dionysos many of the men were still drunk, their heads crowned with ivy wreaths, flushed and merry, waving wine skins. Some of them, arms linked, were dancing in a circle to the music of a flute and drum.

I thought back on the day of Midsummer when I had walked the Sacred Way with the Druids in the grand processional to the sacred circle of the Temple of the Sun on the plain. I remembered the trilling of the pipes and the sun glinting gold from the priest's luluna collars as we made our way to the Great Henge. How could I have imagined then, on the eve of our midsummer rites, I would be taken away, never to see those great stone dolmens again, or share the company of my kinsmen. My heart ached with longing to see Caer Gwyn, to be safe in the shelter of our little straw-roofed hut with Essylt. But it seemed I would never see my homeland again, and I murmured a prayer to the Goddess for at least keeping me safe here with my new guardian, Theon.

Far down by the sea we heard the trumpets blow. I walked close beside Theon, feeling the strength of his presence as I followed his long sure strides along the avenue to the seashore. A great crowd waited at the shore. The harbour was filled with boats of all sizes: fishing boats and ships with carved figureheads painted with god's eyes. Anchored close in, was a fleet of triremes, oars shipped, sticking up like the quills of hedgehogs. My eye caught the flames of fires lit along the beach – fires to honour the sea god.

As we neared the harbour, Theon took my hand and looked down on me with a smile. A gust of wind tugged at his long white robe and tousled his grey hair. Theon always seemed to sense when sadness had overcome me and cheered me with words of reassurance.

"Look, see there? The sea is calm today, a good omen. Poseidon is pleased we come to honour him. See? All the ships have come. There's the king's trireme." He pointed to the largest trireme anchored by a small stone jetty at the shore. From its mast flew a flag with the golden star of the Makedonian royalty.

"Remember our last visit here? How our medicines cured the ailing mariner? When the spring weather comes, we'll sail to the islands. There are many islands, you see. Perhaps we'll go to Samothraki to visit the Temple of the Great Gods. Would you like that, Olwen?"

The idea pleased me, and I smiled back at him.

A throng had gathered around the king and Alexandros, greeting them with wild happy shouts. Surrounding Alexandros were his band of Companions, the chosen few, sons of Makedonian land barons, clean shaven lads, wearing their best clothes, their long hair crowned with ivy wreaths.

Theon and I pushed our way through to where they stood amid a ring of soldiers who protected them from the crush of the mob. I craned to see over the shoulders of the guards. King Filippos stood stolidly, dressed in his polished parade armour surrounded by his bearded generals. Alexandros was next to him, clad simply in a fine linen tunic, a wreath of golden ivy leaves crowning his bright hair. He was like a glittering flame, and always drew eyes. Standing tall, close by, was his friend, Hephaestion. As always, I saw there was something between them, something more than just a friendship. It was almost as if they were one soul in two different bodies, inseparable and firmly committed.

Queen Olympias and Alexandros's sister, the princess Kleopatra were behind the men, surrounded by handmaidens and court women. Olympias stood tall and proud, straight as a spear, lips pressed together. She was elegantly dressed in a crimson gown, her face painted with cosmetics, her reddish hair bound with braids of gold and jewelled clasps. Kleopatra stood in her mother's shadow, her face set in a pout. How must it be, I wondered, to be the daughter of such a domineering woman?

As if she sensed my presence, Olympias glanced across at me. Even at a distance, she frightened me. Her painted mouth curved in a wry smile. I smiled back at her and kept my composure though I felt a chill of trepidation in her haughty glance. Then she looked away, chin lifted as if in contempt.

The people crowded to the shore and threw wreaths into the water, some of them pouring wine for sacrifices. Others had brought votives to offer; small carved boats and dolphins and horses. A purple-robed priest crowned with pine, stood at the water's edge. In one hand, the white-bearded priest held a bronze trident to represent the god, in his other hand a polished silver cleaver. A young acolyte stood beside him holding a tribute bowl. The crowd of celebrants grew quiet as a young bard strummed his lyre and began to sing in a clear treble voice:

191

> *"Poseidon, god of sea, storms and earthquakes,*
> *Tamer of horses and protector of waters.*
> *Poseidon, Earth Shaker, whose palace is made*
> *of gems and coral on the ocean floor.*
> *In storms you save us, great Poseidon.*
> *Your white horses lead us safely to shore.*
> *Save us from the depths."*

The king stepped forward and poured a libation of wine into the water intoning the words of dedication. "To Lord Poseidon who rules everything under the sky, the land and the sea." Every eye was on him. There were murmurs of admiration and cheers. Filippos turned to face the crowds and began to speak to them in his deep-toned voice:

"People of Makedon, today we honour the sea god, Poseidon, and make sacrifices to him. Soon he will guide my royal fleet eastward. I call on your loyalty, my people, for when the seas are calm, we will set sail to Thrace and Byzantium to conquer those people who would rebel against us. Thus we make our offerings to Lord Poseidon."

I heard the whinnying of a horse and saw Alexandros leading a white stallion to the water's edge. Theon had told me that Poseidon protected the sailors, and the white crested waves are the manes of his horses. I remembered how at the midsummer rites the Royal War band of Caer Gwyn had offered a horse as a sacrifice to Nudd at the barrow of the dead warriors. It had been a time of war then, with the death of the ricon's son, Hywel. I had felt the spirits of the dead that day.

I pressed close to Theon and exclaimed: "Is this beautiful horse the sacrifice?"

Theon leaned down and whispered, "Shhh... it is the custom, you see, for the king to sacrifice a white horse before an important sea voyage. Later the men will light bonfires and there will be revelry and more feasting. You must not be alarmed, dear Olwen. Poseidon is lord of the seas and must be revered."

The horse snorted and dragged at the reins, but Alexandros held him firm and spoke quietly to the animal, stroking its neck. The horse shied and his hoofs raked the sand. I saw the priest step up, cleaver in hand, and I looked away. I had seen animals sacrificed. The memory of my white bull, Mithras, still haunted me, and I could not bear to watch this regal animal slain.

Tears rippled in my eyes blurring my vision. I envisioned I was in Caer Gwyn again the day Bedwyr had killed Mithras. I heard Theon's voice beside me, chanting the prayer along with all the other voices.

"Be it so, Lord Poseidon, according to our prayers."

I heard the horse thrash about and someone gave a shout. When I looked again, the great stallion was lying on the shore, a scarlet fountain of blood gushing from the cleft on his mighty throat. As it took its last gasps of breath, Alexandros and his father stood beside it watching the animal's death throes.

My voice trembled when I spoke. "What will they do with it?" I asked Theon.

"It will be butchered," Theon replied in what seemed a matter-of-fact way. "Some flesh will be burned for the god. Some will make a feast for the celebration of Poseidon." He put his hand on my shoulder. "It was a good and noble sacrifice." He stretched out his hand toward the shore. "You see? The waters are already calmed. Very soon the ships will be able to sail."

The smouldering altar was quenched with wine and the crowds began to disperse, making ready for the god's feast. The sun had gone down and the lagoon was dappled with shadows. Torches flickered from the ramparts of the tall stone fortress that stood in the middle of the lagoon. In the darkened sky, the evening star appeared, trembling, white as a maiden, over the sea.

Theon left me and went to greet the king. I stood alone on the beach, the wind whipping my cloak. The sky was tinged coral and reflected on the sea-god's waves that danced along the shore. I shaded my eyes against the glare of the setting sun.

Then I saw a man standing apart from the other seamen on the deck of the royal trireme. He was waving his arms, and I heard him shout: "Little Kelt!" It was the helmsman, Elidi. Since we had met at the harbour when Theon and I had been called to minister to the ailing seaman, I had turned my mind from him, not thinking we would ever meet again.

I watched as he swung himself down from the deck and raced along the shore toward me. My heart almost ceased to beat at the sight of him, his clean-shaven handsome face, his gold earrings twinkling in the firelight.

He greeted me with a wide smile. "So, here we are again, by the sea where we first met. It seems a good omen." His eyes had a mischievous twinkle. He bowed low and kissed my hand.

I could not find the words to express my feelings at seeing him again, re-membering how I had felt ashamed because of the desire he evoked in me when we had first met. In that moment I thought back to being with Teag in the greenwood, how I had loved him. I had been an innocent child then, now I was older, but the feeling sweeping over me, the skip of my heart-beats and the warmth in the pit of my belly frightened me. The words I had learned to chant as a child came back to me. *I am Olwen, daughter of the Raven, the goddess's child.*

"I...I thought you had sailed away," I stammered.

He chuckled. "Not now. Not in winter. Poseidon would not be kind."

"Did the sick man get well?" I struggled for words to say.

"Most certainly, he did. It was your medicines cured him." He looked down the shore to where Theon was engrossed in conversation with Filippos. "You are Theon's helper. He's a good man, a wise physician."

"Yes," I said, "I help him collect herbs and mix the potions. I learned these things from my *modryb,* Essylt. I was going to be a medicine woman like her, a priestess of healing. Now Theon is my teacher and guardian."

Elidi studied me soberly for a long moment before he spoke. "Come," he said. He took my hand and led me farther down the shore of the lagoon, away from the celebrating crowds.

When we were well away from the crowd, he stopped and looked down at me holding my face between his hands. "I thought you may have forgotten me." His voice was soft.

Even in the dimness of nightfall I could see his face clearly, how his hair curled over his brows, the strong, firm line of his jaw. He smelled fresh as the sea. I felt awkward, torn between accepting his affection or retreating to the safe, pure world I had been born to. I hesitated and drew back, but he took both my hands in his.

"I thought we might never meet again," he said, "but you are here and surely it was meant to be." He twined his hand around my braids and brought his face close to mine and kissed my forehead. I forgot everything, heard only the soft slap of waves on the shore. I knew I was wading into the sea's depths. Elidi had beguiled me, made me forget all that had happened in the past, the vast distances that separated me from my home, the sacrifices, the vows I had made to the goddess.

He released me and stood back, studying me solemnly. "My sweet Kelt, I have thought of you so often..." He kissed me again, this time on the mouth. I tasted the sweetness of wine on his lips. I felt dizzy with his closeness and drew away. He stroked my hair. "Do not be afraid, little Kelt. If it is meant to be, it is right."

I remembered that night in Caer Gwyn in my secret covert below the junipers with Teag. *"You are the brightest star,"* he had said. *"the most fragrant of flowers. And that is why the gods have chosen you. It is your destiny."*

All the sad memories of my innocent love surfaced. How in the end Teag had said *"I have wronged you. It is Aeron I love."* Teag had forsaken me and chosen the ricon's daughter. I remembered how devastated I had felt, how my heart had shattered. Could I accept love again? For a moment I was unable to answer Elidi, but presently I found my voice. "I am...You see..."

He reached out and his fingers traced my raven torc. "Yes. You are a Druid's child. I know that. And you are innocent and pure. I know that too." He kissed me again, more tenderly. "Next time, when we meet, we will walk in the palace garden. Would you like that? You will tell me all about your life. You will be safe here, with me." He stroked back a wisp of hair from my forehead. "Perhaps it is the god's purpose that we met."

His face was so intent that I glanced away, afraid if I looked into his eyes again I would give in to the temptation to linger there longer. In my heart I knew I wanted to be with him, to keep him close, but he was a man of the sea. He would sail away one day and perhaps I would never see him again.

We stayed on the beach until the sky darkened and one by one the stars came out. I stepped away from him and looked up into the cold splendour of the starry heavens. Just then, a great shooting star flamed across the sky, its long tail coiling, flaring, twining like a dragon's tail as it plunged into the sea.

The Druid's words came back to me: *Who is the Star-son who twines himself around the universe like a golden serpent? Who is the Dragon who breathes fire across the sky?* Shivers prickled my spine as I remembered my grandfather's portent. *"The Sky Serpent foretells Life or Death. It may be auspicious or it may be ill-omened, but it is a herald of the royal house."*

I shivered and pulled my cloak tight around me. Elidi put his arm around my shoulders. "Are you alright? The star-shower, it is so beautiful. Surely it is a good omen for us, my little Kelt!"

I took a deep breath and looked up at him, my eyes brimming with tears.

"Why are you crying?" He brushed a tear from my cheek.

The Dragons' Fire augured ill, but I could not tell him the meaning.

"The king said as soon as the sea calms the ships will sail. I am sad because we must part and perhaps, we will never meet again".

Elidi stared beyond me out toward the sea. "Yes, Filippos wants to settle scores with some rebel Thracians. Our ships will guard the coastline, but the battle will be on land." He took my hands and looked intently into my eyes. "Will you wait for me, Olwen? After my ship sails east, will you wait for me to return?"

"Yes," I said. "I will wait."

The evening had grown chill and the crowds along the harbour had begun to disperse. Theon would be looking for me, worrying.

"I must go," I said. "Really, I must."

He held me gently against him. "Go then, dear Olwen. But we will meet again. I do not want to dishonour you – never think that. Let it be with us as the gods will." His eyes peered beyond me, toward the dark horizon of the sea. "I will not forget you, my little Kelt. My ship will sail to Byzantium as soon as the seas are calm, and when I return, we will be together again and I will ask for Theon's blessing."

Stanza Two

The night had grown cold. I pulled my cloak tight around me. There were still a few celebrants on the shore gathered around fires singing songs of praise to the god. The beach was strewn with discarded garlands. The altar still smouldered from the sacrifices and the smell of burnt meat quenched with wine lingered on the air. A wooden image of Poseidon, crowned with pine leaves, was placed on a rock surrounded by votive offerings. The remains of the white stallion had been removed – all but the blood stains in the sand. A curl of smoke rose from the altar where the priest had made the sacrifice.

I found Theon searching for me along the shore. He gave me a stern, scolding look. "My dear child, I thought the sea may have swallowed you, or some rascal had carried you away."

I felt my cheeks redden with a blush. "I was with Elidi," I said. Theon raised his brows as if what I said had startled him. "You remember him? The helmsman from the royal trireme."

"Ah yes..." Theon stroked his beard and peered at me soberly.

I saw the stern look on Theon's face and felt a blush warm my cheeks. "He is noble and kind..."

"Yes. And he has charmed you, I see." He looked at me a long time, silent, frowning. "What did you talk about?" he asked finally.

"He asked me... he said... I told him about Caer Gwyn..." I stammered. "Did you see the Dragon's Fire?" I felt a shiver down my spine as I remembered it.

"Yes. A portent I would say – either good or bad."

I wanted to tell him what Grandfather had divined in the Dragon's Fire, to say it augured ill, but felt it best to put it out of my mind.

"The king will set off soon on a new campaign in the east. Pray the gods favour him. Soon the ships will take to the sea Whether they return or not will be the will of Poseidon. Pray all will return home safely."

The off-shore breeze ruffled the water. I listened to the ebb and flow as the waves rolled in tossing sea foam onto the beach. The triremes were dark silhouettes against the pale moonlit sky. I could hear the cries of sailors on the torch-lit decks and wondered if Elidi was there, looking out toward the shore, searching for me.

As if he knew my thoughts, Theon reached out and placed his hands on my shoulders. He looked deep into my eyes. "The men of the sea, they are like feathers on the wind, drifting from sea to shore, isle to isle, port to port. It is their life, you see. They've dedicated their lives to Poseidon and are at his bidding, to go wherever the sea takes them. This man, Elidi, is not a Hellene. He is Phrygian."

Phrygia. It was a place I had no knowledge of.

"Their country, Phrygia, is far to the east beyond the seacoast of Ionia," Theon explained. "Phrygians were allies of the Trojans before we claimed their land. Our great King Midas, the king of the golden touch, once ruled Phrygia. Now their land is ruled by Persia."

As we walked away from the beach toward the torch-lit city with its tall houses and cobbled streets Theon continued his story. "The Phrygians worship an old goddess, Cybele. In the old days they were allies of the Hittites. Do you remember the tales I told you about Troy? Like the Trojans, they were horse-breeders." He chuckled. "Perhaps that is why Elidi has followed Poseidon, the horse master of the sea."

I followed close by him along the shadowy alleyways where melting snow ran in runnels down the gutters. I did not speak, but in my mind, I pictured Elidi – his tanned, taut body, his shiny locks of ebony curls. *Phrygia!* The sound of it conjured something mysterious, exotic. I wondered if perhaps that was the same land my people had come from.

By now we had reached the marketplace. Even though night had fallen the market was doing a lavish business with people gathered around the stalls and under the stoas. Theon stopped to purchase some figs preserved in honey from a grizzled vendor.

"Figs and honey, the food of the gods," he said, smiling. He handed me some of the sticky fruit and bent to kiss my brow. "You are almost a grown woman, no longer as innocent as the child you were when you were first dedicated to your goddess." His grave face broke into a smile. "You are a beautiful young woman and men will be attracted to you like bees to a fragrant blossom. Of course, you might enjoy the flattery. But you must think carefully on the consequences of your desires."

Theon walked silently, frowning as if deep in thought. Finally he stopped and looked down at me. "Do you love him?"

I shook my head. I did not want to think of Elidi in that way, yet I still felt the thrill I'd had when we met at the shore. It was as though the child in me had suddenly blossomed in the way he had touched me, spoken to me. I kept remembering what he had said. *Perhaps it is the god's purpose that we met.*

Theon raised his brows. "Well, my dear child, in the words of our great philosopher Plato: '*Love is the joy of the good, the wonder of the wise. To love rightly is to love what is orderly and beautiful.*' "

We climbed the hill toward the palace. Before we reached the palace gates, Theon stopped again. He spoke to me the way a father would to his daughter. I listened carefully; mindful of his words. "There is the matter of the goddess...It is your *moira,* your destiny, to serve her."

I hung my head, suddenly feeling shamed that I had let myself be so vulnerable, remembering how I was meant to be initiated as a priestess. I thought of how Essylt had never married, but raised me as if I were her own child, and how, in my innocence, I had loved the goldsmith Teag. Could I accept another love now? Should I forsake the will of the gods or follow the path they had chosen for me?

Theon laid his hand lightly on my arm. "Here in Makedon you are free to choose whether you will serve the goddess or choose marriage. Follow your fate, if you will. Elidi is a good man. If it is your *moira* to be with him, then let it be so. But what if he sails away and never comes back? You must think wisely on this and not lose yourself in daydreams."

"I did not think to *marry* Elidi," I stammered. I might not know much about such affairs, but I was not so innocent and knew what might happen – that Elidi might sail away and never return. I knew I should thrust aside temptation and heed Theon's wise words. Yet, those feelings burned inside of me; the memory of Elidi's touch, his tender kiss, the low enticing sound of his voice. I knew he would be impossible to forget.

"I told him I would wait for him," I said.

Theon raised his brows and smiled. "I think perhaps Eros's arrow has struck your heart, dear child. And if that is so, you must follow this dream of yours." He reached out and placed his hands on my shoulders, looking deep into my eyes. "Well my dear child, you must trust Aphrodite for she has beguiled you. You must put your fate in her hands."

I felt tears come to my eyes. The last thing I wished was to leave Theon's side. I felt content here in Pella, though at times I longed for my old life. Theon had become like a father to me. I could not bear to think of leaving him. I felt safe and protected with Theon. Because of him I was able to follow my destiny in serving the goddess with the healing arts.

We climbed the hill to the stairs to the palace gates. I could hear the uncouth shouts and raucous sounds of revelling coming loud and shrill from the great Hall. As we passed through the snow-covered gardens, Theon stopped and looked at me long.

"They say waiting is painful, and forgetting is even more so. But not knowing what to do is the worst kind of suffering. These things we cannot always foresee, but we must not forget. Love is a beautiful thing. It is fickle and like a flower it can blossom then wither. Yet we must not forsake love, for what would we be without it?"

We had reached the door of our small stone house. Theon smiled at me. "Here we are – home! I'll mull us some wine to warm our chilled bones. We will drink to the sea god and to the brave men who follow his will."

"And to Elidi," I said.

"Yes, to Elidi," Theon replied. "And to whatever the gods ordain."

I could not sleep that night. My head was awhirl as I thought of Elidi, his words, and what Theon had said. Elidi was dedicated to the sea and I was dedicated to the goddess. Yet it seemed to me that nothing would make me happier than to be with Elidi. Theon had spoken of Aphrodite, but it was to my own goddess I prayed to Creiddylad, goddess of lovers, daughter of Llyr, our sea god, to ask for a blessing and a sign.

Stanza Three

A Song To Gaia, the Earth Mother

Gaia, healing goddess from whose womb all life sprang.
Gaia, who gave us the gift of medicine and life and healing.
Gaia, who comforts and nurtures.
To you we make offerings.
We are in your hands, Gaia,
Mother of the Earth.

Stanza Four

In the days that followed I was beset with questions about Elidi. At night I lay awake thinking of him, yearning to slip away from the palace and go to the port to find him. I remembered the sweetness of his kisses, the gentleness of his touch. He said he would come to see me, but many days had passed and I had heard no word from him.

You must think carefully on the consequences of your desires, Theon had said, and I respected his concern.

What would happen if I let Aphrodite captivate me? How would I get back to Caer Gwyn again? Because of this I knew I must push away my thoughts of Elidi.

Theon sensed my inner turmoil. "Your *moira* was decided for you long ago, child," he said. "You were meant to be dedicated to the goddess Gaia, to be a healer. You must follow this destiny."

"I had not meant to..." I stammered.

Theon smiled and laid his hand on my arm. "To fall in love."

"He said he would come. We would walk in the garden.

"The ships have gone to Eion, the port near Amphipolis, where they will wait 'til the spring sailing weather," Theon said. He put his arm around me. "You must think no more of him, Olwen, for he is a man of the sea, dedicated to serve Poseidon." He led me over to a chair and motioned for me to sit. He took down a wooden box from the wall shelf and set it on the table.

Inside the box was a heap of scrolls. He chose one, unrolled it, and set it in front of me. It was filled with strange symbols and markings that I did not understand.

"You must take your mind away from fanciful thoughts," Theon said. "What is meant to be, will be. Until then, it is time I taught you the skills of a *pharmacal*, for that is what you were destined to be."

"Yes, I will try not to think..." I stammered, "to think of him. You are right. I must follow my destiny." But my heart ached at the thought of never seeing Elidi again.

"First, you must learn to read Greek," Theon said. "Then you will understand these writings." He smiled and pulled up a stool to sit next to me.

We had no written language in Caer Gwyn, so I had never learned to read, and the strangely shaped marks I saw on the parchment were a puzzle. Theon said it was known as the Greek *alphabeton* and once I learned them I'd be able to read the words. I already knew to speak some of the language and was curious to learn more.

So we began to spend each day with lessons. Soon the mysterious symbols became words, and as I learned to pronounce them, the words took on meanings. The experience was to me more exciting than anything I had learned before, more fascinating than simply picking herbs and learning their names.

I tried my best to keep myself completely immersed in soaking up the knowledge Theon imparted to me. I pushed away any thoughts of Elidi, and as the days of winter passed, soon I could not only speak the words, but write them too.

Theon taught me many other new skills – how to mix the correct purgatives for stomach upsets, how to make potions, how to clean wounds and what herbs prevented infection.

"When I was a young man, I studied at the great Asklepion of Kos where the famous healer, Hippocrates, had his school," Theon said.

Theon's knowledge and dedication to the healing arts impressed me. I thought of my *modryb,* Essylt, who was a respected healer for our people, and how she had tried to impart this passion for learning on me. I recalled the many days we spent gathering herbs and mixing potions. I knew she would be pleased I had found refuge with a physician such as Theon. My thoughts of Elidi were replaced with a desire to learn so I, too, could become a respected healer.

Sometimes Theon let me attend his consultations. People from the palace, servants and sometimes cadets or palace guards came to him with stomach upsets or toothaches and often injuries from practice in the gymnasium or drill field. When he examined a patient I stood beside him and handed him bowls of water, dressings, oil and wine.

"You learn by watching and doing what I instruct you to do," Theon said.

Theon was a stern teacher and soon I was skilled enough to help him with minor surgeries and dispensing proper dosages of medicines. He introduced me to all the *pharmaka* used in healing. He unrolled one of the papyrus scrolls with drawings of plants and roots on it.

"These are the healing herbs. You know most of them, but you must learn their uses for illnesses and for healing wounds," he said. "Remember, as a healer you must first care for yourself. *Let food be your medicine and medicine your food.* Hippocrates taught this. Our daily habits determine the state of our own health. This also gives confidence to the patient. You will minister alongside me, Olwen, and one day you will be as skilled a healer as your aunt was."

He taught me more about the drugs and potions, the seasons and the times of day in which they must be gathered, how to dry them and make extracts from them.

"A physician must be able to prepare his own remedies as needed. The discipline of medicine is divine, gifted by the gods," Theon said. "We worship Gaia, the goddess who birthed the earth and the other healing gods, Asklepios, Apollo, Hygeia and Hermes. You, too, must dedicate your life to serving them."

One day an old, bearded gentleman arrived leading a youth. The boy hesitated shyly at the doorway shuffling his feet. He must have been the age of the cadets or even older, but he had a dull look about him, and only muttered when spoken to. It was clear to see that the boy had little wits.

The older man, his Keeper, led him into the room by the hand, as you would a small child. Theon greeted the old man cheerfully and beckoned to the youth.

"Come, Arridiaios. Don't be afraid. You know who I am. I am Theon the court physician, your father's friend."

Arridaios! I recognized the name of Alexandros's half-brother, though I had never met the boy before. His nose was dripping with a yellow discharge and his eyes were red. He looked around, blinking and held back when his Keeper nudged him forward so Theon could examine him.

"He has trouble breathing," the Keeper explained.

"It's likely just a simple ague," Theon said. "He must have caught a chill." He turned to me. "Olwen, fetch the proper herbs for a cough and watery eyes."

I ladled a cup of the honey, oil, thyme and chamomile that was steeping over the fire embers.

"Drink this," I said, and handed Arridaios the steaming concoction.

He stared at me blankly and pushed the cup away.

"No, Arridaios," scolded his Keeper. "You must drink it. It will help heal you."

"I don't like!" Arridaios said. He screwed up his face and turned away.

"But you must!" urged the Keeper.

I put my hand on Arridaios's arm and spoke to him gently. "Try it," I said. "It's made of honey and herbs. I made it myself and it is very good for you."

He looked at me dully, hesitated and finally he accepted the cup. He took a sip and then another and smacked his lips. "Yes... good!" he said, then gulped down the rest.

"Good boy!" I said. "This will make you feel better."

He grinned at me and handed back the cup. "More?"

"I will put some in a flask for you," I said. "Your Keeper will give you a drink of it as you need it and soon you will be feeling well again."

After they had left, Theon said, "Well done, Olwen. You knew just how to calm him. Usually Arridaios shies away and at times can be difficult."

"He is of little wits," I remarked. "Was he in an accident? Did he fall and hit his head?"

Theon told me about of the birth of Arridaios, who was the offspring of one of King Filippos's wives.

"Arridaios was poisoned, when he was three years old," Theon said bluntly. "And now he has only the wits of a child that age."

I took in a deep breath. "Poisoned? How? Did someone mix the wrong potion for him when he was ill?"

Theon shook his head and shrugged. He had a grim look on his face. "It was no accident. He was poisoned because, you see, he is the son of one of Filippos's war-wives. Olympias was jealous because she thought he might inherit his father's throne instead of her own son, Alexandros." He turned away and began to sort the collection of surgical tools on the table. "You see, Olympias abides no rivals of her own son!"

As the days passed, through Theon's teaching I learned how to recognize diseases both through the body's natural orifices and skin but also from the eyes. Theon taught me how to distinguish between trifling complaints and more serious ones, between ailments of mental and physical origins in order to make an accurate diagnosis. And most importantly, I understood that death holds no terrors for a physician, but for the sick and wounded it is often a merciful friend.

As well as the writings in the scrolls, there were sketches of the human body. I had to memorize the different parts, their functions and uses and the purpose of every human organ. There were also drawings of unusual contraptions and tools. I was curious about Theon's collection of strange instruments.

Theon took a leather satchel down from the shelf and laid the contents on the table in front of me. "These are surgical tools" he explained. "These are pliers, a scalpel and forceps."

I pointed out a strange cup-shaped tool.

"This is a spoon for removing arrow heads," Theon explained. "It's called *the spoon of Diokles.* When the king lost his eye in battle, the court surgeon saved his life by using this, though he couldn't save Filippos's sight."

When he showed me the strange instrument from Egypt used for opening skulls, I gasped. Theon laughed. "It takes a steady hand to open a skull! If the operation succeeded, the physician was well paid, but if it failed, he would be put to death!"

Then he picked up the scalpel and forceps and wrapped a strip of leather around my arm. "It is important you learn how to suture wounds and stem the flow of blood. The most important thing is treating battle wounds and broken bones."

He bound my leg with slats of wood to show how to set a fracture. He felt along my ankle and shin bone and thigh. "This is how you find where the break is." He demonstrated how to trace the bones in my own body and pointed out the places where the important organs were in the stomach and chest. "A wound in these could be fatal, so it is important to know how to treat them."

I felt overwhelmed at the immensity of the knowledge he imparted and the responsibilities he was giving me. I wondered if there was a battle, if I would be called on to use these surgical instruments. Was I brave enough to help the injured or worse, tend to dying warriors? Until then I knew only the uses of the herbs and balms as medicines and nothing of more serious things like treating battle wounds. I had seen the warriors in Caer Gwyn brought back from battle on stretchers and carts and knew that Essylt often went to tend them, but because I was still a child she had kept me from entering the hospital tents.

Theon sensed my lack of confidence. He put his hand gently on my arm. "A bird cannot fly with just one wing, Olwen. I know you are familiar with the healing potions and herbs, but you must learn these other important skills so you will be able to save more lives." He looked at me affectionately. "I cannot tell you everything now that has taken me many years to learn."

All through the winter I sat by the hearth poring over the scrolls, sounding out the words, learning the names and uses of the medicines and practising how to use the surgical instruments. Sometimes at night I dreamed of Elidi, remembered the sweetness of his kisses, the gentleness of his touch, but I pushed away the thoughts of him and immersed myself completely in the world of the healing god, Asklepios.

"One day I will take you to Asklepios's sacred shrine," Theon said. "There you will take the healer's oath, as decreed by Hippocrates: *First, do no harm. The physician must be ready to do his duty, not just for himself but for his patient.* Medicine is a divine art, you see, and it is your *moira* to be a healer."

One morning, as I was memorizing the instructions on how to stem the flow of blood, Alexandros came. His face was flushed from the cold and he brushed wet snow from his cloak.

He apologized for disturbing my studies. "I have come to see Theon. Is he here?" I sensed some urgency in his voice.

When he saw I was bent over the scrolls, he came close to peer over my shoulder.

"How are the lessons? I have heard you are learning the skills of the healing arts."

"Theon's books are difficult," I said. "but I am learning. Theon is a wise teacher."

He leaned over my shoulder and looked at the charts I had been studying.

"Ah...physicians' charts. Yes, I know these. I studied them with my teacher, Aristoteles, who is a physician as well as a philosopher. I'll bring you another book to read," he said with a smile. "*The Iliad* – a story by our famous bard, Homer. You'll learn from it about our gods and warriors." He looked around. "Is Theon here? I need to see him."

"Theon is resting, but I will tell him you've come," I said. I gathered up the scrolls and went to the other room where Theon was asleep on his cot. I shook him awake, "Alexandros is here. He seems troubled."

"More family strife?" Theon muttered. He straightened his robe and shuffled out of the room.

I sat on the cot and busied myself studying a pamphlet that listed diseases, but I couldn't help overhearing their conversation.

Alexandros's voice was low, urgent. He spoke of *'war'* and *'the Persians'* and the Thracian people. "*Barbarians!* They've killed some of our settlers! Father is going to put down the uprising. The northern tribes have been raiding – stealing cattle and sheep. Our ships will set sail for Byzantium as soon as the weather breaks. Father is leaving the seal of authority with Antipatros and me. He says he will bequeath the army to me if he dies in battle."

"*If he dies?*" Theon sounded alarmed. "Has he consulted the oracle?"

"He will," Alexandros's voice sounded strained, pitched high when he spoke. "Father has lofty ideas, as you know. He means to march eastward to fight the Persians who have taken over our lands. He has summoned his generals and made a speech calling for their loyalty. He'll set out for Thrace as soon as the seas allow. If he loses, half of Thrace will blaze up like a fire." His voice rose as he spoke. "He's always on the quest of more lands to conquer. He says he must vanquish the barbarians now, before he crosses to fight the Persians. These tribes of the Tribolli are unruly and threaten the settlements. He can't leave Makedon without first putting his kingdom in order. But should he die in battle, I must take command."

He went on, talking of man and fate; of words he heard in dreams from speaking serpents; of how he had little experience managing the cavalry and infantry. His voice rose, shrill and angry. "And my mother! She nags me relentlessly to attend her more often. How did I abide nine months in her womb!"

Theon had told me how Alexandros often consulted with him because he was frequently at odds with his father and his domineering mother. He had told me: "Olympias wants to control him, make a court dandy out of him. Filippos abhors this and it has caused much strife between them." Alexandros felt some comfort in having Theon's company and advice.

Alexandros was pacing the room, his face flushed, his voice determined. "Father cannot leave the northern borders unattended. I'll go north and stop the barbarian tribes,"

"You're only a young lad, Alexandros," Theon said. "You've never fought a battle or been placed in charge of your father's realm. You must listen to Antipater's wise advice and take heed."

I could understand Theon's trepidation. Just as I had fretted over the new responsibilities Theon had entrusted me with, Alexandros had never been in a battle. He was still a cadet and had no experience on a battlefield.

"I'm nearly sixteen," Alexandros said. There was a sharp edge to his voice. "It's time for me to show my father I am worthy and just as brave a warrior as he is! Because if he dies in battle, it will be me who will take the reins of power!"

Then I heard the door slam shut as Alexandros left, and I heard Theon give a great sigh. He sat staring into the hearth fire, his brow creased with worry.

"He's an impetuous boy!" Theon shook his head. "I wonder...was it a premonition Alexandros had? His father's fate?"

I felt a shiver of trepidation, remembering how on the beach I had seen the sky-dragon and its omen foretelling of a king's death. I thought of Elidi and when I learned his ship had sailed east, I wondered if I would ever see him again. "I heard the talk of war," I said quietly.

"Yes. And it will be soon." Theon sighed. He slouched forward, his face cupped in his palms. "It does not bode well."

BALLAD EIGHTEEN A Celebration Of Winter

Bel, the Sun King, Giver of Life says:
All the sweetness of nature is buried
in winter's black grave.
The wind sings a sad lament.
But listen! Hush!
Spring will come bringing life in its arms.

THE SACRIFICE

Stanza One

Theon said that winter was the bleakest he could remember. Wolves came down to the villages and took the watch dogs. Cattle and herd boys died of cold on the low slopes of the winter grazing. The mountains were blanketed so thick only their great cliffs and the dark clefts in them showed. The limbs of fir trees cracked under their weight of snow.

"Soon we will go to the forest and collect pine boughs for the festival," he said. His mention of a celebration pulled me out of my lethargy.

"What is this festival?" I recalled how our people celebrated the rebirth of Lugh, the oak god and Bel, the Sun King, Giver of Life. We lit bonfires, and the Druids went deep into the forest to cut mistletoe from the sacred oaks.

"When the snow begins to melt we honour the birth of the divine Dionysos, god of wine and gaiety. Once, long ago, it was called Lenaia, the Festival of the Wild Women," Theon said. "They would run wild through the forest chasing a man who represents the god, then they tore him to pieces and ate him. It is a festival celebrating death and birth. The old year dies and soon the earth will give birth to new life."

"Do they really savage a man?" I shuddered, horrified by the image this evoked.

I looked up at him and saw a mischievous twinkle in his eyes. Theon chuckled. "That was long ago, you see, though they say there are still some women who would if they could. Now we call them the Maenads." A smile twitched the corner of his mouth and he winked. "These days it's mostly theatre competitions. Songs of praise are sung to the god and olive branches are hung on the door lintels. If the wild women still celebrate the rites it's just a goat that gets eaten."

I thought back to our own savage rites and remembered that day at the Midsummer when, even though my Grandfather had forbidden these ancient rituals the Druid, Bedwyr, had imprisoned the Wolf Clan's boy in a wicker cage and burned him as a sacrifice to the Oak God. It was a savage act that brought calamity to our tuath.

Theon interrupted my dark thoughts. "There will be feasting and merrymaking and miracles are performed!"

"Miracles?" Surely he was teasing me. I did not really understand the power of his gods.

"Wine miracles," There was a twinkle in his eyes. "The priests of Dionysos seal water in a room, you see, and the next day it will have turned into wine."

"We brew a drink from apples saved from the fall harvest," I said. "It's a great celebration. The women and children bring evergreen boughs and wheat stalks to offer at the shrines. At night a fire is lit from the sacred yew and sacrifices are made to celebrate the passage of the darkness into light."

"There will be fires here too," Theon said. "And much rowdiness. You see, little Kelt, our rites are not much different from yours. Wine will be spilled to Dionysos and sacrifices made on the altars. Now put on your warm cloak and boots. I'll bring the knife to cut the boughs. You carry the basket. We must go into the woods to cut the herbs and bowers."

We bundled in woollen cloaks and set off into the forest beyond the palace. I carried a basket for collecting boughs, Theon brought a scythe. We went out the back gate of the palace and down the hill toward the north wall of the city. An icy breeze from the mountains nipped at my cheeks and my breath steamed from the cold. A bland winter sun shone in the pale blue sky.

A narrow path led outside the city walls toward the woods, trodden with footprints in the snow. I recalled my last winter in Caer Gwyn, how I had gone with grandfather and Essylt to collect rowan berries and mistletoe. I told Theon how the Druids used the rowan berries for charms.

"They are a gift of the gods," I said. "We cut mistletoe that grows on the oaks too and give it as a blessing." I explained the rituals of the winter solstice, how the Druids lit a fire on a log to conquer the darkness and banish evil spirits and made sacrifices to Lugh, the Oak God and to Cernunnos, the Dark Lord who made the earth dark for half the year."

"Many of these rituals are like those of my people," Theon said. "You see, the Druithin, who we called the Magi, came from East, bringing the worship of the *duir,* the oak tree, with them. The oak is sacred to Zeus. Oak trees can stand for a thousand years or more. We will cut some boughs and rowan branches."

We trudged deep into the forest, following the path through winter-bleached bracken. The ancient oaks still rustled with withered leaves and the hollies glowed glossy green between the beeches. We gathered a basket full of pine cones, some silver fir Theon said was sacred to Artemis, some holly and black pine.

The day was growing late when we returned to the palace. The Nubian slave, Xenon, was waiting with a message.

"The Queen invites the Keltic maiden to attend the winter rites in the women's quarters tonight."

I swallowed hard, taken aback. "I'd rather not..." I turned away to hide the blush I felt rise on my cheeks and busied myself by the hearth sorting out the boughs Theon and I had collected. I thought of everything I had been told about the queen, her spiteful nature and how she was possessive of her son, Alexandros. I suddenly felt small and shy, an alien girl, out-of-place in this grand palace. How could I accept an invitation to celebrate with the royalty?

"Olwen, you cannot dismiss the queen's invitation," Theon said sternly.

I spoke out to protest, but Theon continued: "We've just come from the woods, Xenon, so send the kitchen servant with some hot porridge to warm us. And thank the Queen for her invitation. Olwen will be pleased to attend." He put his arm around my shoulders and gave me a reassuring hug. "Now you'll see how the wild women of Pella's court celebrate the winter solstice. Don't worry. There'll be no savagery; no goats ripped apart, perhaps just some serpents..."

"Serpents?" I interrupted.

"Yes. The Maenads use them in their rites. There's no harm. They're not poisonous."

I hoped he was just teasing me. The thought of serpents made my skin turn to goose-flesh. "Is the queen one of those women you call a *maenad*?"

"Olympias is known for her dark powers." Theon's voice dropped to a mysterious tone. "Don't fear her. Her invitation is a courtesy. All the women of the royal court will be there. Consider it an honour she has invited you. It is the custom here for the women to celebrate separately from the men." He patted my shoulder and smiled. "Do not fret. Instead, be pleased Olympias has honoured you with an invitation. Now I must go. The men will be preparing their banquet in the great Hall."

After he had gone, the kitchen slave came carrying a tray with bowls of steaming gruel. She was a young girl, thin as a twig, dressed in simple homespun. I noticed swirls of tribal markings on her scrawny arms. There was a ravaged look about her as if she had been starved and beaten. Her hands shook as she set the tray down on the table. She did not speak but stood back to watch as I sat and began to eat.

"Would you like some?" I asked. It was still strange to me to be waited on by servants as if I was better than them.

"No, Miss. For you." She spoke in almost a whisper, her head bowed.

"Would you like a piece of bread and cheese?"

"No, Miss. I must not..."

"What is your name? Where are you from?" I asked.

She touched her breast. "I am Cale," she said. "From Thrace."

"How did you get here?"

"Men raid my village. Take me."

"Who took you?"

She drew her brows together. Then she took a deep breath and looked up at me with stricken eyes. Her voice shook as she spoke. "The king's men – the Makedoni – they burn my village, kill our men."

"And the women and children?"

She kept her eyes downcast as she spoke. "Bad things. Cruel things. Rape. Soldiers take us away. Sell as slaves. Like me." She put her hands over her face and shuddered.

I remembered how savage our War Band was when they raided rival tribes. I put down my spoon and stared into the half-eaten bowl of gruel, and thought of how Alexandros had rescued me from Sholto. I felt shamed, me being free, this girl being enslaved. Why had I been saved from the same fate? I must have been in the god's favour for my life to have been spared.

The girl put my empty bowl on the tray, picked it up and turned to leave.

"Wait!" I took a small charm from my amulet bag, a stone the shape of a small egg. Essylt had given it to me at the midsummer. "It's a seeing stone," I explained. "If you hold it in your palm long enough and peer into it, the stone will reveal something. Take it, Cale," I said. "Perhaps your luck will change and you will be free someday and find your way back home." As I spoke, my words echoed back to me and I wondered, *Will I ever find my way back to Caer Gwyn?*

She accepted my gift and clenched the stone in her fist. Her eyes filled with tears and she whispered something in her language which I did not understand. She bowed her head and her shoulders shook with sobs. A great feeling of sadness filled me then, and I knew although I had been treated kindly by Theon and Alexandros, somehow I must find a way to return to my own people.

When Theon returned I asked him about the girl. "Why were the women of her village taken as slaves?"

Theon shrugged and said, "Filippos considers Thracians wild and barbaric. He will do anything to subdue them. That is the way of war, my child. Filippos has conquered all the tribes of the north."

I had heard whispers about King Filippos – how he was a brilliant warrior but wanton and debauched. The women in the bathing room said for every battle he took a wife, and especially had an eye for young maidens. I cringed at the memory of how he had reached out and stroked me. I wondered if Alexandros, who seemed so noble to me, would become the same kind of man his father was.

Theon disturbed my thoughts. "Now you must prepare yourself for the celebration," he said. "You must bathe and choose a garment suitable for such a grand occasion. Olympias will look at you with a critical eye, so it is most important you present yourself in garments and a demeanour fit for the royal presence."

I obeyed Theon reluctantly. A servant accompanied me to the bathing room where I was scrubbed and perfumed, my hair combed, brass amulets and crimson ribbons woven into my braids. The servant had laid out the gold-trimmed gown that had been the queen's gift to me, but I wanted to wear something less showy so I chose instead to wear the gold- embroidered Keltic tunic Alexandros had given me.

As I put on my raven's torc I said a prayer to my own gods and asked them to protect me from the dark powers Olympias possessed.

Stanza Two

The palace was so immense it overawed me. The Nubian, Xenon, led me through the maze of garden paths, past the houses of the palace residents, through the courtyards with snow-covered hedges and bare-limbed trees. King Filippos had invited every laird and freeman to attend the men's feast and the din of loud voices singing skolions filled the vast inner court.

A draught of wind shivered the torches in their sconces as I followed Xenon under the shelter of marble-pillared stoas. He led me up the stairs to a fresco-painted hallway. I could hear the shrill laughter of women, voices talking, plates rattling, a lyre's soft strumming.

The queen's maid, Arsinoe, was at the entrance to the imperial apartment, waiting to lead me in. She looked me over carefully, her dark brows drawing together in a frown. Her critical gaze made me feel uncomfortable.

"Why did you not dress in the fine gown gifted to you by my lady?"

"These are Keltic clothes," I said. "A gift from Prince Alexandros."

Arsinoe clucked her tongue. "You are a foreigner here, and you must re-member Olympias is the queen." She tossed her head, the coils of her ringlets bouncing. "Never mind then. Come along. The queen is waiting for you."

Shy and reticent, I followed her into the vast room, my cloak folded around me. The huge room was bright with the lights of a hundred lamps. The walls were painted with friezes of Maenaeds and goddesses. Women lolled on couches around a blazing central hearth. In the centre of the room there was an altar and standing above it on a plinth, a garlanded statue of their god Dionysos. Gathered beside the altar were musicians with *tambors* and *kytheras, sistras* and harps.

The young maidens studied me with curiosity. Some of them whispered behind their hands. No one spoke to me. I lowered my eyes and breathed slowly, my heart pounding. I learned later that among the palace women were several of the king's daughters, born of his campaign wives, and some who were the king's favoured concubines.

Queen Olympias was lounging on a silk-covered couch. A young maiden with chestnut hair sat next to her, a stubborn-chinned girl with grave, sad eyes. "That is the princess, Kleopatra," Arsinoe whispered. "And that other one....' She pointed to a plump glum-faced girl who sat apart from them. "That is Thes-saloniki, a half-sister of Prince Alexandros." She took my arm and led me to-ward the queen. "My Lady, may I present the physician's acolyte."

Olympias looked at me, her mouth curved in a curious smile. She was clad in a flowing black gown and crowned with a diadem of laurel leaves woven with thin clusters of golden berries. A bracelet of a coiled golden snake encircled her arm. Her russet hair was combed and plaited with beads of amber. She uttered a phrase of welcome and inspected me as if I were an oddity. Her eyes were the colour of a mountain pool and hinted at icy depths. I wondered, did she see me as something odious or something pleasing? She beckoned me to come close and leaned out to touch my clothing, inspecting my raven's torc and the amulets that were woven into my braids. Because she was the queen, I bowed, and waited for her to speak.

Olympias peered at me and sniffed. "My son told me you are a Druid's child." Her voice was low and husky.

My tongue stuck fast. I was not sure what I should say or how to begin. I repeated the Greek phrases I had rehearsed with Theon, pronouncing each word, careful not stumble over them.

"My Lady, I am honoured you have invited me here."

Olympias looked at me with surprise. "I hear in the eloquence of your speech that Theon has taught you well. You speak the words clearly enough even with your peculiar accent." She clucked her tongue and patted my arm. "Not to worry, my child. You will learn our language soon enough. You see, I was a foreigner in this court once too, from the kingdom of Epirus."

"Your son, Madam, Alexandros taught me."

"Ah yes," she said. "Alexandros has a gift for languages." She motioned for me to come closer. "Is it true you were an acolyte who was meant to serve at your goddess's shrine? Alexandros says you know the healing arts and can portend omens in the stars."

"That is so, Lady," I stammered. I felt small and insignificant standing there before this formidable woman. "My grandfather was a high priest of the Oak cult, a Druid, my aunt is a priestess and medicine woman. They taught me the secrets of the stars and the healing power of plants."

"Do you know the Mysteries? The secrets of the Oak cult?"

I shook my head. "I know only what I have been taught, my Lady. My aunt was a medicine woman. I was an acolyte of the goddess and was to have been initiated as a priestess at the Midsummer rites, but..." My voice faltered as the memories flooded back.

"What brought you here so far from your homeland?" questioned Olympias.

"I was taken by a renegade warrior chief, my Lady. Alexandros rescued me." I fought to keep my composure, but my voice quaked when I spoke.

"Ah, yes! He has told me this. So now you are here in Makedon. Is this not your *moira* then? For surely you were sent here for a purpose."

"Alexandros put me in the care of Theon, the physician."

Olympias looked pleased. She made a dismissive gesture to the sullen-faced maiden who shared the couch with her. "Kleopatra, harken to what this

Keltic child has to say. She is wise, and surely blessed by the gods." The girl scowled and moved aside. "Come, little Kelt. Sit beside me."

Olympias reached out and pulled me down beside her. I caught in my breath, aware everyone was looking at me. The girl, Kleopatra, cursed me with her eyes. I sat stiffly, my cloak folded around me, shy and reticent. A maiden offered me food from a tray heaped with cheeses and bread. I took a little but refused the wine.

"Come!" Olympias commanded. "I want to hear your tale. My son has told me about you – how he came to rescue you from your captor. So... you are a priestess and you know the healing arts?"

"It is my chosen path as I was instructed by my *modryb*, Essylt," I said. "Now I serve my kind benefactor, Theon. I collect herbs for him and when it is necessary, I help him with the medicines. This is my destiny, Lady."

"And you have come from the far land of the north wind?"

I was aware the room had grown quiet and everyone was listening to me. Some of the maidens whispered and giggled as they jostled to draw nearer, the better to hear. Olympias drew me closer to her. The scent of her perfume had a heady effect on me. I wondered what potions she used, and if they were the elixirs of dark magic. "You must come to Dodona, my home in Eprius. There is a sacred oak shrine. We need a new priestess. The crones who tend it have not much time left to live." Smiling, she handed me a golden cup from a tray a servant had brought. "Drink with us, little Kelt." She lifted her own cup and drank from it, then tossed the dregs onto the floor. "To fair Dionysos, I make this libation."

I accepted the cup and took a sip of the amber liquid. It tasted sharp and was pine scented, not sweet and wheaten like our people's mead.

"It's spruce ale," Olympias explained. "Brewed from the sap of the spruce trees and infused with ivy. It's an ancient *bacante's* drink, one we always have on nights such as this to honour Dionysos, god of wine and revelry."

I did not wish to offend her so I took another sip then followed Olympias's example and spilled a few dregs, echoing the words she had said. "To fair Dionysos..." I knew I must not cross her will or she might cast an adverse spell on me.

It was then I noticed the basket on the floor by the foot of the queen's couch. In it, a serpent was coiled like a copper rope. I had heard the palace gossip – that Olympias was a witch and possessed dark powers. I was afraid if I spoke the wrong words she might ill-wish me. A dark curtain seemed to fall around me, and I felt an icy shiver prickle my skin. Was this serpent part of her cult worship? I said nothing, just stared and took a deep breath to compose myself.

"Are you afraid?" Olympias made a sweeping motion with her hand and the serpent shifted and uncoiled, rippling as though it were a golden chord. It lifted its head and swayed, its cold amber eyes on the queen. Olympias laughed.

"Do not be afraid. Wadjet is harmless. He always accompanies me to the rites." She held out her arm and the snake slithered up, coiling itself around her.

I blinked in amazement and drew away. I heard the princess giggle and say "Look, Mama, the girl is afraid of snakes!"

When she saw I was frightened, Olympias laughed. "He's harmless."

"I have never seen a serpent such as this," I stammered.

"Oh, there are many such things you have not seen. Just wait!" Olympias's smile was mysterious as she leaned forward and whispered, "It will take you time to learn everything. You have come far from your home, and our rites are different here."

I recalled what Theon had said about the women's rites – that they often ended in an orgy. Olympias held her cup out to be filled with more of the spruce wine and motioned to the servant to fill mine. She watched me as I took another sip. Was it my imagination or was my head beginning to spin? A thought crossed my mind that perhaps the wine might be drugged.

"You Kelts are bards, are you not?" Olympias said, gazing at me intently "This night is for celebrating the passage of darkness into light. Tell us a story, Druid's girl. Cast a spell for us. Sing us a song, some words of good omen."

The laughter of the women had died to whispers. I could feel everyone's eyes on me. The girl, Kleopatra, smirked behind her hand. Olympias gave her daughter a harsh look.

I had never sung for a queen, or for anyone except the goddess, when I was alone in the stone circle or sacred grove. I thought of Lleu, how he sang for our ricon and for grandfather.

Hesitating, I accepted the small lyre one of the girls handed me, and strummed my fingers across the strings. The sound of the chords brought back memories to me.

Sometimes Lleu had let me play his harp, but I was not a bard like he was. I closed my eyes and strummed, invoking Lleu's bardic spirit, as I listened to the soft tremulous tone of the notes.

Though I had gained a fair command of Greek, I knew no songs in that language, nor could I tell the queen a bard's tale. Instead, I chose to sing a song I'd known since I was a child. "I will sing you an elegy to winter," I said.

I took in a breath and began, my voice a thin treble. I sang faintly at first, then as I gained confidence, my voice rang clear and true.

> *"I sing of the winter.*
> *Bare are the hills. Snow covers the fields*
> *so the stag cannot feed*
> *and the little birds seek shelter from the icy wind.*
> *The holly is hung with blood red berries.*
> *The reeds have withered.*
> *A fierce wind has torn down the leaves*
> *so the woods are bare."*

I sang on, surprising myself, thinking how proud Lleu would be of me. As the words came they became stronger, clearer, as if the goddess herself had put them in my mouth.

> *"Snow falls on the hillside.*
> *White is the hoarfrost.*
> *Whiter than the breast of a swan.*
> *The wind wails through*
> *the bare-limed willow's harp.*
> *All the sweetness of nature*
> *is buried in winter's black grave.*
> *The wind sings a sad lament.*
> *But oh! Listen, hush! Spring will come*
> *Bringing life in its arms,*
> *strewing sweet clover and flowers*
> *on the hills."*

When I finished, the whole room applauded. Even Olympias seemed pleased. "That song, who taught you? Though I don't know your language, still it was beautiful poetry."

"My grandfather's bard, Lleu, taught me. He often sang it to me."

Olympias set down her wine cup and smiled at me. "Your voice is sweet as a lark's. You have a God-given talent, little Kelt."

I bowed my head and thanked her, then took my place on one of the divans next to the queen's daughter and the other royal women. They ogled me with admiration, all but the princess, Kleopatra, who scowled as I settled back on the cushions. I relaxed, and accepted a honey-drenched sweet from a plate a servant handed me.

The skirling of pipes from an *aulos* and flute began to shrill and some of the women left their couches and began to dance, hair loosened and skirts swirling, jewelled arms entwined as they swayed to the rhythm. Some had donned masks, others, crowns of ivy. The young princess, Kleopatra, carried a wand covered in ivy leaves, topped with a pine cone on a long pole. As they danced, the women sang, but the words were blurred behind their masks.

Olympias rose from her couch and joined the dance, her eyes flashing, crying wildly as she led the women in a circle, twining like a serpent. The room was soon a wild din. I heard the women scream *"Euoi! Euoi!"* Some held their hands out imploring me to join them, but I felt too shy and my head was spinning, dizzy from the spruce drink.

They whirled, their movements frenzied, their voices rising higher like the cries of she-wolves to the moon. They danced to the wailing of the double flute, beating cymbals, trailing long garlands that twined among them as they circled the room. The fine wreath of gold crowning Olympias's hair sparked and trembled in the torchlight. She appeared to be in a trance, her eyes half-closed as she swayed to the sounds of the *sistra* and flute. I watched as she danced. Her skirts swirled and bracelets clashed, her gold-sewn flounces and jewels catching the light.

Two black-clad old crones had entered the room. I guessed they were priestesses. One carried a covered basket in which sacred things are borne. The other stepped into the circle of dancers and cried out in a shrill quaking voice, "We must make the appointed sacrifice."

I wondered what was in the basket. A piglet? A lamb? A hound pup? I recalled what Theon had told me about the customs, that in all the years there is no rite more powerful than the rites of the baccants at the winter solstice.

"It is a solemn day that marks the end of the darkness. If anyone has grief or fear or troubles it will be purified."

The wild skirl of the music died and the women, seeing the crones, gathered around them at the altar. They stood in a ring, hands joined and sang the invocation. The priestess handed Olympias a wine cup. She lifted it to her lips and sipped it, then glanced over the rim toward me, her brows dawn into a frown.

What am I to do? I wondered. *Am I to join the revelry? Will the queen expect me to make the sacrifice? She is a priestess and knows earth magic, so if she curses me, I am doomed!*

Olympias broke from the circle and walked over, holding the golden cup out to me. Her face was flushed, her russet hair glowed. She looked straight into my eyes as if to read an omen. "Drink up, little Kelt," she commanded. "You must join us in the sacrifice to Dionysos."

I saw in her eyes I must obey, and I felt fear. I wanted to refuse, but the queen's formidable stare forbade. I took the cup and sipped the contents. It had a sweet, cloying taste, unlike the tangy spruce wine.

"Drink it all!" Olympias ordered.

I took a long gulp of the strong, unmixed wine. It had a sharp acrid flavour tinged with a muskiness and the scent of fungus. I handed the cup back to her. I expected her to speak, but she walked back to where the crones waited by the altar, her head held high.

Then I noticed, amid the group of baccants and musicians who hovered near the altar, a thin young woman, her clothing torn so she was half naked. I saw the blue spirals on her arms that marked her as a Thracian. It was Cale, the servant girl.

A wave of nausea overcame me and I felt myself reel unsteadily. Theon had told me that in the old days they made human sacrifices to Dionysos on this day. I recalled Dafydd, born away in the wicker cage at the Midsummer. I felt dizzy from the drink and bile rose in my throat.

A dim curl of smoke coiled up from the altar. I watched the crones place the wicker basket on the altar. One of them lifted up a baby goat. The bacchants began to chant, their voices rising shrill as the screeching of gulls. A knife blade flashed in the crone's hand and blood spurted from the kid, splashing the altar. Olympias gathered some blood in her hands and smeared it over Cale's bare skin. I saw the look of terror on the girl's face and heard Olympia's shrill cry, *"We offer thee to Dionysos."*

Dizziness overcame me. The images began to blur, interweaving, inter-changing. I tried to cry out but my voice was only a whimper. The rhythm of timbrels beat faster, the flute shrieked. I stumbled backwards and fell onto a couch. The room swirled and the voices rose into shrieks. Everything seemed to melt and distort; the masked women became frightening animals and hid-eous-faced gods. Suddenly there was a sharp choked scream. The sound tore through my heart. I cowered on the couch, frightened and alone.

Stanza Three:

In the dark before daybreak Xenon came to fetch me. Someone shook me awake and led me, dazed and disoriented, to the stoa where he waited. I stag-gered beside him through the torch-lit gardens. I could hear the shouts and loud singing from the Great Hall where the men still caroused. I shivered from the cold night air so Xenon took off his cloak and draped it around me.
"You drank too much spruce wine, little Kelt," he said in his deep, kindly voice.
"The girl... Cale...did they...?"
"The girl?"
"Yes...the sacrifice to Dionysos...did they?"
Xenon stopped and peered down at me. Against the darkness of his skin, his eyes were wide and white as moons. "A girl for a sacrifice?"
"They slaughtered a baby goat," I said, "And I saw Olympias smear its blood over the servant girl, Cale. She said Cale was an offering to Dionysos."
He put both his big hands on my shoulders and his fingers squeezed them tight. "You must not speak of this," he said in a hoarse whisper. "You must speak of nothing you saw at the rites."
"Did they kill her?" My voice quavered and tears stung my eyes.
"If they did," Xenon said, "not only the wrath of gods will visit the queen."
Theon was not there when we arrived back at the little house in the court-yard. Xenon said he had gone to the theatre and would return soon.
I stumbled to my bed and fell into a deep sleep where strange creatures prowled, and demons threatened. A black-clad crone held up a bleating lamb and began to smear me with its blood. I woke up sobbing, my temples throb-bing.
Gentle hands stroked me and laid a cold cloth on my forehead. When I opened my eyes, Theon was bending over me, his brow furrowed, a look of great consternation on his face.
"I should have warned you... the spruce wine..."
"It was not the spruce wine. It was the drink in the golden cup..." I struggled to sit up but he pushed me back.

"Lie still. You are safe now. Sleep more."

I wanted to tell him all that had happened, but I had been warned not to reveal anything that had transpired in the queen's room. I pressed my cheek against Theon's hand.

"Something in that cup... the queen made me drink it. I was afraid... afraid if I didn't she'd cast a spell on me."

"Well she did, didn't she? She did cast a spell on you." He went to the hearth and brought me a cup of strong chamomile tea. "Drink this. It will quell the queasiness and clear your head. That drink Olympias gave you was potent... too potent for a young girl who knows nothing of the rites. You must beware of Olympias, you see. She is conniving and perverse and not to be trusted. Never mind. You are here with me now and you are safe."

"Did they kill the girl?" My eyes welled with tears as I remembered. "The Thracian girl... was she sacrificed?"

Theon shook his head. "I have heard nothing, though it would not surprise me." He returned to the hearth where a pot of broth was simmering over the flames. He ladled some into a clay bowl and brought it to me. "Drink this. You will recover." He smiled, trying to make me feel at ease. "The chamomile tea and broth and a long rest will cure you." He reached out and lifted my chin, a stern look on his kindly face. "You must not fret over the rites... or the Thracian girl. Perhaps you were only dreaming. Perhaps it was the wine."

But nothing could convince me it was just a dream.

Stanza Four

When snow in the woodland melted with the first thaw, hunters found the Thracian maiden's body buried under a heap of ivy wreaths in the forest beside a shrine to Dionysos, where Olympias and the maenads carried out their wild rituals. They identified Cale by the tattoos still visible on her frozen flesh.

I was serving Theon his morning porridge when one of the palace servants brought the news. I felt faint with shock. Had I been there when they killed her? Gaps in the memory can be merciful. I had only a vague memory of the wild celebration in the queen's quarters. The potions Olympias gave me numbed all my recollection of that night.

I recalled the day I had first met the Thracian maid and had given her the seeing stone charm from my amulet bag and how I had told her *'Perhaps your luck will change and you will be free some day and find your way back home.'*

I recalled how the old crone had given me the stone and the potions and instructed me how to mix them so I could escape from Sholto. I had been lucky when Alexandros rescued me or else my fate might have been like hers.

The news of the discovery alarmed Theon too. "You heard no gossip from the women?"

I did not reply. I only remembered seeing Cale brought into the queen's room and dragged to the altar. After that, the draft of wine Olympias gave me had blurred my vision and numbed my body until all of my memory was erased.

After a long silence, Theon picked up his porridge bowl from the table and got to his feet. "Well, for the moment there is not much to be done. You are safe here with me. I cannot imagine Olympias would harm you, a priestess!" His tone was gentle, comforting. "Do not fret, my dear child. Put all this behind you and take what the gods send."

I wept for Cale's death and thanked the goddess that I had been saved from the same fate. Although I was accustomed to the sacrifices of small animals and had grieved for days over the slaughter of my bull, Mithras, still I could not grasp why humans must be given to the gods. I remembered the day at midsummer when they had burned Dafyyd in the oak king's cage. This human sacrifice was no different from the one my own people had made.

Why do we kill mortals to please the gods? I searched for days in my heart to find a reason and answer for this. It horrified me to think how it might have been me chosen by Olympias to be used in their orgy, sacrificed to Dionysos instead of the Thracian girl. I was an alien here like she was. Was it my dedication to the goddess that had saved me from her fate?

I began to question the gods. For days I grieved, alone with my thoughts. Theon seemed to sense how troubled I was. He gently patted my shoulder.

"We are in the hands of Fate, our *moira*, from the day we are born," Theon said. "You were sent here for a purpose. It was the gods will for you to be dedicated in your goddess's service. This is your home now, Olwen. You must accept your *moira* and live this new life the gods have provided."

I kept silent as he spoke, for he was a wise man. He laid his hand on my shoulder and looked deep into my eyes. "Come now. We will make libations and pray for the Thracian girl."

Theon led me to a small grove near the palace to a little stone sanctuary set in a clearing. He carried a phial of oil mixed with honey and I brought an armful of olive branches, libations for the dead.

"This shrine is for Gaia, the Earth Mother," Theon explained. "From her womb all life springs and all living things must return to her after our allotted span of life is over."

The remains of a recent sacrifice still smouldered on the altar and the smell of burnt meat that had been quenched with wine hung acrid in the air. Theon handed me the phial then raised his arms in a gesture of worship to give a blessing to the dead. His voice was low as he intoned a prayer in remembrance of Cale.

"Oh great Mother Gaia, We are in your hands, Gaia, and to you we make these offerings. We call upon you in our time of grief. Oh, great mother, bring us comfort..."

I held the phial in my right hand as he instructed and poured the wine and honey mixture into the earth. Afterwards I strewed the olive branches over the ground where the libation had been poured, and with silent prayers we departed the grove.

Melancholy hung over me like a dark cloud for days. I wandered by myself, often going back to Gaia's shrine alone. The early spring air was soft and fragrant. Delicate flowers had begun pushing their heads through the melting snow and new buds sprouted on the trees. The grove became my refuge, a place where I said prayers to my people's goddess, Arianrhod, on whose ship the Oarwheel, the dead are carried to the heavenly moon land.

"Arianrhod of the Silver Wheel, goddess of rebirth and reincarnation, I humbly kneel here in the circle. Look down on us from your heavenly land of Caer Sidi. Cast your silver light upon the earth. Keep me safe, and carry the dead safely to your heavenly domain."

One morning as I approached the grove I heard the sound of music. It surprised me to find Alexandros sitting on a log, his head bent over a lyre. His fingers lightly touched the strings as he plucked notes that trembled with a sweet resonance and began to sing, his gentle voice, sweet as honey.

All my melancholy thoughts were displaced by the dulcet tone of the lyre. It took me back to Caer Gwyn, the sweet strumming of Lleu's clarsach.

"I didn't know you were a bard," I said. I told him about the ricon's bard. "He was the bard of our tuath in Caer Gwyn. His name was Lleu. He sang the stories of our people in a voice sweet as yours. You must be a bard too!"

Alexandros gave a little laugh and shrugged. "Not if my father has his way!" There was a bitter tone to his words. "Father thinks it's unmanly to play the lyre. He would rather I wield only a sword." Then he looked at me gravely. "Why have you come here? Where is Theon?"

"I came here to honour the dead," I had an armful of yew boughs and rowan leaves. "The Druids use these for charms. They are a gift of the gods. "

Alexandros watched as I laid the boughs on Cale's grave. "Even a barbarian deserves the rights of passage to cross the river," he said.

"Why did the baccants kill her... that Thracian girl, Cale. Why?"

"Because the god demanded it," Alexandros replied bluntly.

"To kill an innocent girl?" I gasped. "She was like me... a stranger here... taken from her people." Tears welled in my eyes as I thought of my own fate, how Alexandros had saved me from Sholto's wrath. Only because I was a Druid's child had I been spared a fate such as Cale's.

"She was a slave. You are not. You are free to walk the fields and forests. You are a goddess's child, a priestess, a healer. She was a slave, that is all."

I could not speak again. I turned away from him, but he saw I was crying. He lifted my chin and brushed the tears away from my cheeks with his fingertips. "I'm sorry the girl died," he said. "And I am shamed it was my mother's doing." Hearing his words, I felt the good will between us then, and my dark mood lifted. He stood and swung the lyre over his shoulder.

"I will walk with you back to the palace gardens," he said. "You mustn't mourn any longer for the girl. She is in a better world now, free and safe from harm."

BALLAD NINETEEN Paean To Ares

Hail to you Ares, lord of war.
Mighty, valiant Ares,
stormer of cities, killer of men.
Indestructible Ares, unconquered, valiant god.
Your lust for carnage unleashes fear.
Hail to you, Supreme, strong Ares,
Father of war-winning victories.
Give us courage to stand our ground.
From high above shine down on us
and bring us victory.

THE CALL TO WAR

Stanza One.

Spring finally arrived. The snow melted from the passes and the sheep were loosed from their folds to feed on the new growth in the upland pastures. The turbulent sea had calmed so the sea lanes were opened again. In the harbour fishing boats and merchant craft prepared to sail.

I heard no word from Elidi all winter. Each day I watched the harbour to see if the royal fleet had returned. When I asked Theon, he said: "The ships are anchored in Amphipolis port where they're made shipshape for the coming sailing season. They'll return when the king gives the orders." He clicked his tongue and winked at me. "No more fretting over the Phrygian. You've been like a love-sick calf all winter! Fetch your basket, and come with me!"

With the new sprouts greening in the forest, Theon and I went to collect chamomile, thyme and thistle which we would steep in boiling water to make infusions of medicines. We left the forest path the dew-soaked fronds of ferns dampening our clothes as we ventured into the dense thicket gathering plants, content with the deep silence of the woods and the company of each other.

"Now it is springtime will we return to the farmstead?" I asked

Theon shrugged. "Not yet." He looked somewhat dejected. I knew he missed his farmstead as much as I did. He stooped to pick a handful of freshly sprouted chamomile. When he straightened, he gave a deep sigh. "It is the beginning of campaign season. The Thracian tribes to the east have been revolting and the king must put down the rebellion. Filippos will take his court physician with him to the battlefield, so he wants me to remain here until he returns."

I felt a knot form in the pit of my stomach. Elidi had told me the fleet would sail east to guard the coastline. He had said, *When I return we will be together again and I will ask for Theon's blessing.* But I wondered if there was a sea battle would I ever see him again.

I tried to push the thought out of my mind as I followed Theon back along the trail that led to the palace postern gate. I remember what Theon had said to me: *'Elidi is a man of the sea. His life is dedicated to Poseidon and he must go wherever the sea god takes him.'*

During the next weeks, the palace buzzed around us with the news that Filippos's army was preparing to make war against the Thracians. The streets of Pella rang and rattled with the sounds of war. In the palace hall the men sang rowdy skolions and prayers were offered to Ares, the War God.

"This is the month we call Xandikos and a festival will be held. The army will be purified in preparation for their march east," Theon said. He explained that, along with the fierce Thracian tribes, both of the coastal cities of Byzantium and Perinthos had risen up to rebel against the Makedonians. "The Greeks, and even the Persians are siding with the rebels," Theon said. "And the Scythians in the north have risen up."

I could see by his furrowed brows and grim expression that what lay ahead was more than just a tribal skirmish. "This will be a decisive battle, but Filippos has triumphed many times before, and we must trust the gods of war will bring him a victory again."

Each day I heard the sounds of battle preparation, the war songs and paeans to the gods. The ground trembled with the pounding of marching feet and the clash of weapons resounded from the parade grounds beyond the city walls. The king held a war council and performed the purification rites for the army. A black dog was sacrificed to Hades, the god of the Underworld. Our chieftains would have sacrificed a horse and burnt it on a pyre in honour of Gwyndion, our God of War.

I watched the sacrifice with revulsion as the dog struggled and yelped, snapping at the priest's hand as he lifted the sacrificial knife. I was still haunted by the memory of how they had used the boy, Dafydd, as a sacrifice when the warring tribes of the north had threatened our tuath. I wondered if the killing of the helpless dog would bring down the same dire fate on Makedon as Dafydd's death had brought to Caer Gwyn.

Theon took me to watch the ranks of soldiers on the drill field. The king was on the parade ground drilling the men, disciplined battalions of stocky men who moved as one with sharp precision. The noise of war-cries and whinnying war-chargers filled the air. I recalled Caer Gwyn's Royal War Band as they prepared for war against the invading tribes, a fearsome band of unruly half-naked painted warriors, hair spiked with lime, wearing horned and winged helmets that made them look even taller than they were. They'd stand in their wicker war chariots, weapons raised and they screamed war chants as they hammered their blade hilts on their shields. These Makedonians were disciplined and marched in precision, their long sarissas held before them, their cavalry smart in plumed helmets, armour shining.

Within the week, the first troops of foot solders began their march eastward. Soon the king would follow with his squadron of elite warriors and generals. Finally, one morning I heard the heralds announce the royal fleet returned to Pella's harbour. I had been waiting eagerly for news from Elidi, and I had almost given up hope of seeing him again, when a message arrived, brought to me by a ship's boy.

"Elidi, the helmsman, sent me," he said. "The fleet will embark soon for Byzantium. Will you meet with him?"

I rewarded the boy with a silver drachma then went to tell Theon the news. He had left to tend an ailing servant, so I summoned up my courage to leave the palace unescorted.

I made my way past the gate guards and down the steps of the acropolis hill to the city. The narrow streets teemed with people but aside from a few curious glances, nobody questioned me. I ran all the way, past the stone-columned houses, pushing my way through the crowds in the busy market place, down a cobbled lane to where the ships were anchored in the lagoon.

Ahead I could see the royal trireme, it's star-emblazoned flags fluttering in the wind. Elidi was standing on the landing quay. My heart raced as I ran to greet him. He grinned like a youth who had just won his first ivy crown and held out his arms. "My dear little Kelt, I am glad you have come!"

He was taller than I remembered him to be. His tousled mane of black, shiny hair framed his sun-darkened face. He was dressed for travel in a woollen tunic and cape. Shy and reticent, I hesitated before I took a step toward him. "I have come to say goodbye and wish you god's speed on your journey."

Then all the questions that had troubled me burst forth: "The ship's boy brought me your message. Why did it take so long for you to return? And now you are leaving Pella. When will you sail again?"

He put out his hand and took mine in his. "I had no time to come to you before the orders came that we must take the ships to Amphipolis. But I thought of you all winter. I am glad you have come." He pulled me closer.

"But why didn't you send me a message before this?" I pulled away from him. My voice trembled as I spoke. I took a breath, willing myself to stay calm though I could feel the tears brimming in my eyes. "I waited for you but you did not come."

"We had much work preparing the ships. I didn't know when, or if, we'd return to Pella. We were awaiting orders from the king." His face was taut. He looked sad, as though he was withholding something he was afraid to tell.

"Elidi, when there was no word from you, I was afraid I might never see you again. Theon says the king is going to war and your fleet will sail again!" My voice trembled as I spoke. "You will be sailing into a sea battle and Theon told me the Byzantian fleet is far greater than Filippos's." I felt terrified at the thought of what might happen to him and began to cry. "What if you never return? What if..."

He embraced me and brushed away my tears. "Dear Olwen," he said, taking my hand. "You have nothing to fear. It is my destiny, the sea, but good fortune will bring me back to you. I promise I will return." He kissed me, then paused and looked deep into my eyes. "When I return, I will ask Theon permission to marry you. No more will we yearn for each other. No longer will we wait. I will marry you. You will be my love forever."

I felt comforted in his arms, but a cold feeling came over me when he spoke of marriage and I pulled away remembering Theon's words: *Elidi has dedicated his life to the sea god just as you have chosen to follow the path of a healer.* Could I break that trust? I was sixteen and most girls my age were already wed. But could I marry Elidi? If I had been dedicated at the Holy Isle, I would have kept my maidenhood. If I had not, I would have married a man of our tribe. I thought sadly how I still longed for Caer Gwyn and my home with Essylt. Now I had been given a choice – I could stay chaste in the goddess's service with my guardian Theon, or I could bind myself in marriage to Elidi.

I hesitated before answering him knowing my decision would change my life and I could dream no more of returning to my homeland.

"I'll make offerings at the woodland shrine," I said. "And I'll wait for you."

"There is a bond between us," Elidi said. "And I *will* return."

I began to speak but he put his fingers to my lips. I heard the trierarch call his crew to their posts. We walked together back to the landing quay. A light fog had drifted above the shore. The sea was the colour of polished iron, churning the waves into froth. I felt the cool spray against my face.

Elidi took my face in his hands. "Don't be aggrieved, my sweet Olwen. There is time. When I return, we will be together. May the omens be happy ones."

We clung to each other until the sharp command of the trierarch gave orders for Elidi to return to the ship. The triremes were ready to set sail. I watched Elidi mount the skala and take his place at the helm. As the oarsmen plied their long oars and the ship moved out of the lagoon heading seaward, Elidi waved to me and I fought back tears as I waved back at him. When would I see him again? Or would he return?

'He is a man of the sea,' Theon had told me. There was nothing I could do but make offerings and pray the sea god would answer my prayers and bring him safely back again.

The sea was calm and the triremes rode the waves easily, gulls flying overhead. I watched the fleet sail out of Pella's harbour as they grew smaller and disappeared over the horizon. I imagined Elidi standing at the helm of the royal trireme and felt as if my heart would break. I had known him for such a short time, but he had changed my life forever. Nothing would be the same for me again.

Theon was waiting for me in the garden when I returned. "Where have you been? Have you been to the grove?" He peered at me his brow furrowed. "What is troubling you?"

"I went to see the ships sail," I said. "Elidi sent me a message, and asked me to come."

"Elidi, the Phrygian?"

"Yes. He asked me to marry him."

Theon did not speak at first. He stood looking down at me, stroking his beard, his brows furrowed. Finally, he said: "Our wise philosopher, Plato, said love is the joy of the good, the wonder of the wise and the amazement of the gods."

I burst into tears then. "I do not know what I should do. I have given myself to serve the goddess...but I love Elidi. And what if... what if he doesn't return?"

Theon reached out and put his arm around my shoulder. "Dear child, waiting is painful just as forgetting is. But not knowing what to do is the worst kind of suffering."

"What if I don't become a healer?" I sobbed.

Theon held me until I stopped weeping. "You are young, Olwen, but you have been blessed with wisdom." He held me at arms length and looked me straight in the eyes. "Do not think of it now. You will dream and then you will know. Your heart will tell you what is right."

I heeded Theon's words and each day I went to the sacred grove to pray for Elidi's safe return. I prayed to my own goddess, Creiddydad, goddess of love, daughter of Llyr, the sea god, and raised my hands to ask her blessings.

"May he go forth swift and strong as the tides of the sea and bring him victory so he may return home once again triumphant. Great Mother, bring him home, swift and strong as the tides of the sea!"

As I stretched out my arms, I felt the life of the earth and forest enfold me. I wanted to weep but the tears would not come. All I could do was to pray and trust the goddess.

Stanza Two

Over the weeks that passed, dispatches came from Thrace where Filippos was fighting the uprising at Perinthos. Theon explained that the Byzantines had supplied the enemy with their fastest triremes and best troops, so the battle was not going well for the Makedonians.

"The rebels would not stand a chance if the Greeks from the city state and islands, and the Persian satrapies hadn't supplied them with help." Theon explained that the Greeks had sided with the Persians, once their most hated enemies, in order to rout the Makedonian troops. "It will be a long siege! It does not bode well," he said.

The next morning Alexandros came to see Theon. He had returned from a hunt and his face was streaked with dust, his hair dishevelled. He appeared to be agitated, and Theon asked what was troubling him.

"A messenger has come from the east. The Maedoi hillsmen in the north have revolted and are raiding the farms and slaughtering our Makedonian settlers. I must go to fight these barbarians." He began to pace, his voice raised. "If they come farther south into Thrace they'll band with the Tribolloi tribes. I warned father about the Tribolloi, but because he'd already successfully conquered the rebelling Scythians in the north, he shrugged it off. I was right. So, I must stop them or they will block father's return from Byzantium. The Byzantians have the strongest navy and have sent their fastest triremes to blockade father's route to the east. There is a rumour spreading in the south by the Greeks that father's luck has run out."

I thought of Elidi and a shiver of fear overwhelmed me. If there was a sea battle, would he survive?

"Perhaps you should go to Delphi and consult the oracles. Theon suggested.

Alexandros was determined. His lips pressed together stubbornly. "No! I must go to Amphipolis and north up the Strymon River where the Maedoi are raiding," he replied sharply. "I must quell their uprising. Otherwise, they'll cut off father's retreat and block his army in." He wiped his hand across his brow. His face was flushed." I have consulted Aristander, my seer, and sacrificed to the god. The gods spoke to me. It is their will!"

Theon's brow furrowed. "Think carefully on this," he advised. "The Maedoi are savage people, tough as wild goats. Are you familiar with their country? It's as rugged and wild as they are! Your father has entrusted you to learn administration, how to hold war-councils and meet with clan chieftains. If you lose the fight with the Maedoi then Thrace will blaze up and seek retribution. Once this happens your father's lines will be cut."

Alexandros was determined. "By the time I get there they'll already be down in the Strymon valley."

Theon drew in a long deep breath. "You are a cadet still, Alexandros, only sixteen, an *ephebe*. You've never faced combat before. Your father left you in charge here. How can you leave while he is away at war?"

"Antipater has agreed I should counter the attack of the Maedoi. I'm leaving the seal of authority with him. I'm going! I shall leave tomorrow at dawn!"

Theon looked sternly at him. "I know you have been trained as a field officer, but you've never led a campaign, and if you lose, half of Thrace will be ablaze and your father's lines cut."

Alexandros cocked his head and shrugged. "Yes, and if I am defeated father will forever scorn me. Therefore, I have no choice. You can lay your wagers on me, my friend for I will win!"

Theon's grizzled brows met in a frown but he did not comment further.

Stanza Three

At the first glimpse of light the next morning Alexandros rode away on his horse Bucephalus, with his companions and a troupe of elite soldiers, leaving behind a scant few men to defend Pella. I wondered when we would see him again. Theon said these wars could last for months.

After he had gone, the days dragged on. Stories filtered in by courier. Alexandros had led a scouting party against the Maedoi and was victorious, so he had turned east to Perinthos to assist his father with the siege.

We waited for more news, but none came. Finally, one day a runner arrived bearing a message that the king's battle with the Tribolloi had not gone well. His army had clashed with the northern Scythian tribes and defeated them, taking their women and children as slaves. The messenger said Alexandros had gone to Thrace to join his father, and on the army's return to Makedon, the Thracians had attacked their convoy. Filippos was wounded in the fray and was rumoured to be near death.

The news set a dark pall over the palace. Was the king dying? What would happen to Makedon if Filippos, their champion, was taken from them?

I thought back to that day in Caer Gwyn when Hwyel ap Madoc's body had been brought back from the battlefields. How we had mourned that day! I shuddered with apprehension, recalling how his death had set off a terrible war between the Dobunni and Ordovices. What would happen if the king died?

We waited anxiously, and finally, more news arrived: Alexandros was bringing his father back to Pella. The king had suffered serious wounds and needed more care. Theon was advised to prepare to treat him.

I felt some trepidation as I helped Theon assemble the *pharmacae* he would need to treat the king. How serious were Filippos wounds? Would Theon be able to mend them? And what would happen if the king died?

They brought the king back to the palace, carried on a pallet covered with a sheepskin. Alexandros was by his father's side. His face looked drawn and pale. His tall, auburn-haired friend Hephaestion, stood stolidly beside him.

They laid Filippos on his bed. He was lifeless as a corpse and burning with a fever. His head lolled sideways, saliva oozed from his mouth. It was hard to imagine this was the man who ruled Makedon and led a mighty army.

Alexandros was clearly distraught. His hair was tangled, his face smudged with dust. "We rode night and day to get here. I thought he would recover, then he got a fever. I thought if father should die it must not be there, among his enemies. So I brought him home."

Hephaestion, put his arm around Alexandros's shoulder. "In the midst of the battle Filippos's horse bolted" he said. "The king would have been killed by one of the Thracians if Alexandros hadn't run the man through with his sword. Alexandros saved him."

"Father gave me my life. In return I gave him his," Alexandros drew in a deep breath. "They killed his horse under him and when it fell he was trapped under it. He had done everything right. He besieged Perinthos's city walls for days, built towers and battered the walls with battering rams. But Perinthos's walls are sturdy and the Perinthians had called for help from Byzantium. Father kept up the siege day and night and lost a great many men. Then the Persian satraps sent in a force of mercenaries, and the Byzantians supplied their war triremes."

A coldness came over me as I listened. I thought of Elidi on the royal trireme and worried how he had fared during the sea battle.

"Father split his army in two, sent half to besiege Byzantium. He had his best forces with him and might have won Byzantium," Alexandros continued. "He got there fast enough and chose a cloudy night to ride up to the city walls. Then suddenly the clouds parted and the moon was full and high. The town dogs started to howl and this sounded the alarm. It was the dogs and the moon that betrayed father. Whatever sign his diviners gave him was wrong! He should have consulted the oracle at Delphi."

"Perhaps the gods needed appeasing," Theon said.

I recalled how at the sacrifice for purifying the army, the dog had struggled and yelped, then bit the priest's hand. They should have heeded the omens!

"Well, it's done and he's lucky to be alive. The field physician did all he could but I knew we must bring him home or he might die." Alexandros's voice quavered. "Can you save him? Will he walk again?"

Theon examined the king, a grim look on his face. "If sepsis has set in it could kill him. Pray to the god of healing," Theon said. "I will do my best but your father's life is in the god's hands."

Theon removed the wooden splint and examined the shattered bones of the king's leg. Filippos's whole body twitched and he moaned in agony. I had seen Essylt treat wounds from knives or arrowheads, but never a mangled limb such as his.

I gasped in horror at the sight of his leg. "Will you have to amputate it?"

"With skill and the gods' good fortune I hope we can save it," Theon looked up at Alexandros and Hephaestion. "You two hold him down while I treat him. Sometimes with a severe wound like this the opiates don't do enough to dull the pain."

While Theon prepared for the surgery, I stood aside with the basket of *pharmacae*, applied cool wet clothes to Filippos's head and administered potions of poppy tea to sedate him. The king's leg had been bound in a splint and when Theon removed it I could see how the broken bones had pierced the flesh. While I swabbed the mangled leg clean, Theon took the pliers and forceps and jars of medicines from the basket. As he worked to repair the broken bones I handed him the surgical instruments, oil and dressings to staunch the bleeding,

"Will he walk again?" I asked.

Theon had a grim look on his face. "It's a bad wound and it will leave him lame. That will not stop Filippos though. He'll be back on his horse in no time."

Filippos roused slightly. He groaned and opened his eyes. Then he began to thrash about and tried to speak. "Where... where? My horse...."

I held a cup of poppy tea to the king's parched lips. "Drink this, sir. It will ease the pain."

"Your son saved you," Theon said. "It was Alexandros who rescued you on the battlefield. If he had not brought you here you may have died of sepsis."

Filippos moaned and his eyes fluttered open. He looked up at Alexandros and whispered, "You're a good boy, Alexandros!" Then he fell back into unconsciousness.

"He will not admit it was me who saved him. He won't remember how that battle might have been a final defeat..." The shine had gone out of Alexandros's eyes. He looked fatigued, war-weary. He had been a youth when he left Pella. Now he had returned, a man, a warrior.

Hephastion's arm went around Alexandros's shoulders. "Everyone knows it was you who saved him. He does too."

Alexandros took a long breath. "Yes. I know. He gave me my life, now I have repaid him and given him his."

I saw the sadness in his eyes. He had defeated the Maedoi and assisted his father with the siege of Perinthos. His victory against the Maedoi earned him the name of *Basilikos*, the Little King. But to be acknowledged by his father meant more to him.

Stanza Four

Every day I went to the woodland shrine to make supplications to the goddess to pray for the king and ask for Elidi's safe return. One morning as I made my way down the path to the woods, I met Olympias coming alone from the grove. Her coppery hair was covered by a black scarf and she wore a black robe banded with gold.

I stepped aside to let her pass. She stopped and peered at me with narrowed eyes.

"Ah, little Kelt! Are you going to the forest to collect greens?"

"I'm going to make an offering at the shrine," I stammered.

She arched a brow. "To your goddess or ours?" Olympias asked. I sensed the scorn in her voice and her eyes measured me with disdain.

"I pray to your goddess and my own, for the king, and for the ships of the royal fleet that they will return safely," I said.

"Prayers for my husband you say?" She gave a hoarse laugh and tossed her head. It was well known the queen was at odds with the king. Her cheeks flushed and her voice grew harsh. "Filippos is tough as a slab of marble. If a fall from his horse in the midst of a battle didn't kill him, only the gods know what will." Her voice sliced sharp as a dagger blade and I felt a chill like when a dark cloud covers the sun.

"We pray the king will recover, my lady. Theon says he'll walk again, though not without a limp. He's lucky Alexandros was there to save him."

She frowned and shrugged. "Yes, Alexandros...he's impetuous and wilful, but he'll fill his father's shoes well one day." Her voice was measured and deliberate. She brushed past me and strode briskly up the path toward the palace.

I stood for a while looking after her until she passed through the palace gate. Something in her tone had alarmed me. I shivered with a chill and made my way to the woodland to collect fresh violets and rosemary for my offering.

As I entered the grove, the silence of the forest closed around me. A mist had gathered among the trees and there was an eerie silence unlike any I had experienced before. Usually I felt comfort in the grove, but today as I collected my offerings there was an unsettling aura, as if the air hummed with magic.

When I went to place my offering, on the stone altar there was a heap of ashes where a burnt offering had been made. I drew in a slow breath and felt my skin prickle. On top of the ashes lay a strange male figurine made of wax. One of its legs was missing and tied around it was an amulet inscribed with peculiar writing. I drew in a long shuddering breath. Had Olympias left this on the shrine? And what did it mean? Had she cast a binding spell on the king? Surely it did not bode well.

I laid my flower offering beside it and raised my arms, speaking the name of the goddess as reverence decreed, reciting the prayers that give protection from sorcery, then I chanted a prayer to Airmed, my own goddess of healing.

O Airmed, gentle, sweet, great giver. Grant me wisdom to help the king and protect him from the Dark Powers.

Was the queen wishing her husband dead? Had she cast a spell to ensure it? I wanted to believe Olympias had left the votives on the shrine and had asked the goddess to heal her husband. Remembering the Dragon's Fire, I prayed my goddess would intervene and keep the king from harm.

I did not sleep well that night. I did not speak to Theon about the rituals performed in the woodland shrine. I lay awake wondering if I should tell him about my meeting with the queen and the strange votive I found on the shrine.

For several days the king lay close to death, drained of blood and delirious with pain. Each day I went to his chamber to change his dressings and rub honey and healing balms on to his wounds. One morning, as I made my way through the palace garden to go to the king's chamber, Alexandros called to me from the painted colonnades of the stoa. As he strode toward me I could see the look of concern on his face.

"You are going to tend father? How is he? Is he recovering well?"

"He is recovering slowly," I said. "It will be some time before he can stand or walk, but his wounds will heal."

"You know what happened– how the dogs and the moon betrayed him. You know the rites. He should have consulted the oracles." He looked around the garden furtively as if searching for an intruder. "Have you seen anyone in the woodland? Has anyone been to the shrine? Have you seen my mother there?"

I thought of the morning after they had brought the king home when I had met Olympias coming up the path from the forest.

"I saw her once – on the path that leads from Gaia's shrine."

I thought, *Should I tell him of the strange wax figure and the amulet?*

Alexandros drew in a long breath. "If she comes to father's bedside and brings him medicines, wine or cake, keep them from him!"

His words alarmed me. I remembered seeing the Dragon's Fire the night of the celebration of Poseidon on the beach. Should I tell him of that portent? I did not trust myself to speak more of his mother lest I blurt out something unseemly. I had grown fond of Alexandros, looked to him as if he were a brave older brother. Fate had intertwined our lives. I owed my life to him. I simply replied, "I will tell Theon."

"Yes, you must!" Alexandros said. Then he turned and walked away.

That evening, as we sat eating the barley soup Theon had prepared, I told him about my encounter with Olympias and how I had found the wax figure with the strange amulet inscribed with the peculiar markings on the shrine.

Theon paused a while, his brow creased. "It sounds like Egyptian magic," he said. "You see, Olympias practices such things and has since her youth."

He told me how Olympias had been influenced by an Egyptian shaman pharaoh who had come to Pella to ask Filippos's help in driving the invading Persians from his land.

"She embraced his beliefs," Theon explained. "From then on she began to worship their god, Ammon." He leaned back in his chair as he related the tale and stroked his beard. "She was a young girl then, your age, and newly married to the king. This shaman – Nectenabo was his name – convinced her she would be visited by the golden snake of Ammon and give birth to a miraculous child. Soon afterwards, she gave birth. That child was Alexandros." Finally he said, "Perhaps she wants the king healed – or perhaps not. We must be aware. Olympias is a spiteful woman, one never to be crossed."

The weeks dragged on. The king mended slowly and gradually his strength returned. One morning when I came he was propped on his pillows drinking a cup of wine. He looked fresh, his eyes bright and alert, his face ruddy, his russet hair and beard newly trimmed. He smiled and greeted me, lifting the wine cup in a salutation.

"Sir," I scolded. "Theon said no wine until the wound is completely healed."

"Nonsense!" Fillipos snorted. "Where is Theon? Tell him I want to leave this bed!" He struggled to sit, his wounded leg stiff in its wooden splint.

"You must not, sir."

But he was determined, and when he tried to stand he fell back, wincing in pain.

I stood by the bed and asked, "Is there anything else you need, my lord?"

I felt Filippos's eyes on me. He stroked his beard with a sly smile and said, "You must know me well, little Kelt."

As I tried to put a clean sheet of linen under him, he grabbed me by my waist and pulled me to him, his hand fondling me. "You would make a pretty bed mate," he said.

I felt a surge of boldness and gave him a long, clear look as I pushed away from him.

"Sir! I serve in the name of your god Askelapios and Airmed, my goddess of healing. I am here to tend your wounds!"

He seemed taken aback by my forthrightness and pulled his hand away. Then he chuckled and said: "You're a brave girl, my pretty little Kelt. I like your spirit. You serve me well!"

I remembered the palace gossip – how the king had taken many wives, some young enough to be his daughter. The house maids said he liked maidens, and boys too.

Just then, Theon arrived for his morning visit and saw Filippos sitting on the bedside.

"Whatever are you doing, sir?" he scolded. "You know it is too soon for you to stand!"

I sighed in relief that he had come. "The king wouldn't listen..."

"You'll damage your leg further, sir." Theon helped Filippos back and examined the bandaged leg. "The wound is healing but the bone has been badly shattered. You will walk again, but never the same as before."

"Nonsense!" Filippos grumbled. "A lame leg won't stop me! Girl, pour me more wine. And one for the physician."

I brought him the wine as he had bidden and he settled back against the pillows.

"You almost died this time, Filippos," Theon told him sternly. 'You're not a young colt anymore and you need to take care. Alexandros saved your life. You're a fortunate man to have a brave son such as he is."

"Yes, he's proven himself. Defeated the Maedi and drove them out." He set down his wine cup and looked up at Theon with a broad smile. "Quite a boy, Alexandros." He took a long draught of the wine and wiped his hand across his lips. "His mother wants to make a fancy boy out of him but he has proven he's worthy of inheriting the kingship. Now, if I can keep his mother from interfering in his life..."

I thought of my meeting with Olympias on the forest path, and how I had found the strange votives on the goddess's altar. How would she react when she learned Alexandros was in his father's favour?

BALLAD TWENTY A Prayer To The Sea God

We offer our praise to Poseidon,
master of the waves.
O god who carries us from land to land,
friend of sailors, merchants and traders,
Poseidon, earth shaker, ancient, mighty one!
We pray you guide our fleet safe to shore,
calm the rough waves.
Accept our gifts as we thank you, Poseidon,
for bringing our ships home safe.
We honour you with reverence and joy.

THE RETURN OF THE FLEET

Stanza One

My days hung heavy as I waited for Elidi's return. Each day I waited anxiously for news. Months went by, the snow melted on the hillsides, and the winter-browned grass was growing tall and green. Soon Spring would arrive.

The days seemed endless as I waited, with more heartache than hope, for the royal triremes to arrive back in Pella's port. It troubled me that perhaps Elidi's ship had been one that had gone down in the sea battle at Byzantium. Theon reassured me, telling me the royal triremes had put in at Amphipolis's port for repairs. But still I worried, and wondered if I would ever see Elidi again. How could I ever bear waiting for him each time he set sail never knowing if he would return to me again?

Finally, on a fresh, blowy spring day, the fleet returned. The sea shone blue, crested with waves that glinted silver. I hurried down through the city to the lagoon, pushing my way through the mobs of excited, shouting people. The whole city had come to greet the triremes and their crews. Pella's lagoon shimmered in the sunshine. In the middle of it, the island fortress that held the treasury and dungeons was lit with great cressets and the Makedonian royal standards fluttered from the ramparts.

Beyond the wide curve of shore, over the swathe of wetlands that surrounded it, shore birds swooped and soared, their shrill cries heralding the arrival of the fleet. Out in the harbour, beyond Pella's shallow lagoon, I saw the war triremes, sails furled. As the fleet came into view the people began to sing a paean honouring the sea god.

All praise to Poseidon, great god of the deep,

Lord of the waves, currents and tides.
We revere you and offer you praise!
  I watched as the ships skirted t
he narrow mouth where the lagoon met the sea. A cluster of small fishing boats escorted the triremes toward the lagoon. They glided in easily until they nudged the shore. I watched them row into the harbour, craning for a glimpse of Elidi on the deck.

The royal trireme was first in, sails furled, oars shipped. I could see the men on its deck, dark heads bent over their tasks. The smaller galleys banked their oars to let the royal trireme through. Ropes were flung and hitched, the stone anchor heaved overboard making a loud splash and the gangplank clattered as it fell to the shore.

The crowd surged forward preparing to greet the trierarchs and their crews. I nudged my way through to get closer, searching for Elidi at the helm. I pushed my way past to the edge of the lagoon and strained to see the men who were aboard the royal trireme's deck. The cold hand of despair gripped me when I did not see Elidi. Why was he not at the helm? Had some misfortune befallen him? Even the people had fallen silent. Many of them, like me, did not know if their loved ones were among those who had returned.

Fitted out in parade armour and plumed helmets, the trierarchs were the first to leave their ships, striding proudly down the *skalas* saluting the cheering crowds. The crowd roared and cheered, a deafening sound. Then suddenly they grew silent. There was a hum of wonder and cheers from the throng. "Alexandros!" Then another cheer, louder than before, and a gasp of wonder as Alexandros and his troupe of Companions arrived on horseback making their way toward the shore.

Alexandros looked splendid, dressed in burnished parade armour, carrying a shield emblazoned with the Makedonian eighteen-pointed star. He wore a helmet with a crest of red and white horsehairs, the hinged cheek flaps embossed with lions. His horse, Bucephalus, pranced and snorted in fine spirits.

I hardly recognized him as the same youthful huntsman who had rescued me that Samhain night in the dark forest. Alexandros truly was a prince! As always, Hephaestion, confident and proud, his tousled coppery hair framing his face, rode beside him on a chestnut steed. Behind them, rode the other Companions, well-born, fresh-faced youths, decked out in parade regalia, riding glossy horses with silver cheek rosettes, their bridles sparkling with gold pendants.

The crowd hailed him with cries of *"Basilakos!* Little King! Bravo, Alexandros!" The people's voices rose in a thunderous cheer when Alexandros saluted them. "Alexandros! Alexandros!" It was clear they adored him.

Alexandros and his Companions cantered their horses to the shoreline. Alexandros swung off his horse and came down into the crowd to greet them, calling some of the trierarchs by name, speaking to them in their Makedonian tongue.

"I bring a welcome from my father Filippos, the king," he called over the din of the townsfolk. "Brave men of the sea, my father wishes to honour you! There will be a celebration in the Great Hall tonight."

I stood in the crowd, still searching the deck of the royal trireme for Elidi. My heart felt empty as a tomb; I pressed my palms against my eyes to hide the tears. Finally, I turned away, full of despair. And then, I heard someone call my name, and saw Elidi striding down the *skala* to the shore. My heart leapt in my breast at the sight of him.

He strode over to me and took my hands, smiling. "My dear Olwen, how thankful I am to see you again!" He held me at arm's length and inspected me, brows lifted. "You are as beautiful as a young goddess...golden-haired and ravishing as Aphrodite!" When I blushed, he tweaked my cheek and bent to kiss me. "When I left you were still a maiden. Now you truly are a woman!"

He clasped me in his arms and I pressed against him. I felt so relieved that he was back safe I began to cry. Elidi lifted my face and wiped the tears from my eyes. "Do not cry, my Olwen. I am here now, and all will be well."

I gazed up at him, unable to speak. I had forgotten how beautiful he was. His hair fell in rough curls around his sun-browned face. His dark eyes were grave and gentle. He looked leaner and more weather-beaten. His homespun clothes were bleached by the sun and sea-spray, yet he carried himself with the style of a highborn laird.

"Father Poseidon brought us safely home," he said.

"I have waited so long for you to return. At last you are here!" I tried to hide the tremor in my voice and blinked back my tears.

"There were storms," Elidi explained. "Then we put into Amphipolis's port to repair battle damage to the ships. I am sorry, dear Olwen, if you despaired. I thought of you every moment."

"Why didn't you send me a message? I was so afraid. I offered votives at the shrine every day!" I pressed close to him, comforted by the warmth of his presence. "Thank the gods you have returned safely home."

He led me through the crowds of townsfolk to a stone bench by the edge of the lagoon. We sat in silence awhile, not speaking, just gazing at one another. I could see he was war weary. He did not speak of the naval battle at Byzantium. He listened quietly as I spoke of the healing arts, how I had spent my time helping Theon tend the sick. I felt the warmth of his arm around my shoulders, saw the tenderness in his smile. Elidi had beguiled me. I had known him for little more than a year, but it seemed a lifetime to me.

As we sat in quiet contemplation on the bench, we had not noticed the crowd had grown quiet and began to disperse. Then I saw Alexandros striding toward us.

Elidi rose to greet him, fist to brow. "Alexandros! It is an honour."

"Greetings, Phrygian!" Alexandros returned the salute. "My father is proud of you and your shipmates. The royal triremes fought a mighty battle at Byzantium." He greeted me with a smile and put his arm around my shoulders. "This

234

girl, Olwen, the little Kelt, helped save my father's life. She is an honourable maiden. You must treat her well." He smiled at me and said: "You have chosen well, little Kelt. The Phrygian is an honourable man!" He saluted Elidi again. "Tonight, you and your shipmates will be honoured at the feast! My father wishes to pay tribute to the crews." Then he turned and walked away to join his Companions.

An honourable maiden. Alexandros's words filled me with pride yet struck a chord in me – a feeling of uncertainty I had struggled with from that night on the beach when Elidi had professed his love for me. I thought of my life, of gods and fate. What if Alexandros had not rescued me? What would have become of me? From my birth I had been dedicated to serve the goddess as a healer. Before he had departed for Byzantium, Elidi had said he would ask Theon for permission to marry me. Could I forsake my pledge and marry him?

Stanza Two

We left the lagoon and made our way into the city. Pella's marble temples and grand houses sparkled in the afternoon sun. We pushed our way through the crowds in the sprawling, busy marketplace and along the narrow streets then up the cobbled road that led to the palace on Pella's hill.

By the time we reached the palace, we could hear the raucous voices of the celebrating men. The spirited music of flutes and drums, the sound of laughter and paeans of victory erupted from the Great Hall. The king's rowdy celebration to honour the trierarchs and their crews was well under way.

The king had mended slowly and though he was impatient to walk again he heeded Theon's orders. Theon had made it clear to him that he must not attempt to stand too soon, or he would damage his leg beyond repair. In spite of Theon's warnings, Filippos attended the feast, hobbling on a crutch, matching cup after cup of wine with his generals.

We walked past the Great Hall, under the shade of the palace's painted stoa, to the gardens where the first blossom of spring flowered in carved terracotta urns. When we reached Theon's house at the back of the palace grounds, we stood outside in the courtyard for a while, not speaking, as if both of us felt the same trepidation and were stalling the confrontation with Theon.

"Will you go to join the celebration?" I asked Elidi.

"We must talk to Theon first," Elidi said. "If he approves, and gives us his blessing to be wed, then I will celebrate!"

"What shall we do?" I asked finally.

"It has to be your decision," Elidi said.

Thoughts of the past came crowding in on me and I suddenly felt shaken and breathless. My voice caught in my throat. I remembered back to the day I had gone to the great stone circle on the Plain to join in the rites of the Midsummer. How afterwards, when I was destined to leave Caer Gwyn to serve the goddess on the Holy Isle, Fate had intervened. I had witnessed Sholto's brutal murder of his brother and from that moment on, my whole life had changed. If Alexandros had not rescued me that Samhain night in the forest, I would not be alive now to pursue my destiny. The seers say you cannot deny what has been portended. I felt wretched and small. It seemed as though I was continually searching in the depths of my being for an answer. My heart pounded with the enormity of the decision I must make.

I took a sharp breath. "I was born a child of the Druids and from birth I was meant to serve the gods. I have known no other life."

Elidi took my hands in his. Through his touch I felt the warmth of his confidence and love and leaned against him, his arms enfolding me.

"You are right, Olwen." Elidi said gently. "You must serve the gods as you were born to. Learn all you can from Theon and follow your destiny." He looked deep into my eyes. "I serve the sea gods, you serve the healing gods. But that does not stop us from loving one another. And truly, I believe we are meant to be one. Aphrodite and Eros have willed it."

I took a few moments to compose myself. I thought deeply over what he said. It was true, the god of love had brought us together. Surely it was meant to be that we should marry and still serve our gods.

I raised my eyes to look steadily into his. "Yes, I want to marry you," I said. "But first we must speak with Theon. He is my guardian and counsellor. If he gives his permission, it will be so."

Stanza Three

Theon was at his table studying his scrolls. He looked up, his head tilted, his brows creased.

"Where have you been? I have been waiting to show you this book I found that explains the procedures for removing arrow heads from wounds." He laid down his scroll and stood to greet Elidi. "Ah...so finally you have returned! We heard about the sea battle at Byzantium. Olwen feared for you; I am pleased to see the gods brought you back safely."

"Yes, sir," Elidi said. "Many ships were lost, and it was good fortune ours was one that survived the battle." He looked at me and smiled. "I have come to ask for your blessing, sir."

"A blessing? From me?" Theon seemed puzzled. Then he studied our faces and his stern expression softened, but he remained silent, gazing from Elidi to me.

Elidi spoke up boldly. "Yes sir. We wish to marry and for this we need your blessing."

Theon hesitated for a long moment as he considered what Elidi had said. Theon was always frank. "Have you thought this out well?" He peered at me under his dark brows. "How old are you, Olwen? You know, Greek girls are given in marriage as young as twelve. You must be well past the age of most betrothals."

"I'm seventeen at the next midsummer, and I love Elidi," I stammered. I felt my cheeks blush red.

Theon tilted his head, his brows creased and he nodded. "Ah yes – a maiden well ripe for marriage." He turned to Elidi. "And you, Elidi? You are no longer a youth but are you ready to take a wife?"

Elidi reached out and took my hand. "Yes sir, one that I love."

Theon stroked his beard and looked at both of us sternly. His expression was sober and solemn. "Love is fickle – especially for one such as you who lives his life on the sea. I know the life of the seamen – women in every port, enough to suit your fancy."

Elidi's face reddened. "I...I promise, sir," he stammered. "I promise I will be faithful!"

Theon's countenance grew more solemn. "And you, Olwen, what about those long months Elidi is at sea? What then? And will you forgo your vow to serve the goddess as a healer?"

"I will be with you when Elidi is away, and I will tend the sick with you."

Theon paused, as if seeking words. He looked at Elidi straight in the eyes. "I trust you. I know you are a good man."

He glanced at me warily, his brow furrowed, then he put out his hand and took mine. "Very well, if you wish it to be so, I will give you my blessings." Theon reached out and offered his hand to Elidi. "As Olwen's guardian I give you per-mission to wed."

My heart-beats raced and I took a deep breath. I tried to respond but my words would not come. Theon smiled at me. "You have chosen well."

"And I will not forsake you, Theon," I said, grasping his hand in both of mine. "You are like a father to me, and you are my teacher. I will still serve you, and the goddess, for that is my calling."

A smile lightened Theon's face. "Olwen is a virtuous maiden, and a wise, quick learner. I have entrusted her with knowledge of the healing arts. She has been a willing student and has proven herself adept as my assistant in tending the sick and injured."

Elidi put his arm around me. "For this I am proud of her, sir. Truly, Olwen is dear to my heart, dearer than anything. Thank you, sir, for your blessing. I know you will care for Olwen when I am away at sea."

Theon cleared the table of his scrolls and took three silver goblets from the shelf. He poured wine in them and passed one to each of us. "We will drink to Eros and Aphrodite, and ask for their blessings."

We raised our cups and spoke the words of blessing together:

"O Immortal Aphrodite, hear our prayers.
Bestow blessings on our hearts.
Eros, god of desire, we call on thee.

> ***Smite our hearts with your golden arrow.***
> ***May our love be enduring."***

I added a blessing for my own goddess as well.

> ***"Branwen, goddess of love and beauty,***
> ***weave a circle of light around us***
> ***and grant us thy love and protection."***

Elidi raised his cup. We drank the wine in silence and spilled the dregs. There was no need for more words.

A blast of trumpets came from the courtyard and the mighty roar of cheers.

"The men are honouring the King," Theon turned to Elidi. "You must join your friends in celebration, for the gods have brought you safely back to us."

Elidi hesitated, but I pushed him toward the door. "Go now. And enjoy the festivities. We will have time to celebrate our good fortune tomorrow. You know I will be here waiting for you."

He kissed me and saluted Theon. "I thank you, sir, and I will offer a tribute to the gods on your behalf for your kindness." He looked down gravely at me. "I promise to cherish you and to be true to you, my dear Olwen."

"Will you join the celebration in the Hall?" I asked Theon. "The king will expect you to attend."

Theon laughed. "I tired of the king's banquets long ago," he said. "They'll drink until they are at each other's throats – old scores will be settled before the night is through, in spite of the feasting and joyful songs of victory and praise. And without a doubt Filippos will announce his next campaign."

I went with Elidi to the edge of the garden. Dusk was falling and as I watched him walk toward the banquet hall, I wondered how many times I would say goodbye to him, always wondering if he would return again. Yet I knew I loved him, and I was happy Theon had given us his approval.

I returned to the house and sat quietly while Theon bustled about preparing our evening meal, silently contemplating what had gone before.

Theon looked up from the pot of barley soup he was stirring. "We will leave Pella soon to return to the farmstead," he said. "It has been too long since we left there... two winters!. My service to the king is done for now. The crops must be sown, the animals put out to pasture."

The farmstead! I had longed for the quiet solitude of the countryside. Part of me worried, though, that I would be leaving Elidi, not knowing when we would be together again.

Theon must have sensed my trepidation. He set down his ladle and came to sit beside me, putting his arm around my shoulders. "No need to fret. The ships will stay in the port until the king declares another war. We will celebrate your marriage at my farmstead at the midsummer. We will invite friends from the palace and Elidi's shipmates. It's best we are away from the palace..." He gave a little cough. "And Olympias's meddling."

Although I was a foreigner and not part of the royal court, I was a guest-friend of Alexandros's and to ignore his family would be considered a slight. I thought back on the celebration for Dionysos, remembered the drugged wine, the Thracian maiden, Olympias's ancient witchcraft and I understood the wisdom in Theon's advice. I knew if Olympias should disapprove of my marriage it would cause a tempest in the women's quarters. I didn't want my wedding to be turned into a cult orgy such as the one I had witnessed at the winter rites. Would ignoring the royals be considered a slight?

"The queen wouldn't dare meddle, would she?"

Theon sighed. "Perhaps not. You are a guest in the palace and Elidi is the king's helmsman. But if we hold the nuptials at my farmstead..."

"But what about Alexandros? We must tell him. What if he tells her?"

"Alexandros knows his mother's wiles," Theon assured me with a smile. "Olympias need not know. It will be a family affair – my friends will be invited, not the palace sycophants." He gave me a comforting pat on my shoulder. "Don't worry. Olympias will not meddle in your marriage and the king is too occupied with his battle plans."

Theon went back to the hearth and scooped a ladle of soup into a clay bowl, handing it to me. "Barley soup," he said," Hearty and healthy. Soup soothes the soul." He patted my shoulder and pulled up a chair to sit at the table. "Don't fret. You have chosen well Olwen. Elidi is a man of noble purpose, and he will be a faithful husband, I am sure. But you must be prepared for those long months he will be absent, and you must not grieve for this."

"What if there is another war?" I asked

Theon put down his spoon and paused, a frown creasing his brow. "There is quarrelling among the Greek city states and I know the king is determined to take control. I expect, as soon as he's well enough..."

"Well, if it's a land battle perhaps he won't need his navy for that," I replied, trying to sound cheerful.

"Oh yes, he will!" Theon said. "The king will use his war galleys to guard the coast and fend off the Greek navy."

"The royal fleet is in the sea god's favour," I said bravely. "I must trust that Elidi will always return to me."

Theon let out a long slow breath then turned his gaze toward the flames on the hearth. "Yes, you must believe he will always return."

That night I lay awake thinking of the marriage tryst Elidi and I had made. It was my choice to be Elidi's wife, but memories of Caer Gwyn flooded my mind. If only Essylt were here to share my joy. I had always dreamed one day I would go home again, but if I married Elidi I knew that dream would never be realized. I fell into an uneasy sleep, haunted by the longing I always felt for my homeland.

I dream I am hiding in the glade of trees below Caer Gwyn's high fortress, the same place I hid when I witnessed Sholto murder his brother. Someone is calling to me and I know it is Essylt's voice I hear – Essylt, my

239

aunt and protector, my assurance of safety. From my hiding place I see her running down the path. I try to call back to her but she cannot hear me.
Stanza Four

The God speaks and says: I am the shining tear of the sun. I am the dew that falls on the grass. I am the nourishing rain. Who, but I, knows the secrets of the season?

In the month of Artemesios, when the spring rains began to fall, as I was busy packing up our possessions in anticipation of our return to the farmstead, news came from the palace that the king had called a War Council.

"Filippos's ambition is to control Greece," Theon explained. "The Greek City States have been quarrelling and he must secure their loyalty before he makes war on the Persians. He has announced he's sending envoys south to negotiate with them. The king must use all his bargaining power if he hopes to make peace with Athens."

"If there is to be another war will Elidi have to leave?" I thought of our marriage plans for the coming midsummer. Would the Fates intervene and take Elidi away from me again?

"It is a diplomatic mission," Theon assured me. "The royal fleet will not be deployed unless the talks fail. If there is to be a war, it will be a land battle."

Even though Theon tried to reassure me, the sounds of war rang through Pella's cobbled streets. The king's wounds had mended and he was again able to endure a day on horseback. Every day he rode to the drill field with his men, drilling the phalanx. Each day councils were held as the generals prepared for war.

One morning Elidi came to tell me the triremes were setting sail to patrol the Makedonian coast. "I will return by midsummer," he assured me. He put his arm around me and drew me close. The pain of parting twisted inside of me. I took a long breath and started to speak but he put his finger on my lips.

"No, Olwen. Do not speak. Our paths must separate for now, but we will be together again soon."

"I will love you forever," I said. My voice quavered. I felt sad to see him leave again, but I remembered Theon's words: *'The men of the sea are like feathers on the wind, drifting from sea to shore. They have dedicated their lives to Poseidon and must go wherever the sea takes them.'*

This time I took comfort knowing Elidi was not sailing into a sea-battle, and if the king's mission to the Greek city of Corinth was a success and the Greeks agreed to his terms, he would return home soon.

I spent the days helping Theon prepare for our move to the farmstead. I was happy to be leaving Pella and returning to the farmstead, away from the conflicts in the palace and talk of war. Two winters had passed since we had left there, and I knew Theon was anxious to return to his quiet life in the countryside.   There would be new lambs in the fold, and crops to be sown. I, too, longed for the tranquility of the countryside, far from the palace intrigues.

The night before we left Pella I paid a last visit to the woodland shrine to leave a tribute, and pray for a safe journey. The shrine had been a comfort to me during our stay at Pella. I prayed to my Keltic goddess, Branwen who like me had left her homeland and fallen in love with a man from a faraway tribe.

"Branwen Goddess of love, it is a heavy burden I bear. Goddess, protect Elidi and let him return safely."

I felt full of trepidation, worried perhaps this time, something dire might befall Elidi's ship. Yet I knew I must trust the goddess, so I quickly put the thoughts out of my mind.

Stanza Five

The day of our departure, before the sun rose, Alexandros came to bid us farewell. With the king planning his new conquest, we had seen little of him. His face was flushed, and I sensed his eagerness. He said he had been away at the old palace of Aigai studying his father's battle plans and training a squadron of peltasts.

"Father has formed two new squadrons and has given me command of one. He is determined to take Greece. It's been a boiling cauldron for years, but until now the city states haven't dared to challenge him." He paused for a moment, his brow creased as if in deep thought. "Perhaps, after Perinthos and Byzantium and because of his almost fatal wound, they think he's weak and will be easy to vanquish. Just watch! Father is not one to shirk a challenge!"

What Alexandros said concerned me. Once again I felt those nagging trepidations, worrying about Elidi. Theon must have noticed my concern and put a comforting arm around my shoulders.

"Do not fret, Olwen," he said. "All will be well."

Alexandros escorted us out of the palace to the north gate of the city, riding on his horse ahead of our mule-cart, his faithful hound Peritos loping at the Bucephalus' heels. He promised to visit us. "I will come and bring you quarry from my hunts once I am free from my soldier's duties," he assured us, "Father has kept me busy drilling the peltasts so there has been no time for hunting."

We bade him farewell. I watched as he rode back toward the city. I was glad to be leaving Pella, but I would miss our visits with Alexandros.

As we set out from Pella, the sun had started its journey across the sky leaving behind the city and the palace that crowned the acropolis hill. It was a splendid day, cool and clear. Beyond the city, the land stretched out in green pastures where a river flowed through marshy wetlands thick with reeds where storks and herons nested. The land was dotted with ash groves and small copses of terebinth and oak trees. Yellow mallow and blue iris bloomed on the grassy slopes. Flocks grazed among the olive groves and vineyards by stone-built farmsteads. I thought of Caer Gwyn. At home, the alder would be in bloom and the winter floods receded. It would be the Ash Month and the gorse would be lit on the hills honouring the shepherds, as the new shoots would provide food for their sheep.

Theon told me stories as the mule cart rumbled along the rutted track. "I will tell you the story of Demeter, the earth mother, and her daughter Persephone who was enticed by Hades to his dark realm of the Underworld." He swept his arm out toward the fields. "All the crops and blossoms, the leaves on every tree, died the day Persephone left earth. So great was Demeter's grief that the land became bleak and cold. No seeds sprang up, no crops grew. Everything perished." He paused, looking out toward the fields again. "Zeus, the father, knew of Demeter's grief and sent his brother Hermes to escort her to Hades to plead for Persephone's release. When, finally, Persephone returned to Earth, everything began to grow again. That is why Persephone is known as the Goddess of Springtime. She brings new life to the earth."

I blinked away a tear as Theon related the tale. I recalled my childhood in Caer Gwyn when Essylt would tell me the stories of Blodeuwedd, our Goddess of Springtime who was created by magic out of flowers. "Blodeuwedd was also known as Olwen, the name I was given," I said.

Far ahead the summits of the distant mist-shrouded mountains were still snow-capped. I sat at the front of the mule cart, a light warm breeze blowing through my hair. I breathed deep, inhaling the sweet fragrance of herbs in the green fields, feeling the presence of the land.

It was our delight when, after a day's journey, we saw the homestead in the distance. Theon and I looked at each other joyfully. Theon cheered. "We are home at last!"

As we drew closer, I felt a sense of relief. The farmstead had become a comfort to me, a safe place away from the turmoil of Pella and the frightening talk of war.

The young man who had been sent by Alexandros to tend the farm during Theon's absence came out to greet us. "Welcome! It has been my pleasure to share your hearth, sir. Your flock has been well tended. There are six new lambs born this spring and the hens are laying. I've tilled the garden plots and sown the seeds. There will be a good crop to fill your larder this year!"

Theon paid him generously for his help "My home is always yours,' he said. "There will be a wedding at midsummer." Theon looked over at me and winked. "You must come with your family to help us celebrate. Olwen will marry Elidi, one of the king's helmsmen. It will be a grand affair, befitting a maiden who has been like a daughter to me."

I blushed when he said "daughter'. In truth Theon had become to me like the father I had never known. It seemed a long time ago that I had been taken from Caer Gwyn and I realized then just how much I had grown to love Make-don and this man who had become my protector.

While Theon unpacked his medicine and surgical chests, I went out to the field to gather fresh thyme and oregano and a basket of wild roses to make a concoction of honey, bee pollen and oil used for healing potions. I thought back to the days when I went with Essylt to collect herbs for healing. The rumblings of war in Pella were far behind us here, though I still remembered those days when Caer Gwyn had been clouded by war-talk, and threats from invading tribes and cattle raiders.

There was a peacefulness in the Makedonian countryside that set it apart from the world we had left behind. I sang as I collected sage to smudge the cottage and offer blessings. Although I longed for my homeland, the gods had brought me here to dwell with Theon and serve them as I had been destined to do. By midsummer, Elidi and I would marry. This was my home now. I was safe here and I felt blessed.

BALLAD TWENTY-ONE A Midsummer Marriage

A Hymn to Branwen, Goddess of Love.

Branwen, daughter of Llwyn, goddess of love
bless this new beginning.
Your love is all encompassing, unwavering.
Help me to stand strong.
Give me the gift of hope.
Fill my heart with love.
I feel your compassion, dear Goddess.
You have wiped away my tears
and opened my eyes,
so I feel the joy and beauty around me.
I honour the power of your love
with gratitude and blessing.

A BALLAD FOR LOVERS

Stanza One

At last, mid-summer arrived with its fruitfulness. The hills were bright with yellow gorse and the fields lush green. In our garden, the orchard was abloom with pink and white blossoms. Far across the fields I heard the bleating of the sheep and the cries of a plow man encouraging his oxen. The Spring days had passed quickly yet it seemed I had been waiting forever for Elidi to arrive from Pella. Soon it would be our wedding day.

The wedding rites would be held at Theon's farmstead. We decorated the cottage with gilded garlands and pots of fresh flowers. Amphorae of wine had been delivered from the local vineyards and Theon hired some of the local farm wives to prepare a lavish feast.

I waited anxiously for Elidi to arrive from Pella. Word had come from the city that the king was planning a new campaign and I worried Elidi might be sent back to sea.

Then, one morning, on a day the rain had fallen and everything was fresh and smelling sweet, as I stood gazing out across the fields I heard the hoof-beats of an approaching steed. A lone rider galloped toward the homestead and as he came closer, my heart raced when I saw it was Elidi.

He reined in the horse and dismounted. I ran to him and we embraced.

I leaned against him and felt the dampness of his clothes. "You rode here through the rain?"

He held me at arm's length. He lifted a lock of my hair, then raised it to his face, breathing in its fragrance. "Yes," he said. "To be with you."

I reached up and ran my hand over the stubble of beard on his face. He looked fatigued. His face was pale and his eyes were weary.

"Your clothes are wet. Come inside and I'll light the fire so you can dry off." I took his hand. "I waited for you every day!"

His teeth flashed in a tired grin. "Is there a pot of warm broth on the fire?"

"Yes," I said. "And wine. Come, Theon will be waiting for news from Pella."

He let his horse loose to graze and I led him through the garden to the house.

Theon greeted Elidi with a warm embrace and the two sat talking while I prepared them bowls of steaming broth.

"What is the word from Pella?' Theon asked.

Elidi sighed wearily. "More war talk. Filippos is negotiating with the Greeks. Rumours are he plans to invade."

Invade! That very word sent shivers down my spine. I set the bowls of steaming broth down in front of them. "No more talk of war," I said. I tried to sound cheerful, but my heart clenched at the thought of another war which would mean Elidi would once again be obliged to sail away. "Let's talk about our marriage."

Elidi set down his spoon and reached out to grasp my hand. "Well most certainly, my darling Kelt. It will be a grand celebration." He turned to Theon. "Will you see that the villagers are invited? And we will have guests from the palace."

"Will Alexandros come?" I asked.

Elidi shrugged. "That will depend on Filippos's war plans."

"War plans or not, this will be a grand celebration." I tried to sound cheerful, but the thought Elidi might be called back to sea, sent a chill through my body, spirit and soul.

Elidi reached out and took my hand. "Nothing will hinder us from marrying, my love. Not even the king!"

Stanza Two

It was the custom in Makedon to share the days before the wedding with friends. Theon explained that the Makedonian marriage celebrations lasted three days.

"First," he said, "there is the *prouaulia*, the wedding preparations. Then the *gamos* which is the wedding ceremony. And afterwards there is another cele-bration called the *epaulia,* your wedding night."

Our Cymry weddings were different than the Makedonians. We would gather in a circle outdoors under the yew trees, barefooted to be close to

245

Mother Earth and make offerings to Branwen our goddess of love, and Brigid, bride of the Earth and keeper of the hearth.

Theon invited his neighbours from the nearby farmsteads and several choice guests from the palace at Pella including the Nubian Xenon and Aricia. who would act as my bridal attendant. Each day the house was full of people. There was music, singing and laughter. Because I had no dowry, the country women brought rolls of weaving, trinkets and necklaces they heaped on the table. Aricia brought a gift of perfume, an exotic incense from a world far away.

"You'll smell like the wind in springtime- sweet, flower scented," she said.

Theon made a simple speech and lifted a golden goblet to pour a blessing, offering a silver drachma to Aphrodite for a fruitful, happy marriage.

"Immortal Aphrodite, weaver of wiles, come hither, with thy divine countenance. Bring blessings, stir the lovers' hearts."

The guests cheered and lifted their cups in response, calling out blessings of good fortune, as they sang a wedding song honouring Hymen, god of wedlock.

> *Sing the hymn.*
> *Wedlock must be honoured.*
> *Sing to Hymen, Apollo's song,*
> *to Hymen, god of wedlock.*
> *Raise up your voices,*
> *wedlock must be honoured.*
> *Sing to Aphrodite, goddess of love.*

Stanza Three

My wedding day began with a nuptial bath of scented oils. Fresh water was brought from the spring, carried in a clay vase by a farmer's child who was given the special honour of bringing the bath water to the bride. I was a modest girl; it made me blush being surrounded by all the village women as I sat naked in the tub while I was scoured and scrubbed. An old village crone dried me with towels of soft fleece and anointed me with fragrant rose-scented oil.

"Ach, my child," she crooned, "This mystical bath consecrates your maidenhood and ensures you will give birth to healthy children."

The women fussed over me. I was veiled and dressed in a gown of ivory silk and a robe of scarlet. Aricia braided my hair and placed a crown of roses on my head.

"The veil means purity," Aricia explained. "It shows that you are an unblemished girl, pure and chaste."

I looked at myself in the mirror and saw an older face than mine – a stranger's face, a girl older than I remembered. My steady grey eyes looked back at me, and I smiled. So much had happened since I had come into

Theon's care. I had been a frightened girl of fifteen then. I was still a modest girl, but one who was much wiser.

Because it was our Keltic custom, I had convinced Theon to hold the wedding ceremony outdoors, He agreed, and just as it would be in Caer Gwyn, our guests would form a circle under the spreading branches of the plane tree, joining hands around me to celebrate Mother Earth, giver of life and sustenance. The day was warm with a gentle breeze wafting from the hills and birds trilling from the tall shade trees.

As it was the custom, before the wedding Elidi had gone to stay with his friends at the neighbouring farmstead. I had not seen him for several days until that moment when he stepped into the circle and came to stand beside me. He looked like a vision of Eros dressed in a blue trimmed white tunic, his dark hair crowned with a wreath of flowers.

I felt a glow of happiness surround me. The sound of flute music swirled around me as the women pulled me forward toward him. He held out his arms to receive me while a group of village maidens sang the wedding song.

A shaven-haired priest dressed in white linen robe waited in the centre of the circle holding a basin of sacred water. Elidi and I stood before him as he prayed to Aphrodite, willing her to bless us.

The priest asked, "Do you come willingly to this marriage?"

"Yes!" Elidi said in a loud, firm voice.

I replied in a quieter voice, finding it hard to speak aloud. "I do... come willingly."

"Do you vow fidelity to one another? Will you care for each other for the rest of your lives?"

I repeated the wedding vows, looking into Elidi's eyes as I spoke the sacred words. "I give my body to you, so we might be one. I promise always to love you as you love me."

Elidi smiled and said, "I promise always to be true as I offer myself to you. May we be together 'til death parts us asunder."

The incense in the golden censor was lit and the sweet smoke swirled heavenward. Then the priest poured libations from a golden cup and spoke the names of the gods. I whispered the words with him, though the rites were not familiar to me.

The priest anointed us with the sacred water and more prayers were said. As was their custom I offered a lock of my hair to the goddess Artemis, who would provide a smooth transition from my youth to my new life as a wife. It was laid on the altar while the priest intoned hymns in a droning sing-song voice. I also said a prayer to my goddesses, Branwen, Goddess of love and Brigid, Keeper of the Hearth.

Elidi lifted the veil from my face and bent to kiss me. "Dearest Olwen, we will be together until the end of time," he whispered.

I clung to him, wishing his embrace would never end. "I will love you forever," I whispered.

A lavish wedding feast had been prepared by the neighbour women. There was a profusion of dishes – baked fish, sweet greens gathered on the hillside, and honey cakes. Amid the heaps of bride goods, the torch-lit room was full of merry-making guests. The music shrilled, everyone shouting over it. The wine flowed freely. As the goblets were emptied some of Elidi's friends began to sing a skolion. When Theon brought in the ritual wedding loaf they cheered.

"Blessings on you! We raise our voices to honour you and bless your marriage!"

Elidi sliced the loaf with a knife and broke off a piece for me to eat. I savoured the taste of honey and spices, then waited as Elidi tasted his.

The guests rose to cheer us. We were now man and wife. Elidi leaned close to me and gazed at me with tenderness. "You are my beautiful bride, my little Kelt. I promise to always love you."

I raised my cup to him. "To my love. To Eros and Aphrodite." I gazed around with glowing eyes at the room full of friends. I had never felt so happy.

As twilight fell it was time to mount the mule-drawn carriage that was decorated with floral wreaths. It was our transportation to the neighbouring farmstead where the owner, a land baron of some renown, had agreed to let us spend our nuptial night.

Elidi's face shone as he smiled at me and took my hand to lead me to the wedding cart. The guests gathered around, their torches burning bright in the evening dusk, accompanied by the spirited music of flutes and drums.

A light breeze murmured through the quivering leaves of the trees. The gleaming stars shone all about in the sky. A silver moon flooded the shadowed earth with peaceful light. Elidi lifted me into the carriage and it started down the road followed by a torchlight procession while the music of flutes and *kitharas* played, the tasselled mules harnesses tinkling with little bells.

The celebrating crowd followed the wedding cart, across the fields toward the little stone house where we would spend our wedding night. The guests carried baskets of flowers and fruits and threw wild rose petals over us as we alighted from the cart and entered the cottage. The maidens sang special songs which Elidi said were to scare away evil spirits and help us have a male child. I blushed as I realized then, my maidenhood was over. I was now Elidi's wife. What would the future bring? I prayed it would bode well for us.

It was time for us to enter the marriage chamber where a bed had been prepared with fresh linen sheets and hand-woven blankets of soft wool. Outside the door a chorus of maidens sang the bridal song. Others flocked into the house behind us tossing rose petals around the room as they sang a marriage hymn and a song they called an *epithalamon,* a hymn, to escort the bride to the marriage bed.

> *"Eros, sweet god of love and dance*
> *loose an arrow and pierce their hearts*
> *with enduring love."*

"It is a bedding song," Elidi winked and pulled me close. "A song of love and lust."

I stopped at the doorway of the bedchamber and faced the guests. I lifted my veil and let it drop to the ground. Elidi laughed as he picked me up and carried me over the threshold, kicking the door shut behind him.

The room was permeated with the fresh scent of perfume.

"A special essence for lovers' delight," Elidi explained.

I could hear the laughing and singing outside. Elidi sealed the shutters to keep out the prying eyes. We stood listening until their voices faded away and we heard the footsteps of the departing guests. At last we were alone. For the first time, I felt scared.

Elidi took my face in his hands. "You need not fret. You know I love you, and will always be by your side." He drew me close and kissed me. "My sweet Olwen." He took an object from his belt pouch – a gold cross inset with blue lapis. It had a loop at the top like a teardrop.

"This is my wedding gift to you. This is an *ankh* and it will protect you. It's a talisman from Egypt. It symbolizes earthly life and the after-life. May the omens be happy."

I held it out to admire it. I had never seen anything more beautiful.

"When I was a boy," he said, "before I became the king's helmsman, my father was a trader who sailed to Egypt. When I was old enough, he took me with him. I carried this talisman myself and now it is yours." He embraced me and kissed me so deeply I could scarcely breathe. "My dearest little Kelt, how I love you!"

He led me tenderly to the wedding bed strewn with rose petals. I hid my face against his shoulder.

Elidi smiled and smoothed a strand of hair back from my face. "Are you afraid?" He held me close against him. "There is nothing to fear," he said softly.

Gently he undid the shoulder clasp of my gown and unbound the girdle so the garment fell loose. I stood naked and shy. My heart beat fast as he drew me against him. I had no skill, no experience with men except my long-ago innocent childhood tryst with Teag. I felt anxious and vulnerable, but Elidi was very gentle with me.

"You are beautiful," he said. "You are my Beloved." He tossed aside his tunic. I had never seen his body naked. His bronze skin glistened with scented oil, a mat of dark hair curled across his chest. He was a vision of a Greek god, like the finely carved marble statues I had seen. Truly, a vision of Eros!

He turned up my face in his hands and kissed me. I trembled at his touch. He touch was delicate. His hands traced the contours of my body. I hid my face against his shoulder and ran my hands down his body hesitantly.

Elidi whispered softly in my ear as he laid me down. We lay together, my head on Elidi's shoulder, his hands gently caressing me. All the reluctance that had troubled me before my wedding night was gone now, even as I gave in to passion I kept my modesty and tried not to cry out, but when he entered me, I had a sudden memory of Sholto – his brutal attack that Samhain night in the forest.

Elidi sensed my fear and spoke softly in my ear, calming me. "What is troubling you?" I won't hurt you, my dearest Olwen."

I had never told him about Sholto, how he had attempted to violate me, perhaps kill me or at best sell me as a slave. How could I put into words the nightmare that had followed me ever since. My mind went back, far back, to that terrifying Midsummer day when I had witnessed Sholto murder his brother and because of it, he took me as his captive and luck-piece as he fled across the Narrow Sea. I recalled the day Sholto had slain the ship's boy who had been my only hope of rescue – and all the times I had tried to escape until he had put such fear in me that I succumbed to my fate and followed him like an obedient dog in his quest.

"What was his quest?" Elidi asked.

"To join the king's army. He was a warrior and a fearless one. He heard there was a king in the south gathering an army. An old crone we met knew something was amiss. She gave me a potion to put in his drink, so when we were near the border and I feared he would sell me as a slave, I put the potion in his mead. When he fell asleep I tried to escape, but he woke and caught me. He would have..." I began to shudder at the memory.

Elidi put his comforting arms around me. "I cried out and somewhere in the forest there were hunters. And then... he came... Alexandros, and saved me."

Elidi held me tight and wiped my tears away. "You are safe now, my little Kelt. You will never again have to fear. I am here to protect you."

I closed my eyes and gave myself up to the sensation of pleasure as he caressed me. As we lay together, I felt what we had done was not love making, but was a magic act of passion transforming me. Never had I felt so content. I was loved, and all of my past seemed to vanish away, as if receding to a distant shore. Elidi and I were one. The joy of it was overwhelming. I could not recall being happier than I was then. I felt safe and loved. The bewildered child in me had grown into womanhood, and I felt secure and content with my chosen path.

The next morning, when I observed my reflection in the mirror as I combed my hair, there was a rosy glow on my cheeks, a sparkle in my eyes. I was in love, and life could not have been better.

Stanza Four

Of all the others I could remember that summer was the most blessed. Each day Elidi and I spent together, sometimes tending chores around the farmstead, sometimes hiking the hills in search of herbs to fill Theon's medicine chests.

The days were full of sunshine and joy and I could not recall being happier than I was then. The bewildered child in me had grown into womanhood and I felt secure and content with my chosen path. I thought less each day of Caer Gwyn and no longer dreamed of returning there. I had Elidi now and his presence and love meant more to me than reviving the old memories.

One morning toward the end of summer, after Elidi and I had herded the sheep up the hillside, we climbed farther up the mountain path, scrambling over boulders and brambles to collect baskets of the pungent herbs growing among the rocks, herbs Theon used to brew healing teas. We picked busily for awhile, content with the deep silence and the company of each other. Once our pouches were stuffed full, we sat enjoying the silence. The air was fresh with the scent of sage and sweet chestnut. Below us the green fields and vineyards spread across the plain where a sparkling river snaked across the marshlands toward the sea. Birds chirped from the woodland and far off on another hillside, a shepherd's pipe sounded. As I sat on the rocky outcrop, Elidi's arm around me, I felt such serenity and happiness.

Suddenly, disturbing our reverie, Elidi raised his hand. "Listen!"

I heard the distant sound of hoof beats and saw, far down below on the road, a cloud of dust. Someone was riding toward the homestead. As the horseman drew closer, I could see he was carrying a banner with the emblem of the royal star.

"Look there!" Elidi said, squinting against the sun's glare. "It's a king's courier. What message is he bringing from Pella?"

A sudden chill passed through me. I gripped Elidis's arm. He patted my hand. "Don't fret, little Kelt. Perhaps they need me back at the port to oversee the new helmsman." He stood and waved at the approaching horseman, then he started down the hill. I followed him reluctantly. Elidi's cheerful reassurance could not quell the deep sense of foreboding I had. I thought of the king and Alexandros. Had there been some misfortune? What dire news was this horseman bringing us?

We reached the farmstead just as the courier rode up. Theon had already come out to greet him. "You have ridden long and hard on this hot day," Theon said. He offered the rider a flask of water to quench his thirst. "What news do you bring?" Theon was smiling but his voice was tense and I knew like me, he feared the news was not good. "Is it a message from the king?" he said. "Has Filippos fallen from his horse?"

"No sir," the horseman replied. He caught in a deep breath and steadied himself as he dismounted. "The king is well. But all is not well in the kingdom. Forgive me for disturbing you, sir, but the king has sent for you and the helmsmen, Elidi. You must both return to Pella at once. "

The courier looked over at Elidi. "Are you Elidi the helmsman?"

"Yes, I am the king's helmsman," Elidi said.

The courier handed him a scroll from his belt pouch. "You must return to your ship. The king has declared war on the Greek states and has ordered the royal fleet to sail south to Thermopylae. These are your orders. You must return at once."

I saw the troubled expression on Elidi's face. "When will they sail?" he asked.

"In a few days. While it's good weather, before the autumn storms."

Elidi glanced at me. He looked concerned as he handed the document back to the courier. "Tell the king I will come straight away."

I wanted to cry out to Elidi *You are married to me now, not the sea!* but I knew, like my vow to serve the healing gods, he had dedicated his life to Poseidon.

"So, Filippos has decided to wage war on the Greeks." Theon's grim expression bespoke his thoughts. His brow was creased, and his cheeks reddened. "This has been a war long in the making. He's always vowed to take over the Greek states. It's sure to be a battle that will surpass all others."

"Filippos is preparing the troops to march south to Chaeronea," the courier said. "You are also ordered to return to Pella. The king's aim is to control Greece. He has already sent a platoon to treat with the Thebans but so far, the news has not been encouraging. The Thebans are determined to take a stand against him. There is a rumour Persia has supplied them with weapons. I fear the other states will join them. Now, I have delivered you the message and I must return to Pella."

"Why has the king commanded me to come?" Theon asked.

"To help in the hospital tents, to treat the wounded," the courier said.

I felt a tremor shudder through me. "The hospital tents? On the battlefield?"

"I have a duty to serve the king," Theon said.

I took a deep breath and stepped forward beside him. "You are my father and mentor and you will not go without me. You must not. For you have taught me all I know and the goddess has blessed me with these gifts of healing. So I will go with you."

Theon reached out his hand and took my arm. "Olwen you need not. You will stay here and tend the farmstead."

"No!" I spoke in firm determination. "I must go with you. It is meant to be."

"As it is my duty to serve the king, I'll go back to Pella with you," Theon said to Elidi. He turned to the courier. "Tell the king I will return to Pella to serve him as he wishes."

The courier mounted his steed and we watched him gallop away across the field toward the next farmstead.

"Will you really go to battle too?" I asked. I was shocked at the idea Theon would put himself in jeopardy.

"I must. They will need me on the battlefield," Theon said. He had a grim look, his brow creased with a frown, and he bowed his head uttering a deep sigh. "Filippos is a warrior unlike any others. He will stop at nothing to rule all of Greece. There will be many, many casualties in this war, I can swear on that. More than ever before. And nothing is going to stop him!"

"But… but… you are old now…" I stammered, and caught his arm. "You cannot risk your life on the battlefield."

"I have a duty to serve the king. So I must go!" Theon said. He turned toward the house, his shoulders slumped. "I *must!*"

"Then I will go too. I will assist you as I always have," I said. "You cannot go without me. You must not. For you have taught me all I know and the goddess has blessed me with the gifts of healing, so you must take me too!"

"Olwen, this is *war!* A real war! It is no place for a woman," Elidi said. "You must stay here and tend the farmstead."

I caught my breath, felt a surge of blood rush to my cheeks. My eyes burned with tears. "I will not stay! I must go with Theon. It is my duty to be by his side as he tends the wounded. I will *not* stay here and tend the hearth. I have made a vow to the goddess to help those who needed me and I will never forsake my oath!"

Elidi stared at me, his dark eyes wide with alarm. "You are my wife! You *must* stay here! A battlefield is no place for a woman!"

In my mind I recalled the women of my tribe: brave Aeron, the ricon's daughter and Talia, the swords woman, her black hair adorned with hawk feathers, riding on her pony beside scar-faced Sholto. Thoughts of Caer Gwyn flooded my memory: Madoc's red-caped War Band, in their chariots. Tall, fearless warriors, a terrifying sight, bronze helms gleaming, some with hair spiked with lime, screaming curses against their enemies and crying the war paean as they rode out across the plain.

I put my hand to the gold raven torc I wore round my neck to show I was a Druid's child, and I remembered Lleu's words: *"Remember who you are! You are Olwen, Child of the Raven"*. The words of the bard's song came back to me:

> **"I am a child in swaddling clothes.**
> **I am a sword in a warrior's hand.**
> **I am the cry of the raven in the field of battle.**
> **I am Olwen, Child of the Raven."**

Elidi took my hands and looked deep into my eyes. "I know you, little Kelt. I know of your people. They are fierce warriors. And I see you have inherited their spirit. But you must think wisely on this. It will be a battle to end all battles, and Filippos will hold back nothing to make sure it is. You have never seen a battlefield. You have never stepped into the depths of Hades. It is no place for a woman."

Perhaps I had not been part of a battle, but I had witnessed enough to know what it meant. I recalled clearly, as if it was that day long ago, the ricon's carts heaped with the dead, the wagons with the wounded, the cart bearing Hywel, the ricon's favoured son, home from the battle, his body bloodied, the cries of woe and prayers to Dyrmwch Gawr, our god of war.

In spite of Elidi's pleas, I defiantly stood my ground. "I am Olwen, Child of the Raven. The Raven is a war goddess! *I won't stay here*!" I said firmly. "I will go wherever you and Theon must go."

"You must think carefully," Elidi said. "Do you want to risk your own life for the sake of an ambitious king's dream?"

I took a deep breath. "Yes," I said firmly. "I owe everything to Theon and I have given myself to you. I will not forsake either of you." I pulled away from him and ran after Theon into the cottage.

Our idyllic time together was over. That night I clung to Elidi as he whispered endearing words to me, trying to comfort me. "I cannot bear to be apart from you. But the king has decreed it and must be obeyed. We will be separated for a while, but not forever."

"Yes... you have been commanded to go." I took a deep breath, my voice thin as a drawn thread.

He drew me closer. "All we wanted was to be left alone," he said quietly. "Freedom is such a small request, yet the gods have willed it otherwise."

"Will the war last long?"

"Only until Filippos defeats them." He nestled beside me, his face buried in my hair. "Olwen, please, I beg you to stay here where you will be safe."

"No. I must go with Theon!"

"The battle ground.... the hospital tents... it is no place for a woman."

"But I am Olwen, and I serve the goddess." I said firmly. My voice trembled even though I tried to sound brave.

He sighed. "You are brave and stubborn," he said. "But I fell in love with you because of that. So, go if you must, and may the gods keep you safe."

Outside the window, the moon shone, a hard silver orb in the dark night sky. Its beams flooded into the room. I rested against Elidi, feeling the comforting warmth of his body.

"What is to become of us?" I asked.

"Only the gods know the future," Elidi replied.

The next morning, we poured a libation of wine to the gods and said our farewells. I was determined not to cry, not to let Elidi see me sad. I didn't want to spoil those happy days we had spent together that summer. But though I hid my face from him so he would not see my tears, I thought I might burst. I clung to him, not wanting to say goodbye, not wanting him to see my despair.

"You are a man of the sea," I tried to sound brave, but my voice trembled. "You must go. It is your duty to serve the king." I stroked back the dark hair that framed his sun-browned face.

"We will be together again when the gods will it," Elidi said. He held me close and kissed me once again, then mounted his horse and spurred it down the trail. As I watched him ride away, my heart felt like an empty tomb. I walked back to the cottage, not looking back, unable to keep the tears from spilling.

BALLAD TWENTY-TWO The Oracle

Sing goddess of the wrath of Makedon.
One man will flee the battlefield.
Another will be victorious.

Preparing for Battle

Stanza One

Theon and I spent the next days preparing for our departure. He hired the neighbour's son to tend the flock and gardens and I helped him load the mule cart with all our provisions: jars of medicines, bags of herbs, pliers and forceps, syringes, scalpels and other medical equipment we would need to tend sick and wounded soldiers. There was little time to think about Elidi. Still, I held some hope he would not have departed from Pella and I might see him again before the fleet sailed.

Within a week, we were on our way heading across the plain back to Pella. The late summer weather was hot, the wind still, the air redolent with the scent of ripening grapes and mowed fields where stacks of barley and wheat had been harvested.

We met other travellers along the way, mostly men and youths who were also going to Pella. They toted packs of personal items, and some carried short, curved swords or lances. Theon said they were going to join Filippos's army.

"He has a strong force of *peltasts*, mostly made up of men from the countryside. They're tough and strong and make good foot soldiers."

"What about the boys?" I asked. "Will they go to war too?"

"Every youth dreams of being a cadet in the army," Theon said. "They will go along to serve the soldiers and learn the art of war."

There were no women among them. Often the women from Caer Gwyn fought alongside the men, or at least followed them into battle. The Cymry were fearless women, unafraid to face the wrath of their enemies.

Theon left our mule-cart at the city gates with a driver who would take it up the back road to the palace. When we entered Pella, the city was in pandemonium. Excited crowds gathered in the agora and along the lagoon shore.

My heart sank as I scanned the harbour looking for the royal triremes. A troop of soldiers marched past us followed by a gang of excited youths. Weeping wives and mothers watched from the roadside and fathers stood proudly, arms raised to salute them. Other than a cluster of smaller boats, the king's ships were not in the port and I knew Elidi must have already sailed. I prayed to the god of war to keep him safe and bring him back home to me.

We made our way to the palace gate where we were greeted by more confusion. Royal women and servants stood huddled in groups in the courtyard watching as men streamed out of the Assembly Hall where the king had been holding a war council. By the looks of despair on their faces it was certain the news was dire. Theon was told a courier had arrived from the south announcing a marble tablet in Athens, that signified a peace treaty, had been torn down and the Greeks had declared Filippos as nothing more than a drunken barbarian. Filippos had used all his bargaining powers to make peace with the Greeks, but the Hellenic states had united and were assembling a large army.

Alexandros came out of the Council Hall followed by Hephaestion and some of his other companions. He looked surprised when Theon greeted him.

"Your father has ordered me to tend the hospital tents," Theon explained. "Olwen insisted on accompanying me"

Alexandros looked at me and frowned. "Women do not go to battlefields... unless they are camp followers." Then he smiled, his grey eyes sparkling. "But I know you, little Kelt. You will follow the goddess's wishes and will assist Theon with the wounded. For this you will be blessed."

A shrill cry from the entrance to the women's rooms interrupted. Olympias came down the steps followed by her handmaidens. She was dressed in a white bathing robe, her russet hair loose, spilling over her shoulders. Her handmaidens gathered around her, but she shrugged them off and strode angrily toward Alexandros.

Her voice was as piercing as the cry of a kite's. "So! Filippos has named *you* to lead the Royal Band. In the name of all the gods! He's assigning *you* to the front lines? Alexandros, you are still a boy! Filippos is deliberately putting your life in danger!" She threw out the name *Filippos* as if it was a curse.

Alexandros turned to face her and said calmly. "Mother, I *must* go, and you know it!"

She fixed Alexandros with a fierce stare and replied in a tone of bitter reproach. "So, you are a man now? I am your mother who bore you. I fought for your rights when Filippos would have shunned you like a stray dog in favour of any of his bastards. I have lived for you, have gone to any length for you to entrust you were given your rights. And now you take Filippos's part, and not mine! Now he has put you on the front lines where you might easily get killed!"

Her angry voice made heads turn and I heard breaths drawn from the Companions and the buzz of shocked voices.

Alexandros said nothing, but I could see her words had angered him. His fists were clenched and a crimson flush spread up his face, but he replied to her in a calm, firm voice "Mother, I serve my father willingly."

Olympias's voice dropped to a deep undertone as if she was uttering a curse. "Don't call that man your father! The day will come when you will learn who your true father is!" Then she turned and ran back toward the women's quarter, her face wet with tears.

Alexandros strode away with his Companions, calling back over his shoulder to us. "We will meet again, and may the gods keep you safe."

As Alexandros departed, Theon said: "Alexandros has only been in small skirmishes and border patrols before." His brow furrowed and I could tell he was concerned. "He rode at the head of his troops when he was sixteen but that was not the same as this battle...those were highland skirmishes. This time he's riding with his father and it will be a full-fledged war!" Theon had a worried frown on his face. "If Filippos doesn't move fast enough, the Greeks will invade his territories. The Thebans control the southern route into Athens and Athenian ships are already ranging the coast."

This news brought a chill rippling down my spine. What if the royal triremes were engaged in a sea battles? Would I ever see Elidi again?

Theon sensed my concern and put his arm around me. "Don't worry. Filippos is a master of war and his fleet is commanded by the best of his trierarchs. They'll block the Athenian ships from coming farther north. The real battle will be on the land. Just like *this* battle!" He gave a wry smile. "Since he was born Olympias has been waging a war with Alexandros over Filippos, trying to turn Alexandros against his father. Only the gods know how it will end!"

Stanza Two

We set off from Pella a little after sunrise, travelling in the hospital carts behind the army. The route went along the coast road, past fields where sheep and goats grazed peacefully in the meadows. Magpies and crows perched among the heather and scrub and set up a raucous crowing as we passed. Little shrines with offerings to the gods stood at every cross-road. Country folk waved laurel leaves and called blessings on the passing troops.

Soon the fields unfolded into little hills that sloped down into the inky blue sea where whitecaps, stirred by the wind, splashed onto a long stretch of narrow beach. We passed villages where stone houses clung to the hillsides People came out to cheer and offer food and wine to the weary soldiers.

The long trail of men straggled along the shore road, bearing southward.

In Thessaly we were joined by allied cavalry troops who Theon explained were expert horsemen. At night, cook-fires blazed through the camp. We shared a meal of bean soup and bread with the men, washing it down with wine. Their men's voices sounded around the camp as they laughed at jokes and sang songs, recalling old battle tales.

Days passed until we reached a place called Thermopylae, where there was a gap between the mountains and the sea. The army stopped here to pay homage at the grave mound of a famous spartan general.

"This is known as the Hot Gates," Theon explained. "Long ago an army of Spartans and Greeks came this way led by a brave general named Leonidas. His three hundred Spartans defeated the Persians here."

Dawn glimmered over the low hills. Along the road the stony heights were topped with remains of an old fortress once used to command the passes. I lost count of the days as we travelled farther south. The march seemed endless; the pace of the men slower.

As the sky lightened over the great bulk of a mountain Theon explained, "That is Mount Parnassus. On that mountain is the sacred oracle of Delphi where the gods dwell. We will stop at the sacred site," he said. "The king will make a sacrifice there and consult the oracle."

"What is the oracle?" I asked.

"She is the priestess who makes the prophecies, "Theon explained. "The king must consult the oracle before he goes into battle. She is always consulted before wars and at other times, because her words are sent right from the gods."

The thought of being in such a holy place made me forget any of the fears I had about facing the battlefields. "I pray the oracle will provide wise counsel for the king and the omens will be fortuitous," I said, trying to sound cheerful.

Theon sat under an oak tree, leaning his back against the gnarled trunk. His face was haggard with weariness. I handed him a cup of wine and a hunk of flat bread. Young as I was, I also felt my strength ebbing from the endless trek.

The marches were long and the pace slowed as we climbed the steep mountain tracks. By nightfall, we were too weary to talk.

I knew Theon was concerned for me. He felt my brow. "Your face is flushed. Do you have a fever?"

"It is burned from the sun," I said. I did not tell him every bone in my body was aching with weariness.

The army was encamped around us and the smoke from their fires filled the glade with haze. The sound of men's voices surrounded us. Amidst the low rumble someone strummed a mournful tune on a lyre. I was reminded of Lleu, the bard, and the memory of him playing his clarsach saddened me. I thought about my homeland, counting the months and seasons since I had left Caer Gwyn. Almost three years had passed! During that time I had grown to womanhood, acquired knowledge of the healing arts from Theon and married a Phrygian helmsman. Now, once again, I was facing an unknown future. A battle! Would I live to return to Theon's homestead and reunite with my husband?

A day's march later, the army reached the towering marble heights of Mount Parnassus where Theon said the ancient temples stood. The sun was setting behind the highest peak in a blaze of pink and magenta. We made our camp in the valley, below the grand pinnacles of the mountain range near a river.

"The king holds all the passes," Theon explained, "The army will stay here and wait while Filippos makes his visit to the holy shrine."

The river gleamed in the moonlight. Along its banks watch fires blazed. Alexandros rode up to our camp and greeted us. "Father is giving an audience to the Boeotian land barons," he said. "They're eager to give him the enemy's plans since the Athenians have betrayed them." He gazed out into the dark silence as if lost in thought. After a while he started to say something of the coming battle, then stretched out his hand toward Theon, his brow creased. He began to speak, then hesitated.

"Father has appointed me to head the right flank of the cavalry," he said. His face was flushed and I sensed his excitement and pride.

Theon's brows lifted. "For your first battle?"

Alexandros gazed as if in deep contemplation into the firelight. "Yes. My steed, Bucephalus and I. Our first big battle." He patted the horse's neck. "He's trusting me to vanquish the Theban Sacred Band."

I had heard the soldiers talk about the Sacred Band, an elite regiment of three hundred. Lovers, they said, each man, dreading disgrace in the eyes of his beloved partner, would fight together like one possessed. If one fell, the other would stand by his comrade 'til the last.

"Father will put an end to the Greek's dominance. We Makedonians, who Demosthenes of Athens curses and calls phony bastards, will be the conquerors," Alexandros said.

"You were born to perform great deeds, and you will accomplish this," Theon replied. But as Alexandros rode away, he shook his head and looked up toward the heights of the mountains. Delphi. "Aristoteles says: *The man who has an aspiration to excess is called 'ambitious'* Still, the boy is his father's son He is well trained in the art of war. So I pray he succeeds with his ambition."

Stanza Three

We left the river camp before dawn the next morning, following the king and his escort up the steep mountain track toward Delphi's sacred precinct. There the king would make a sacrifice and consult the fabled oracle about the coming battle.

Far beyond the deep ravine, a river wended through a valley lush with olive groves. In the distance, the sun glinted off the sea. When we reached the trail that led to Delphi's sanctuary the sky had lightened and the sun touched the high peaks like a flame, turning the snow-capped mountain peaks to gold.

We left our cart to walk up the path toward the sacred site. Two pairs of blue-tinted cliffs towered on each side of the sanctuary, their rock surfaces dazzling in the glow of the sun. I gasped in wonder at the first sight of the many shrines and temples that clung to the steep slope of the mountain, the sun glinting on the mellow old marble and painted pediments, bathing them in a golden light. I could never have imagined anything more beautiful! A feeling of serenity surrounded me. Truly, I could feel the gods there!

Below the terraced slope of the trail, there were more shrines and a circular temple that clung to the edge of a precipice. As we walked along the path, Theon pointed each one out to me.

"That is the Tholos and the Temple of Athena Pronoia. Those small buildings are where the priests dwell. Farther down the slope, there is a gymnasium where the Pythian Games are held. It is not only a great festival of running, leaping, wrestling and other feats of prowess, but also a festival of music, poetry and eloquence."

Some of the temples were painted. The sun glittered off the white marble and golden cornices of others. I had never seen anything so beautiful!

Theon led me farther up the trail. We came to a shaded glen where a spring of water cascaded from a cleft in the rocks into a mountain pool. The steep vertical cliffs surrounding the glade were clothed with ivy, the banks of the pool fringed with terebinth and laurel. Carved into the cliff-face beside the spring was an ornamental building with marble facade and niches for votive offerings. A young maiden sat under the laurel tree strumming on a lyre, its sweet sound soothing as a balm.

"She is a priestess of Gaia," Theon said. "That is the fountain house where the priestesses of Gaia dwell. This is the Castilian Spring. Before we enter the sacred site we must cleanse ourselves in the water and make an offering to the god, Phoebus Apollo."

He beckoned for me to sit under the shade of a gnarled olive tree. "We will rest here awhile," he said.

I was glad to rest after our long morning's trek. I sat under the shade of a plane tree and leaned my back against the trunk. I closed my eyes as I listened to the lyre's sweet notes and gurgling of the waterfall, and tried not to think of Elidi and what lay ahead.

Theon sat on the grass beside me. "Let me tell you the story about Phoebus Apollo," he said. "He is the most beautiful of all the gods. He came from the island of Delos. The laurel is his tree, and the dolphin and crow are sacred to him. Once this sanctuary was dedicated to Gaia, Mother Earth." Theon continued. "Her son, the serpent Python, dwelled in a chasm nearby. The young god, Phoebus Apollo, came here in the form of a dolphin from Delos. He slew Python, so now it is dedicated to Pythian Apollo, and the temple sanctuary is called Delphi. This is why the oracles are communicated by the Pythia, a priestess named for Python."

He stood and motioned for me to follow him to the edge of the pool. "Before we enter the Sacred Precinct, we must bathe in the sacred stream and purify ourselves. You see, Apollo is the link between gods and mortals, guiding us to know the divine will. Here we learn how to make peace with the gods, for Apollo is the purifier, the cleanser. Even those who are stained with the blood of their own kindred are cleansed.

Two temple maidens greeted us as we approached the spring and gave us sprigs of laurel to place at the shrine. One of them, who carried a painted clay ewer, beckoned for me to follow her to the spring. While a flautist blew on a double pipe, she scooped water into the ewer, poured it over my head and intoned: *"The gods be exulted. Let us praise them! Praise Gaia, Pythia and Apollo!"*

The icy coolness of the spring water sent a healing tremor through me. I felt all the weariness of the journey wash away in the soothing stream. I scooped some into my hand and drank, refreshing my thirst.

After the libations were made, the priestess dried me and another maiden brought fragrant oil made from the laurel to anoint me, murmuring a prayer to Apollo as she poured it over my hair and rubbed it into my scalp and temples, gently massaging my forehead while she whispered in a soothing voice: *"Phoebus Apollo, most beautiful of the gods, here at your throne where shadows darkened the truth. With unshaken faith we honour you."*

After the purification, Theon and I continued our walk up the hillside. The cloud-patched towering peaks of Parnassus loomed over us; a pure refreshing pine-scented breeze wafted from the mountains. The path from the spring led to a small agora with porticoes and stalls selling votive offerings. We entered the Sacred Way through an ornate archway and stepped onto the thick marble paving stones that led up the hill. On each side of the road were votive monuments and hundreds of gold, bronze and painted marble statues of the gods and heroes, including a large bronze bull and a massive serpent column that supported a tripod commemorating a famous battle. In the midst, towered the ancient temple of Apollo, its thick Doric columns bathed in sunlight.

Theon spread out his arms as he looked up at the majestic sight and proclaimed "This is the centre of the world. Apollo's oracle!"

The temple stood high atop a stone platform. Its ancient, blue-tinted columns, worn by time, were decorated with golden wheel-shaped ornaments.

"Those are oracular wheels," Theon said. "They are magic wheels called *inges.*"

A ramp led up to the Temple's entrance. "Inside, there is an underground chamber" Theon said. "There's a crevasse where the Pythia sits on a tripod, chewing laurel leaves while she inhales the mystical vapours from the chasm. Whatever the Pythia predicts will infallibly come to pass."

I wished I could go into this mysterious chamber to consult the wise old priestess. Perhaps she would convey a message to me from my people, from Essylt and my grandfather Maelgwyn's spirit.

"May we enter?" I asked.

Theon shook his head. "Women are not allowed inside"

"Who is Pythia?" I asked. "And why are women not allowed to consult with her?' I had hoped I might ask the priestess for a special prayer for Elidi, just as I might have consulted the priestess of my own people.

"She is a wise old crone selected from the village who has the ability to commune with the gods," explained Theon. He smiled at me. "Perhaps, like you, women often have more sense than men and do not need a Pythia to tell them what is best for them."

We climbed the steep path to the terrace. A group of men, some of them commanders and others ephebes who were the king's escorts, were gathered in front of a great stone altar. Some temple maidens gathered nearby in twittering groups while a flautist played a sacred hymn on his double pipe.

The remains of a black bull-calf smouldered on the altar. My mind went back to thoughts of my bull, Mithras, and that Beltane day when he had been sacrificed by the Druid, Bedwyn. All of my past life seemed so far away now, so long ago, and yet the images, the scars on my psyche were still raw when I thought of it

"This is the altar of Apollo where sacrifices are made before the Pythias is consulted." Theon said. "The king has already made his sacrifice and has gone inside the temple to consult with the priests before he meets Pythia. She will give him the oracle."

I could feel the tension in the excited buzz of the crowd as they waited for the king to emerge from the temple. Everyone knew whatever the Pythia told Filippos would somehow determine how the coming battle would fare.

I wondered where Alexandros was and while Theon spoke with the men to inquire, I wandered further up the trail. The path was lined with clusters of violets and cyclamen, the forest clearings loud with birdsong. Below me was the great curved arch of the theatre with its tiers of stone seats and high *parados*. I sat quietly, breathing in the sweet pine-scented air, and let my mind drift to thoughts of Elidi. I wished he could have been there with me. It seemed so long ago we had been together, it was hard to imagine it had ever been anything but a vague dream.

My reverie was disturbed by the sound of voices. A troupe of young men were coming down the path. I recognized them as Alexandros's Companions. They were laughing and jesting with each other. Alexandros was in their midst, his coppery hair tousled in the breeze, his sea-coloured cape fluttering around him. He didn't see me where I sat in the shade, turning as he passed to speak to his friend, Hephaestion.

I heard shouting from the temple grounds below, so I hurried down the path after them. The king had emerged from the dark secrecy of the temple. He stood on the top step of the temple portico, a sturdy man with a neatly trimmed beard, a leather patch over his blind eye. His body-guard, Pausanius, rushed up the steps to greet him but was quickly rebuffed.

The crowd cheered and cleared a path for the king as Filippos hobbled down the steps straight toward Alexandros who was waiting there with his Companions. Filippos was smiling, his face flushed. He put his arm around Alexandros's shoulders and drew him aside. The two spoke quietly together, then walked back down the Sacred Way, their escorts following close behind.

I noticed Pausanias lingered behind, standing in the shadows cast by the temple pillars. He was speaking to another youth who I recognized as Kassandros, the Regent's son. The two of them had their heads bent, whispering furtively.

Something about them sent a shiver of trepidation through me. I had seen the look of anger on Pausanius's face when Filippos rejected him, and recalled how I had witnessed his violent outburst the day the king had sent him out of his quarters. I had heard the palace gossip, that Pausanius had fallen out of the king's favour. Filippos's rejection of him on the temple steps made that clear.

As we walked back down the mountain trail, Theon was silent and thoughtful, his head bowed.

"What is troubling you? Is it what the Pythia told the king?" I asked.

Theon stopped and sighed. He laid his hand on my shoulder and leaned down as if to impart a secret. "I know only what was told to the men who were close to him," he said. He took a deep breath. "I do not know for certain whether it is true or how to interpret it." He spoke almost in a whisper. "Apparently, the Pythia, the Oracle, told the king *'Your sword is strong and bright. But there is another that is stronger and brighter.'* I wonder how Filippos has interpreted this?"

He paused, his brows drawn together, "The Athenians have a strong army. The most formidable of all is the Theban Sacred Band."

"Are they the Sacred Band that Alexandros will lead the cavalry against," I asked.

Theon fell silent awhile, then took a deep breath and spoke. "Yes. The Sacred Band of Thebes. It does not bode well."

BALLAD TWENTY-THREE Paean To The God Of War

Ares, God of ruthless fury,
invincible God of War,
bellow the battle cry and drive fear
into the hearts of our foes.
Gods of Terror, Destruction and Strife
whose fury never slackens,
make our steeds to be surefooted
on this day of battle.
Embolden the spear-men,
make them fearless as a charging boar.
From them may no man escape.
Slay those who have slain our brave warriors.
May vultures sweep the battlefield
stained with blood from our fallen.
Atone our deaths by their deaths.
Shed their blood for our blood shed.

The Battle of Chaeronea

Stanza One

We did not stay long at Delphi. By late afternoon we started back down the mountain, to where the army waited by the River Kephesos. The autumn winds blew chill down from the heights. Our pace was slower than the troops as we followed behind, riding in our mule-drawn carts that were stocked with hospital tents, medicine and surgical instruments.

The road went east, along the river through the mountain pass. Some days later, we arrived at a great plain that stretched for miles, flanked on each side by mountain slopes. From the hillside I could see the breadth and length of the plain.

The wide space of green field was dotted with olive trees and covered with barley stubble. A river, sparkling brown in the sun, wended across the expanse between the poplar and plane trees. Sheep grazed in the meadows, bleating as their herdsmen drove them up to the hillsides. On one side of the plain, the fortified acropolis of Chaeronea stood on a rise. Opposite was a steep mountain slope. I saw the town folk watching from the hillside outside of the town, mostly women and herdsmen guarding their flocks.

The plain was cut by a stream that flowed into the River Kephesos where the Athenians had made their camp, their right flank by the river, their left wing under the citadel on the hillside. The Makedonians camped by the stream which Theon said was called the Haemes, "Blood River", an ominous sounding name.

I had never seen so many troops. The entire army led by King Filippos and Alexandros with his elite cavalry, numbered thousands of men, regiment after regiment. There were hundreds of hoplites in phalanx formation, clad in protective cuirasses and bronze helmets. They carried short-bladed swords, spears held high. They were followed by the light infantry made up of farm boys hired as peltasts who could hurl a dart or sling a stone, and squadrons of cavalry riding sturdy horses bred especially for combat

"Chaeronea is a theatre of war," Theon said. "Many men have bled and died here."

Far across the plain I could see the glint of spear-tips and armour where the Athenians had encamped according to each city and state. A rumour circulated the enemy numbered as many as forty-thousand men. Their infantry was between eight and sixteen shields deep across the entire front line. The elite regiment of Thebes – three hundred men, the Sacred Band, and the boldest of all, were formed in their battalions, ready to confront Alexandros and the Makedonian cavalry. Filippos's Makedonian troops numbered far less.

Theon must have sensed my concern. "The Makedonians are fierce fighters, disciplined and fearless," he assured me. "They are driven by *adiantropa*, the brazen will to fight. Nothing else matters to them. They have no fear, only the love of glory. Filippos has trained them well – Alexandros too. He has inherited his father's bravado."

The king granted his troops a few days of badly needed rest as they waited for the siege train to arrive with the catapults and other siege equipment. The horses and mules were let loose to forage and the men huddled around campfires. In spite of the dangerous and arduous battle that lay ahead, the men were in good spirits. Some of them exchanged stories while others danced to the music of kitharas and flutes.

Theon and I made our camp under a patch of trees below the hillside. While he helped the soldiers set up the hospital tents, I busied myself sorting the *pharmaka* - herbs, potions, bandages, splints and all the surgical instruments we would need to lance, suture and bind wounds. Earthenware jars of water and wine were brought in to quench the soldiers' thirst.

By the third morning, the camp was seething with action. Orders were issued and the regiments formed into their battalions ready to face the oncoming foe. Before the battle a sacrifice of a white bull was made to Herakles, with whom the Makedonian royalty claimed kinship, and a black dog to Hecate, goddess of the Underworld. The diviners accepted the blood offerings, examined the entrails and proclaimed the auguries were good. The soldiers cheered; their spirits buoyed, they poured libations of wine to honour the gods. As Theon and I laid sprays of olive branches on the altar I whispered a prayer to my own war gods, Dyrnweh Gawr and Gwyndion, to ensure our safety. I thought of Elidi, somewhere out at sea at the helm of the royal trireme, and I said a prayer for him too.

Orders were issued and the troops marched forward to the plaintive sound of the paired aulos, yelling, lances drawn, swords flashing. The field was wide, so Filippos had divided the troops accordingly, on his right the infantry phalanx, six brigades with nine thousand men and three regiments of Royal Guards men, one thousand in each. On his left, others of lesser rank.

Theon and I climbed the brow of the hill where we could see the layout of the plain. He described the battle plan to me and pointed out how they would engage the enemy's heavy infantry first.

"Warfare is like theatre and the essence of theatre is feigning, acting out, trickery. There's a good deal of play-acting and treachery in war," Theon explained. "The Athenians may be audacious, but they aren't necessarily courageous. They're amateurs, citizens recruited to fight, and it has been twenty years since they took to the battlefield. Filippos is an old hand at warfare. He is cunning and relentless in battle, so he won't let go. His phalangites will bear down on them and terrorize them so they'll lose their heads in fright. The brigades of foot soldiers will advance on them and the others will seal the breaches."

"And Alexandros? Where will he be in the battle?" I felt overwhelmed but tried to hide my trepidation from him.

"Alexandros and his cavalry troops will charge the Theban regiments and the Sacred Band. The Thebans don't understand our method of warfare. They despise the cavalry and hold the horse troops in contempt." He gave a wry smile. "Their hubris will be their defeat."

The flood of men spread out across the plain, their burnished silver helmets and cuirasses glinting in the sun. The Makedonian regiments were far away but I could hear the sound of trumpets blaring and war cries roaring from thousands of throats. In the distance, faint yet distinct, war hymns and anthems responded from the enemies. The cavalry was running like racehorses, stampeding toward the foe, charging with lances lowered and sabres drawn. I heard voices crying out as commanders shouted orders.

Not in all my life, or even in my worst nightmares, could I ever imagine witnessing a scene such as this. I had seen our fierce Keltic warriors, naked bodies painted with woad, hair streaming in the wind as they galloped their ponies to confront their foes. But this was a battle scene with armies lined in precision, warriors wearing armour, horses bedecked. I was overcome with terror but put on a brave face as I prepared myself for the battle, the bloodshed and the carnage.

The din of the onset resounded over the fields. The noise filled the valley. Even from a distance the sound was deafening; men yelling, some screaming as if in agony, shields clashing, horns blaring and above it all, the battle paean rose while trumpets shrilled. The press of men and horse's hooves churned the ground until a thick cloud of choking dust rose over the fields.

On the left, the Makedonian phalanx shoved forward doggedly lunging toward the Athenians, the points of their sarissas bristling like porcupines.

Through the haze of dust I glimpsed the glint of helmets and shields. Behind the phalanx the cavalry waited their horses fidgeting, whinnying at the sound of battle. The smell of blood mingled with the dust in the air. The din resounded over the fields as the armies crashed through the olive groves and vineyards yelling to one another or screaming curses. Shields clashed; horses squealed. Each corps of men shouted its own battle paean, while officers barked orders, and trumpets blared. In the distance a paean to Ares could be heard. Amidst the shouts of "On to Athens!" I heard the agonizing screams of wounded men and the fitful moans of the dying from where they lay in the stubble field among the trampled vines and wildflowers.

Theon and I set about preparing for the first wounded to be brought in. I sorted the instruments for surgery, clean cloths for bandages, herbs, salves and ointments, poppies needed to sedate and ease the pain of suffering. By evening the wounded were carried off the field on shields. There was much work ahead for us. Spears and arrows inflict horrible wounds.

They brought in one peltast with three arrows protruding from his bloodied body: one in his throat and two in his chest. I found myself fighting tears as I laboured with Theon in the lamplight. The boy was an ephebe, no older than I was. I knew he was past help, yet I bent over him and spoke to him as I worked with Theon to remove the arrows. His eyes were glazed but his lips moved and he spoke a blessing to me just as he died, his fingers closing around my hand. I knelt beside his body. His eyes were open. I closed the lids and covered him with his bloodied cape. I felt a wave of nausea sweep over me and poured fresh water in the basin to wash my hands of the blood, swilling some over my face.

A hoplite was brought in bleeding from a dozen wounds. I cut away his bloodied clothes. While Theon tried to stem the flow of blood, I mixed a brew of poppy tea for the man to help ease his pain.

I recognized another soldier as one of the king's elite officers. A long spear shaft protruded from his side. His face was white as chalk, his lips parched as he drew in painful breaths. He was mumbling something about the king, but there was no time to worry whether Filippos was safe. The spear had pierced the soldiers' lung. His face was white, and blood dribbled from his mouth as he drew in painful breaths.

"Cut the shaft!" Theon ordered as he cut away the man's bloodied chiton.

I used a sharp knife to slice through the shaft.

"I'll have to cut the shaft head out," Theon said. He slowly and carefully tugged the stump of the shaft until the shaft head came out, followed by a gushing stream of blood. The air whistled softly as Theon removed the spear head from the gaping purple hole in the man's side. His head lolled and he lay still as a marble statue, drained of blood, too weak to cry out as I helped Theon bind the wound.

More soldiers staggered in, splashed with blood. Others were carried on friend's shoulders and laid on the ground, groaning in pain from their wounds. Theon gave me more exacting tasks than ever before. I learned that festering wounds had to be burned, while others were dressed and bandaged. I not only attended the injured but also the mortally wounded, calming their fears of death so they left their life and faced their mortality with serenity.

By nightfall the first day of battle ceased. The sky had darkened in the west. Where the sun had dipped low behind the hills, blood red clouds consumed the sky like fire. I stood outside the hospital tent, exhausted. Just then a meteor flared across the sky. I felt shivers down my spine. Was it a portent? The dragons-fire? The words of one of our Keltic war songs came to my mind: *"See the blazing star bright on the Dragon's crest? It tells when warriors meet to die!"* Quickly I collected myself. This was not the time to be dismayed, to fear disaster may befall us all.

I calmed myself and quietly prayed. "Goddess, I do not ask it for myself, only that the battle will be won."

Exhausted, I wanted to lie down on my bed forever. Young as I was, I felt my strength ebbing. As I sank onto my cot my head was spinning and I choked back the acrid nausea that rose in my throat.

Theon brought a damp towel and wiped my forehead. "You are exhausted, my child. It has been an overwhelming day, and I am proud of your stamina and courage. Truly, you have served the healing gods well."

I began to retch, and he handed me a bowl. My hands trembled as I held it. My head swirled. "It's nothing serious. It will pass."

Theon tucked a blanket around me. "Sleep, my child. By tomorrow you'll feel better." He brought me a cup of hot chamomile tea, but the taste of it made me feel even worse.

I slept fitfully that night, the sounds of battle and cries of the wounded still vivid in my mind. As I slept my dreams were filled with fearful glimpses of what I had witnessed, what I had heard – the cries of the wounded and moans of the dying disturbed me more than anything in the past ever had. But I knew I must force myself to go on, because of my respect for Theon and my promise to the goddess.

In the cold darkness before dawn I woke suddenly with a cry and lay sweating, my hands gripping the blankets covering me. My heart thumped and I shuddered with dry sobs thinking of all those dead men's souls drifting over the battlefield, the heaps of dead, the carrion birds hovering above, the wolves and jackals already tearing their bodies apart.

I reached for my amulet bag and found the *ankh* Elidi had given me on our wedding night. As I clutched it in my hand, I repeated words we had said in our wedding vows:

>*"May we always be together 'til death part us asunder.*
>*I vow to love you through all hardship, darkness and pain."*

I lay in my cot weeping silently. I dared not tell Theon of my worries. It had come to me earlier that day when a wave of nausea swept over me. I had been so distracted by the war I had not noticed I had missed my menses. I was pregnant with Elidi's child.

Stanza Two

The battle raged on for days. There was much work for me to do so I had no time to think about the child I was carrying. Each day I laboured in the hospital tents listening to the cries of the wounded. I helped Theon wash and stitch together gaping wounds, bodies pierced by javelins. I treated men with smashed skulls, replaced torn flaps of scalp, set broken bones, dressed wounds and thrust entrails back into gashed bellies. To those whose death was certain, I administered opiates and held their hands, so that they might pass away in peace. To the wounded I gave wine mixed with poppy tea to sedate them and soothed them with quiet words of comfort. The soldiers trusted me even though I was a young woman, a barbarian, a Kelt. Sometimes they teased me as if I were a little sister, but I knew they respected me for my knowledge of the herbs and potions. Some even consulted me about omens.

At night I bathed myself, washing the dried blood from my hands, and changed my blood-soaked tunic for a fresh, clean chiton. I saw more death those days than I could ever imagine and treated wounds so horrid the memory of them would never fade away.

I woke one morning to the sound of the battle cry from our camp on the hillside, the clashing of swords, frantic neighing of horses, screams of men. The distant shouts drew closer and through the clash of sword blades I heard the cry: "We are going to die!"

I rushed outside with Theon. We could not see much from our camp, but heralds kept shouting the news so those troops in the rear could hear the commands.

"Alexandros and his generals are on the left wing with the pike men. The phalanx has been sent forward smashing into the Athenian left wing. Alexandros is attacking the Thebans with his cavalry...."

I was rigid with fright; my whole body shivered. I took a breath to speak but Theon silenced me. He wrapped his arm around my shoulders and folded me into him.

"What if he dies?" I wept, my face pressed against his chest.

"Don't worry about Alexandros. He is in the gods' favour." Theon stroked my hair; his touch and gentle words soothed me. "Olwen, I am sorry you have to experience such pain..."

"But I wanted to come," I cried. My voice trembled like a plucked lyre. "I did it because of you and because of my promise to the goddess"

Then I heard the herald's voice. "Demosthenes has fled and taken the Athenians with him!"

Just as Theon had predicted, because of the Makedonians superb tactics. Though they outnumbered the Makedonians, the Athenians were not mighty enough to vanquish them. All of them, which included Athenians, Thebans and Achaeans, had suffered heavy losses. They had fought on, even after one of the king's officers rode down the line to tell them if they surrendered Filippos would spare their lives.

Everyone, even the badly wounded men, arose from their cots and cheered. Soon the sound of Makedonian drinking songs came from the camp as the men celebrated their victory. The Athenians had turned back, fled from the field. Demosthenes, the orator who had spoken out against Filippos and rallied the Athenians to make war, was the first to flee. Now Filippos, with the aid of Alexandros, controlled all Hellas.

The Athenian army was in disarray. The roar of battle changed to an exultant shout: "The enemy is in retreat!" And the proclamation: "He is through! Alexandros has broken the Theban line. The Sacred Band is standing firm, but they are cut off beside the river!" The Athenians had not reckoned on what would happen when Alexandros, leading the left wing of cavalry, confronted the Theban Sacred Band.

The soldiers in the hospital tents who were conscious, heard the jubilant cry and, feebly at first, then stronger, began to cheer. "The gods be thanked!"

Soon a courier rode into the camp bearing the jubilant news: "The Sacred Band is dead- all of them – they died together! Alexandros has annihilated them! Three hundred of them, all dead!"

King Filippos rode down the long stretch of battlefield surveying the carnage as a courier galloped through the field and proclaimed the Makedonian victory. The field was scattered with the dead, the prisoners put under guard and the wounded carried away. Those who were not taken prisoner or killed in the onslaught took their own lives. Only two score of them survived, those mostly maimed or disabled. Many of them begged to die, some even opening their wounds to spill more blood.

Alexandros rode his steed, Bucephalus, through the camp up to hospital tent, helmet off, hair shining copper in the sun, scarlet cape unfurled, sword drawn. Hephaestion, handsome in armour of burnished silver, rode behind him, his chestnut steed wheeling and stamping as Alexandros made his proclamation of victory.

"The Thebans faced us, locking their shields. They fought bravely, their backs to the river, but against our cavalry they were unable to sustain their line." He paused to take a breath and wipe beads of sweat from his brow. "They all fell, two by two, until the whole Sacred Band was down. All three hundred of them!"

He accepted a flask of wine handed to him by one of the soldiers and made a tribute to the brave Thebans. "They will be honoured as they should be, because they were the bravest warriors. I called on them to yield but they would not, and fought until the very last one fell."

That night the royal tents were open, and a victory celebration was declared. The rhythm of old Makedonian drinking songs, clapping, and cheering as the men danced, their heads crowned with wreaths of olive leaves could be heard across the plain. An unsteady line of men, torches waving, danced through the camp.

The king, with his personal guard, Pausanias, by his side, was surrounded by a group of laughing, drunken, torch-bearing men. Swaying and limping, he lurched at the head of the line, arm in arm with Pausanias. His face glistened red in the torchlight as he bawled out the paean. Alexandros, blood-splattered and smeared with ash in honour of the Makedonian dead, joined the line, his arm around Hephaestion's shoulders. I saw Filippos push Pausanias aside as Alexandros took his place beside his father. As the *komos* wove its way around the campfires Pausanias stood abandoned and alone, his faced reddened by the king's rebuff. Then he pushed his way into the crowd of celebrants and disappeared into the darkness.

Theon watched Alexandros and the king with a faint smile on his weathered face. "Alexandros has always been jealous of his father, fearing he would achieve such great glory there would be nothing left for him. He has achieved a great goal today, defeating the Sacred Band. There is no doubt someday he will be greater than his father!" His eyes glittered in the firelight. He reached out and put his hand on my shoulder, meeting my eyes. "I can never thank you enough for being my assistant, Olwen. May the gods bless you, dear child, and your infant on the way."

Before I could question him, he smiled, "Yes, I suspected it. I am a physician, after all. A woman who is with child has a certain aura about her, a sparkle in her eyes, a blush on her cheeks." He tilted his head, bent close to me and said in a whisper: "And, of course, because of the times you were nauseous, when I knew you had no fever!"

I stepped closer to him and took his hand. "I did what I could for you – and in the service of the gods."

Theon's voice cracked when he spoke. "I know you have suffered more than I could imagine, but we are safe now and it will be good to see you happy again."

Stanza Three

The trek back to Pella seemed endless. We had left Chaeroneia when the mountain passes had patches of snow. By now, in Makedon, the crops were almost ready to harvest in the parched fields and in the vineyards, the grapes ripe for picking.

All of us were weary after the war; the soldiers longed for their families and I was anxious to return, hoping Elidi would be waiting for me. The king and Alexandros had gone south to Hellas to claim their victory and treaty with the Athenians and Corinthians; it would be a triumphant return for the army.

I rode in the ox-cart leading the wagons laden with the hospital tents. Theon watched over me all the way, making sure I was able to bear the jolting wagon, and fed me broth when I suffer the discomforts of my birth-sickness. He told me about the goddess Ilithyia, who came from a far-away land to the island of Delos to help Leto bear her labour and give birth to the god Apollo.

"You need not fear. Trust in the goddess," he said. "The midwives are experienced in delivering healthy babes. And I will be there to provide assistance and *pharmacae* should you need it."

My worries were not so much about giving birth, but if Elidi had returned safely. I couldn't bear the thought of birthing our child if he was not there to share my joy. Theon assured me the royal fleet should already be in the port. I was overwhelmed with excitement at the thought of being reunited with Elidi. I stroked the growing bulge of my belly and smiled, thinking of him, and how blessed we were to be given this child.

At night we pitched the tents in an oak grove. I welcomed a chance to sleep but worries still beset me. What if I should miscarry after such an arduous journey? As I dozed, I thought I heard Essylt's voice. *'You are a strong, brave girl. The gods have blessed you and they will keep you safe.'* Startled, I awoke certain I could feel her presence there beside me. I did not feel strong and brave. I felt weary and vulnerable. But her words stirred something in me.

I must not let the horrors I have seen or the dangers I might face in the coming days deter me. I must stay strong, for the sake of this child I carry within me.

The long train of soldiers and carts rumbled through the pine groves where streams spilled over boulders, travelling through the uplands until the road flattened and we reached a pass that opened to a narrow plain. Beyond it, between the low green hills, I saw the glint of the sea. We had finally reached the coast! The flood of men, spurred by the sight began to cheer. I whispered a prayer to thank the gods for bringing us safely this far. Before us, the road led north along the seacoast. The trek would be easier now. Soon we would reach Pella.

Finally, far ahead, the sturdy walls of the city came into view. As we drew closer, I could see the sun's reflection on the lagoon where the boats took shelter, and I wondered if Elidi's ship would be moored there. Some of the soldiers broke rank as we drew closer and rushed ahead to greet their wives and families. I could hear the sound of celebrating from the shore.

The army's return was greeted by the blowing of horns. Pella's streets resounded with cheers and the shrill of women's voices as they greeted their men. I had never seen such a joyous public display. People were dancing in the streets to the piping of flutes, and surrounded the army's ranks waving laurel and pine branches.

A shiver of goose-flesh brushed over my skin as the crowds surged around us. I strained to see if Elidi was among them, my heart racing with anticipation. And then, over the excited din, I heard Elidi call: "Olwen! My darling Kelt! At last you have come home!"

My heart skipped with happiness at the sound of his voice.

Theon reined in the oxen and stopped the cart. Elidi pushed his way through the crowd and held out his arms to me. I climbed down into Elidi's arms and leaned against his strong chest. I had forgotten how beautiful he was with his careless air and the way his dark eyes sparkled. I stepped back from his tight embrace to look at him. His skin was bronzed from the wind and sun, his hair falling in rough curls around his ruddy, clean-shaven face.

His arms tightened around me. Tears welled in my eyes as I clung to him. "I was afraid – afraid we would die on that battlefield – afraid you would not return from your voyage.."

His voice was warm in my ear. "Hush," he said. "No more talk of battle and dying. We are together again. The gods have looked down on us with favour."

He held me at arm's length. I knew I must look care-worn and exhausted from our long journey. His hand brushed the curve of my belly. He looked puzzled for a moment, then surprised. "You have changed. You are a woman now…I can see that…" He brushed a strand of hair from my forehead and bent close to kiss me.

"I… I am with child," I stammered.

He did not speak for a long moment, and I wondered if he was pleased or just shocked. After a long silence he smiled, then gathered me tight against him. "My beautiful wife. How blessed we are!"

"I was so afraid we would not be together again," I whispered, leaning closer to him.

"Hush, my sweet one," Elidi said. He embraced me close to him. "It is over," he whispered. "You are with me now. I promise I'll be here for you – always."

"The goddess will provide for us and our child," I said. "She has protected me when all around me was chaos and everyone was dying and…"

"You are safe now," Elidi whispered. "The goddess has blessed you. We will be together forever."

All the blessing I needed was to be home again, with him.

When we returned to Theon's homestead things were much as we had left them. The house and flocks and gardens had been well-tended by the boy Theon had hired. The neighbours arrived bearing welcome gifts of wine and fresh-baked bread. After those arduous months away it was a comfort to be back in that place where Alexandros had first brought me to the safety and loving care of the physician, Theon.

During the next weeks I rested while Theon and Elidi tended to the farm duties. Still exhausted, after the long months of war and the arduous trek back to Pella, I lay on a divan under the oak tree and watched them. Theon always made sure I had plenty of fresh fruit from the groves and vegetables from the garden. "It is important that you remain in good health, Olwen, if you wish to give birth to a healthy child." I knew what he meant. So many newborns died within a few days of birth. I obeyed him, and ate well, determined that my baby would be strong and healthy.

Stanza Four

A Prayer to Ilithyia, Goddess of Child Birth

> *Hear me, Ilithyia, Birth Goddess.*
> *A woman will bring forth a worthy child.*
> *Alleviate the travail of her childbearing.*
> *Sing her your sweet song.*
> *Spin your divine wiles*
> *so this maiden will be joyful.*
> *Ease her birth pangs.*
> *May she be joined in love with her beloved*
> *and give praise to thee, O Goddess.*
> *For her prayers will be answered*
> *and her babe born.*

The birth pangs began one morning. While Theon went to summon the midwives, Elidi tried to soothe me. He looked worried and pale under the fine dark olive of his skin. I caught my breath as another wave of pain wrenched through me and tried to laugh as he held me.

"It's nothing...only childbirth," I said, trying to be brave though spasms of pain wrenched through me.

Elidi stayed with me until Theon returned with the midwife and a clucking group of village women who descended on the room busy as hens inspecting everything and fussing over me making signs of good fortune. Theon explained they were looking for anything that was tied in a knot, because that was a maleficent sign that could delay the birthing.

It was the custom that men did not attend the birth. I held tight to Elidi's hand, wishing he could stay with me. "I will be waiting... outside the door!" he said.

After he left, the room felt empty even though the village women fussed about and birth pains throbbed through me, rhythmic as my heart-beats.

Toward evening I felt a gush of water and knew it was time for the baby to be born. I was moved from my bed to a birthing stool. The midwife bent over me massaging my belly while another woman crouched below to catch the newborn.

By nightfall, the pains came closer together and although I tried to sleep, or at least doze, I could not. The midwife gave me a cup of chaste-berry tea to calm me. I wished Elidi had stayed with me, but it was not proper for men to attend a birthing.

I prayed to Ilithyia, goddess of Child-birth to help me bear the pain that swept over me, breaking like a wave. I groaned and pushed, hard, as the infant's head thrust out of me. Then I heard a baby's weak cry and rejoicing from the women in the room. I must have drifted off while the cord was cut, and the afterbirth delivered. When I opened my eyes, the midwife was standing beside me holding up a tiny, red-skinned creature wrapped in swaddling cloths.

"You have a son!" she said joyfully. "A fine, healthy son!" She lifted the infant up so I could see him. He was wizened and red, still with the bluish birth cord attached.

She placed the newborn in my arms. He smelled sweet from the rose water he had been bathed in. I touched the soft silken flesh of his cheek. He opened his eyes and seemed to look at me. His eyes were blue and sightless, but I knew in time they would become dark as Elidi's. I stroked the damp fluff of black curls on his tiny head. He would be dark, a Phrygian like his father. I kissed him and he nuzzled against me as if searching for my breast.

The midwife called Theon and Elidi into the room. Both of them were beaming with happy smiles.

"A son! We have a son!" I held up the babe for them to see.

Elidi embraced me tenderly. I ran my fingers thru his tangled hair. He looked pale and somewhat gaunt. "Did you not sleep well, my love?"

"Theon and I stayed up all the night waiting for the child." He looked down at the small babe in my arms, peering into the infant's crumpled rosy face. Then carefully he reached out and laid a finger against the tiny lips. The baby turned toward his touch making a suckling sound.

Theon leaned close and pulled back the baby's swaddling to inspect him. "He's a fine healthy boy!" he exclaimed. "Praise to Ilithyia!"

"He's a strong little man," Elidi said, smiling with delight. He bent to kiss my brow. "Oh, my beloved Olwen. Fortune has given us this child. I thank Ilithyia, the birth goddess for this wonderful gift!"

He grasped my hand in his. "I am glad beyond words," I smiled at him. "He'll be just like you!" I snuggled the baby and he instinctively found my breast. Smiling, and still nursing our child, I slipped into sleep.

In a dream, my grandfather Maelgwyn came to me. He appeared as I remembered him, the long grey beard, dressed in his white Druid's robe with the hammered golden torc at his neck. He was studying his star charts and looked up as I approached him. "Have you seen it, my child? Have you seen the Dragon's Fire?"

"Yes grandfather," I replied. "I saw it fall over the battlefield at Chaeronia, and many times before that."

He looked dismayed by my answer and placed his hand on the top of my head as if in a blessing. "Pay heed to the omens. Do not be afraid," he said. "There is a storm coming. But if you follow the stars they will take you home."

I woke to the sound of the baby's soft mewling cry. The dream puzzled me, yet the vision of my grandfather was comforting. I looked down into the face of my sweet new child and said a prayer of thanks to the gods. Whatever might happen now, my life was complete with this precious gift they had given me.

Stanza Five

The next morning Theon announced he was preparing a naming ceremony for our child.

"It's our custom. I have invited our neighbours and a few friends from the palace," he explained. "There will be a ceremony called an *amphidromia* to name your child, performed by a priest and then a feast to celebrate the little one."

On the day of the celebration, we decorated the house with olive branches which Theon said was a symbol of family and connection to ancestors. Our guests arrived from the nearby homesteads bearing gifts for our child, blessing him with warm greetings. They filled the courtyard where Theon had set out tables of sweets and wine. The women arrived with platters of food for the feast that would be held after the purification ceremony.

A priest from a nearby shrine arrived with his acolytes, all dressed in white robes and crowns of olive leaves. Theon explained that the *amphidromia* was a purifying ceremony to bless the newborn child with good health and fortune.

Everyone gathered inside the house, circling the hearth. The midwife who had assisted in the birth was there to carry the newborn around the room because I didn't have a nurse.

I thought, *If only Essylt were here. She would be the nurse for my child just as she cared for me when I was found at the Standing Stones.*

The baby was wrapped in a newly woven blanket of white sheep's fleece made by the midwife herself. As she carried the baby around the room, stopping solemnly by the house shrines to dedicate him to the gods, the people sang and danced joyously.

Elidi and I stood before the priest and waited until the midwife circled the room and finally handed our child to me. The priest anointed the baby with sweet-scented oil and intoned a prayer of gratitude that our little one had survived, praying he would grow into a healthy, strong man.

"What will you name him?" he asked.

I had thought he should have a Cymry name such as Maelgwyn, after my grandfather. But Elidi explained it was their custom to name the child after the paternal grandfather.

"We will call our son *Nikos*," Elidi said, "Nikos was my father's name. His name will be Nikos Elidimis - Nikos, son of Elidi."

Nikos Elidimis. The name had a sweet, almost magical sound. I looked down into the face of the little one I held cradled in my arms. He was so like Elidi, the dark sparkling eyes, the fluff of ebony hair and olive-tinged skin. "Nikos Elidimis!" I repeated the name over. "Yes! This will be our son's name! And he will carry it proudly to the ends of the earth!"

A strange feeling came over me when I said that. It was hard to imagine this fragile little creature bundled in the sheepskin to be a warrior or a wanderer who would travel the world. But whatever he chose to be, he would be brave and wise, perhaps a seaman like his father, travelling to distant lands, or perhaps a caring, wise healer like Theon. The gods would surely bless him and lead him onto the right path.

BALLAD TWENTY-FOUR Plea To Hades

*Fearsome Hades, you enrich yourself
on our sighs and tears.
We offer our best black bulls and rams to you
Hades, ruler of the Underworld.
We beseech you to bestow mercy on us,
dark-cloaked Hades, god of death and darkness.
Accept our sacrifices. Appease our fears.*

The Invitation

Stanza One

In the month of Boedromion, when the crops were ready to harvest, a festival was held, and sacrifices were made to Apollo and Gaia to honour the dead. Black bulls were sacrificed and offered to Hades and Persephone who rule the Underworld where the spirits of the ancestors reside. I recalled our Keltic tradition of offering a black bull to the gods, and with a pang of regret, I remembered my pet bull Mithras and how he was taken from me for the sacrifice.

Theon explained that Boedromion was mainly a festival to show respect to parents who had passed over the River. So I said prayers for my grandfather, Maelgwyn, who had found me as a babe in the Stone Circle and Essylt, the woman I called *modryb,* my aunt, who were the only parents I had known.

Elidi and I watched the rites performed near the farmstead in the field. I held tight to my child as they were performed. At five months, Nikos was already an attentive child. His rosy cheeks dimpled with a smile, and he waved his arms with excitement when he saw the bull taken to the alter.

Later that morning a messenger from Pella arrived at the farmstead with news for Theon. The man was dishevelled, as though he had ridden without stopping. I felt my heart clench with a feeling of foreboding. What dire news did he bring? Had something happened to the king, or worse, to Alexandros?

The courier leapt from his horse and wiped the sweat from his brow. "King Filippos and Alexander have returned to Makedon. The king's alliance with the Athenians and Corinthians went well. He has consolidated the Greek states and declared an official victory." His hand trembled as he handed Theon a royal scroll. "The king requests you return to Pella to attend his wedding,"

Theon's brows raised in surprise." Wedding?"

"Yes. To celebrate his victory, the king is taking another wife."

Theon frowned as he took the scroll from the messenger. He unrolled it, scanned it quickly. He stood quietly stroking his beard, a look of concern on his face. "This is troubling news," he said.

The courier nodded and gave a wry smile. "It has caused some chaos in the palace," he said. "You must return as soon as you can!"

It wasn't until the courier had departed that Theon spoke again. "This new bride... she is the niece of Filippos's friend, Attalos, a land baron who lives near Pella. She's a young girl, no more than fifteen." Theon glanced over the message again. He shook his head and muttered a curse.

"Apparently on their way back from Hellas, the royal party were guests at Attalos's home. Filippos saw the girl, and after a night of drinking, he proposed marriage to her. Of course Attalos would not deny the request. It seems Attalos has convinced the king he should have a lawful, true-born heir." Theon threw down the scroll and sighed. "This does not bode well for Alexandros."

"What does this mean for him?" I asked.

"The girl is a Makedonian, and any male child they have would consolidate the baron's connection with the royalty." I could see by the look on his face he was displeased.

Elidi also looked concerned. "And what about Queen Olympias?"

Theon shook his head. "I am certain the queen has been in a rage ever since the news was made known. She's a dangerous one and will not stand for this betrayal. Nor will Alexandros. He's a strong-willed boy."

"Must you attend the wedding?" I asked.

"Yes, the king expects me to give him a blessing." Theon gave a deep sigh. "As for Alexandros, I will see if I can advise him how to settle the dispute between his parents. His mother's wrath must not be reckoned with. Who knows what she will do. Her jealousy knows no bounds. This is sure to stoke a blood feud!"

His words rang true. The following day Alexandros rode into the farmstead. I was sitting under the plane tree rocking baby Nikos in his cradle when I saw the horseman galloping across the fields. Even from a distance, his hair shining like copper in the sun, I knew it was him. I called to Elidi who was tending the garden. "Look! It's Alexandros. I wonder what news he brings?"

Alexandros gave no word of greeting to us when he rode up. His face was flushed, his hair tangled from the wind. It was obvious by his distraught expression, the ruddiness of his cheeks, that something was deeply troubling him. Without so much as a nod, he leapt from his horse, leaving Bucephalus to graze, and barged past us into the house where I knew Theon was at the table sorting his *pharmacae.*

From where we sat in the garden, through the open door, we could hear Alexandros's voice clear and hard, pitched high with anger.

"Father has betrayed us... all for this girl...this *child!* It was a drunken brawl and he has made a foolish mistake. Attalos put the girl out as bait to tempt father so he could put himself in a better standing with the royalty."

"Didn't Antipater or any of his other generals try to dissuade him?" Theon asked.

"It's Attalos who has convinced him to wed her. You know father, give him a year and he will tire of her and take another younger one!" I could hear the despair in Alexandros's voice. "Even his body-guard, Pausanias, tried to convince him it was wrong. So father threw Pausanias out and told the stable boys they could have their way with him."

I gasped at the mention of the name. Pausanias, the king's personal guard, the dark youth who always accompanied the king and was rumoured to be his lover. I recalled the scene at Delphi when Filippos had rejected him, and again at Chaeroneia when he was rebuffed by the king. A shiver of foreboding pricked my skin. '*A storm is coming,*' my grandfather had said in the dream. Could this be the 'storm' he meant?

I heard Theon gently try to calm Alexandros, but to no avail.

"Father has no shame, especially when he's drunk! He has wronged my mother. Attalos has convinced him to wed the girl to provide Makedon with a legal heir – one of true Makedonian blood. How can anyone respect a man like that? He's an impotent old man, blind drunk most of the time." Alexandros's voice was choked with sobs. "He expects mother and I to attend his marriage. What an insult! My mother has always said he is not really my father, but I didn't believe her. She said my real father was an Egyptian shaman-Nektanebo – who came to plead with Filippos to help him in his war with the Persians. Mother says she took him as her lover – and that is how I was conceived. Now I believe it to be true."

Theon responded in a gentle voice. "Alexandros, there is no proof of that. It's a tale concocted by your mother, is all. Filippos *is* your true father. Sit down! Stop your pacing! Here, have a drink of wine. Calm yourself! Take some time to think about this. Of course your father has the reputation of being a brute, but he is a respected king and has won many battles."

I heard the sound of a goblet being thrown down. Elidi saw my look of concern and put his arm around me.

"I understand why Alexandros is enraged," he said quietly. "His mother is not Makedonian. She's an Epirote. This means Alexandros's standing as heir to the throne will be in jeopardy if the king's new wife gives birth to a boy child who is a full-blooded Makedonian."

He reached into the cradle and lifted baby Nikos up to hold him close to his chest. "Our boy will never have to face such a dilemma... to be estranged from his father and face an unknown future. "

"And for this, I thank the gods," I said.

The debate inside the house went on for some time, then finally there was quiet. Elidi and I waited under the plane tree trying to appear as though we had not heard the drama. When he stepped out of the house with Theon, Alexandros appeared calmer and greeted us, then turned to Elidi.

"Phrygian," he said, his voice gruff with a tone of authority. "You must return to Pella. My father is preparing to sail east in the Spring. He is sending some of the fleet to the coast off Ionia."

"Is the king going to war?" Elidi asked.

"It's a reconnaissance voyage to treat with the Persians. Everything must be made ready," Alexandros responded curtly. Then he leapt on Bucephalus's back and spurred his horse away.

Clearly Alexandros's words disturbed Elidi. His face flushed red and he took a deep breath. Finally, he said: "This means I'll be called back to man the helm on the royal trireme." He looked at me with concern and reached out to stroke baby Nikos's cheek. "I'll have to leave you and our son... for who knows how long."

"Perhaps not for long if it's just a reconnaissance voyage." Theon's words were meant to comfort, but I heard the concern in his voice. He looked around at the fields and gardens. "It is time to leave the farmstead. Winter will soon come and we always spend the coldest days in Pella." He must have seen the worried expression on my face and reached out his hand to me. "Do not fret, my child. If Elidi must leave, it won't be for long. The ships will not sail till the winter weather calms, so you will still have time together."

I blinked back the tears that had welled in my eyes and clung tight to my child. I did not want Elidi or Theon to see my trepidation, but the thought of Elidi leaving again frightened me. Somewhere deep inside me, I knew it did not bode well.

Stanza Two

I felt reluctant to leave the farmstead, but we had no choice because of Theon's invitation from the king and Elidi's order to return to his ship. The crops had been harvested and Theon employed the neighbour's son to tend the flocks, so the next morning at sunrise, we piled the mule cart with our belongings and Theon's baskets of potions and set off across the fields for Pella.

An early morning breeze was blowing carrying with it the pungent scent of ripening grapes and freshly mowed crops. The fields were bare after the harvest, but thyme and bracken grew along the roadside among the smooth boulders. The surrounding mountains were already crowned with the first snowfall and mist shrouded the foothills.

We travelled southward, along the river valley where poplars and silver birch lined the rugged path. We rode most of the day travelling at the mule's pace, jostled together in the cart, barely speaking for most of the journey. There was no other sound but the clip-clop of the mule's hooves on the stony path and the far-off cry of crows and other birds scavenging the stubble of the fields.

Finally, the walls of the city came into view. By then, the sun had set, and a chill wind blew in from the sea. As we grew nearer, I glimpsed the glint of gold from the gilded ornaments on the palace's tall pediments. Below the palace, wisps of smoke rose over the terracotta rooftops of the city houses. In the distance, the darkening sea reflected the moon's pale light and Pella's great salt lagoon, with its island fortress, glimmered with torchlight. The day had declined into evening. Lamps glinted in windows as we made our way through the narrow city streets. Only a few people were about, returning home late from the agora.

We drove up to the great northern gate where the guards came out to greet us. Theon ordered one of them to take the mule cart to the palace stables. As we walked up the steps to the palace, Theon stopped. His countenance was solemn and he hesitated a long moment before speaking.

Finally he spoke, in a solemn whisper: "Remember, we must all keep our decorum. Do not reveal anything you may have overheard Alexandros say, or discuss our opinions about the king's choice to rewed." He studied my face as if reading my expression which must have betrayed my feelings of trepidation. After a long, thoughtful moment he said: "Trust that all will be well. Alexandros is angry at his father, and with good reason, but that will pass. He's a wilful boy, but also one with a good spirit. He *is* Filippos's son and rightful heir. It is natural he should be enraged over his father's choice. But this all will pass."

Without another word, he turned and started up the steps. I followed Elidi, without speaking, contemplating Theon's words. It was comforting to have Elidi beside me, carrying our child. Nothing mattered to me more than we were together, and I vowed I would not let the king's business interfere with our lives.

The paved courtyard of the palace garden was empty, the coloured marble flagstones scattered with windblown twigs, sparkled with frost. Clay urns of rose bushes and trailing plants lined the path. No one was stirring except the palace slaves. When we arrived at the cottage at the back of the palace grounds, Elidi didn't wait for anyone to attend us. He began opening the fretted shutters that had been closed during our absence. I followed Theon into the dank, dusky house and set baby Nikos down on the divan.

"Where's the wine jar?" Theon looked around and found some wine stored in a clay cask, pouring us each a cup. I was tired from the long journey, aching and cold, and the wine was a soothing balm that warmed my blood.

There was a stir at the door and the Nubian slave, Xenon came in, our possessions heaped in his muscular arms. "Master Theon, sir, welcome back to Pella!" He turned to Elidi and me and saw the child beside me on the divan. His dark face shone and he grinned. "And blessings to you both and your babe. I am here, as always to serve you." Then his cheerful demeanour turned dour, reminding me clearly of the events that had caused us to return. "There is turmoil in the palace, sir," he said quietly to Theon. "You have heard of the king's decision to wed?"

Theon nodded. His look alone told of the gravity of what would come to pass. "And Olympias?" he asked finally.

Xenon shrugged and shook his head. "As I said, sir...there is turmoil."

I felt a tenseness, a dark cloud of anxiety. I was worried, not only because Elidi had been called back to his ship, but the feud between Alexandros and his father could have an ominous outcome.

While I was unpacking, the servant maiden, Aricia, arrived, carrying an armload of late blooming wild flowers "To brighten your abode," she said. "Welcome back to the palace! I am here to serve you." When she saw little Nikos she laughed in her carefree way and scooped him up in her arms. He startled with surprise and whimpered, so she fussed over him and soon had him smiling back at her. "A fine little man! And he looks just like his father!" She smiled across at Elidi who was helping Theon unpack his *pharmacae*.

"You have a fine son, sir!"

I was happy to know I would have Aricia's company again. She would not only help me tend little Nikos, but she would share stories with me and keep my spirits light with her bright demeanour and kindness. There was nobody to whom I could relay my innermost feminine thoughts. Although she was a servant, a slave in the royalty's eyes, Aricia was my closest confidant and friend.

Stanza Three

Our house at the palace was quiet, but I did not feel at peace. I wished to be on the farmstead, away from the royal dramas, back in the garden of Theon's home with Elidi and my son. But it was not to be. Within a few days after arriving, Theon left to attend the king's wedding feast at Attalos's country estate, and Elidi was ordered to work on the trireme, coming back only on occasional evenings.

As I had grown older and was more accustomed to the way of life in Pella's palace, I realized there was always a scandal brewing, not just among the servants and soldiers, but among the royalty as well. I had known for some time about Filippos's penchant for young cadets and servant girls. The king had a lascivious eye and I remember how he had leered at me when I was first introduced to him, and when I was caring for him during his recovery from war wounds. But this was much more. It was a clan and court dalliance! So when Aricia came one day to share the gossip about the drama unfolding in the queen's quarters, it was not a surprise.

"The queen is in a rage. She is packing up and going back to her home in Epirus" Aricia said. "Something must have happened at the wedding. Olympias has asked me to fetch you. She needs some potions."

I was not surprised to hear the news that Olympias would leave Pella's palace because of her husband's new marriage. But why had she requested my presence? It had been months since I had last seen the queen. She mostly kept to herself, and as I was not one of her servants, I was not invited into her presence. This suited me after the few encounters I'd had with her. Frankly, the woman terrified me. I felt she held some evil powers that, if crossed, she could easily unleash. So it was with great trepidation I agreed to answer her summons.

Carrying my basket of medicines, I followed Aricia to the royal quarters. The shutters were closed in the queen's room, and only a few lamps were lit casting an eerie glow. Olympias was propped against the pillows on her bed. Next to the bed I saw a basket with a coiled snake – Olympias's serpent *daimon*. I hesitated to approach, but she beckoned me to come closer.

I could see she had spent many sleepless nights. Her eyes were ringed and blood-shot, her face gaunt and ashen, lined like an aged crone, her russet hair was dishevelled and fell in a tangled mass over her breasts.

"What is it you wish, my lady?" I asked.

"You are a healer, are you not?" Olympias croaked.

"Yes, my lady. I am the physician Theon's assistant."

"I am in need of an elixir. You can see I am not well... That bastard, Filippos..." Her voice caught with a dry sob and she uttered a curse. "He has betrayed me! He will live to regret this perfidy..." Her voice trailed off and she pulled herself upright, her fists clenched. I heard her mutter an oath under her breath.

"What have you got in your medicine basket that will ease my pain?" she croaked.

I knew she was crafty. Theon had told me the Epirotes were *mystai* who worshipped at an old oak tree. There was no doubt in my mind Olympias held the dark powers and could wreak vengeance.

I administered her an elixir of willow bark mixed in a cup of warm water. "This will calm you, lady" I said, and backed away from her bedside. "I will leave some other medicines for you as well. It is all I can do. I am sorry, lady, for your distemper."

She pulled herself upright onto her elbows and began to ramble on about her son, Alexandros, how he had been betrayed just as she had, and how she would seek revenge against the king.

"Alexandros is the rightful heir. He has the blood of Achilles in him. He's blessed by the gods. How can Filippos abase my son like this?" Her grey eyes had dilated and looked almost black. Her mouth had whitened, her face flushed red. She threw out her words as if they were a ritual curse, her voice rising.

"The day will come when he will know my vengeance. Yes! He will learn Alexandros is greater than he could ever be!" Her sobs turned into a high-pitched shriek.

I stepped farther back, stifling my terror. It frightened me to hear her rave so vehemently, and it sent cold shivers up my spine.

She screamed out the words of a curse, one I knew was from Hekate, a spell portending death. Her face had become like a terrible mask, like a gorgon's head. I stiffened, my flesh pricking at the vile words that spewed from her mouth. I drew in my breath and stepped farther back. I could feel myself trembling but tried not to show her how frightened I was. Her voice was so shrill it startled her snake daimon. It uncoiled and lifted its scaly head, spitting as if in agreement with her curses.

"Filippos has insulted me and for this he will pay! Marrying a virgin of fifteen! In a year or two he'll tire of her and find a younger one, the filthy old goat! He has slighted not only me and our son, but the royal house of Epirus. Yes! He will learn my son is greater than he will ever be!" Her sobs turned to a high-pitched shriek. Her hands clenched into fists and she beat her breasts. "Why have the gods been unjust to me?"

I stepped farther back, stifling my terror, muttering a prayer.

She's mad! I thought. I recalled that time in the grove when I had found the votive she had left on the shrine from her secret rites.

What will she do? I wondered. *How terrible will be her revenge?* I had witnessed the barbaric vengeance of my people, the Kelts, but even that had not frightened me as much as the queen's vicious anger.

At last her shrieks quelled and she lay back on the pillows, weak and drained from the outburst.

"Poor child!" she said, and beckoned me closer. "It must have been a sickness that befell me. You know...I'm not really mad, though the man who is my husband says I am. Say some prayers to your gods," she implored. "Ask for a sign – some revenge for what the bastard has done to me and my son! I am a woman of honour and cannot let this pass."

I stepped closer cautiously, put my hands on her temples and whispered a prayer of healing. Then with careful courtesy, I disengaged myself, leaving her with the only words I could muster: "My lady, I will make a sacrifice for your well-being and pray the gods will give you strength and healing."

When Elidi returned from the ship that night, it was plain for him to see I was still upset by my encounter with the queen. "I gave her some physics," I said. "They will do her more good than I could. She's worried about Alexandros – thought I could say some words to charm the goddess. Her head is so full of hatred for her husband it is no surprise she is ill!" I told him about Olympias's tirade. "I was so afraid. It was as though she was possessed by a demon. I fear what she might do to take revenge on the king!"

Elidi heard the terror in my voice. He took me in his arms to comfort me. "Don't worry. She will not harm him lest the blame fall on Alexandros."

I grasped the folds of his chiton. "What should I do? Should I tell Theon? Will he tell the king? If the queen learns I told...will she have *me* killed?" I couldn't stop the sobs in my voice.

Elidi stroked my hair and kissed my forehead. "You need not be frightened. I heard Alexandros has sent some of his cadets back to Pella to fetch her. He's taking his mother to Epirus. Her brother is king there and she will be out of harm's way. What can she do from Epirus?" He held me closer in his arms to comfort me. "Be brave dear Olwen. Sacrifice to the gods. They will protect you."

By the time Theon returned to the palace several days later, Alexandros's companions and the queen had already left Pella. Theon was travel weary and I could see that he was obviously worried. Once he was rested and had been served a cup of wine, he related the events of the wedding to us.

"It was a fine wedding – there were heaps of splendid gifts for the dowry. Guests from all around the kingdom. The young bride seemed shy and somewhat frightened. Filippos was drunk, blaring out army songs with his friends." He paused, wiped his brow, and took a long drink of wine from the cup Elidi held out to him. "I could see Alexandros was trying his best to maintain some decorum. He and Hephaestion stayed on their own, observing. I had hoped Hephaestion would defuse any spark of Alexandros's anger but as the day went on Filippos and his friends grew drunker and rowdier. Then Attalos got up to make a speech – going on about the married couple conceiving a true born Makedonian heir. After Attalos had spoken, Filippos staggered to his feet and made a speech, saying he hoped the union would bring him a 'legitimate' son." Theon took a long breath and shook his head. "That was when Alexandros sprang from his dinner couch and threw a wine cup at Attalos. He shouted something about being called a bastard, then turned on his father and berated him – calling him a filthy old drunkard."

"What happened then?" I asked. I looked over at Elidi and saw he was standing, mouth agape, obviously as shocked as I was.

"Filippos leapt off his couch and lunged at Alexandros. He had his sword out, intending to attack his son, but Hephaestion stepped between them to protect Alexandros. Then Filippos staggered forward, fell on his bad leg, and crashed to the ground!"

"And Alexandros?" Elidi asked.

"He said he was taking his mother back to Epirus. To see his mother shamed, his father making a drunken show with a girl of fifteen." he shrugged and shook his head. "Most of his companions stood by him and said they would go too. They will always be faithful to him. Hephaestion tried to urge him to make amends with his father. I tried to talk to him too, to calm him, but he shrugged me off and sent his friends back to Pella to fetch his mother."

I told him about my meeting with Olympias and her fit of wrath. "Will Alexandros return here? Or will he stay with her in Epiros?" I asked.

Theon shook his head. "He won't return unless Filippos makes peace with him. He's a strong-willed boy and will not tolerate humiliation. His mother holds a lot of influence over him and one thing he will not do is to betray her!" He paused and wiped sweat from his brow. "And there is more troubling news."

Theon's countenance grew more solemn. "The King is making plans for his invasion of the Persians in the Spring. He is sending his general, Parmenio, to lead the reconnaissance. He's got control of Greece. Now he wants the rest – and he will start with the Greek cities on the coast of Ionia."

I gripped Elidi's arm. "This means you will be called back to sea!"

"Yes," Elidi said "I will have no choice, if it's the king's will. And if he invades the Persians, it will be a long war."

My expression must have betrayed my concern. Theon was studying my face as if reading my thoughts. "Will Alexandros return to Pella to serve with his father?" I asked.

"It will depend on Filippos," he shook his head and shrugged. I could see the concern on his face. Theon continued,"Alexandros takes no pleasure from his father's conquests. He'll say there will be nothing left for him. And now he is estranged from his father. Ach! I fear the intrigues and feuds of the royalty will not have a good outcome. Even kings have no right to wrong men. Filippos has settled many blood feuds in his reign, but I fear now he has started one himself."

BALLAD TWENTY-FIVE Cry To Eris

Eris, daughter of Nyx, mother of hardship,
goddess of strife and descent,
You are Darkness.
Your wrath is relentless.
You hurl bitterness and anxiety on men.
You are chaos.
You incite murder and calamity.

The Assassination

Stanza One

The Spring winds of March warmed the hills melting the snow. Roads once deep with mud were passable again. The air grew mild and gentle breezes blew. The sea calmed. It was sailing weather, and I knew Elidi would be called back to his ship. Frequent news had come from the east reporting the Persians were moving farther along the Ionian coast and there were rumours the king was sending some of his fleet to Ephesus where the Persian Royal Road came to the sea.

Filippos's attempts to negotiate a treaty with the Persians had failed. So he decided to send his head generals to Asia Minor to assess the best methods of attack and as the campaigning season opened, he was preparing his troops. The king would send his generals, Parmenio and his new wife's uncle, Attalos, with an advance force of Makedonian troops to cross into Asia Minor and make preparation for the invasion that would follow.

Elidi returned to the palace with the news he had been awarded a new position on one of the triremes. I had not seen him so elated since the day our son was born.

He was flushed with excitement and his dark eyes sparkled. "I have been promoted to *kybenetes,*" he said. "That's the navigational officer! I'll no longer be at the helm. I will be the captain piloting the ship!"

I couldn't help but share his excitement, though I still had trepidations about him setting sail again. But when he offered to take me on board to show me his new ship I couldn't refuse.

"We'll take our boy along!" Elidi said. He lifted little Nikos onto his shoulders. "Do you want to see my new ship? I remember when my father showed me his ship when I was a boy. You will see, my little man, what the life of a sailor is."

I recalled Elidi's tales of sailing with his father. Did I wish for my son to follow his father's footsteps? Deep down, I had imagined Nikos might become a physician like Theon, but I could not deny Elidi's enthusiasm and was glad for his prestigious promotion.

We walked together from the palace on the acropolis, down the long-paved avenue through the city to the port where the ships were moored. We made our way between the fine houses with gilded roof cornices and painted marble pillars and through the lively marketplace where vendors hawked their wares.

Some of the fleet was docked at the quay in Pella's lagoon. Elidi pointed out the trireme he would pilot - a long, sturdy vessel built of pinewood with eyes painted on the bow and a bronze ram shaped like a winged goddess on the bow.

"That's a Siren," Elidi explained. "Our ship is named after her." I knew the story of the sea-nymphs who charmed sailors with their seductive songs. Theon had told me the tales of Odysseus' long voyage home after the Troy wars when he and his crew were lured by the Sirens. In the story, the enchanted sailors had thrown themselves into the sea. I shrugged off the thought. It was a fable, after all.

Elidi pointed out the three banks of oars the rowers used to propel the vessel through the sea.

"We will have almost two-hundred rowers," Elidi explained. "And a battalion of hoplites in case we are challenged to a battle."

He led me up the gangway onto the deck where some of the crew were preparing for the voyage. "Let me show my son the helm." He set little Nikos down and took his hand.

Nikos cried out with excitement and pulled away from Elidi's firm hold, taking several tottering footsteps forward.

Elidi cheered. "His first steps alone! He knows his place –– on the deck of a ship – just as I did when I was a child."

I watched my son as he toddled toward the helm. Would he be like his father and follow the sea gods? I wondered. Or would he grow to embrace the knowledge of medicines and become a healer like I had?

Soon after, the news I had been dreading came. The king had ordered the royal fleet to sail. When Elidi told me, I couldn't hold back my tears. He put his arm around me and drew me close. I took a long breath and started to speak but he put his finger on my lips.

"No, Olwen. Don't speak. Our paths must separate for now, but we will be together again."

I held him for a long time, trying not to cry. In spite of Elidi's show of confidence, I tried to be brave and not show my own feelings of trepidation.

It was a warm April morning, when they set sail. A cloud caught the hidden sun and glowed above us. The sea was clear blue, dazzling in the sun.

Elidi's ship was moored by a stone jetty in the harbour, its oars already shipped and sticking up like the quills of a hedgehog. The trireme's twin square sails with their lion of Makedon emblem billowed in the breeze. The rowers had already taken their places on the three banks of oars. Hoplites and infantrymen, dressed in heavy bronze armour, crowded the deck waving fare-wells to their families.

A great host of people had gathered on the shore of the lagoon to watch the departure of the fleet. The priests were there to pour libations to the sea gods as the ships glided smoothly out of the shelter of the harbour. I stood in the crowd with Theon and Aricia who had accompanied me to help tend Nikos. I felt despair at Elidi's leaving but tried not to show it, and tried to keep a pleasant face, though my eyes were blinded with tears. My mind was in turmoil: *Will he come home again? What if he doesn't return? How will my child and I survive without him?*

Elidi looked at me steadfastly and said, "Wait for me, and I will return by the time the grapes are ready to harvest."

I did not leave his encircling arms until he released me. His eyes met mine and he stroked my hair. "Do not fear, dear Olwen. When our mission is over- and I'm certain it will be successful – I will be back with you and Nikos." He leaned forward and kissed me, then he lifted Nikos from Aricia's arms. Nikos giggled when Elidi kissed him and reached up to grasp a handful of his father's hair. "When you are grown, my little man, I will take you sailing with me, just as my father did for me." He turned to Theon who was standing nearby. "Take care of my wife and son. I know they are safe with you. You will give them a good life while I am gone."

As he mounted the skala, he turned once to wave at me. Through my tears I took one long last look at him, his pleasant, bronzed face framed with curling dark hair, his warm smiling mouth and steady brown eyes. Elidi and I had been together for such a short time, but that time together had changed my life. Nothing would be the same again. I tried to collect myself, but the tears would not stop falling. Elidi was everything to me. Nothing would be the same until he came home again.

As the warships sailed out of Pella's harbour, I felt as if part of my life was departing. I stood watching, my palms pressed into my eyes to stop the tears. When I looked up again the ship had left the lagoon.

Cheers sounded across the water as fleet rowed full speed seaward. The wind gusted, and a surge of waves thundered in, smashing against the jetty. As I turned away from the shore, a wave from the wash of the ships came and sent a spray over me, chilling my flesh. A thought came to me, grandfather's words *"a storm is coming."* I heard it plainly as if it was a sign from the gods I pulled back from the water's edge. Elidi was in Poseidon's hands now. I stretched out my hands said a prayer to the sea gods, to their god Poseidon and mine, Lyr.

"Great gods of the deep, Lords of the waves, currents and tides,
keep my beloved one safe and bring him home to me again."

Stanza Two

We had hoped to return to the farmstead before the summer solstice, but that was not to be. The new queen, Eurydike, was with child, and as we were preparing to depart, a message came from the king asking Theon and I to remain to attend his new wife's birth. Reluctantly, Theon agreed to stay.

A few days later, a letter from Alexandros was delivered to the palace, sending greetings to his father.

"Does this mean he will reconcile with the king?" I asked.

"It seems they have struck a bargain," Theon said. "Now that Filippos is making plans to make war with the Persians, he needs Alexandros. After Alexandros's victory at Chaeronea, Filippos knows he can rely on the boy."

"And the queen?"

"She has agreed to return with him. Olympias never lets Alexandros far out of her sight."

I wondered how Alexandros would receive the news of the new queen's pregnancy. And what would his vengeful mother do when she learned a new heir would be born?

"Filippos will send his new wife and newborn babe to the old palace of Aigia, out of harm's way," Theon explained, though I could tell by his furrowed brow and the tenseness in his voice he was as concerned as I was. "Alexandros will be welcomed back. But Olympias..." He shook his head. "If she returns, it will not bode well."

I remember Olympias's rage at the king's marriage to the young girl, her unbridled wrath and how she had cursed them both. Surely no good would come of it!

On that day the new queen's birth pangs began, Theon and I were called to her royal quarters. As we approached the woman's stoa, Filippos was there, waiting for Theon and me at the entrance to the woman's stoa. He didn't appear as war-weary as the last time I had seen him. He was dressed in a short white tunic and looked tanned and robust. His dark, grey-streaked hair and beard were neatly trimmed and he wore a gold-studded patch over his blind eye. We followed him along the stoa. He limped on his bad leg, but he looked strong and fit – younger than his forty years.

He was obviously excited but also seemed somewhat wary. Theon assured him all would be well with his young wife and he would stay near the birth room and assist the midwife if it was necessary. "Olwen is experienced in these things" he said, glancing at me with a smile. "She will be ready to assist and make certain the birth goes well."

Filippos scrutinized me at first with a frown, then his countenance brightened and he smiled. "Ah yes, the little Kelt healer. I heard you did well at

Chaeronea with our wounded. There was a lot of praise for you – your kindness and expert healing skills." He turned away abruptly before I could respond.

My skin prickled as a steward led us through the palace to the door that led to the queen's quarters. Even though the old queen was gone, I could still feel her sorcery.

"The king and I will wait here," Theon said. He laid a reassuring hand on my shoulder and nodded a greeting to a dark-skinned maiden, the queen's attendant, who was waiting at the entrance. "Attis has come to take you to the birthing room".

I followed the maiden into the room. All the nooks and crannies seemed to hum with voices, every shadow moving as though possessed by spirits. Although the room had been cleared of Olympias's belongings, this was still her domain, and she had made certain the spirits she had conjured would remain. I remembered her anger on my last visit there and how she had cursed Filippos: '*The day will come when he will know my vengeance for this betrayal!*'

I wondered: *What will Olympias do now that his new wife is giving birth?* Even now the memory of her demonic outburst made me shiver with fear. How will she avenge the birth of this new heir to Makedon's throne?

The new queen, Eurydike, lay white and still, propped on the birthing chair. She was a young girl – no more than fifteen summers. Seeing her brought back memories of my own youth – how fragile and vulnerable I had been. A sudden thought pierced me, of that day in the forest when Sholto had attacked me. I was no more than her age then, and as virginal and innocent as a child. If he had raped me, for certain he would have cast me off later and sold me as a slave.

If Alexandros hadn't come and saved me... I shook the terrible memory from my mind.

The midwife was a plump, elder woman. She looked me over with a critical eye. "I know you are a healer," she said," but have you assisted in a birth?" I told her what I knew about the birthing. "I gave birth myself a year ago," I said. "And I have knowledge about midwifery. The king requested I attend."

"Well then," she said in a stern voice. "You will bide by what I tell you and assist me when the babe is ready to come. Meanwhile, you can bathe her and try to soothe her. The girl is frightened and needs comforting."

I knelt beside the birthing chair and held the girl's hand. She was trembling, her face ashen and tear-streaked. I offered her an infusion of herbs to ease her pain. When she cried out in fear as the contractions wracked her body, I said a prayer to Eleuthyia, the goddess of childbirth.

I assisted the midwife, showing the girl how to move and relax. The midwife called for her assistants to bring more water and warm cloths. As the pains came closer the girl's shrill cries grew louder. I tried to comfort her, remembering back to my own birthing.

Finally, after a struggle, the child was born. The birth cord was tied, the afterbirth delivered. I helped wash the young queen in warm rose-scented water as the midwife held the small red crumpled infant in her arms.

"It's a girl!" she said. There was acclamation of praise from the servants and other midwives as she lifted the child to view.

The king was called into the room. The midwife held out the tiny infant to him. He took the babe in his arms and pulled back the swaddling clothes. Filippos's bearded face cocked sideways as he peered at the baby out of his one good eye. "A son?"

"No sir, you have another daughter!" the midwife exclaimed.

I saw his look of dismay. Clearly, he was disappointed, "A girl!" His face reddened and he thrust the infant back into the midwife's arms. "I had dreamed of another son!"

"She's a fine, strong girl, sir. She'll grow to be a beauty like her mother." She put the babe gently into Eurydike's arms. "Do not fret," she whispered. "He'll grow to love her just like he loves you."

Filippos looked over at his young wife and shook his head. At first I thought he might storm out of the room. Instead he walked over and bent down to kiss Eurydike.

"My lord," she cried. "I'm sorry – I'm sorry it was not a boy child. I know you wanted another son."

It was plain to see he was disappointed by the birth of a girl. 'No matter," he said, his voice gruff. "We will try again." He peered again at the babe in her arms. "We'll call her Kleopatra."

"But my lord, that is the name of your other daughter," Eurydike said.

"Then we'll name her Eurydike, after my mother... and you," Filippos said with a wry smile. "It's a regal name. And this girl is a true Makedonian."

He bent and kissed the young queen with no more affection than he would have shown his elder daughter, and left the room before she could reply.

Stanza Three

Not many days passed before news came that the king was moving the new queen and the newborn to the old palace at Aigai. I was concerned he would consider taking the fragile young mother and her baby away from Pella, but Theon explained it was only a few days journey.

"The old palace was used by Makedonian kings for many years, but now Filippos and Alexandros only visit there during hunting season. It's in the hills near the royal tombs, and it is a quiet retreat for them." Theon shrugged and shook his head. "Besides, with Olympias returning to Pella, it is the safest place to be for the new queen and her child."

There had not been any recent news about Alexandros and Queen Olympias, but a few days after the royal entourage had left for Aigai, the palace was astir: Alexandros and Olympias were returning from Epirus.

Theon and I went with the others to the palace compound to welcome them. To the fanfare of trumpets and lutes, Alexandros strode up to the dais with his friend Hephaestion close beside him. He was wearing simple homespun clothing, unadorned, and looked tanned and in good spirits. His arm was around his friend as they stood amidst his other companions. Although Hephaestion was slightly taller and darker than Alexandros, it was as though he was Alexandros's shadow. They moved alike as though they were one in spirit and mind.

They mounted the small dais in the courtyard together to make a welcome speech. The queen stepped up beside them. Slender as a willow, Olympias wore a plain garment of soft embroidered wool. She was still young in appearance, her face blushed with cosmetics. She stood next to Alexandros, straight as a spear, her head held high, her glossy chestnut-coloured hair falling over her shoulders. She smiled, standing proudly aloof as she accepted the welcome praise of the palace servants and the king's regent, Antipator, who had come to welcome them in the king's stead.

"I have returned with my mother to our rightful place," Alexandros announced. "We are happy to be back in Pella. I will serve with my father, the king, as he plans his campaign against the Persians who have over-run our land in Ionia."

The crowd cheered, shouting his name, "Alexandros! Alexandros!" There was no doubt he had their support. Everyone was happy to welcome him back.

When the king returned alone from Aigai, it seemed as though peace might once again reign in the palace. Then one morning Theon was summoned to Filippos's audience room. I waited anxiously for his return, wondering what news he would have about the king's reunion with Alexandros and Olympias. However, when I saw the dour look in Theon's face, I knew there must be more troubling news.

"Filippos wanted me to attend to his older son, Arridaios, who has complained of a fever and runny nose. It seemed just a minor ague, nothing of great concern. What did concern me was Filippos's plans for Arridaios."

Theon sat on the bench in the courtyard, his head in his hands, pausing for some time before he spoke again. When he looked up I could see the concern on his face.

"Filippos has been sending secret envoys to spy and report to him on Karia, one of the most powerful satrapys on the Asian coast which is under rule of the Persian Shah. They told him that Pixodorus, the king of Karia, has a daughter of ripe marriage age. So Filippos has sent a message to the king asking to betroth his daughter to Arridaios." He muttered an oath. "I have advised Filippos that Arridaios should mingle more with the people to help stir his wits. But for him to wed? To force a young woman to wed this incompetent dolt? Filippos is doing this simply to seize control of Karia, and because the king is an ally of Persia. He has given no thought to the outcome." He shook his head. "He's using Arridaios until his new wife gives birth to a boy. Arridaios is twenty years old and has grown a beard, but he still wets himself and has fits. He may have a strong body but he has a useless mind. To engage him to the daughter of the Karian satrap – a move designed to consolidate their houses - is a mistake. Unfortunately, Pixodorus has agreed. Clearly he has no idea of what Arridaios is capable of. How can Arridaios be a spouse to this young girl?"

I fell silent with shock. I had seen Alexandros's older brother sometimes wandering the palace gardens with his Keeper. He appeared to be like other young men, though he was obese and rarely spoke. I knew the story of his birth – how he was the son of one of the king's lesser wives and had been poisoned at a young age, supposedly by Filippos's jealous new queen, Olympias - leaving him with no more wits than a three-year-old.

"It will be a marriage of proxy and designed for the king to gain a hold on Karia." Theon said. "I tried to dissuade him against it, but Filippos is adamant, insisting the marriage will win him Karia. Nothing will deter him."

A day later, Aricia came to see me, her cheeks flushed, bursting with excitement.

'You must come to hear the king's news, my lady! There is a rumour that he has found a wife for Arridaios!"

Theon looked up from the scrolls he was studying and gave a long sigh. "Filippos is a fool! You go, Olwen. I prefer to stay here and read the wise words of Hippocrates."

A small crowd of palace residents and servants had gathered in the compound in front of the palace as Filippos led Arridaios to the palace parade ground. Filippos mounted the podium, Arridaios stumbling after him, his Keeper urging him on as if he was afraid. Arridaios's mouth gaped open, saliva dribbling into the thin wisp of his reddish beard. He was carrying a toy horse in his hand. He was much like his father, favouring Filippos's dark complexion. He was somewhat taller than Alexander, but obese and awkward, dressed in a cuirass and greaves. I had only seen him wearing a plain tunic, so it seemed his father had something important planned for him.

When Filippos made the announcement that he had engaged his son to the daughter of the king of Karia at first there was a bewildered silence. I saw people nudging and whispering to each other. Then they began to cheer, hesitantly at first, then loud enough to make Arridaios begin to tremble in fear.

Filippos put a comforting arm around him and said, "My son is overcome with joy that he will be wed to the daughter of the Karian king. This marriage will help us consolidate our campaign against the invaders from the East."

The crowd cheered again, this time louder. Filippos grinned and raised his hand in a salute. "I have won us Karia by the marriage proposal," he said.

A few days later, as I sat in the courtyard under the plane tree by the fountain, watching little Nikos play with his wooden toys, I saw Alexandros coming down the path through the palace gardens, his dog, Peritos, following at his heels. Oddly he was without his companion Hephaestion.

I turned my attention back to my son who was growing into a curious and active child, sturdy and brave. So like his father, I thought, as I watched Nikos, his tousled dark hair bent over a toy ship he was sailing in the fountain's pool. I missed Elidi. No word had come from him. It would be months before there would be any envoys returning from Ionia with news.

As I sat there, Alexandros passed right by without seeming to notice me, and shouted Theon's name at the door. Then, without waiting for a reply, he went straight into the house. I could hear his voice, strained and shrill with anger.

"What is my father thinking of, marrying the idiot off to a Karian princess? My mother has found out about it and she flew into a rage. I have convinced her we should send my friend, Thetallos the actor, to Karia to convince the satrap that *I* should marry his daughter instead of Arridaios."

Theon's voice was firm yet gentle as he tried to calm Alexandros, but to no avail.

"Hephaistion is against the plan, but it's the only way I can assure I keep my hereditary right!" Alexandros retorted. "Father has betrayed me by passing me over in favour of that brainless dolt."

Theon reproached him for behaving so foolishly. "Why do you wish to marry the daughter of a mere Karian who is no more than a slave of a barbarian king?"

There was more discussion, but I had turned my attention away to play with Nikos. When Alexandros eventually came out of the house, he did not look my way and strode determinedly back toward the palace. I was certain Theon had counselled him with strong words, not just a scolding. I hoped he had taken heed.

After Alexandros departed, Theon came out to the garden. He sat down on the stone bench beside me, shook his head, and sighed. "Alexandros has gone too far this time. He's impulsive and rash. He must learn to rein himself in to avoid trouble with his father. It is foolish for him to interfere."

"Who is this Thetallos whom Alexandros has sent to Karia?" I asked.

"He's an actor and a citizen of Athens and has no rights here," Theon explained. "He could be hung for this treachery, but he's an artist of Dionysos and his person is declared sacred. This does not bode well. No good will come of it." He opened his mouth as if to say more, then shut it again. Some things are best left unsaid.

Theon's words rang true. Within days the buzz of gossip spread throughout the palace. Filippos had found out what Alexandros had done. He flew into a furious rage because his plans for a diplomatic marriage to help his forthcoming Asian invasion had been thwarted.

"Filippos accused Alexandros of treachery and called him a traitor and a fool. In doing what he did he has lost his father's chance to win Karia. Filippos has sent a formal letter to Pixodoros with Arridaios's signature, withdrawing from the foolish betrothal. He told Alexandros that while he and his mother were here in Makedon, he must keep his hands out of his mother's plots or both of them could go back to Epirus and stay there."

"How can he exile his own son?" I asked. "Alexandros is heir to the throne!"

"Yes, it is unfair," Theon agreed, "but Filippos is his father, and Alexandros has wronged him. He has lost Karia, one of the most important ports on the Middle Sea. He should have had more sense than to let himself become a Persian vassal. Filippos has banished Alexandros's friends and forbidden them from meddling in palace affairs. And he has ordered Thetallos to be thrown into prison when he returns. The parody is, it turns out the girl is only a child – barely eight years old. But I fear Alexandros has created enough mischief to severely put a rift in his relationship with his father."

Amid the strife, the most serene place I could go for comfort was the god's shrine in the woods below the back wall of the palace. I had not visited for some days and wanted to make an offering to the gods to plead for Elidi's safety on his voyage.

As I went down the path leading to the grove the words came to my mind: *'I am a wave breaking on the shoreline. I am the threatening roar of the sea. I fill men's hearts with terror.'*

As I drew closer I sensed a shadow in the grove and felt my skin prickle. The air seemed to hum with magic, and I felt something tug me back, slowing my footsteps. When I looked again, I saw it was not a shadow, but a figure dressed all in black. Perhaps it was a palace crone come to make an offering at the shrine? I could not be sure, and I stopped in my tracks and hid behind an oleander bush to watch.

The woman had set a lighted torch in the altar slot, and when she stood back, I saw that she was holding a small black pup in her hands. She pulled back the shroud from her head and loosed her hair from its clips; a tumble of chestnut hair fell loose over her shoulders. It was Olympias!

I watched as she held up the tiny pup by its hind legs. It wriggled and squealed as she hacked at its throat with a knife. Finally it stopped twitching and she put it on the altar where it lay still. Then she knelt before the altar and raised her hands in supplication to the god. Her hands were drenched with the dog's blood. She began to beat on her breast calling out to Eris and Hades in a wild, frightening supplication. I heard her cry the words *Filippos, Thanatos!* She was calling a curse on her husband, a curse of death! What dire consequences could this have? Surely her curse was one of grievous intent.

I kept myself hidden until she was gone, then trembling with fright I made my way back to our cottage. I was so shaken by what I had seen I could not even speak about it to Theon. I was afraid if Olympias knew I had spied on her in the grove I could put my own life in jeopardy.

Stanza Four

I was beset with worries after what I had witnessed in the grove. What if Olympias learned I observed the hateful rites she had performed? Would she turn her spitefulness on me and put a curse on me? So it was with great relief when, one morning, Theon said, "We must return to the homestead!'

I sensed he was as deeply troubled as I was. His face was pale and drawn the lines on his brow deeper, his hair and beard had grown more grey. We were both weary of the drama, the tension among the royal family. And I still held the secret of what I had witnessed in the grove, terrified it would be made known to Olympias.

"There is no real need for us to remain any longer in Pella," Theon said.

Alexandros had been assigned to train the young ephebes for his father's army, so we seldom saw him. The king was away in Aigai tending to his newly pregnant wife and planning the marriage of his elder daughter, Kleopatra, to her uncle, Queen Olympias's brother, who was the king of Molossia.

The more modest life of the country appealed to me more than the palace where there was always treachery and intrigue afoot. Although the thought of returning to the tranquility of the farmstead filled me with happiness, I still waited hopefully to hear news from Elidi.

Theon sensed my concern. "Elidi's fleet will not return until Parmenio and Attalos have secured a peaceful pact with the Persians and expelled those who are occupying Hellenic lands. There is no need for us to stay here any longer. I think we have served the king very well."

So, we packed up the mule cart and set off.

It was still early in the season. We would be home well before midsummer. As we turned our backs away from Pella, heading north toward the distant snow-capped mountains, I felt a stirring of excitement, a relief from the stress and gloom that had languished in the palace. Perhaps this change of pace would bring good fortune.

We followed the road along the river across the marshlands, past grazing flocks, fields ablaze with poppies and mud-brick farmhouses.

By early nightfall, we reached the homestead. I felt a surge of excitement and held up little Nikos so he could see. "Look, Nikos! Here is your home! See the sheep? And there's the horse you can ride when you get a bit older."

Nikos bounced happily on my knees and clapped his hands. "Horse? Sheep?"

"Yes, and there are chickens too... and a rooster."

He laughed and made a crowing sound. He was happy, and I was too. We would be comfortable and safe here while we waited for his father to return.

The hired boy had carefully tended everything. The cobbled courtyard was strewn with fallen blossoms from the plum tree. Against the pink-washed stone wall of the thatched roof cottage, the pots of wild roses were ready to bloom. A few stray hens pecked among the remnants of last year's crop in the garden and in the vineyard the vines were budding.

I set Nikos down under the plane tree and went to help Theon unload the cart. Nikos had turned three at midsummer. He was growing fast, a plump sturdy child with softly curling black hair and delicate brows. I could see his father in his wide dark eyes. He had learned to speak quickly. He spoke Greek and I taught him some Cymru words too and told him stories of my childhood in Caer Gwyn. He would soon be old enough for other lessons Theon would teach him.

He asked incessant questions. "Why" and "How" and sometimes he asked for his father.

"Your papa is at sea, and he will return soon," I said,

I spoke to him about Elidi often so he would not forget his father. "You are Nikos Elimidis," I said. "That is the name your papa gave you."

I was pleased to see how he would often emulate something that mirrored Elidi – the tilt of his head, a gesture, and smile. He seldom said the word 'Papa' but when he did it was with a smile and usually when he was playing with his little boats in the pond.

"Your papa is far away at sea," I said. "But the sea gods will bring him home to us soon." He was still too small to understand how much I missed his father, but when he played with his toy trireme I knew he was aspiring to be like him.

That summer, we spent our days in the meadow. I took Nikos with me when I went to collect herbs just as Essylt had taken me as a child. Like Essylt, I taught Nikos the names of the herbs and what they were used for.

Theon had become like a grandfather to Nikos, just as Maelgwn had been to me. He introduced Nikos to the farm animals, let him ride the mule and help herd the sheep, and showed him how to collect the hens eggs without smashing them. He even built a small pond for Nikos to sail his toy boats in.

We were playing with Nikos's boats in the pond one day when Alexandros came by, riding his fine steed Bucephalus, his faithful dog Peritos loping behind him. When Nikos saw the horse and rider approaching us his eyes opened with surprise and he cried, "Papa? *Patera mou?*"

I was as surprised as he was. At first I had thought it was an envoy until I recognized the rider.

"No my boy, it's Alexandros," I said. "Prince Alexandros."

I hadn't seen Alexandros for months. He sat straight on his horse, looking lean and handsome. He was clean-shaven and tanned his coppery hair tangled from the wind.

He alit from his horse and strode over, smiling to greet us, holding out his hand, calloused from spear-shaft and sword, to clasp mine.

"You came alone," I said. "Where is Hephaestion? You're always together."

"I left him in charge of the ephebes" he said. "I have brought a message for Theon." He looked down at Nikos who was gazing up at him, wide-eyed, and bent to scoop up him in his arms. "Ah! You're a fine little man!" He examined the toy trireme Nikos held. "And I see you like sailing boats just like your father."

Nikos held out his toy boat and smiled. "I like boats!"

"You'll make a good seaman like him then," Alexandros said, and set the child firmly down on his feet. He turned to me and smiled. "You have raised a fine son!"

The dog ran up and nuzzled Nikos. "That's my dog, Peritos," Alexandros said when he saw Nikos shy away. "Don't be afraid. He's a gentle soul and he won't hurt you! I got him when I was as little as you are."

"When I'm big I'll get a dog, and I'll teach it to fetch things!" Nikos said. He wrapped his arms around Peritos's neck and let the dog lick his face.

Alexander looked around and inquired, "Where is Theon? I have brought a message from my father – an invitation to my sister's wedding."

Theon had heard the horse gallop up and came out of the house. "Alexandros! What a pleasure that you have come."

He invited Alexandros in for a cup of wine. I took Nikos's hand, and we followed them into the house.

"Father wishes you to attend my sister's wedding," Alexander said. He handed Theon a rolled piece of parchment. "Here's the official invitation. He is marrying my sister to our uncle, Alexandros king of Molossia. It will help father consolidate our kingdoms."

I had rarely seen his sister, Kleopatra. She was younger than I, probably no more than fourteen. I wondered how it would fare for her, marrying a man who must be much older than her, just as her father had married the young niece of Attalos. But such was life in Makedon, a life so different than mine would have been in Caer Gwyn. At her age I would have been dedicated to the goddess and sent to the Holy Isle to learn more of the healing arts if Sholto had not stolen me away. At least, I thought, marrying an elder uncle may not be as horrid a fate as being stolen away by a renegade chieftain.

As Alexandros rode away back to Pella, Theon laid down the scroll and turned to me. The lines on his face had deepened. "I will tell you the story about the man who will become Kleopatra's husband," he said. "The Molossian tribes of Epirus are powerful and rule the whole western seacoast. They come from a famous lineage – that of Achilles – and Filippos has traded with them for years. When their king, Olympia's father, died and her brother Alexandros was too young to become king, Filippos brought him to Pella. As soon as he was old enough, Filippos named him king of the Molossians." He got up from the table and stood silently for some time gazing out the doorway toward the fields. Finally he spoke again. "When Olympias went back to Epirus after the king rejected her in favour of his new bride, she tried to provoke her brother to make war on Filippos, but he would not. Instead, he made an alliance with Filippos in exchange for an agreement to marry Kleopatra. Filippos is a crafty man. He's done this so he will have more control over the Molossians."

His words had an ominous sound, but I quickly put them out of my mind. Even though it would only be for a few days, I felt reluctant at the thought of leaving the quiet solitude of the farmstead to return once again to the turmoil I was sure we would encounter back at the palace. But we must go, or it would slight the royal family.

Stanza Five

The next day, in the dark before dawn, we left to return to Pella. As we approached the city I saw a meteor flare across the sky toward the west, its yellow glow and fiery tail plunging into the abyss. I felt a chill. Was this dragon's fire an omen of ill will?

Theon sensed my unease, and said: "Call it an omen or not, the gods will be at Aigai."

I turned my attention back to my son. "You see? There's the ocean, and the city where the king lives."

"And the ships?" Nikos asked. "And Papa?"

I hugged him tight. "No sweet child, Papa isn't there. But he will come home soon."

Aigai was only a short journey from the royal city so we would arrive there for the marriage rites that would begin by mid-morning. The road from Pella led west, toward the mountains, a narrow-rutted trail that wound through the foothills where oaks and chestnut trees shaded the way. We were not the only travellers on the road. The king had invited land barons and allies from the area to attend the wedding, so there was a stream of wagons and riders on horse-back, some already celebrating, lifting wine cups as they rode with cheers of "Long live King Filippos!" and "Blessings to the bride!"

I had expected to see a city as grand as Pella, but Aigai was not much more than a collection of scattered villages loosely connected around the palace which stood on a high rise fortified by a defence wall that was lit with torches.

Coloured banners fluttered from the ramparts. Below it, in a shaded grove, was the theatre, set on a low slope overlooking the fields and hills.

A fragrant breeze from the forest and the scent of burning pine from the torches filled the air along with the sweet aroma drifting up from the altars where priests in white robes were tending the sacrifices. Theon explained that on the first day there would be a festival honouring the bride and groom. Filippos had planned a grand processional to pay tribute to them and the gods.

"The king has sent his chief diviners to Delphi to consult with the oracle," Theon said. "The diviners said the oracle told them *'The bull is garlanded, the sacrifice is ready. The end fulfilled and the slayer too is ready.'* Filippos thinks the 'sacrifice' means the Persian king, Darius. So once the wedding is over, he will prepare to go to war against the Persians."

I thought over what Theon had said. *The bull is garlanded, the sacrifice is ready.* I recalled the dragon's fire I had seen in the sky falling in the direction of Aigai. Was it a portent of good or ill?

Any thoughts of foreboding I had were quickly dispelled as we entered the theatre and a steward led us to our seats in the curved row below the podium where the king had set up his throne, flanked with chairs for his new son-in-law and his son, Alexandros.

The small theatre was packed with people: soldiers, tribal lords and chiefs of the hill people. In the upper tiers were the noted athletes, charioteers, singers and musicians who would compete in the Games after the wedding.

I was surprised to see the king's former bodyguard, Pausanias, among the guards. I remembered how rumours had circulated in the palace after the infamous falling-out at Filippos's wedding to Attalos's daughter. I had heard Filippos had replaced him with a new favourite, but Theon explained the king had appeased him by promoting Pausanias to Commander of the Guard.

The crowd began to cheer as King Filippos, dressed in a purple cloak, crowned with golden laurel leaves entered and stood before his throne. Beside him was the groom, Alexandros of Molossia, a handsome man, still youthful in appearance, his beard neatly trimmed, coppery hair curled and cut to the nape and crowned with a wreath of gold oak leaves. On Filippos's other side was Prince Alexandros dressed in a white chiton and a blue cape clasped with a gold pin. Like the groom, he also wore a crown of gold oak leaves.

Just below the king's throne, Queen Olympias sat straight-backed in a tall chair beside her daughter, dressed in a clinging saffron-coloured gown. There was a flush on her cheeks and a slight smile on her face. Her dark russet hair, crowned with a wreath of golden oak leaves shone in the sunlight. Even at a distance she exuded an aura of sorcery, as if the dark powers surrounded her. Alexandros bent down and spoke to his mother. She whispered something back, a smug smile on her face.

Kleopatra, the young bride, sat beside her mother looking somewhat bewildered. Wearing an elaborate bridal gown of white and gold; except for her red hair she favoured her father's stocky build. She was no more than fourteen, the same age I had been when I was enchanted by the goldsmith Teag. It made me smile to think of him. How vulnerable and innocent, how devastated when he had chosen Aeron, the ricon's daughter, even though I was promised to serve the goddess and ready to be sent to the Holy Isle. I had almost forgotten the coins Teag had given me – the gold coins embossed with the image of King Filippos. I still kept them in my amulet bag as a kind of talisman. How could Teag or I ever have guessed his coins, would lead me here to Makedon!

I looked for the king's new queen, but Theon explained she was not on the royal podium as she was confined to the palace awaiting the birth of a child.

Down in the theatre's orchestra, fires glowed on a circle of twelve altars set up to honour the gods of Olympus. There was a bellowing of trumpets as a garlanded sacrificial white bull was led up to the altar by the King's chief diviners, the priests of Apollo and Zeus who had brought Filippos the oracle from Delphi.

Little Nikos clapped and squealed when he saw the bull. I enfolded him and stroked him, to shield my son from the rites, afraid the sight of that magnificent animal being sacrificed might haunt him forever the way Mithras's sacrifice had haunted me.

Once the sacrifice was made, a blast of trumpets heralded a splendid parade of twelve floats honouring the gods that entered the theatre through the tall gateway of the parados. Each cart was drawn by brightly caparisoned horses. First came King Zeus, on a gilded throne, garlanded with his staff and eagle.

I pointed out each one to Nikos. "There's Zeus on his throne. And Apollo, the musician. See his golden lyre? And there's Demeter crowned with a sheaf of golden corn."

Nikos shrieked with excitement when he saw Queen Hera with her peacocks, and Artemis the hunter with her stag.

"And there's Athena! See? She is holding her spear – and here comes Ares the war god, and Hermes the messenger." When the float with Aphrodite seated with Eros on a flowered throne went by I thought of the young queen Eurydike, who was in the lying room recovering from her birth, and Kleopatra, the new bride. What would be their destiny?

Nikos shrieked with excitement when I pointed out Poseidon on his sea horse chariot. "Yes, Nikos, that is your Papa's god – Poseidon!" I felt a pang of sadness when I thought of Elidi. If only he could have been there with us to share this special day!

Finally the last of the floats entered through the gate greeted by a deafening fanfare of trumpets. On it was the life-like image of Filippos wearing a Persian tiara, sitting on an eagle-headed throne, his feet resting on a winged bull.

"That represents the Persian King Darius!" Theon whispered to me. 'Just a clever reminder of Filippos's intentions to overthrow the Persians!"

After the parade of floats, all the invited chieftains and lords of Makedon marched into the theatre to the beat of the deep-toned pipes. The Royal Guard led the march. Pausanias swaggered at their head dressed in his parade armour, waving to his friends in the crowd.

There was a blare of trumpets, and the crowd cheered "Long live the King!"

I glanced up to the tier where the bridegroom and Alexandros stood beside Filippos's empty throne. Olympias was staring straight before her toward the parados.

Pausanias, standing alert with the Royal Guard, looked straight ahead toward the doorway of the theatre as the king entered through the parados riding on a white horse. Pausanias barked an order to the Guards and Filippos walked his horse up toward them and saluted. He reined in his steed, and as he dismounted, Pausanias moved forward to assist him.

As he stepped down, Filippos stumbled on his lame leg and Pausanias offered him his arm. Then, so swift that it was hardly noticeable except for the quick glint of silver off a blade, Pausanias stepped back and the king fell. There was a long moment of disbelief as the crowd waited for Filippos to struggle to his feet. He moved once, then fell back.

At that moment Pausanias made a dash toward the gate as one of the other guards ran forward screaming: "He's killed the king!"

Now I could see clearly there was a dagger protruding from Filippos's chest. His white tunic was drenched with blood. After a moment of shock, Theon leapt down from the tier and raced toward the fallen king. The screaming of the crowd had frightened Nikos and he began to cry. As I comforted him, I looked up and saw Olympias. She seemed unmoved, standing motionless, still staring ahead, a smug smile on her face, her eyes fixed on the turmoil. Her daughter, Kleopatra, clung to her arm wailing and tearing at her hair.

The words I had heard Olympias cry out in the grove came back to me: *Filippos, Thanatos!* She had called a curse on her husband. Surely the dragon's fire I had seen in the sky, falling over Aigai, had been an omen of ill will!

Alexandros had run down from the royal tier to the orchestra and was bending over his father's body. I heard his anguished cry: "My father is dead! The king has been slain!"

Theon was on his knees beside the king's body. I knew he would do what he could to help. But it was too late.

Alexandros's friend, Hephaestion, and a crowd of guards, chieftains and soldiers had gathered around them. From the parados gate someone shouted. "They've caught the killer!"

The entire theatre was in chaos with people crying and calling on the gods. Theon was still bent over Filippos's fallen body while Alexandros stood beside them. He looked pale and his voice shook as he cried out to the crowd. "My father is dead – murdered. But the killer has himself been killed and rest assured I will find out who paid him to commit this evil deed!"

The guards lifted Filippos's body and carried it to the gilded float that held the king's image. The noise of the crowd died to a shocked silence as the cart was led around the theatre and out the gate where it would be taken to the palace and prepared for burial.

Theon looked shaken and pale when he returned to our place on the tier. The king's blood stained the front of his chiton and there was still some on his hands. "I hoped I could save him," he said, his voice trembling and choked with tears. "But the dagger had pierced his heart. It was a Keltic dagger."

A Keltic dagger! I was too shocked to speak. I recalled that day in the forest after Alexandros had rescued me from Sholto – how he had taken Sholto's weapons and later at the hunter's campsite had given the dagger to Pausanias. Was it Sholto's dagger that had killed the king?

"Pausanias tried to flee, "Theon said "but they say he tripped on the roots of a vine and fell. One of Alexandros's Companions, Perdikkas, killed him. Some of the guard are angry because they wanted him alive to confess who paid him to do this terrible deed."

I wanted to tell him of the curse I had heard Olympias utter in the grove, but I was too afraid and shocked to repeat it. I remembered that day in the queen's bedchamber when she had learned of Filippos plan to marry Attalos's niece. *"He has betrayed me. He will live to regret this perfidy!"* What if she had arranged her husband's death? What if Alexandros also knew of the plot to assassinate his father?

Stanza Six

The murder of the king brought chaos to the entire country. The roads into Aigai were jammed with people coming to pay their homage. Theon and I took shelter in the old palace while plans were made for the burial.

Meanwhile, gossip spread like a brush fire. Who was responsible? Was it Queen Olympias? Did Alexander have a part in it? Or did Pausanias, enraged because of his rebuff by Filippos, do it as revenge? Some even suggested the Persians had arranged it and paid Pausanias to carry out the deed, in retaliation for the Makedonian's threat to make war against them. Or could it have been the Athenians? They hated King Filippos as well.

Theon brooded for days after we returned to the palace, even though I did my best to try and give him solace. Eventually he was ready to speak about it, though reluctantly. His voice trembled when he mentioned Filippos's name. Theon had been a physician of the court in Makedon for years and was a friend of the king. What did he think? Did he believe the queen was the instigator? He knew how enraged Olympias had been when Filippos took his younger bride and knew if she were to give birth to a boy child, it would put Alexandros's role as heir to the throne in jeopardy.

"Olympias is an Epirote, not a Makedonian," Theon explained. "She feared he would choose a new full-blooded Makedonian heir over her son." He sighed, and his shoulders sagged. "Filippos and Alexandros have been known to quarrel bitterly over this, and then there was that ridiculous episode when Filippos wanted to marry Arridaios off to that Karian child princess. The rift between father and son has been evident for some time." He leaned his elbows onto the table and put his head in his hands. I put out my hand and gently stroked his shoulders.

"I cannot believe Alexandros would..." I began, my voice trembling with emotion.

Theon looked up and I could see the despair in his eyes. "Nor do I want to believe it. But he may have been influenced by his mother. She has always held a strong control over him." He shook his head. "These nefarious plots are famous in the Makedonian court. The royalty is well known for its treachery."

Theon stood and paced the floor for some time before speaking again. "They should never have killed Pausanias. I am told there were horses waiting for him to aid him in his escape, so surely there were others involved in the plot. He was humiliated by Filippos to be sure, but it seems like he was paid by others to carry out this deed. This appears to have been a calculated and well-executed murder." He went to the side-board and poured himself a cup of wine which he gulped down quickly. "Perhaps we will never know who the guilty ones are, but one thing is certain: Alexandros will carry on his father's plans to raid the Persian lands. If there was animosity between him and his father, Filippos certainly trained him well." He poured another cup of wine and sat back down at the table. "Alexandros has made his mark since he was a youth of sixteen and his father allowed him to *'Found'* a city in his own name after the successful attack on the Thracians. He also joined his father for his campaign against the Scythians. And of course, at Chaeroneia he commanded the cavalry in a successful defeat of the Sacred Band. He's more than ready to step into his father's shoes. I just hope his mother doesn't meddle in his affairs like she has tried to do for most of his life."

King Filippos's funeral was a lavish affair. As was their custom, the king's body would first be cremated along with his favourite steed.

I left Niko in the care of a palace servant and went with Theon to watch the rites. I recalled the day I had accompanied Essylt to pay homage to the ricon's son, Hywel ap Madoc, when he had been killed in battle. Everyone from the humblest peasant to the richest chieftain had assembled for the burial rites. We had made offerings to the gods, especially to Gwyn ap Nudd, the ruler of the Otherworld.

Our burial barrows were in the fields below Caer Gwyn's hill fort, simple mounds heaped with shale and earth. All the members of the Royal War Band and other nobles were buried there. The wains carrying the dead prince's bier were pulled behind the ricon and his Royal War Band. Hywell's bier was made of polished bronze, studded with jet-stone and amber. All of his best weaponry was placed in the barrow with him. His body had been accompanied by one of his young squires who was a willing sacrifice to serve his master on the journey to Annwn, in the Otherworld. There would be no such human sacrifice made at King Filippos's grave.

Just as in Caer Gwyn, a column of mourners filed down the path from Aigai to the site of the royal tombs. As I watched King Filippos's funeral parade, I remembered the song the bards had sung as the auguries were made the day of Hywel's burial:

"We will light the candles on the shrines.
We will spill the wine dregs to the gods;
and after the wine-feast,
we will weep for our brothers and bury the dead."

The gods were lauded by the priests who attended, but there was no dancing to the rhythm of timbrels or the mournful dirge of pipes as Filippos's remains were carried to the funerary pyre. There was no rejoicing that his soul had crossed the River Styx to Hades, that dark, fearsome place of the dead. Our Otherworld, Annwn, is not a place of gloom. We Kelts believe the souls of the dead will return to us when the time is right, so once the dead are safe inside the barrow there is always rejoicing and feasting.

Alexandros stood perfectly still beside the pyre. His face was flushed, and although he kept his dignity, I saw the shine of tears on his cheeks. Beside him stood Olympias, her eyes fixed on the cremation mound. She exuded an aura of perverse triumph. Did I detect a smug smile on her face? No doubt exaltation in the knowledge her son had inherited his father's throne.

The king's body lay on a pallet, shrouded with a purple cloth. It seemed as if he was sleeping, though his face was ashen and gaunt. The priests intoned their funeral rites and declared their king a man worthy of being acclaimed a god.

When the torch was lit and ready to set the pyre alight, I looked away. The stench of burning flesh soon filled the air along with the sobs of onlookers. When I looked up. Alexandros was kneeling by the fiery mound, his body shaking with sobs. Olympias still stood unmoving, her eyes fixed on the flames as they consumed her husband's body.

I heard the frightened neighing of a horse and saw the stable-master leading a tall chestnut stallion toward the pyre. The horse pranced and kicked out with his hooves as the horse master led it toward the pyre. As they came closer, the stallion reared up and shied as if it sensed its doom.

"That is Filippos's favourite war horse," Theon whispered.

The white robed priest intoned the words of the funerary invocation and lifted a thick bladed cleaver. I averted my eyes when the priest raised the cleaver over the horse's neck. It shrieked and tossed as the priest hacked at it. Blood gushed everywhere as the horse collapsed on the pyre. When I looked up again, it was engulfed in flames.

Theon put his hand on my shoulders to steady me. "We must not grieve," he said quietly. "The stallion will ride to the Elysian Fields with the king."

The king's body was cremated hurriedly, burning only the flesh off of the bones. The remains were placed in a golden casket which would be interred inside a tomb filled with extravagant grave goods including artisan's work depicting hunting scenes, drinking vessels, personal items and a vast array of weaponry. I thought back to our own Keltic traditions – how our warriors were buried in simple barrows along with their weaponry, a more modest way of honouring dead heroes, instead of deifying them as they did with King Filippos.

It was usual for Games to be held after the funeral. There would be athletic competitions at Aigai's gymnasium, and dramas and music performed in the theatre. I was curious and eager to attend, but instead Theon insisted we must leave. I could tell by the deep furrows of his forehead and tight set mouth that something dire had made him change his mind about staying – something more than his concern about returning to the farmsteads

I learned the reason for his anxiety. After we had left the theatre, Pausanias's body had been dragged in and hung on a murderer's stake for all to see and curse. Later, Olympias had it taken down and burned it over the same pyre where Filippos had been cremated. There were malicious rumours as to why she had done this. Was it to punish him? I wondered. To send him to Hades with Filippos where he would be tormented for his evil deed?

Then, on the day we left Aigai, Theon told me Olympias had built a shrine to honour Pausanias near the site of Filippos's tomb. It seemed more certain than ever then, that she had a hand in her husband's assassination.

Stanza Seven

The funeral was barely over, and without waiting to observe the funeral games that would be held in the king's honour, we left Aigai to return to Pella. The westering sun was behind us. Autumn had arrived. The oaks and chestnuts in the foothills were turning colour and the rutted tracks of the road were wet with fallen leaves. Shadows crept over the fields. As we drew closer to the city I felt a stirring inside of me, a change of destiny.

We reached Pella at eventide. The setting sun gleamed like an orange flame behind the palace on the city's acropolis. The streets, usually still teeming with people out to enjoy an evening stroll or to sit in the taverns under the trees, were all but deserted. On the corners, some men were gathered in huddles, talking in low tones. I supposed they were discussing the fateful event of Filippos's assassination, probably gossiping over who was responsible for the evil deed.

We made our way to Pella's acropolis where the gate guards greeted us sombrely and a boy was called to take our cart and donkey to the stables.

There was a strange aura inside the palace walls, as if a dark curtain had been drawn. The paved courtyard was scattered with windblown twigs; the pots of flowers and rose bushes wilted. Even the painted colonnades seemed to have lost their lustre. The palace servants shuffled about wordlessly, some barely raising their hands in greetings.

Xenon, the Nubian, met us without his usual cheerful smile. He looked dark and glum as he led us to our abode. Theon grasped his hand in a silent greeting. "We are only here for a few nights," he said. "It's time to leave here to harvest the crops," Theon sighed and gave a weary shrug. "But the official crowning of Alexandros is something we must not miss, Alexandros will expect us to be there."

I was anxious to leave Pella too. The homestead had become my place of solitude and peace and the chaos of the palace did not sit well with me. Yet I knew Theon was right. We must attend the crowning of the new king.

Xenon inquired about Alexandros. He had served in the palace most of his life so I knew he must be grieving the king's death, but nothing was spoken about the assassination or the funeral. Not even a question as to who or why the dreadful deed had come to pass.

"The queen?" When Xenon uttered the word it had a bitter tinge.

"Olympias will return with Alexandros after the funeral games to prepare for the formal ceremony to name him king," replied Theon. Nothing more was said. It was as if everyone was afraid to speak Filippos's name.

I summoned Aricia to prepare our baths. Even she was silent, her usual cheerful demeanour stifled under the curtain of grief.

Little Nikos had already fallen asleep and whimpered when I woke him. "Hush, my little man. You are here in the king's palace but soon we will go back to the farmstead."

He fussed as Aricia undressed him for his bath. She spoke to him in her gentle way and soon he was splashing in the little tub. His childish laughter seemed to brighten the dour mood and soon Aricia was laughing too and chattering to him in her cheerful way. After Nikos was bathed she combed his tangled hair and dressed him in an embroidered tunic of soft wool, then brought him his toys and a tray of sweets.

I was grateful for Aricia's attentiveness and friendship. Except for her, I always felt alone in the palace.

The ceremony to crown Alexandros as king was held in the palace throne room. I had never been inside the throne room, and as we stepped over the marble threshold I gasped with amazement. The vast room was crowded with guests and soldiers, some spilling out into the courtyard. The walls were hung with deep-dyed tapestries and old weaponry polished until they gleamed. The pebble mosaic floors had designs of lions and centaurs and richly painted friezes adorned the walls. The heavy marble colonnades had been entwined with laurel boughs and a lush carpet led to the dais.

The priests had made their offerings, and the altars smouldered with sweet, scented smoke. I knelt beside Theon, close to the rostrum.

Olympias was seated on the dais on a high-backed chair, her lips pressed together. She was dressed in a robe of purple bordered with gold, her hair bound and draped with a silk veil. She sat rigid and unmoving on a sphinx-headed chair. Even without her gaze on me she frightened me. I could feel the touch of her evil and shivered. A dark chill enfolded me. I felt a coldness in the pit of my belly. My skin crawled and I felt my scalp tingle. I made a sign against evil and hoped she didn't see. I thought about Filippos's murder and remembered what she had said to me that day in the bed chamber: *He has betrayed me. He will live to regret this perfidy.* Did she orchestrate her husband's assassination so her son could take the throne?

The tall doors opened, and the crowd cheered as Alexandros entered the palatial room, escorted by Antipatros, the tall grey-haired regent. Alexandros wore a robe of state, woven of wool and dyed a rich purple, the breast and back emblazoned with gold lion masks with glittering emerald eyes. Theon whispered to me that this regal robe had been handed down from former kings of Makedon.

Alexandros's face flushed, he smiled and lifted his hand to salute the crowd. Everyone cheered: "Alexandros! Alexandros! Long live Alexandros!"

Stumbling along behind was his half-brother, the lack-wit Arridaios, an ungainly dark-haired youth, overweight and clumsy. He had grown a beard that made him resemble his father, but clearly he could never achieve maturity and as always, carried a toy in his hand.

As the regent took his place on the rostrum, the crowd cheered again. Antipatros was a well-seasoned warrior, now retired from active combat, and he had been Filippos's regent for several years. He had lost some of his sprightliness but still commanded himself like the esteemed general who had served the king for all the years of Filippos's reign. His voice boomed with the same resonant timbre as when he had commanded his troops. He spoke of Filippos, his voice quavering with emotion. But his voice lifted with enthusiasm when he spoke of Alexandros, reminding the crowd of his blessed birth, and how Filippos had groomed his son well for the kingship.

"Alexandros will follow in his father's footsteps and make Filippos proud," he said. "He has been well trained by his illustrious father and will be victorious in any quest, making us proud Makedonians under his kingship."

He lifted the golden olive-leaf crown from the carved oaken casket a youthful ephebe handed to him. The audience stirred and chattered, then a hush fell over the throne room as he placed the crown on Alexandros's head.

"Alexandros, son of Filippos, I name you king of Makedon and Hegamon of the League of Corinth!"

The accolades of support were deafening. As the cheers increased, Alexandros tilted his head and raised his clenched fist. I could not hear what he said because the sound was so deafening. "Alexandros! Alexandros!" was all I heard.

Hephaestion stepped out of the crowd and mounted the rostrum to stand beside his friend. I saw Alexander clap Hephaestion's hand and raise it with his, smiling down at the crowd.

One of the generals came forward and beckoned to the regent. Antipatros's grizzled brows lifted and his face beamed with a smile. He held up his hand to silence the audience.

"Father Zeus has sent a sign from his heavenly throne!" The crowd grew silent, as if waiting with bated breath. "Yes, Father Zeus, our heavenly protector, purveyor of omens, has sent one of his golden eagles – it is circling above the palace."

There was a gasp, then another cheer and everyone pressed toward the door to clamber out into the courtyard. Alexandros stepped down from the rostrum, Hephaestion beside him, and strode out past his bodyguards. Theon and I and the other guests followed.

Outside, just above the palace rooftops, a great golden bird circled, swooping so low it was almost possible to glimpse the glint of its amber eyes. The crowd gasped and cheered. ,I clung to Theon's arm.

"It truly is an omen!" I whispered. "What do you suppose it means?"

"Victory!" Theon replied tersely. "Alexandros will follow his father's footsteps. The Persians will be vanquished!"

A few days later, some shocking news came from Aigai. Filippos's young wife and the boy child she had recently given birth to were dead – murdered! There was a dark whisper snaking about the court. Who knew what maliciousness it would reveal?

"Olympias must have ordered this heinous deed," Theon said. He paced the floor restlessly, his face flushed, fists clenched. "There is no way she would have allowed a boy-child to live – one who was full-blooded Makedonian who might contest Alexandros's legitimacy to inherit the throne. There has been word that Eurydike's uncle Attalos is dead too – supposedly killed in an encounter with the Persians at Troy-Ilium. Undoubtedly it was likely part of a heinous plot!"

The rumours were quickly squelched when word came from the north that the Illyrians and Thracians had revolted.

Theon's brow creased with worry. "They have taken advantage of the turmoil caused by Filippos's assassination and have risen up against the Makedonian troops who were stationed there," he said.

Alexandros gave up his usual autumn hunting trip and wasted no time sending out the command to the generals to prepare for war. Theon and I went to the parade ground where the troops were assembling. Ranks of men flooded the grounds, gathering around the rostrum from where Alexandros would address the troops. The men were packed shoulder to shoulder in formation, armed with their long sarissas and swords. Behind the foot soldiers, the cavalry sat erect and proud on their war stallions.

Alexandros rode out on his horse, Bucephalus, surrounded by his Bodyguards. He dismounted and stepped up to the platform followed by Hephaestion and his other Companions. His face was glazed and shining. He clasped Hephaestion's hand and raised it with his, smiling down at the troops addressing them for some time, explaining the situation in the northern tribes.

When he announced he would lead them against the rebels, the cheers were deafening. As the roar of the soldier's voices increased, Alexandros tilted his head and raised his clenched fist. He stepped down from the rostrum, his Companions following. He shouted to the troops, and they mounted their horses, galloping away toward the palace.

I couldn't hear what he had shouted to the troops. "Alexandros! Alexandros! Alexandros" was all I heard. There was no doubt he had their allegiance.

The next day, Alexandros led his army north, leaving the regent, Antipatros, in charge of palace affairs. It was the first act of his reign as king. I said a prayer to the gods of war that he would be victorious.

The morning before we left to return to the homestead, Theon went down to the lagoon where the king's royal trireme was anchored. When he returned, he told me he had spoken to the trierarch and because of Filippos death, some of the fleet that had been sent to Asia Minor would return by Spring.

"As Alexandros is the new king, he will want to revive the fleet and prepare it for the invasion," Theon said.

I was elated to hear the news. I had lost count of the months since my beloved husband had set sail. Now that I knew he would soon return to us I could return to the farmstead full of new hope. The crops would be ready to harvest and the grapes ripe for picking. Once our farm chores were completed, Theon said we would return to Pella for the winter, as we always did. We would stay there until Elidi's ship returned.

BALLAD TWENTY-SIX A Prayer To Persephone

Persephone, daughter of Demeter, the earth mother,
gracious goddess who guards the door of the Underworld.
Persephone, nourisher and death bringer,
you were stolen from your bed by powerful Hades.
We offer these sacred olive branches to your captor,
and pray he will release you from the depths of the earth.
Persephone, you are Springtime, you bring the light,
you appear in the fragrant meadows
and the blossoming branches of the trees.
Hear our prayers, Persephone.
We wait for you to return to our realm
and send us the fruits of our harvest.

A Celebration for Hades and Hekate

Stanza One

Autumn 335 BC

It was late autumn when we set off to return to the farmstead. Mist shrouded the hills. I could smell the ripening grapes on the gentle breeze. The clearings rang with birdsong and the orchards were bright with fruit, the crops ready to harvest.

The afternoon light was fading, and clouds billowed over the mountains when we arrived. We unpacked our bundles, and while Theon went out to tend the animals and chickens, I prepared a pot of steaming barley soup. The boy Theon hired to care for the farmstead came with a basket of fresh eggs and fruit from the orchard, so there would be food for us while we tended to the farm chores and harvested the grapes. I felt such peace being back.

Before we left Pella, Theon had spoken to the trierarchs and they said because of Filippos's death, some of the ships would return by Spring. I had lost count of the months since my beloved husband had set sail. Now that I knew he would soon return, I had returned to the farmstead full of new hope.

The next morning I took Nikos with me to gather the herbs we used for medicines and teas. We collected wild rose hips and the red chestnuts that had fallen from the trees. As we picked the tisane, chamomile, mint and fennel for the teas, and the other herbs that cured winter colds, I told him about my Aunt Essylt. He was old enough now to know about my childhood, and to learn about his Cymru ancestors.

"My *modryb* is a healer, like Theon. She taught me everything I know about the plants we use for healing. She is a wise woman, and in our *tuath*, she is much respected."

"What's a *tuath*?" Nikos asked.

"That is my clan. We are from Cymru, the Essyltyr clan, the people of the Raven. Our warriors are the fiercest and bravest. We call our king a *ricon*. His name is Madoc."

We stopped for a while to sit in the shade. "My grandfather was a high priest. His name was Maelgwyn and he was a Druid."

Nikos frowned. "What's that?"

"Druids are star seers," I said. "They can foretell the future in the heavens."

Nikos set down his basket of herbs and looked up at me wide-eyed. "Are they sorcerers? Do they know magic?"

"They worship the oak trees," I explained. "They are very wise men!"

"Can we visit them? Your people. Can we go there?"

I sighed. "No, Nikos. My village, Caer Gwyn, is far away beyond the mountains and across the narrow sea, on a great plain. There is a big circle of giant stones there where we worship our gods."

Nikos's eyes widened. "Can Papa take us on his ship?"

I tousled his hair and smiled. "It's too far away, Nikos. Far, far over the mountains."

As we sat to rest, I told him more of my story. "When I was a baby I was left at the stone circle. My *tadcu,* Grandfather Maelgwyn, found me and brought me home to my *modryb,* Essylt. She became like a mother to me."

Nikos frowned. "Where is your real mama?"

"She must have died when she gave birth to me," I explained. "Someone, probably my father, left me at the stone circle."

He puzzled a moment over this. "Why?"

"He knew the Druids would care for me," I said.

"Why are you here?"

I took a deep breath, and hesitated, not certain I should tell him the whole tale. I simply said, "The gods sent me here... to find Theon and your father..." I set my basket of herbs down and knelt to give him a hug. "And so I could have you, Nikos!" I wrapped my arms around him. The wave of sadness I'd felt when speaking about Essylt and Caer Gwyn quickly vanished as I held my child close to me. "Yes, it was because the gods wanted me to find your father and have you for a son!"

His brow crinkled as he puzzled over what I had told him. Then he asked: "Where did you find Papa?"

"I met him on the king's trireme, when Theon and I went to tend a sick sailor. Your father comes from Phrygia, a country far to the east." I pointed in the direction of the eastern hills. "He became a seaman when he was young and came here to sail on King Filippos's ships."

His face crumbled and his eyes glistened with tears. "When will Papa come back?"

"He will be back as soon as winter is over, in the springtime when the seas are calm."

"Can we go to his ship?"

I hugged him close. "Yes, Nikos. And then Papa will come home with us to the farm."

Stanza Two

The harvest moon waned as October drew to a close. In Caer Gwyn, it was called Onn, the Ash month, and the bards would be singing at our shrines in the ash groves. Furze fires would be lit on the hills so the sheep could graze on the new shoots after the winter.

In Makedon, a festival was held to honour Persephone, daughter of Demeter the Earth Mother, who was abducted by Hades. There would be a torch lighting ceremony in the village and a feast for the goddess, with prayers and votive offerings so Demeter would grant a good harvest. Although it was mostly a women's festival, I took Nikos with me to the enjoy celebration.

As I told him the story of the Earth Goddess's daughter who Hades stole and took to the Underworld, Nikos's eyes widened.

"Why did Hades take her, Mama?"

"Persephone was a beautiful maiden, the only child of Demeter, the Earth goddess," I explained. "Hades saw Persephone and wanted her for himself. So he snatched her from her bed one night and took her with him."

"Why?" Nikos asked, wide-eyed.

"Hades was a cruel man. He ruled the kingdom of darkness, the place where people go when they die."

As I told my little son the story, memories flooded my mind of how, like Persephone, I had been snatched away by an evil man, Sholto. "Once you are taken by Hades to the Underworld you cannot return to Earth." I said.

Could I ever return to Caer Gwyn? I wondered.

I swallowed the lump in my throat and continued the tale. "When her mother discovered Persephone was gone, Demeter began to wander the Earth looking for her. She wandered day and night across the whole world but couldn't find her daughter. The earth became bare, everything died. That is why, when the Harvest Moon shines in the sky, the earth goes to sleep. All the plants die and the trees lose their leaves."

Nikos's eyes brimmed with tears. "Can't she go home?"

I put my arm around him and held him close as I continued the story. "Zeus learned what had happened and demanded Hades send Persephone back to the Earth. Hades agreed, but first he made her eat a pomegranate seed and told her she could only go home for a little while. When she did return to the Earth all the crops grew and the trees grew new leaves."

Nikos clapped his hands and laughed. "And the flowers, apples and grapes."

"Yes, my darling," I said, "That is how we have the springtime! And after Persephone returns to the Underworld it is winter again. But there will always be Spring and soon your papa will come home, and we'll be together again!"

Stanza Three

The first cold winds of autumn had begun. It was the moon of Apellalos, the Hunter's Moon, when the Greeks celebrated the fearsome goddess of the by-ways, Hekate, guardian of Hades. It was always a dark time when the people gathered outside under the moon and sacrificed a black dog in honour of the goddess. In November, the sun descended, and the lords of the Underworld roamed the earth.

It was also an important day for the Cymry and the Kelts as it was *Calan Gaeaf,* the moon of Samhain, when we honoured our ancestors. In Caer Gwyn fires were lit on the hills and the bards and Druids worshipped in the oak grove.

I wanted my son, Nikos, to know the celebrations I enjoyed as a child, so Theon agreed we should have a small festival in the courtyard.

The sky was grey all that day, The autumn winds whispered through the leaves of the trees sending the last leaves spiralling down. The night was chill, so when the sun went down behind the hills, Theon gathered dried branches and twigs then built a small fire outside. We sat around it, the flames burning brightly to warm us.

"The fire keeps the bad spirits away," I explained to Nikos. "Samhain is a time when even fearless warriors are afraid, a time when the sun descends to the underworld and the spirits of our ancestors roam the earth. And some say a fearsome black sow comes with a headless woman to catch the bad people." Nikos's eyes widened and I put my hand on his shoulder. "Don't be frightened, because I will say some spells to protect us. On Samhain eve we sit by the fireside and listen to the elders tell their tales. This is the beginning of the dark side of the year, the black time, when the earth sleeps. It's a time of mischief when the spirits of the dead revisit our world."

Nikos clapped his hands. "Tell me, Mama, about the spirits and black sow."

"I don't want to frighten you," I said.

"Will your grandfather Maelgwyn visit us?"

I smiled and took a deep breath. "I think my grandfather is always near, I feel his spirit and I know he is happy I have found Theon, your papa, and you."

More than five Samhains had passed since I was taken from Caer Gwyn. I had tried to put those fateful memories out of my mind, but this year I was determined not to be frightened and to share the experience of our Keltic tradition with my child. This Samhain would be different. There were no evil spirits here on the farmstead. I was safe here with my son and Theon. But, as I gazed into the flames, I could not help but remember my past and the memories flooded back...

I remembered witnessing Sholto brutally murder his brother and take me captive, the voyage across the narrow sea, and the ship's boy who had befriended me. How Sholto told him we were going to Carnac and when the boy led us to the trail, how I had whispered a message to him to take to Caer Gwyn, and how Sholto killed him and the wayfarer too.

When I thought of the killings I felt an icy chill. It was hard not to forget the brutal days and months of travel by horse and foot across the Keltic lands, and the times I tried to escape Sholto's threats.

I remembered the old crone who had perceived what was the truth and gave me the potions to put in his mead. And that Samhain night in the forest, when I had tried to flee hoping the potions had worked their spell on him.

Even now my body clenched with fear when I recalled Sholto's anger and violent attack; and I whispered a prayer of thanks to Alexandros, who had saved me. I was determined the visions that had been haunting me all these years would now be forgotten forever.

Theon must have sensed my thoughts. He handed me a cup of hot, spiced wine.

"Drink this," he said with a gentle smile. "You are a brave woman, Olwen. You have more courage than anyone. You are the child of the Raven, the goddess's child."

Yes, it was true. I had proven to myself I was a strong woman. Theon had taught me so much and because of him I was much stronger now, and wiser.

I set down the wine cup and took Nikos's hand. "Come, my son. Let mama tell you about how my people celebrate the harvest. On Samhain we dance around the fire and toss white stones into the flames, one for each person." I took a clove of garlic from my amulet bag. "First, I'll say some runes to chase away the fearsome black sow."

I took Nikos by the hand and Theon held mine. Together we skipped around the fire. When we stopped skipping Nikos squealed and clapped his hands with delight as I sang the Samhain song from my childhood.

"Run home at once, or the black sow will snatch you and eat you!"

Afterwards as we sat around the fire again, I said a prayer to my goddess, Cerridwen, our Celtic goddess of nature, and asked her to give us an abundant crop in the springtime.

"In the presence of the goddess I bear offerings... from the Holy Kindred these gifts I offer." I took four small white stones from my amulet bag. "Each stone is for us... one for Theon, and one for you, Nikos, one for me and one for your Papa." I tossed the stones into the fire and said a prayer to the spirit of my Druid Grandfather, Maelgwyn. "May these stones give us long lives...and guard us under the midnight sky."

Theon and I drained our cups silently and poured the dregs for the goddess. Nikos had fallen asleep, so Theon carried him into the house. I sat for a while watching the flames die until only the burning embers remained.

As the Samhain moon beamed it's light down on me, I raked through the coals to find the four white stones. I found three, but one was missing. A strange chill came over me. Was it true that if one of the stones was missing that person would die? And it if was true, who would it be? I thought of Theon. I had noticed how his hair had grown thin and grey. He had aged so much the past months. My little son, Nikos, was a hale and healthy child, and my husband, Elidi... I sighed, remembering the tautness of his muscles, his strength.

I quickly shook off the troubling thoughts. It was a childish ritual after all, something I had played at Samhain once, a time long ago. All would be well. And when it was springtime Elidi would return home!

Stanza Four

Not long after the ominous celebration for Hekate, we heard news from Pella that Alexandros had put down the northern uprising, but there was trouble farther south in Thebes. A man came riding to the farmstead on a beautiful chestnut horse, a grizzled old soldier, no doubt a messenger. He dismounted and walked up to Theon. "Sir, a message from the regent, Antipater."

Theon thanked him and watched him ride away before unrolling the parchment. I could tell by the dour look on his face it was not good news.

"Antipater has summoned me back to Pella," Theon said. "I must return to treat some of the soldiers who have been wounded in Alexandros's campaign in the north."

Even though I knew I must assist Theon, I was reluctant to leave the tranquility of the farmstead.

"Soon the first snows will fall and the roads will become impassable. We must go now." His voice had an urgent tone. "There are rumblings from the city of Thebes in the south. That rascal politician, Demosthenes has been proclaiming in Athens that Alexandros was killed in the siege. In fact, he *was* wounded but..."

I caught in my breath with shock. "Alexandros was wounded? Is it a dangerous wound?"

Theon shrugged. "Likely just a slight flesh wound – the graze of a sword-blade or arrow- nothing life-threatening. He has good-healing flesh like his father. However, the Thebans heard the rumour and are taking it as an opportunity to revolt. I've been told they have received Persian money, and Demosthenes contributed as well. He purchased weapons and donated them to the Thebans. Two Makedonian officers were killed and the Thebans have declared their independence from Makedon." He rose wearily from his chair. "I have no choice but to return to the city."

He must have noticed my look of dismay, and said, "No need for you to leave here Olwen. Stay here with little Nikos. All will be well."

I knew I couldn't let him go alone. He would need me to assist him as he had at Chaeroneia. However, it was with some regrets that I helped him pack the medicines and scrolls for our departure. I dreamed of the day we would no longer have to leave the farmstead. It had become a home to me, my place of solace and safety. But I knew Theon must obey the regent's bidding.

We arrived in Pella the next day as the dying sun reflected gold in the darkening sky. Just as Theon had feared, the news that greeted us at the palace was dire. The Thebans, whose city had been occupied by the Makedonians since the battle of Chaeronea, had staged a major rebellion.

"They resent the rules Filippos imposed on them" Theon explained. "In particular that they had to become a part of the League of Corinth. They prefer to be independent of the other Greek states. So, when they heard Alexandros was in the north with his army, they saw it as an opportunity to rebel." He shook his head. I had never seen him look so downcast. He covered his eyes with his hand and sighed. Then he pushed himself away from the table and began to pace about the room.

"Alexandros tried to make a treaty with them. He has sent several emissaries to see if it could be resolved peacefully, but the Thebans have resisted. Alexandros needs the allegiance of all the city states before he can launch his campaign against Persia. If the Thebans resist, they will face the consequences."

A hospital tent had been set up on the drill field outside the city walls. I left Nikos in Aricia's care in the women's quarters while I went with Theon to tend the wounded soldiers. Most were men who came to have their wounds cleansed and stitched and their broken bones set. While Theon tended those with the most serious wounds, I was kept busy mixing concoctions of honey, bee pollen and oil which would help heal wounds from arrows and sword blades. I steeped herbs in boiling water to make infusions using flowers, seeds and herbs – thyme, chamomile, bilberry and rowan berries which Essylt said had magical powers of healing. I made mixtures of poppy and willow bark to sedate and blunt pain and helped Theon pack wounds with crushed yarrow and honey.

I recalled our days in the hospital tents at Chaeronea, how anxious I had been, horrified by the men's gaping wounds and haunted by the cries of the dying. This time was different. Certainly there were frightening war tales, and some men had suffered serious wounds, but I was calmer, more at ease while I helped Theon.

"You are indeed a full fledged *pharmakes!*" he said. His eyes twinkled when he smiled at me. Was he making a jest? I didn't consider myself a *sorceress*, though I was grateful I had achieved this honor.

"It is because of you, Theon, that I have learned these skills." I thought how pleased my aunt, Essylt, would be if she had heard his words.

Stanza Five

One day, word came from the mountains, that on the march to Thebes, Alexandros had gone to Delphi to seek council from the oracle. The messenger said when the priestess, Pythias, told Alexandros he could not consult the oracle in winter, he had dragged her from the temple, insisting she *must* give him an omen. According to the story, all she had said to him was *"You are invincible, my son."*

"What does that mean?" I asked.

Theon shook his head and muttered a curse. "It was wrong for Alexandros to force the oracle out of her temple. That is hubris! As he is planning his campaign against the Persians this does not bode well!"

The whole palace was on edge as we waited for news from the south. When finally a dispatch came, it was greeted with both celebration and dismay. Alexandros's campaign against Thebes had been rapid and fierce. On his orders, the army had completely annihilated the city and burned it to the ground.

"He has killed or enslaved all the people," Theon said. He sat silently, his head in his hands. When he looked up again there were tears in his eyes. "The only people left alive or free were Pindar the poet and his family. The rest of them... all of the citizens of that city... gone!"

The news shocked me, though I could recall stories of our own people burning down whole villages and slaying whoever they did not take as slaves. "Why only the poet?" I asked.

"Because he wrote odes praising Alexandros's royal ancestor, the first Alexandros."

I didn't understand the full consequences of this news, although I remembered how our fierce tribes of Essyltyr were known for their relentless raids on villages, the blaring of the war horns that terrified the enemy, their unmerciful killings, the walls of the ricon's hall decorated with the skulls of their adversaries.

Theon gave a weary sigh. "I wish we could return to the farmstead, Olwen, but the roads north are no longer safe for us to travel in our mule cart. We must stay until springtime. Alexandros will soon make his triumphant return to the city. It is proper we are here to welcome him home."

Stanza Three

It was the time of the midwinter moon, Audnaios, when the sun wanes and offerings are made to the winter gods. On this night we Cymry celebrate the rebirth of our winter god, Lugh, the Oak God, giver of life, who warms the frozen earth. The oak tree, *duir,* is our sacred tree. I often accompanied my grandfather Maelgwyn to perform the rites and had learned the divinations from him. I remember him, dressed in his white robe and golden torc set with jewels. To honour his memory, and our winter god, I went to the grove to collect dried oak leaves, acorns and some sprigs of rowan berries, just as I would have done in Caer Gwyn to prepare for the winter celebrations.

The snowy pathway to the shrine in the grove was well-trodden by the footsteps of those who had come there to offer tributes. I could smell the pungent odour of smoke from the altar. As I approached, I felt the presence of ghostly spirits and stepped back into the shadows.

Then I saw Olympias standing in front of the shrine, an ivy-twined wand in her hand. I had not seen her since Filippos's funeral rites. She was dressed in a fine robe of purple bordered with white and gold. Her glossy auburn hair was bound with a gold fillet and draped with a veil of sheer silk. Even from afar, I could feel her witchcraft.

The altar smouldered from the flesh of some small animal she had used as an offering. I hesitated to approach, embarrassed that I had intruded on her rites. Somehow she sensed my presence and turned to face me.

"I... I'm sorry, my lady," I stammered. "I have disturbed your rites. I am sorry!"

She inspected me with narrowed eyes. I felt a shiver and wished I could run from the grove. "Ah, the little Kelt. Have you come to make an offering? To whose gods?" She made a gesture of disdain. Her voice was sharp, her face set in an expression cold as stone.

"Why, to yours as well as mine," I said. "I will offer to Lugh, our oak god, an offering for the winter, my lady." I held out the basket of oak leaves and rowan I had collected. "He conquers the darkness and banishes evil spells."

"Do you know the secrets of the mysteries? The dark arts?"

I shook my head. "I know only what the Druithin have taught me, my lady. I will pray that Lugh brings luck for the coming year. I will pray he gives Alexandros victory in battle."

"Ah yes, my son, Alexandros," she sighed, and her voice softened. "The oracle told him he was invincible! But he's more than that. And when he returns from his conquest, I will reveal to him the truth about his birth."

I puzzled over what she said. What did she mean? Was Filippos not Alexandros's father? I gathered my courage and said, "My lady, I'm sorry for your husband's cruel death..."

She threw back her head and laughed. "My husband was a drunken boor, rutting whenever it was his pleasure." Her tone was crisp and cold. There was a flush on her cheeks and her grey eyes widened. A prickle shivered down my spine. I had never seen eyes that looked so dangerous.

Although I faced her boldly and tried to hide my fear, the thoughts kept invading my mind. *Did she have her husband killed so her son could reign? Is that why she killed his new wife and her boy child, so there would be nobody else to claim the throne? And what did she mean, 'Alexandros's true father?'* I remembered what she had said that day in her bedchamber: *'Filippos will live to regret his perfidy!'*

I turned away from her, bewildered and afraid. I could feel my heart pounding in my chest.

"My son has the blood of Achilles," Olympias said. Her eyes widened. She laughed and tossed her head. "He is invincible because he is descended from the gods."

The thought struck me that she may have taken some potion before making her sacrifice.

I drew in a long breath before I dared speak. I stared straight into her eyes as if I was charming a snake. "Yes, surely he will be victorious," I stammered, and tried to put the thought out of my mind. After all, does not every mother think her child is a gift from the gods?

"One day long ago a man came to Pella," she said. "An Egyptian shaman. Nectenabo. He was a learned man and taught me many things. He told me I would be visited by the god and gifted with a child – Ammon's child. There were God-given omens at Alexandros's birth – two eagles appeared over the palace, a portent that he was from two worlds." She tossed back her mane of chestnut hair and turned to leave the grove.

As she walked away, she swept around to face me again. "Truly, Alexandros *is* god-begotten," she said. "He *will* be victorious, and his name will be known throughout the whole land!"

I watched her slither away up the path, but her presence seemed to linger long after she had gone. *She's mad!* I thought *What potion has she taken to cause such fanciful ideas?*

I made my offerings on the shrine, scattering the dried oak leaves over the charred remains of the creature she had sacrificed.

I knelt before the shrine and prayed to Lugh, the Oak God who conquers darkness and banishes evil spirits, and to my goddess, Brighid, the Great Mother, to help me see things more clearly. I stayed at the altar for a long time. I could feel the goddess's presence, as if she was pulling me to a place within herself that was also within me. I prayed she would guide me through the winter months until it was springtime and my beloved husband would return.

BALLAD TWENTY-SEVEN A Plea To The Sea God

Poseidon, Earth Shaker, god of the waves,
king of the broad blue seas,
all praise to you, great god of the deep.
We honour you, and offer you praise.
Calm the billows, still the winds,
Poseidon, Savior of ships,
hear our prayers
and bring the seafarers safely home.
Highest god, Lord of the sea-battle,
Lord of current and tides,
we honour you and offer you praise.

A Winter Festival

Stanza One

The winter festival for Poseidon was held in the moon of Peritos. I left Nikos at the palace with my handmaiden Aricia, and joined Theon for the processional that led to the altar on the seashore where we would honour the god.

It was a bright morning, the sun flashing in and out of the clouds, white waves roaring in on the shore. A horse had been sacrificed, its remains still smouldering on the ritual pyre. I listened to the priests singing the paeans, the wind tossing their voices about like the scattering of leaves.

"We call on Poseidon, great son of Kronos, lord of water, king of the broad blue seas. We offer you praise and seek your blessing."

As they strummed their lyres and sang, I thought of Caer Gwyn's bard, Lleu, and remembered the songs he sang of Llyr, our god of the sea, patron of sailors. I whispered a prayer for Elidi.

"Llyr, rider of the maned beast. The waves are your horses, your great war spear stirs the raging ocean. Lord of the currents and tides, still the storms and bring my husband home safely to me."

After the songs of praise and the libations were made, each person in the processional threw barley onto the alter as they called on Poseidon, lord of waters and king of the seas.

"We honour you and pour sweet wine in reverence and love, O great one. Hear our prayers, Poseidon, grant us your blessings. Praise be to you!"

After the rites, when dusk was falling, the smouldering altars were quenched with wine, the townspeople gathered together on the shore. The garlanded women stood in whispering, tittering groups while the men lit bonfires. Wine and food had been provided for everyone to share. Poseidon was known as the lustful god, so there was much revelry, feasting and debauchery in the sea god's name.

I looked up at the sky to see a brilliant star shining over the sea. Sirius, the Dog Star, blazing red in the sky, brighter than all the others. A potent omen, brilliant and beautiful, but one full of menace.

I pointed it out to Theon. He sensed my concern over the omen, but shrugged and said: "Sometimes it brings pestilence and fever and woeful diseases. If this is true, perhaps we will be kept busy this Spring." Then he smiled at me. "But do not concern yourself, Olwen. It will not come to pass. It is the thing of fables!"

At the edge of the crowd nearby, I saw Olympias accompanied by her servants and guards. I felt a chill enfold me as I recalled our last meeting in the glade. She looked over toward me, her eyes narrowed, her mouth tight and thin. I could feel the touch of her evil and shivered. My flesh crawled and I felt my scalp tingle, but I held my ground, my feet planted firmly. Suddenly she turned and with a scornful glance, stalked away, past the guards who closed around her. I felt a coldness in the pit of my belly. Then I heard Theon's voice.

"Come Olwen, let us join the others at the feast." He put his arm around my shoulders. "You must not let her frighten you!"

"You saw?" My voice trembled when I spoke.

"Yes. But you need not fear her. After all, you are Olwen, the Raven's child" He smiled and took my hand to lead me through the crowd of merry makers.

Stanza Two

It was a fine day, the time of the Gamelion festival in February, when Alexandros and his army rode back into Pella. The winds blew chill from the snow-capped mountains, but the promise of Spring was displayed with new buds on the trees. Long before dawn, people had begun to gather outside the city walls, spilling out over the vast field of winter-brown grass. The air was fresh and cool with the salt tang of the sea on the breeze.

The streets of the city rang with shouts of jubilation as we walked down to the parade field.

"This is an important day for Alexandros," Theon said. "Not just a celebration of the defeat of Thebes but preparation for Alexandros's campaign against the Persians. There will be a sacrifice and speeches."

We made our way closer so Nikos, who was riding on Theon's shoulders could get a better view.

Nikos was wide-eyed and chattered excitedly. "Will papa come?"

"Papa will come soon on the ships," I said. I tried to sound hopeful. "When the Spring weather opens the shipping lanes, we will all go to the harbour to meet the ships. It will be a great celebration, just like today!" In my mind, I counted the days 'til the royal triremes would return. One more full moon and finally Elidi would be home!

As we reached the edge of the throng of people, a splendid parade came into view. The column of men seemed to stretch for miles, the spirited music of trumpets and double flutes accompanying them.

Alexandros led the troops on his spirited horse, Bucephalus, sitting erect on a scarlet saddle cloth. He wore his bronze battle armour and a winged silver helmet, and shield adorned with a gold lion mask. His faithful hound, Peritos, loped at the horse's heels. The Companions followed, led by Hephaestion, riding caparisoned horses, their cuirasses and helmets gleaming in the morning sun as they led the long line of foot soldiers across the stubble field. Behind them the cavalry rode on their sleek battle chargers, bridles sparkling with gold and silver.

As I watched the troops approach I thought of our Cymry warriors who went to battle half naked, with lime-bleached hair, their bodies painted with woad. I remembered the shrill, dreadful din of their terrifying battle shouts and the frightening blare of their trumpets.

The disciplined squadrons of the Makedonian phalanx marched in long formations, eight men to a row, wearing burnished helmets crested with red or white horsehair, each wielding long a *sarissa*. The pennants on their lances fluttered in the wind. They were followed by the phalangites dressed in chain mail, armed with painted round shields and short curved swords.

When they reached the centre of the field, Alexandros raised his sword to salute the crowd. He swung off his steed and mounted a platform where the tall, imposing white-robed regent, Antipatros, waited to formally welcome the army home.

Alexandros's strong voice carried over the field as far as the crowds who had gathered outside the city walls.

"Men of Makedon, you fought bravely to vanquish the Thebans who sought who betrayed us! Makedonians! We have won Thebes! Now all of the Greek city states are under Makedon's rule and soon, when the spring winds calm the sea, I will lead our army east to take the Persian lands. The gods are with us, and we will be victorious!"

He ordered sacrifices to Herakles and rites to purify the army. A docile black dog was led up to the altar were a priest performed the rites.

Nikos squirmed and hid his face against Theon's shoulder. "It is an offering to Hekate," Theon explained. "Don't cry for the dog. It has lived a worthy life and died a brave death for the blessing of the army."

I had always tried to shield my son from observing the animal sacrifices. I recalled clearly the day in the field at Caer Gwyn when my beloved bull, Mithras, had been taken from me. How could I explain to Nikos that these sacrifices were made to honour the gods, and the animals had been chosen especially for that purpose.

That evening every laird and freeman attended the victory feast. I had been reluctant to attend, but Theon said it was expected. I sat on my couch, my cloak wrapped around me, feeling shy and out-of-place. I'd have much rather stayed in the comfort of our hearth with my son Nikos, but Theon had insisted I must join the women for the festivities.

Usually the female members of the royal family gathered together in the woman's rooms, but tonight the royal family attended. Olympias, her daughter Kleopatra and Filippos's daughter Thessaloniki, along with other royal ladies. Several young daughters of lairds and wealthy landowners had also been chosen to attend. They clustered together beside the royal women, whispering and tittering.

The sound of music and roars of bawdy laughter filled the palace's vast inner court. Alexandros and all his best friends and Companions were the honoured ones. Crowned with victory wreaths, they lounged on supper couches tended by young servant girls. Wine goblets were emptied and quickly filled again. The men's voices grew louder, their faces flushed as they argued and bragged and sang skolions.

I ate little and refused the wine. Once I saw Olympias watching me from her place, her eyes narrowed and the creases deep on her brow. I smiled across at her and kept my composure.

Will she announce tonight what she told me in the grove, and disclose who Alexandros's true father is? I wondered.

To shouts of acclamation, Alexandros rose from his couch to make a speech, thanking his companions and the other generals for their faithfulness. He complimented them on their success in defeating the Illyrians, Thracians and the Thebans. And he spoke of the exploits of his father Filippos. "But we will conquer more lands than he did!" he bragged. "We will conquer the world."

Later, when I returned to our house, Aricia was sitting on the divan holding Nikos while she swayed and rocked him, humming a quiet tune.

"He's a beautiful boy," she said as I took him from her arms. "He has your beauty and the strength and spirit of his father."

I told her about the feast and all the young maidens who attended. She said: "Olympias wants to see Alexandros marry a Makedonian girl." She rolled her eyes. "His mother does not like the tales about him – how he prefers the company of Hephaestion to a woman. And if she has her way, she'll see he is married off before he leaves on campaign."

Stanza Three

One quiet afternoon soon after, Alexandros surprised Theon and me with a visit. He arrived alone, without his companion, Hephaestion. I had not seen Alexandros since his triumphant return from Thebes and we had not spoken since his father's funeral. His days were separate from ours, kingly and filled with duties we had no part of. He looked tired and battle weary, his russet hair tousled like a lion's mane. Even though he was still a youth of nineteen, he was king now and had the responsibility of the army and all his father's kingdom.

Theon and I made him welcome; I poured the men cups of wine. Theon raised his wine cup and said: "We'll spill the lees for luck – for your good fortune – and your victorious conquest of Persia."

"It is my good fortune having a wise man such as you to entrust my wounded to." He smiled over at me. "And you, little Kelt... you have served my father and me well. I have not forgotten Chaeronea."

"What about the wound you got in Illyria?" Theon asked.

"Nothing more than a slash wound on my thigh," Alexandros said. He lifted the edge of his tunic to show the scar.

Theon offered him a chair, which he refused. "I did not come just to talk about the war," he said.

It was clear Alexandros wished to have a private conversation, so Theon led him to the andron, the inner room where they could talk privately. I could hear their conversation through the open door, but tried not to pry, though at times Alexander's words sparked my interest.

Their talk was mostly about Thebes, of man and fate, of Alexandros's ambitions and plans to confront the Persians.

"Mother wants me to marry before I go on campaign," he said. "She's tried to interest me in several of the laird's daughters."

"Don't be troubled by this," Theon replied. "All mothers like to see their sons wed, so they can welcome grandchildren."

"When the time comes for me to wed, I will choose someone worthy – not just a country laird's daughter," Alexandros said. "I have no time for marriage. There is business to attend to – envoys, petitions, army matters – and worlds to conquer."

Then Alexandros said something that made me move closer so I could hear every word.

"You have known me since my birth,' he said. "Filippos was my father, was he not?"

I recalled the conversation with Olympias at the grove. What did she tell him?

"Mother insists I was born of a god! Was this one of her insane dreams? Or could it be true?"

I heard Theon chuckle. "Your mother does have unusual dreams!" he said.

Alexandros's voice was pitched high, urgent. "I know we are descended from the seed of the heroes Achilles and Herakles, but she says I am the son of Zeus Ammon! What did she mean?"

Through the open doorway I saw Theon's face redden. He shook his head and spoke in a cautious tone. "Alexandros, your mother is a cultist. Pay no heed to her ramblings. When your father met her at the sacred grove of Samothraki, she was just a young girl, and already revelling with the Mystai who worship Hekate. She has kept snakes as her daimons for as long as I've known her, indulges in potions and the potent delusions caused by the mushrooms she ingests. Filippos *was* your father. That is all I know." He put his arm around Alexandros's shoulders. "All things are known to the gods, and if your mother's words are true, then one day it will be revealed to you."

Alexandros pulled back from Theon's embrace and began to speak bitterly of his father's marriage to Attalos's niece.

"It was a dangerous insult to my mother and me. Mother never accepted that my father would take a younger girl for a wife – one who was barely fourteen! When we returned to Epirus, mother consulted the Oak shrine and I knew she made some oaths against my father. Then, the way she honoured Pausanias after father's murder! I wondered whether it was she who had ordered father's assassination."

"And the killings of the young queen and her newborn," I thought. *Did she use Egyptian poison to work its magic on them?*

When Theon replied, his voice sounded tired, his patience short. "You must not dwell on these things, Alexandros. You must keep your mind clear as you plan your campaign. Your mother is a complicated woman – delusional sometimes, as well as being ambitious. You cannot let her actions control you. You are the king now. And you have a mighty kingdom to rule."

"Yes," Alexandros said. "And they know who is in command now. Not my father!"

I hurried back to tend the hearth before Theon led Alexandros back into the kitchen. I didn't want them to know I had listened.

Theon offered Alexandros more wine and they sat for a while by the hearth in a quiet, more carefree conversation. The shadows threw darkness across Alexandros's face but I could see his eyes, bright in their sockets, watching me intently.

He beckoned me over to the hearth side and reached out to take my hand. "Make a divination for me, little Kelt," he said.

To comfort him I spoke from remembered prophecies Essylt had given to the warriors of our tuath:

May you enjoy every journey. May no day be grievous to you.
Sure footed be your steed and may you win every battle.
May the power of the eagle be yours."

When I reminded him the oracle at Delphi had said he was invincible, a slow flush spread up his face. "The Pythian told you that you are invincible and you will achieve your dream. She is the most powerful oracle, and the oracle speaks the truth."

What I said seemed to satisfy him. He looked into my eyes, paused a moment, then he took a deep breath and said, "That is all I wanted to know."

The last rays of light had left the courtyard and the sky was tinged with the colours of sunset when, without saying more, Alexandros thanked us again, and left. From the doorway, I watched him go, striding though the wilted plants of the winter garden. I knew no matter what happened, even if I should never see him again, I would always carry him in my memory.

"He's an intelligent, sensible young man," Theon said. "He always said his father would leave him nothing more to do, but he will outdo his father and achieve what Filippos always dreamed of – and more. Alexandros will conquer the world!"

Stanza Four

Winter passed. Spring arrived in the valley through the mountain peaks still dazzled with snow and the wind blew chill from the north. Xandica, the Moon of March is the beginning the campaign season and the whole garrison was ordered back to the parade ground to train for battle. Alexandros called war councils and consulted with his tribal lords as he prepared his campaign in the east.

The sea stayed rough all that month, as if the winter did not want to loosen its grip. The waves roared and the wind whistled through the dried reeds along the shore of the lagoon. When the seas finally calmed, once the royal fleet returned to port, the army would leave Makedon for the campaign against Persia.

It wasn't until the Moon of Artemisios in April, that finally, one morning, word came that the royal triremes had been sighted offshore.

Excitement surged in me and my heartbeats quickened with excitement. At last, Elidi was coming home!

The sun rose in a cloudless sky that morning. The wind had died, and the sun glittered off the water. Gulls swooped and soared over the sea. The sea was calm, and far offshore oars flashed as a fleet of triremes rowed toward the shore.

Alexandros's staff officers had assembled, their weapons and armour polished to a shine, their maroon capes and corselets bright in the morning sun. As the fleet came into view they raised their voices in a paean for Poseidon.

We watched as the fleet approached the shore, the rowers straining to keep the boats on course. I took Nikos for a closer look.

"Papa's ship is coming!" I pointed out the curved prows with the figure-heads of serpents and gorgons. "Watch for the Medusa," I said. "That will be Papa's ship!"

A roar went up as the first triremes manoeuvred into the crowded harbour. Ropes were flung and hitched and gangplanks clattered. The throng of people, who had gathered, cheered as the first trireme docked. Women dressed in brightly dyed gowns gawked brazenly at the bare-chested muscular crewmen.

By mid-morning the fleet had landed, but with all the people crowding the shore I could not see Elidi's ship.

"I'll go down to the landing dock," Theon said. "You wait here, and when I find him, I'll bring him to you."

I watched as he pushed his way through the celebrating throng who had swarmed around the disembarking crews.

"Can we go too?" Nikos tugged impatiently at my hand. "Is Papa coming? Can we see his ship?"

I held tight to his hand. "Yes, my son. Papa will be here soon."

Then I saw Theon returning from the shore and a chill came over me. He was alone. Where was Elidi?

Theon did not speak at first but led me to a stone bench. "Sit here," he said. A look of sorrow shadowed his face.

"Where is he? Did you find him?" I clutched Nikos close as I searched the shore where the crews were gathering to greet their families. I hoped to see Elidi among them. "Is he still on the trireme? Will he come ashore soon?"

"I have spoken to one of the trierarchs," Theon said. His face looked haggard. He put his hand on my shoulder, bowed his head, then spoke in a soft, strained voice. "There was a storm at sea. Elidi's ship went down!"

His words dropped like cold stones inside me. I felt dizzy. Horror crept over me, and I cried out: "No! Tell me he is safe!" I felt my face pale with shock and screamed hysterically, clutching Theon's arm. It was like a terrible, dark dream. I leaned against Theon as he embraced me. "No! It cannot be. Tell me it isn't true – it *can't* be true!"

Theon answered, a tremor in his voice. "There was a fierce storm. One of the other ships sighted a wreck. It was the *Medusa*, Elidi's ship. All of them – the entire crew – were lost at sea."

The entire crew... lost at sea! My vitality drained from me like water from a cracked pot. I felt dizzy and held firm to Theon's arm. Everything seemed to dazzle and spin before my eyes. My world began to crumble and everything whirled as if the earth was spinning.

Theon tried to console me, but nothing could prove to me it was not just a bad dream. There was no proof – no bodies, no pieces of a wrecked ship. Nothing. I could not believe Elidi was dead.

I sat clutching little Nikos to my breast. Nikos, our son, the only proof I had that Elidi had existed. I buried my face in Nikos's curls and felt sorrow wash through me in unending waves, not only for the loss of Elidi, but I felt as though the goddess had deserted me.

How much time went by, I cannot remember. Grief lay over me like a black shroud. One morning at dawn I finally rose from my bed, dressed, and put on my amulet bag, the soft embroidered pouch of kidskin Essylt had given me when I was a child. In it I kept all my sacred treasures. Silently, so as not to disturb Nikos, I went out into the garden. Birds were waking in the trees, but it was still too early for anyone to be around.

At the foot of the stairway by the entrance gate, a guard leaned wearily on his spear as I passed by. He lifted his brows as if to question me but said nothing.

I went down the hill from the acropolis. The streets of Pella were empty. There was no sound but the distant crowing of a rooster and the barking of a dog. I walked through the silent streets to the shore. Once there, I stood awhile looking out at the vast blue sea. The surge of the waves drew me closer. I felt drawn to throw myself into the brine, to let the waves carry me away. Then, as the sun rose over the eastern hills, those hills of the far away place where Elidi had once dwelled, I thought of our son, Nikos. It was not only for Elidi that I wept, but for our son.

I thought, *Now I have a child to raise, a son who will grow to honour his father.*

I remembered what Elidi had said when I told him I was going with Theon to serve in the hospital tents at Chaeronea. *You are brave and stubborn, my little Kelt, and I fell in love with you because of that.*

I knew for our son's sake, I must live up to Elidi's words.

I sat on the shore and emptied my amulet bag of all the treasures that were my luck charms: the small, dried bundle of sage Essylt had given me when I had reached my maidenhood, the acorn from the sacred oak where grandfather worshipped, a small pebble I'd collected from the Stone Circle, the gold coins given to me by the goldsmith, Teag, the gold and lapis ankh Elidi had given me on our wedding night.

I put all the talismans except the ankh back into my amulet back, then I walked down to the edge of the sea. As the waves lapped around my feet I looked toward the east and said a prayer to the memory of my husband. I remember Elidi telling me *"I will never leave you, Olwen."*

I held out the ankh. Elidi had said: *"The ankh is a symbol of life."* Now he was dead, taken by sea. How could I live without him?

I pressed the ankh to my lips against the lapis surface. Then I hurled it into the sea and collapsed in despair on the shore.

When I returned to the palace, Theon was waiting in the courtyard. He stood to greet me when he saw me but said nothing for a moment.

"I have been to the seashore," I said. My words caught in my throat as I spoke. "I have said my final goodbye and…"

I could say no more. I walked by him into the house and straight to where my son was happily playing with his toys. I bent over and stroked Nikos's cheek, then I picked him up and cradled him in my arms.

He looked at me, his dark eyes bright like his father's, and put his arms around my neck to snuggle close. "Mama? Why are you crying Mama?"

Theon stood by watching me a long time without speaking. Finally he said: "I know your suffering. I was married once, you see. My wife died. Even I, a physician, could not save her. These tragedies we cannot always foresee, but we must not forget."

In all the years he had cared for me, I had not known he carried his own sorrow.

He put his arm around my shoulders then said, "Love is a beautiful thing. We must not forsake love, for what would we be without it. You have lost the one you loved, but you must let go. Only then will you heal. As my friend, Aristoteles, says: *'It is during our darkest moments that we must focus to see the light.'* "

I felt Theon's hand on my shoulder, strong and firm. "Alexandros will soon leave on his campaign to the East. The regent, Antipater, will be left in charge of royal duties here. Olympias is already quarrelling with him, and she no doubt will return to her home in Epirus. There is no need for us to stay here. Perhaps it is time for you to go home."

Home! Did I want to leave behind the memories of Elidi and the life I had grown to love? Could I ever go back to Caer Gwyn? If I did, how would Nikos grow to know his father's people?

Theon looked deep into my eyes. "Do you miss Caer Gwyn? Don't you think it is time for you to return?" Yes. Theon was right. It *was* time. Time for me to return to my own people, to take back with me all I had learned and to start my life anew. Time for Nikos to know my people, the Cymry. But how? I had been taken from Caer Gwyn by a ruthless Essyltyr warrior, forced to follow him across all the Keltic lands, through forests and over mountains. Almost ten years had passed since I had been taken from my home in Caer Gwyn. My thoughts went back to the gruelling journey with Sholto – the nights spent in forests or trekking mountain trails. Was it possible I could travel back to Caer Gwyn safely with my child?

Theon put his arm around my shoulders. "Olwen you have been to me the child I never had You are like a daughter to me. I would never let you go alone. I will take you there."

I raised my head and peered into Theon's compassionate face. I realized then how much he had become the father I had never known. "Oh, Theon! What would I have done if it were not for you! What would have become of me?" I thought of the farmstead, that place of sanctuary, where Alexandros had brought me and put me into Theon's care. "But how can you leave the farmstead? That is your home. How can you leave it? Would you be happy in my country?"

"As the philosopher has said: *Happiness depends on ourselves.* I will give the farmstead to the boy who tends it for me. He's a good boy and has served me faithful."

"But you have served the king and his army and the people."

"I can still practice my *pharmacae* in your land," Theon said. "And you can too. I have taught you all there is for a healer to know. You will take that knowledge back to your people."

Home! Did I want to leave here, leave behind the memories of Elidi and the life I had grown to love? Could I ever go back to Caer Gwyn? Yet I knew Theon was right. After all my years away, life at Caer Gwyn would be strange and sometimes difficult, but it was still my home, and I knew it was time for me to return.

BALLAD TWENTY-EIGHT A Wayfarer's Prayer

Hermes, fleet-footed god of wayfarers,
guide me safely on my journey.
The by-ways will be perilous.
Protect me from danger.
Hear my supplication, Oh blessed Hermes.

THE DEPARTURE

Stanza One

The word spread quickly throughout the palace that Theon and I were leaving Pella. When Aricia heard the news, she came quickly to see me. Her flaxen hair was loose from its braids and fell over her shoulders in a tangled mess. There were dark circles under her eyes and tears streamed down her cheeks as we embraced.

"I have heard you are leaving Pella, going back to your people. How will you travel so far with your son? "She looked at Nikos who had come to greet her.

"See 'Ricia?" he held up his toy boat. "A boat like Papa's"

Aricia's voice trembled. "It is a long and dangerous journey, Olwen. And by ship...."

"Don't cry," I said. I knew she was thinking of Elidi and the fate that had befallen him. I felt the words choke in my throat. "We are in the hands of the goddess. She will protect us. It's time for me to leave here..." I held her tight and after a moment she stopped sobbing.

Aricia and I had become close friends over the years I stayed at the palace, the only woman friend I ever had. Like me, she was a hostage, one of Filippos's war prizes taken from her tribe, little more than a slave. At the palace I had always been treated like a guest friend, but Aricia must stay to serve the royalty. So saying farewell to her was a sad time for me and I regretted she could not come with us.

Aricia straightened and brushed her tears away. "I will serve you until you leave," she said. Then she bent and lifted Nikos up. "Come with me, little man, and we will sail your new boat in the fishpond."

I said a blessing for her as I watched them walk out of the portico into the garden, Nikos happily chatting to her as they made their way to the fishpond. Aricia had been a friend to me, like a sister and an aunt to my son. We would never meet again, but I would never forget her kindness and companionship.

A few days later, Alexandros came. We had seen little of him since his return from Thebes. Most days he was on the parade grounds training his young cadets for the coming invasion of Ionia. He had come from the horse field, dressed in a dust-stained homespun tunic, unarmed except for his sword belt. He was unshaven, his coppery hair tousled and unkempt.

He strode into the atrium where Theon and I were packing our *pharmacae* and surgical equipment. He clasped Theon's hand, then embraced him.

"I have heard you are leaving Pella. Why? You have served as physician here for many years."

"I'm escorting Olwen back to her people," Theon said.

Alexander's brows lifted and he frowned then glanced over at me with a look of concern. "You have lost your husband, little Kelt. And we have lost one of the best helmsmen in the royal fleet." He reached out and put his hand on my shoulder. "You must not grieve long. It is a tragedy, but you must remember only the best of what it was." He looked at Nikos who was standing beside me gazing at him in wonderment. "The boy will carry on in his father's name."

"Just as you have done," I spoke softly. "You are the king now and following your father's path. I wish you well and may the gods look on you with kindness."

He turned back to Theon. "Athens is a city divided in allegiance to Makedon, but still, a magnificent city." He took a leather pouch from his belt and handed it to Theon. "Here. Take this. It's enough gold to pay for your journey. I will send two of my best men to escort you. There are brigands on the road through the mountains and my men will keep you safe. When you reach Athens they will take you to our garrison and help you find safe lodgings and passage."

Although Alexandros was known for his generosity, still his kindness overwhelmed me.

"Did you know our friend Aristoteles has established a new school in Athens?" he asked Theon. "The Lyceum. If you visit him, tell him I will convey messages to him from Persia and send him specimens of the flora and fauna to examine. We are leaving on the next full moon," Alexandros said. "I have sent advance troops east to ensure our safe passage across the Hellespont."

"What about your mother?" Theon asked.

Alexandros frowned. "She's going back to Epirus. It's best for her to leave here. She resents me for leaving Antipatros as regent. It would only create conflict in the palace if she stayed."

"And Arridaios?"

Alexander spoke kindly of his pitiful half-witted brother. "For his own safety he will come with us. It is best for him."

As he turned to leave, he smiled at me, then reached out to take my hand and bent to kiss me gently on the forehead. He looked into my eyes and said: "You are a brave woman, little Kelt. You have served us well in the court of Pella and on the battlefield at Chaeronea. The journey ahead of you is a long one – just as mine will be – but you will persevere. And when you get back to your people, tell them about Alexandros, the king who will conquer the world!"

It was a bold statement, yet I believed him. Alexandros always achieved what he had his mind set on, and I had no doubt one day we would hear about his victories.

He embraced Theon again. I saw there were tears in his eyes. "I will make a tribute at the god's shrine for your safe passage." he said. "You have been like a father and mentor to me. I pray the gods will speed you on your journey."

Without another word, he turned and went out, striding in his proud manner through the gardens toward the palace. I could not help but feel sad saying goodbye to him, but I knew he would live in our hearts and minds for all time.

Stanza Two

Theon had hired a covered ox cart and a driver to carry us on our journey.

"It will be a long and arduous adventure," he said. "It's best we have some comfort along the way."

As we were preparing to leave, Xenon the Nubian, came to help us carry our belongings and medical chests to the cart for the journey. There was a frown on his dark face instead of the usual beaming smile.

"Master Theon, we regret the news that you are leaving. You have served here for as long as I can remember."

Theon reached out and clasped Xenon's hand, a friendly gesture usually reserved for friends, not slaves. "You have been a good and faithful servant, Xenon," Theon said. Xenon's eyes glistened and he managed a smile.

I remembered when I had first met him. I had never before seen such a dark-skinned giant of a man, and I had been intimidated by him. But during my stay at the palace Xenon had always been the gentle giant who cared for me. I remembered the night of Olympias's wild orgy when she had served me the drugged wine, and how Xenon had cared for me and kept me safe. I whispered a blessing to him as we parted, holding back tears. I could only hope now Alexandros was leaving Pella, perhaps Xenon would be given his freedom.

We set off as dawn reddened the eastern sky, escorted by the two soldiers Alexandros had sent to accompany us. One, who was named Ajax, was a highlander, bold and brazen, with swarthy skin, his arms marked with war scars. He had a thick beard, a mat of tangled black hair, and a broken nose that gave him a formidable demeanour. He said he was one of Alexandros's personal guards, assigned to join the Makedonian garrison at Athens, and assured us no harm would befall us on our journey. The other was a young cadet named Cleon, a freckle-faced boy with chestnut hair, the son of a horse-trader from Thessaly. He would ride with us as far as Thebes.

The two yoked, sturdy brown oxen plodded slowly, their hoofs clicking on the flag-stones as they trudged through the streets. Belos, the driver, a hawk-nosed, straw-haired man with a darkly tanned face ran alongside with his prod. The city was silent as we made our way to the gates, the streets hidden in shadows. Beyond the gates we passed a few caravans on the road, merchants heading to the city, their carts laden with goods to sell in the agora and farmers trudging beside their donkeys that carried bundles of hay and produce for the market.

As we rode out of Pella, I could not help but feel some regret in leaving, remembering the happy years I spent on the farmstead with Theon and the kindness I had been shown by Alexandros and the servants at the palace. I felt a stirring of destiny, a change in my fortune. Was I making the right decision in leaving on such a difficult journey with my small son? Would we be able to safely make our way over the sea, worlds away, to Massalia, and then through the Keltic lands to the passage of the Narrow Sea? And what would I find when I got back to Caer Gwyn? Recalling the war-like nature of our tribe I wondered if the settlement still existed, and if it did, what had become of Essylt and the others? I could only trust in the gods, and in Theon's guidance, and as I held Nikos close to me, I prayed all would be well.

The road led by the sea where little fish boats bobbed in the sea-swell. We kept close to the shore, skirting the mountains As the day declined to evening and the sun was low over the western hills, we made camp for the night in a stone-built shepherd's bothy where herds of sheep and goats grazed in the glade. Belos unhitched the oxen and led them out to pasture. I unpacked our food and prepared a meal of goat cheese, black bread and olives.

We sat around the fire feasting while the guards passed round their wine flasks. The guards talked idly, told tales, recalled old jokes. Ajax, his face red from the wine, sang old army songs for our entertainment.

"I remember when I first went to war with Filippos,"Ajax said to Cleon. "I was just a lad, your age." He spoke of King Filippos, whom he had served since he was a youth, and went on to recount tales of tribal wars and blood feuds.

Belos joined in, his voice harsh, face flushed with anger. "The Skopjan raiders came to steal our cattle. They set our fields on fire and pulled us from our house. They killed my father and raped my mother. That's the way it is in the back country."

Ajax clapped Cleon on the shoulder. "I have been a soldier most of my life. It is the only life I've known. When I was eighteen, I rode in the cavalry when Filippos fought the Illyrians. I got my first war wound there – broke my arm when I fell off my horse." He laughed and took another long swig of his wine. "Ah, but that battle was nothing compared to Chaeronea. That was a blood bath! It's a brutal business finishing off someone who tries to resist. You have to imagine it, boy! We had three brigades of sarissas, all upright with their shiny silver spears. I led one of them. Alexandros led the cavalry. It was his first battle, and he defeated the Sacred Band!"

Cleon's grey eyes widened. I could see he was transfixed by Ajax's tales. I was glad my son, Nikos was too young to understand.

Cleon questioned Ajax about Alexandros's war plans. "Do you think he can drive the Persians away from the Greek lands on the coast? How long will the campaign last? Will the army travel farther than the coast? I have heard King Darius has a mighty army!"

"Alexandros wants this war with Persia, and he will succeed," Ajax put his hand on Cleon's shoulder and looked at him straight in the eyes. "This will be your first campaign, boy! Are you ready to pledge yourself to fight?"

Cleon took a deep breath. "Yes, I am, "he replied. His freckled face was ruddy from the wine.

"You must have *dynamos,* the will to fight, my boy, and the *ardor,* the soul. This is how a great soldier is made. The more battles you fight, the stronger you will be," Ajax bumped Cleon playfully with his fist. "Look, don't worry, little brother! You have your whole future ahead of you. I joined the army when I was your age. I've served Filippos and I've served his son. It's hard, I know how far the army will go to pursue victory, but the farther you march, the more battles you fight, the stronger you will be. This is what makes a good soldier!"

Theon was sitting quietly and had not spoken. I saw the stern look on his face. Finally he stood and said, "Alright lads, let's have no more war talk." He glanced over to where I was huddled by the fire holding Nikos. "This young woman here... and her child..."

"Enough talk then," Ajax stood and raised his wine cup. "Let's drink to you, Cleon. To you, my boy, who will go with Alexandros and fight like our brave companions did on the field of Chaeronea."

Cleon gave a cheer and tipped the dregs from his wine cup. His face flushed with pride, he said, "From you, Ajax, I have learned the skills of war. It is my honour to accompany you with the good physician and the Kelt. And I will serve Alexandros as bravely as you fought for Filippos."

Ajax strode over to Nikos who was playing with a toy wooden horse. "Do you like horses?" Nikos eyed the big man who stood before him suspiciously at first, then he held out his toy and said: "My horse!"

Ajax lifted him up and carried him over to where the horses were tethered under a tree. He set Nikos on one of the horse's backs. Nikos squealed with delight.

"Soon you will be big enough to ride on him yourself!" Ajax said. He let Nikos sit for a while, stroking the horse's mane, then carried him back over and sat him down on the log by the fire." Now I will tell your son the story of how Alexandros tamed his horse, Bucephalus." Ajax sat beside him and put his arm around Nikos, then he began to relate the story.

"You see, Bucephalus was a wild steed, a fine horse, high spirited. None of the men were able to mount him. Even the horse trainer couldn't control him. But Alexandros – he was just a young boy then – he wasn't afraid. He had watched and saw what scared the horse. It was a shadow."

"A shadow?" Nikos's eyes were wide. "It scared the horse?"

"Yes," Ajax said. "Alexandros bargained with his father to let him ride the horse."

"And did he? Did he ride it?"

Ajax chuckled. "Yes, my boy. Alexandros knew horses, even though he was a young lad. He walked round, making sure his shadow was behind him, then he grasped the reins and mounted!"

Nikos gasped and clapped his hands. "And did the horse throw him?"

"No. Everyone was afraid it would. But it was as if the horse knew Alexandros. Alexandros grasped onto the horse's main, kicked his heels and off they rode together. It was an amazing sight to see! And now, Alexandros will ride Bucephalus to the Persian lands."

Nikos clapped his hands. "One day I shall have a horse like that!" He turned to me, "Are there horses in your land, Mama?"

"Yes, the Kelts have many fine horses," I said "Epona is our horse goddess. She rides a magical white mare that nobody can catch."

"Can I have one – a horse like Bou...ke...?" He stammered over the name.

"There are no other steeds as fine as Bucephalus," I smiled at him. "But one day, when you are old enough, maybe you will find one almost as brave!"

After two more days of travel, ahead of us the majestic peak of the holy mountain, Olympus, still crowned with snow, sparkled in the sun. Beyond the groves of oak and chestnut trees, rose a magnificent limestone precipice known as the throne of Zeus, partly encircled by mist. We stopped at a roadside shrine and offered a tribute with a prayer for a safe journey.

Our pace was swift. The spring sun warmed the hills. The road along the coast was well-trodden because of the many times the Makedonian armies had marched that way. Almost a week passed before we finally reached the narrow Pass of Thermopylae, the Hot Gates, named for the warm springs, where Theon said we would stop to bathe.

The road had narrowed, traversing between the precipitous mountain slopes and the sea. Oak, chestnut and plane trees grew along the lower levels while higher up, pine forests stretched to the snow-line. As we entered the Pass, the narrow trail became dank and mossy. Below us, through the trees, the sea sparkled. A winding trail led from the Pass to the beach where Leonidas and his 300 Spartans had perished holding off the forces of the Persians. I recalled stopping here on our return from Chaeronea, and the memory brought back thoughts of Elidi again.

I looked down at little Nikos who was sitting next to me on the ox-cart bench. Almost three years had gone by since his birth. I put my arm around him and held him close. How could I have imagined then that I would be left a widow with a little child to care for, and a long, arduous road ahead of me, as I followed my destiny and endeavoured to return to my own people.

At Thermopylae we stopped just long enough to lay a tribute at the mound honouring brave Leonidas. After a refreshing bath in the hot springs we were on our way again. Beyond the narrow, shadowy Pass, the road opened up to a valley with sunlit fields where cattle and sheep grazed and farmers tilled the soil preparing their summer crops. I heard the sound of crowing cocks, the bleating and lowing of cattle, the cries of shepherds driving their flocks up the steep hillside.

We turned westward travelling through the hills and grasslands of Boeotia. Ahead, loomed mighty Mount Parnassus, its peaks glistening with snow. Nestled somewhere below those stony heights was the sacred sanctuary of Delphi.

"Will we stop to visit there?" I asked Theon. The idea of paying a visit to Delphi was comforting, for surely the oracle would bless us on our journey.

"Certainly. We *must!*" Theon replied. "No wayfarer passes by this holy site without stopping to say a prayer and make a votive offering."

Shafts of light shone through the green foliage and brightened the way along a narrow path lined with myrtle, arbutus and broom. As the sun set behind the snow-capped peaks, we made camp in a beech grove by Delphi's sacred river, the Kephissos, where we had camped four years before on our way to Chaeronea.

I remember how the soldiers had lit fires along the River God's banks, and how Alexandros rode into the camp, flushed with eagerness, and proclaimed his father had appointed him to lead the cavalry. We were both so young then, just seventeen, yet Alexandros had done what no other had before him. He led the Makedonian cavalry into battle and destroyed the 300 members of Thebe's Sacred Band and won the war for his father.

Theon's words to him still resound in my memory: *"You were born to perform great deeds and you will accomplish them."*

Would Alexandros succeed in his war against Persia? Perhaps I would never know, but I prayed he would succeed.

Stanza Three

The next morning, as the first rays of sun glimmered through the trees, we set out again, up the track that led through the pine forest. The mountain path grew steeper until at last it opened to the familiar road that led up to Delphi's sanctuary. As we neared the sanctuary, there were throngs of people on the trail. We left the ox-cart beside the road with the driver, Belos, and joined the two guards who followed behind the other supplicants who had come to pay homage at the shrine.

At the spring of Kasalia, we stopped to rest and cleanse ourselves of the grime of our travels before climbing the hill to the sanctuary. There were many other supplicants in the grove, so we sat on a stone ledge under the shade while we waited for the temple maiden to come and lead us to the pond.

The soothing sound of water burbled from the cleft of the rocks fed from the ice melt on Mt Parnassus slopes. Nikos was eager to run ahead and splash in the pool.

"We must wait here for the priestess to give her blessing. And while we are waiting, I will tell you the story of how Apollo came here and slew the evil serpent named Python who lived in a cave on the mountainside."

"A real python?" Nikos asked, his dark eyes wide.

"Yes, a real python." I related the tale to him, just as Theon had told it to me on my first visit.

"Python was a frightening, evil monster and beautiful, brave Apollo came from his island, Delos. That is why this place is called Delphi. He killed that evil Python with arrows he shot from his silver bow."

"Was Apollo a god?"

"Yes. He was the son of Zeus. He was a healer too, and he taught men the healing arts just as Theon taught me. Apollo is the god of light and truth. No false word ever falls from his lips."

A young rosy-cheeked temple maiden had come to greet us and lead us to the spring. We stood quietly while she made her ablation and blessed us before we washed ourselves. Nikos splashed in the pool even though the water was icy from the melted snow that spilled down from Parnassus's peaks.

Theon lifted him from the water and wrapped him in his cloak. "We must be clean before we enter the Sanctuary, but it is a sacred pool, not one for play."

"W-what is sanct'ary?" Nikos shivered, his lips tinted blue from the cold.

"We will make an offering to the gods there so we will be safe on our journey," Theon explained.

He set Nikos down and took him by the hand. I followed them out of the grove and up the road of black marble paving stones that led under a tall, carved arch to the Sacred Way and into the sanctuary. The air was scented with sweet pine and the spring flowers that bloomed along the path. Monuments and shrines smouldering with votive offerings lined the road. Nikos squealed with delight at the sight of all the garlanded statues.

I pointed out the great bronze bull. "They are all offerings to the gods from cities in Greece."

When we reached the great serpent column Nikos pulled back and held tight to my hand. "Is that the python Apollo killed?"

"It's a monument to a famous battle," I explained.

"This place, Delphi, is the home of Gaia, Mother Earth," Theon said. "People come here to pay her homage and leave her offerings."

Nikos's cheeks flushed with excitement. "I will leave her one of my toy boats!"

Theon lifted him up and pointed out the majestic temple set on the terrace slope. its marble columns glistening in the sun.

"You see, we are here in the centre of the world, my child," he said. "And there... do you see that big temple? That's the Temple of Apollo where Pythia gives her oracles."

"Can we go inside and see her?"

"Only grown men may go inside," Theon explained. "King Alexandros came here and so did his father. And the oracle advised them what they should do."

His words reminded me of that day four years before we left for Chaeronea, when I had stood in that same place, surrounded by Filippos's men while the king was inside the temple consulting the oracle. I remember the excited anticipation as we waited to hear what Pythia would predict. The visions were clear in my memory, how the crowd had cheered when Alexandros, his coppery hair tousled, blue cape fluttering around him, climbed the steps to greet his father when Filippos came out of the temple; how Filippos's bodyguard, Pausanias, had run up the steps to join the king but was rudely rebuffed, and Filippos's bold announcement that Pythia had said: *Your sword is strong and bright, but there is another stronger and brighter.* Now Filippos was dead, murdered by Pausanias, and Alexandros was the king.

We made our offerings at the shrine by the temple where Filippos had sacrificed a black bull, said our prayers, and burned sage for cleansing and laurel in honour of Apollo. I took the cup of barley seeds Theon handed me and lifted the cup to spill the stream of translucent amber grains onto the glowing embers on the altar. A swirl of fragrant, blue smoke rose toward the sky as I offered my prayer to Gaia.

> *I offer my prayer with respect and gratitude,*
> *Great deity of the earth, Mother goddess.*
> *We praise thee for the seeds we sow in springtime,*
> *the winds that whisper through the pines and mighty oaks.*
> *Oh Mother Earth, we praise thee*
> *for all things you have given us.*
> *Keep us from harms way, Gaia, our protector.*
> *Calm our hearts, enfold us with your tender love.*
> *Keep us safe, I ask you.*

As I chanted the words, I could not help but wonder what our future held. Was I right in agreeing to return to my people? Was I putting my small son, Elidi's child, in jeopardy?

After our offerings and prayers were made, Theon went to visit friends who he knew at the Council House. I took Nikos by the hand and walked down to the grassy slope below the sanctuary.

We sat under the trees, overlooking the vast chasm, green with olive groves that spread below us toward the distant sparkling sea. Nikos lay on his back beside me gazing up at the clear sky. It had been an exciting but tiring day for my little son and I hummed a tune to soothe him as he drowsed.

Suddenly Nikos sat up and cried out, disturbing the silence. "Look mama! Look!" He pointed up at the sky where two eagles were circling above us.

"Those are Zeus's eagles!" I said. "Zeus is Lord of the sky and he must have sent his eagles to look over us!"

We watched as the majestic birds swooped and circled then soared down gracefully over the Temple of Apollo. I could not help but believe, after all my trepidation, that they had been sent as a good portent, a sign that this journey I was on with my young son was truly meant to be and we would safely return to my home, Caer Gwyn.

Stanza Four

We left Delphi the next day, travelling east along the river Kephesos through mountain pass. Four days later we arrived at the entrance to the great plain where the battle of Chaeronea had taken place. Ahead, the valley flattened and widened. The river, gleaming in the light of the paling sky, burbled through the lush, green meadow. Along the river, stone-built houses stood on the terraced slopes and farmsteads where sheep and cattle grazed among the olive groves.

We made our camp at the throat of the pass near the same place where we had set our hospital tents before the battle. A deluge of memories flooded my mind. Chaeronea had been days and days of carnage and death I had tried to forget, but now, it all came back to me. My thoughts became a tangle of images. I trembled as I remembered the battle cries, the clash of weapons, the screams of wounded men, the hospital tents filled with bloodied soldiers moaning in pain, crying out to the gods for mercy, many of them opening their wounds to spill more blood so it might hasten their death and release them from their agony.

Today the valley was quiet and peaceful. Only those painful memories remained. I shook off the horrible images and tried instead to remember the triumph of the Makedonians: King Filippos riding across the field declaring victory, Alexandros, on his horse Bucephalus, helmet off, his copper hair shining in the sun, scarlet cape unfurled as he proclaimed his cavalry had defeated the Theban Sacred Band.

Cleon lit a fire; and I put on a pot of lentils while Ajax opened his wine flask and poured each of us a cup.

"We must spill the dregs to the gods for our safe journey," he said, "and remember our comrades and friends who fought and died here." He turned to his companion. "Cleon, you were too young to have fought at Chaeronea, but every Makedonian boy knows about the brave warriors and how Makedons defeated the Athenians."

Ajax lifted his cup to make a libation, his yellowed teeth glimmering in the firelight. With his scarred face and grizzled black brows and beard he made a fearsome sight. "I raise my cup to you, my Lady," he said to me. Then he turned to Theon. "And to you, sir. For I owe both of you my life!"

I was taken aback, and he could see that. He stepped closer to me and lifted his tunic to display a jagged scar where a spear had pierced his flesh. I caught my breath in shock, remembering how they had brought one of Alexandros's officers to the hospital tent, a spear shaft protruding from his side. As if it was yesterday, it all came back to me – how I had used a knife to cut through the wooden shaft, and how Theon had dug out the spearhead.

"I would not have survived if it had not been for your care," Ajax said. His face softened, and I saw tears glint in his eyes. "I cannot go to fight the Persians with Alexandros, but he has given me charge of the garrison at Pella in his absence. And he entrusted you to my care, because he knew I owed my life to you."

That night, once again the memories of the battle haunted me. Then, as if his spirit had come to console me, I felt Elidi's smooth strong hands caressing me. I remembered how I had lain awake at night in the hospital tent, frightened and worried because I knew I was pregnant with his child. I wept as I remembered our wedding vows: *May we always be together till death part us asunder. I vow to love you through all hardship, darkness and pain.* I knew I would never forget that vow, and I would honour it for our son's sake, no matter how many difficulties lay in our journey back to my people.

We set off early the next morning. A soft breeze was blowing across the meadow. The fragrance of lavender and herbs sweetened the air. While Belos unyoked the oxen and led them to graze, Cleon built a fire. The guards had hunted along the way and Ajax placed two plump hares on a spit to roast while I prepared a pot of wild greens I had picked from the meadow.

Across the meadow from our camp loomed the great heap of earth and stones that marked the grave of Chaeronea's fallen warriors. Nearby stood a massive stone lion that Theon said was a tribute to the brave warriors of the Sacred Band of Thebes.

I remembered how the field had been strewn with shields and helmets, broken spears, the dead and dying lying everywhere as vultures circled overhead. The Makedonians had collected their dead, but the others, the Athenians and Thebans, had been left until their cities bartered for their return. I recalled how, when Makedon's victory had been declared, the Makedonians had celebrated, dancing a *komos* as the wine poured freely.

I was glad the next morning when we left that haunted site and made our way to the road that would lead us to Thebes. We travelled through the heath lands, along the foot of the hills through oak groves and woodlands where larches trembled in the breeze. The road began to narrow until it was not more than a steep, stony track winding up through the dense forest.

I was lulled by the sound of the oxen's hoof beats on the rugged track, cradling Nikos in my arms, when I heard the oxen bellow and suddenly the wagon gave a lurch. A large black boar had darted out of the underbrush in front of the team, snorting as it charged across the road into the forest.

"The boar has spooked them!" Besos shouted. He leaped from the driver's seat of the cart onto the road and ran ahead shouting at the ox team. There was a sharp cracking sound and the wagon began to sway. I held tight to Nikos.

Theon turned from where he was sitting in the front of the wagon. "The oxen have broken from their yoke!" he cried. "Hold on!"

There was a sharp jolt and I felt myself tipping as the wagon tilted sideways and crashed over on its side. Still holding Nikos as tightly as I could. I felt myself hit the ground and heard him cry out. Then, for a while there was only blackness.

When I finally opened my eyes, I was lying on the edge of the trail. My body ached and my head swirled. I rose up on my elbow and reached out to find my son who was lying beside me, not moving or crying.

'Nikos! Nikos!" I managed to scramble up and cradled his limp body in my arms. "My Nikos! Oh gods...no!" There was a bruise on his forehead and a stream of blood trickling from his scalp. "Please gods ... No!" I began to sob and pray, sure that my child was dead.

The guards had dismounted, and Cleon rushed to my side. "The boar startled the oxen, my lady." He knelt beside me and wiped Nikos's forehead with the hem of his cloak.

I couldn't stop my tears and Cleon put his arm around me. "Don't worry, my lady. He's alright ... Look!"

Then I saw Nikos's eyes flicker open and he let out a weak cry. "Mama..." I kissed him and soothed him, my own tears splashing down on his dirt-smudged little face.

I brushed back his hair and saw the cut on his scalp was just a small gash. I wiped away the blood and dust from his cheeks. "Oh, my Nikos! How lucky we are! The goddess, our protector, saved us ..."

I looked around to find Theon. He was standing on the other side of the trail beside the tipped cart, leaning on Ajax.

"The physician has injured his leg," Ajax called to Cleon. "How is the woman and her child?"

"Has he broken a bone?" I asked. If Theon was lamed it may mean we could not be able to travel farther than Athens.

"I will do what I can," I said, trying to calm the tremor in my voice.

I set Nikos in a safe place under the trees and limped over to tend Theon. There was blood trickling down his leg from a deep gash on his thigh. He was able to stand but could not take a step without crumbling, his face contorted with pain.

"Cleon, fetch the box of medicines and surgical supplies from the cart." I knelt beside Theon and wiped away the blood with the edge of my cloak. It was a deep gash and no doubt would leave a noticeable scar.

When Cleon brought the medicines, I rubbed a soothing salve on the wound and bound it up with a clean cloth.

"I'm alright," Theon assured me. "What about you and the boy? Don't worry. I am sure I have no broken bones. Just scrapes and bruises." He looked around at the upturned cart and pointed to Besos who had caught the wayward oxen and was leading them back.

"The oxen's yoke is broken," Besos said. "I will try to fix it well enough so we can continue our journey." He glanced over at Nikos and me, then at Theon's wounded leg. "Are you sure you are alright, sir? And the young lady and child?"

"Just a few cuts and bruises," Theon said, and chuckled. "I might walk with a limp for a while, but it won't stop me. With Ajax and Cleon's help you will get the cart upright and the oxen yoked so we can proceed." He smiled reassuringly at me. "Just a mishap of travel, my girl. And I hope it is the only one."

Stanza Five

The road to Thebes wound down a steep path between the pines. It opened onto a wide plain crossed by a river that flowed through olive groves and pasture lands.

"Another day's journey across the plain," Theon said. "Then we will reach the city of Thebes. One day there to fix the oxen's yoke and repair the cart, then we will be on our way to Athens."

We made our camp under the shade of an oak grove overlooking the stone walls of what appeared to be a ruined temple.

"That is the Sanctuary of the Kabeirion," Theon said. "We must pay homage to the Kabeiroi there."

"What are the Kabeiroi?" I asked.

"It's an ancient cult," Theon explained. "Come with me, and I will tell you the story." He beckoned for me to follow as he limped slowly down the stony trail. Sometimes he stopped to lean on the cane Ajax had made him from the branch of an old oak. I saw him occasionally wince with pain.

It was a steep track. At the bottom was a moss-covered stone wall. Past the stone wall Theon pointed out the remains of a small marble temple, its pillars twined with ivy.

"That is the Kabeirion. It's been there since time out of mind." He winced when he sat on the remains of the old stone wall to rest. His face was flushed, his brow glistening with sweat.

'Are you sure you are well?" I asked.

He shrugged off my alarm and forced a smile although I could tell he was in pain.

"Your leg? Perhaps we shouldn't have walked so far."

"No, no," Theon said. "It's good to exercise. I will be fine. A bit of poppy tea and the pain will be gone. Let me tell you about the mysteries of the Kabeiroi.

It is an old tale about a secret cult. Some say they were related to Dionysos and Hermes, others believe to Persepolis and Hades."

Theon was a wise man, and I always believed what he told me, but I could see there was a twinkle in his eye when he spoke of this mysterious cult.

"Some even say they are other-worldly, divine creatures associated with Gaia, the Mother Goddess. They have been worshipped here, and on the island of Samothraki at the Great God's shrine since time out of mind."

I was puzzled by the unusual tale. "I have not brought any votive offerings. What offerings shall we leave for such strange creatures? Why should we pay homage to the Kabeiroi if they are only a cult?"

Theon smiled. "Because they are said to protect seamen and sailing ships. So we will honour them because our sea journey will be a long one and we need the gods' protection - *any* gods."

I followed him somewhat reluctantly through the stone arch into the mysterious sanctuary, Nikos ran ahead to romp in the field of tall grass that surrounded the old temple. Strewn in the grass and weeds, there were shards of old wine cups. I picked up a piece of the broken pottery and saw it was painted with strange, fat, dwarf-like figures with over-sized genitalia. As well as the broken wine cups, I also found some small clay sculptures of bulls.

"What are these for?" I asked.

"Those are gifts dedicated to Kabeiros and Pais, the deities who dwell here. The Kabeiroi also protect the vineyards and animals. The bulls represent an initiation into manhood so there was always an orgy during which much wine was drunk."

I laughed at the thought. "I can see there has been much frolicking and celebration here. But has that made the Theban men any stronger than all the others?"

"They have fought many wars, and won them," Theon said. "One of their greatest generals was Epaninandos. Alexandros's father, Filippos, was a guest friend here when he was a boy and learned many of his war skills from him." Then he paused and his voice took on a graver tone. "Of course there was the Sacred Band... their bravest fighters of all ..."

I thought of the brave three hundred men of Thebes' Sacred Band and how the Makedonian cavalry had killed them, leaving their bodies strewn on the field of Chaeronea. I picked a few wild flowers from the meadow surrounding the temple and when we reached the old altar, I placed them there and said a prayer for the Sacred Band.

We stood in silence for a few moments, each of us making our own supplications to whoever these strange gods were. I could only hope, if they really were the protectors of sailors and ships, our journey from Athens by sea would be a calm, safe voyage.

Stanza Six

It was almost sunset the next day before we reached Thebes city gates. The streets were deserted; and torches lit the gloomy sight of ruined buildings and the widespread destruction. I recalled the stories that had been told of the Makedonians' revenge against the city after the Thebans betrayed them by swearing their allegiance to Athens. In the revolt, they killed some of the Makedonian soldiers Alexandros had posted there after the battle at Chaeronea. So, in retaliation, Thebes had been stripped and plundered, all the men killed, the women and children sold into slavery.

As I looked around at the ruined city, I wondered why men create such carnage to destroy the lives and property of people. I recalled the raids our Keltic tribes made – burning villages, stealing herds of horses and cattle and enslaving the inhabitants. I thought of my last day in Caer Gwyn when the Dobunni tribe had attacked and I wondered if my village, like Thebes, still existed.

Once we were inside the city gates, we dismounted from the ox cart to say goodbye to Cleon, our young escort guard, who would join the troop of cadets at the garrison. When Theon stepped down from the cart he faltered and stumbled, then leaned heavily on his cane. Ajax, who had dismounted from his horse, reached out and caught him. "Are you alright, sir?"

"Yes, yes," Theon said. "Just a misstep."

I shook Cleon's hand and said a blessing for him. I thought of him going off to war with Alexandros. He was still a youth, the same age I'd been when Sholto kidnapped me. What would his future be? Would the Fates allow him to return once again to his family just as I hoped to return to mine?

"I will make an offering to ask the gods to protect you," I said. Cleon's face flushed and he gave me a cocky grin, then turned to Theon. "Take good care of them, sir," he said. "May your journey to Athens be safe and your sea voyage swift."

Theon took him by the shoulders and peered at him like a father counselling his own son. "You are a fine boy!" he said. "You will make your father proud."

We watched Cleon ride away toward the barracks yard, Belos following with the ox cart. Ajax said he would take us to meet the garrison commander who would provide us with lodgings for the night. We followed Ajax as he led his horse through the ruined streets. Theon leaned heavily on his cane, his breathing laboured. There was sweat on his brow even though the evening air was cool.

"Are you sure you are well?" I asked.

He shrugged and sighed: "I'm just tired from the journey."

We continued along the road through the wreckage of buildings that had been destroyed during the war. I expected our lodgings would be in a rough barracks dwelling, but we stopped in front of a beautiful old mansion with vine-covered white marble pillars that must have once been the home of someone of great importance. Ajax told us we were to be lodged there for the night because we were the commander's guest friends, an honour bestowed on important people who were in the king's favour. We waited on the road while he went to speak to a servant who was standing in the courtyard, then returned a few minutes later with a stocky, grey-bearded man who he introduced as the garrison commander, Petros. The commander greeted us warmly. He explained he had been an old friend of King Filippos, so he had been entrusted with the command of the barracks at Thebes after the uprising.

We followed him through a garden abloom with purple anemones, yellow chrysanthemum, cyclamen and roses. In the midst of the flower beds stood the statue of a beautiful maiden holding a lyre.

"That is the muse of poetry, Erato," Theon said. "This must be the house of the poet Pindar!" He looked around in obvious delight. "It was the only house they did not destroy, because Pindar once wrote a eulogy for one of Alexandros's ancestors." He stood in silence for a moment, then spoke again. "'*What is man but the shadow of a dream. But there comes to some a gleam of splendor, a gift from heaven that bathes them in the light of glory and blesses their days.*' Those are Pindar's words. He was one of our greatest poets!"

Petros led us past a shrine to Hestia, the hearth goddess, into the inner courtyard, a large open room with a mosaic pattern of ceramic tile on the floor and walls decorated with paintings of what Theon said were the feats of Heracles. "They say Heracles was born in Thebes," Theon explained.

Several soldiers lounged on couches around a central hearth, drinking wine from silver cups. Commander Petros introduced us and offered us wine and food from gilded plates. The wine was barely watered. I took a cup, but did not drink, and sat with Nikos listening to the men's talk. They were full of ardour talking about the coming raid of Persia by Alexandros's army, and reminiscing about tales of the destruction of Thebes.

I soon grew weary of all the war talk, and Nikos was growing restless. I turned to Theon and noticed he was nodding too, and did not seem attentive. I whispered it was time for Nikos's bath. He did not respond at first, then he took a long breath and said wearily, "Yes, the boy needs his sleep."

"And what about you?"

He shrugged and gave a sigh. "I must stay with the men. It is expected of me. Petros will have a servant show you to the women's room."

The servant led me up a flight of marble steps to what once was the women's quarters. The room seemed to exude some mysterious spirit. There was a musky scent of bath oil, incense and pine ash from the bronze hearth basket. I felt the presence of spirits. Could they be the spirits of the women who had once dwelt there? Theon said all of Pindar's relatives had been allowed their freedom. I wondered where they were now.

A single lamp, hung on a tall bronze standard provided a dim light. On the walls were paintings of nymphs and satyrs that somehow amused little Nikos.

He ran about laughing while I prepared a bath for him in a large basin decorated with dolphins.

I bathed and dried him, wrapped him in a blanket, and carried him to the bed. The bed, which was covered with a purple edged blanket trimmed with bullion, had legs inlaid with abalone shells ending in gilded sea-bird's feet. Nikos found this amusing and clapped his hands in delight. I wondered if it had once been the bed of Pindar's wife who had resided there long ago. I tried to imagine what it must have been like before Thebes was destroyed.

After I had bathed myself, and blew out the lamp, I settled on the bed with Nikos cradled beside me. I lay for awhile contemplating the devastating fate of Thebes and its inhabitants, until I fell into a deep slumber and dreamed.

I am running through the narrow streets of Caer Gwyn. Some of the cone-shaped straw roofs are burning and the streets are filled with smoke. I hear the sound of men shouting, women screaming, swords clashing. Someone shouts: 'The Ordovices are attacking us! They want vengeance for their prince who was stolen and sacrificed at the midsummer.' I run outside through the village gate along the path below the hill fort and into the shelter of the oak grove. When I look back, the village is engulfed in flames...

I woke suddenly, my frightened cries disturbing Nikos. He whimpered softly beside me. "Mama? Mama?"

I held him close. "It's alright, my child. Mama just had a dream..." But I lay awake wondering what I would find when I returned to Caer Gwyn. The Keltic tribes could be just as ruthless as the Makedonians had been. Perhaps the Ordovices *did* destroy my village. Perhaps it was an impossible dream to think I could ever be reunited with Essylt and the other people of my tribe. Was I wrong to risk the sea voyage in hopes of returning to my people? Should I have remained at Theon's farmstead where life was simple and safe?

I drifted back to a troubled sleep and was wakened by the sound of men's voices and the clatter of weapons from the parade grounds. Nikos was still asleep beside me. I let him be and waited for Theon to come with the news that the ox yoke and damaged cart had been mended so we could safely continue our journey. But Theon did not come. Instead it was Ajax who burst into the room. He looked distressed.

"Come quickly, my lady. It's the physician. He is not well!"

I called for the servant and asked him to take Nikos to the garden to play, then I hurried with Ajax to the *andron*, the men's quarters where no women were usually allowed.

Theon lay on a couch covered with fox skins. I could see he was shivering yet dripping with perspiration. I felt his brow. His face had a yellow pallor and his flesh was burning hot, his breath coming in gasps. I grasped his wrist and felt the pulse beat.

"Just... a fever..." Theon gasped and winced in pain. "My leg ..."

My stomach clenched. *It is more than just a fever,* I thought.

I pulled down the cover to examine Theon's leg and ordered Ajax to bring me the medical supplies which we had stored on the ox cart. When I un-wrapped the cloth from the wound I could see that it was seeping and inflamed.

It could be sepsis! The thought frightened me. I knew I must act quickly or his condition would grow more grave. If the infection was not treated correctly and immediately he might not survive it.

It did not take Ajax long to return with the *pharmacae.* He was breathing heavily as he had run all the way to the barracks to find Belos and the ox cart.

"What is it, my lady?" He bent over to take a close look at Theon and gasped when he saw the open wound. "Can you heal it?" His brow was furrowed with worry.

"That cut on his leg. It could be sepsis," I tried to sound calm but my voice shook when I spoke. "I will have to treat it quickly or it will spread to his blood-stream and he could... " I could not bear to even think of the word *"die."*

I laid everything out on the table: the herbs and other medical concoctions, the surgical tools: pliers, forceps, bleeding cup, scalpel. The thought occurred to me, if the wound failed to heal, I might have to amputate Theon's leg. I had watched him perform surgery on soldiers. I knew how to remove arrow-heads and sew up sword wounds but I never imagined I might have to perform such a thing as an amputation.

I put Ajax in charge of handing me the jars of medicine, scalpels and for-ceps. Lancing the infected wound was something I had watched Theon do many times, but this was the first time I would attempt to undertake it without his guidance.

"Shall I call for the garrison commander, my lady?" Ajax asked.

I looked up and nodded, "Perhaps. We may need his help."

Theon's eyes were closed and his breathing shallow. I poured water from an ewer into a small basin near the bedside, washed my hands and carefully dabbed at the wound, cleaning away the blood caked on it. His leg was red and inflamed, a hideous wound. I washed and dressed it, cutting away the infected flesh and scraped away the pus that oozed from the open sore. I knew he might die if the infection was not cleansed from his body.

I mixed a concoction of agrimony, burdock and rosemary and slathered it over the wound. A servant came with a hand lamp and tinder box to kindle the standing lamp and light a fire in the hearth. I brewed some tea with arti-choke and honey and hoped it might bring down Theon's fever. I lifted his head and put the cup to his lips. He sipped some but then lay back, too weak to take more.

Ajax returned with the garrison commander. Both men looked worried and after seeing Theon, stood talking quietly.

"I have done all I can." I rinsed my hands and dried them, and tucked the covers around Theon, making sure he was comfortable and warm. I shook Theon gently and spoke to him but there was no response.

"You are young, my lady, but surely the gods have blessed you with wisdom," the commander said. "We will provide for you until the good physician is well enough to leave his bed."

"We must not travel until he is well..." I remembered Theon saying, *"With healing we must be patient. The body will heal itself in time."* Could I live up to the physician's creed?

Later that day, Ajax returned with Nikos and the servant, who had brought us a roasted duck to share. Ajax carved the meat and handed a plate of it to me. The aromatic smell reminded me I had not eaten since the previous day.

Ajax must have noticed my distress. "You must eat, my lady, or you will fall ill yourself." He put a comforting hand on my shoulder. "You have done your best, my lady. The good physician taught you well."

Over the next days, I tended Theon carefully, cauterizing the wound, packing it with a concoction of honey, bee pollen and oil and poultices of agrimony leaves crushed with pork fat for healing. I gave him tea of vervain and artichoke to bring his fever down and tried to feed him lentil soup. He slept most of the time and barely responded when awake. I worried his time might be over and I prayed, *"Please my lady goddess, let him live."*

Ajax consoled me when he saw how careworn I was. He brought me sweets from the market and offered to tend Nikos during the day while I kept watch over Theon. At night he sat with Theon while I slept.

Each morning Ajax would hoist Nikos onto his shoulders and take him to the stables to see the horses or to the training grounds where Cleon was drilling with the other cadets. He was one of those men who, in spite of his demeanour, would have suited the role as father and he did his duty as if Nikos was his own son.

As the days passed, I found comfort in our friendship. Sometimes I spoke to him about Elidi although afterwards, I would feel myself sink into despair. But I knew I must keep my mind on healing Theon.

Ajax was a rough man, and though his scars were a reminder that he was a warrior, he was kind, and respectful. One day I asked him: "Are you married? Do you have children of your own?"

A dark look crossed his face, like a cloud covering the sun. "My wife died in childbirth," he said. "I had no desire to take another." Then he brightened. "Of course, there are women – lots of them. It's a soldier's life!" He paused and sat quietly watching me as I mixed potions for Theon's wound. "And you, my lady, I know how you came to be in Theon's care and your husband was lost at sea. But why do you want to leave our country? Can there be a better life for you than the one you have here?."

"You need not call me 'my lady'," I said. "My name is Olwen."

Ajax thought on what I had said for a moment, then replied: "Alexandros always called you the little Kelt."

"I *was* just an innocent maiden when he met me," I said, "But I am older now. My grandfather named me Olwen, after the goddess of springtime because it was springtime when they found me at the Stone Circle."

A broad smile lit up is dark face and he said my name again: "Olwen! "repeating it slowly as if relishing the sound. Then he smiled and said: "Now, lady Olwen, tell me about your people, the Cymry."

I hesitated at first, then I began to relate my story to him – how when I was an infant, I had been found at the Stone Circle and cared for by the Druids.

"The chief Druid, Maelgwyn, was like a grandfather to me, and the healer, Essylt, became my mother. My people are a brave tribe of warriors. I am an Essyltyr, from the Clan of the Raven. Our *tuath* – that is our town - is called Caer Gwyn. It is a beautiful place beneath a hill fort on the heath, near the great Stone Circle where we honour our gods."

Ajax thought on this a moment, then asked: "Why did you leave your people?"

I hesitated before allowing myself to go back in my mind to that dreadful day. "I was stolen away by the ricon's son. He took me because I had seen him slay his brother and he thought, because I am a Druid's child, I would be his luck-piece and keep him from harm. So he fled with me across the Narrow Sea and across the Keltic lands."

"Then Alexandros rescued you?"

"Yes." I paused, withdrawing into myself, not wanting to dredge up more of those dark memories. Finally I said: "Alexandros saved my life. I might have been slain or sold as a slave."

"And the good physician, Theon, he has become like a father to you."

I looked over to the bed where Theon was sleeping. "Yes. Yes he has," I said.

Ajax sat quietly in thought, his brow furrowed. "What will you do if he…" He paused before saying the dreaded words. "If he dies."

I felt my stomach clench at the words. My throat felt dry, and my heartbeats quickened. What *would* I do? Theon had given away the farmstead. Could I go back to Pella? I knew I would not be welcomed by Olympias in the palace without Theon. Could I continue the journey home by myself and my son?

Ajax reached out and put his hand over mine. "You are a brave woman, my lady. A warrior woman. Your people will be proud of you and welcome you home."

That night I laid awake until the flames on the hearth fire guttered and sank. My skin prickled with cold I felt as it did in moments of mortal danger. Careful not to waken Nikos, I got out of bed. I took some sage out of my amulet bag and went to the hearth shrine. The sprig of sage lit easily from embers on the hearth. I said a healing chant to my Keltic goddess, "Bone to bone, skin to skin, flesh to flesh, blood to blood. Oh Airmud, gentle sweet, Goddess of healing, giver of life. Honour my gifts. Heal the physician. Give him back his life."

By the seventh day the fever had subsided. and it appeared Theon was finally recovering. I began to breathe more easily. Each morning I gave him stimulants and cleansing draughts of rosemary and vervain to hasten the healing. He was more alert and was able to prop himself up and enjoy the bowls of barley soup the servant brought. He even asked for wine, which I served him mixed with rosemary. When I dressed his wound, I saw the infection responded well to the poultices and his wound was no longer raw and red.

"You are more than a healer, my girl," Theon said. "You are truly a physician, and when you return to your people they will honour you." He insisted we must leave Thebes soon. "The days are passing quickly and we must be in Athens in good time to get a ship for Syracuse."

"We will not travel until I am sure you are well enough," I said to him sternly.

"When I am well enough to at least walk with my cane!" he said. I saw that familiar twinkle had returned to his eyes and his face brightened with a smile. "Until then, I will obey the good *physician*!"

BALLAD TWENTY-NINE Ode To Athena

Beautiful, golden Athena,
your graceful form glimmers down on us.
Lovely Athens, standing over the city.
Watch carefully, Athena.
Look down on us from your holy temple
and grant us your blessings.

CITY OF THE GODDESS

Stanza One

The road from Thebes led west, over the hills, skirting the foot of a pine-forested mountain. We passed through arid fields of new crops, olive groves and orchards. Across the fields I could hear the crowing of cockerels, the bleating and lowing of farm stock and the cries of shepherds driving their flocks up the mountain paths. In places the road grew steep, winding between the hills toward the coast. A few goats grazed in the bracken on the hillside; and in the distance I heard the sound of the goat herder piping like the trill of a bird.

The road sloped down past fields bright with Spring poppies and ahead I caught a glimpse of the sparkling blue sea. We had reached the coast. Belos, the ox-driver, told us this was the last stretch of our long journey by road, but it would take several more days to reach the city.

Farmers and tradesmen, merchants and wayfarers crowded the well-trodden road, all of us going to the same destination. Athens. The road led by the shore. The refreshing breeze was invigorating. I breathed deep of the salt air and soon forgot all the troubles we had gone through at Thebes. As the days passed, I began to shed the mantle of grief that enfolded me after Elidi's death and my spirits soared.

Theon was well now and seemed as excited as I was to see the great city of Athens. As we rode along, he told me stories of the city as he remembered it, when he lived there in his youth.

"Athens is a glorious city!" he said. "For some years there was strife among the city states until Filippos united them. Since then, Athens has thrived."

Ahead, at the foot of a rocky cleft, I saw the painted columns of a temple and around it other pillars and gilded statues. "Is that Athens?" I asked.

"This Eleusis is a most holy place dedicated to our goddess, Demeter!" exclaimed Theon. "It is here the Sacred Mysteries are celebrated."

As we drew closer, he asked Belos to pull the cart over and stop by the roadside.

"Olwen, we must visit this place," Theon said. "Even though the rites are held in the month when the crops are sown, it is important to pay homage to the goddess."

We dismounted from the cart. Nikos was asleep so I left him with Belos and Ajax and followed Theon up the path to the sacred shrine. As he led the way, Theon told me the story.

"Every year the priestesses of Demeter and Persephone lead a great procession from Athens, along the Sacred Way, to pay tribute at the shrine," Theon said. "There is much celebrating and rejoicing, dancing and revelling."

He led me past small marble temple buildings and garlanded shines, up stone steps to the foot of a stony bluff where there was a gaping hole in the rock.

"Persephone's cave!" Theon exclaimed. "Every springtime, the goddess's daughter, Persephone, returns from the Underworld where Hades has kept her prisoner. This is the place where she appears!"

I stood before the sacred place and whispered a prayer.

"To *Demeter, Earth Mother, and your daughter, the lovely Persephone. What a miracle when every Springtime you return to make the flowers grow and the fields green.*"

I thought of how I was named after Olwen, our Celtic goddess of flowers and springtime and how, like Persephone, who is released from Hades each year, I had also been rescued from captivity.

When we returned to the ox-cart, Theon told me the road we would travel into Athens was known as the Sacred Way. "It leads all the way to the agora and the temple of Athena."

Stanza Two

The road was dusty, the hills around, parched brown. Theon pointed out a dense grove of olive trees.

"That is the sacred grove leading to the gardens where the philosopher, Plato, had his Academy. I attended there when I was a youth. I met my friend, Aristoteles at the Academy. Later, I went to the Asclepeion of Hippocrates to learn more about medicines."

All along the road past the Academy were monuments to mark the graves of famous soldiers. As we neared the city it was thronged with people coming from the country – travellers, merchants - some from other lands bringing wares, and farmers with cart loads of fruit and vegetables to sell in the market. The narrow, unpaved dirty streets were littered with refuse. Plain white brick houses with shuttered windows, and little shops selling votive offerings lined the roadway. Some of the houses had paintings of Apollo, bringer of health, painted on the walls.

We came to a large graveyard. There were tombs and painted grave steles, some faded with age, others freshly decorated with grave wreaths. A narrow river flowed through it, the reedy banks abloom with lilies.

"This is known as the Kerameikos," Theon said. "These are the tombs of great soldiers and statesmen of Athens, and some of wealthy families, too. It is a place of tribute and remembrance."

Ahead were the tall stone towers of what Theon said was the Dipylon Gate. He asked Belos to halt the cart. "Olwen and I will walk into the agora," he said. "We will meet you and Ajax at the south gate."

I held tight to Nikos's hand as we walked along the rocky path.

"Where are we going, Mama? We stay here now?" he asked.

"Just for a few days, Nikos, until we find a ship to take us away."

We entered through a gateway along a wide stone path that led into a massive marketplace. "This is the Panathenaic Way that leads to the Parthenon, Athena's temple. Ahead is the agora, the assembly place of Athens where all the citizens meet," Theon explained. "It's mainly a place where business is transacted and philosophy discussed. Later in the afternoon it will be less crowded, as people will go to attend the gymnasium or drama competitions."

Elegant marble public buildings flanked the outer edges, separating the market area from what Theon explained were places of assembly for the citizens and politicians. There were ornate fountains, altars to the twelve gods smouldering with sweet incense and beautiful painted stoas, one depicting battle scenes and a display of bronze shields that Theon said had been captured from the Spartans.

"The city has been treated with favour by Alexandros because of his teacher, Aristoteles," Theon said.

As we pushed through the crowds of traders and city administrators who mingled with the ordinary folk who had come to market, little Nikos's eyes were wide with wonderment. He gazed around in delight and tugged at my hand when he saw a dolphin fountain spouting bubbly water. "Can I play with my boat here?"

"Hold tight to Mama's hand now," I scolded. "If I lost you in the crowds what would I do?"

Ahead towered a steep cliff crowned with a magnificent painted temple. As I lifted my eyes I saw a glimmering of gold from a tall statue and drew in my breath in amazement.

"That is the Sacred Rock, and the Temple honouring the city's goddess, Athena," Theon pointed up toward the great golden statue that looked down over the city. "Athena is the guardian of Athens."

I found myself rooted to the spot and tears welled in my eyes. I had never imagined such a glorious sight as this.

"Has Athena bewitched you, my girl?" Theon chuckled. He looked at me, cocked an eyebrow, and winked. I saw the twinkle in his eye. "Athena will do that – and you will never forget her."

Theon guided us along to a roadway where another smaller temple on a small hill commanded the other side of the agora.

"The Temple of Hephaestus," Theon said. "We will meet Belos and Ajax at the boundary stone near there. First, I want you to see where the generals and city officials meet. The agora is the centre of all the politics and business of the city"

He led us on, stopping now and then to point out buildings of importance and monuments to heroes. Past the Temple of Hephaestus we came to a long building with a pillared porch that faced the Sacred Rock.

"Here is the Bouleuterion, the Sanctuary of the Mother of the Gods. The Assembly meets there to draft the city's laws. And that round building ahead – the one that looks like a hat – that's the Tholos where the city officials meet."

By the time we met Belos and Ajax at the gate, my head was awhirl. I had thought the palace of Pella was lavish, but what surrounded me here, in the Agora of Athens, was something I had never imagined. I thought of my humble village of Caer Gwyn with its cone-shaped thatched roofs and mud-built houses and wondered how I would explain this to my people.

A cobbled road led along the foot of a hillside into a grove of pine trees. "This is the *Mouseion*, the Hill of the Muses," Theon said. "The garrison is here on the hillside, guarding the road."

When we reached to gated entrance to the garrison, we got down from the ox cart and gathered our bundles.

'I'll take my leave of you here, sirs," Belos said to Theon and Ajax. He turned to me, and bowed. "To you, my lady and your child, I bid you a safe onward journey."

Theon paid him with a generous handful of gold coins. "Where will you go now?" Theon asked.

"I'll stable the oxen while I pick up some wares in the agora and find some travellers who are going north."

We thanked Belos and I said a blessing for him as we watched him drive the oxen back down the road toward the agora. Belos had brought us safely to Athens from Pella, and I was grateful for that. He was a good man, and I hoped his trip back home would be swift and safe.

The garrison was built on the brow of the hill. Ajax said he would go alone to speak to the garrison commander and we should wait for him by the road. So we took our bundles and found shelter in a grove of pine trees.

It was quiet in the grove. The warm spring sun slated through the trees. The fresh scent of pine sap permeated the air, birds trilled in the trees, and occasionally people strolled by on the road. Through the trees, I saw a rock face with a gaping opening that must have been the entrance to a cave. As I looked closer I noticed it was enclosed by an iron gate.

"What is that?" I asked Theon. "Is it the entrance to a cistern?"

"That is a prison," Theon said. "It was the place where our great philosopher, Socrates, was held after his trial."

"His trial?"

"Yes. He had disagreed with some of the city's laws. Socrates was one of our greatest philosophers. Plato was one of his students."

"If he was a respected philosopher, why would they imprison him?" I asked. I thought of our Druids and how they were held in such great esteem.

Theon paused for moment, then he said: "You see, years ago, after the wars with Sparta, people began to question Athens's democracy and morality. Socrates was one of them. This upset many of the Athenians and they turned against him, accusing him of wrongdoing. Some of his friends pleaded with him to leave the city, but he wouldn't, even though he was morally and politically at odds with many of the Athenians." Theon stood, and faced the cave entrance, standing silently, his brow wrinkled as if deep in thought. "Socrates was always loyal to Athens, but he also praised Sparta, Athen's rival," he said. "He questioned the idea of whether giving a show of might and engaging in warfare was the correct path to follow to make things right. He believed just because men thought themselves to be wise, it did not mean they actually were. He disagreed with many of the Assembly's policies and thought they were wrong."

"So for this he was condemned?"

"They found him guilty of corrupting the minds of the youth of Athens with his teachings, and of impiety toward the gods. So they put him on trial for heresy." He pointed toward the cave. "This is where he was held until he was convicted of his crimes and forced to drink a mixture poisoned with hemlock."

I tried to understand the depth of Theon's words. How could a notable, respected man of such great intellect as Socrates be executed for his beliefs?

While I was pondering this injustice, Ajax arrived accompanied by a tall man, fair-haired and ruddy-cheeked, dressed in a white chiton, his head crowned with a silver helmet.

"This is Commander Phaon," Ajax said.

The Commander shook Theon's hand and smiled at me. "You are welcome here," he said. "Ajax has told me of your arduous journey from Pella."

His friendly demeanour was charming. "You will come to my home and be welcome there," he said. "I have the orders from Alexandros to find you passage to Syracuse," He swept out his hands and looked toward the agora and the Sacred Hill. "But you can enjoy Athens for as long as you wish."

Ajax hoisted Nikos up on his shoulders and carrying our bundles, we followed Commander Phaon along the stone-paved road. We passed through a gateway where several elegant painted houses were built along the brow of a ridge overlooking a ravine. Below, along the tree clad slope, a long high wall protected a road that led toward the west.

"This is the Hill of the Nymphs. Once many famous men lived here, "Theon said. "That is the Koile Road It leads to the seaport where the ships are docked."

Commander Phaon led us through the gated entrance of the first house to a courtyard overlooking the ravine. Two children were playing in the garden with hoops and balls. When they saw the commander, they left their play and ran to him crying out in delight. He saluted the boy and picked up the little girl.

"These are my children, Milos and Maia," he said. They were beautiful children, fair and rosy-cheeked. The girl was about Nikos's age, the boy a little older.

Phaon motioned to Nikos who was standing shyly beside Ajax, pressed close to his side. "Children, this little boy has travelled all the way from Makedon. Why don't you take him to the garden with you and show him how to play hoops?"

The children smiled at Nikos and the boy held out his hand. "Come and play with us," he said.

At first, Nikos held back shyly when they greeted him, but with a little coaxing he raced after them into the garden laughing in delight. It filled me with joy at the sight of him playing with other children. In Pella he had no playmates, so this was a new adventure for him.

A woman, who the commander introduced as his wife, Chryse, came out of the atrium to greet us. She was a beautiful woman, dressed in a saffron linen chiton and sandals with amber clasps. Her upswept golden hair was carefully set with jewelled pins. To me, she was almost as beautiful as a goddess.

She welcomed me with a smile and asked my name. "Olwen." She repeated it carefully. "Not a Greek?"

"No, I'm a Cymry," I said, "from the Keltic lands."

"But you speak Greek?"

"Theon taught me many things," I replied.

She looked surprised, then Phaon explained to her that Theon and I were physicians from Pella and friends of Alexandros. "They wish to sail to Syracuse," he said. "Alexandros has asked me to find them passage on one of our ships. They will stay with us until arrangements have been made."

"And you are travelling all that way with your child?" Chryse exclaimed. "You are certainly a brave woman. That is a long journey, and sometimes the seas can be stormy."

"We are going back to my people in Cymru," I replied. "I was taken from them and because of Alexandros, I found refuge with Theon."

"You must be weary from the long journey down to Athens," Chryse said. "Come with me. I will have my servant prepare a bath and you must rest awhile." She looked over where the children were playing. "I'll see your son is cared for. He will be happy with my children."

She called to a young bronze-skinned girl who came from the atrium. "Tey, mind the children while I take our guest to the atrium. And later bring them in for their baths, the little boy, too. His name is?" She looked at me for a reply.

"Nikos," I said. "His name is Nikos Elidimis. His father was a Phrygian helmsman on the king's trireme. His ship went down in a storm."

Chryse put out her hand and touched me arm. "Dear girl," she said softly, "Surely the gods must look on you with pity."

I followed her through the atrium where a servant had prepared a tray of bread and oil, cheese and olives. Chryse offered me a plate and poured me a cup of watered wine. We sat a while by the hearth talking as we ate. She asked me more about the journey and about myself.

"You are a healer, like Theon? How did a Keltic girl like you come to be in his care?"

I told her my story, how I had been raised by the Druids and meant to be a healer. "Then I was stolen from my village and taken far away. Now I must go home again," I said. "When my beloved husband died, and since Alexandros is leaving on his campaign, Theon suggested we should leave Pella. He has taught me everything about the healing arts and I wish to take that knowledge back to my own people."

The day was growing late. A bright glow of golden sunset flooded the western sky.

"Come," Chryse said. "It is time for you to rest awhile. Don't worry about your child. I will see he is cared for with my own children."

She led me from the atrium to a room with a mosaic tiled floor, the walls painted with murals of the nymphs. There was a couch and a table draped with an embroidered cloth, on top of it a tray of fruit and a pitcher of wine. An ornate lamp stood beside a bed of carved wood, a coverlet of fine wool on it.

"This will be your room while you are my guest," Chryse said. "The men have gone to the andron to discuss their business. I will have my maiden, Hippolyta, prepare a bath for you and then you must rest."

Hippolyta helped me change out of my travel-soiled homespun tunic and gave me a linen robe to wear to the bathing room where a bath of steaming water had been prepared. I lay in the tub half dreaming as the servant girl scrubbed me with a scented sponge and hummed a tune to soothe me. When the bath water cooled, she helped me up and dried me with a soft towel, then led me back to the bedroom.

I had not expected such lavish care once we had left Pella, and being here, in Athens, in this lovely home with my friendly hosts, was more than I had ever imagined. I lay in the bed and let myself drift into a serene dream knowing my child and I were safe.

Stanza Two

When I awoke the next morning, I found Theon in the garden watching the little boys play with their toy boats in the lily pond.

"Nikos is happy with his new friends." he said. "This morning I will take you to the Sacred Rock. The servants will see he's well cared for while you are gone."

The Sacred Rock! I felt as giddy as a child at the thought of visiting the goddess's temple.

I bent down beside my son and kissed him. He had been carefully tended by Tey and was dressed in a fresh new tunic of saffron wool. I put my arms around him and sank my nose into his tousled hair. He smelled of sweet jasmine oil.

Nikos looked up at me with shining eyes. "I'm sailing my boat like Papa,".

I felt a pang of sadness when he mentioned Elidi but said nothing. It made me glad to know he still thought of his father, perhaps even believed Elidi was still living. I kissed the nape of Nikos's neck. "Mama is going to the Sacred Rock with Theon." He looked up, then pushed away and went back to his play.

I followed Theon down the cobbled path to the boundary stone that marked the entrance to the agora and a building where Theon said the generals met, then we turned along a road that passed by a well-guarded building.

"This is the prison where Socrates died after they condemned him," he said. He pointed ahead toward a cliff that lay below where the Sacred Rock rose over the city with its magnificent temples. "And that is the Areopagus Hill, dedicated to the god Ares. Trials are held there, and criminals are judged and condemned, then sent to this prison to await their fate."

I still puzzled over why a man such as Socrates should be executed for his beliefs, I thought of Caer Gwyn, the swift, merciless punishments meted out by the ricon, the severed heads of his antagonists and enemies atop the poles of his lodge. There were no trials, no justice served. Only revenge.

We walked along in the shade of the long-painted stoas, past monuments to gods and heroes and into the busy marketplace. The morning crowd was mostly men, citizens of Athens and dignified senators dressed in white girdled tunics fastened at the neck with pins wrought of gold, farmers wearing wide-brimmed hats plying their produce, some slaves, and foreigners who Theon called *metics,* clad in long robes and turbans.

"They are wealthy merchants who have come from lands far away," he explained.

There were few women in the agora. Chyrse had told me most Greek wives stayed in their homes and sent their servants to the market. A few old crones plied their wares of herbs and potions, and young maidens dressed in clean plain tunics carried baskets of fruit and produce on their heads. I noticed a few women in the busy crowd who were dressed in colourful himations with beautifully embroidered borders. Some wore shawls, others carried parasols. Many of them mingled with the men in the shade of the stoas while others gathered by the shrines and fountains. Theon said they were *heitaras,* women who offered their services to men.

We stopped to purchase some olives and lemons and sweet-smelling herbs to offer at Athena's shrine. At the Panthaenaic Way, we turned up toward the hill, past a row of bronze statues of famous men. As we started up the steep path, Theon related the story about the Parthenon.

"It was built as a symbol of triumph after the Greeks' victory over the Persians at Marathon," he said. "It is dedicated as a sanctuary to Athena Polias, protector of the city. Her statue guards the place where Athens' treasures are stored."

On the trail we stopped to rest on a ledge enjoying the peacefulness of our surroundings. The marble was warm from the sun and the hillside dappled with shade from the pine trees on the slope.

Theon continued his story. "You see, once there was an older temple there that had gone to ruin. It was Pericles who planned to build the new one, and only the best architects and most eminent sculptors in Athens were hired to carve the pediments and friezes. It's an artistic masterpiece of Pentelic marble, the pride of Athens. In fact, the pride of all Hellas."

As we climbed the steps toward the Temple I looked up to the High City. The polished marble stones and the golden ornaments on the pediments gleamed, reflecting the sun. We were close enough to see the painted pillars, some a rich golden colour, others deep blue and gilded, some sparkling white. The pediments were carved with scenes depicting the birth of Athena, the chariot of the Sun, and images of mythical battles.

There, beside it on the north gable surrounded by a bronze barrier, stood the golden figure of Athena, glimmering in the sunlight. I had never seen a sight more wondrous than this. I felt my eyes well with tears.

The statue was almost as tall as the temple. The Goddess stood upright, clad in a dress that reached her feet. On her breast was a head of Medusa, the serpent goddess, wrought in ivory. in her right hand, she held a crowned Victory and in the other, a spear. Her face, hands and feet were ivory, her eyes inset with precious stones. On her helmet was a sphinx, with griffins on each side. A shield with a relief of the battle of the Amazons lay at her feet. Near the base of the spear she held a golden serpent coiled.

I stood in awe looking at Her. I had never imagined a goddess so beautiful, standing so regally, the gold shimmering in the sunlight.

"She was made of molten gold and designed to glow in the darkness," Theon said. "She is the guardian of the city. Her name is Athena Parthenos."

There was an altar near the gate. "We must make our offerings here," Theon said. "No one but priests and priestess are allowed within the sacred precinct."

We laid our offerings on the altar and I said a prayer.

"Athena, protector of the city, wise in all things. May your blessings fall on us. Hear my prayers, Goddess, protect us, show us the way, grant us fulfillment and good health."

I looked up again at the tall golden figure of the strong, beautiful goddess. She seemed to smile down at me, and I felt a surge of strength and renewed determination that my quest to return to my people would be fulfilled.

Stanza Three

When we returned to the Commander's house later that day, the servant, Hippolyta, met us in the courtyard.

"The Commander and my lady, Chryse, have planned a feast to welcome you," she said.

Theon exchanged a look of surprise with me and gave a wry smile. "I am certain some of my Athenian friends want to know what I think of Alexandros's plans of conquest and his peace terms with Athens." He shrugged, shook his head and went into the atrium.

I looked around to see if Nikos was in the garden. Hippolyta sensed my concern and said, "The children are safe in their room. Tey has fed them and will tend them. Come. I will help you bathe and dress. The guests will arrive soon."

A steaming bath had been poured. Hippolyta helped me out of my clothes, and I stepped into the water letting the fragrant steam enfold me as I sank into it. I lay there awhile, soaking in the scented pool as Hippolyta scrubbed me with a sponge. I let myself drift off into a daydream, thinking of the marvellous sights I had seen that day – the golden goddess on the Sacred Hill, the magnificent temple in her honour.

Hippolyta dried me and rubbed scented oil into my skin. She had taken my homespun clothes away. In their place was a beautiful white gown trimmed with blue and gold and a pair of new sandals with lapis clasps. She helped me dress and combed my hair, braiding it into coils woven with threads of gold. When I looked at myself in the mirror I could not believe it was my own image. My cheeks were flushed, my eyes bright, all the weariness of the long journey gone. I looked like a young girl again. I thought back to the day when I had married Elidi, remembered my image in the mirror that day. This was the same innocent young maiden I had been then, flushed and happy, the young girl who was about to become a bride, a woman. A tinge of remorse touched me, but I shook it off. This was a new time now, a time to start a different life. And I knew Elidi would approve.

I went out to the terrace to find Theon. The guests had begun to arrive: Makedonian soldiers from the barracks dressed in their short tunics, Athenians scholars and politicians wearing fine linen chitons, colorful mantles thrown over their shoulders. Some of the men had brought their wives, elegant women dressed in gowns of fine linen, their sparkling jewellery and fashionably styled hair showing their wealth. I had not seen such elegance since attending Queen Olympias in Pella.

Ajax greeted me and gave a little bow. He was clean and shaven, looking much handsomer than before, wearing a new blue chiton stitched with gold. He seemed surprised when he saw me and smiled a broad happy grin.

"My lady Olwen, you are as beautiful as Aphrodite!"

His words made me blush. I looked away shyly and followed Theon into the atrium.

It was my first banquet, and I was dazzled. The servants had prepared a lavish feast. The tables were laden with plates of barley bread with oil and wine for dipping, bowls of olives, lentils, wild greens and platters of roast quail, fish and eels. Dinner was served on ceramic plates decorated with fish and octopus. A bowl of well-watered, chilled wine in the centre was generously ladled into silver wine cups. The men reclined on elegant couches in the atrium, their food placed on low tables. Usually the women dined alone in the women's *gynaikon,* but this night we sat apart from the men at tables in a quiet corner, distanced from them, but still close enough to watch and listen to their friendly banter.

There was quiet talk at first, discussions of philosophy and politics and speeches praising Alexandros. Libations were made to Dionysos and accolades given to Alexandros. Everyone was anxious to hear Theon's news from Makedon about Alexandros's plans to invade Persia.

Theon stood to address the group. His greetings were brief. He told them what he knew of Alexandros's plans.

"Alexandros sends his good will to the Makedonian garrison here and the people of Athens, and praises you for your support. He has chosen not to stay in Pella while the Persians overrun our frontiers. He has amassed a great army and soon they will cross the Hellespont and confront the Persian invaders."

The soldiers shouted their approval, raised their wine cups and cheered. "Alexandros! Alexandros! Long live King Alexandros!"

When the cheers subsided, Theon continued: "Alexandros asked me to say this to you, Makedonians: 'My father united you and made you masters of Greece.'"

There was a pause and a low sound of whispers among the Athenian guests. Theon turn to address them, "And to you Athenians, Alexandros said to tell you this: 'Now you have peace as the quarrels between your city states are reconciled." Then they, too, cheered.

As the evening proceeded the men's talk grew rowdier, their raucous laughter filling the room with merriment. Occasionally I looked over to where the men were lounging on the couches and saw Ajax watching me, smiling. We exchanged silent glances, but I looked away, trying to be discreet, even though I felt a warm tingle when he caught my eye.

After the food was eaten, the tables were removed and the servants brought around basins of water so the diners could wash their hands. Chryse led the women out to the garden to sit under the almond tree's cloud of pink blossoms. The servants had set out trays of honey-drenched cakes and figs. The women were curious and eager to hear my tale of how a Keltic girl came to their country. We sat awhile together laughing and relating stories. The sun had set, and the western sky was tinged red. The servant lit the torches in their sconces, and they burned with bright flames. Then the quiet was disturbed by the raucous laughter of the men singing drinking songs and Chryse suggested they should return to the quiet of the women's room.

I chose to linger for a while in the courtyard. Stars blazed down out of the night sky. The air smelled of wild herbs and sweet-scented blossoms drifted from the trees. Below, along the Koine Road, lights twinkled from the houses and torches blazed along the Long Wall. From somewhere nearby I heard the thin, treble piping of a flute. My thoughts returned to earlier that day, the thrill I had felt standing at the gateway to the Parthenon looking up at the golden statue of Athena. I had been destined to go to the Holy Isle, to serve our Keltic deities, but instead the gods had sent me here to this city, Athens, a city protected by such a magnificent goddess.

The sound of footsteps crossing the terrace startled me out of my reverie. I turned to see it was Ajax. He came to stand beside me.

"My lady Olwen! Have you been charmed by Athens? Has she captivated you?"

"It is a place I could not have imagined, even in a dream," I said.

"You could stay if ..." he hesitated, his brow furrowed, his voice low. "It's a long sea voyage from Hellas shores to Massalia and there may be dangers ahead. Would you not like to stay here instead of risking such a journey?" He halted, as if too shy to speak. He took my hand and spoke with the greatest gentleness. "My lady, Olwen, may I ask you... Would you marry me?"

His words took me by surprise, and I was too taken aback to reply. He leaned down and kissed me gently on my forehead. I caught my breath in and withdrew my hand from his. His dark eyes sparkled, reflecting the torch light. "It is your choice to go or to stay. I know you would be happy here with me. The garrison commander's wife will be a good friend and Nikos will have playmates."

I thought back on the long journey from Pella, how Ajax had guided and protected us, those days in Thebes when he had been such a comfort and help-mate. He had shown me a side of himself I had not expected – a kind, loving man, one who had taken care of my son as if Nikos was his own. I stood staring down at the patterns of the mosaic tiles on the courtyard floor. What should I say? Should I forsake my love for Elidi and forgo my journey home to embrace a new life with this other man?

As if he understood my dilemma, Ajax stepped back and said, "I know it is a difficult choice for you, but I will wait for your answer. You know, I have grown to love you as we travelled together. I have not forgotten how once you saved my life at Chaeronea, and saved the good physician's life. I admire you and have fallen in love with you."

As I struggled to find the words to reply, I heard footsteps behind me.

"My lady!"

It was Hippolyta. "My lady Chryse has sent me to fetch you.." I breathed a sigh of relief.

"I will await your reply," Ajax said. He turned away and went back to the atrium.

I followed Hippolyta to the *gymnaikon* where the women were seated at tables playing a game with stone dice. There were plates of honey drenched cakes and cups of watered wine. I declined the sweets from the tray Hippolyta offered me. I was troubled by what Ajax had suggested, and sat quietly, deep in thought.

Chryse looked up from the game, peered at me and said, "Are you well dear girl? You seem perplexed."

"Just tired," I replied. "It has been a long day." The truth was, Ajax had set my mind in turmoil.

"Then perhaps you should rest," Chryse said. She studied me intently, then ordered Hippolyta to escort me to my room.

Alone in my chamber that night, I lay in my bed and thought of Ajax's kiss, and what he had proposed to me. All night I scarcely slept. I shut my eyes, but Ajax's words kept echoing in my mind. What should I do? Should I risk the long sea voyage and endanger my child? Or should I stay here, in this beautiful city where I could live happily in the shadow of the Sacred Rock?

Stanza Four

The next morning I rose late and went to the courtyard to watch Nikos and the other children playing with their hoops. My mind was still in turmoil from Ajax's proposal, and when Theon came from the andron to tell me he wanted to take me to visit his old friend, Aristoteles, I would have preferred to stay with Nikos. I thought about feigning a headache, but I knew it was an important visit. Aristoteles had been Alexandros's teacher, and Theon had spoken so often of his friendship with the philosopher. So I agreed to go.

As we walked along the road, past the Hill of Muses toward the Sacred Hill. I looked up and caught a glimpse of Athena's golden armour glinting in the sunlight. With Ajax's proposal still on my mind, I prayed:
Athena, Give me strength and wisdom to make the right choice.

We passed a theatre in a grove of firs under the stony heights of the acropolis and walked down a narrow-cobbled street of painted houses with lavish porticoes and gardens abloom with flowers; and farther along we passed more modest homes. As we walked, Theon told me more about his friend, the philosopher.

"Aristoteles's father was the physician to King Filippos's father, so Filippos and Aristoteles were friends from childhood. That is why Filippos asked Aristoteles to be Alexandros's tutor. There is no better man than Aristoteles. Filippos chose the shrines and caves at Mieza for the school and invited Alexandros's friends to attend as well. From his childhood Alexandros admired Aristoteles more than his own father. You see," Theon went on, "Alexandros was always devoted to learning. He had been brought up with a pedagogue who taught him the stoicism of the Spartans and this helped shape his character and made him a strong man. Aristoteles taught him many more things too - philosophy, science, even medicine, because Alexandros wanted to be able to tend to his friends if they fell ill or were wounded in battle."

Although I tried to concentrate on what Theon was saying, my mind kept drifting back to the previous night, Ajax's proposal, thoughts of Nikos and our future.

We had entered a quiet grove of ancient trees where a river flowed through a wide swath of grass.

"This is the Lyceum," Theon said. "It was a gymnasium. I understand that Aristoteles wished to buy it, but because he's Makedonian and not Athenian citizen, he was not allowed to. However, the owners offered it to him to use as his school."

Across the field I saw a man dressed in a white tunic, a blue cape thrown over his shoulder, followed by a group of boys. Once in a while, they stopped walking and gathered around the man who, by his gestures, was lecturing them on something important.

"Ah! There he is! Aristoteles! "Theon exclaimed. "And those boys following him are the *Peripatetics*, his students. They are named this because they walk while they discuss philosophy and life's matters."

He hurried his footsteps, while I trailed behind. When the man saw Theon approach, he stopped and dismissed the boys who ran off across the field toward a stone-built oval building which I supposed to be the gymnasium.

I watched as Aristoteles approached Theon, his brow furrowed. He was a lean man, short of stature. He had a kindly face, greying wiry hair, and a neatly trimmed beard. As he got closer to Theon his piercing eyes lit up with recognition and he opened his arms in a greeting.

"Theon! My friend. What has brought you to Athens?"

"I bear greetings from Alexandros," Theon said, returning Aristotele's warm embrace. "It has been some time since you left Pella, but I see that fortune has been with you." He looked around at the tranquil grassy glade. "As you have this new school, Alexandros wanted you to know he will send you specimens from his travels – plants, animals - things for you to study."

"Yes, I am writing some studies on animals and plants," Aristoteles said. "How is the boy? With his father dead, and his mother ..." he scowled, then went on in a sober tone. "And now he's off to conquer the Persians. He is barely twenty and he's taking on the whole world."

"He will do well to be out of his mother's domain," Theon agreed. "Olympias has tried to control him for most of his life. It is good to see him take up Filippos's challenge to wrest the control of Ionia from the Persians. It would make his father proud."

"The Persians have beset our country for many years and destroyed so much. Alexandros will punish them for this and take our lands back," Aristoteles said.

"He has assembled a great army," Theon told him. "They will set off across the Hellespont before summer. He hopes to take back all the Ionian lands first. But, even if he does, that won't stop him. Alexandros is determined to take over all of the Persian world."

Aristoteles mused for a moment on what Theon had said. He frowned, and stroked his beard, then replied: "It is not enough to win the war," he said. "It is more important to organize peace. Alexandros told me once how he wanted to forsake philosophy for war. I taught him and his friends, you can never do anything in this world without courage. It is the greatest quality next to honour. Alexandros thinks because of the honour of his rank, nothing he does will go unnoticed, making the hardships easier to endure." He paused, stroking his beard as though deep in thought, then smiled and said: "The boy always thought he was invincible because he was born on an auspicious day – the day Filippos had achieved two victories - that same day, the Temple of Artemis in Ephesus burned down and the seers foretold this was an omen that declared the end of Persian domination."

With my simple Greek, I did not understand all that was said. I held back, standing behind Theon, as the men went on discussing in their scholarly way, things like philosophy and stoicism and the importance of education. My mind drifted back to my own thoughts until something Aristoteles said broke my reverie.

"It is important to be educated," he said. "The roots of education are bitter, but the fruit is sweet, and it can enable a man to rise to great heights in the world."

His words resonated with me. What kind of life would my son have if we returned to Caer Gwyn? I thought of the boys from our tuath, Ned and Bran. Would Nikos grow up to be like them, a stable boy, or a goat herder? I wanted more than that for my son – a life of learning and wisdom. The Hellenes were intelligent people with a rich history of philosophers and physicians, men of wisdom like Theon and Aristoteles. In my land, the bards were our story tellers, the Druids our wise men and Star Seers. The healers were mostly crones or elders like my Aunt Essylt. If I took my child away from here, back to my people, would I be depriving him of an education and rich future?

Then I heard Aristoteles ask Theon. "What are your plans? Will you stay in Athens or return to Pella?"

"No," Theon said. "I have given up my farmstead and I will not return to Pella."

"And this young maiden? Who is she?" Until then I was not sure Aristoteles had noticed me as I had stayed out of sight behind Theon. He peered at me closely, his brow furrowed. "She is not a Greek," he said.

I felt too shy to speak, supposing he thought I was Theon's handmaiden.

Theon put his hand on my shoulder and nudged me forward. "This is Olwen," he said. "She is Cymry, from the Keltic lands of the north. Alexandros rescued her from a warrior who had kidnapped her and he brought her to me. I have taught her the healing arts. Now I am taking her back to her people."

"Ah, the Kelts!" Aristoteles exclaimed. "They are brave people and fear nothing except if the sky should fall on them."

"We will travel by sea as far as Massalia," Theon said. "Then overland to the northern channel, and cross to reach her people on the Great Plain."

Aristoteles raised his brows. "That is a long, arduous journey!" Then reached out his hand to take mine and drew me closer to him. His grip was warm and strong. "Like your people, you are a courageous girl, and that is an admirable quality."

His words resonated with me. *You are a courageous girl.* Was I, really? Could I give up my dream and stay here instead returning to my people?

After more talk about our journey, we said goodbye to Aristoteles. As we left the Lyceum, on our way back to the agora, Theon stopped, and addressed me in a stern, serious tone. "What is troubling you, my girl. I have sensed all day there was something you wanted to tell me, and yet you are afraid to speak of it."

"Ajax asked me to stay in Athens and marry him," I blurted out.

Theon said nothing at first. Then he looked into my eyes and said: "Olwen, this is a grave decision only you can make. You must know, however, Ajax is a warrior – a soldier – and it is his sworn duty to keep faith with his men and serve the king. Ajax is a good man. But you know the life of a soldier. You have also observed the women's life here. Although it may seem luxurious to you, it would mean you would not be able to practice your healing arts. Once married, you would be expected to tend your house and child."

He said no more, but walked on, head down, as though deep in thought. I followed after him, mulling over what he had said: *You will not be able to practice your healing arts. You would be expected to tend your house and child.*

Had I become so enraptured by Athens, and seduced by Ajax and his proposal, that I was willing to give up all my hopes and dreams of returning again to my people?

When we returned to the commander's home, Nikos ran from the courtyard to meet me. He took my hand, excited to show me how Milos had shown him how to play knucklebones, a game the older boys played with a tossed dice and pieces of bone. I went to sit with Chryse in the garden to watch the children play. The sun was shining, birds twittering in the trees.

Chryse wanted to hear about my meeting with Aristotle but I was still mulling over my thoughts about my son's future and the things Theon had said. I was anxious to ask about her son, Milos, and what his future would be.

I looked over where Milos was standing beside my child, showing him the way to hold the hoop so it wouldn't fall when he tapped it with a stick to send it twirling over the cobblestones. He was a sturdy boy and even at the age of five, he was clever and well spoken. Nikos had grown attached to him, imitating things Milos said and did.

"When will Milos go to school?" I asked.

"When he is seven," Chryse said. "He will have a *pedagogue* first, who will accompany him to school where he will be taught reading, writing and mathematics. After that," Chryse explained. "He will have a *ketharistes* who will teach him how to play the lyre and a *palaestra* to teach him sports at the gymnasium."

"I saw the boys today, with Aristoteles. After he sent them away, they went to the gymnasium."

"Yes," Chryse said. "An important part of a boy's time is spent at the gymnasium. When Milos is older, we will hire a tutor for him, someone very wise. Remember how Alexandros was taught by Aristoteles? It is important for boys to gain a good education."

"What about girls?" I asked. "Are they educated too?"

"Education is only for the boys. Our girls are taught at home," Chryse said. "We teach them how to keep a good household, to serve their father and later their husband, how to raise children, prepare food, how to weave cloths for our clothing. This is our life's work."

I thought of our Cymry women – most of them toiled in their homes, some, like Essylt, were healers, others were warrior women. "Do your women go to battle?" I asked.

Chryse looked surprised at my question. "No, of course our women do not go to battle! Except the Spartans. They are expected to run their *polis* while the men are away at war, so they know the art of war. Greeks believe in the education of the mind, body and imagination. Music and literature and dance and sciences are important, as well as philosophy, rhetoric and sophistry."

"Sophistry?"

"That is the art of arguing, using deception and reasons to persuade the public to agree with a certain point of view," Chyrse said. "When boys turn fourteen they receive teachings from the Sophists and philosophers. Athenians believe intellectual education is important for a person's identity and reputation. Then, when they are eighteen, boys become an *ephoebes* and receive military training."

I thought more about our Cymry boys. Most were expected to take up arms for the ricon. Education wasn't as important as bravery on the battlefield. Is that what I wanted for my son? Would he end up being a warrior in the ricon's War Band?

As I sat contemplating the things Chryse had told me, she reached out and took my hand.

"You seem troubled," she said.

I blurted out to her what Ajax had proposed.

"My dear girl! I saw the way he kept looking over at you during the feast," she said, "But you must not lose yourself in daydreams. Do you love him? Consider what is best for you and your child. Ajax may say he has fallen in love with you, but is it true love? Men can be fickle – especially a man like him who has been a soldier all his life. You know a soldier's ways. Their allegiance is to their king before all else. Suppose Ajax gets called to join Alexander's campaign. What then?"

She spoke with unexpected gravity. My eyes blurred with tears and she reached out and stroked my hair. "You have learned to make your own life. You are a healer now, not just a mother, and you must not make an unworthy choice and waste those precious things Theon has taught you. Is marrying Ajax what you truly want? Theon has taught you the skill of a physician, which you have said you were dedicated by your people to do. You cannot let that learning be wasted. You are a healer, not just a mother."

Tears burst from my eyes and trickled down my cheeks as she spoke.

"Your people need someone with your knowledge," Chryse said. "If you stay here and marry Ajax, you will be bound to your hearth and home like all women here are. You will be alone with your child, because Ajax is a soldier and he will not always be by your side."

Had I become so enraptured by Athens that I was willing to give up all my hopes and dreams of returning again to my people? For how many years had I had longed to return to Caer Gwyn? Now my destiny was clear if I chose to remain here.

"I am... *hiraeth,*" I said the word aloud in my own language *"Hiraeth –* I am homesick!" I had forgotten how I had dreamed of returning to Caer Gwyn ever since that day Sholto had stolen me away.

I had made an oath at the Midsummer rites at the Stone Circle that I would follow the path destined for me and become a healer, and I knew I must keep my oath. I drew a long breath. My voice trembled. "I must honour the goddess," I said in a whisper. "I cannot stay here. I must go home."

Chryse took my hand in hers. "Follow your heart, my sweet child," she said. "Listen to the advice Theon has given you. I believe your people need your knowledge. Listen to your heart and the gods will bless you."

The next morning I met with Theon in the atrium and told him about my talk with Chryse and the decision I had made to continue my journey home.

"Am I doing right?" I asked. "I want my son to have a good life, an education like the Greek boys. What will there be to offer him in my homeland?"

Theon looked at me, his brow creased. "My dear Olwen, you know that just as I have taught you, I will teach Nikos philosophy and science and all the things he needs to know." He reached out and took my hand. "You have grown into womanhood and learned the healing arts. This was your chosen path. The journey to your home will be long, and there may be dangers ahead, but I am glad you have made the choice to go."

Stanza Five

Our days in Athens had slipped by as in an idyllic dream. Spring passed into summer. The gardens burst with new blooms. The days were warmer and brighter as the gods delayed the moon's course to lengthen the days. The air grew mild, the breezes gentle. It was sailing weather.

Word came from the north Alexandros's army had set forth on their campaign against the Persians. The soldiers from the fort revelled at the news. All night we were kept awake by their victory songs and accolades.

Then, the next morning. Commander Phaon came with the news.

"I have found a ship that will take you to Syracuse. It will leave in two days time. It's one of our ships – a trireme – sailing to Syracuse with the news of Alexandros's departure for the Persian campaign. The trierarch said you are welcome to board. They will transport you safely to Syracuse."

Theon told me about the Greek colony of Syracuse on a far-away island. "The Corinthians settled there, hundreds of years ago," he said. "Since then it has become a popular place for the Greeks to reside. Even Plato lived there once, before he came home to open his Academy. I have a friend who lives there and we will be made welcome."

The news gave me a feeling of hope, that I had made the right decision to return home.

"It is a long journey by sea, but it's the best way to get back to your people," Theon said. "And once we get to Massalia, the overland journey is not too difficult. The roads north lead through Keltic lands to the wide passage. Hopefully, if the seas are calm, and the overland trip is not too treacherous, we may reach your home by late in the autumn."

I called to Nikos who was playing with his friends in the garden. He pouted and reluctantly left his play.

I held out my arms to embrace him. "We are going on a ship, Nikos. One like your papa used to sail."

"On a ship? I don't want to!" He looked over at the other children. His face flushed; his eyes filled with tears. "I want to stay here!"

"You will have new friends," I said.

"Will Papa be on the boat?"

"No Nikos. Papa is far away." I gathered him up in my arms. "Papa's ship ..." I couldn't bear to think of how Elidi's ship had gone down at sea and tried to keep a brave face. "This ship is just like the one he sailed on!"

Just the mention of Elidi seemed to cheer him. He looked at me gravely. "Can I sail it like Papa?"

"Perhaps, when you are older," I said.

His expression brightened and he ran off to tell his friends he was going on a ship – one like his papa's.

That night, Chyrse and the Commander held a farewell feast in our honour. Ajax's proposal was still on my mind and when Chryse told me her husband had invited several of the men from the fortress, I knew I would have to confront him with my decision.

The banquet guests were soldiers of high rank from the garrison, clean shaven, dressed in military garb. I saw Ajax among them. We did not speak, but he nodded and smiled at me. I felt my cheeks redden and looked away.

A dozen couches were arranged around the atrium. The hall was warm with lamplight and pleasant revelry. A splendid array of delicious food had been prepared: ducks, fish and a lamb roasting on a spit. Wine goblets were filled freely, and platters heaped with food were passed round the guests.

Chryse hired an acrobat to entertain the children, and we talked, watching them romp and play. She reclined gracefully on her couch next to mine.

"I understand how difficult it must have been for you, how you must long for your own homeland. You have been a welcome guest friend here, but now it is time for you to return to your homeland." She looked at me with affection and reached out to hand me a small silk bag. "This is for you... for luck, and remembrance."

Inside the bag was a dolphin pendant of shiny silver and lapis.

"It's a luck charm," Chyrse said. "Dolphins are a good portent. It will keep you safe on your perilous journey."

Tears welled in my eyes as I put the pendant around my neck. "I will wear it with gratitude," I replied. "I will never forget your kindness to Nikos and me."

I had grown fond of Athens and Chyrse, and part of me still wanted to stay. Yet every day I had been away from my tuath had been a day of *hiraeth*, nostalgia, a longing for my people and Caer Gwyn, a home I thought I had lost forever. Now I had been given this opportunity to return, and no matter how dangerous the voyage, or difficult the trek overland, I knew I must risk it.

After the feasting the men began bawling army songs and making speeches praising Alexandros and his campaign, Chyrse went to thank the entertainer while the nurse, Tay, led the children off to their room. I watched as Nikos skipped along beside his friend, chatting happily. It had been good for him here in Athens, too, and I still felt some regrets that I must take him away from his new friend and the opportunities living here would bring him.

I saw Ajax watching me as I went out to the courtyard. A profusion of flowers spilled from the terracotta pots their fragrance heavy in the warm evening air. The setting sun painted the sky a brilliant tinge of red and gold. I stood in the garden by the stone fountain looking out at the ravine with the long road that led toward the port.

I closed my eyes and listened to the cooing of the collared doves nested under the roof pediments. *Tomorrow,* I thought, *we will journey down that road to the port and board our ship.*

The sound of footsteps interrupted my reverie.

"My lady, OlwenOk."

It was Ajax. I took a deep breath and turned to face him, my eyes peering steadily into his. He smiled at me and reached out to take my hand.

"I have been waiting to hear from you," he said. His face was flushed from the wine.

I drew in a long breath. My voice trembled when I spoke. "I cannot marry you, Ajax," I said.

I saw the look of disappointment cloud his face. He did not reply at first, then said, "I know you are destined to be a healer." His voice was soft and husky. "And you must follow your destiny. But it is a long and dangerous journey you are going on. What about the boy? How will you survive all those days sailing when it is difficult even for men of the sea?"

"From childhood I was dedicated to serve the goddess as a healer," I said. "Theon taught me everything, and I must take this learning back to my people."

Ajax looked at me with sadness, then bent and kissed me on the lips. "If it is your duty, then you must go." He clasped my hands in his. "You are a brave woman, Olwen. May the gods give you a safe and peaceful journey."

I turned away from him, and without saying more, walked back into the atrium to join Chryse.

The following morning, soon after sunrise, we said our farewells as Chryse and her children set off for the port. Commander Phaon hoisted little Nikos up onto his shoulders and two of his men helped carry our packs down the long road that ran along the high stone wall protecting Athens from invaders.

The day was bright, with a fair wind blowing from the west. The wide curve of the harbour was crowded with naval ships – three tiered triremes and double-tiered biremes with bronze battering rams and eyes painted on their bows. While naval officers barked orders, the sails were furled and the decks became a hive of activity with mariners and rowers going about their work.

Commander Phaon led us to the ship, a stoutly built vessel with a hull of pine wood, a carved figure of a sea nymph decorated the bow. There were three banks of oars and the vessel was large enough to carry a crew of two-hundred men, officers, mariners and rowers.

As I followed Theon and the trierarch up the gangway, I recalled how, the last time I had seen Elidi when he had sailed away, it had been on a trireme like this. I would never forget his handsome bronzed face, curling dark hair or his smile as he waved to me from the deck and how he had called out:

Wait for me. I will return to you when the grapes are ripening.

But he had never returned!

The trierarch, Captain Demos, was a burly, bearded man, his skin bronzed and weathered from all his years at sea. He greeted us kindly and said we would share his quarters for the voyage. While Theon went with Commander Phaon to stow our belongings, I stood on the deck with the trierarch, holding tight to Nikos's hand and watched the rowers take their places as the trireme prepared to set sail.

When the crew were in place, we said our farewell to Commander Phaon. The sails were furled, and the rowers bent over their oars. The bow officer shouted his command, "Cast off!" and the three banks of oars dipped and splashed, propelling the trireme out of the harbor.

As the shoreline slipped away, I looked back at the port and tried to stop my tears.

Captain Demos must have sensed the reason for my sadness. He reached out to touch my arm, "Are you alright, my lady?" He laid his hand on my shoulder. "Do not be afraid. It will be a safe sailing. I knew your husband, my lady," he said. "I sailed with Elidi on many voyages." He looked down at Nikos and took his hand. "Come with me my little man, I will show you how your papa steered his ship."

I remember Elidi's excitement when he had done the same, how Nikos had taken his first steps to grasp his father's hand, and how Elidi had said: *He knows his place on the deck of a ship, just as I did when I was a child.* Did I want my son to grow up to be a seaman? In truth, I hoped for a better future for him, one like the Greek boys had. I could not visualize him working in a cattle pen or riding into battle as a warrior like our Cymry boys did.

Once under sail, the trireme leapt forward like a great seabird taking flight. The wind was stronger now. Water splashed over each side of the prow and the oars jumped and shook in the rowers' hands. Sunlight sparkled off the water that dripped from the oar blades as the trireme moved steadily away from the port. The ship strained against the swells and the masts groaned as the square canvas sails, with their lion emblem of Makedon, fluttered and billowed in the breeze. We were out of the harbour now, the sails billowing out as the trireme flew over the sea. I sat silently for a while watching as Hellas's shoreline disappeared. The wind was favourable and soon we were far off shore, heading south down the coast.

BALLAD THIRTY Homeward Bound

A PLEA TO THE SEA GODS

> *To mighty Poseidon,*
> *master of the water,*
> *and Lyr, the Cymry sea-god,*
> *lord of the thrashing waves.*
> *I beseech you to calm the seas*
> *as we travel homeward.*
> *Keep us safe and serene*
> *within your watery realm.*

THE VOYAGE

Stanza One

The rolling motion of the ship was soothing. The oar master sang as the ruddy-faced rowers bent over their oars. His voice seemed to rise like a breaking wave with each oar-stroke as the rowers laboured through the sea.

There was a steady wind. A family of plump grey sea creatures leapt through the wake of the bow wave, blowing glittering spray, a pod of six skimming the surface playfully in pursuit of a shoal of fish,

Nikos whooped with excitement. "Look Mama!"

"Those are dolphins," I said. "They are messengers of Poseidon. If they come to visit your boat it's a good omen."

Occasionally we saw smoke on the shore and long ships beached there, likely merchants.

We sailed along the rock headland until, ahead of us, a tall cliff of jagged rock rose from the sea. On its summit the setting sun dazzled off the marble pillars of a temple.

"That is the Temple to Poseidon," Captain Demos said. "We will anchor here for the night and make offerings to the sea god. We have a long voyage ahead!"

That evening, the sun set over the sea, glimmering off the temple's pillars. A full moon rose in the west, making a twinkling pathway in the sea. Surely it was a good omen!

In the morning, after oblations of wine were made to Poseidon, a good wind took us westward. The sea was calm, the only sounds the slap of ripples on the hull and the swish of the oars. I looked up to see a gull swoop over the ship. Like that free-flying seabird, I was homeward bound and with the blessing of the sea gods, it would be a safe voyage.

We were four days sailing from Sounion, off the coast of the Pelops when a ferocious gust of wind from the south sent waves splashing over the trireme's deck. The oars jumped and shook in the rower's hands as the ripples on the surface of the sea grew larger with each gust, creating whitecaps. Water splashed over each side of the prow blowing salt spray into my face.

Nikos began to cry, holding his stomach.

"He must be seasick," Theon explained.

I found some dried mint in my amulet bag and mixed it with a cup of water for him to drink, holding tight to my son as we huddled together on the deck.

Theon's face was pale and drawn. I could see by his furrowed brow that he was concerned." This is a dangerous passage, "he said. "There have been many ships wrecked here."

His words alarmed me and I held tighter to little Nikos.

The oarsmen kept to their tasks, bending over the oars, straining against the power of the wind. The oars flashed as the water was churned by the rising gusts. The breeze increased, turning into a fierce wind blowing from the southwest. The waves slapped onto the belly of the ship and sent spray over the bow. The ship groaned as if the timbers might tear apart. It dipped and sent another stinging arc of sea spray over us soaking us through.

Theon and I huddled close together on the upper deck, sheltered against the trierarch's cabin. I clutched Nikos close to me, terrified he might be swept away. My stomach clenched with every heave of the ship. Nikos began to cry and screamed in terror as the water splashed over him. The wind gusted and the sea swells sent spray over the deck drenching both of us. Theon kept calm and tried to reassure me, but I felt his concern.

The sea seemed to have risen. The ship lurched and waves almost as high as the mast crashed over the bow. I was sure the sea would engulf us and sweep us away just as the storm that had taken Elidi's ship down. Were my son and I destined for the same fate? As I clung to my son, I prayed to Poseidon, and to Lyr, my Keltic sea god to save us from being swept to our deaths.

The mast cracked and threatened to break and as the crew tried to furl the sails a great surge of waves and wind tore at them bearing us closer to the off-shore reefs. The towering rocks loomed ahead and I thought we would crash against the cliffs. A whirlpool spun, glittering, a great churning abyss drawing the ship toward it. The sails flapped wildly as the ship lurched toward the rocky crag. Were the gods angry? Would we perish at sea?

The storm completely unnerved me. I sheltered on the deck holding Nikos close to me, my stomach churning each time the trireme lurched showering me with sea spray. I began to have regrets about making this journey. Should I have listened to Ajax's warnings and remained in Athens? Had I put myself and my child in too great a peril? We were only on the first part of what would be an endless sea voyage and what harms could befall us? Besides the danger of storms, I had heard stories of renegade ships who plied the great sea beyond Syracuse – pirates who raided the trading ships and enslaved the crews. Had I risked being taken captive with my child? What would become of us before we reached Massalia's shore?

Then, just as suddenly as it had gusted, the wind died and the sea calmed. The sea gods had answered our prayers! There was no sound but the crying of gulls and the splash of water against the side of the boat. I looked up to see the twinkling stars. It seemed as though I had lost the sense of passing time. Captain Demos shouted orders ordering the helmsman to head north to the island of Zante. Later, he explained why we were sailing north and not west.

"We must make repairs to the ship," he said. "The mast has been splintered and the hull battered enough that it needs to be resealed with tar for safe sailing."

That night I saw the Dragon's Fire fall over the sky toward the east exploding in a brilliant spray of golden fragments. I wondered what portent it meant. I said a prayer for Alexandros who must have been well on his way to conquer the Persians, and one for our safety on our long voyage into the unknown that lay ahead.

Stanza Two

The ship ploughed north, The wind was fair, the calm sea a dark blue of lapis. We could see the shoreline rising to low mountains. We made stops each night along the way, sometimes anchoring off-shore, other times we put into ports while the crew loaded supplies of food and wine. After several days of sailing we pulled into a wide bay of brilliant turquoise water, white sand lining the curve of the shore. The trierarch said we would drop anchor so the rowers could rest, for they had been over-tasked by fighting the sea storm.

Although the voyage up the coast had been pleasant, with calm seas, I continued to worry. Perhaps Theon guessed at my inner turmoil, for after the ship lay anchored and we went ashore, he suggested we should take a walk to see the palace of a once great king.

"It will be a long walk," he said, "but after all these days onboard the ship, it will be good for us all to stretch our legs and see the countryside. The walk will be good for your psyche. We will walk from here and be back by sundown."

I agreed, somewhat reluctantly. I was worried about Nikos. "Is it a long walk? Should I leave him with the captain?"

'The walk will be good for him too,' Theon said. "He needs to run and play. And we will stop for rests along the way."

We set off down a dusty road, passing stone-built farmhouses where flocks of sheep grazed in the lush green fields. As we trudged along, breathing in the pine and herb-scented fresh air, Theon related the story of the long-ago king who had once ruled over this land.

"His name was Nestor. He was a kind man and highly esteemed for his generosity when he sent ten of his ships to the Troy wars."

Of course I had learned of the Troy wars, but I had not paid much heed. However, something in Theon's story intrigued me.

"When the famous Troy hero, Odysseus, failed to return home, his son Telemachus set out to find him and gather information about where his father might be. His first stop was here, where he went to make a plea to King Nestor."

I recalled the story of the Troy hero, Odysseus, and his arduous voyage back to his island home on Ithaka.

"Did he find news of his father?" I asked.

We had stopped under the shade of a grove of trees to rest. Nikos romped happily in the grass, chasing a butterfly, while Theon continued his story.

"Odysseus had been missing for many years," Theon went on. "Telemachus found Nestor and his friends on the beach, and the king invited him to the palace." Theon pointed up the slope of the hill ahead of us. "See? Up there is where Nestor's palace was. We are walking the same road they must have walked. So, shall we continue?"

I was hot and tired, but Theon's story intrigued me. I called to Nikos and we set off up the hill toward the place where the ancient palace once stood.

The palace ruins were on the top of the hillside. All that remained were crumbled walls with faint painted murals that had once adorned them, and some tiled floors. It must have once been a grand palace. We sat to rest while Theon related the rest of the story.

"Nestor was a kind man, known as the shepherd of the people, and he received Telemachus into his house and gave him a kindly welcome. Just as a father might his own son who after a long time had newly come from afar:"

"Did Nestor have news of Telemachus's father?" I asked.

"No, Nestor knew nothing of Odysseus's fate because they had not left Troy together. But he knew his friend Menelaus of Sparta would know. So he provided Telemachus with a chariot and offered to send one of his sons who knew the way overland, which was faster and safer than by sea."

A thought crossed my mind. *Had anyone from Caer Gwyn set out to search for me?*

"Did he ever find his father?" I asked.

"Not for many years. His voyage was delayed by many dangers including a shipwreck. One day Odysseus found himself on a shore he did not recognize.

Telemachus saw the old man on the beach and approached him. He thought Odysseus was a cast-away beggar, but Odysseus recognized the young man and said, "I am your father!" After all those years, Odysseus was home!

What will it be like when I return? I wondered. Who will be there to greet me? Will they know me? Did the Dobunni and Ordovices destroy Caer Gwyn? Perhaps Essylt is gone – passed into the Otherworld like my grandfather.

Theon was a perceptive man. He understood my trepidation and I realized that is why he had brought me here to tell me of Telemachus's search for his father and Odysseus's long ordeal at sea.

He reached out and took my hand. "Do not worry yourself, my child." His voice was soft and comforting. "The journey will be long and sometimes dangerous, but remember, you are a Druid's child, and you must trust the gods to lead you home safely." He smiled then, and said: "Just as Odysseus prevailed, so will you, and your people will rejoice to see you again just as his did."

"But it took him twenty years!" I said, trying to sound light-hearted.

Theon chuckled, "Yes, but he *did* get home and was welcomed by his family. And so will you!"

After another day of sailing we reached the island of Zante and dropped anchor. We would stop there while the mast was mended and the trireme's prow sealed with tar.

Zante was a welcome paradise. The island was lush with greenery and fragrant with flowers. The shore was lined by shallow bays and sandy beaches with steep cliffs. But past the shore was a wide plain with olive groves, orchards and vineyards.

I took Nikos to the beach to play in the sand and paddle at the water's edge. We collected shells and built fortresses in the sand. I had been so worried about my child's safety during the voyage, but his laughter and carefree nature dispelled my fears. He was a strong child, brave and resilient, just as his father had been.

One afternoon as Theon, Nikos and I strolled the beach I told Nikos the story of my childhood. When I began to relate to him how we Cymry people celebrated midsummer, I suddenly stopped, unable to continue. Theon noticed my reluctance to go on with the story and asked what was troubling me.

All Theon's comforting words of the past had not completely allayed my fears. As I spoke of the midsummer, I recalled the raid of the Orodovices and Dobunnis on Caer Gwyn the day I was kidnapped.

"I'm afraid they might have destroyed my village. I wonder if Essylt and the others will still be there?"

Theon reassured me. "You are no longer the child who was taken, Olwen, but a woman with a child of your own, and lots of learning. You have seen cities they could never even imagine, you have served in the hospital tents in one of the biggest battles ever fought. You have learned the art of healing, met with Aristotle, a famous philosopher. You have all this knowledge to offer your people. I am certain they will be there to welcome you home." He reached out and put his arm around me, embracing me like a father would a daughter. "I am here. No matter what, I will be here, your mentor, your friend."

A few days later, the repairs were done and a cargo of tar from the island's pitch wells, used to seal the cedar hull of the ship, was loaded into the hull in copper vessels to be transported to the shipyards in Syracuse. We sailed away from Zante with Poseidon's blessing. The sea was calm, but soon after we left the shore, a breeze blew up from the east so the sails were unfurled and the rowers allowed to rest. From then on, I hoped it would be smooth sailing.

Stanza Three

The next days passed serenely. The wind favoured us, and the rowers shipped their oars as we moved ahead. At sunrise we rounded a cape.

Theon said, "This is the island of Trinacria. It is called that because there are three headlands. And look there! That is Mount Aitna!"As I stood astern with Nikos and Theon, ahead I saw the cloud shrouded slopes of a majestic snow-capped mountain rising high above the sea.

Theon lifted Nikos up for a better look "There's a monster trapped under that mountain. His name is Typhon."

Nikos's eyes widened. "A monster?" He squirmed with excitement in Theon's arms.

"Yes, he's kept prisoner there by Zeus, god of the sky and thunder. And under the mountain Hephaestas has his forge. When Typhon gets angry he sends fire and brimstone raining down on the earth."

Captain Demos joined us at the stern as the ship plied its way into the harbour. He clapped Theon on the shoulder. "We'll soon drop anchor in Syracuse's port, Ortygia."

"I have an old friend living in Syracuse. Nikanor is a wealthy merchant," Theon said. "I'm certain he will find us a ship for our voyage to Massalia."

The trireme threaded the busy shipping lane. The rowers banked the oars and manoeuvred the ship into the crowded harbour. The ship dropped anchor. Ropes were flung and hitched, the gang plank lowered. It was time for us to disembark. The voyage from Zante had taken nearly thirty days. Nikos was squealing with excitement, and I knew he was as anxious I was, to feel his feet on the land again.

Captain Demos wished us well as we prepared to depart. He saluted Nikos and said, "You remember all I have told you on this journey, my boy! Perhaps you will be a seaman like your papa was one day." As a parting gift, he gave Nikos a small wooden trireme. "So you will always remember you sailed on a ship like your papa did!"

We thanked him and the crew for our safe passage and disembarked to enter the fortified town.

At the end of the causeway was a fortress. Tall, fortified walls surrounded the port of Ortygia. We walked along the causeway toward the tall stone walls and guarded gates of a massive fortress.

"Syracuse is an ancient city," Theon said. "Over many years it has grown and prospered and now is one of the most powerful Greek cities, rivalling Athens. It has been a Greek colony since the Corinthian Greeks settled here hundreds of years ago."

We entered Syracuse's port of Ortygia through a central gate guarded by a crouching stone dragon. As we walked through the dusty cobbled streets, Theon related more stories about the city.

"The fortress was built by the tyrant Dionysos the Elder to protect the city against raids. The Carthaginians besieged the city many times, but because of this strong fortress, they have never succeeded," Theon said. "Many years ago, when he was a young man, our philosopher, Plato, lived here. He often told us stories of his life in Syracuse. Once he disagreed with the tyrant and was sent to prison. Dionysos, the tyrant, threatened to sell him into slavery!"

We left the port and entered the city of Syracuse. It was a market day, and the narrow, cobbled streets were bustling with merchants hawking their wares. Theon asked one of them for directions to the home of his friend, Nikanor

Nikanor, was a trader, a *metic* who owned several ships and was a prominent citizen of the city. We had no trouble locating his home in the lower town, a square white house facing the sea. The courtyard was surrounded by thick stone walls, the garden green and lush, kept cool by a spring that gushed over the rocks at the rear of the garden. The terrace was covered with coloured marble mosaics. There were pots of flowers and sweet-scented shrubs and a trellis with a grape vine.

A servant led us to the stoa where low couches with white linen cushions embroidered with Egyptian scarabs surrounded a central fountain. Somewhere close I could hear a boy singing a lilting song accompanied by a kithara.

A well dressed, silver-haired man with a kind, gentle face came to greet us.

"Theon! How many years has it been since we last broke bread and drank wine together? We were young men then." He looked Theon up and down and smiled. "I see the years have been kind to you. What brings you to Syracuse?"

"We are sailing to Massalia, then travelling to the Keltic lands."

Nikanor looked surprised at Theon's answer. "So you have travelled from Athens, and before that from Makedon?" He shook his head.. "That is a lengthy journey. And you say you are sailing to Massalia with this maiden and her child and you are going to the land of those barbarian Kelts?" He raised his brow and looked over at me, seeming to notice me for the first time. "Who is your travel companion? Your daughter? A servant girl?"

"She is a Kelt. Olwen is like a daughter to me and I'm taking her back to her people," Theon explained.

"A Kelt?" He scowled.

"I am Olwen," I said politely, careful to speak my best Greek. "I am from Cymru. I am an Essyltyr of the Raven clan."

"From Cymru? My ships have sailed there to take on cargoes of tin. The Keltic tribes are barbarians! What brought you to Hellas? Why did you leave your own people?" His words had a patronizing tone and I felt their sting.

Theon explained to him how it came to be, that I had been taken from my home, and that he had taught me the healing arts. and was escorting me back to my land to share this knowledge with my people. "I am told you own several merchant vessels," Theon said. "I hoped you might help us find passage to Massalia."

"To Massalia?" Nikanor frowned. "Do you not think this long journey is a risk?" He glanced over at Nikos who was sailing his boat in the fountain pool. "And with a child?"

"We were given passage here on one of the Makedonian triremes from the naval port at Athens, and I hoped you might help us find lodgings and passage to Massalia," Theon said.

"You can stay here until I find you passage on one of my ships. There is a merchant vessel in port now that will be sailing soon. I will speak to the captain. Now come, rest, you must tell me about more news from Hellas!" He beckoned to his servant who waited nearby. "Milos, fetch some food and wine for our guests. They have come on a long journey and will rest here awhile."

We made ourselves comfortable. The men exchanged news, discussed Alexandros's Persian campaign and why we had left Pella, and how we had made the long oxcart journey to Athens, then the voyage to Syracuse.

The servant returned with a tray of sweet cakes and an amphora of wine. Nikanor poured the wine into decorated clay cups and raised his. "To you. Both of you – I wish you a safe journey, and may Zeus protect you."

The next day, Theon took me to explore Syracuse, a splendid city that seemed just as cultured as Athens. There was a theatre where Theon said the famous dramatist Aeschylus once performed, a gymnasium for the athletes, and several temples which Theon said were built by the Corinthians.

"I am taking you to visit the Temple of Athena the Corinthians built to honour how she gave them strength to fend off the many Carthaginian raids."

The streets were hot and dusty. We walked along a narrow, cobbled path past stone-built houses, some with painted walls and trellises of sweet, scented flowers. The hills around the city were parched and brown, but farther past the outskirts it was lush with vineyards and orchards spread across the lower slopes of the mountain and the broad plain at the city's outskirts.

As we walked, Nikos skipped happily ahead, and Theon told me more stories about the city.

"Once, long ago, there was a young woman who came to this island. She wasn't a hostage like you were, but a political prisoner – exiled here when she opposed the tyrant who ruled her island. Her name was Sappho of Mytilene. She had a child, too."

I had heard Sappho's songs sung but knew little of her.

Theon began to quote fragments of a verse. *"'I have a beautiful child, graceful, as golden flowers, my precious Kleis.'* She was one of our greatest bards."

"Did she ever go home again?" I asked.

"Yes, once the tyrant was deposed, somehow she found her way back home."

I wanted to ask more about Sappho, how she survived the long sea voyage, was she reunited with her child? But Nikos, who had run ahead, was calling me.

"Look, Mama ... Look there!"

Ahead just past the rows of houses on the knoll of a hill overlooking the seaport and the sparkling blue sea, was a beautiful temple with painted columns, its gilded cornices sparkling like a beacon.

"Ah! There it is, the Temple of Athena!" Theon exclaimed.

As we climbed the path up the hillside, Theon told me the story of how the temple was built by the Corinthians to honour Athena after the Syracuse people won a battle with the invading Carthaginians.

The temple was smaller than Athena's temple on the Parthenon, but still majestic, with white marble columns inset with ivory and trimmed with gold, and a fountain at the gate with lion's heads spewing water into a pool of lilies. There was an ornate alter at the entrance in front of a smaller temple decorated with golden pediments and a copper shield. Theon said it was dedicated to the goddess.

Nikos and I collected wildflowers from the hillside to put on the altar at the entrance. As I placed my offering on the altar, I remembered the day in Athens when I had prayed to Athena for a safe journey. We were still far away from my homeland, and there would be many more perils facing us along the way, but I prayed again, asking the goddess for guidance and safety.

Stanza Four

We had to wait for some days until Nikanor found us passage on a ship that was carrying a cargo of wine amphorae from Nikanor's vineyards and pottery from his shops to the market at Massalia. The vessel was tied up to a small stone jetty in the harbour, its masts already raised, its oars shipped and sticking up like the quills of a porcupine. It was a sturdy merchant galley with a broad pine-wood hull and an eye painted on the prow. It had a single tall mast as well as oars which Theon explained were only used when there wasn't enough wind. Both the bow and stern posts were raised and there was a canopy on the midships deck where the crew slept at night. We were told we could shelter there during the day and at night we'd sleep on the deck on straw mats just as we had on the trireme.

The ship master was a big sun-browned man with black hair and a curly beard. His demeanour assured me that, like all ship masters, he had a command of seafaring. He put up no protest when Nikanor asked him to take on three extra passengers and assured us we would be treated kindly.

Some of the twenty crew members stood by talking in low voices, staring at us curiously as we stepped aboard. Most were rugged men who had probably spent most of their lives as sea. Besides the crew there were fifty oarsmen, dark skinned, wild-looking men with shaggy hair and huge shoulders, their bare, muscular arms marked with tattoos. Among them I saw some with the russet hair of Kelts.

We bade farewell to Nikanor and thanked him for his hospitality. A crewman took our belongings to store them in the captain's cabin, and we settled ourselves under the shade of the tent on the deck.

The captain shouted an order, and I heard the slap of ropes and the ship moved, thrusting away from the jetty, the prow pointing to the open sea. The water in the harbour was as smooth as a silver plate. A drum began to beat and the oars began to move in perfect unison, down and up like a bird's wings, scarcely ruffling the surface of the sea.

Soon we were out of the harbour. The ship tacked sharply as a gust of wind caught the sail as it was unfurled and seemed to wallow in the brine. I held tight to Nikos's hand. The sail flapped, billowed in the wind showing its image of an eagle, and Nikos cheered in delight. Soon Syracuse faded from view, only the massive cloud-shrouded Mount Aitna was visible against the sky.

That night as I lay outside on the deck, I saw in the sky a strange, brilliant glimmer on the horizon. I flung off my coverlet and got up, quietly so as not to waken Nikos, and went to stand at the prow. I held on to the bow rail, my eyes focused on the vast, empty space beyond the bow where the sea and sky seemed to merge. When I looked again, I saw it wasn't a star I had seen. It was a Dragon's fire, it's tail, a track of twinkly sparks glowing in the dark night sky. As it passed across the western horizon I felt within me it was a message from Elidi. He said he would never leave me, that he would always be with me and our son. I heard his voice in my ear, a soft whisper – or was it just the sea-sound and my imagination?

"All will be well," he said. **"You must be brave! I will shield you from harm. You must always stay strong for our son!"**

I lay back down, snuggling close to my sleeping child and looked up at the stars twinkling in the blue-black sky arching over me. For the first time since Elidi had left us, I felt a sense of joy and new resolve. The gentle rocking of the ship soothed me. I was homeward bound and with the blessings of the sea gods it would be a safe voyage.

Stanza Five

The fair weather held so we sailed easily toward the west. The shoreline was low and thickly forested rising to distant mountains. Each night the ship dropped anchor, sometimes at a small port near a village where we put ashore for fresh water and to take on more supplies. All the crew was armed as the captain said some of the people in those villages were ship-robbers.

Some evenings we disembarked and camped on the beach. The ship-master posted guards, because he said the Kelts who lived there were fierce hunters and plunderers. Some of the sailors fished during the day and the crew lit fires to roast the fish they had caught. Much to his delight, they sometimes took Nikos with them along the beach to collect clams which they tossed into the embers along with the fish.

This morning we had set sail early. It was a bright day, the sun glinting off the blue sea, the wind fair and steady. The sail was unfurled and the sound of the vessel splashing through the waves soothed me. We had been at sea for twenty days and would soon reach the port of Massalia.

Theon and I rested under the shade of the canopy while Nikos napped. I was starting to doze when shouts from the helmsman startled me. I jumped up to see what the commotion was about when one of the crew came running toward the stern crying out: "There's a ship following us!"

I saw a small black craft with a serpent headed prow sailing close behind. I could just make out the men on the deck, brown-skinned men, some with cloths wrapped round their heads. They were a wild-looking crew wielding spears and swords. One man, standing apart from the others, shouted orders to an archer who had his arrow fitted to his bow, aimed toward our helmsman. The sight of them made me tremble with fright.

Some of the other merchant crew raced past toward the helm, weapons drawn, shouting "Brigands! Brigands!"

Theon rushed to stand beside me as I watched the strange ship draw nearer.

"This does not bode well," he said. I saw the look of alarm on his face.

"Who are they?"

"It looks like brigands."

"Brigands?"

"Yes. Pirates!"

"What does that mean?" I asked Theon.

"They are plunderers!" he said. "They rob the merchant ships of their cargo and take the crew as slaves!"

Just as he said this, the Ship Master came running from the stern, his face taut and reddened. "Quick! Get inside my cabin!" he shouted. "You must stay there well hidden! They are a band of Carthaginians sailing under the guise of a fishing boat. You'll fetch a good price if they kidnap you and sell you into slavery. But do not fear. My men know how to fight. If there is to be a battle with these brigands, we will win!"

We followed the captain's orders and hurried into his cabin. Theon blocked the door with a table and we crouched on the floor. The captain's words had alarmed me and I huddled on the cabin floor, my arms tight around Nikos who was whimpering in fright. The word "Carthaginians" had struck fear in me. I had heard many stories about these people and one that frightened me most was they were known to sacrifice children.

Theon sat stolidly beside us. When he noticed I was trembling he leaned closer and put his arm around me. "You must not fear, Olwen. You must trust the gods. They have brought us safely this far."

His words were of little comfort. I thought of my life, the good and the bad times, the gods and fate. Once before I had been taken and might have been sold as a slave or killed if Alexandros had not rescued me. What if everything I had experienced and learned was all for naught? If the brigands took us what would become of me and my child? If they should come aboard and take us would my son and I be sold as slaves. Was this to be my *rhan,* my fate?

Outside on the deck we could hear the sound of a bitter battle, clashing swords and men shouting curses. There was a loud crashing sound and the ship lurched. I heard stomping outside the cabin door and I put my hand over my mouth to stifle a scream, cringing in fright, as I clasped Nikos close to my breast. Theon leapt to his feet and tried to block the cabin door. My breath caught in my throat as the door was pushed open.

Praise be to Zeus! It was the Ship-Master, dishevelled and blood splattered.

"We've beaten them, killed the lot, the sea scum! We rammed a hole in their ship and sank it with all hands. Some of my crew are injured, but we are safe now. As you are a physician, sir, could you help tend the wounded men?"

"It is my duty," Theon replied. He glanced over to where I still sat huddled in a corner with Nikos. "And the young woman, for she is skilled as a healer too." He smiled at me and said, "She helped the wounded at Chaeronea and she saved my life at Thebes."

We set up the captain's cabin as our hospital and unpacked all our surgical tools and medicines. One of the crew took charge of Nikos and promised to take him to the helm while we tended the wounded. They brought us the most seriously wounded first – men with deep knife wounds, some pierced by javelins or arrows.

Theon and I worked together. I prepared potions of mandrake to dull the pain, and herbal teas to reduce blood loss. After I cleaned the wounds, I handed him his instruments as he needed them. Theon probed and extracted arrowheads and splinters of bones with his forceps then stitched the edges of the wounds together, binding them with cloth.

That evening the Ship Master held a victory celebration on board for the crew.

Theon made a speech thanking the crew for keeping us safe. "It is said that courage is the first of human qualities because it is the quality which guaranties others. You men have shown great courage. We owe our lives to you; and it was an honour for us to tend your wounds. Thank the gods we have not lost a single man!"

The men thanked him and praised the Ship Master, lifting cups of wine in his honour for keeping the ship and its crew and cargo safe and made offerings to the gods – Poseidon, god of the sea and Zeus Xemos, protector of travellers, for sparing us.

Stanza Six

Several days after escaping the pirate's attack, with the light of morning, we arrived at Massalia. It was the month of the August moon. We had been at sea for thirty days since leaving Syracuse. Theon, Nikos and I stood together at the forward deck of the galley and watched the shore draw closer. The big square sail sagged limp in the morning breeze. The oarsmen propelled the vessel cautiously keeping their eyes on the Ship Master who directed them toward the wharf and the dark stone ramparts of the city walls that loomed beyond the wide curve of the harbour.

"Massalia has been a Greek settlement for hundreds of years," Theon said. "The city has been plundered several times, but, somehow, she always rises from the ashes. Nothing has crushed her! It is one of the most important Greek trading ports. Ships from many countries come here to load cargoes of wine, olives, fish and other goods. It is also a trading port for the Keltic tribes from Iberia and the north who bring copper, tin and amber to trade."

When he spoke of the Kelts, I thought of Teag, the goldsmith. He had come from Massalia. I remembered the day I met him at the Standing Stones. It made me smile to think of him, how vulnerable and innocent I was then, how disconsolate when he chose the ricon's daughter, even though I had been promised to serve the goddess on the Holy Isle. I remembered the gold coins he gave me - coins stamped with the image of King Filippos. I had thrown one into the sea and thanked the sea gods for bringing me to Hellas and giving me my husband, Elidi. Now here I was in the very city Teag came from. Was this an omen too? Would he still be in Caer Gwyn? Would he remember that day we met at the Standing Stones?

Massalia's busy harbour was dotted with fishing boats and sturdy merchant vessels. The great sail of our vessel was lowered, and the oarsmen rammed their oars in the water to slow our approach. The anchor was lowered astern and fastened securely then we tied up at the stone jetty.

The wharf was bustling with porters transporting goods to and from the ships. A throng of people crowded along the edge of the harbour. Some women were gathered on the shore, dressed in brightly-dyed dresses. They gawked brazenly at the taut-muscled, bare-chested crewmen who were hauling barrels of salted fish, olives and large bronze vessels of wine and cargo onto a ship that was anchored by the pier.

I felt a stir of excitement as our ship docked, yet I was still cautious, unsure of what the next step of our journey would bring.

We bade farewell to the Ship Master and his crew and thanked them for keeping us safe on the long voyage. Theon paid a porter to carry our bags, and we followed him through the tall iron gates into the city.

Inside the walls, a wide-open square, brimmed with a mix of people: finely dressed Greeks, bronze-skinned Carthaginians and Egyptians, russet-haired Iberians, Nubians and even a few men who I recognized as Kelts with their hooded cloaks and long, dishevelled hair and beards.

Massalia's narrow streets were jammed with crowds of jostling people. I held tight to Nikos's hand and followed close behind Theon and the porter strode ahead to clear us a path along the cobbled road. Past the square we entered a street of armourers, a tannery, timber yards for shipwrights, and goldsmith shops.

When we came out of the square we entered a street of marble stoas with gilded pediments and columns of coloured marble, and elegant painted houses, some with steep pitched terra-cotta roofs to throw off the winter snow. Massalia was so different from Athens and Syracuse. I saw few temples and shrines. It seemed to be a city of revelry and I wondered if the people of the city paid heed to the gods. When I questioned Theon, he said: "The Massalians worship Dionysos, god of wine. Their vineyards produce plenty of grapes and they trade in wine."

There were many women on the streets, finely dressed, who greeted us as we passed. It seemed as though the women's lives here were not as strict as in Athens. The Massalian men were dressed differently than the Greeks from Athens, in colourful garments belted at the waist, their hair long and tied back in a somewhat feminine style.

Theon laughed and said, "The Athenians joke about them and question if they have lost their manhood."

When we left the marketplace there were fewer crowds. The porter led us to a quiet, clean inn, a modest house built around a courtyard. I felt a pang of nostalgia as I thought of Theon's farmstead, remembering all those happy years I spent there.

A silver-haired innkeeper welcomed us. We sat under the vine-covered trellis while he served us watered wine and poured Theon a cup of honey mead.

"Honey mead?" Theon asked. "I've not tasted this for many years."

"Yes," the innkeeper said. "We trade good wine to the Kelts for it." He raised his glass. "It is our custom to welcome strangers. It is *philoxenia*. We have not forgotten our Greek roots."

"We are journeying north," Theon told him. "We have travelled from Makedon and our destination is the land of Cymru across the Narrow Sea."

"Into the Keltic lands?" The innkeeper seemed aghast. "Why are you venturing so far?"

"We are returning to this woman's home. Olwen is a Cymry from the Essyltyr people. She was stolen from her home years ago and it is her desire to return."

The innkeeper smiled at me and reached out to tousle Nikos's hair. "That is a long journey for a woman and a small boy. You are brave!"

He directed us to go to the home of a wealthy merchant who might be able to help.

"His name is Timonides of Samos," the innkeeper said. "He made his fortune trading with the Iberians in amber and gold, and trades in oil and wine with the northern Kelts. He is a Pythagorian. There are many of them here in Massalia, all of them wealthy. They are much esteemed in our city."

"What is a Pythagorean?" I asked Theon.

"They are scholars who studied the philosophy of Pythagoras, He was a philosopher and mathematician from Samos island," Theon explained. "Pythagoras also studied the heavens which showed men how to use the stars to navigate the seas."

"He studied the stars, like the Druids?"

"Yes. He used that knowledge to enable sailors to navigate the seas safely. He had a great following of scholars. Many of our philosophers like Plato and Aristoteles were influenced by his teachings."

The innkeeper's wife, a stout little woman, carrying a tray of food, greeted us and offered us a humble meal of barley cakes and goat cheese.

"My name is Vera," she said. "You must be weary travellers. I will prepare a room for you, and a bath." She looked closely at Nikos. "Is this your child? What is his name?"

"Nikos," I said. "We have been at sea for many days and he has endured many things along the way." I sighed. "It is so good to be back on land again!"

Vera bent and tweaked Nikos's cheek. "You're a good young seaman then!"

"My papa's a helmsman and I am too!" Nikos said proudly. I felt a twinge of nostalgia when he mentioned Elidi.

Vera chuckled. "Then after you've rested you must tell me your tales!"

After we had dined, Vera showed us to a room off the courtyard where she had prepared a bath for Nikos and me. I felt happy to be free of the worry of the many perils we had endured on our long voyages. The kindness of the innkeeper and his wife set my mind at ease. They had shown us the same true spirit of friendship we had experienced in Athens. I felt certain all would be well and with good fortune we would find safe passage north.

Stanza Seven

The next day we set out to find the merchant's home to ask if he could provide us passage north.

Past the bustle of the city, the road wound through a quiet meadow then sloped up a grassy hillside. The innkeeper had said the merchant lived in a villa overlooking the city.

The square white house hugged the edge of a bluff, facing the sea surrounded by vineyards and olive groves. We were met at the gate by an elderly servant. He regarded us with a critical glance and asked why we wanted to see his master.

"We have come from Syracuse and have been told your master has means of transport to the north." Theon spoke softly.

The servant stared hard at Nikos and me and frowned. "You are travelling north with the woman and child?"

"Yes, through the Keltic lands. We were told your master may provide us with transport."

The servant shrugged and reluctantly led us into an inner courtyard, then he shuffled away to announce our presence to the merchant.

While we waited, I looked around at the rich surroundings. The merchant's home seemed even more luxurious than the palace at Pella. The terrace was paved with coloured marble, strewn with colourful carpets. There were urns of flowers and scented shrubs. Couches with tapestry cushions were placed around and next to elaborately carved tables of olive wood, decked with lanterns that gave off a sweet fragrance.

Soon the servant returned with the merchant, Timonedes, a tall man with piercing blue eyes, his ash-grey hair tied back framing a handsome clean-shaven face. He was dressed in a loosely belted tunic of rich woven linen like some other Massalian men I had seen.

He greeted Theon graciously. "My servant says you are travelling north and require transportation?"

"Yes," Theon explained. "We set out from Pella months ago, after Alexandros left on his campaign. We are bound for Cymru. Our innkeeper said perhaps you might help us find transport to the north as you trade with the Kelts."

"Why are you going north?" the trader asked. "It may not be a safe journey for you and the girl." He looked at me and frowned. "And you are travelling with a child!"

"This is Olwen. She is Cymry. She is like a daughter to me," Theon said. "I am escorting her back to her people."

"A Kelt?" When Timonides spoke, his voice matched his haughty demeanour and his smile turned into what seemed like a sneer. "How did you come to be in Hellas. Are you a slave?"

I kept my composure and smiled politely. "I was stolen from my home,"

"Stolen?"

"Yes. And Alexandros was my saviour."

Timonides looked at me with amazement. "Alexandros?"

"Yes, King Filippos's son, Alexandros. He rescued me from the man who had stolen me from my people."

Timonides turned his attention to Nikos who was clinging to me shyly. "And the boy? Is he your child?"

"Yes," I replied. "His name is Nikos. His father was a helmsman on the king's trireme,"

"Ah! A seaman! There's nothing grander than sailing a ship. When I was a boy that was what I wanted to do." He reached out and stroked Nikos's hair tenderly. Nikos fidgeted and held tight to my hand. "Your father must have been a noble man!" Timonides said.

Theon interjected, "Olwen has been in my care for many years. This is a brave girl, one worthy of honour. I have taught her all she knows about the healing arts and now she will impart that knowledge to her people. "Theon pointed to the gold torc I wore around my neck and continued, "She is a Druid's child."

For a long moment Timonides didn't speak, then he looked at me, this time in a kindlier manner, and said: "A Druid's child, and a healer. Then you are a woman of high esteem. May you be honoured by your people. I wish you a safe journey home."

Timonides frowned and paused in thought. "Perhaps..." he took in a long breath. "It is a long journey, sometimes dangerous. And I only trade with the people of the Arverni, so from there you would have to find your own way."

The servant brought a tall jar of wine and Timonides poured a cup for Theon and himself. As the men talked I played with Nikos in the courtyard, but I listened to what they were saying.

"My family were noted astronomers who studied with the great mathematician, Pythagoras," Timonides said. His tone had a touch of arrogance.

"When I was a youth I studied the philosophies of Plato, "Theon said. "Then I learned the healing arts from the teachings of Hippocrates." He took a deep draft of the wine. "The innkeeper told me many of the mariners and traders in Massalia are Pythagoreans,"

Timonides mused for a while then went on. "There is one young *ephebe*, Pytheas is his name, who talks of sailing to the Tin Islands one day." Timonides chuckled. "He has great aspirations, but if he makes good on his dream it will open up many more trade routes for us."

The servants had prepared a feast and set the tables with plates of fruit, platters of squid and oysters, wild greens in olive oil and fish stew prepared with saffron and thyme. Timonides motioned for us to sit at the couches in the atrium.

"I would like to hear more about your journey. I invite you to share a meal with my wife and me. Come, sit, and partake of the feast with us!" He turned to one of the servants, "Tell Lydia we have guests for our meal today!"

A woman entered the courtyard. She had lustrous coppery hair and was clad in a silk garment the colour of purple cyclamen bordered with a pattern of woven gold threads. Her cheeks were coloured with blush, her eyebrows blackened and painted with shadow. She smiled, but her eyes, observing me, were hard as green stones.

I felt a cold shiver prickle my skin. The sight of her brought back a tumult of unpleasant memories. *Olympias!* I thought, but I smiled graciously and waited discreetly for her to speak.

Although she greeted me politely, her tongue was sharp as the sting of a wasp. "The servant tells me you and your companion are travelling north?"

'Yes," I said. "We were told your husband might provide us with passage. My name is Olwen," I held out my hand in greeting, but she did not respond.

For a moment she eyed me, then she pointed to Nikos. "And who is this?"

"This is my son, Nikos Eladimis."

"Hmm... Is he Greek?"

"His father was Phrygian," I said.

She inspected Nikos with a critical eye. "Come here child." She beckoned Nikos closer, but he held back, clinging to my hand. "Does he speak Greek?"

"Yes my lady, as well as my own Cymru language."

"You are Cymry?" She clicked her tongue. "A *Kelt*?" She spoke the word as if it was a curse.

"Yes, my lady."

Her eyebrows arched in surprise. "And you are travelling with your child to the land of those barbarian Tin People?"

I felt the colour rise in my cheeks. "My people are not barbarians, my lady. We are from Cymru. My people are the Essyltyrs of the Raven Clan from the *tuath* of Caer Gwyn on the Great Plain."

She studied me, the frown lines between her eyes deepening, then she raised her jewelled hand, pointing to one of the couches.

"Come, sit!" she commanded, and led us to one of the couches apart from where the men were dining.

She strode to the couch in a haughty manner and reclined gracefully against a bank of embroidered silk cushions. "Come!" she ordered when she saw me hesitate. "The child too!"

I settled myself reluctantly on a couch next to hers, pulling Nikos close.

"I have a son," Lydia said, "He is grown now, and like his father he's a master trader. What will become of your boy once you return to your people?"

"He will be educated by Theon and taught how to be a good man," I said.

Lydia tossed her head. "Do you not think it is foolish to make this journey with your child? The Kelts are barbaric... savages!" She spit out the words as if they were laced with poison.

"They are not!" I protested. "I am a Druid's child. My grandfather was a chief Druid. Theon has taught me the arts of healing and I am returning to my people to share this knowledge with them!"

Lydia's brows lifted. "Do you really trust those brutish, vulgar people to give you safe passage through their lands?" she scoffed.

I could feel the heat of anger rising within me. I stood, grasping Nikos by the hand. "It is late, my lady. We must go now."

I walked away, back to the courtyard, my heart pounding in my breast, my cheeks flushed with anger at the woman's unkind insults. Theon saw me leave and I heard him say to Timonides, "This day has been long and we must return to the inn. I bid you farewell. We thank you for your generosity."

After we left Timonides' house and were alone again, I commented to Theon how different from the Athenians these Massalians were."Some of them seem to have lost their *philoxena.*"

Theon peered at me knowingly under his thick brows. "Lydia? Yes. The Massalians are different from the Athenians. They came here from Ionia to make a new life for themselves and found riches in trade. It is the bane of the wealthy to look down on those who have nothing. I noticed how arrogant and perhaps unkind his wife was, but I believe Timonides is a good man, and he was a generous host. I trust his word, that he will find us a safe passage north."

That night I could hardly sleep. Lydia's sharp words haunted me: *Don't you think it's foolish to make this journey? Do you trust those brutish, vulgar people to give you safe passage through their lands?* I worried I might be putting myself and Nikos at risk. I was still full of expectations and questions even though Theon had tried to allay my fears. I trusted Theon. He was my guiding light, my protector. I had to believe he would help me reach home safely.

Stanza Eight

A few days later, we were roused by the innkeeper who told us Timonides had sent word that he had a convoy of wagons bearing merchandise leaving next day for the north.

"He said there will be room to transport you. The wagonage will wait for you at the city's north gate."

As we prepared to leave Massalia, I had a feeling of trepidation. We had reached Massalia safely, but what lay ahead? It would be a long journey overland and a voyage across the wide channel before I would reach home. I dared not think what might happen along the way,

Theon assured me all would be well. "Timonides is a well-known trader and you can be sure his convoy of merchandise will be safely guarded."

Timonides was waiting for us when we arrived at the city gates. He greeted us warmly and showed us to our transportation, a covered ox cart. There were five other ox-drawn wagons all loaded with clay amphorae of oil and wine, accompanied by a wagon master, guards, drovers, and a team of pack mules bearing baskets of other produce. Theon offered to pay him for providing us transport but he smiled and said, "You will need your gold to pay for your passage across the Narrow Sea."

He introduced us to the wagon master and drovers. "These people have travelled far and I have assured them you will provide safe passage as far as the Averni lands." He turned to Theon and held out his hand to wish him farewell. "The Averni people are friendly. I have been trading with them for many years," he said. "They will welcome you and help you reach your destination."

Beyond the city's outskirts the hillsides were rich with olive groves, orchards and vineyards. The road north led between tall cypresses and across wide fields fed by a river. The late sun dappled the trees that were shedding their colourful leaves. The land was dotted with a few small copses but it was mostly bare, open fields.

A light drizzle of rain began to fall. I wrapped a blanket around Nikos, fastened my woolen cloak and drew up the hood. All day long the wooden wagons rolled up the road. The journey was slow, the road slippery with mud from the rain which increased as the day wore on. In spite of it, the drovers sang as they plodded alongside the oxen.

When we came to a sheltered place in a grove of trees, they pegged the mules, unharnessed the oxen and made camp for the night. The rain trickled through the canopy of trees. I was tired, aching and cold. One of the drovers passed around a goatskin of wine, another baked oat cakes on the hot stones of the crackling fire.

That night was spent in the ox-cart under the shelter of a grove of trees. It was cold, damp and miserable. I sniffled and sneezed all through the night, dreaming of Theon's warm homestead.

The next morning, the rain had ceased, the sky was clear and the sun shone warm and strong. The road wound along a river and through a valley where the trees on the hillsides flamed red and gold. We were following the trade route road, past fields where long-horned roan cattle and herds of sheep grazed. Here and there shepherds and cowherds hailed us to talk and ask for news. There were other merchants with pack mules and ox-carts – copper smiths, leather workers and jewellers from Massalia, and bearded Keltic traders, dressed in tunics and leggings bound with leather thongs. The wagon master told us the Kelts were loyal friends of the Greeks, and came to bargain in exchange for amber, copper and gold.

Along the way we saw settlements protected by wooden palisades and deep ditches. The houses were round with walls built of wattle and daub with domed thatched roofs. The sight of them stirred so many memories of Caer Gwyn.

Outside the settlements shaggy ponies and cattle grazed in fields. There were sheep and goats in pens guarded by grizzled dogs with matted fur. As it was early autumn the slaughtering had begun in the flatland by the river. Occasionally the cattle herders came to greet us. I told them, "We are going north across the wide channel. I am *Ynys Prydein.* My people are Cymry." I felt such pleasure speaking my own language again, though these people were Kelts of a different tribe and their language was not quite the same as mine.

On the fourth day, we reached the Averni settlement where the traders would exchange their goods. As we crossed the bridge over the moat to pass through the palisade gates, a pack of snarling mastiffs greeted us snapping at the oxen's hooves and frightening the pack mules. The drovers chased them back, hurling curses at them.

Inside the circular wooden ramparts, the village houses were grouped together surrounding a low hill topped by a stone-built hill fort. Sheaves of hay were stacked on wooden platforms beside some of the houses, and grain was stored in wicker granaries on stilts.

A tall, stoutly-built man with braided raven-black hair came out of one of the houses and called a greeting to the wagon master. I knew by his coat of ermine pelts and the gold torc around his neck, he was a man of importance and wealth.

The wagon master introduced us to him.

"This is Brion. He's the chief trader of the village. Brion, these people have come with us from Massalia. They are on a long journey north. Can you give them lodgings?"

The Keltic trader smiled and held out his hand to Theon, greeting him in Greek. "You do not need to fear my people. We will respect you and make you welcome."

"We are grateful for your hospitality," Theon replied.

The Kelt peered at Theon closely, noting the white tunic he wore. "You are a priest?"

"I am a physician," Theon replied.

"And this young woman and the child?"

I answered him in my own language. "I am *Cymry*," I said. "My people are the Essyltyrs."

The trader peered at me closely. "So, you are a Kelt?" When he noticed the raven torc around my neck; his brows lifted in surprised. "You are a priestess?"

"My grandfather was the Chief Druid of our *tuath,* and my *modryb* Essylt, was a *vate*, a diviner. Theon is my guardian and teacher," I explained. "He taught me the healing arts and is taking me back to my home in Cymru on the Great Plain."

"Ah, so you too, are a priestess of the healing arts?" the trader looked down at Nikos who was hiding shyly behind Theon. "And the child?"

"He is my son, Nikos. His father was lost at sea. He was a helmsman on the king's trireme."

Brion grinned and reached down to tousle Nikos's hair. "Ah, you are a brave boy and will be a warrior one day," he said. "We Kelts are great warriors!"

Nikos shrank back staring in awe at Brion, who must have seemed like the giants in tales I had told him.

Brion turned to the people who had gathered around us and spoke to them in his loud, resonant voice: "People of the Averni," he shouted, "These people are healers. They have come from far away and are going north, across the Narrow Sea. We must make them welcome."

At the sound of his voice, the door skins of the houses parted and more men came out of their houses, sturdy, swarthy men with braids and black beards that hung to their chests. Behind them, olive-skinned, dark-haired women followed, dressed in brightly patterned tunics.

I greeted the women in my own Keltic tongue and they smiled, surrounding me, touching my cloak, bidding me welcome. They looked at Theon with respect and fussed over Nikos who drew back shyly from their touch.

Brion called to one of the women. "Neala, these people are travellers from Massalia. They will be our guests. Take them to our house and prepare a feast!"

The trader's wife led us through the village to a large round stone and mud house near the foot of a trail that led up to the hillfort. The smell of roasting pork fat met me as I entered the house. On the central hearth, a pig was roasting over the coals, the smoke curling up through the roof vent. The house was larger inside than most. Tin pots hung on a rack near the hearth, shields, lances and iron swords were hung around the walls. The floor was strewn with hay and animal pelts. In one corner there were straw mats covered with sheepskins for sleeping and some low stools where the woman said we could sit.

So many years had passed, I had forgotten how rustic life was in a Keltic village and wondered, after living such a privileged life with Theon enjoying the comforts of life in Hellas, if I could return to such a base way of living as this.

We were seated comfortably by the hearth when Brion arrived, bringing with him a group of men and their women. He introduced them as his neighbours; some of them traders, others were craftsmen. Most of them spoke Greek and were eager to make conversation with Theon while the women hovered around me, curious, asking me many questions. "How did you, a Kelt, come to live with the Greeks? Why did you travel so far from your home?"

They were surprised I spoke their language, even though my tongue was somewhat different from theirs.

When I answered them they were shocked and wanted to hear more, but Neala was ready to serve the feast. Some of the women helped her dish out the pork on flat wooden trenchers along with bronze bowls of nettles, beans and black bread while Brion poured flagons of honied mead for the men.

"Come! Eat!" he said, "Then we will talk, and you will tell us of your travels."

After we had eaten our fill, more flagons of mead were poured, Brion wiped his moustache on his sleeve, put down his bowl and turned to me. "Now you must tell us about your people and how it came to be you were taken away."

I had not spoken of my last days in Caer Gwyn since Alexandros rescued me and took me to be with Theon. The memory was one I had chosen to hide away and now, revealing it again, was reliving a terrible nightmare. As I spoke about it, I could feel my stomach knot and my throat ache.

"It was Midsummer and we were returning to our tuath from the Great Stone Circle when they came, the Wolves of Cymbeline, those men of the Dobunni. They swarmed on us like demons. They had taken our ricon, Madoc, as a hostage and demanded their ricon's boy, Dafydd, who had been stolen by Madoc's eldest son, Sholto, be returned to them. But the boy had already been sacrificed after the rites at the Stone Circle on the orders of the Druid, Bedwyr who was an evil sorcerer and threatened to harm anyone who disobeyed him."

I felt myself tremble as I spoke and the long-forgotten memory of seeing Dafydd being driven to his death in the wicker cart brought tears to my eyes. "My *modryb*, Essylt, told me to run and hide, because our village was on fire. She was afraid the Dobunni warriors would kill us all. So I went to the sacred grove to hide and it was there I saw it happen." I stopped to take a long breath. "I saw the ricon's son, Sholto, murder his younger brother because Sholto blamed him wrongly for killing a warrior woman he had stolen from another tribe." I felt the tears splash down my cheeks, but I went on.

Brion and his friends leaned closer, listening, "When Sholto saw me, he was going to kill me too, but instead he took me away... far away... and that is how ..." I was unable to go on speaking so Theon finished the story for me.

"Alexandros, our young prince, was hunting in the forest and found them. He slayed the Kelt and rescued the girl, then brought her to me to care for. And that is how Olwen came to Hellas and learned the art of healing. Now we are returning to her home so she can share her knowledge with her people."

For such a big man, Brion was gentle. He reached out his hand and took mine. "You must not fear," he said. "For even if the Dobunni destroyed your tuath, you will always find a home somewhere among your own people. You have put yourself in the gods' path, so they will go with you." He turned to Theon. "You must stay here with us until you are rested, then I will provide you with a mule and wain to carry your belongings. It is a long journey to the north."

He took a sword from a sconce on the wall "Do you know how to wield a sword?" he asked Theon.

"I have not wielded one since I was a young plebe," Theon said.

"I will provide you with one for your safety. There are rogues in the northern tribes, robbers who lie in wait for travellers like you." He turned to me. "Here..I will show you how you wield it." He placed the sword in my hand and explained how to get a proper grip on the hilt. "You place your thumb here... into the hollow of the blade. Now lift, and thrust."

It seemed strange to me to be holding a weapon. I thought of Talia, the warrior woman who had accompanied Sholto to our tuath, and other women I had known who were as fierce and brave as the men, not afraid to go into battle. But for me the sword felt alien and unwieldy. I could only hope there would be no need to use it.

Stanza Nine

A few days later, after bidding farewell to Brion and his wife, we set off. The covered mule cart he provided was small, but large enough to store our belongings, and if it rained we could stay dry. Nikos rode in the cart, while I walked alongside it with Theon. It would be a long and sometimes arduous trek so we were grateful to Brion for providing us with transportation.

The trail from the Arveni tuath led along a river through the hills. By the end of that day we had reached flat-lands of green pastures where cattle and sheep grazed, and fields of wheat stubble where farmers were stacking the newly harvested sheaves. We waved and called a greeting as we passed by. They watched us pass, eyeing us with curiosity, but did not return our greetings. Not far ahead, there was a hilltop fortress and below it the wooden stakes of a fenced tuath.

"This must be the lands of the Bituriges," Theon said. "Brion told me they were mostly peasants who live off their land. We will stop here to replenish our food. Perhaps we can find lodgings for the night."

Two scrawny youths dressed in ragged tunics greeted us as the gates of the tuath. The tallest boy, a skinny youth, half naked with woad tattoos on his chest, pointed the way to the market. A pack of mangy curs came to greet us, snuffing at the wheels of the wain as we rode into the village. There was an acrid odour of manure in the street and the houses looked ill-kept. The two boys followed us along the narrow-cobbled road-way past the dilapidated houses made of mud and sticks. In front of some of them were posts with skulls mounted on top. They reminded me of the mounted skulls around the ricon's meeting hall in Caer Gwyn. Nikos gasped in fear when he saw them.

"They are the skulls of enemies killed in battle," I told him.

The market was a few rustic stalls with fruit and vegetables where a group of shabbily dressed women had gathered to gossip Theon and I had put away our Greek garments for the journey. He was wearing a short, belted tunic like the men of Massalia, and I wore breeches and a tunic. I spoke to the women, but my language was different from theirs and they did not reply and made no friendly gesture but whispered behind their hands as they stared at us.

We loaded up the wain with the produce and set off without so much as a friendly gesture from the folk in the marketplace. The two youths who had followed us were huddled together, whispering. I had noticed them hovering around Theon, watching him as he took coins out of his bag to pay for his purchases. I meant to draw attention to them, but Theon had stopped one of the townsmen to inquire if there was an inn where we could spend the night. The man eyed Theon suspiciously, grunted and pointed toward a rustic shack near the town gates.

"These people seem like unfriendly sorts," Theon said. "I think it's best we don't stay here. Perhaps we should spend the night under the stars."

We continued down the trail until we came to a grove of beech trees near the banks of the river. We unhitched the mule so it could graze. I helped Theon unpack the wagon and left him dozing under the trees while I took Nikos down to the river to bathe.

The riverbank was thick with rushes and water-lilies floated on the surface. There were a few ducks and swans swimming among the lily pads that delighted Nikos. I left him in the shallows watching them and waded out into the stream. The water was cool and refreshing after our long day's journey. As I let myself sink into the depths, a memory came back to me, a long-forgotten memory, of my kidnapping.

I was submerged in a river, my arms spread wide letting the current tug at my clothing, cleansing me from the filth of travel, of Sholto and his sneering evilness. I wanted to let myself sink, hoping I would be carried away by the current, but something made me push to the surface. A cob of swans circled around me as though they had come there to protect me.

A loud shout from Theon disturbed my reverie. I waded to the shore and climbed up the embankment where I saw the two youths who had followed us in the marketplace. One had wrestled Theon to the ground and was tying his hands behind his back. The other was crouched over him, a knife in his hand.

I led Nikos to a safe place under the willows and told him to wait there for me. "Theon needs me. You stay here until I come back to get you."

I remembered the sword Brion had given us for protection was in the donkey cart. I made my way up the embankment, creeping as stealthily as I could across the grass toward the wain and retrieved the sword. It felt heavy in my hand. I pressed my thumb into the hollow of the blade the way Brion had shown me and came up behind the youth with the dagger. The other younger boy who was crouched by Theon, saw me wielding the sword. His eyes widened with fright and he shouted a warning.

The older youth turned to face me. I could feel my heart pounding but threw off my fear as I thrust myself forward wielding the sword. He lunged toward me with his dagger drawn. I lifted my foot and kicked him as hard as I could just below his belly. He staggered backward, and bent over howling in pain, dropping his weapon. The younger boy yowled in fright and fled back down the trail toward his tuath.

The older youth, still wincing in pain, stood to face me. I thrust the tip of my sword on his breastbone until a thin trickle of blood dribbled down his chest.

"You have threatened a Druid's child and healer. I will put a curse on you and your tuath if we are not allowed safe passage through your land. Now, begone from here! You are nothing but scum! If you dare return I will put a curse on your people!"

He backed away from me then fled down the trail. I hurried to tend to Theon who was crouched on the ground, his hands still tied behind his back.

"They meant to rob you," I said. My voice trembled when I spoke. "I saw them watching you in the market ... filthy swine!" I untied the leather thongs from his wrists and helped him to his feet.

"You are a warrior woman!" Theon said. He smiled when he said it. "I am proud of you for your bravery."

"I wasn't going to let him harm you... or us!" I said. Then I heard Nikos crying and turned to see him hiding under the wagon. "Nikos, are you alright? Why didn't you wait under the willows?"

"I saw you with the sword, Mama. I was scared."

I cuddled him in my arms. "Don't be frightened. The wicked boys have left and won't return."

"We'd best not stay here for the night," Theon said. He hitched up the mule and put our belongings back on the wain. "We cannot take a chance that the ruffians will return. I had a bad feeling about that tuath. The people were so ."

I knew what he meant. There was no kind spirit in that tuath. They were poor, oppressed and suspicious of newcomers. I could only hope for the rest of our journey we would not meet with any more like them. I longed to consult with a seer, someone who would tell the omens and set my fears at rest.

Stanza Ten

Before sunrise the next day, Theon and I loaded the wain with our belongings and set out on our journey north. Nikos rode in the cart while Theon and I walked beside it. We journeyed the whole day, the mule cart travelling slowly through the dappled woods. When twilight deepened into night, we made camp under the trees. The flickering flames of the fire Theon had lit cast eerie shadows in the grove. I lay awake on my pallet, with the soft sound of Nikos breathing beside me. I lay wrapped in my cloak watching the moon rise over the thicket watching the heavens. I had lost track of time, but by studying the heavens, I sensed it must be early in the month of the harvest moon. My thoughts went back to Makedon, and Elidi. I remembered his kisses on my lips, our bodies pressed close together. Again I felt the ache of regret. Had I made the best choice in trying to return to Caer Gwyn. What future would there be for our son? What future was there for me?

Day after day we travelled north trudging over hills, through woodlands and across fields. Wisps of mist clung in the valleys. A cold wind had sprung up tearing the crisp brown leaves from the trees. There was new snow on the distant mountains and once the sun went down, the chill of evening rose from the damp, frosty ground. Theon gathered dried bracken to build a fire, and we camped under the stars with the moon hanging over us.

For days, at each sunrise, we set off again fording streams, through more woodlands and across fields. We found watering places along the trail, occasionally stopping at farmsteads where Theon purchased provisions. We trudged along in silence, following a track beside a patchwork of fields with recently harvested crops of grain stalks, scythed and gathered in stooks. The farmers should have been in their fields, but everything was deserted. There was not even a single traveller on the road.

Days passed and I lost track of time. Then, one day, late in the afternoon, I saw, ahead of us, the straw roofs of several houses with smoke curling from their thatch. As we came closer, I noticed that although there was a ditch, there were no defence walls around the village, only a wooden fence guarding a collection of wattle huts.

"We must stop here," Theon said with a weary sigh as he plodded along beside me. "Perhaps they will give us shelter for the night." He was breathing heavily and shivering, his cloak pulled tightly around him. I could see by the lines on his face and his stooped shoulders how exhausted he was. My own body ached with weariness. My legs were trembling with fatigue. We were tired and unkempt and I knew we could not go much farther without stopping for the night. I could only hope these people would be friendly.

We crossed the little wooden bridge over the ditch and entered through the open gate. A pack of dogs barked at us, sniffling at the mule's hooves. They followed us into the enclosure, crowding around, snuffing and whining a greeting. Theon pushed his way through them, and I followed beside the wain where Nikos was sleeping. Wakened by the shrill yaps of the excited dogs several men parted the door skins of the huts and came out of their houses. One of them came forward toward us. He was a tall, grey-bearded man wearing a red and yellow striped cloak pinned with a silver brooch. I saw by his bronze arm bands and the torc around his neck that he appeared to be one of the tuath's elders. He spoke in a different tongue, but not so different and it was easy to be understood. He asked who we were. Theon replied in the few words of greeting he knew. I told him we had travelled by ship from far away Hellas, to the trading port of Massalia.

The man raised his brows in surprise. "You are Greeks? That is a long journey you have made. What brings you here?"

"I am from Cymru, from the clan of the Essyltyr, the Raven's clan," I said. "My companion is a Greek physician. We are going north to the narrow sea."

He smiled and held out his arms in greeting. "We are the Belgae people. My name is Evander, I am an elder of my village. You must be weary after such a trek! I will take you to our tribal chief."

I lifted Nikos from the wain and one of the men unhitched the mule so it could graze. We followed Evander through the circle of huts. We could smell roasting meat and hear the laughter of women. Several children came out and ran along beside the pack of dogs.

He led us to the centre of the village where there was a large round house with stone walls and a thatched roof. Beside it was a grain silo, several other buildings and a paddock where several shaggy horses were tethered.

"This is our tribal great-house," Evander said.

We followed him into a room spacious enough for the village people to gather for safety. It was warm and dry inside, with the scent of pine resin from the torches. The thick walls were reinforced with sturdy beams of oak and decorated with hanging bowls bearing disc designs, and bronze scabbards and swords. Brightly woven tapestries hung on the walls and the roof beams were carved with images of animals. The floor was covered with thick layers of rushes and animal pelts. The feel of them underfoot indicated wealth.

In the centre of the room, a log fire crackled, its pungent smoke hanging thick about the roof vent and thatched ceiling. The tribal chieftain sat by the fire with several other men. He was much younger than I expected, a tawny-haired handsome man not much older than I. When Evander explained to him who we were he lifted his brows and stared at us then said, "You are going to the Narrow Sea?" He waved his arm. "It is not far from here!"

"They need a place to rest for the night, my lord," Evander said. "It has been a long, perilous journey they have made."

The chieftain looked at me and pointed to Nikos. "I see you have a small child!"

"He is my son," I said. "His name is Nikos."

He smiled. "I have a son too, one like yours!" He motioned for us to sit next to him by the fire. "My name is Urien. I am the tribal chieftain. We are friendly people here and of course you are welcome to stay. Here, come sit by me and tell me your tale."

I drew in a long breath as if I had just woken from a troubled sleep. I sat beside the chieftain with Nikos snuggled in my lap. I felt relieved, and mur-mured a prayer of thanks to the goddess, grateful for the kindness and hospi-tality of these Belgae people. Theon was welcomed too, and took a place to sit by the other men who seemed eager to question him.

Some of the villagers had followed us into the chieftain's hut and squatted around the room gazing unashamedly at us, the bedraggled, road weary trav-ellers. A beautiful young woman with coppery hair who introduced herself as Luneda, the chieftain's wife, brought us cups of hot honey mead. Another woman brought a trencher of barley cakes, roast pork and fresh garden greens.

"Now, tell me about your travels," Urien said after we had finishing dining. "What took you so far away from your own people?"

I related my tale to him while he listened attentively. When I mentioned that Theon was a physician, he interrupted and gave a deep sigh. "I wish you had been here when my father took ill," he said. "My father, who was the tribal chieftain before me, died of an ague. Our healer's medicines did not help him." He went on to tell us about his tuath. "The Belgae of my tribe are not warriors. We are farmers. We don't live huddled together, but prefer small farmsteads, each with his own chieftain." This explained to me why there was no hill fort, no skulls mounted on posts around the great house, no weaponry hanging on the walls, giving it the sinister air of the ricon's dwelling in Caer Gwyn. These people were not warriors but peaceful people dedicated to their land.

"I will send Evander to escort you to the coast," he said. "It is not far, only a day or two. You will stay here tonight so you can rest." He called to his wife. "Luenda, show our guest where she can sleep tonight."

Nikos had already fallen asleep, wrapped in my woollen cloak. I carried him, following Luneda to the far side of the great house where there were beds made of heaps of straw covered with warm furry hides. She had provided a basin of warm water and watched me as I bathed, then helped me brush the tangled knots out of my hair.

"You are a beautiful woman, my lady, blessed by the gods, a wise, brave woman, and a good mother to your son."

As I settled myself down, somewhere a harpist began to play, strumming on a clarsach. The plaintive sound of his sweet tenor voice made me think of Lleu, Caer Gwyn's bard.

> *Enjoy the sweet and goodly mead,*
> *sweeter than any honeyed food.*
> *Drink from the burnished cups.*
> *Commune ye with your loved ones*
> *while sweet music strikes on your ears.*

It was an old song, one I had often heard Lleu sing. As the harpist's fingers plucked the strings, I closed my eyes, letting the notes wash over me as I drifted off to sleep, imagining I was in another place, a quiet grove, amid the standing stones.

We set off before the sun was high in the heavens. Evander was a pleasant companion on our trek, regaling us with stories of his people and asking questions about ours. He was most fascinated by Theon's tales.

"I know we make trade with the Greeks," he said." But I have only met seamen on the coast, rough fellows, not so highly esteemed as you. I am certain you will be regarded well." He turned to me with a smile. "And you, my lady, your people will herald you and hold you in great honour for you are a brave woman, one who will make her tuath proud!"

Two days later, we reached a shore settlement near the shore of the Narrow Sea.

"That is a village of fishermen," Evander said. "They know the sea well so we will ask them to find you a safe passage across."

I stood on the shore, looking out over the dark expanse of water. Somewhere over there was my home. I had no other home anywhere in the world.

Yet so many years had passed since I had been stolen away, and now I was returning, a mother with a child. What if Caer Gwyn was no longer "home" to me? What then?

As I watched the rough seas and foam-crested waves, recalling long-forgotten memories, Evander interrupted my reverie. "Are you sure you do not want to wait until it is better sailing weather?" He pointed at the sky where a dark cloud had blown over the sun. "The sea is treacherous at this time of year."

Theon agreed. "Perhaps it's best we wait till the storm season is over."

I knew the sea was running high, but I would not be deterred. I had come this far and I was determined to cross to my homeland.

"No. We must go now," I said. "I will make an offering to the Sea gods and they will give us a safe journey."

The next morning, Evander took us to search for a vessel. The shore village was a settlement of little stone houses with low thatched roofs. Rafts and small round coracles used for shore fishing were strewn on the beach and there was a larger wooden hulled ship tied to the quay. Evander asked the captain if he would give us passage. Theon offered him a handful of silver coins.

The captain shook his head. "We have just come across with a cargo of tin," he said. "The sailing season is over; and we won't make another voyage until springtime when the sea is calmer."

I felt a pang of disappointment. There must be a way for us to cross, perhaps another vessel. The fishermen were still sailing out each day. There were some on the beach hauling their leather-hulled currachs ashore. I urged Evander to ask if one of them could transport us.

There was a currach tied up to the stone quay. It was a wooden, plank-bottomed fishing craft covered with animal hides and had a single sail, The captain was a thin, dark man with black hair and a bushy beard. Some of the crew stood nearby staring at us curiously. I was certain by their swarthy appearance and muscular builds they were Cymry or Britons.

Evander spoke to the captain and when Theon offered him the silver coins, the captain readily accepted taking on extra passengers. He pointed across the sea toward the distant fog-shrouded shoreline.

"We stopped here to mend our nets," he said. "We will sail back tomorrow. The sea may be rough, but we fish in any weather." Then he glanced over at me, where I stood with Nikos. "But ye're crossing with a woman and a child? Are ye certain ye want to ..."

"Yes! I am going home!" I replied, surprised at the curt tone of my voice. "I am Cymry. My home is Caer Gwyn near the great stone circle of Cor Gawr. My people are the Essyltyr. I am from the Raven Clan."

"Ah, the stone circle... and those *Cymry!* Your people are a fierce tribe...strong, fearless." He turned to Theon. "The sea is running high, but the journey across is not long – the best part of a day, with my six men plying the oars. But are you willing to risk the journey…" he glanced over a me… "with a young woman and a small child?"

"We've been told the passage can be dangerous," Theon said. He turned to me and said: "Are you certain you want to go now?"

"Yes, perhaps you'd be best to wait till springtime," Evander agreed.

But I remained adamant in my resolve. "I *must* go now," I said. "I want to be home to celebrate Samhain with my people."

Evander's brows lifted. "But why Samhain?"

"Because the spirits of the dead return to us on that night, and I want to honour my Druid grandfather, Maelgwyn, and my husband, Elidi. And to pay tribute to my friend, Alexandros, because he saved my life on a Samhain night."

Alexandros! I had not spoken his name aloud for a very long time and just saying it now seemed to fill me with renewed courage. I remembered him, the handsome fair-haired young hunter, who had rescued me from my captor on that haunted night in the forest so long ago. I will never forget him. I owed my life to him!

The captain shrugged. "If you must. Then meet us here tomorrow at daybreak." He looked out over the water. "Just pray your gods will still the waves for a safe crossing."

That night, I studied the heavens, the way Grandfather Maelgwyn had taught me. *The stars are the messengers of the Gods,* Grandfather said. *Look for your portents in the stars.*

I searched among the constellations, watching for a sign, but none appeared.

BALLAD THIRTY-ONE Song Of The Raven

Let me sing you this song.
I was taken from my tuath,
Caer Gwyn, on the Great Plain
where my people guard the sacred Stone Circle.
I have journeyed through forests and over seas.
I have been a shield in the hand of a warrior.
I have served in the court of a king,
spoken in a language that was not my own.
The gods gifted me with knowledge to comfort and heal.
I have travelled the world,
worshipped at the shrines of gods that were not my own.
I am the Raven of the sacred grove.
I am the Raven, borne by the wind.
Where will I go? Where will I dwell?
I am a healer and a mother.
Beauteous is the land from where I was taken,
that noble land of my people the Cymry.
I am Olwen, daughter of the Raven.

This is my song.

THE CROSSING

Stanza One

We said goodbye to Evander the following morning. Theon tried to pay him for his kindness, but he refused the gold coins he was offered. "You will need them to pay the captain of the currach." He looked out over the water and shook his head. "I pray you will have a safe crossing."

He watched us as we took our places, huddled at the prow away from the stench of the baskets of fish and heaps of nets at the bow, and waved a final farewell. The captain stood at the prow shouting orders as the six fishermen plied the oars. And so began our perilous journey across the Narrow Sea.

I could not remember much of my first crossing when I was Sholto's captive. I vaguely recalled the sleek black trader's craft with a griffon carved on the bowsprit and yellow standards bearing the crest of a two-headed crimson bird fluttering from the mast. The currach was a simple fishing vessel and not built for long voyages and stormy seas.

As we pulled away from the rocky shoreline I prayed to the sea gods to give us a safe passage and murmured an ancient charm.

May I be an island on the sea.
May I be a hill on the land.
May I be a star when the moon wanes.
May I be a lamb safe in a fold.

Though there were rain clouds in the distance, the wind was favourable when we set off. The currach rode low, plunging into the waves, the motion churning my innards. Seabirds cried in our wake as the fishermen bent over their oars. Once we were out of the harbour, the wind blew stronger and dark clouds had hidden the sun. The sail billowed and the currach bounced over the waves. The fishermen sang as they rowed. The sea seemed to have risen and the swells became so high that spray splashed over the prow. I held tight to Nikos who was trembling with fear. I was frightened too, nauseated from the rolling of the vessel, but determined not to let Theon or the crew know.

I sat silently as I watched the coastline disappear behind us. Some of the crew began yelling, their voices muffled by the sound of the wind. I thought I heard the words *storm* and *danger* but the captain shouted back the orders to keep rowing.

Theon leaned over and shouted over the sound of the wind and sea: "The captain claims it is only a day's journey across. Let's hope this is true." His face was flushed, and I could feel him trembling. I was sure he was as frightened as I was. I said a prayer to our god of the sweeping waves, Manawdan ap Lyr, pleading he take us across safely.

We were far from shore now. The wind had picked up and ahead of us the sea churned and roiled, the waves growing higher. A great wave crested over the prow soaking us through and I heard Theon cry, "Poseidon, spare us!"

I thought of how foolish I had been for insisting we make this journey. What had I done? Would we all drown as a consequence of my selfish decision? How could I have put my child and my mentor in such peril? Had the gods allowed it in order to teach me a lesson in humility?

I do not know how long I crouched there, clinging to Nikos while the tired oarsmen tried to row the currach out of the gale. Nikos was screaming and I cried out in terror, certain we would capsize. The boat quivered. I heard the cracking of wood breaking and felt something strike my head. A spume of icy water washed over me and I felt myself fading from consciousness.

I regained consciousness and I opened my eyes, the sky had lightened and ahead I saw high white chalk cliffs rising out of the churning sea. Perhaps I was dreaming. Or had I drowned? I was cold as ice, soaked with brine, and my head ached as though it would burst.

Theon was beside me, comforting me. "It's alright. A piece of the spar broke loose and hit your head."

I groped next to me, looking for Nikos, but he was gone. Had he been washed overboard? I screamed his name. "Nikos! My baby! My son!"

Then I heard one of the fishermen speak in my own language. "Do not fear. The child is safe!" I looked around and saw he was holding Nikos in his arms.

The captain shouted a command and the fishermen shipped their oars. The wind had changed and the sky brightened. To my relief, we were near land, gliding toward a small rocky beach at the foot of the cliffs. Fortune was with us. Somehow we had reached landfall without capsizing. The sea god had allowed us a safe journey to the other side of the Narrow Sea. I was back in my own land!

Some of the men leapt out of the currach and pulled it onto the shore.

"We will stop here to rest,' the captain said. "There's a shore village not far from here."

A cold wind still blew off the sea and the fishermen brought us blankets and dried our cloaks by the fire. Nikos had fallen asleep, his head on my lap. I stroke his hair and looked at him feeling an ache in my chest, chastising myself for putting him in such danger. Theon sat near me, staring into the fire, his jaw set, a grave look on his face. He did not speak, remaining stoic.

We stayed by the fire on the stony shore until we were rested and dry. The fishing crew had begun unloading the baskets of fish they would take to the market at the nearby shore settlement The currach captain said he had a friend in the village, a peddler, who might provide us with lodgings.

The roll of the sea had not yet left me so I clung to Theon's arm to steady myself as we followed the crew along the sandy shore to the settlement.

The shore settlement was little more than a collection of houses built of reeds and timber surrounded by a wooden stave fence. Beyond the sandy shore were low green fields where sturdy brown cattle and goats grazed. As we entered the village gates the fishermen yelled and cursed at the pack of snarling mastiffs who snapped at our heels and snuffed at the baskets of fish.

"These Shore people are friendly folk," the captain said. "They always greet us kindly when we arrive with our catch of fish. But their dogs..." he laughed. "They keep 'em to guard the gates. They'll chew yer leg off like it's a mutton bone if ye let 'em."

The market was crowded with merchants and village people who greeted us as we passed their stalls of farm produce and other goods. As soon as the fishermen set down the baskets of fish a crowd swarmed around eager to make a purchase.

The captain told us to wait with his men. "I'll go and fetch my friend. He'll give ye lodgings. He's a peddler and can take ye as far as the river."

Nikos was restless and eager to explore, so while we waited, I took him by the hand and walked around the market stalls. When I returned, I was amused to see Theon was handing out fish to the townspeople who had come to purchase them.

I burst out laughing. "Who would imagine a scholar and physician like you would be found selling fish in a Keltic market?"

He rolled his eyes. "Yes, and I'll stink to the heavens before this day is done. But we must exchange one favour for another," he said with a smile.

By the time the captain returned, the fishermen had sold all the fish in their baskets. They bid us farewell and left to return to their currach for another day of fishing. Just as they left, the captain came with his friend, the peddler.

"This is Arrak. He's an old friend of mine," the captain said. "He says he can help ye."

The peddler, Arrak, was a gentle mannered man with kindly eyes and a thin, pock-marked face. It was plain to see he was not a wealthy man like the merchants and traders. He was dressed in a grey woollen tunic that hung loosely on his slender frame. His breeches were baggy and mud-spattered. His only ornaments were a bronze torc and the copper bracelets on his arms.

"The captain tells me ye need a place to stay and a ride to the river," he said. "Ye're welcome in my house and I'll be heading to the river tomorrow to market my wares."

We bade farewell to the captain and followed Arrak through the village to his home. The house was an old, low-walled, ill-kept hut with a pointed roof of shabby thatch. There were cockerels and chickens pecking in the fenced yard and corn drying on racks by a rough-hewn shack where a shaggy pony was tethered.

"Come in!" he said. "Welcome to my home."

When we entered through the door skins I was surprised to find the inside of the house was cozy and warm. There was a jug of mead on the table and an old lamp that sent a stream of blue smoke up to the ceiling thatch. The floor was beaten earth, trodden until it was flat and smooth strewn with pieces of pottery and wicker boxes filled with other goods.

"Look Mama!" Nikos had spied a ginger cat curled up by the hearth and ran over to pet it. The cat yawned and rolled over on its side so he could stroke its belly. It pleased me to hear him giggle with delight after all he had endured.

"Come! Sit ye down!" Arrak said. "Eat and drink with me while you share your story. Ye'd best fill your bellies while you can. I've a pot of pork stew on the fire and plenty of black bread and mead." He nodded toward Nikos. "And honey-cakes for the boy!" He spooned us each a trencher of steaming stew from the pot on the hearth. "Tell me about yer'selves. What is your business? Why have ye come here?" He filled Theon's cup, then his own and sat back waiting for Theon to speak.

When Theon finished telling him our story, Arrak took another long draft of his mead, looked over at me and said: "You are brave to have journeyed so far with this young woman and her child."

He leaned close to peer closely at my raven torc. His eyes widened. "Ah...your torc... A priestess are ye?"

"I am a Druid's child who was meant to be a priestess. My grandfather, Maelgwyn, was the chief Druid of our tuath," I said. "I am a Cymry, from the Raven's Clan of the Essyltyr who dwell on the Plain."

He gave a sigh. "When I was a boy I wanted to study with the Druids. But my parents were poor, so I had to work, and I became a peddler." He nodded toward Nikos. "And the child? Where's his father?"

I had not spoken of Elidi for some time and the mention of him brought a lump to my throat and tears to my eyes. Arrak sensed my distress and patted my arm.

'Ne'er ye mind. Ye're a good mother to the boy. Yer husband would be proud of you. The gods only go with ye if ye put yerself in their path, and that takes courage."

"We are going to the chalk trail on the plain that leads to the Standing Stones," I said.

He raised his brows. "The Great Stone Circle?"

"Near there. To the tuath of Caer Gwyn"

He frowned and rubbed at his chin stubble. "Caer Gwyn? The Essyltyr tuath?"

"Yes. That is my home."

"Ye've been gone for a long time?"

"Ten years," I said. "I am returning to my people."

He shook his head. "I've heard of that place... yes, there was a great battle there long ago.

I felt my heart skip and my body clenched. "Yes. That's when I was taken." I was afraid to ask him more but gathered my courage. "Was the settlement destroyed?"

"They say so. Those Ordovices and Dobunni are fierce fighters and it is said they set fire to the tuath and killed many of the people. The story goes that it was a revenge slaughter." He gave a sigh and leaned back in his chair. "But I believe the tuath may still there – some of it - though I don't go across the river to trade with them Cymry."

I was greatly alarmed by what he said. Had I come all this way only to find my tuath no longer existed? Was this journey all in vain? What had happened to the people? Would I find Essylt?

He reached out and took my hand. "Never mind," he said. "Ye're safe here. Ye've had a long journey and what ye find when ye return will be in the hands of the Fates. I'll gladly give ye transport to the river crossing. It's a long journey there if ye don't have a horse and cart."

Nikos had climbed onto my lap and fallen asleep. The warmth of his small body stirred something in me. For the sake of my son I knew I must not give up hope. I held him tightly, stroked his hair and kissed his forehead. I did not find consolation in what Arrak said but no matter what I found when I reached Caer Gwyn, I must be strong and resilient and make a new safe home for my child.

Stanza Two

I woke to the crying of a cock in the farmyard. Arrak had already hitched his pony and loaded the wain with wares.

"Best we make an early start," he said. "There will be stops along the way and I reckon it'll take two or three days to reach the river."

We started out just after sunrise, travelling toward the west out of the settlement, along a rough track littered with beechnuts and acorns from the trees growing along the track's edge. The trail led into a woodland of hawthorns, hazels and blackthorns. It was cold and dark among the trees. The briers, bushes and ferns shimmered with the early morning dew. Soon the trees thinned out and we came out onto an open heath of brambles, juniper scrub and tall tawny grass.

The journey across the heath was pleasant. The air smelled of cypress and rosemary. The wheat and barley fields had been harvested and ploughed and the heath was green from the autumn rains.

The countryside was dotted with small settlements. We waited in the wagon while Arrak stopped to ply his wares. Along the way there were watering places and farmsteads where we purchased provisions. Each night we found lodgings at a farmer's home or inn for wayfarers.

Soon we crossed a ridge that sloped toward the downs. Between the birch and yew trees I could see the gleam of water as the sunlight reflected on it.

"There's the river ahead," Arrak said. "I'll leave ye there. There's lots of boats crossing so ye'll easily find passage over."

We reached the river by mid-morning. There was a fleet of coracles paddling along the shore, little round vessels made of wickerwork covered with skin used for fishing in the streams. Each craft was only large enough to hold two men. How could we cross in one of those? I whispered a prayer to Diva, goddess of rivers begging her to take us safely across.

Then Theon pointed, sailing from the other shore, a large currach made of bright coloured skins and two men aboard rowing toward us. As they drew close I could see by their swarthy features and thick, dark hair they were Cymry.

Theon waved to them and called out. They waved back and steered their craft toward where we were waiting. When they came close Arrak shouted, "Will ye give my friends a ride across? They're going to the Chalk Trail!"

"We are going to Caer Gwyn," I called out in our language. "Can you take us across? We will pay you well!"

The tallest man at the prow of the vessel grinned and waved. When the currach got closer to shore he called out a greeting to us. "Cymry are ye? *Croeso!* To the Chalk Trail, eh? Then surely ye must be heading north to the Great Stone Circle to celebrate *Calan Gaef!* Welcome! Certainly we'll take ye across.

He flung a rope to Arrak who caught it and pulled the currach toward the riverbank. Once the boat was moored, the boatman held out his hand to lift Nikos onto the craft and then helped Theon and me to step aboard.

We waved goodbye to Arrak as the currach pulled away from the shore. The boat skimmed easily through the overgrown reeds and the sailed calmly out over the river.

I was overcome with emotion as the distant shore grew closer. I raised my hands palms toward the sky and whispered a prayer. I could feel my throat tighten with tears. At last I was almost home!

Stanza Three

When the boat touched the other shore, Theon paid the boatman a handful of coins and we prepared to set off. Mist curled from the river, and I heard the wind murmuring in the reeds. As I stood on the river's shore breathing in the fresh scent of the damp soil, I felt a shiver down my spine. I looked out across the vast grassy plain. Almost ten years had passed since I had been taken from my home. I was certain they had mourned me as dead. Now, as I set my feet on the solid earth of my homeland I was overcome with emotion. Warm tears splashed down my cheeks as I gazed out over the wide expanse of the plain and gentle hillsides toward the distant blue rim of Cyrmy's mountains. Somewhere in those hills was Caer Gwyn. In just a few more days, we would reach the Chalk Trail that led to my tuath.

The fields were still green and full of grazing sheep and stout brown cattle. As we trudged across the heath, memories began to flood my mind. I remembered how I used to get up at dawn to wander those fields with Essylt picking yarrow, comfrey and chamomile for medicines, and mandrake to use in our mystic rites. I recalled helping her tend the sick and going to the stone circle afterwards to say prayers to the goddess. My life had been dedicated to these tasks ever since my Druid *tadcu*, Grandfather Maelgwyn, had found me at the Stone Circle when I was an infant. Without him I may not have had a good life, which, in spite of tribulation, was a life so rich and I vowed to spend the rest of it serving my people the way Grandfather would have wanted me to.

We walked all day until the sun went down over the western hills reflecting gold in the darkening sky. Before nightfall, we found shelter in an abandoned hut. Theon built a small fire to warm us and we sat around it, feasting on the last of the barley cakes.

"Tell me about this festival *Calan Gaef*," Theon said. "What makes this eve so important for your people? Is it like our Themosphoria when we honor Demeter, how she searched for her daughter, Persephone, who was stolen by Hades, God of the Underworld?"

"*Calan Gaef* is the chief of spirits and it is our most important festival marking the beginning of our winter; the end of the harvest when we enter the darkest half of the year," I explained. "Some Kelts call it Samhain. It is a celebration of mystery and magic when the ghosts of our ancestors return from Annwn, the Otherworld, and wander the land, just as Persephone returns from the Underworld every springtime in Greece. The Druids are wise men, philosophers and seers. They teach us that after death our souls still live on in another world. Annwn, the Otherworld, is a land of beauty and pleasure where sickness and decay is unknown."

"Are there really ghosts, Mama?" Nikos's eyes widened and he moved closer to me.

I put my arm around him. "Yes, but not the frightening kind of ghosts. These are the souls of the people we loved who have gone to Annwn. We light fires on the hillside and it is between the fires that our ancestors walk. That is why it is important for me to pay homage to my grandfather this night, and to thank the gods for bringing me safely back home."

"Will Papa come to visit us?"

I hugged my son closer to me. "We must never forget your Papa," I said. "We will light a candle for him and leave a plate of food to welcome him, and perhaps he will come." I had put Elidi out of mind for so much of this arduous journey. Now, I as I looked at our child, I could visualize him and hoped Nikos would grow into as brave and kind a man as his father was.

"What of the others of your tuath? Have you thought of those who may not have survived the enemy's raid?" Theon asked.

His question disturbed me. I thought of my *modryb* Essylt, Lleu the bard, and the others – my friend Tog the cattle steward and Teag. the goldsmith. Had they survived? Would they still be there? I sat staring into the dying fire, fighting back the tears welling up in my eyes.

Theon saw my distress and put his arm around me. "You must trust the Fates, dear Olwen. Whatever will be, you are a strong and resilient woman. And you know I will always be here to guide and comfort you."

I looked up at him. The dying firelight flickered on his face, and I saw how the lines of his brow had deepened. He looked haggard and exhausted, his hair and beard greyer than before. We had gone through so much together. Theon was my saviour and wise counsellor. Without him I would have never reached my homeland.

The fire burned to embers and the night grew darker. A silver moon had risen above the trees and Sirius, the Dog Star beamed, brightest of all among the stars. I studied the sky the way Grandfather had taught me, searching the constellations watching for a sign. As I gazed at the heavens suddenly a brilliant blaze of fire streaked over us, like a pulsating golden serpent falling toward the north.

"Look mama! A star is falling!" Nikos exclaimed,

"That's a Fire Dragon, my darling," I said.

"A Fire Dragon?" Nikos eyes widened with wonder.

"Yes. It is a messenger from the gods." I repeated the words my Grandfather had taught me. *"Who is the Dragon who breathes fire across the sky? I am the Star-son, the golden dragon, the Firedrake, the Sky Serpent. I foretell your destiny."*

"What does that mean, Mama?"

"It means the sky gods have sent us a sign," I said. "It is leading us home."

Stanza Four

The next morning we started out after sunrise. Soon we reached a well-trodden pathway, the Chalk Trail, that would lead us to Caer Gwyn. The trail led over the meadows and through a glade of trees. As we walked beneath them, they stirred in the wind, shrugged off their russet leaves, and sent them drifting down to scuttle at our feet. There was something familiar about that glade, something that stirred long-forgotten memories. I thought of my secret covert where I often hid, safe from the turmoil that had beset our tuath. I remembered the day when Teag and I had met in the beech grove on a tryst. I recalled the way the sun caught in his tawny hair giving it a sheen the colour of honey, the green-gilt of his eyes, how our bodies had touched. When he kissed me his mouth had tasted as sweet as berries. "Your life is in the goddess's hands," he had said. *"You cannot choose another destiny. You must be pure and chaste, a sacred vessel for the Earth Mother."* What he said was true. My life had been dedicated to the Goddess and I knew I could never denounce her. Yet I still felt the pang of hurt in my heart I had felt the day I learned he was wooing Aeron, the ricon's daughter.

Beyond the woods the trail opened onto a clearing with a small ring of grey stones. I felt my heart pulsing in my chest. This was the stone circle where I had so often honoured the goddess when I was a young maiden. It appeared to still be well-kept. There were bundles of sage and other votive offerings at the foot of the head-stone. I could feel the presence of Modron, the Great Mother.

I reached into my amulet bag and found the last of the gold coins – those same coins Teag had given me the day we first met at the stone circle. They felt warm in the palm of my hand as if the gold was on fire. I studied them – the gold staters with the engraving of King Filippos and on the reverse side, the head of Apollo who I had once thought to be Alexandros. I thought how they had been my luck charms that had led me to Greece and my new life. Now I offered them with the other votives at the shrine. I said a prayer to Modron, our mother goddess, and thanked her for my safe journey.

Just beyond the stone circle was a hill surrounded by a deep trench and on its crest a stone-built hill-fort. The pennants were flying from the corners of the stockade which meant the ricon was present. Below the fortress, surrounded by a stockade, nestled a village of round, thatch-roofed houses. I felt my heart race. Was this the tuath of the Raven Clan, Caer Gwyn? Then I heard a raven's cry and knew it was welcoming me home.

We entered through the stockade gates. The village square was empty except for a pack of stray dogs that barked and snarled at us as we approached. I supposed the village folk were already making their way to the Great Stone Circle to celebrate Calan Gaef and prepare the bonfires.

The cattle sheds looked different than before. There was a new building with a stone wall and fresh thatch on the roof. I wondered if Tog, the cattle steward, still tended the herd. I remember the nights I spent there with my bull, Mithras, and how Tog had comforted me after the bull was sacrificed at Beltane. What had happened to him and to Galen, that miserable stable boy who enjoyed taunting me?

Past the cattle sheds, on the far side of the compound, was the blacksmith's hut. The door skins were down and there was no sound from the forge. Was Teag still the chief blacksmith of our village? Had he left Caer Gwyn, or perhaps been killed in the Dobunni's siege?

Most of the village was just as I remembered except for a few unfamiliar stone-built huts. We passed the harness-makers, the tanners, the market place. When we reached the centre square there was the round stone walled building with the thick thatch of roof, my Grandfather Maelgwyn' lodge! As we got closer, I could hear the soft, lilting tone of a clarsach and a sweet tenor voice singing a ballad. Could it be Lleu, the bard? As though it were yesterday, my mind travelled back to those evenings when I had sat at Lleu's feet while he strummed his clàrsach and sang the beautiful ballads that told our people's story.

"This was our home," I said. My voice quavered when I spoke. What would they say? Would I be a stranger now or welcomed? All the way home I had thought of those days long past, a little afraid at returning. Theon must have sensed I felt reluctant to go to the door. He put his arm around me reassuringly. "You have come all this way and now, no matter what you find, you know the journey was not in vain."

He waited with Nikos while I approached. I stood outside the door-skins, hesitating afraid of what I might find. I wiped a tear from my cheek with the hem of my cloak and waited outside the door for a moment, leaning against the lintel. For ten years I had dreamed of returning home. Would it be the same now that I had returned? Would anything be the same? Finally I called out, my voice trembling. "Lleu? Essylt?"

The singing stopped. I heard soft, padded footsteps approach the door and the door-skins brushed aside. I knew the man who stood there was Lleu. He was still as handsome as I remember him. His face was haggard, he had grown a beard and his tawny hair looked more ashen, but I knew it was him.

"Lleu! It is me, Olwen!"

His eyes narrowed and he bent near to peer closely at me. "Olwen?' His face flushed red and then he stepped back, his mouth agape, as if he had seen a ghost. "*Our* Olwen?"

'Yes," I said. "I have come home. It has been a long journey, but at last I am here." I turned to beckon Theon to come closer with my child.

"You are *really* our Olwen?" Lleu stood at the door sill, peering down at me.

"Yes!" I pointed to my gold priestess's torc with the raven's symbol. "It is me, Olwen, the Druid's child!"

He kept staring at me as though I was one of the ghosts of Annwn. "We thought..." he stammered "We were sure you were dead or had been taken as a slave by the Dobunni. We searched for you... never gave up hope that somehow..." Then he regained his composure and nodded toward Theon, peering intently at him. "And who is your companion? Is he a magi? A priest?"

Even though his garments were soiled from travel and his hair and beard unkempt, Theon always had a priestly look. He chuckled and stepped forward holding out his hand to grasp Lleu's. "No, I am not a priest. I'm a physician."

Lleu seemed puzzled when Theon spoke in our language. "You are Cymry?"

"No," Theon explained. "I am Greek – from Makedon. Olwen has taught me some of your language, though I do not speak it well."

"Greece?" Lleu exclaimed. "Is that not a country far across the sea? I have heard the stories of their poets and bards."

"When Sholto stole me away he took me far south to this country, Makedon, where he heard a king was looking for soldiers for his army," I said. "I was rescued by a young man, Alexandros, who happened to be the king's son." I reached out to take Theon's hand. "Alexandros took me to Theon, who became my guardian. It is because of him I was able to come home."

"And the boy?' Lleu pointed to Nikos who was hiding shyly behind Theon. "Is he your child?"

"Yes, he is my son, Nikos."

Lleu studied me closely as if trying to imagine me as the young girl he had last seen on that Midsummer night almost ten years before. "You are not the innocent maiden I remember. You are a woman now, and you have travelled far with your child," He held open the door skins. "Come! Essylt is here. I have been caring for her." He spoke in a quiet tone. "She has been ill, and I fear she will not live long. All the chaos of the past years... the destruction of our tuath, the loss of so many friends... especially your disappearance. Essylt has all but given up hope."

We stepped inside. The old house still looked much like when I had lived there, the walls hung with pelts, woven blankets, and cooking pots. A fire blazed on the hearth and the room smelled of smoke.

Lleu led me toward the bed where Essylt lay propped on a heap of pillows. In the shadows she looked almost like a corpse, her thin frail body covered in a linen sheet.

"Essylt," Lleu whispered. "It is Olwen. She has returned to us."

I stood beside her bed, heartsick and afraid. She was scarcely breathing and I thought for a moment she was dead. Then she opened her rheumy eyes and blinked. Her face was pinched and pale, creased with lines of age and worry. Her eyes searched my face.

I bent closer. "Yes, it is me, Olwen!"

Her eyes widened and her blue-veined hands reached out to me. She reared her head to peer closely at me and said in a cracked, shaky voice: "Olwen?"

I knelt beside her and took her hand. "Yes, my m*odryb.* It is me, Olwen!" I leaned closer. "I have come home to you."

Her fingers dug into my arm as though she wanted to hold me there forever. "You are home now?" Her grip tightened. Her thin, quavering voice cracked when she spoke. "I have waited a long time for you to come. You must never us leave again!" Then her grasp relaxed and she gave a sigh. Tears trickled down her cheeks. I saw her lips moving in a silent prayer and knew she was giving thanks for my return.

I beckoned Theon closer to the bed. "This is my saviour and guardian," I said. "Theon is a physician from Greece. He is the man who has cared for me as though he were my father and taught me the healing arts."

Essylt reached out her hand toward Theon. "I have prayed to the gods to send us a good man who could help my people. I am too old now. My healing powers are gone."

I remembered the times when I was a child and she had taken me to the oak grove where the Druids worshipped at a secret shrine, how we had gathered vervain and rowan berries as offerings and kept the votives lamps burning on the sacred altar. I recalled her saying to me: *"You are an honoured child. I am the sorceress, the High Priestess of the Earth Mother and you are her acolyte. Together we will honour Her!"*

She looked up at me, squinting as she peered closer. "You have grown into womanhood in those years you have been away. You were born to be a priestess, a healer and given the gift of sight and the love of healing."

"And I shall use those gifts to help my people," I said.

Essylt had noticed Nikos who was hiding shyly behind me. "Who is the child?"

'This is my son, Nikos," I coaxed him closer and lifted him up to sit on the bed beside her. "His father was a helmsman for the king's fleet but a storm took him away from me."

Essylt smiled and reached out her arms to embrace him, but Nikos held back, a wary look on his face. "Do not be afraid, child," Essylt said. "I am your mother's *modryb,* I am her Aunt. You may call me *nain,* Grandmother." She wrapped her arms around him and held him close.

Lleu had set the table with a trencher of roast pork and black bread. He beckoned us over. "Come. Sit. Eat. You must be weary from your travels. The distance has been long indeed, and these are dangerous times."

He poured us flagons of hot wine mixed with spices. I held mine between my hands and brought it slowly to my lips, murmuring a blessing. As we ate, I told him about our journey, how we had travelled from Athens by trireme and a merchant ship from Syracuse, then the long trek overland through Belgae lands to the Narrow Sea.

"You were brave to cross the Sea by currach," Lleu said. "Surely the gods were with you all the way on your journey!"

I asked him about the raid by the rival tribes. "We were told by the peddler who brought us to the river that Caer Gwyn had been destroyed. I was afraid there would be nothing here when I returned."

"Yes," Lleu took a long draft of his wine and sat back, musing before he spoke. "They came down on us like the wraiths of the gods, those fierce Ordovices and Dobunni. The Wolf clan of the Ordovices wanted vengeance for the death of their chief's son, Daffyd, who Bedwyr burned as an offering at the midsummer rites. And the Dobunni sought revenge because Sholto had stolen the chieftain's wife. They threatened to kill every man, woman and child in our tuath." He set the flagon down and sighed. "They burned most of the village and killed many of our people. Some were taken as slaves." He sighed and reached out to grasp my hand. "That is what we thought was your fate."

I felt a shiver as I recalled that day, how I had run to hide in the grove and witnessed Sholto murder his brother. I quickly put the unpleasant memory out of my mind.

"Tog, the herdsman, is he still caring for the cattle?" I asked.

Lleu shook his head sadly. "We found him in the cattle shed, poor fellow. He was trying to protect the sacred bulls. His heart must have just stopped."

"What about that slow-witted stable boy, Galen?" I asked. "And little Bran... what became of them?"

"That young scamp Galen?" Lleu said. "Yes, he is still here but he won't be making trouble now. Almost lost his leg, he did and might have died if Essylt had not been there to treat him. The young lad, Bran, he's still helping in the stable."

"Our ricon, Madoc, did they kill him too?"

"Yes, Madoc was tortured and died the shameful death. It was his *rhan,* his fate. And that evil Druid, Bedwyr, was sent away by the Council in disgrace. A trouble-maker he was. The people of the tuath blamed him for all our tribulations."

"Who is the ricon now?" I asked

"The Council chose Ifor the Red," Lleu said.

The name brought back another unpleasant memory of that fateful day when the Dobunni chieftain's wife, Tallia, had been killed. Ifor the Red was a kinsman of Madoc, a fearsome warrior. I recalled how, when he killed Tallia, it had stirred up more animosity between our tribes.

"Why did they name a man like him as ricon?" I asked.

"He was the only kinsman of Madoc left alive," Lleu explained. "The Council had little choice but to name him ricon. Fortunately, since then, he has shown regret for partaking in the feud between Sholto and the Dobunni chieftain. And now we have a new Druid as well, a ricon's son from Senghennyd who studied at the Holy Island – a good man, a peace-maker, and one who has helped give our tuath and our village new life."

"What about Madoc's family - his daughter, and wife?" The mention of Aeron brought back memories of Teag again, how he had bewitched me. I remembered that day I had found Aeron, half naked, in the smithy, how she had pressed against Teag shamelessly. I have never forgotten his words to me: *"I have wronged you, little spirit. I do adore you. But it's Aeron who I love."* I wanted to ask about Teag. Had he married Aeron?

Before I could ask, Lleu continued his tale. "None of Madoc's family survived. The girl, Aeron, was killed in the raid along with Madoc's wife. They found his youngest son, Ned, in the woodland. His throat had been slit. Nobody knows what became of that other one- the one who started this feud. Sholto. Perhaps they killed him too."

My stomach clenched at the mere mention of his name. "It was Sholto who stole me away," My voice quavered as I spoke. "I saw him kill Ned. That is why he took me. He said I was a luck charm because I was a Druid's child."

I told him about my abduction, how we had crossed the Narrow Sea on a merchant vessel, how I tried to send a message back to Caer Gwyn with the ship's boy, and the long journey by horseback to the Makedonian lands. As I spoke tears welled in my eyes and trickled down my cheeks. Lleu reached out and took my hand to comfort me as I recounted my terrifying ordeal.

"It was on the night of Calan Gaeaf, a Samhain night, when I thought for certain he would kill me, but a young hunter appeared and rescued me. His name was Alexandros. He was the son of Makedon's king. He took me to Theon, the physician, and asked Theon to care for me." I looked over at Theon and smiled. "That is how Theon came to be my guardian and teacher. He taught me the healing arts and now I am home again I want to help my people."

"You have been given many blessings in spite of your ordeal," Lleu said. "And the gods have brought you back to us to help our people!"

While Lleu and I were talking, Theon had gone to Essylt's bedside to question her about her frail condition. He was showing her some of the packets of medicines he had brought from Hellas.

Nikos had fallen asleep beside Essylt, so I went to sit by Theon at her bedside. Theon asked Lleu to bring him a bowl of hot water from the hearth. Lleu poured water from the cauldron into a bowl and brought it to Theon. I watched him mix a fragrant concoction of healing remedies: basil for her memory, rosemary for her heart and juniper for the stiffness in her joints.

"Essylt, I think your ague is likely something we can easily cure," he said. "These medicines will at least give you back your strength. With healing we must be patient."

When the herbs had steeped enough, Theon handed me the cup of the steaming infusion and I held it to Essylt's lips as she sipped it. Silently, I said a healing chant she had taught me when I was a child: *"Bone to bone. Skin to skin. Blood to blood. Flesh to flesh."*

She drank the brew willingly and almost at once I saw a change in her. She lifted herself from her pillow and gave a deep sigh. It was as if the frail old woman had been brought back to life! She soon became more talkative, asking questions about my journey, telling me about some of the people who were still living in the tuath.

"Has Lleu told you we have a new Druid?" she said. "A handsome man, gentle and kind. He has made our tuath the blessed place it was when your grandfather was chief Druid – before that wretch Bedwyr brought such pestilence on us!"

Lleu had been strumming his clarsach while we talked but set it aside. "Our new Druid was sent to us by our god, Duw. He has delivered us from our darkness, taught us his truth and liberated us. And because of him our tuath is thriving again."

"He will want to meet you," Essylt said. "I have told him about you." She had a mysterious twinkle in her eyes as if the potion Theon had given her was causing her to have some inner visions.

"We will go first thing in the morning then," I agreed. "Must I request the Council's permission to enter the Great House?" My memories of the Great House had invoked many nightmares through the years. When Madoc was the ricon I was terrified of the Great House. I shuddered at the thought of entering that dark chamber again, where those posts with the skulls of slain enemies surrounded the room, the place that held so many frightening memories of the evil Druid Bedwyr.

"He and the ricon have already gone to the Great Stone Circle with the other villagers to prepare for the rites. Tomorrow you will meet him," Essylt said. She lay back on the pilows and gave a great sigh. "The gods have sent you home to us and the people will welcome you, especially the Druid." There was something in what she said, and her mysterious demeanour that left me wondering.

That night I lay on a pallet by the hearth, while Lleu strummed his clarsach and sang a song I remember from my childhood.

> *My dreamy-eyed, enchanted child*
> *what charms cast ye*
> *that keep me bewitched?*
> *What dreams spin ye, my darling one?*
> *Your laughter is the sound of field spirits*
> *piping melodic tunes, making me dance.*
> *You weave spells,*
> *like gossamer threads binding me.*
> *You are Fair as sunshine.*

> ***You are the daughter of the Hawthorn,***
> ***a fey spirit, a wood nymph, a sprite.***
> ***You are Olwen, the Goddess's Child.***

As I drifted off to sleep, I thought of what Lleu and Essylt had said about the new Druid, and I remembered the words my Grandfather often spoke: *"Wisdom, love, truth and courage are the most important qualities of the soul of man. We believe in the coming of one who has all of these virtues, for he will be the one sent by the gods."* Perhaps this new Druid was the one sent as a gift from the gods to teach my people the love of everything good, charity, and the love of peace. A man like that would truly help to heal our tuath from the evil, destructive fate Bedwyr had brought upon my people.

Stanza Five

I woke at dawn to the sound of my son's laughter. He was still on the bed beside Essylt where I had left him sleeping the night before. Essylt seemed to have regained her strength and was sitting upright, the luck stones, bones and charms from her amulet bag emptied onto her lap.

"Look Mama! Grandmother has magic stones!" Nikos's eyes sparkled, wide with wonderment.

"Those are divining stones," I explained. "Grandmother uses them to tell people their fortune and to help with healing people who are ill."

He held up one of the bronze coins. "She says with this one she can talk to people who have gone to the Underworld. Can she talk to Papa?"

I went over to the bedside and put my arm around him. "'Tis Annwn, Nikos, and perhaps. Come now, my boy. You must bathe and dress, for this is a special night – a big celebration."

There was a chill in the room. An autumn wind rustled the thatch and the leather door skins had been pulled aside letting in the frosty morning air.

"Where are the men?" I asked.

"They have gone to the paddock to fetch a horse and cart," Essylt said. "It's a long walk to the Sacred Henge, so they will carry me there on the cart."

"But are you well enough to go?" I felt her cheeks with my hand. She was flushed, but not feverish. "You have been so ill, Auntie."

"I *must* go!" Essylt insisted. "I have never missed celebrating Calan Gaef! Not in my entire lifetime."

"You must take care!" I scolded. "If you fall ill again..." I worried about her going on such a trek in the chill of autumn.

"I will not!" There was a stubborn edge to her voice. "And if I do – you are a healer, and so is the physician, Theon. It is because of him I have gained enough strength to attend the rites." She gave me a quirky smile. "And if I *should* die my spirit will return from Annwn to attend the rites next year!"

The fire on the hearth had burned to ash, but there was still warm water in the cauldron. I filled a basin and bathed Nikos, dressing him in a clean tunic. Then I sat him at the table with a bowl of barley porridge. "We are going to the Sacred Stones," I said. "It will be a long day's journey."

"Are there really ghosts there, Mama?" Nikos asked. "Grandmother says they light big fires and the dead people come."

"Yes, but the ghosts are not frightening ones. They are the souls of the people we loved who have gone to the Otherworld."

"Will Papa visit us?"

I put my arm around him and held him close. My throat tightened when I thought of Elidi. Would we feel his presence?

"Perhaps he will," I said. "We will light a candle for him."

I cleansed myself and put on a long tunic of honey-coloured wool and a shawl with a bright-woven pattern of blue and amber. I looked at my reflection in a mirror as I brushed my hair and saw an older, more careworn me, and a much wiser woman than that innocent child who I had once been.

After Essylt had bathed I helped her into her ceremonial robe of white linen and wrapped her blue woollen cloak around her frail shoulders, clasping it with a raven-shaped pin. As I spread the end pieces of her raven torc and slipped it around her neck, she said, her voice strong. "Do not worry about me, Olwen. One must trust the gods. I know when I wear my torc, I walk with them." Her eyes searched my face. "My child, you have found your true place in the world. I am old now, and frail. I cannot heal the sick but you, my child, can serve the people of our tuath. The Mother has given you great gifts. They are yours to use the best way you know how."

I heard the sound of men's voices and the rattle of cart-wheels outside the hut. Nikos rushed to the door to greet Theon and Lleu who had returned from the paddock with a straw-filled cart and a shaggy pony.

"Mama says we are going to the place where the dead people are!" he exclaimed, his dark eyes wide with excitement. "There will be big fires and maybe my Papa will be there!"

"We light the fires to chase the bad spirits away," Lleu said. He reached down and tousled Nikos's hair. "And surely, because only the good spirits come to visit, your Papa will find you there."

The early morning air was crisp with the first frost. Theon helped Essylt into the cart and I wrapped a blanket around her then lifted Nikos up to sit beside her. It was just past dawn as we set off, following the chalk trail north, occasionally passing other villagers who were making their way to the Stones. The rising sun had warmed the frost from the grass but there was still a chill in the air. Sheep grazed in the meadows. The last of the wheat had been scythed and brought in from the fields, the grain collected, and the chaff tied into stooks of straw. We heard the low of cattle. At Calan Gaef the farmers slaughtered some of their herds to provide food for winter and others were brought from their summer pastures and herded together in wooden palisades.

424

"It is a long day's journey to the stones," Lleu said. "We should arrive there by the time the midday sun is up."

The trail led into a grove of ancient oak trees where magpies and jackdaws called a shrill greeting as we passed. The path was strewn with chestnuts and acorns and dried leaves scuttled under our feet. We stopped to rest in a clearing where Essylt and I picked sprigs of evergreen, rowan berries and mistletoe to use as offerings at the rites.

We came out of the oak woods into open pastures. All day long we travelled up the chalk road, following the path across the fields until it came to the place where two rivers met. A short way up the bank there was a raft large enough to hold the pony and cart.

"We believe this river is part of the ritual passage of life to death and in crossing it, we are celebrating those who have died," I told Theon.

"Like the River Styx?" Theon asked.

"Perhaps. But I hope it doesn't take us to Hades," I teased.

We paid the rafts-man a handful of copper coins and he took us across to the trail that led to the Sacred Stones.

We finally arrived at the end of the trail. Ahead of us rose the enormous circle of bluestones that stood higher than any man, like silent giants, surrounded by a wide greensward of fields and gently rolling hills. The sun was high in the sky its rays glowing over the great Head Stone that leaned at the entrance to the Sacred Circle. I recalled, as a young girl, how I had felt its power sear my flesh.

The sunlight played over the bluestones making shadows, so it seemed as though they were moving. It had been nearly ten years since I had last attended the rites at the Druid's Circle, and in that time I had seen many wonders built by men. The massive stones didn't have the regal splendours of the Parthenon with its painted columns and pedestals of gold. It was an age-old circle of monoliths that had stood there from time out of mind, a place where the Druids gathered to read the omens in the skies; a place haunted by the souls of the dead.

A long line of torches crossed the field and I heard the throbbing of drums and the thin, plaintive tone of a flute. Farther across the meadow a crowd had gathered around stacks of tinder to be lit that night for the rites.

Lleu led the horse forward and tethered it to a wooden post. I lifted Nikos down and took his hand. Theon helped Essylt offering her his arm. We approached the Stones in silence along the broad torch-lit avenue that led up to the pair of gigantic granite monoliths that formed a gateway into the inner sanctuary. A group of white-robed Druids were gathered in the Inner Circle, their voices droning as they made their supplications. Some were young men, others aging white-haired sages like my grandfather who had served the gods for all their lives. Many were venerable wizards who lived solitary lives in the mountains worshipping the spirits and the gods of thunder and lightning.

Essylt whispered to Theon: "These men are the Druids. They all know powerful magic, and all the Mysteries since time began."

Theon stood in awe gazing at the sight. "Tell me about this holy place," he said.

"This is Cor Gawr, the great circle of the Holy Anointed Ones, a place of kings and priests," Essylt replied. "This is the domain of the dead. We bury them facing the noontime sun. It is also a place of healing and where we worship our ancestors." She paused to take a breath. Her voice quavered when she spoke again. "On Calan Gaeaf we celebrate the rebirth of Lugh, the Oak God, he who is the sun King and Giver of life. We make offerings here at the altars and light the bonfires to invoke the gods: Calan Gaeaf, chief of spirits, Cerridwen, the goddess of wisdom, mistress of the cycle of change and Morryar, the raven goddess of our tuath."

"Then it is much like our autumn festival, the Panosian when our goddess Demeter's daughter Persephone is taken to the Underworld by Hades," Theon said. "In the springtime, we celebrate the Thesmophoria when she returns and brings life back to the earth."

Essylt clutched Theon's arm and as we walked toward the tall lintel stones she continued her explanation of the rites. "We also believe in the after-life," she said. "The Druids teach us that the soul passes from one body to another." She stopped a moment to catch her breath. "After death our souls continue to live in the Otherworld, a place where sickness and decay are unknown, a land of enchanting music, and an abundance of food and drink." Her voice took on a mysterious tone. "The dead return from Annwn on this night. It is our most important festival and for some, the most frightening night of the year because of the spirits of the dead. On Calan Gaeaf, sometimes even the bravest warriors are afraid."

"Why are they making two fires in the field?" Theon asked.

"We light the fires to confront the darkness and banish evil spirits," Essylt said. "It is between the fires that our ancestors walk. We make offerings to their spirits, asking for peace, harmony and love, and they appear to us bearing messages of hope from the Otherworld."

She leaned heavily on Theon's arm and stopped to take a breath. "The fires are the divine eyes through which the gods communicate with us. Although darkness may dim the light of our world, there is something to be seen in this darkness. So we celebrate it, dance to the fire, and bless the season when darkness enfolds us."

When we reached the entrance of the sanctuary. Essylt let go of Theon's arm. "Olwen and I must make our offerings. You go with Lleu and the child to the field. We will meet you there after we have made our supplications and offerings at the Great Altar Stone."

"Can I come Mama?" Nikos asked.

"The Inner Circle is only for priestesses and Druids," I explained. "You go with the men to the field and later Mama will come."

Theon took Nikos by the hand and led him away while Essylt and I walked up the path toward the great dolmens at the sanctuary. When we reached the entrance, I stood still, staring up at them.

Treasured memories rushed to my mind, as well as unsettling ones of my last visit on the Midsummer years before. Midsummer was always a joyful time, but that year it had been a time of war. I recall our dismal processional to the Stones and how Essylt had tried to reassure me. Why, on that day, had we not seen in the runes the tragedies that were about to befall our tuath?

I recalled how Essylt had said: "This day is the end of your childhood. You were brought to the Stones as a babe. Now you shall return as a woman."

In truth, it *had* been the end of my childhood. I thought back on everything that happened since that Midsummer day Sholto had taken me away. My life certainly *had* changed and I truly had returned here as a woman – one who had lived through perilous times, faced death, learned the healing arts, had married and given birth to a child.

Before entering the sacred place, we prostrated ourselves, then joined the priestesses who had also come to make their offerings. A group of Druids were gathered by the Altar Stone, their voices droning as they made their supplications. Next to the altar, a young black goat was tethered waiting to be sacrificed. The Druids had placed bundles of mistletoe and sheaves of wheat on the fire which blazed, filling the air with the tang of smoke mingling with the strong scent of burnt offerings.

There was a silver horn on the altar containing honied wine. Essylt and I both drank from it and as we placed down our bundles of evergreens on the fire, we intoned the words: *"From the Earth, From all that is given, I give this in return."*

As I laid my offerings down I chanted a prayer. *"On this day I invoke Cerridwen, Goddess of wisdom, Keeper of the cauldron of transformation, mistress of the cycles of change. Grace me with your blessing, Goddess. Watch over, protect and guide me."*

Then I said a prayer for my Grandfather whose presence I felt. I remembered when I was a child how I stood by this alter with him while he made his supplications, and how afterwards he told me the story about how he had found me on the altar when I was a baby.

The altar fire crackled as the offerings were made. The pungent smell of burning herbs and evergreen filled the air. One of the Druids came to the altar bearing an armload of rowan branches. He stood, his head thrown back as he supplicated the gods. When he had done with the incantations, he turned to greet us. He was a tall, handsome, older man with russet-colored hair and beard and a kindly face. He was dressed in a white robe and a blue gold-trimmed cloak. Around his neck he wore a crescent shaped disc of gold set with jewels, a *lunila,* that showed he was a Druid of high rank.

He greeted Essylt with outstretched arms. "My lady, Essylt! Praise be that you are well enough to attend the rites."

"Yes, truly it is a miracle," Essylt said. "And Blessed be! Because of the god's mercy my girl has returned home!" She turned to me. "This is the Druid who has helped to restore our tuath."

He peered down at me, a puzzled look on his face, his brows drawn. "This is the girl? The one you have searched for all these years?"

I made a deep curtsy. "Yes, my lord Druid..." I stammered, "I am Olwen. My grandfather was the Druid Maelgwyn and Essylt is my *modryb,* the one who taught me the rites and cared for me."

"There is no need for formalities between us, my lady. My name is Heuil," He reached out and grasped my hand. "The gods have brought you back for a reason. Essylt told me how you had been destined to go to the Holy Isle to be initiated as a priestess, and how at the Midsummer your tuath was raided by the Ordovices and Dobunnis, and you had disappeared."

"I was abducted the day of the raid," I said, "The ricon's wicked son, the one who had caused the tribulation between our tribes, took me across the Narrow Sea."

"I am from the tuath of the Ordovices, the elder son of the Wolf Clan's ricon," Heuil said. "I am the older brother of Dafydd, the boy who was taken as a hostage and burned here on the Midsummer by the wicked shaman, Bedwyr."

It shocked me when he said Dafydd's name, and brought back frightening memories of that last Midsummer. Now I understood Essylt's mysterious look when she had told me I must meet the new Druid.

"Essylt told me how you had befriended Dafydd and comforted him," Heuil said.

I felt tears come to my eyes as I remembered that day, seeing Dafydd in the wicker cage, dressed in a scarlet sagum like those worn by the Princes of Caer Gwyn when they went to battle, a gold diadem of oak leaves crowning his head. I recalled how horrified I had been when Bedwyr had ordered him to be burned as a sacrifice.

"I did not know about the feud until some years later," Heuil continued. "I had left my tuath to go to Caer Troia, the Holy Isle, to study with the Druids. I went there because of who I am. I was not born to be a warrior, but a peacemaker. But when I returned, I heard about what happened to my brother and the calamity that befell your village. The people of your tuath, the Essyltyr, and my people, the Ordovices – we are all Cymri,' Heuil said. "I knew I must try to unite out tribes, atone for the killings and make amends for my people. That is how I came here to be the Druid for Caer Gwyn." Heuil looked down and smiled at me. "A brave maiden like you who knows the healing arts and portents is truly a gift worth more than gold. You understand the power of the stones and the messages of the runes. Today we will praise the gods for your return."

"I feared for my life, but the gods spared me," I said. "I was rescued and found a safe haven, in a far away country called Makedon. My guardian, Theon, who is a physician, accompanied me on the long, dangerous journey back to Caer Gwyn. Thanks be to the gods, I am home again!"

The chanting of the priests had grown louder as they poured the last of the oil from their offering cups for the gods. The sun had dipped lower behind the hills casting a golden glow over the Head stone. From the fields I could hear the cry of the celebrants as the fires were lit. Dusk was falling. The first evening star had appeared glimmering in the sky.

"Now it is time for us to attend the fires," Heuil said. "When we have finished the rites I would like to hear more of your story."

The sky glowed as the waning moon rose over the ridge of the hills shining above the Sacred Stones with a silver light. Essylt and I followed Heuil and the Druids and priestesses out of the holy sanctuary along the torch-lit path toward the meadows where two fires blazed. Swarms of people were gathered around close to the fires waiting to pour their offerings of oil and grains onto flaming pyres. There was a babble of excited voices, women's chatter and loud shouts. There were people from tuaths near and far, along with their ricons: Essyltyrs, Ordovices, Dobunnis and others from farther away. Women wearing ankle length tunics woven in bright colours, their long hair in braids, carried their children and hovered around fires gaping at the priestesses as they made their tributes. Men wearing knee length tunics, leather breeches and hooded cloaks passed around flasks of wine and cups of honey mead.

I heard the sound of a horn and I recognized Caer Gwyn's flaming-haired new ricon, Ivor the Red. A troupe of young men followed him carrying armloads of offerings to the fire. I looked for Teag among them, but he was nowhere to be seen in the crowd of revellers.

Theon, Lleu and Nikos were waiting for us at the crowd's edge. Nikos ran to me and grasped my hand. "Mama, see the fires? Will Papa's spirit come?"

"We will look for him," I said. "I will make an offering."

The fires blazed. Torch lights flickered in the dark. The Master Druid, Heuil, blared on a curved horn calling on the chief of spirits, Calan Gaeaf, while the others sang and recited as they made their offerings carried in bronze bowls.

After their offerings were made Heuil cast his auguries, offering apples, the fruit of immortality, for those who had departed. "We offer these apples, the fruit of this sacred land, so the departed will know they are loved and remembered. Ancestors, come close to us, let us hear your whisper in the flames. Let us remember the past and its lessons and gather a harvest of wisdom."

I watched as Essylt walked carefully toward the pyre, leaning on Theon's arm for support. When she took her place with the other seers to make her offerings I realized, with a sense of sadness, perhaps this might be her last time to administer the rites.

She raised her arms and began to chant a prayer. Her voice and hands trembled, but proudly, she held her head high. She stared into the flames, her hand cocked by her ear as if listening.

"Hear the god's voice in the roaring flames," she cried. "Tell us the tales of our ancestors. Show us those who have passed before us." After she was through blessing the dead, she raised her eyes and turned to Lleu. "Bard, sing us their tale."

Lleu bowed his head and stepped forward, his hand hovering over the strings of his clarsach. Then he began to strum the first few notes. He sang, quietly at first, then his voice grew louder, his sweet tenor rising in a treble. slowly gathering resonance as the notes transformed into harmony. It was a tale of good against evil, life over death. The music washed over the crowd and the babble of voices grew silent as he sang.

Ever since I was a child, no time had been more magic to me than Calan Gaeaf. I shivered as I drew my cloak closer around me, recalling the last Calan Gaeaf I had celebrated in the woodland when I had tried to escape from my captor. Tonight I did not feel that same kind of fear.

I held Nikos's hand as we crept closer, listening as another bard sang his mysterious songs. He was a wizened old man, clothed in ragged homespun robes, one of the mountain seers who possessed untold wisdom and magical powers. He sang tales of mountain lore where wolves and wood nymphs cast bewitching spells on mortals.

We stood close to the pyre, listening to the hiss and crack of the burning offerings. The flames leapt up, like a dragon's fire sending their glare over the gathering. As the flames leapt high and higher, the crowd grew more excited. A wild uproar of shouting and bellowing broke out.

I could feel the singe of heat against my flesh. From my amulet bag I took out two sprigs of evergreen and gave one to my son. "This is for you to make an offering and say a prayer for your father," I said.

Nikos pressed close by my side, drawing in his breath, his fingers clenching the sprig of evergreen. "Will Papa come then? Will I see him in the fire?" His eyes were wide, glistening in the firelight.

"Listen as Mama says the prayers. Then you can make your offering."

I tossed my sprig of evergreen into the flames and said a prayer to Morryar, the raven goddess of war, asking for victory for Alexandros when he went to battle, for I owed my life and my freedom to him. I peered into the fire, hoping perhaps I would see the shape of him in the flames.

"O gods, grant him protection, strength and victory in his conquests," Then I said a prayer for Elidi, so his spirit would rest peacefully in the Otherworld.

Nikos watched and listened alertly as I made my offering. He seemed to understand and stepped up closer to the fire. He lifted his hand with the sprig of evergreen and uttered the words of an oath he had often heard me say as he tossed it into the flames.

When we stepped back from the pyre I noticed the Druid, Heuil, was standing nearby watching us. Nikos looked up at the tall man, eyeing Heiul's white robe and glittering lunila. His eyes grew round with wonder.

"Are you one of the spirits?" he asked.

Heuil laughed and reached down to tousle Nikos's hair. "No my boy! I'm the one who lays them to rest."

"I'm looking for my Papa in the fire," Nikos said.

"Is he your child?" Heuil asked.

"Yes. He's my son, Nikos. His father, my husband, died at sea. That is why I returned to Caer Gwyn. My saviour, King Alexandros, went off to war and there was uncertainty and conflict in Makedon, So, my guardian, Theon, escorted me back to my people. It was sometimes a dangerous journey, and many times I felt guilty for putting my child through so much strife, but I thank the gods we arrived here safely."

Heuil looked down steadfastly at me, his grey eyes peering into mine. The light from the fires illuminated his face, his high brow, the angle of his cheekbones, the copper sheen of his hair. His strong dark brows drew together as he spoke to me in a low tone, his voice gentle.

"You are a brave woman, Olwen, a braver person than I. When I was young, before I left to go to Segnhydd and the holy Isle, I was married. I was very young then and when my wife died in childbirth, I did not know how I could care for my child. My people, the Wolf Clan, are warriors and I knew her life would be one of strife. So I brought the babe to the Stone Circle and left her on the altar in the sanctuary. I knew a Druid would find her and she would be cared for."

I caught my breath. "How long ago was that?" I asked.

"Some twenty years ago. I have always felt guilty," Heuil said."I was as young as you are, but I was not brave enough to raise a child on my own. For all these years I have felt regret at abandoning my child, and I suffered for it, always wondering what had become of her."

My heart was thudding against my ribs. I tried to speak, but I was breathless. ***Was this man my father?***

Heuil reached out and caught my arm. "Are you alright, my lady?"

My voice trembled. "Did you know that? Did Essylt tell you I was that child? I was the babe found at the altar. Grandfather Maelgwyn found me at the Stone Circle and gave me to Essylt so she could care for me." I stepped closer and pulled down the neck of my tunic to reveal the tear-drop mark on my shoulder. "See this? It is the mark of my birth! A tear-drop!"

I heard him gasp and he leaned closer to look at the birth mark. "Then it must be you... you are my child!" he said. "She had just a mark on her... the mark of a tear shed at her birth." I saw he was crying, and I was too.

"The gods have brought us together here at the Stones for a reason," he said. "I have found my daughter. You have found your father. We are blessed!"

"I must tell Essylt…" I said. But I wondered if she might have already known. I remembered how mysterious she had sounded when she first told me about the new Druid. Essylt had the Sight and perhaps she had guessed Heuil was the father of the child she had raised as her own.

"We will announce it at the hill fort tomorrow so all the tuath will celebrate with us." He took my hands in his and looked deep into my eyes. "We are here tonight to welcome the spirits of those who have passed to the Otherworld. But sometimes we forget there are those living who we have lost, until they return to us. Tomorrow will be a day for us to start a new life." He put his arms around me and held me close. Both of us were crying, but they were tears of happiness.

The first rays of the morning sun had risen in the east, turning the sky rose and gold. The autumn skies were clear, and the dew-wet grass shimmered in the early sunlight. The torches guttered out, and smoke rose from the smouldering fires, leaving only heaps of ashes. Most of the villagers had packed their bundles and set off back toward their tuaths. I went to join Essylt and the men. Lleu had hitched the pony to the cart and Theon was waiting with him. Essylt was already sitting in the cart. Nikos had fallen asleep beside her.

"I saw you talking to the Druid," Essylt said. "And embracing him."

"Auntie," I said. "Did you know his story? Is that why you wanted me to meet him? Did you know it was Heuil who left me, his child, on the altar at the Stone Circle?"

I heard Theon and Lleu gasp when I spoke.

"Your father?" Lleu exclaimed. "Truly?"

"Surely this is a blessing from the gods!" Theon said.

Essylt caught in her breath and closed her eyes. Her hands clutched her robes. Perhaps she was praying, but she made no sound or movement. After a few moments, she spoke.

"I had an insight, something he told me about Dafydd and his life with the Ordovices. How his wife had died in childbirth and he had left his tuath to study with the Druids. Something in my heart made me suspect he might be your father, but I wanted you to find out yourself. He's a fine man, Heuil, worthy of a daughter like you."

As we walked away from the Sacred Circle, I stopped for one last glance back at the Circle. As I passed by, a flash of russet and slate blue caught my eye. A hawk was circling over the blue stone dolmens, alighting on the Heel stone. *Guenhwyvar, the hawk!* Birds are portents and have links with the Otherworld. Was this a message from Elidi? I remembered the hawk tattoo on his shoulder. Had he come to guide and comfort me?

I roused Nikos who had fallen asleep beside Essylt in the cart. "Look at the hawk, Nikos. It's him, your father!"

He opened his eyes and looked toward the bird on the bluestone. "Papa?" He smiled, snuggled closer to Essylt then fell back to sleep. I put my cloak around him and bent to kiss his forehead.

I lagged behind the cart on our journey back to Caer Gwyn. I wanted time alone, time to meditate and reflect on what had happened – the fires, the offerings, how my true father had come into my life, Elidi's spirit appearing as a hawk. Had he come to reassure me? It seemed unreal, as if it were a dream.

The autumn day was bright. The hawthorn bushes glowed copper red with berries and the fields were still green for grazing. I made my way up the Chalk Trail, stopping now and then to rest and contemplate.

As I walked across the meadow toward the village, I heard distant voices, laughter, the bleating of sheep and bawling cattle being herded into the fields.

A lone rider was trotting his shaggy pony down from the hill fort. I watched in the reflection of the sun's glow, turned back in time, remembering that other lone rider on the road to Pella, the glow of the sun bathing him in gold.

"Alexandros" I whispered. His name caught in my throat.

As I walked toward the village with its simple thatched-roof houses, I thought of the white temples of Athens High City, how they appeared like a jewelled crown bathed in the glow of the sun. I was conscious of the tinkling of goat bells and the sound of a shepherd's flute but they were drowned out in my mind by the clicking of cymbals and the strum of kitharas. The music of that other world went round and round inside of me. Could things ever be the same for me again?

I belonged to other worlds now, not just this one. I always dreamed of being a priestess and a healer and now my dreams had come true. But what mattered most of all was I had found my true father. Just as Essylt had said, everything that happened was meant to be, and it was determined long ago.

The man on the horse was closer now and I could see the tawny colour of his hair and beard and the sun's reflection on his face. I couldn't be sure if I knew him. Was this the moment of returning I had sometimes dreamed of, the reunion, the coming home? Could it be him, Teag?

At that moment the rider pulled his pony to a sudden stop. He waited silently as though he was transfixed, peering closely at me as I came closer. He looked careworn and he frowned as I approached. Then, as I came near, I saw him smile.

I caught my breath and walked up to him slowly. "Teag!" I said. "It is me, Olwen. I have come home."

EPILOGUE

Listen to me, I am Olwen, child of the Raven clan, daughter of the Druid. I am an honored child.

> *I will be the pine cone clinging to the branch.*
> *The wind will not dislodge me.*
> *I will be the coral on the sea reef.*
> *The waves will not displace me.*
> *I will be the stone dolmen of the Sacred Henge.*
> *Neither time nor elements will disturb me.*
> *I will be the willow bending in the wind.*
> *I will be the wave uncurling on the sea.*
> *I will be the mountain, my pinnacle crowned with sun.*
> *Steadfast I will stand.*

GLOSSARY

Welsh words:

Cymru: the country that is now Wales
Cymry: the people of Cymru
Cymri: Welsh
Ynys Prydein: Britain (also known as "The Tin Isles"
rhan: fate
cwtches: hugs
cyhryraeth: a ghostly specter
dewer, dor: oak
curraches: small wooden hulled boats sewn over with hides.
tadcu: grandfather
modryb: aunt
Calan Gaeaf: Samhain
Ysprdnos: Beltane, the Day of the Fires.
hiraeth: homesickness, nostalgia or longing for a home.
Derwydd: Druid
sagum: the collar worn by the Druids.
clarsach: a string instrument like a lyre.
Annwn (ah-noon): the Otherworld (death)
vates: diviners
tuath: clan or village
ricon: chieftain
clarsach: an instrument like a small harp
Samhain: (pronounced So-ween by the people of Cymru)
postern gate: rear gate

Greek words:

pharmaka: surgical goods
pharmakes: sorceress (or woman healer)
chairetai; welcome
moira: fate
astronomia: astronomy
hetaera: a woman of pleasure.
tambors, kytheras, sistras, aulos: musical instruments
baccantes: celebrators at the rites.
Mt Aitna: Mt Etna.
Basilikos: king
daimon: luck charm
philoxena: hospitality